ELINOR CLARE;

OR,

THE HAUNTED OAK.

COMPLETE, WITH NEW AND BEAUTIFUL ILLUSTRATIONS.

LONDON:

PUBLISHED BY EDWIN J. BRETT, 173, FLEET STREET, E.C.

1886.

ELINOR CLARE OR THE HAUNTED OAK

THE DISCOVERY OF THE BODY OF WALTER COPELAND.

CHAPTER I.

"There is oft told
A melancholy record of this grove."

"Do, pray, let us go back, dear Isabel; I am frightened to death. How dangerous it is! The gipsies have pitched their camp not half a mile from here, and should any of them discover us—and there is the Haunted Oak right in the path we are going; and, besides, if my poor father should wake and find that we have left home——"

"I will *not* go back, Annie; I told you before we came out that I had a firm belief that I should find him here, dead or alive, and I will not go back while I have strength to continue the search."

The person who uttered this speech was a fine, tall girl, with a dark, expressive countenance, and eyes that seemed to flash with fire, as she spoke, while her lips quivered with emotion. She to whom her speech was addressed was much younger, and of a less marked character; her fair complexion, blue eyes, and flaxen ringlets, bespeaking nothing but mildness and timidity; but there was a third, who was silent, whose beauty far surpassed that of the two sisters, while the earnest gaze which she from time to time cast around her, and the evident total abstraction of her thoughts from the conversation of her companions, showed that her mind was deeply interested in some important subject.

Elinor Clare, the cousin of Isabel and Annie Copeland, was only in her seventeenth year, though early sorrow and habits of deep reflection had given her lovely features a tinge of pensiveness, that to a cursory observer made her appear older. Not so tall as Isabel, she was just the height that best becomes a female. Her form, moulded with the purest symmetry, was only exceeded by the intellectual beauty of her face, which, faultless as were the features, owed its chief charm to the look of blended sensibility and sweetness, which, when she was at ease, dimpled round her mouth, and added lustre to her brilliant yet dove-like eyes. Nothing, indeed, could equal Elinor, when she was in a pensive mood, except Elinor in moments of sportive mirth and archness, and those, though "few and far between," did even now, when she had "fallen upon evil days," sometimes occur to startle and fascinate the beholders.

At the moment we have chosen to introduce them to our readers, the two sisters, with their cousin, were in the very heart of a wood, so vast, that it might almost have been entitled to the name of a forest. It was a fine summer night, and the moon, now struggling through the thick and interlaced boughs, seemed shedding a silvery shower on the green sward beneath, and then, where there was open space, threw a broad flood of light over every object, rendering the surrounding darkness the more black and impenetrable.

To those, however, who were threading the seeming labyrinth of this secluded spot, every path, almost every tree, was familiar. Isabel and Annie were born in the farm-house which their father still tenanted on the edge of the wood, and Elinor was too young, when first she became an inhabitant of her uncle's house, to retain any distinct recollection of another home. They had passed many happy summer days, engaged in the various sports of childhood, under the umbrageous shelter of those leafy recesses, and many a moonlight night had they "made the woods vocal" with their joyous voices and ringing laughter. Alas! with what different feelings did they now pace along the intricate paths, peeping on each side into the nooks, now starting at a shadow, and then stopping and holding in their breath, in the expectation of hearing some sound repeated, which had indistinctly reached their ears, and which would sometimes prove to be only the flitting of a night-bird, disturbed from its haunt by their unwonted presence, or the distant bleat of sheep on the common.

They had proceeded in this manner for nearly half a mile, when Annie's courage failed, and she entreated her sister, as before related, to return, but in vain.

Isabel still kept on determinately, Annie clinging to her arm while Elinor followed silent and thoughtful.

Suddenly Annie uttered a scream; she had seen a figure glide across the path, she declared, only a few paces ahead of them, and as if going towards the Haunted Oak which stood a little out of the path on their right hand.

"I cannot go on, I cannot pass it for the world!" she exclaimed, trembling, and speaking with difficulty. "Oh, Isabel, dear Isabel, do not ask me to go any further if you do not wish me to lose my senses."

"It would be cruel to wish it, I am sure," said Elinor, warmly, advancing at the same time and raising the terrified girl from the ground on which she had thrown herself at the feet of her sister. "Do, Isabel," continued Elinor, "be persuaded to relinquish your wild project and return home."

"You may go if you please, Elinor, and take Annie with you," returned Isabel, coldly. "I knew, though she persisted in coming with me, that she would only be an incumbrance; for myself, my mind is made up, and I will proceed alone."

"Listen to reason, Isabel," replied Elinor. "During the day your father and his men have searched every part of the wood without success. Is it likely that what they failed to discover in the full light of day will be revealed to you by the uncertain light of the moon?"

"Elinor, it is in vain to talk; Walter is within the boundaries of this wood, and I will find him before I return home," exclaimed the headstrong and fearless girl.

"Merciful Heaven, preserve her!" softly ejaculated Elinor; "grief and anxiety have unsettled her brain. And this poor child, too," looking at Annie, who, with her frock thrown over her head to shut out all surrounding objects, sat weeping and trembling at her feet on the grass. "Will you go back part of the way, then, Isabel," she demanded, "with your sister, and wait while I see her safe to the door; and then I will hasten back to you and accompany you wherever you wish to go?"

"No, I will not go back; but I will sit down here, if you will, and await your return," said Isabel. "As to danger, I do not fear any to me——"

"But I saw some one, indeed I did, Isabel," interrupted the fearful Annie, "and for what purpose, but that of mischief, could any one be wandering about in such a place as this and at such a time of night?"

"They might say the same of us," returned Isabel; "but, however, you may set your mind at rest, that which you saw can threaten no danger to me, for it was only a poor pony, strayed, I suppose, from the gipsy camp; and look, here it comes again to prove that I am right."

It was with difficulty that Annie was persuaded to look up at the harmless object of her recent alarm, which was quietly grazing along under the trees; but when she did so, instead of acknowledging the folly of her fears, she shook her head and murmured—

"That was not what I saw, it was a tall figure, not——"

"This is sheer obstinacy, Annie," observed her impetuous sister. "I saw from the first what it was; but do pray rise and let Elinor see you home as she has kindly proposed, for every moment that you remain here is so much time lost."

Annie was too long habituated to obey the commands of her sister to protract longer her stay; with Elinor's help she arose, and, clinging to the arm of the latter, declared that she was ready to go.

"But, oh! Isabel," she continued, in a tone of pathetic entreaty, "do promise that you won't move a step from this place till Elinor comes back. You are so daring, and so thoughtless; but Elinor is quite the contrary, and she——"

"Yes, Elinor is the contrary," interrupted Isabel, with something of bitterness in her manner, "for Elinor is not looking for a dear, a beloved brother, a more than brother. Oh! Walter, Walter," and she wrung her hands and burst out in the accents of despair, "none, none can feel your loss like your unhappy sister, Isabel."

"I will say nothing of your injustice to me, Isabel," observed Elinor, calmly, in reply; "but I *will* ask you to remember the greyheaded parent, bereaved of his only son, and still in uncertainty of his fate, before you *parade* your affliction, and recollect, too, how much his sufferings will be increased should his daughter endanger, by any foolish act, her own safety. Come, Annie, let us no longer lose time," she continued; "I will see you to the outskirts of the wood, to the tree where our swing used to hang in those happy days, that have, I fear, gone for ever, when none accused Elinor of indifference to her friends, and especially to the brother of her adoption."

She turned away without waiting for Isabel's reply, and half leading, half forcing Annie forward, hurried through the path by which they had come.

Numerous were the instructions, and most impressive the charges, which Eleanor poured into Annie's ear, as to how she was to act when she got home to avoid awakening and alarming her father, who, after a night and day's fearful and harassing exertion, had been persuaded to retire to bed, and had, from absolute exhaustion, fallen into a deep sleep before they had ventured to leave him.

"I will be very careful, indeed I will, Elinor," returned the gentle and simple-hearted girl; "but, oh! dear, I cannot help thinking how unjust anybody must be to accuse you of not caring——"

"Hush, hush," interrupted Elinor, putting her hand on Annie's mouth, "that will be all set right one of these days. God bless you, dear girl, I will leave you now, for you will not, of course, be afraid to cross the field in the open moonlight, and I must hurry back to your sister."

"Oh, yes, and I will run as fast as I can across the field, I shall be almost home before you are out of sight," replied the timid Annie, who did not altogether like being left, even though she was within sight of home.

Elinor, however, waited not to hear any more, for she was too anxious to return to Isabel, and as quick as her light feet could run, she set off back again through the wood, fearless of all danger to herself, though certainly quite as much, in reality, exposed to it as her whom she was so desirous of protecting.

She had nearly reached the spot where she had left Isabel, when the moon became obscured, and at the same moment some person darted across her path among the trees. For an instant, she hesitated whether to proceed, but a faint thought crossed her mind that she recognised the figure to be one with which she was well acquainted, and, determined to be satisfied, she exclaimed—

"You need not avoid me, for I know very well who you are."

"Elinor, dearest Elinor," returned a voice, and in an instant, the speaker, a tall young man, bounded to her side; but at that moment several persons were heard, conversing, as they seemingly approached the spot, and the young man, in apparent agony, exclaimed—

"Ha! they have missed me already; I cannot stay, Elinor, to inquire by what chance you are here alone at this time of night; but for Heaven's sake hasten home instantly, if you value your safety, your very existence. I would go with you, but that would be to draw danger upon you which you may otherwise escape. Elinor, I am, at this moment, one of the most wretched of created beings, do not ask me why; promise me only one thing, that should we never meet again—but no, forget me, Elinor; forget that such a wretch as I ever existed."

"Edward, what is the meaning of all this?" demanded Elinor, with the most violent agitation, "speak, tell me."

"I can tell you nothing, Elinor," he replied, hastily; "Heaven protect you."

He was rushing away, in spite of the weak attempt she made to detain him, when a sudden thought seemed to strike him, and he turned back.

"You are not alone here, are you, Elinor?" he hastily demanded.

"No, Isabel——"

"Ah! I guess how it all is," he interrupted her, before she could finish the sentence. "Walter—Yes, yes, I know all about it; but promise me one thing, Elinor; solemnly promise that you will not tell—that you will not reveal to any one that you have seen me to-night."

"I will—I do promise," returned Elinor, "if it is your wish; but why this mystery, Edward? why should you shun——"

"Ask me no questions, Elinor, if you do not wish to drive me to distraction," he replied, and then starting, he added, "Hark, they are coming; I must prevent it by hastening to meet them. Farewell, Elinor, a long, it may be a last farewell."

He strained her violently to his bosom, and then rushed from her, while Elinor, rivetted to the spot, stood lost in alarm and amazement. By degrees the sound of footsteps and voices, which she had plainly heard approaching, receded, and all was still again.

Calm and collected as Elinor usually was in the most trying

circumstances, her fortitude and self-possession on this occasion entirely failed her; a thousand dreadful surmises rushed into her mind, but one thought, one master-grief usurped dominion over all others. " Edward had gone, had bidden her farewell for ever, and had avowed too that he was miserable." To Elinor it seemed as if there could be no sorrow in the world to equal this, and for some minutes she gave way to the full tide of her anguish.

" What a selfish, unfeeling creature I am," she suddenly exclaimed, starting, " I have forgotten Isabel, and she thinks, probably, I shall not return."

Not another instant did she hesitate, but darting down the path soon reached the spot where she had left her cousin, and where the latter had promised to wait for her; but no Isabel was there, and again reproaching herself for having lingered until she exhausted the patience of her impetuous relative, she proceeded onwards in the path which she considered the latter had most likely taken, stopping every two or three minutes to listen; but not a sound reached her ear, except the sighing of the wind through the branches, and the heavy black clouds that from time to time flitted across the moon's pale face, and obscured her light, gave notice of a coming storm. It was at one of these moments when, by the intervention of a cloud, all around her was veiled in thick darkness, that Elinor approached the Haunted Oak, so well known as the object of fear to herself and her companions in childhood, and which even now was regarded with awe by the simple peasantry of that neighbourhood, who would sooner make the compass of the wood than pass " The Oak " after twilight. In Elinor's mind not a vestige of superstition existed; but there was a tale of horror connected with this tree, which she had often heard repeated by the rustics in her uncle's kitchen, until it was engraved on her memory, and always caused an involuntary shudder, when, as upon the present occasion, accident compelled her to pass it.

Pre-occupied as her mind was now, by a series of melancholy and harassing circumstances, and anxious as she was to overtake the rash and headstrong Isabel, she might probably have passed the spot without bestowing a thought upon it, had not her attention been suddenly arrested by a noise resembling the low whine of a dog, followed by that of the accents of a human voice, which, though scarcely above a whisper, appeared to her attentive ear to utter a command to the animal to be silent.

" Merciful God, protect me," mentally prayed the startled Elinor, who now trembled so violently that she was unable to proceed, and was compelled to lean against a tree for support. A pause of utter silence ensued; the affrighted girl could hear nothing but the throbbings of her own heart, which she vainly tried to still by forming various conjectures as to the sounds she had heard; but the moon again shone out with unclouded lustre; it poured the full splendour of its rays on the large open space in which stood the monarch of the wood, the " Haunted Oak," and involuntarily she turned up her eyes towards it. " Power of mercy! could it be possible; was she not dreaming?　Oh! no, too surely, surely it was true : it was Walter Copeland, her dear Cousin Walter, lying at the foot of the tree, senseless, immoveable.　Alas! too truly her fears predicted—he was *dead*." Yet not till she had raised his head in her arms, had knelt by him, and called distractedly on his name, and conjured him to answer her, and found the face cold, the form rigid, and the ear deaf to her voice, could she give up all hope; but it was indeed no longer to be doubted, and in an agony of grief she sunk down by the corpse on the grass, unable to collect her thoughts or resolve how to proceed.

" His father, his poor father," she murmured, with trembling lips; " this will indeed be an awful termination to his suspense; and Isabel, how will she bear the confirmation of her worst fear for her beloved brother ?"

A flood of tears came to her relief, as her imagination depicted the sorrow and anguish of the heart-broken father, thus bereft of his son, who was the pride and solace of his declining years, and to whom he looked as the protector and guardian of the two motherless girls, Isabel and Annie, when he should be laid low in the grave; but from these thoughts Elinor soon wandered to a more appalling subject.　That Walter had been murdered was the dreadful suspicion that crossed her mind, and a slight examination of the body but too forcibly confirmed the suspicion. The hands were clenched, and the features distorted, while even by this uncertain light she could discover that his shooting dress was torn, and soiled with blood and earth, as if he had been dragged along the ground to the spot where he now lay.

Not there had he been murdered, for there must have been evidences around of the death struggle, yet there nothing was disturbed, and as he lay with his face upon the verdant turf, he looked so calm and peaceful that a passer by might have concluded he was sleeping.

That he had been brought there, and *recently* brought by his murderers, was Elinor's fearful conviction.　Until the twilight had put an end to the search, the father of the unhappy young man, his servants and neighbours, had all been engaged in the fruitless search for him. Every corner of the wood had they explored, and it was an utter impossibility he could then have been lying there, not ten yards from the beaten path, without their discovering him. Nor was it, indeed, probable that Isabel could have passed the spot without seeing the object of her anxious search. He must have been brought there, then, within a few minutes—perhaps, even now, the murderers were lingering within a short distance of her. The voices she had heard recurred to her mind, and with fearful anticipation she raised her eyes and gazed around; but the next moment she sunk down again and clasped the cold lifeless form of Walter, as if he could protect her, for her eyes had met the dark glare of the assassin from behind the tree, and at a few paces only distant from her. The next moment she heard his retreating footsteps plunging through the thick underwood, crunching it beneath his feet, and tearing away the branches that impeded his progress.

An inspiration of thankfulness burst from Elinor's throbbing heart, and she arose from the ground resolving to return home instantly, and summon the assistance of the farm-servants to convey the body of Walter to his late home, and take what measures they thought advisable for the discovery of the murderer.

"But Isabel, where can Isabel be?" was the thought that suddenly darted into her mind, after she had proceeded a few paces, and was followed by a thousand dreadful surmises. But one course, however, could she pursue, for it would, she felt, be madness were she alone to attempt to discover what had become of Isabel, and on the wings of terror she flew back to the farm, and succeeding in rousing Philip, Mr. Copeland's principal man, who, almost as much interested in the affairs of the family as if he had himself been a member, had, for the two nights that Walter had been missing, refused to retire to bed, or to pull his clothes off, but lay stretched on the settle before the kitchen fire, "that he might be ready," as he said, "to start up at a moment's warning, if he was wanted."

It was with difficulty Philip restrained within bounds his expressions of consternation and surprise, when he awoke from the heavy sleep which the day's fatigue had induced, in spite of grief and anxiety, and beheld Elinor standing before him, with a candle in her hand, displaying her features ghastly pale, and her eyes beaming with horror and dismay; but still more difficult was it for him to repress his exclamations, when, with quivering lips, she related to him her discovery of the body of

Walter, and Isabel's strange disappearance, entreating him to lose no time in calling up the men to accompany her to the spot where the corpse lay.

Fortunately for Elinor's plan, as she thought of concealing from the bereaved father the extent of his misfortune until the morning, when it could be gradually broken to him, the servant men slept in a building detached from the farm-house, so that Philip was enabled to get them together without disturbing his master, though even after they had all, to the number of seven, passed through the gate, in to the lane which led to the wood, the former could not divest himself of the idea that either Elinor had dreamt what she had told him, or that grief and anxiety had deranged her mind, and she had fancied the tale she had repeated to him, and he hesitated to follow her, until he had prevailed on her to repeat all she had witnessed.

"It must be true," he exclaimed, when he found that she did not vary from what she had before told him; and directing the men to keep close together, and make as little noise as possible, he hurried on to the wood, Elinor, in spite of his entreaties to the contrary, keeping by his side.

A burst of lamentation and threats of revenge broke from the men the instant they beheld the corpse of Walter, which was lying precisely as Elinor had left it. There was no motive here for repressing the full expression of their feelings, and the wood echoed with their noisy exclamations and suggestions. On one point only they were agreed—that the murder had not been committed there; for on the very spot where the corpse now lay, had their master (the father of the unfortunate murdered young man) chosen to rest that very afternoon, when he sunk overpowered with fatigue and sorrow.

"Yes, yes, I know the place well enough," observed one of the men, shuddering, and casting a fearful glance around him. "I didn't mind it then," he continued, "though I tried to persuade master to come a little further towards home, even when it was daylight, but it's awful now."

The panic seemed to spread, and even Philip appeared afraid to look around, while he gave directions to the others to form a litter of boughs, which they tore down from an opposite elm, avoiding, as by mutual consent, touching the tree which had been so long the object of their awe.

Upon this the corpse was placed, and the mournful procession was about to move, when a sudden exclamation was heard, and the next moment Isabel rushed among them, pale and speechless, and evidently in a state of the most violent excitement.

"My prayers have been heard!" she exclaimed, "I have found him, and I have found his murderer too; he has escaped for the present; but I knew him, and will pursue him to the world's end."

Every voice was instantly loud in demand, how or where she had made the discovery, and who was the person she alluded to; but Isabel was deaf to all their questions, her eyes were fixed on Elinor with a look of fearful meaning, and when they at length moved on towards the farm she seized the arm of the latter, and in a low voice, whispered—

"Elinor, 'twas Edward Hatherleigh who basely, foully murdered my brother."

For a moment Elinor was struck dumb; a thousand circumstances corroborative of this assertion rushed upon her mind; but it was but for a moment; the next she exclaimed—

"It is false, Isabel; false as heaven is true."

"You will see, Elinor," she replied; "for the present, indeed, he has escaped; but vengeance will overtake him, and ere long. I knew it was," she continued, "my heart told me that there was but one person in the world who could have the wish to injure Walter Copeland."

"That person was not Edward Hatherleigh, Isabel," returned Elinor, firmly, "he would sooner have sacrificed his own life for him."

"It is well for you to say so," returned Isabel, with bitterness. "You have not lost a brother; on the contrary, the death of Walter has relieved you from what you call persecution."

"This is cruel, Isabel, cruel indeed," commenced Elinor, in a faltering voice; but she recollected herself, and suppressed all further expression of her feelings, in pity to her cousin's distracted state of mind, whom she continued to support, though her own frame was sinking with agitation.

From the moment they emerged from the wood the utmost silence was observed by the mournful band; for they were aware, that in the stillness of the night, their voices could be heard for a considerable distance; and they were mindful of Elinor's advice, that, if possible, the death of his son, the sad confirmation of his worst fears, should be kept from the unhappy father as long as possible.

But her excellent counsel was doomed to be defeated; for, softly as they trod, the measured fall of the men's footsteps, as they bore the corpse, had reached his ear, and at the very moment they were passing under his window, he threw up the sash, and beheld the melancholy procession.

"It is he! he is dead!" he exclaimed, in a frantic tone. "Is it not so?"

The groans and sobs of Isabel, which could no longer be repressed, was the only answer, for though aware he could not now be kept in ignorance of Walter's fate, all shrunk from confirming it to him.

"We had better take the poor boy into the best parlour, Miss Elinor," observed Philip, who seemed to look up to her as the only one calm and collected enough to give directions. Elinor assented, candles were procured, and the pale, ghastly form was extended upon the long, oak dining table, that table at which he had often sat, the gayest of the festive party who were used to assemble round it. In a few moments, Mr. Copeland, the bereaved father, entered the room, and those who were before crowding eagerly round to examine the body, shrunk back in silence; even Isabel hushed her groans and exclamations, and Annie, who glided into the room after her father, hid her face in her hands, and stifled the gush of terror and grief.

Long and earnestly the old man gazed on the face of the corpse; he put his hand on the breast, as if to ascertain whether it heaved, and then, turning round his eyes, glanced with a wild stare from face to face, as he uttered, in a breathless whisper, "He is dead, yet there is no wound; he could not have killed himself."

Philip shook his head mournfully as the old man's eye rested on him.

"No, no, master," he replied, "there's been foul work, and I doubt more than one or two has had a hand in it; but there's been no fire-arms used, nor no sharp weapons neither. Here," and he parted the thick clustering curls that shaded the manly brow of the corpse, and showed a deep and frightful wound, "here is the blow that caused his death, and that has been given by a heavy bludgeon."

"Yes, and a bludgeon he had in his hand," exclaimed Isabel, "when I saw him."

Elinor started and thrilled with horror; she had noticed that Edward Hatherleigh had a large stick in his hand when she met him, and she now scarcely breathed, as she listened to Isabel's replies to the questions that her exclamations drew upon her.

It appeared, that after Annie and Elinor had left her, Isabel had remained sitting on the root of a tree, the thick branches of which threw a heavy shade over her, while the path for some distance was quite light. The sound of footsteps approaching alarmed her, and she sat still, and presently beheld a person whom she recognised as Edward Hatherleigh, coming towards her from a cross path in the wood.

"I did not speak," continued Isabel, "for I was aware that he did not see me, and I was struck by the strange wildness of his looks. I will confess the truth," she added, looking at Elinor, with an expression, half imploring pardon, and half defying; "I will acknowledge that I suspected Edward all along to have had a hand in the disappearance of my poor brother. It was this thought, then, that made me sit still, determined to watch him. He came up almost close to me—so close that I could hear him sigh repeatedly—and then he stood still, and seemed to be either listening or to be undetermined whether he should go on or not; at last he turned back into the same path he came by, and I glided from tree to tree, still keeping him in sight, until I unfortunately stumbled over something, and I suppose the noise alarmed him, for he instantly darted off, and before I could recover my feet he was out of sight. Disappointed in this," she continued, "I turned to go back to the spot where I had promised to wait for Elinor, but I missed the path, and came round by the Haunted Oak, and there I beheld——"

A burst of tears and sobs prevented her finishing the sentence.

"But you wasn't there, miss, when we came up," observed Philip, who had been intently listening to her account.

"No," she replied, "I had scarcely ascertained that it was my poor brother, and that he was, indeed, beyond all human help, when a dog, that I instantly knew to be Edward Hatherleigh's Brenda, jumped on me. I drove it hastily away, and almost immediately after heard a low whistle not far from me. The thought that, perhaps, the wretch who had been guilty of one murder would not hesitate at another to prevent discovery, suddenly darted into my mind. The dog still hovered about me; I expected every instant to see his master rush upon me; and at last, frantic with fear, I plunged into the thickest of the wood, on the opposite side of the path, thinking I could find my way round to meet Elinor, but I was so bewildered by fright, that I lost myself, and was wandering distractedly about, till the voices of Philip and the men guided me to them."

During this recital, Elinor had recovered the self-possession which had nearly deserted her at the first outset. She knew now the worst of the charge against Edward, and she was thankful it was no worse, though it must have been a great deal worse before it could have induced her to have suspected him of such a crime.

Without uttering a single word, Copeland had listened to his daughter's narrative, but when it was concluded, he turned his keen eye full on the countenance of Elinor, with an expression that made her tremble and cast hers to the ground.

"Truly, indeed, did she, who is now in her grave, prophesy," he observed, "that I should rue the day that made you one of my family. Yes, this is your gratitude; this is my reward for rescuing you from the beggary that would have been your portion. You have robbed me of my boy, my pride, my glory. Yes, you," he continued, his vehemence rising into frenzy, "it is you who have been the cause of this brutal, barbarous murder; but mark me, girl, I will pursue the villain to the world's end. He shall die on the scaffold, as sure as my poor Walter now lies there before me, and you shall witness it. Do not attempt to interrupt me," he exclaimed, dashing Philip away, as the latter hastily stepped forward, and was about to speak. "I swear it, by the blood of my murdered boy, I will have vengeance upon all who have had a share in the deed that has ruined my hopes for ever, and will send my grey hairs with sorrow to the grave. Isabel, Annie, stand off, why do you hang about her who has been the cause of your brother's death," he continued, as the two sisters (frightened at the fixed eye and attitude of Elinor, who stood like a marble statue, without seeming even to breathe during this denunciation from her uncle) both rushed to her, Annie throwing herself on her neck, while Isabel, seizing her cold and passive hands, and pressing them in hers, whispered—

"Forgive me; Oh! Elinor, forgive me, it is I who have caused all this, but do not look so dreadfully, and I will never again——"

A strange smile passed over Elinor's countenance, but that which the sympathy of her cousins failed to do, in recalling her to herself, Philip's plain warm-heartedness effected.

"Cheer up, Miss Elinor," he exclaimed, "and lean upon me. There's nobody can suffer but the guilty, and they must be *proved* guilty first. As to you, even if we were sure that this sad piece of business rose out of jealousy, as I s'ppose master and Miss Isabel mean to say it did—" ("Oh, no, not I," faintly exclaimed Isabel; but Phillip continued without heeding her), "why, they must be cruel indeed that could blame you for it; but I don't believe a word of it, indeed I don't, sir," turning to Mr. Copeland, "and I'll go over to Beechgrove myself as soon as it is day-light and fetch young Hatherleigh here, and I am very much mistaken if he don't give a satisfactory account of all that looks suspicious now."

" You will not leave this house without orders from me," observed Copeland, turning fiercely upon his free-spoken servant, whose long residence in the family, and faithful services, placed him rather on the footing of a humble friend than a mere menial. " If you do," added his master, " you will return here no more."

Philip's heart seemed to swell at this peremptory command; his lips opened to utter a remonstrance, but Elinor's expressive look withheld him.

" Leave to the Great Being who rules all hearts the vindication of Edward's innocence of this foul deed," she observed, with comparative calmness; " for myself I need none, for I know that even while my uncle uttered the words of accusation against me he was conscious that I did not deserve them."

Elinor quitted the room as she uttered the last sentence; but neither her words nor her departure seemed to be noticed by Mr. Copeland, who was again leaning over the breathless corpse of his son, and bewailing his loss.

CHAPTER II.

O, happiness !—In vain we chase
Thy shadow, and attempt to trace
 Its ever changing dances :
Like the horizon's line thou art
Seen on all sides—but sure to dart
 From every one's advances !—ANON.

SIXTEEN years previous to this period, at which those events took place which were narrated in the former chapter, Mr. Copeland purchased and took possession of the farm on which he now resided. Of his previous history, nothing was known by the persons among whom, it appeared, he intended to pass his future life. As he paid three thousand pounds down, however, for the house and lands, and, in forming his establishment, gave very convincing indications that he was as generous as he was rich, it was concluded by his neighbours that he was a person of great respectability, a supposition which was certainly rather confirmed than infringed by his conduct during his after residence at the Grove, as the farm was called.

Those, indeed, who knew Farmer Copeland most intimately, were disposed to think him much more calculating and cautious than he appeared to a superficial observer ; but on the whole he was generally liked and respected, and in money matters, though it was generally observed that he knew how to drive a hard bargain as well as most people, and was always alive to his own interest, yet he was considered highly honourable and conscientious.

Affairs had for the first three or four years after he settled at the Grove, appeared anything but flourishing with Mr. Copeland; crops had failed, he had a wife who was perpetually ailing, and who yet, every year, added to his family a son or a daughter; he lost too, considerably, by some speculations he made, yet there seemed no diminution in the substantial style of comfort in which the family lived, nor was it ever known that the farmer failed in an engagement, or was in the slightest degree less punctual in his payments. His resources, therefore, were judged to be much more considerable than he avowed; yet there were many who blamed his imprudence, when, for years after his taking possession of the Grove, he voluntarily added to his large and increasing family, by bringing from a distant part of the country the orphan daughter of his sister, to bring up with his own family.

Elinor Clare, the child in question, was at this time a pale, delicate, timid girl, about five years old. She had never known her parents, for her mother died in giving her birth, and her father, who was then abroad, was drowned on his voyage to England.

Elinor was therefore entrusted to the care of a woman, whom she was accustomed to call her " Granny," but whom she afterwards learned was only her nurse. The woman was fond of her, and kind to her, as far as she could be, but she was very old, and wretchedly poor; and poor Elinor's infancy was passed in loneliness and privation.

The cottage or rather hut, which her nurse inhabited, was situated half-a-mile distant from any other, and the poor creature's deafness, and other infirmities of old age, made her society seldom sought by her neighbours. The cottage stood on the edge of a bleak moor, and so far from any road or pathway, that days sometimes elapsed without a single person being seen by its inmates; and except that once a week the old woman took her with her to the next village to purchase the few necessaries that her limited means would command, poor little Elinor would have scarcely known that there was a world beyond the moor, or anybody in it, except her " Granny " and herself. The old woman's illness, and impending death, was the means of releasing the poor child from this miserable state. The wretched pay of three

ELINOR CLARE.

EDWARD ENTERED FROM THE ADJOINING ROOM.

shillings a week which she received for the support of little Elinor, was nearly all that poor old Granny Brown had latterly to depend upon; and when illness came upon her, the poor creature found it so insufficient for her wants, humble as they were, that she was compelled to apply to the parish for some assistance. This led to an investigation into the claims of the little orphan. Granny Brown was very deaf, also very stupid, and moreover, very unwilling to answer any interrogatories on the subject; but at last she was compelled to acknowledge that she knew nothing about the child, except that when it was apparently only a few weeks old, it had been placed with her by a man and a woman, who agreed to give her the sum before mentioned for its maintenance, had paid her a twelvemonth's stipend in advance, and had regularly transmitted the money due every quarter since. It would be tedious to relate by what means Farmer Copeland was at last traced out by the parish authorities; but so it was, and his reply to the letter addressed to him on the subject, was a sufficient sum enclosed to pay the little girl's expenses by the coach to the market town nearest his own residence.

With many tears the child quitted the poor old woman, who was now an inmate of the workhouse, to which she had been removed some days before. "Granny" was the only friend she had ever known, and cross and stupid as the old woman was, her little heart clung to her with all the energy of youthful affection which had never known another object.

Elinor's first interview with Farmer Copeland was not calculated to lessen her regret for poor "Granny;" the manner in which he grasped her thin little arm, and led her up to the candle to stare in her face, and then muttering, as he flung her from him with violence, created an impression of terror in her childish mind which was never effaced by his after kindness.

But, if Elinor's first feelings towards Mr. Copeland were not very conducive to her happiness, still less were those with which she was impressed towards his wife.

Mrs. Copeland, indeed, was by no means remarkable for kindness or sensibility towards any one beyond the circle of her own family; but towards the orphan Elinor, she seemed to feel an absolute aversion, from the instant she beheld her, and many were the bitter lessons of mortification and humiliation which the poor girl was doomed to suffer for the first four years of her residence at the Grove.

At the end of that time, Mrs. Copeland died, and Elinor's situation became considerably ameliorated.

The family of Farmer Copeland, at the time of his wife's decease, consisted of one son and two daughters. Walter and Isabel were twins, and three years older than Elinor, while Annie was as many years younger. The rest of the numerous family which Mrs. Copeland had brought her husband, preceded her to the grave; and it seemed as if the loss of so many had endeared to the father those who remained, for never, perhaps, was a parent fonder or prouder of his children than Farmer Copeland.

But Walter was his favourite; Walter, the manly, active, high-spirited and impetuous youth, was the idol and pride of his father, although the latter was by no means insensible to the merits and attractions of his daughters.

It is singular, but no less true, as those who have looked on the world with an observant eye will acknowledge, that many persons, who, towards the world in general, appear utterly destitute of all the kindly feelings—who are hard, insensible, and unfeeling to all the claims of man upon man—in the bosom of their own families appear to possess the keenest sensibilities.

So it was with Copeland.

In society, he was cold, callous, indifferent, insensible to social sympathy; at his own fire-side he was kind, sensitive, tremblingly sensitive to all that could affect his children. And they requited his love, for never were children more tenderly attached to a parent than they to him.

Among this family, Elinor Clare grew and flourished. Good air, plenty of substantial food, healthful exercise, and, above all, the affection and cheerful society of her playmates, soon effected a wonderful change in the person, as well as manners, of the poor little pinched, brow-beaten, and stinted child.

Yet, though she grew up beautiful, healthy, and comparatively cheerful, Elinor still retained a delicacy of appearance, a pensiveness of feature and manner, that forcibly distinguished her from her more robust and vivacious companions.

No one who ever marked Farmer Copeland's look or manner towards Elinor, could suspect him of regarding her with any undue share of affection; yet his conduct towards her was such as defied the world's opinion.

At the time of Mrs. Copeland's death, she was just nine years old. Up to this time, indeed, she had been but little regarded in the family, where her sole occupation had been waiting on the capricious fancies of the invalid.

Elinor was sent to the same school with Isabel, whom she was now taught and allowed to call her cousin, and for five years continued to share all the advantages afforded to the former.

At fourteen, Elinor returned home, if not perfectly educated and accomplished, at least with as much education as put her in the right road to obtain more—as many accomplishments, perhaps more, than were suitable to the station of life in which she appeared destined to move.

Walter, and, of course, Isabel, his twin sister, were at this period nearly seventeen, and never, perhaps, were brother and sister more strongly resembling each other or more affectionately united.

Walter thought none equal to his spirited sister, Isabel;

and Isabel, in her turn, was never weary of sounding the praises
of her handsome, lively, bold, and active brother; but in nothing
did the brother and sister more cordially agree than in their
fond devotion to their cousin Elinor, whom both looked upon as
the first of created beings.

Elinor, however, was nearly sixteen before she had made the
unwelcome discovery that there was a vast difference in the
species of affection with which she was regarded by the brother
and sister.

At the distance of half a mile from the Grove stood a large
ancient house secluded from the road, which passed at no great
distance in front of it, enclosed by high walls and a heavy iron
gate, and bearing the designation of the Nunnery, which, indeed,
it more resembled than a mere dwelling-house.

It had been so long neglected and suffered to fall into decay
that very few of the apartments were habitable; but in those
were established a widow lady named Hatherleigh, who, with
her only child, a son one year younger than Walter Copeland,
had become a resident there much about the same time that
Mr. Copeland took possession of the Grove.

There were at first many strange stories and dark hints circu-
lated in the limited circle of the neighbourhood respecting the
lady's motives for thus secluding herself from all society and
living in such a dismal mansion; but by degrees they died away,
and Mrs. Hatherleigh's kind, benevolent disposition, her mild,
unassuming manners, and unaffected piety, rendered her universally liked and respected.

Between Edward Hatherleigh and Walter Copeland an
intimacy commenced in their boyhood, which, as they grew
up, ripened into the most ardent friendship.

Yet no two could be more dissimilar than these almost
inseparable friends.

Walter—a fine, athletic, manly youth—was rash, impetuous,
and headstrong; he was the best cricketer, the most expert at
single-stick, the swiftest in the race, and the lightest in the
dance, for many miles around. Devoted to field sports, and his
dog and gun, or mounted on the hunter which his father indulged him with, he soon distinguished himself as an unerring
shot and fearless rider, while his open good-humour, and
companionable qualities, made him an ever welcome guest at
every table, from the squire's downward.

Edward Hatherleigh, on the contrary, though tall and finely
formed, it might be said elegant in person, was much less

strongly knit and robust than Walter; his clear olive complexion too, except when heated by exercise or under the influence of excitement, had little of the ruddy tint with which Walter's hale, honest countenance glowed, and he was much oftener seen, in boyhood, musing with folded arms and thoughtful countenance, or absorbed in the contents of some favourite volume, when mingling in any of the boisterous sports in which his companion delighted.

As the boys grew to manhood this contrast became more strongly to be marked, and it was with considerable superciliousness and self-satisfaction that old Copeland was accustomed to remark it.

He had little of what he called book-learning himself, and held it in contempt in others.

"Whatever will that boy be fit for?" he would remark, speaking of Edward. "Books, books, books, from morning till night. If his mother had it in her power to make a parson of him, it might do very well; but, as it is, I take it she had better put him to the plough-tail, or bind him 'prentice to som honest trade, than to let him be idly wasting his time in thi manner."

There was one whose fair cheek never failed to crimson at these or similar remarks—and that was Elinor Clare; yet were both she and Edward totally unconscious of the feeling that united them, until Walter Copeland thought proper to declare, "that the love he felt for his beautiful cousin was not merely the cold affection of a relative, but that his happiness depended on making her his wife."

Mr. Copeland seemed at first thunderstruck at this declaration; but a little reflection apparently reconciled him to it, and Walter received his father's permission to communicate to the favoured object of his affection the honour he intended to bestow upon her.

What was Walter's astonishment, his rage, his despair, when calmly, gently, but at the same time most firmly and decidedly, Elinor rejected him!

As a relative she told him he would ever possess her affection and esteem, but as a husband she could not think of him.

Eagerly Walter flew to confide to his friend Edward the disappointment of his hopes; but even while he spoke, a suspicion darted into his mind that he had discovered the cause of Elinor's coldness to him.

"You have betrayed me, Edward!" he exclaimed, as he

marked the sudden flush of the latter's cheek, and beheld the unequivocal expression of delight that sparkled in his full dark eye. "You love Elinor yourself, and you have treacherously supplanted me in her affections. Oh! yes, I see it all; fool that I have been, not to suspect it before."

For some moments Edward's agitated silence seemed to confirm the truth of this accusation, but at length he spoke, though the very first words he uttered were such as rendered Walter more frantic than ever; for they contained a confession of his love for Elinor, though he denied the imputation of treachery.

But Walter was not to be convinced; he was furious with rage and despair, and only for Edward's better and calmer temper, a scene of violence would have ensued.

This, however, Edward shunned by tearing himself away from the infuriated youth, and leaving him, as he hoped and said, "to recover his reason by reflecting on the injustice he had been guilty of."

This occurred about three months previous to the period at which our narrative commenced in the first chapter; Walter and Edward never met again as friends, nor was the latter ever allowed to enter Mr. Copeland's house, the old man stigmatising him, whenever he was mentioned, as "a sly, undermining, smooth-faced villain," taking credit to himself, at the same time, for having always had an instinctive dislike to him.

Poor Elinor, bitter were the sufferings she was compelled to endure between Walter's continued importunities, Isabel, his sister's, persuasions and entreaties, and the old man's hints and threats of the consequences, if she persevered in making his son miserable.

"And all for what," he would angrily demand, "for a proud, idle beggar who cannot support himself, much less provide for a wife and family."

To all Mr. Copeland's observations and vituperations, on this subject, Elinor invariably opposed but one defence—silence.

She well knew that nothing she could say in Edward's defence would avail ought with his accuser, and she wished not to add by a single word to the vexation and disappointment felt by her uncle, to whose bounty she owed everything.

But to Walter and Isabel, she was much less reserved, for she defended Edward with spirit from every charge they brought against him of treachery and deceit.

"Not one word Edward ever breathed of love to me," she observed; "but if he had ——"

" Yet you love him," interrupted Walter, vehemently. Elinor crimsoned to her very ears.

" This is cruel," she observed; " why am I to be thus questioned, or why am I to be less at liberty to——to—— ?"

" To make your own choice, I suppose you mean to say," observed Walter, in a fierce tone, finding she hesitated to finish the sentence, which would certainly have implied more than she was willing to confess. Her not contradicting the construction Walter put upon her silence, was, however, quite sufficient, and from that time the young man ceased to press his suit by words, contenting himself by keeping a jealous eye upon Elinor, that no communication should take place between her and Edward, towards whom his hatred appeared to be implacable.

In spite, however, of his vigilance, and that of Isabel, who entered with all the warmth and impetuosity of her kindred nature into her dear brother's disappointment and resentment, Elinor and Edward had met and had discussed their present situation and their future prospects (which, to say the truth, were dismal enough) more than once.

Edward Hatherleigh had grown up without scarcely knowing what was his real situation or what was the source of his mother's scanty income; for scanty it was, though her prudent management, and the pride of keeping up appearances, made her submit to many privations in her solitude, that were little known beyond its gloomy, comfortless walls; but when it came to his knowledge that Elinor's home was no longer a happy one, when the deprivation of her society became so irksome to him, that he could not pursue his usual studies, could neither eat, sleep, or in short, do anything but hover about the neighbourhood of the Grove, like a miser hovering about the spot that concealed his buried treasure—in short, when he discovered that he was deeply in love with Elinor, and had reason to believe that love returned, then it became of importance to him to understand rightly from his mother what he had to depend upon, and to consult with her on the possibility and propriety of his immediately entering into some pursuit which would add to their income, and enable him to make a home for a wife as well as a mother.

Poor Mrs. Hatherleigh had for a long time felt in her secret heart the propriety of the advice which her neighbour, Farmer Copeland, had always enforced upon her, whenever they had any casual conversation, to think seriously and set about getting her son into some way of earning his bread; but though an amiable, kind-hearted woman, Mrs. Hatherleigh was also a weak one; she still delayed the evil day, and when Edward himself pressed her on the subject, with tears deplored that he was so eager to leave her.

"But why must I leave you, dear mother?" was his frequent reply; "why are you so wedded to this place? Surely you could live as cheaply in a town, or if not quite as cheaply, what I should soon earn would more than suffice to make the difference."

Mrs. Hatherleigh could not make any reasonable reply to this, yet she still persisted in saying that she would not leave her present abode; and in short, every conference of this sort came to the same end in delaying what she considered the evil day.

Edward's love for Elinor opened to him a thousand new-born ideas, and he determined at once to come to an explanation with his mother on many subjects, which his kind feelings for her had induced him not to persevere in when they had been started, because they appeared painful to her.

Full of these thoughts, Edward, after a long solitary ramble, sought his mother; of the conversation that ensued, we are not now going to give a detail, but at the end of three hours Edward rushed from the house in a state of fearful excitement, nor was he again seen either at his home or in the vicinity of the Grove until that fatal evening, when Elinor, as has been related, encountered him in the wood.

Of the causes that led to Walter Copeland's disappearance not the most distant conjecture could be formed by his distracted family until after the discovery of his murder.

A few days previous a large party of gipsies had established themselves on a piece of ground on the edge of the wood, which had been from time immemorial the place of their encampment, though their visits had been both irregular and "few and far between."

It was now nearly five years since they had been seen in this part of the country, but Walter, who had little compassion for follies or frailties that differed so entirely from his own, could not be at all reconciled to the vicinity of these "free denizens of the earth."

"A set of idle scamping vagabonds," he exclaimed, when he announced to his father, at dinner-time, that he had accidentally discovered their camp, which they had pitched there the preceding evening. "I should have liked to have gone in among them, and scattered the whole crew. There are two or three among them as regular hang-dog-looking fellows as ever disgraced a gibbet; one, in particular, stood watching me with a scowl, as if he could read my thoughts, and knew that I hated such skulking drones. They had best not let me catch any of them on our grounds, for if I do, man, woman, or child, it will be the worst for them."

"Pooh, pooh, what is the use of being so hard on them?" observed Mr. Copeland, who was much more disposed to be lenient to the wanderers than his son. "I never yet found any harm from their being in the neighbourhood, and I don't believe half the tales told of them."

Walter, however, was not to be persuaded out of his prejudice; and a circumstance that happened a day or two after the arrival of the gipsies served strongly to confirm it.

A poor man who rented a cottage about two miles from the Grove, had, by a long course of industry and self-denial, accumulated upwards of fifty pounds, which he foolishly kept by him, and still more foolishly was in the habit of boasting of.

During his absence, the cottage was broken open, and the store ransacked, though hidden where no other eye but his own was ever likely to discover them.

Many years had elapsed since a robbery of any magnitude had taken place in that part of the country. It was then unequivocally traced to some of the members of the vagrant tribe, one of whom had been hanged, and the others transported, and it was now, therefore, with one voice declared by the whole community that there could be no doubt that poor Ralph Harrowby's money had been taken by some of the same gang.

None, however, were so loud and so positive on the subject as Walter Copeland; he was earnest in his advice that the magistrates should be applied to for a warrant to apprehend the whole of the vagabond tribe; and when it was pointed out that, as not a single article was taken but the gold, it was not likely it could be traced to their possession, he grew angry, and swore that the people around were a set of superstitious fools, who were afraid of the gipsies' supposed power, and contented to be robbed rather than run the risk of offending them.

There were some, however, and among them one or two best able to form a correct judgment on the subject, who strongly suspected that the person or persons who had robbed the cottager were those much more intimately acquainted with his circumstances and habits than these vagrants, who had been so short a time in the neighbourhood, and were not likely to have heard the wealth spoken of, which there were certainly no outward indications of in the humble cottage which the unfortunate Harrowby inhabited.

The poor man himself, who was always rather of weak intellect, was so totally overpowered by his loss that he became completely deranged, and was removed from his cottage to the parish workhouse early on the morning of the very day that Walter Copeland so unaccountably disappeared from his home.

During his breakfast, which he had taken, as was his custom, in the kitchen, with his father's men, Walter had been loud in his invectives against the wretches who had brought this misery on poor Ralph, who was universally liked for his quiet, sober habits, and when the meal was concluded, he had taken down his fowling-piece from where it hung over the chimney-place, and observing, that he should do no good if he tried to work, left the house without saying which way he intended to shape his course.

Walter was afterwards seen by one of the labourers making his way towards the gipsies' camp, but from that hour no tidings could be gained of him, until his lifeless body was discovered as related.

Suspicions had of course fallen upon the gipsies, and their huts were carefully searched, and the whole of the men, seven in number, closely examined, but their account of themselves appeared so clear and honest, and they showed so much readiness to assist in investigating the mysterious affair, that even the most prejudiced were compelled to think them innocent.

Never, however, had such a thought suggested itself to any one except Isabel, to implicate Edward Hatherleigh in the affair, until the moment of her disclosure.

So far, indeed, was any other of the family from suspecting that Edward could be guilty of so foul a deed, that more than once his absence had been mentioned with regret even by Mr. Copeland.

"If Ned Hatherleigh was here," he had observed once or twice, "I know he would trace him dead or alive, for, though they were not friends just now, I am sure Edward would forget all to serve poor Walter, and he has more thought and ingenuity than any of us."

When, however, Isabel frantically uttered her accusation, the whole horrible truth seemed to rush upon his mind at once, and the farmer, instead of pausing to weigh the probability of her being deceived, or even suggesting a single doubt, instantly decided that the young man was guilty, and blamed, as he said, his own stupidity, for not having suspected before what now appeared as clear as the sun at noon-day.

There was, however, more than one present when this declaration was made, who differed with Mr. Copeland on the subject, though they did not think proper at this moment to avow it; Philip, indeed, had boldly stepped forward in vindication of his young favourite, and, though compelled to silence by his master's peremptory order, while in the presence of the latter, he no sooner quitted it than with emphasis he uttered—

"The lad is no more guilty of the murder than I am; Edward Hatherleigh would not harm the meanest worm that crawls beneath his feet, much less would he take the life of one that he loved like a brother. No, no, he couldn't do it—he didn't do it."

"It will go hard with him whether or no, Philip," observed an elderly female, who had, since Mrs. Copeland's death, acted as housekeeper to the family, and at this moment entered the kitchen to give orders. "I trow there's been many a one hung upon less evidence than there seems against Edward Hatherleigh."

Philip started. It was not that his faith in his young friend's innocence was shaken by this observation, but the extent of Edward's danger seemed for the first time to strike him, and most heartily did he wish that he could see the youth, if only for a few minutes, to warn him of the charge against him, and prepare him to meet it, as he hoped he could, with immediate refutation.

His master's denunciation, however, checked Philip's friendly intention, and he was compelled to confine his sympathy to a repetition of good wishes, and the reiterated expression of his perfect belief in Edward's innocence.

CHAPTER III.

Tho' dews upon her forehead rise,
No tears are in her large wild eyes,
She starts, some strange and sudden thought,
The crimson to her cheek has brought;
Her bitten lip is yet more white,
Her blue eye fills with eager light;
Some wish, on which she dare not brood,
Has risen on her feverish mood!
Some thoughts there are, that may not brook
Upon their own resolve to look;
The grief which acts is earlier borne,
Than that which weeps—the loved and lorn;
And urged by love, and love's despair,
What is there woman will not dare?—L. E. L.

THE spirit which had sustained Elinor while in the presence of her unjust and prejudiced relative, vanished the moment she found herself alone, and in the agony of horror, misery, and despair, she threw herself on her bed, and stifled her convulsive sobbings in the pillow.

This paroxysm, however, soon passed away.

Elinor had been tutored by necessity to subdue the expression of her feelings, and soon began to review with comparative calmness the awful and extraordinary events in which she had been engaged, and to endeavour to form something like a rational conclusion as to their causes and consequences   Alas! the more she reflected, the more inexplicable appeared the whole affair.

That Edward could be guilty, not for a moment would she admit; yet how could she interpret, otherwise than as a confession of guilt, what he had said to her in the wood?

His wild looks too, his haste to be gone, his fear of discovery, all—all seemed fatally to corroborate the suspicion.   The whole world would have condemned him on such proofs, but Elinor did not.

"He is innocent; with my life I would answer for his innocence," she perpetually repeated to herself; "he could explain, I am sure he could, all that now appears against him."

A thought suddenly darted into Elinor's mind, and in an instant she resolved to act upon it.

"I can reach the Nunnery," she thought to herself, "before

daylight; he has certainly returned home, and I can easily rouse him, even if he has gone to rest, and when I tell him the construction that has been put on his conduct, he cannot then refuse to explain."

A thousand other reasons suggested themselves to Elinor, while she hastily prepared for her expedition, to reconcile her to its seeming impropriety.

Her being previously prepared for it would in some measure disarm the shock Mrs. Hatherleigh would receive from such an accusation against her son. They would both, too (mother and son), be better enabled to refute the charge, by being aware of it beforehand, and in no way could her interference do harm to any individual.

There was little difficulty in Elinor's getting out of the house unobserved, for the recent awful discovery still occupied the attention of the whole household.

She paused and shuddered as she reached the parlour-door, and heard the suppressed sobs of the two girls, and the deep groans of the bereaved father, who were still mourning over the lifeless corpse, but her purpose admitted of no delay, and she hurried forward.

It was not until she had entered the fatal wood, across one corner of which lay the nearest path to the habitation of Edward Hatherleigh, that a thought of personal danger entered Elinor's mind; but the moon was now gone down, the wind was sighing among the branches, and scarcely would the path have been discernible to any one to whom it was less familiar than she, who now with trembling steps glided along it, shrinking even from the beating of her own heart, and casting around her, into the deep obscurity, looks of the most trembling scrutiny and alarm.

All, however, was silent as the grave, and Elinor stopped not even to take breath, till she stood before the high, gloomy and dilapidated wall of the mansion she sought.

Not a ray of light was visible in any of the windows, nor would any one not previously aware of the fact, have suspected from the outward appearance of the place that it was inhabited; but Elinor was too well acquainted with the place to be deceived by these appearances, and after a moment's pause to recover herself, she climbed a part of the wall which had fallen down, so as to afford her an easy means of gaining admission, and crossing the court-yard, proceeded to the back of the house, where were situated the only habitable apartments.

Light as her footsteps were, however, they reached the ears of Edward's spaniel, who came running to meet her; and convinced from this, both that he was at home and had not retired to rest, she proceeded with more confidence towards the room which they had made a kitchen, and from the windows of which she could discern a faint light streaming through the chinks which time had made in the heavy shutters.

For an instant Elinor paused to reflect how she should announce her being there at such a strange time of night; and naturally anxious to ascertain whether Mrs. Hatherleigh was still up, a circumstance which she felt would save her much embarrassment, or whether Edward was there alone, she applied her eye to one of the before-named chinks, which was of sufficient width to enable her to command the whole of the apartment within.

Mrs. Hatherleigh was there, and Edward was there; so far all was right, but Elinor recoiled from the window in utter consternation, at the discovery that a third person was present, and that one a stranger.

Never since she and her cousins were first admitted within the walls of Mrs. Hatherleigh's gloomy habitation had she known of any other person being allowed that privilege.

The house, or rather the ruin, for it was little better, had been from time immemorial the property of an ancient and distinguished family, the last heir of which had totally neglected it, and suffered it to fall into its present state of decay.

It was said, indeed, that many years had elapsed since he had quitted England, and had never been heard of since; but one thing was certain, that no one had demanded rent of Mrs. Hatherleigh since she resided there, and the distance and reserve she preserved towards the people around her prevented her being ever intruded upon under the pretext of friendly visiting.

It was, therefore, an event so utterly unlooked for that she should behold a stranger seated by their domestic hearth, that it was of itself sufficiently startling, but when to this was added the unreasonable time of night, almost, indeed, verging upon morning, and the appearance of the stranger, so inconsistent with the almost fastidious refinement both of the manners and habits of the lady of the mansion, Elinor was indeed surprised and puzzled.

The person who had given rise to these sensations, was a tall, athletic man, whose deep olive complexion, raven locks hanging in wild profusion, and piercing black eyes, would have induced any one to pronounce him a native of a warmer climate than that he now inhabited.

His features were particularly handsome, and his whole figure, in spite of the meanness of his dress, imposing; but there was a look, as he raised his eyes to reply to some observation of Mrs. Hatherleigh's—who sat opposite to him, and consequently with her back to the window, so as to conceal her countenance from Elinor—that made the latter shudder, so strongly was it expressive of vindictiveness and ferocity. The lines, too, around his mouth were indicative of craft and cunning, and altogether his appearance was so repulsive as, for a few minutes, to cause her to waver in her intention of making known to them her vicinity.

From the face of this stranger, Elinor's eyes, when she returned to the investigation, wandered to that of Edward, who was sitting between his mother and the former, his elbow resting on a small round table, and his cheek resting on his hand, as if in deep abstraction from the scene around him.

Elinor could only see his profile, yet she was instantly struck with the resemblance between the lineaments, though not the expression, of the stranger and him. The same high, expanded forehead, the Roman nose, short upper lip, and finely-cut mouth and chin. In the expression alone lay the difference, but that difference was so great, that had Elinor seen them apart, it would never have entered her mind that there was a resemblance between them.

Doubtful how to act, and in her surprise and astonishment, for a moment, forgetting the urgency of her errand, the trembling girl stood with her eyes intently fixed on this mysterious being, until aroused by the tones of his deep voice, as, with a look of angry reproach, he addressed some observation to Edward, and starting on his feet pointed to the old-fashioned clock, which was ticking in one corner of the kitchen.

What it was he said Elinor could not hear, but the effect seemed to be to plunge Mrs. Hatherleigh in the deepest grief, while Edward's countenance, as his mother threw herself into his arms, expressed equal sorrow and anger.

The stranger had, in the meantime, thrown on his outer covering, a large loose coat, reaching to his feet, and confined round the waist by a broad belt, while a broad-brimmed hat drawn low over his brows, so as entirely to shade his features, completed the singularity of his appearance.

Elinor felt that her mission must no longer be delayed, for it was evident that Edward was preparing to accompany this strange-looking being, and that it would be no temporary absence was plain, by Mrs. Hatherleigh's unwillingness to part with him.

All the consequences of his leaving home at this critical moment instantly rushed into her mind.

"They will say that he has fled from justice," she murmured to herself, as she laid her hand on the latch of the door.

The fierce bark of a large dog, which, it appeared, had been until then lying quietly on the mat just within the door, betrayed instantly the approach of some one to those in the room.

Elinor retreated a few paces in alarm, and then heard the voice of the stranger speaking to the dog, whose barking was now altered into a low growl.

Terrified lest the door should be opened, and the dog let loose before they knew that she was there, Elinor now called loudly upon Edward and Mrs. Hatherleigh.

"I must see you directly; pray secure that dog and let me in. It is Elinor Clare," she exclaimed.

There was a momentary bustle, the light from the candle disappeared, the dog's growls were silenced, and the door was cautiously opened by Mrs. Hatherleigh, who looked doubtfully out into the darkness, and then catching a glimpse of Elinor's white dress, which was only partially concealed by the cloak she had thrown over her, she exclaimed—

"It is indeed her! Elinor, in the name of Heaven, what can have brought you here at this hour?"

It was some moments before Elinor could utter a word; but her eyes darted eagerly round the kitchen, now lighted only by the fire.

"I must see Edward," she at length articulated, having ascertained that he had retreated, together with the stranger.

"Good God! what is the meaning of this?" demanded Mrs. Hatherleigh. "What new misfortune threatens me?"

Elinor entered the kitchen, having by this time ascertained that the dog, whose fierce bayings had so alarmed her, had disappeared with his master.

"This is no time for dissimulation," she observed, sinking into a chair. "Edward, I know, is within hearing, and I must see him."

Before Mrs. Hatherleigh could frame a reply, Edward entered from the adjoining room.

ELINOR CLARE.

HE SEIZED HER ARM WITH A GRASP THAT PAINED HER.

Elinor's eyes eagerly scanned his countenance, but there was no expression there beyond extreme surprise and anxiety, as his eyes dwelt on her agitated countenance.

"He is innocent," again she mentally ejaculated. "Yes, I am right, he is innocent."

In as few words as possible, Elinor now proceeded to demand of Edward if he was aware of the dreadful fate that had befallen Walter Copeland.

Edward's looks betrayed the most unequivocal surprise, while Mrs. Hatherleigh remarked:

"Alas! how selfish have mine own sorrows made me. I had forgotten until now, Edward, that Walter has been missing from his home, and that——"

"He has been found," interrupted Elinor in a solemn tone, "found murdered, and within a hundred yards, Edward, of the spot where I saw and spoke to you to-night."

For some moments Edward remained motionless, gazing into Elinor's face, and yet as if his thoughts were totally abstracted from the present scene.

"Murdered!" he at length repeated, with a wild and shuddering glance around him, as if fearing that the words he uttered should be heard beyond the confines of the room. "Walter murdered!" he again repeated, "who could have done the deed? He, who had not an enemy in the world."

"There are those who are cruel enough to say that Edward Hatherleigh was his enemy," observed Elinor, shrouding her face with her hands.

"But you do not believe it, you have never believed it," exclaimed Edward impetuously, seizing both her hands, while Mrs. Hatherleigh, with a loud groan of anguish that showed how fully she comprehended all that Elinor had to communicate, sank into a seat, and remained with clasped hands, and looks of utter despair, awaiting the remainder of this heartrending communication.

"Had I believed so, Edward," returned Elinor, struggling to speak with calmness, "you would not have beheld me here. But I am aware how often innocence is the victim of appearances, and I am come to put you on your guard—to tell you how singularly your appearance in the wood to-night, so near the spot where my poor cousin was almost immediately after found——"

"But there were none who saw me but you, Elinor," he interrupted, "and you surely——"

"Isabel beheld you," she replied, with emphasis, "and even before she saw you there, she declares her suspicions had lighted on you as the cause of her brother's disappearance."

"Cruel, unjust, unfeeling girl," exclaimed Edward, while his before pale countenance lighted up with the deep crimson of strong resentment; "and has she dared then openly to charge me with the commission of this horrble crime?" he demanded.

"She has," returned the agitated yet now gratified Elinor.

"And Mr. Copeland—Annie?" he hastily demanded.

"I have come over here, Edward, to warn you," she replied, "that in a few hours you will be called on publicly to free yourself from this horrible suspicion, by declaring the cause of your absence from home for some time past, and your motives not only for being in the wood at such an unreasonable hour, but also not merely avoiding, but flying from Isabel. These are the questions your enemies will put, Edward," she hastily added, observing the flash of resentment that kindled in his eyes. "For myself," she continued, "I rely so firmly on my own conviction that you are utterly incapable of harbouring even a thought of malice against——"

"You have but done me justice, Elinor," he articulated in broken accents. "Heaven is my witness that Walter was as dear to me as a brother, and that were it in my power, by any sacrifice, to bring to justice his inhuman murderer, I here swear——"

A sound, which evidently proceeded from the adjoining apartment, interrupted this sentence.

Elinor cast her eyes fearfully towards the door, expecting to see the stranger, whose appearance had impressed her with so much terror, enter; but the room still remained closed, and Edward, as if suddenly recalled to some reflections, even more painful than those which she had pressed upon his attention, stood apparently doubtful whether he ought not to obey that which was evidently intended as a signal to him.

Mrs. Hatherleigh, in the meantime, had raised her head from the table, on which she let it drop, in unresisting agony, as she comprehended the full purport of Elinor's mission, and Edward's wild wandering glance now rested on her countenance.

"Mother, can you wish me to go with such a charge hanging over my head?" he demanded, with intense earnestness. "Is there any one," he continued, raising his voice, "who professes to feel any interest in me, who can wish me to quit this spot, until I have cleared myself from this foul suspicion?"

"And how can you do it?" demanded the stranger, throwing open the door, and advancing into the room without seeming to heed the presence of Elinor.

Mrs. Hatherleigh shrieked and hid her face with her hands; while Edward, less occupied as it appeared at that moment, with his own individual interest than that of others, looked anxiously at Elinor, as if to discover what effect the stranger's appearance had upon her.

"Rash boy," continued the stranger, "reflect for a moment on the consequences of what you propose. Imagine that you remain here to meet the charge of which you say you are innocent——"

"Say!" repeated Edward, furiously, "of which I am innocent, of which you know me to be innocent."

"But will my testimony avail you aught?" demanded the stranger, with a bitter sneer. "Would you wish to remain here, that I may in the court of justice testify that——"

"Oh! no, no, no," interrupted Edward, in a despairing tone, "not even," he added, while his whole frame shook with agitation, and his voice sunk to a scarcely audible whisper—"not even if I were sure of suffering the penalty of a crime, of which my soul revolts from the bare contemplation."

For a moment, the stranger's countenance seemed to undergo a complete revolution. The fierce and bitter expression which had deformed his fine features vanished; his eyes dwelt on Edward's face with a look of tenderness, and his lower lip quivered with strong emotion; but the next instant, he seemed as if stung with some sudden recollection, he smiled as in disdain of his own weakness, and in a tone of coldness observed—

"This is not a time, young man, to yield to romantic feelings. You know as well as I do, that it will be impossible for you to give such proofs of innocence as will acquit you in the eyes of those who have already adjudged you guilty. It is very evident," he continued, glancing at Elinor, "that this young woman, who appears to be truly your friend, is well convinced of the danger you would run by remaining here; she would not have exposed herself to so much hazard and inconvenience to warn you of it."

"I came to prepare him for the charge, that he might disprove it, not fly from it," observed Elinor, firmly yet timidly.

"And he knows he cannot disprove it," returned the stranger, in a tone of deep sarcasm, "without, indeed, he resolves to commit a crime of even deeper dye."

Elinor's agonised look sought in Edward's countenance an explanation of this horrible assertion, but he only turned from her with a gesture that said it was but too true; and then in a low tone addressed some words to his mother.

"If you do not wish me to expire at your feet, Edward," she replied, "you will fly while there is time. Remember the consequences that may ensue, not only to yourself, but——"

The glance which she directed towards the stranger, spoke more significantly than words could have done her meaning.

"There is no time to devote to debate longer on this subject," observed the latter, moving towards the door; "at all events I go."

Edward's features betrayed the agony he suffered from the conflict in his bosom; but at the instant the stranger was leaving the house he decided on the course he should pursue.

" Elinor," he exclaimed, " I must go, though it should brand me for ever with the name of murderer.   You know me innocent, continue to believe me so, and the rest I can bear.   Farewell."

He rushed out of the house, and was gone before Elinor could sufficiently recover from her astonishment to utter a word of remonstrance.

The grief in which Mrs. Hatherleigh appeared to be plunged prevented the former from uttering that which her heart dictated. She would have asked her, if there could be any circumstances paramount to the duty Edward owed to himself, of vindicating his character from the dreadful imputation that would hencefor- ward rest upon it ; she would have prayed her, if she had the power, to have recalled him before it was too late ; but the un- happy woman's expressions of despair, though she understood not their cause, disarmed her, and Elinor remained silent.

The bright rays of the rising sun eclipsing the feeble light within, reminded the latter that unless she quickly returned to the Grove, her absence would be discovered, and she arose to depart.

" Would that I could—that I dare explain to you, Elinor, what I am conscious must appear to you most incomprehensible," observed Mrs. Hatherleigh, also rising ; " but I cannot, and I must trust to your kind good heart not to reveal what you hav witnessed here."

" It is not my wish that it should be known that I have been here to-night," returned Elinor ; " of course, therefore, you secret is safe with me."

" But if you are questioned ?" returned Mrs. Hatherleigh, with extreme anxiety.

" There is no probability of that," returned Elinor, with some- what of disdain in her manner at the pertinacity of her companion ; " but of this be assured," she added, after a moment's silence " that as far as depends with me your secret is safe."

" Heaven bless you, Elinor," exclaimed Mrs. Hatherleigh, as she unclosed the door to let the former pass out.   " Oh, if you knew with what horrible fears and presentiments my heart is torn."

Elinor did not reply ; she could not, indeed, command her voice to speak, or she would have said, that it was impossible any one could feel more wretched, more utterly despairing than she did ; but she suppressed the expression of these feelings, and pressing the hand of Mrs. Hatherleigh in silence, hastened to regain the path to the Grove.

CHAPTER IV.

I've seen,
Hours dreadful, things strange; but this sore night
Hath trifled former knowings.—MACBETH.

On her smooth brow her chesnut hair
Descends, and makes a twilight there;
As softly shadowed and as sweet,
As that when light and darkness meet
On that pure tablet, grief hath laid
Her hand, but not one furrow made;
On that unsullied page as yet,
No impress of her seal is set.
From those rich tresses to the view
That dark eye takes a darker hue.—ANON.

THE shutters were still closed when Elinor reached the farm, although the sun was now above the horizon, but the hope she indulged at seeing this of being enabled to reach her own room, was frustrated; for, at the very moment she entered the passage, the door of the parlour which fronted her was opened by Annie, who had a candle in her hand, and at the same instant Mr. Copeland raised his head from the table on which he had been resting it, close to that of the corpse, and his eyes and Elinor's met.

He started up, and with a look of fury advanced towards her.

"Where have you been?" he sternly exclaimed, seizing her arm with a grasp so firm as to make her recoil with pain—"but I need not ask you," he continued, throwing her from him with violence; "of course you have been to warn your paramour that his guilt is discovered. You *have*. Well, then, now mark me. If through your means he has escaped from justice, so sure will I charge you as his accomplice. Do you know the penalty you have incurred? Answer me, girl: are you aware of the penalty you have incurred? Do you know that for assisting a murderer to escape, you may be committed to prison, and tried, aye, and you shall be, by——"

"Oh! father, dear father, do not speak so harshly to her." exclaimed Isabel, laying hold of the infuriated old man, while Annie, terrified at his looks, tried to draw Elinor from his grasp.

The farmer, however, resisted both their efforts.

"Answer me," he repeated with vehemence. "Do you know what you have been doing?"

"I know that if Edward Hatherleigh were what you say, sir," replied the trembling girl, "I should be——"

"If, if, if," he repeated furiously. "Come here," and he dragged her to the side of the corpse, which still lay in the same state and position in which it had been first placed. "If!" he again ejaculated, with emphasis, "look there, and tell me, tell me, as you value your salvation, was there a creature in the world who was an enemy to that poor boy?—was there one who could have had the slightest motive to commit the barbarous deed, but the villain, who thought, in getting rid of him, he was removing the only impediment between himself and you?"

"Edward Hatherleigh never regarded Walter Copeland in that light, sir," returned Elinor, summoning all her spirit to her aid, though her tremulous voice and shaking limbs betrayed the violence of her agitation. "He knew otherwise," she continued, gaining courage from his silence, "for he knew well, that had there been no such person in existence as Edward Hatherleigh, I should never have looked upon Walter Copeland with any other feelings than those I have entertained towards him. As a dear brother I regarded him, as a dear brother I lament his loss."

She bowed her head upon the pale face of the corpse as she spoke, and burst into tears; the first she had shed since the awful discovery had frozen their source.

For some moments Mr. Copeland stood regarding her in silence. It seemed as if, for the first time, he was struck with his own injustice towards her, and was revolving in his mind how he should bring about a reconciliation between them. Suddenly, however, a new thought seemed to strike him.

"If he is innocent," he observed, looking suspiciously at her, as she raised her head, and with her eyes still fixed on the pallid face of the corpe, essayed to wipe away her tears, "he will fearlessly face the charge. Is he prepared to do so, or will he not profit by your intelligence to escape? Answer me," he continued, raising his voice, as he beheld the change that passed over her countenance at this observation. "Do you not know that he has already fled?"

"I know that circumstances have compelled Edward to absent himself for some time," she faltered, "but I do most solemnly affirm, that I believe this unhappy event has nothing to do with it, and that his departure was decided upon long before he knew even of the dreadful death of his poor friend." Elinor's eyes, which had been raised to his with a look of perfect ingenuousness as she uttered this, dropped to the ground as she observed the expression of withering scorn and incredulity which stole over the old man's countenance at her admission that Edward was gone.

"I see full well," he observed, after a few moments' silence, "that it is useless for me to hope to hear the truth from your lips. We shall see, however, what account you will give to the jury; only this I warn you, that you need expect no favour from me, if you continue to shield the villain who has robbed me of my poor boy—my only hope—my pride."

Too sincerely did Elinor sympathise in the anguish which wrung the unhappy parent's breast, to offer to interrupt the ebullition which for many minutes rendered him insensible to everything but the sad spectacle before him.

From the moment Elinor acknowledged that Edward was gone, Isabel's manner towards her had altered; her dark eyes seemed to flash fire, and she angrily pushed her sister Annie away, who was evidently trying to sooth and remonstrate with her.

"Do not tell me," she exclaimed with vehemence, in answer to some suggestion of the latter, "if she did not herself know that he is guilty, she would have been the first to have persuaded him manfully to meet the charge. No, she is guilty as he is."

"You are in the right there, Isabel," Elinor gently observed, "if Edward is guilty, then am I so; but the time will come when you will look back with shame and sorrow at these unjustifiable assertions."

She moved towards the door as she concluded the sentence, but Mr. Copeland hastily stepped forward, and prevented her leaving the room.

"I will take care," he observed, "at any rate, that you do not give me the slip; you leave not my sight until it is decided one way or the other."

Elinor, with as much calmness as she could command, seated herself: she would have given the world to have been alone and free to have given vent to the emotions that swelled her bosom to suffocation, but she would not offer the slightest resistance to Mr. Copeland's mandate, and leaning her head on her hand, she tried to conceal her feelings from all present.

A long and painful silence succeeded. Mr. Copeland had

resumed his despairing contemplation of the features of his departed son; Isabel, seated on a couch opposite to Elinor, kept her eyes fixed on the face of the latter, with an expression of mingled doubt, sorrow, and resentment; and Annie, who had crept unconsciously as it seemed towards Elinor, stood hesitating and watching the looks of her father and sister, as if fearful of offending them by her sympathy with her beloved cousin.

"It is daylight," at length observed Mr. Copeland, raising his eyes to where the straggling sunbeam had found its way through an aperture of the closed shutters, "we must lose no longer time. Isabel, you and your sister had better go to your room, and try to rest, if it be only for an hour or two, I shall not be longer absent; and Dorcas and the women will keep watch here; I can safely trust them now it is daylight. Nay, I will have no objections," he continued, seeing Isabel about to speak, " you will be ill if you do not get some sleep; and God knows, you will have need of all your strength now, both of body and mind."

Isabel rose reluctantly, and Annie with still more evident hesitation followed her example; both of them, as if influenced by the same thoughts, turned their eyes from their father to Elinor.

" I understand you," he observed, nodding his head significantly. " I will take care of that—send Dorcas in."

The two girls quitted the room. Annie, who lingered last, contrived, as her sister bent over the corpse, to impress a passing kiss upon its cold lips, to slide her hand into her cousin's, and by a warm pressure assure her of her sympathy; and this simple expression caused the tears, which extreme anguish had suppressed, to stream in torrents from the eyes of poor Elinor.

" You will go to your room for the present," observed Mr. Copeland, turning to her, " and I shall take the liberty of securing your staying there, by turning the key upon you; and now for your own sake, unworthy as you are, let me give you one caution, and that is, on the inquest where you will be called as a witness, be careful that you tell the truth, and nothing but the truth. You are little aware of the awful situation you stand in, if it should be discovered that you make any attempt to screen the murderer."

" I cannot, sir, be in any danger of doing so," returned Elinor, " for I again repeat I know not the murderer. He whom you call so is innocent."

" Let him prove himself so, then," returned the old man.
" He will soon have others to judge him than me ; those who
will not be either impartial or unjust."

The entrance of the old housekeeper, Dorcas, prevented his
proceeding, and having given his directions to her and another
female servant, to remain in the room with the corpse, until his
return from the magistrates, whose assistance he meant to seek
to detect the murderer, he followed Elinor, who had, in obedience to his signal, gone up stairs, and repeating to her that
his absence would not be long, locked the door upon her.

For a little while Elinor thought nothing of this temporary
imprisonment; she was too glad to be alone—to be able,
without interruption, to review all that had passed on that
eventful evening, and endeavour to form some rational conclusion as to the probable consequences of the impending inquiry
into the circumstances of Walter's awful death ; but when hour
after hour passed away without her hearing any indication of
Mr. Copeland's return, or at least, of his coming to release her,
she felt a cold damp strike to her heart at the reflection that
this was, perhaps, but the prelude to a far more rigorous imprisonment, if Mr. Copeland should put his threats in execution, and charge her with being accessory to the escape of the
supposed murderer.

" And he would be but too glad to get rid of one whom he
has always hated," she despairingly ejaculated. " And yet,
why should he hate me ?   It cannot be merely because I am
poor, for though he loves money, I sometimes think, overmuch,
yet he has always been rather liberal to me than otherwise."

The thought brought with it a train of reflections, which for
a short time banished the recollection of the immediate cause
of her uneasiness. " What could have induced Mr. Copeland
to undertake a charge which was evidently so distasteful to
him, since he certainly could not have been compelled to do
so ?" Then again—" Why did he so scrupulously interdict her
asking any questions respecting her parents ? With regard to
other members of his family he showed no reluctance to speak."
Of his father he often told anecdotes. His mother's careful
and industrious habits were frequently expatiated upon to his
daughters, as guides for their conduct. His brother, too, who
had died under peculiarly distressing circumstances, was often
the subject of his conversation. It could not, therefore, be
supposed that any excess of sensibility deterred him from
speaking of his sister (Elinor's mother), or her husband, and

yet he did shrink from the subject, and except the bare facts, that her father had died at sea, and her mother in giving her birth, leaving no inheritance but her poverty and her sorrows behind, the poor girl knew nothing of those to whom she owed her birth.

" There is some mystery," she had often said to herself, " some strange mystery in Mr. Copeland's shunning to speak of my poor father and mother. Why, too, does he always object to my calling him uncle, if he is my uncle?" At the present moment these thoughts recurred with added force, for she felt that, if, as she had always suspected, there were hidden reasons why Mr. Copeland disliked her, he would now eagerly seize upon the means of getting rid of her without blame to himself.

Poor Elinor! she knew little of the world, how should she, reared and educated as she had been; yet the little she did know, was sufficient to make her tremble at being thrown upon its mercy.

That she could not be found guilty when she was innocent, she was *quite* sure; and that she was innocent of anything resembling the crime she was charged with, she was equally certain. Of the final consequences, therefore, of any investigation of her conduct, she felt no fear; but of its effects, as alienating her from those to whom she had been attached from her childhood with all the fervour of affection which had never known any other objects, she could as little doubt. How could she ever bring herself to enter again the doors of one who could bring such a charge against her, or how could he ever bear to receive as an inmate one towards whom he had harboured such a suspicion?

Such were the thoughts which occupied and harrassed the mind of the unhappy Elinor, until the sound of strange voices, and an unusal bustle in the room beneath her, recalled her to what was more immediately passing.

The voice of Annie outside the door at this moment met her ear.

" Elinor, dear Elinor, do not be frightened," said the affectionate and kind-hearted girl. " all will be right. I am sure it will be. Do be calm, pray do. Oh, how I wish I could unlock the door! Even Isabel is hurt, and vexed beyond description, to think that my father should treak you so. We did not know it till just now; but he will be home directly, and then ——"

The sound of Mr. Copeland's voice, speaking to some one as

he entered the house, interrupted her, and Annie hastened down stairs.

A considerable time elapsed, however, before any further notice was taken of Elinor, and then the room door was opened by Dorcas, who informed her that she must prepare herself to go before the jury, as the coroner was every minute expected, he having been most opportunely in the neighbourhood when Mr. Copeland applied to the magistrate, and had immediately given the necessary orders for the inquest.

"And do'ee, Miss Ellen," observed the old woman, in a persuasive tone, "do'ee make up thee mind to tell all that'ee knows about it, for only consider, if young Ned Hatherleigh be such a barbarous monster, it isn't fit that you or I, or anybody should screen him from his rightful punishment; and if so be as he did not do the deed, you know —— They do say there be a warrant out against him a'ready," she continued, dropping her voice as if communicating a secret she had been forbidden to speak of, "and a whole posse of 'em are gone over to the Nunnery to take him. I'm sure I pities the poor mother to my very heart, poor creter; but, then, you know, as master always has said, what could she expect bringing a lad up in such idleness?"

The bright colour which had for many hours previous deserted Elinor's fair cheeks, rushed into them again at this observation. Frequently had she, indeed, heard it made from the lips of Mr. Copeland himself, and never without feeling strongly tempted to confute the assertion that Edward ever deserved to be called idle, but to one so prejudiced and ignorant as her present companion, she felt no disposition to enter into any vindication of him, hurt as she was at hearing him thus unequivocally condemned.

"Tell, Mr. Copeland I shall be ready whenever I am called upon, Dorcas," she mildly remarked, turning away from the old woman, and standing at the window, in hopes she would take the hint to go.

Dorcas, however, still lingered.

"I beg your pardon, Miss Ellen," she at last observed, "master told me I wasn't to lose sight of you for a minute 'till you're called for; now, you see, it's very ill-convenient for me to be staying up here and leaving everything at sixes and sevens down stairs, so if you wouldn't mind sitting in the kitchen a bit, it will be ——"

"It is all the same to me, Dorcas," returned Elinor, who

though she felt indignant at the humiliation she was exposed to by Mr. Copeland's orders, still retained her usual gentleness towards the old woman.

"Ah, you're always considerate, I will say," observed Dorcas, leading the way with alacrity down stairs. "We won't go past the parlours," she continued, looking very sagacious, "for there's such a lot of 'em there, some of 'em in the best parlour with the poor dear murdered boy, and the rest in the common parlour, eatin' and drinkin' as if it was a feast they'd come to, instead of such a molloncholy thing."

Elinor, without any remark, followed her round the backway, which led by a circuitous route past the stables to the kitchen, but she quickly repented that she had done so, and would have retreated, had not Dorcas held her fast by the arm, as a group of men at that instant came up, among whom she instantly recognised the constable of the village, and, therefore, readily guessed they had been on an errand to the residence of Mrs. Hatherleigh, which Dorcas had spoken of.

The first words uttered by the latter confirmed this supposition.

"Ah! what 'ee haven't cought him, then?" she eagerly exclaimed, without seeming to notice Elinor's extreme agitation, and evidently only desirous to satisfy her own curiosity, without regard to the feelings of her charge, or indeed any thought about her (Elinor) except the determination to obey her master's commands by not for a minute losing sight of her.

"No, we haven't caught him, indeed," returned the man to whom Dorcas addressed her question; "but it's no more than we expected, after what we heard from poor Farmer Copeland." His eye, turned on Elinor, gave full meaning to his speech, and before Dorcas could throw in her ready observation, he continued, "No, it wasn't likely he'd stay there, though we thought it our duty to search the house, and make all the inquiries we could, to see if we could make anything out of the old woman."

"And did you find out anything? and what did she say?" demanded the curious housekeeper.

"Why, we found out one thing," he replied, "as had a mighty strange look with it, especially as Mrs. Hatherleigh didn't choose to give us any account of it."

"And what was that?" demanded Dorcas, with breathless impatience, while Elinor's eyes betrayed her deep interest and anxiety.

"While we were searching about in the room, that she said was her own bed-room, I took it in my head to pull the bed out and look behind it. It wasn't that I'd any suspicion, and yet I thought somehow she seemed restless and uneasy like, whenever we went that way. I'd looked under the bed, and pulled the clothes off, and the bed off the mattress, and still nothing, so then, thinks I, I'll have a look behind it. I cast my eyes on Mrs. Hatherleigh's face the moment I called to somebody to lend me a hand to pull the bedstead out from the wall, and I saw that I had hit the right nail on the head, though she tried to look mighty careless, and walked away, as if she didn't think it worth while to stay any longer with us. Before she could get out of the room, however, I'd found out that there was a low narrow door behind the head of the bed, and I directly called to her to come back and give us the key to open it."

"'She'd no key,' she said, 'we might be sure she made no use of the place, or else her bed wouldn't have been placed against it, and as to keys, she never thought of locking the house-door, and hardly that.'

"'But this is locked,' said I, 'and from the look of it, it's not very long since it's been used, for there's no sign of dust about it, and I should like to see the inside of it. Pray, ma'am, is it a closet or what?'

"'It is a passage to those rooms that are uninhabitable,' said she; 'you have, I believe, examined them already.'

"I knew she was trying to bamboozle me, by the very tone of her voice, so I told her at once, that as she hadn't got the key, we must make bold to open it in the shortest way. It wasn't so soon done as talked of, however, for a precious job we had before we could burst it open, and when it was open, we could see nothing, it was so dark; but I soon got a light, and then we found that the door led through a narrow passage, into as snug a little chamber as you'd wish to see, except that it had no windows; but what was the oddest part of it, there was a bed that I could swear had been slept in, within a night or so; there was   water in the jug, and basin, and soap and towel, and everything to prove that somebody had been using the room, and that it wasn't young Edward, we're sure, because we had been in his room before; now, nobody ever heard of Mrs. Hatherleigh having any visitors, and besides, if she had, why should she hide them in the dark room, when she'd plenty of light ones to choose. Hey, Mrs. Dorcas?"

"To be sure, but what did she say?" demanded the housekeeper, with breathless eagerness.

"Say! why she said she should not answer any questions; that it was no business of ours who had slept there; suppose she had herself indulged a whim of sleeping sometimes in one room, and sometimes in another, she did not know that she was bound to acquaint us, or, indeed, anybody. I saw that she was terribly frightened though, for all that she pretended to carry it with such a high head; however, all I could do, either by fair words or foul, could get nothing out of her, and so we came away as wise as ever."

"And didn't 'ee find out, then, after all?" observed Dorcas, with extreme vexation and disappointment depicted in both her looks and voice.

"No we didn't," replied the man, and was turning away when he caught Elinor's glance, which unconsciously expressed satisfaction at his acknowledgment, that neither cunning nor insolence had succeeded in drawing from Mrs. Hatherleigh the secret, which, though she (Elinor) knew not why, she was convinced was of infinite importance to Edward.

"We didn't get at the bottom of it," repeated the man, with a look of malicious meaning at Elinor, "but Mrs. Hatherleigh, as well as other people that's in the secret, will soon be brought before their betters, and they'll be made to find their tongues and speak out then, I'll warrant me."

Elinor turned away without a reply, though no one could doubt that this observation was levelled at her, but Dorcas's curiosity was now satisfied, or rather she found there was nothing more to be learnt, and she therefore suddenly recollected that she had got, as she expressed it, "the world and all to do in-doors," and therefore hurried her passive companion into the kitchen.

Hour after hour dragged slowly and heavily away, and Elinor still remained under the *surveillance* of Dorcas. Isabel and her sister had evidently been forbidden by their father to hold any intercourse with the forlorn girl, whose spirits sunk lower and lower, not only from the constraint and humiliation she was enduring, but from the exhaustion consequent on so many hours' watching and exertion, without having taken any refreshment.

Dorcas had, indeed, been thoughtful and considerate enough to set a breakfast before her, but Elinor's heart was too full, and at the first morsel she attempted to put into her mouth

such a crowd of recollections rushed upon her mind that, unable
to swallow a mouthful, she burst into tears.

With Elinor, indeed, not one creature seemed to sympathise,
or have one feeling in common; none seemed to recollect that
she had feelings to be wounded, or that, in reality, she had
perhaps at that moment more cause for sorrow—more claims
of compassion than any one. In Walter she had lost one whom
she ever regarded as a brother, while by the manner of his
death, she had not only been placed in jeopardy herself, but
beheld her every future prospect of happiness blighted for ever.

With the family of Mr. Copeland she could not live—she
could not submit to remain after the termination of the present
inquiry, and then what was to become of her? None was less
selfish than Elinor, yet in the midst of a thousand other causes
for grief, these questions would recur with startling force :—
What am I to do? What is to become of me?

The arrival of the coroner was at length announced, and
Elinor was, after a very brief interval, summoned to the parlour,
where he held his inquiry. Every eye was turned upon her as
she entered the room. There were few indeed present who had
not frequently seen her before, for of course the jury was composed principally of the neighbours of Mr. Copeland, yet all
gazed on her with intenseness, as if they had sought to read in
her countenance an explanation of the awful and mysterious
circumstance they were met to inquire into.

Elinor's downcast eyes were for some moments hidden under
their deep fringed lids, but the momentary colour that mounted
to her pallid cheeks betrayed that she was aware of the observation her appearance excited.

She was desired to tell all she knew respecting the deceased,
and she did so, relating, though in a tremulous tone, yet with
clearness and distinctness, her discovery of the body, and all its
attendant circumstances.

When she mentioned her being roused from her first agony
of grief, by hearing the whine of a dog, and the low accents of
a voice commanding it to be silent, there was a low buzz of surprise among the hearers, but when she added, that she had, on
rising from her knees, distinctly seen a man looking at her from
behind the tree, and heard him hastily retreat through the
bushes, there was a simultaneous expression of horror and
astonishment.

" Did you know that person—can you describe him ?" were
the questions eagerly uttered by several voices.

ELINOR CLARE.

"WHAT ARE YOU DOING HERE, GIRL?" EXCLAIMED MR. COPELAND.

"I did not, nor can I describe his person," returned Elinor, "for I only saw his face for a moment, as he looked round the tree at me. I saw, indeed, that he was very dark and coarse-featured, and that he had a bright red handkerchief round his neck, and an old white hat on, with, I think, black crape round it."

"Do you think you should know him again if you should see him?" some one asked.

Elinor replied, "that she should be sorry, from such a momentary view, to be positive, yet she thought she should."

"And pray did you tell all this when you first came home?" demanded an old man, whose eyes had been fixed upon her, with an expression of incredulity, the whole time she had been speaking.

Elinor saw instantly that he meant to imply a doubt of the truth of what she had uttered, and she could not doubt that the source of this was, that he had been already prejudiced by Mr. Copeland into the belief of Edward Hatherleigh being the murderer, and was unwilling to believe that it could be any one else.

Indignation, therefore, gave decision to her voice, as she replied,

"I did not, sir, for no one listened to me when I attempted to speak, and, indeed, in the horrible surprise and confusion that attended the affair from first to last, I then forgot to mention what I had seen."

"Strange, indeed!" was the reply, delivered with a sneer.

Elinor, however, was not to be disconcerted, and she awaited with firmness the effect of the whispering consultation that was carried on among the jury, until one of their number, a shopkeeper in the adjoining village, arose and addressed the coroner, observing, "that he begged leave to say, that a man, exactly answering the young woman's description, had about seven o'clock on the preceding evening, consequently some hours before the discovery of the corpse, been in his shop purchasing several trifling articles.

"I noticed him particularly," he continued, "because I thought he was a most ill-looking fellow, and he seemed as if he had lately been fighting, for one of his eyes was swollen, and his knuckles were cut and bruised on one hand. He had a fierce little cur with him too, and I fancy that he belonged to the party of gipsies that I knew was in the neighbourhood."

Philip, Mr. Copeland's man, who was in the room, now stepped forward, and begged to be heard. " He too had seen the man in question with his dog, in one of the lanes near the Grove, and was quite sure he did belong to the gipsies, though he recollected perfectly that he was not seen at the tents among the rest of them when the search was made there by himself and others, to ascertain whether they were concerned in the disappearance of his poor young master."

These were certainly very strong corroborations of Elinor's assertions, and it was very evident that they created a sensation greatly in favour of her veracity, and consequently, of the murder having been, as was at first suggested, the act of some of the vagrant tribe, a belief that was certainly favoured by the fact that not a farthing of money was found in his pockets, though it was well known that Walter was never without money, and it was believed he had, at the time he quitted his home, three or four sovereigns, besides silver.

It was, indeed, rather singular that his watch was left untouched, and his fowling-piece was left by his side; but this was accounted for, that they were fearful of these well-known articles leading to detection if they detained them. But all that had seemed to lead to this conclusion was speedily forgotten when Isabel appeared, to relate what she had seen in the wood. Elinor, who was now seated behind her, trembled as she saw the change which Isabel's testimony effected in the minds of the jury. The few questions they put to her, all indicated their conviction that Edward Hatherleigh was the criminal, and they scarcely went through the usual forms of consultation, before the foreman announced the verdict, " Wilful murder against Edward Hatherleigh."

Prepared to hear this, and possessing sufficient knowledge to be aware that this was not a final tribunal, but that Edward's guilt or innocence would become the subject of a far more solemn and deliberate inquiry, before he could receive either sentence of punishment or acquittal, Elinor sustained the blow with calmness and fortitude; Isabel looked alarmed, even at the completion of what she had so earnestly laboured to bring about; and Annie, to whom such forms and proceedings were new, and who imagined she heard in these words sentence of death pronounced against poor Edward, threw herself on Elinor's neck, uttering a succession of exclamations and lamentations.

" Oh, Elinor, what shall we do to save him? He is not guilty; no, no, though Isabel and my father say it, I will never believe it. Oh! why did you persuade him to go? If he had but come here, and told these people and my father why he was in the wood, and why he ran away from Isabel—and that she could be so cruel, too, when she knows how kind and gentle-hearted Edward always was, and how dearly he loved us all. Yes, even to the very last, I am sure, he loved poor Walter as a brother, and would ——"

" Let me have no more of this," interrupted her father, roughly pulling her away. " You are a fool, child," he added, as he led Annie away; " that girl is the worst enemy you have, and you ought to rue the day that ever she entered this house. Your poor mother said I should, and she was right."

This was the second time, within a few hours, that Elinor

had heard this observation. Certainly, all her recollections of Mrs. Copeland corresponded with the description thus given of the sentiments of that person; but why it should be so, Elinor could form no idea, and more forcibly than ever did the thought occur to her now:—" Why should I be the object of such enmity? By what action of my childhood could I have deserved that she should have uttered such a prediction? She could have had no cause of enmity against my parents, if Mr. Copeland had."

From the train of thoughts which were thus engendered in her bosom, Elinor was aroused by the discovery that she was alone. The persons engaged in the melancholy duty of the inquest were all departed. Mr. Copeland and his daughters, at last yielding to the demands of nature, were taking the first meal they had tasted since Walter's disappearance had first alarmed them; but Elinor, poor Elinor! neglected and forgotten, as it seemed, by all, was suffered to be unnoticed, as if she no longer formed a part of the family, in which, with the exception of the heads of it, she had been hitherto so tenderly cherished.

" They mean me to feel so," thought the unhappy girl, as she arose from her seat, and looked wildly around her. " Yes; indeed an outcast, and alone in the world."

With faltering steps she left the parlour, and proceeded to her own room, but when she entered it, a thousand terrifying apprehensions, partly induced, and certainly greatly increased by physical exhaustion, completely overpowered her, and she sank fainting on the bed.

CHAPTER V.

Though all at once, unheard, reprove me,
    Left alike by friend and foe,
I will not shrink, if thou but love me ;
    No hand but thine can strike the blow.
I fear not censure's bitter sneer,
    I heed not envy's venomed tongue.
*   *   *   *   *
And e'en though wrong, if thou canst love me
    Or friend or foe may frown on me,
Their barbarous rage shall never move me,
    If blest by one kind word from thee!   ANON.

It seemed as if hours had passed over her in that brief sleep, so
strongly resembling death.   When Elinor awoke to remembrance,
some one was at her side with kind words, pressing her to
swallow the cordial that was held to her lips, and Elinor complied, not that she was altogether conscious that she required,
or had any wish for nourishment, but that it was her disposition
and habit invariably to yield to the voice of kindness.   The
effect of the draught was most powerful, and she almost instantly
recognised her companion to be a young girl, the daughter of a
cottager in the neighbourhood of the Grove, who was occasionally employed by Dorcas in the domestic affairs of the
household.

" Is it you, Betsy?" she faintly observed.   " How came you
to think of me, my good girl ?"

" I'm sure I'd be very ungrateful if I didn't think of you,
Miss Ellen, when the very gown and apron I've got on you
made for me out of your own," returned the simple girl; " but
I'll tell the truth; it was Miss Isabel that told Dorcas to mix
the wine and spice, and send me up with it, for she said she was
sure you must be quite faint and weak for want, if nothing
else, and so sure enough you was; for I'm sure I was almost
frightened to death when I found you lying here so cold and
pale."

Tears stole silently down Elinor's cheeks, and Betsy's compassionate looks and silence rather increased than otherwise the
weakness which she had in vain endeavoured to check.

" I've got something to tell you, Miss Elinor," observed the girl, after carefully looking outside the chamber door to see that no one was listening. "You know," she continued, "that I've been for a week over at my uncle's, at Stock Newton (this was a little hamlet about six miles from Farmer Copeland's residence, the Grove) and only came back about two hours ago."

Elinor nodded assent. She knew nothing about it, or had forgotten altogether a circumstance so insignificant, but she was anxious to learn what Betsy had to communicate, and therefore would not interrupt her narration.

"Well," continued the girl, "I was in the fields this morning, afore it was well daylight, looking for one of uncle's pigs that had strayed the overnight, and who should I see crossing along the path that leads into the London road but young Mr. Edward Hatherleigh, and another man. He didn't see me at first, but I called to him, and the minute he heard my voice he stood still, but the other man ran away like mad."

"And did Edward say anything?" demanded Elinor.

"Yes. I asked him first after friends, and 'specially them at the Grove, and he seemed so hurt like, and could hardly get the words out as he said, ' They're in dreadful trouble, Betsy ; poor Walter has been found dead in the wood. It is said that he is murdered, but I have not seen him myself.' You may be sure, Miss Elinor, how dreadful sorry I was, for though Mr. Walter was used to be a little rough and passionate, and wasn't to be compared to Edward, yet——"

"Pray do go on, there's a good girl," interrupted Elinor, impatiently. " What else did Edward say ?"

" I was going to tell you, Miss, that he asked me when I was going over to the Grove; and when I told him I was going directly after breakfast, because Mrs. Dorcas always wanted me on Saturday, he seemed quite in a flurry. ' Betsy,' said he, ' can I depend upon you to do me a great service?' I told him to be sure he might; for I never could forget how kind his mother was to me, and all of us, when we were lying down with the fever, and how he used come and bring us nice things she made for us when we were getting better, and sit and read to us, when we might have been out in the fields like others."

Elinor's looks again betrayed her impatience; and Betsy passed over the rest of her eulogium on Edward's merits, which though at another time would have been a grateful theme, she saw was now quite the reverse.

" Well, Miss," she continued, " he told me then, that Mr.

Copeland and Miss Isabel had been cruel enough to accuse him of having a hand in the murder. ' And though,' says he, ' Betsy, I am as innocent as the child unborn, yet I cannot stay to be put in prison and the like of that. I hope, therefore, you'll not mention that you've seen me at all, as it will, maybe, put them on the track after me; and if you see Miss Elinor, as of course you will, tell her—but, stay a minute; I will write a few words, if you promise to give them to her unknown to anybody.' And so, Miss Elinor," continued Betsy, " he took and tore a leaf out of his beautiful pocket-book, and he put his hat on the stump of a post, and wrote it with a pencil; but his hand shook so, that I'm afraid you can hardly read it."

Elinor, indeed, had some difficulty to decipher the contents of the rumpled paper, which the simple girl produced from her bosom, where she had hidden it for fear, as she observed, " that she should drop it out of her pocket, among so many things as she kept there;" but at length the former contrived to make out the few sentences as follows :—

" I cannot let this opportunity pass, dearest Elinor, without again entreating you to let no circumstances shake the belief I know you feel of my entire innocence of all participation in poor Walter's horrible death. A fearful mystery hangs over my fate, Elinor; yet, I can bear it all with fortitude, so that I do not lose your love. Elinor, I can scarcely believe my senses, that I am flying from my home a wretched fugitive— that I am compelled to sue even to you that I am not a murderer. Yet, even now, a ray of hope breaks through the gloom, and tells me that the time will come when I shall be cleared from this undeserved disgrace. Believe so with me, Elinor, and believe, too, that in all circumstances, let what will betide me, to the remembrance of you I shall ever turn as my haven of hope—as one precious treasure, of which I know the world cannot deprive me, and which I will never forfeit by my own ill-conduct.

" God bless and preserve you,

" EDWARD HATHERLEIGH."

" You have not, of course, Betsy, mentioned to anybody that you have seen Edward?" observed Elinor, when she could speak, which was not till some minutes after she had folded this precious piece of paper, and deposited close to her heart.

"Lor, Miss Elinor," returned the girl, reproachfully, "I hope you don't think so bad of me as that; I am sure if I could get all the heap of money—fifty pounds they do say it is —Mr. Copeland will give to anybody that takes him, I would not even point my finger the way he is gone."

Elinor shuddered. How many, she thought, there were even within the small circle of her acquaintance who would be unable to resist the temptation of such a sum; even to this poor girl, Betsy, who had never, in all probability, in her life, been the possessor of a single guinea, what a sum it must appear.

"God will reward you, Betty," she uttered, with emotion, grasping her hard, horny hand, "and, if ever my fortune should change, so as to enable me to show how much I feel indebted to you——"

"Oh, don't talk so—pray don't, Miss Elinor," exclaimed poor Betsy, beginning to cry most piteously. "I'm sure a poor girl like me can do——"

The bed-room door suddenly opened, and Dorcas thrust her yellow withered face forward, as if afraid to venture farther until she ascertained the state of affairs within-side first.

"Goodness, I thought I heard somebody sobbing, and I was frightened as something had happened," she observed.

"Here's enough happened I think, Mrs. Dorcas," returned Betsy, rather pertly, "for here's poor Miss Elinor been lying here just like a dead thing, and nobody caring anything about her."

"I'm sorry, I'm sure," returned Dorcas, coming close, and evidently struck with Elinor's pallid looks; "but, there's been such a to-do down stairs, and——but, Lor' bless me, I shall go and tell master how ill you are. I'm sure he can't be so unnatural as to——"

Elinor eagerly stopped her.

"Don't, Dorcas," she exclaimed, "don't mention my name to him now, it will only irritate him; I am better now, much better. I will stay here to-night, and try and get some rest, and then to-morrow I shall be able——"

"Stay here to-night!" repeated both Dorcas and Betsy in a breath. "Stay here to-night!" reiterated the former, as if but that moment she was awakened to a true sense of Elinor's situation.

Dorcas was not destitute of feeling, though a naturally sharp, shrewish temper, and the necessity she fancied existed of ruling with despotic authority over the men and maids of Farmer Copeland's establishment, had given harshness to her manners, and made her often appear worse than she really deserved.

Elinor had always been a favourite with her, because she was ever anxious to spare the old woman trouble, and to assist her, without in any way trespassing on her authority, while Isabel, on the contrary, whenever she interfered in domestic affairs, which was only by fits and starts, was too apt to make Dorcas feel that she considered herself mistress. The old housekeeper had, too, as she always professed, a fellow feeling with Elinor, because she also had been early left an orphan, and brought up by a relative who had made her eat the bitter bread of dependence, until she was able to get her own living.

"You will stay here many nights, child," she resumed, after drawing a long breath, and peering into Elinor's face, as if she would read her very heart. "You mustn't take it amiss what's been said to you," she continued, "for you know Mr. Copeland is always harsh and rough when he's crossed, even to them he likes best, and goodness knows he's got enough now to make him so, and there's nothing to be done but to bear it patiently till the fit's over; I know in his heart he can't blame you altogether for trying to screen Edward, though everybody thinks him guilty."

"No, I don't, Dorcas," interrupted Betsy, impatiently, "and I'm sure he arn't neither, because——"

She caught Elinor's eye, and suddenly stopped.

"Because what?" demanded Dorcas, contemptuously, "what do you know about it?"

"I don't know anything," returned Betsy, looking very foolish, "only I'm sure Miss Elinor wouldn't——"

"Oh, there, hold your tongue, and don't purtend to judge of what you know nothing about," interrupted Dorcas, sharply. "Get you down stairs, and see if you can't find something to do there."

Betsy complied in silence, though her looks betrayed her unwillingness to quit Elinor: and, indeed, after she had left the room, she turned back to remind Dorcas that the former had had neither dinner nor tea.

"Nor I shouldn't wonder breakfast either," she muttered, as Dorcas, uttering a thousand excuses for her forgetfulness, hurried down stairs to repair her neglect.

It was not Dorcas, however, but Annie, who a few minutes afterwards brought Elinor some tea.

"Isabel told me to come to you, dear Elinor," she exclaimed, seeing, by the countenance of the latter, that she was about to utter some remonstrances against her (Annie's) exposing herself to the danger of displeasing her father and sister by this visit. " Isabel is, I know, as sorry for you in her heart as I am," continued the affectionate girl; " but you know, dear Elinor, how obstinate and high-spirited she is. She cannot bear, when she has said anything, to own herself in the wrong."

" Do you believe, then, that she thinks so in the present instance, dear girl?" demanded Elinor, with solicitude.

" I cannot say that she is convinced that she is wrong altogether," returned Annie; " but I am almost sure that in her heart she wishes Edward may escape. Oh! it cannot be possible that she who was always so partial to him can have changed so all at once, as to wish to see him brought to shame and—I saw her shudder a little while ago, when father said something dreadful about Edward: and when she bade me come to you just now, she told me to tell you not to give way to despair. And you won't, will you, dear Elinor?" continued the kind-hearted girl, twining her arms around Elinor's neck, while the latter affectionately returned her embrace. " Dorcas said you were talking of going away from us, Elinor," she timidly added, looking earnestly in her face; " but you would not mean it seriously. You would not surely desert Isabel and I now? If we were to lose you, you as well as poor Walter——"

A burst of tears followed this mention of her brother, and prevented her proceeding, while Elinor took the opportunity of explaining that it would not be a voluntary act her quitting the Grove.

" But you know as well as I, Annie," she continued, " that your father never regarded me with any affection. But for your love and Isabel's towards me, indeed, it would have been impossible I could have borne the cruel coldness he has ever shown towards me. Often has my heart sunk beneath the withering frown, or the bitter sneer with which he has repressed any attempt on my part to conciliate him; and to your mother, Annie, I was still less indebted for kindness; she hated me, and did not scruple to tell me so. Why it should be so, why it should be so is a mystery that——but, I forgot, dear girl, this was not exactly what I intended to speak of; I meant to say, that if my presence here has been so unwelcome to him, when there was no reasonable plea for his dislike, can it be possible that he will bear the sight of me now that he lays to my charge——"

"Oh, no, he cannot, he will not believe anything wrong of you, dear Elinor, when he becomes himself again," interrupted Annie. " Grief has so distracted him, that he knows not hardly what he says now, but when this dreadful shock— dreadful to all of us, but as you said last night, before we knew the full extent of our misfortune, to none could a father's feelings for the loss of his only son be compared. Surely, then, you will make allowance for him, if he seems cruel and unjust to you now. He will be, when he comes to himself, as Isabel always is, sorry I know in her heart to have given you pain."

"Isabel loves me," returned Elinor, in a dejected tone, " but your father hates me."

Annie was beginning to say that it was impossible—that no one could hate Elinor, when, as if to prove her error, the chamber-door was suddenly opened, and Mr. Copeland, in a voice of rage, exclaimed—

"What are you doing here, girl? Is this the way you show your love and respect to your brother, by comforting and associating with the creature who has been the cause of his death? I guessed I should find you here, for her heart——"

"Oh, no, father, do not say so," exclaimed Annie, " I came here entirely of my own accord; Dorcas told me that Elinor was ill, and besides that she was talking of leaving us to-morrow, and——"

'Leaving! and pray where do you intend to go?" demanded Mr. Copeland, hastily.

"Anywhere, sir," returned Elinor, bursting into an agony of tears, "any place would be preferable to remaining here; I would rather beg my bread, starve, die, than submit longer to depend upon you. You know, sir," she continued, hastily drying her eyes, and becoming more calm as she spoke, "you are well aware, that I have never wished to eat the bread of dependence. You well know that years ago, as soon as ever I attained to an age that I could make myself useful, I wished and offered to do so; I would have gone to work in the field, rather than have been condemned to bear your frowns, to be reminded as I am every hour that passed, that I had no claim but on your charity; but you would not let me go when I could have got a living for myself, you were angry that I dared think of such a thing, and I yielded because I thought it would hurt your pride, that the child of your sister, *if* such is my relationship to you——"

Mr. Copeland's eyes fell beneath her piercing glance as she

uttered this, and his countenance betrayed surprise and confusion.

"If," he repeated, striving to recover himself, "what motive could I have—what reason can you have to doubt that you are —that such is the relationship between us?"

"Only, sir, your conduct towards me," returned Elinor, half frightened at her own temerity in having said so much, yet feeling that now was the time to pursue the advantage she had gained. ' I confess, sir," she continued, "that I have often been tempted to believe I am no way akin to you, for it seems so unnatural that one so near as a brother to my mother——"

Mr. Copeland, however, had by this time completely recovered his presence of mind.

"Oh! and pray, then, who do you think you are? or what motive do you suppose I can have had for being burthened with the care and trouble you have been to me?" he interrupted, with a malicious smile. "Or, perhaps, you think the honour and pleasure of bringing up such a choice specimen, is quite sufficient to repay me. But, be that as it will," he continued, "you certainly show extreme kindness and discretion in choosing the present moment to display your ingratitude, and add to the grief that is already weighing me to the earth."

Elinor was herself struck with the justice of the latter reproof.

"I acknowledge," she observed, "that I might have chosen a time more suitable to have spoken of this; but, I cannot but feel that your treatment of me this day has confirmed what I have often before felt, though I have ever been unwilling to acknowledge it even to myself, that you would eagerly seize any opportunity of getting rid of me with decency."

"Indeed!" replied Mr. Copeland, with a sneer, "then, I can assure you that you are mistaken. Heaven knows," he continued, "that no one ever had a better reason for hating the presence of another than I have towards you, for never shall I look upon you again without remembering that to you I owe the loss of my poor boy; yet, I do not wish to part with you —I will not," he continued, with peculiar emphasis. "No, you shall stay and witness the misery and devastation you have brought upon me; and you shall stay, too," he added, with a bitter smile, "to see the villain Hatherleigh brought to justice."

"If only justice is done towards Hatherleigh," murmured Elinor, as Mr. Copeland left the room, closing the door with violence behind him, "it is all I wish. It is the fear only that he will not meet with justice from his prejudiced foes that terrifies me."

Annie had, at her father's first appearance, crept from the room, and Elinor, once more left to herself, yielded to the impulse of exhausted nature, and retired to bed, to try to lose for a short time, at least, in repose, the memory of the complicated evils that had befallen her.

Every means which were adopted by Mr. Copeland to trace the supposed murderer of his son proved of no avail. Poor Walter's remains were committed to their final resting-place amid the tears and regrets of all who knew him; and except Mr. Copeland and his immediate connections, the excitement occasioned by the awful circumstance we have related gradually died away.

The rapid and rather premature approach of winter had driven the gipsies (who were still, with many persons, the object of suspicion) to break up their camp, and seek shelter in their wintry retreat; but that which occasioned the most talk and conjecture was the departure, none knew whither, of Mrs. Hatherleigh from the Nunnery.

That a solitary woman should feel unwilling to remain in such a dreary habitation was certainly nothing surprising; and when to this was added the misery of knowing that she was, and would be, henceforth the object of suspicion to every one, and would be liable to all sorts of insults, not only from the low and ignorant people with whom necessity brought her in contact, but also from those whom she had been used to consider her friends, it would have been much more strange if she had chosen to remain, especially as she possessed not a single tie or connexion, as far as was known, to render the place preferable to any other.

The cheapness of the necessaries of life, and the quiet and simple manners of the natives, had been, as she then declared, her only motive for settling in the neighbourhood; and though at that time there were not a few whispers and conjectures as to her real reasons for seeking such utter seclusion while yet in the prime of life and possessing striking personal charms, time, however, and the total unobtrusiveness of Mrs. Hatherleigh's mode of life, had gradually silenced the voice of scandal; or if there ever by any accident was raised a conjecture as to her former situation of life, and the motives which had induced her to withdraw so entirely from society, it always ended in every one expressing their conviction that she had been an unfortunate, in all probability an injured woman; but no one ever presumed to doubt that she was an innocent one.

Recent events, however, especially the certainty that she had had a secret visitor at the Nunnery, for so of course the discovery of the dark chamber was interpreted, induced a very different opinion of Mrs. Hatherleigh's character to be formed than she had hitherto borne; stories were now told of the lights having been casually seen at the most unseasonable hours moving about in the Nunnery. A strange-looking man who had once or twice been seen in the dusk by some of the villagers, and whose appearance had at the time caused considerable alarm and wonderment, was now confidently said to have been the person whose visits Mrs. Hatherleigh received, or whom she had concealed there; and, in short, the most terrible rumours were afloat respecting the Nunnery and its inhabitants, even before it was suspected that the last one had quitted it.

A week's almost unintermitting rain had kept nearly every inhabitant of the neighbourhood in doors for that time; and, as may be supposed, of course one of the principal subjects of conversation was the late transactions, and the persons concerned in them.

It was in a circle of this kind, at the kitchen fire-side of a farmhouse, about a mile and a half from the Grove, and rather less distance from the Nunnery, that they were speaking especially of the latter place, and its inhabitants.

A conjecture had just been raised whether Mrs. Hatherleigh would ever have the courage to show herself again in her pew at church, from which she had never been known till now to absent herself a single Sabbath.

The three which had elapsed since the death of Walter Copeland, and the flight of her son, she had not been there; but then it was known that she was ill, so ill as to have been compelled to have a doctor and a nurse to attend her, the latter an old woman who lived at the cottage nearest to the Nunnery, and had been for years occasionally employed by its mistress, indeed from the time the latter first resided there.

The question was therefore, whether, now that the lady was well again, she would venture to show herself?

They were still discussing this important subject when Alice, the old woman alluded to, came into the kitchen on some errand.

"We were talking about your missus, over at the great house, Alice," observed one of the men

Alice shook her head.

"Aye, you may talk now," she observed, "for all you may say can do her no harm."

"Why, she arn't dead, is she?" exclaimed two or three voices together.

"No, no, she's not dead," returned the old woman, "but she's gone away clear out of this country altogether, poor thing; gone where no lying tongues can reach her. God bless her, say I, wherever she's gone, and so say many more besides me, in their hearts, if they be'n't afeard to speak out; but that I ba'n't, no, not if there was twenty Farmer Copelands persecuting her, and thof he be rich, and I be poor, I be'n't afraid to speak my mind; and I say he's a cruel man, for as to Master Edward ever harming any living creature, no, I'd never believe it, if Farmer Copeland was to take fifty bible oaths of it. A sweeter, kindlier, gentler-natur'd lad never breath'd the breath of life than him, and as to his mother, she was the most of an angel that ever——"

"Aye, aye, Alice, praise the bridge that carries us safe over," interrupted one of the servants; "but do tell us, when did she go, and where?"

"Them are questions easier put than answered," returned Alice, significantly. "I won't say I didn't know she was going, for when she lay ill she told me that if she got better she was going away to a foreign country, where she hoped to meet her poor injured boy again; and when she discharged me she gave me a lot of things to take home with me that she said she would never want again. I shall keep 'em like treasures of goold for her sake. Howsomever, I'd no misgiving that she was going directly. I asked her if I should come over next day and if she wanted anything, but she said, 'No, not to-morrow, Alice.' I couldn't take a liberty with her for the world, to do what she told me not, there was such a grand way with her, gentle and meek as she was; and so, though I was very uneasy all the day, and longed to see how she was getting on, I didn't go till the next morning, and when I went, what should I see but the place all closed, shut up, and a padlock on the door. How she got the things away, or whether they be left there, passes my knowledge."

"Oh, no, you're quite innocent of it, I daresay," observed the man who had first spoken on the subject; "but this I say, Dame Alice, that you nor nobody else can't persuade me that Mrs. Hatherleigh could move off in that manner without its being pretty well known to everbody round. I'll be bound, if you chose, you could give a fair guess, both how she got away, and where she's gone to."

The doubt thus thrown upon the old woman's veracity brought forth an angry reply from her. Alice was, indeed, noted for the sourness of her looks and the tartness of her speech, and, as usual with persons of her qualities, she was frequently doomed to make sport for those who delighted to bring them out.

In the present instance the contest became so violent as to reach the ears of the master of the house, who came into the kitchen to demand the cause of it.

The news of Mrs. Hatherleigh's flight appeared, however, in a much more serious light to him than to be made the subject of idle jesting, and he recommended Alice to go over without delay and acquaint Mr. Copeland with it.

Alice had no good will to the task, for she considered the latter as having been, as she said, the instigation of her losing the best friend she ever had in Mrs. Hatherleigh; but the hint she received that she might get herself into trouble for having kept the secret so long decided her to go at once as she was recommended.

For the first time since the death of Walter the whole of Mr. Copeland's family were assembled together at the tea-table when the old woman reached the Grove. Mr. Copeland had, after seeing the remains of his son committed to the earth, returned home and retired to his chamber, where he had remained insensible to all consolation, and totally neglectful of all the duties of life, until that very morning, when the receipt of a letter bearing the London post-mark seemed in some measure to rouse him from the lethargy of grief into which he had fallen, and he yielded to his daughter's persuasions to come down stairs and mingle once more with his family.

" Where is Elinor ?" was his first inquiry, as he looked round the room.

" Elinor has been ill, father," returned the trembling Annie, " so ill, that we were afraid she would have died."

" Afraid !" he muttered to himself. " Why was I not told this ?" he demanded aloud.

" Isabel mentioned it to you once, father," said Annie, " but— but she did not like to trouble you again."

The fact was, Mr. Copeland had on that occasion burst into such a torrent of invectives against Elinor that neither of his daughters had ventured to mention the subject a second time.

ELINOR CLARE.

ELINOR KEPT HER EYES FIXED ON THE MAN.

"Is she not able to come downstairs, then?" he demanded.

"Yes, she came down yesterday for the first time," returned Annie, "and she would be down now, I believe," she added, with some hesitation, "only that she is afraid that you——"

"She need not be afraid of me," he somewhat hastily interrupted; "besides, I wish to see her."

Annie flew to Elinor's room with eager haste to convey this unlooked-for change, as she conceived, in her father's sentiments, and in a few minutes the latter was once more in the dreaded presence of Mr. Copeland.

Elinor had indeed been ill—very ill; and as she now tottered into the room, supported by Annie, Mr. Copeland almost started

at the alteration which had taken place in her appearance. He
replied, however, to her timid salute only by a stiff bend of his
head, and then, turning to the fire, fixed his eyes upon it in apparently gloomy abstraction.

The tea was brought in, Isabel entered with it, and they took
their usual places at the table. It was the first time they had
done so since Walter's death, yet no one seemed to recollect that
circumstance but Elinor, or at least there was no perceptible
difference in the settled countenances of sorrow they all wore.
With Elinor, however, it was different; Walter had always been
accustomed to take his seat at her elbow, and his cheerful laugh
and mirthful eye, beaming with good humour and vivacity, were
at that moment so strongly present to her imagination that she
looked round as if expecting to behold him, and then, struck with
the awful contrast, burst into tears.

Mr. Copeland fixed his stern eye upon her, but it was evident
he mistook the cause of her emotion.

"I am quite aware, Elinor," he observed, addressing her with
somewhat more of softness in his manner than was usual with
him on such occcasions, "I am quite aware that your situation
is not a very pleasant one, and that there is very little probability
of you ever being comfortable among us again. For my own
part, I tell you candidly, that never shall I look upon your face
without recollecting——"

"Father, dear father," interrupted both the girls in a breath.

"Well well," returned the old man, "I shall say nothing more
on that subject; what I meant to tell you is, that I received a
letter this morning from a relation of mine, who has been some
years living in America. He has been compelled to come with
his wife to England to settle some affairs, and is now in London
but will go back in a few weeks. Now if you choose to go with
them I can settle the matter advantageously to you, and shall
write to invite them to come down here; but mark, I do not want
to be troubled with their visit unless I am first certain that you
will accept the offer; therefore, I shall expect you to give me a
decided answer, and abide by it."

A slight flush of resentment for a moment visited Elinor's
pale cheek at this abrupt and unfeeling proposal, but it was
succeeded by a burst of anguish, as she thought how utterly
unfriended, how desolate was her situation, when it could be thus
proposed to her to exile herself for ever from her native land
to become a dependent upon utter strangers. Even Isabel's
countenance betrayed shame and sorrow at her father's unfeeling

proposition, and Annie's lips quivered with emotion as Elinor's eyes and her's met.

It was some moments before the latter could command her voice to reply.

"It is almost too much to require of me, sir," she at length faltered, "to decide upon such a step without knowing something of the persons you speak of. To be thrown on the mercy of strangers in a foreign country is——"

Mr. Copeland was on the point of angrily interrupting her when the door of the room was suddenly opened, and old Alice was unceremoniously hurried in by the housekeeper, who was breathless with impatience to hear what was the intelligence the old woman had brought.

Elinor's agitation became so excessive that it was with difficulty she could keep herself from fainting as Alice commenced her circumlocutory account of Mrs. Hatherleigh's disappearance from her abode.

It was very evident that Mr. Copeland was as much disappointed as Elinor was relieved by the conclusion of the old woman's narration. Both had anticipated information of much more importance.

"I was in hopes you were come to tell me that the villain was within my reach," observed the former, in a disappointed tone, "but though this is certainly a proof that he will not venture into his old haunts again, I will not despair. And you say she talked of going abroad, eh, Alice? Where could she get money to go abroad?"

The contemptuous manner in which he uttered this seemed to rouse old Alice in defence of her late mistress.

"I don't know, sir," she replied; "I never see no want of money there. I know when missus paid the doctor I saw that she'd got a few golden guineas in her silken purse."

"Aye, indeed," returned Mr. Copeland, "but did she tell you how she came by them?"

"I know she had money to take every quarter at the bank at Newton Regis, though she didn't trust every one with that secret," replied the old woman, with the triumphant air of one who felt her consequence increased by having been trusted in such an important affair.

Mr. Copeland, however, made no reply to this; he was in seeming reflection upon the subject.

"To America did you say she was gone?" he at length demanded, looking up.

"She didn't mention Ameriky, sir," returned the old woman, "but I think it's likely, because I've heard her talking about that place to Master Edward many's the time."

Alice was dismissed to the kitchen to make some refreshment, and Mr. Copeland, turning to Elinor, with a malicious sneer observed,

"This news, I expect, will go near to reconcile you to my proposal, as there may be a chance of your meeting your friends again there; that is, if he succeeds in escaping the officers of justice."

Elinor made no reply to this taunt. She felt too happy, indeed, in the strong conviction which had taken possession of her mind, from the moment she learned Mrs. Hatherleigh's departure, that Edward was already beyond the reach of his pursuers, to care for anything that could be said; and not anxious for any renewal of the subject, she took advantage of Mr. Copeland's temporary absence in the kitchen, whither he had gone to put some further questions to Alice, to return to her room, leaving Isabel and Annie to excuse her on the plea of her still-remaining weakness.

CHAPTER VI.

But this was not a moment when the head
Could trifle with the heart! The cloud that spread
Its chilling veil between them, now had past—
Too long awaking—but they woke at last!
He rushed where clung the fainting fair one—sought
To soothe with hopes he felt not, cherished not;
And while in passionate support he pressed,
She raised her eyes —then swiftly on his breast
Hid her blanched cheek—as if resigned to share
The worst with him ;—nay, die contented there!
That silent act was fondly eloquent;
And to the youth's deep soul, like lightning sent,
A gleam of rapture—exquisite, yet brief.
                                        ANON.

THE agitation which Elinor had suffered, in the first place, from Mr. Copeland's abrupt and unfeeling proposal, and in the second from the intelligence of Mrs. Hatherleigh's departure, produced a relapse of her disorder, a nervous fever, and for three weeks Elinor was again confined to her room. During this period affairs had returned much to their usual course in Mr. Copeland's family. The old man had resumed the active superintendence of his farm, and though his head drooped lower than before, his hair became more silvery white, and his stern brow never for a moment relaxed its severity, it was evident that he was regaining health and vigour, and that the blow, heavy as it had fallen, would not be mortal.

Could those who made this remark have read the old man's heart, they would have seen that the burning desire for revenge which reigned there counteracted, in a great degree, the sorrow which would otherwise have preyed upon it.

He thought less frequently of the loss of his son than he did of him through whose means he believed he had sustained that loss; and morning, noon, and night, did he breathe the same fervent prayer, that he might live to behold the murderer of his son in his power.

And there was one shared these feelings, while she more than shared his sorrow.

Warm in her affections and attachments, generous and liberal in her sentiments, Isabel resembled her father only in positiveness and vindictiveness; there she was truly his own child.

During Elinor's illness, Isabel's affection towards her had revived in its full force, and nothing could exceed her kindness and attention to the invalid; yet never for a moment had Isabel relaxed in her bitter feelings towards Edward Hatherleigh—never had she ceased to pray that he might be brought to punishment. However, to Annie she dissembled these feelings, in compassion to what she considered the weakness of her gentler sister, into whose bosom not a spark of that fiery spirit which inhabited her own had ever entered.

But there existed a secret motive in Isabel's heart which embittered her feelings towards Edward that none besides herself suspected—one which she would have blushed to have owned even to herself, and yet which still unconsciously influenced her in the highest degree.

Isabel had never forgiven Edward his preference of Elinor. It was the first her vanity had received, and it sank deep. From her earliest childhood she had looked upon Edward as superior to every other living being. The idea " grew with her growth, and strengthened with her strength," and never did such a thought intrude into her bosom as that it was possible Edward could prefer another to her. From this dream she was rudely awakened by Walter's discovery of the mutual attachment between Edward and Elinor, and though her pride induced her to smother her disappointment so effectually that not one suspected it, yet, from that moment, hatred, far more intense than the love she fancied she had felt for the unconscious Edward, took possession of her heart, and under the pretext of espousing her brother's suit with Elinor, she secretly sought to revenge the insult her imagined superiority had received.

"There is no fury like a woman scorned," is the language of the poet, and Isabel might justly be cited in proof of the truth of the assertion; but when to this secret cause of hatred towards Edward was added the conviction that his hand had deprived of life the brother to whom she was so ardently attached, no words can paint the fierce passion of revenge which took possession of her every thought.

Towards Elinor her feelings had, however, undergone a complete revolution. While she had considered the latter in the light of a happy and successful rival, Isabel's feelings towards her had been scarcely less vindictive than towards Edward, but Elinor was, now that not the smallest hope could survive in her bosom of being ever united to the object of her affection, only an object of pity, and her kindness towards her was resumed to its fullest extent, though they mutually avoided ever mentioning the name of him who had divided them.

Elinor, indeed, though far from suspecting the secret of Isabel's disappointed love, was intuitively aware that the former, however guarded in her speech, was still Edward's bitter enemy, and that nothing she could say would have the effect of removing the dreadful prejudice her cousin indulged against him.

To Isabel, therefore, his name was never breathed by Elinor while she retained her recollection; and when, in the delirium of fever, she would fancy she was addressing him, or would pathetically plead in favour of his innocence, Isabel would fly from the room and leave her to the care of Annie, as if fearful of listening to anything that might tempt her to forego her fearful desire of revenge.

During Elinor's confinement, in consequence of the relapse of her disorder, some circumstances occurred which appeared to add mystery to mystery respecting the disappearance of Mrs. Hatherleigh from her residence.

One of Mr. Copeland's men, who had been sent to the market town, and remained there drinking till a late hour, on his way home mistook his path in the darkness, and for some time wandered about at random, until he found himself, to his no small alarm and vexation, close to the dilapidated walls of the Nunnery.

A heavy shower of rain and wind, which came on at this moment, rendered almost any shelter welcome; and, in spite, therefore, of all the superstitious fears which were connected with the place, he determined to try whether he could get admission at one of the out-buildings.

The lock of the stable-door readily yielded to his efforts; he entered, and finding some straw scattered about, drew it together in a heap, and threw himself upon it to await the clearing of the weather.

The door of the stable he had drawn to after him, but not entirely closed, so that he could command a full view of the whole of the court-yard and the back of the house, as far as the darkness of the night would allow; but what was his astonishment and terror when he heard the creaking of a door on the hinges, and a moment after a man came out of the house, carefully closing and locking the door after him.

"Do not frighten yourself, dear Elinor," said Annie, when she related this story to the latter, "Watkins (the man who had seen this) says that he is quite sure it was not Edward. He was a great deal more stout, and an older man, he was sure, by his walk, as he passed the stable door; and Watkins could thus see his figure distinctly, though he could not make out his features. My father was very angry at first," she continued, "and called Watkins a cowardly fool for not seizing hold of him, and insisting upon knowing what he was doing there, and how he got admission into the house; but as the poor fellow said, 'How did he know how many more there might be within hearing; and, besides, what right had he to question anybody, especially when it was plain the man had got the key to let himself in or out?'"

It appeared, however, that Mr. Copeland had thought the circumstance of so much importance that a second warrant had been procured to search the house, which had been broken open for that purpose. Nothing, however, of any importance was elicited by this, except that a number of the heaviest articles of furniture belonging to Mrs. Hatherleigh remained in the house—thus removing in part the apparent mystery of how she had got away, and inferring, on the other hand, that she intended, at no very distant period, to return.

Watkins' story of the stranger he had seen would have been totally disbelieved, the deserted appearance of the rooms seeming to contradict the assertion that anyone had entered since its inhabitants had quitted it, but for the discovery that a lantern, with part of a candle in it, and some matches, were placed on a bracket just within-side the hall-door, evidently to afford facility to some person to procure a light as soon as he or they entered.

Various were the conjectures to which this gave rise; but on one point all concerned in the solution of the mystery were agreed, namely, that a watch should be kept for some nights for the mysterious nocturnal visitor.

On the first night Mr. Copeland himself had remained there all night with the constable, without, however, any result. On the second he was persuaded by the entreaties of his daughters, who saw the ill effects of the damp, and cold, and anxiety, to relinquish the task to the others; but though on that and three subsequent nights they persevered in their gloomy and wearying watch, and, as they declared, adhered strictly to Mr. Copeland's instructions, remaining in perfect darkness, and never speaking to each other but in a whisper, nobody came, all hope of detecting the intruder by this means was reluctantly relinquished, and the doors, both in front and at the back of the house, by order of the magistrate, were securely fastened up.

Such was the story Annie related to Elinor as soon as the latter became able to attend to it.

But though the former assured her over and over again that Watkins was quite positive the person he saw was not Edward, Elinor could not divest herself for some time of the belief that it was him, or of the shuddering terror it excited in her bosom, to think that he had been so near falling into the power of his enemies.

A few words of conversation with Watkins, however, as soon as she was able to go down stairs, and could find an opportunity of speaking to him, removed this impression from her mind, though it increased the mystery which had before puzzled her.

Watkins was one of the few who remained unconvinced of Edward's guilt; though he acknowledged, to use his own phrase that "matters looked very black against him, and he was afraid it would go hard with the poor lad if he was taken."

The sympathy, however, that existed between him and Elinor on this subject made him readily comprehend what she aimed at in questioning him as to the particulars of the circumstances which Annie had related to her.

"Don't frighten yourself at all about it, Miss Elinor," he observed; "it wasn't young Hatherleigh I saw, that I'll take my oath of; though, if it had been him, I wouldn't have hurt a hair of his head; but it wasn't him, it was a man old enough to be his father, and as queer-looking a fellow as ever I saw in my born days, with a great hat, and a coat down to his heels, just like a conjuror that I saw at last Newton Regis fair. Master says I was drunk, and saw double; but I wasn't though, for if I had taken a drop too much, the walk and the rain, and my losing my way, aye, and getting within a stone's throw as I did of the Haunted Oak, before I struck into the path that led me to the Nunnery, had properly sobered me. The clouds had just cleared away too, and the moon partly shone out at the very minute the man came out of the house, and I saw his dark-looking face, and his black locks hanging round it, quite plain; and, as I told you afore, he was old enough to be Master Edward's father. I should have thought he was one of the gipsies, indeed, only I know the vagabonds have been clean gone out o' the country these three weeks. So don't make yourself uneasy, Miss Elinor; the lad will have sense enough, I'll warrant me, to keep out of the reach of his enemies; and as to me, if it was a hundred pound instead of fifty, I wouldn't lay a hand upon him if I saw him to-morrow."

A few shillings, nearly all Elinor possessed in the world, slipped into Watkins' hand, bespoke her approbation; and Elinor retired to muse over the intelligence she had received, which, while it relieved her on one point, increased considerably her uneasiness on another.

In the description that Watkins had given of the midnight intruder at the Nunnery, she instantly recognised the stranger, whose appearance in company with Edward and his mother had occasioned her so much surprise on the night of her last visit.

Who this man could be, and what mysterious influence he could possess over both mother and son, became once more the subject of her deep reflection; and again, though most unwillingly, was Elinor compelled to come to the same conclusion as she had done before, that, in the stranger, she beheld the husband of Mrs. Hatherleigh and the father of Edward, though what circumstances could compel him to adopt this secrecy, or what motive induced him to appear in such a strange and degrading habit, it was impossible for her to form the most remote idea of.

At the time, indeed, before spoken of, the same idea had suggested itself to her, that it now appeared had occurred to Watkins, that the stranger, from the darkness of his complexion, the cast of his features, the raven locks that hung in such wild profusion around them, and the coarseness yet singularity of his attire, might easily have been taken to be one of the vagrant tribe, who were looked upon with such a mixture of contempt and awe by the rustics in the neighbourhood of the Grove, and whose strange habits and manners had often excited Elinor's surprise and curiosity, though her good•sense preserved her from being the dupe of their imposing pretensions.

But to suppose that Edward Hatherleigh could have any connection with, much less that he could be the son of a gipsy, was too degrading a thought to be voluntarily admitted by Elinor, though in vain she tried to banish the idea, which everything seemed to confirm.

Even Edward's unaccounted for absence from his home previous to the death of Walter, might be connected with the appearance of the gipsies in the neighbourhood, which took place about the same time; her meeting with him in the wood and at so great a distance from the encampment; his expressed fear to her that *they* were approaching, thus evidently connecting himself with several persons whom he dared not, or at least wished not, to name, all seemed to confirm the idea which she wished to prove false, but was compelled to fear was but too true.

During all her illness, whenever she was capable of reflection, it had been her consolation to think that, from what Alice had communicated, and the utter disappointment of all Mr. Copeland's attempts to trace them, Edward and his mother had succeeded in embarking for a foreign country, and had thus successfully eluded the pursuit of their enemies.

But what she now heard awakened her fears that such was not the case, but that they were still lingering, and probably at no great distance from the spot which was naturally endeared to them by years of peaceful and apparently happy residence.

Too soon was this supposition confirmed.

It was now the eve of Christmas, but the season was unmarked by any of those joyous preparations at the Grove which were usually carried to excess.

All was silence and sorrow, for none could forget that he, who used to be the life and soul of every sport, was mouldering in the grave. The weather, however, was not in unison with these gloomy feelings, for it was as warm, as clear, and genial, as the beginning of autumn.

Elinor, who began to feel a renewal of strength, and had been so long confined to the tedious monotony of a sick chamber, was delighted to be able to stroll in the open air, though she was compelled to go alone; Isabel not being inclined, and Annie, too much afraid of exciting her father's anger to become the companion of one who still lay under his frowns.

Since the time he had first mentioned the subject, Mr. Copeland had never directly alluded to his proposal to her to go to America with his friends; and, as may be supposed, Elinor herself had no disposition to recur to it; but it was very plain, from many hints, that the former had not relinquished his intention that she should leave his family, though he forbore to speak more openly of his views, not out of regard to her feelings, but to avoid the remonstrances of his daughters, who could not hear an allusion to Elinor's quitting them for ever without manifesting the most decided grief and reluctance.

The uncertainty in which she was thus placed as to her future fate, was of course an additional source of uneasiness to Elinor, and never, perhaps, had she felt it more strongly than when, on the day in question, she took her solitary walk through that part of the wood which used to be the scene of their childish pastimes, when she and her cousins and Edward Hatherleigh would steal from their respective homes, and beguile a long summer's day in their various sports, without a single thought or fear, except, perhaps, the transient one of being chided on their return home, for being absent at regular meal-times.

Here their swing had been fixed by the united efforts of Walter and Edward. The same hands had constructed a rustic seat and table at a short distance, which served alike for their simple repasts and the purpose of study, and a few paces further they had contrived to divert the course of a little rill, the waters of which, pure as crystal, was to them the most delightful of beverages.

Elinor turned away and burst into tears as a thousand recollections crowded into her mind; but she started and quickly returned to the spot, as her eyes caught a glimpse of a folded paper which was lying on the rude table before mentioned.

What could it be? She stood in doubt, for well she knew that none of the family had visited the spot since the night that Walter's lifeless form had been discovered at the foot of the Haunted Oak.

Then Annie had rested a few moments on the bench, while Isabel and she were consulting which path they should take, and then she (Elinor) was sure no paper was there.

There was no regular path through that part of the wood,

and seldom, indeed, was it visited, except, perhaps, a strolling urchin or two from the village, whose intrusion Walter would resent, while Edward would purchase their absence by a few pence and a recommendation to go to some other part, where they would find chesnuts or beechnuts in far greater abundance than there, a *ruse* which seldom failed to rid them of the trouble-some intruders much quicker than Walter's blustering threats.

The place, in short, had almost been held sacred to the young people; and though Elinor felt that never again could it be the scene of their innocent enjoyments, she could scarcely reconcile herself to the belief that it would be altogether deserted and become common to every foot that should choose to trespass on its hallowed bounds.

But to return to the paper that had excited not only her curiosity but astonishment how it could have been placed there; for it could not, she thought, after a moment's reflection, have lain there long, since the breeze, gentle and genial as it was, would certainly have wafted it away from its present position.

The first glimpse of the paper, as she took it up, confirmed this impression; while it made her start and thrill with terror, for it contained verses in the handwriting of Edward Hather-leigh, addressed "To Elinor." It had evidently been recently written, and was as follows:—

> Not when the gaudy light of day
>   With yellow radiance gilds the scene—
> Not when the moonbeams' milder ray
>   Shed silver lustre o'er the green—
>   Not then, not then I'll meet thee.
>
> Not when the spring-time decks the grove,
>   And fragrance loads each passing gale—
> Not when the birds with notes of love
>   Make vocal every hill and vale—
>   Not then, not then I'll meet thee.
>
> But when the winter rains fall fast,
>   And blinding snows drive o'er the plain,
> When keenly blows the blighting blast—
>   'Tis then that we shall meet again;
>   Yes then, oh! then l'll meet thee.

" Merciful Heaven! what madness! what imprudence is this?" exclaimed Elinor aloud, as her eye glanced rapidly around, expecting every instant to see Edward himself appear from behind some of the trees that surround the spot.

Nobody, however, replied to her involuntary exclamation, and she threw herself on the seat to try to recover from the dreadful state of trepidation into which she had been thrown by this unexpected intimation of the vicinity of one who she had hoped was far removed from the danger that threatened him.

From time to time, as the breeze rustled among and showered down the few dry leaves that yet remained on the trees, she started and fancied that she heard the whispering and sound of voices, or the noise of footsteps; but she soon became convinced these were only the inventions of her fear, for the solitude around her remained undisturbed; until at the very moment she had made up her mind to rise and return home, lest her long absence should have been noticed, and might lead to an enquiry where she had been, a sound different to those occasioned by these natural causes met her ear, and raising her eyes, she beheld a man at the end of the long and now leafless avenue which led from the open glade into the very heart of the forest.

Elinor's trembling limbs refused to bear their weight when she attempted to rise, and she sank down again, keeping at the same time her eyes intently fixed on the person whose appearance had thus excited her.

The man, in his turn, seemed to be regarding her earnestly, though he did not attempt to approach her; but all her terrors and apprehensions subsided into something very strongly resembling disappointment, when she discovered that the person in question was a clownish rustic in a smock frock, with an axe on his shoulder, at once declaring the purport of his being in the wood.

He passed on, and Elinor considering it certain that Edward, if he had been there (which, that he had, could scarcely admit of a doubt) would certainly not have remained at the risk of being discovered by the woodman, quitted her seat, and returned home as fast as her weak and trembling limbs would allow her.

Before she reached the house, however, the necessity of concealing that she had met with any particular occurrence was forcibly brought to her mind by her seeing Mr. Copeland enter, he having apparently just crossed from the stables. She delayed, therefore, long enough to be pretty certain that he would be seated at the fireside; and then, assuming as much calmness as possible, she went round by the back way to the kitchen, where she remained for some time by the fire with Dorcas, observing that, fine as the weather was, she felt completely chilled.

"You've been in the wood, Miss, hav'n't you?" demanded

Philip, who was at that moment employed in some little job for the housekeeper.

Elinor replied in the affirmative; not, however, without betraying some slight confusion.

"I wouldn't advise you to be too venturesome, Miss Elinor," resumed Philip, with a significant shake of the head, "there's something uncommon strange to me about the place. I had to cross to get into the Newton road the night before last, and though the moon was shining bright enough, and I could see my way before me, I declare I never was so glad to get out of any place in my life. I fancied every now and then that I heard somebody stealing about among the trees, and heard voices whispering; and I wasn't much out either, for at last, a strange dog, I knew it belonged to nobody about this neighbourhood, came smelling up to me. I didn't half like the creter, but I thought I'd speak him fair, and so I said, 'Hollo, old fellow, where do you come from?' but the very minute I spoke, there was a loud whistle, I'm sure not fifty yards off, and away went the dog; so that it was plain somebody was lurking about, and for no good purpose, you may be sure."

Elinor felt rather disappointed than alarmed at the conclusion of Philip's adventure, for she had hoped to learn something more decisive as to the person or persons of whom he was apprehensive. She suppressed, however, all expression of peculiar interest, and merely replied that she was thankful for the caution.

"Though I do not know," she added, with a deep sigh, "why I should fear any one, since they could have no motive to molest me."

Philip appeared to be on the point of saying something, but, as he raised his head from his work for that purpose, he suddenly stopped. Struck at his confused and significant look, Elinor turned round to ascertain the cause of it, and discovered that Mr. Copeland was standing behind her, and had evidently, from the expression of his countenance, heard what had passed.

He said nothing, however, on the subject; and Elinor in a few moments quitted the kitchen and went to her own room again, to read over the verses which had so mysteriously come into her possession.

That Edward had adopted this mode of letting her know that he was in the vicinity, and should seek an interview with her, she could not doubt, and that he had done so in the form of verse was undoubtedly in case the paper should have fallen into the hands of any of the rustics in the neighbourhood, who would neither have comprehended it or have suspected it could convey any intelligence in that shape.

But while her heart throbbed with emotion at the thought of once more beholding him whom she loved with all the fervour of first and undivided affection, she could not conceal from herself the fearful risk at which this indulgence must be purchased; and almost could she at that moment have resolved to sacrifice even the hope of ever again seeing him, could she have been assured that he was safe beyond the reach of his enemies.

In a short time her reflections were interrupted by the entrance of Annie.

"How you could venture into the wood, Elinor, alone," she observed, "or how you could bear to go there at all I cannot think; I am sure I would not venture to enter it for the world."

"How did you know I had been there, my dear girl?" demanded Elinor, rather from the necessity of replying than any consideration of what she asked.

"My father mentioned it," replied Anne, "and I thought seemed rather displeased about it; at least he asked very particularly how long you had been absent, and if we knew whether this was your first visit there? and when Isabel said, 'she did not know whether it was your first visit or not, but that you were out yesterday, though she had not inquired which way you went,' he said, speaking to himself, 'I am right—I am sure I am; it is not chance that carries her there.'"

"Isabel tried very hard," she continued, "to get him to explain what he meant, but he would not; he only said, 'Let her (meaning you) alone, girl and it will all come out;' and so I thought I would just give you a hint, though I'm sure I cannot think what father could mean."

Elinor, however, could readily guess that Mr. Copeland had made some discovery connected with the subject that so deeply occupied her thoughts at that moment; but while the conviction struck terror to her heart, she felt most thankful that, through Annie's affection and unsuspiciousness, she was made aware of it in time to prevent her either falling into the snare or being made the means of entrapping him whom she would have died to save.

She disguised, however, her thoughts from Annie, and merely observed "that she would certainly not go again within the boundaries of the wood."

"Though it is hard," she added, with a deep sigh, "that I

cannot even take a solitary walk to the spot where I have been
happier than I can ever hope to be again, without exciting your
father's anger and suspicion."

"I am sorry, dear Elinor, very sorry it should be so," returned
Annie, in an apologising tone; "but you connot wonder," she
added, with a melancholy look, "that my father hates the place
that has been the scene of such heavy misfortunes to us. I do
not think he likes to hear even the name of the wood mentioned;
and he said just now, after he had been a long time silent, and
Isabel and I thought he had forgotten altogether how angry he
had been, 'that he wished it was his own property; he would
set it all on fire, and burn every tree down, even if he was sure
that the farm and all he is worth in the world would perish in
the flames.'"

Elinor shuddered at the vindictive spirit which had prompted
this observation, but which the simple-minded Annie interpreted
so differently.

During the whole of that night sleep never for a moment visited
Elinor's pillow, for she was incessantly occupied in forming plans
—no sooner indeed formed than rejected from the impossibility
of carrying them into execution—to remove herself from the
power of Mr. Copeland, whom she every hour learned to fear
more and like less.

Love towards him she never could feel, and never had felt;
but there had been times and seasons when she had felt herself
bound by the ties of gratitude to respect her benefactor, for such
she then believed him to be.

But it was not merely selfish feelings that induced her so
earnestly to wish for a speedy removal from the Grove.

The fact was that, unwilling as she was to believe that she
could be in any way accessory to Edward's being betrayed into
the hands of those who were so inveterately prejudiced against
him, she felt terrified that such might, if not now, at some future
period be the case if she remained there.

If she were gone — it was not vanity that suggested the
belief, but her knowledge of Edward's ardent and adventurous
disposition—he would no longer have any inducement to risk
his safety by venturing.

Oh! how often did she wish, during the perturbed reflections
of that night, that she possessed some means of communication
with him, if it were only for a few moments, that she might
warn him that Mr. Copeland's suspicions were awakened, to beg
of him, as he valued her happiness, her peace of mind, nay, her

ELINOR CLARE.

AT THAT INSTANT A FIGURE BOUNDED TO THEIR FEET.

very existence, to shun the vicinity in which he was exposed to such imminent danger, and trust to Providence to clear him in its own good time from the dreadful imputation that lay now so heavy upon him.

The verses, which she had read over and over again, indeed till every line was imprinted on her memory, seemed only to hint to her a future meeting, but still who could have placed them there but Edward himself?

She recollected, indeed, the description of the person whom Watkins had seen coming from the Nunnery, and who, she could not doubt, was the same man that she had beheld on the eventful night in company with Mrs. Hatherleigh and

Edward, and whose influence over the latter had certainly induced him to adopt the resolution—the fatal resolution, Elinor considered it—of not appearing boldly to face the charge, and vindicate himself from it.

But even if that person were now in the neighbourhood of the Grove, Elinor thought there was little probability that Edward would have confided to him an embassy of love, or that he, so stern, so rude, so almost ferocious, as he appeared to her on that night, would have undertaken it.

The morning came, and found her as much perplexed as undetermined, and as miserable as ever. She exerted herself to appear to maintain an appearance of calmness, and by mingling more with the family, and avoiding as much as possible being alone, to disarm the suspicions of Mr. Copeland, who she saw watched all her actions with a jealous eye, though he avoided as much as possible letting her see that he ever noticed her presence, and never addressed a single word to her.

In this miserable state of restraint another week passed away. Every day that passed lessened in some degree Elinor's fears, for she did not think it possible that Edward could have remained so long in the neigbourhood without something having been heard of him, and that there had been nothing she was well convinced, since, if Mr. Copeland had chosen to keep it a secret, Isabel's looks would have betrayed it, even if Annie's fond attachment to Elinor, and her firm conviction of Edward's innocence, which she never hesitated to avow to the latter, though she was compelled to be silent on the subject in the presence of her father, had not induced her to reveal anything which she might have considered important to him.

The weather for the last two days had become very inclement; keen easterly winds had brought them drifts of snow and sleet, rendering it impossible for Mr. Copeland to pursue his usual out-of-doors avocations; and this was also a considerable relief to Elinor, who had hitherto never seen him leave the house without feeling a sickening sensation of terror, lest before he returned he should have made some discovery respecting Edward.

The freedom, indeed, from these immediate causes for fear was dearly purchased, by being subjected to so many hours of penance, as she was now compelled to pass in the society of the farmer; but painful as this was, Elinor bore it patiently, and endeavoured, by the most unaffected meekness, and unobtrusive kindness, to prove that she was not deserving of the persevering resentment which he still displayed towards her.

Less, however, did Mr. Copeland's forbidding sullenness give her pain than the restraint which it imposed upon Isabel and Annie, who seemed afraid to utter a word more than was absolutely necessary to her in his presence.

Hour after hour, therefore, was she condemned to sit, mechanically plying her needle—to read was a crime at all times with Mr. Copeland, who held book-learning, as he called it, in females, in utter abhorrence—without a single word being addressed to her, unless it immediately applied to her occupation; and even then, if Annie so far forgot herself as to add to her request for the scissors, thread, &c., "dear Elinor," as had been her wont in happier days, or Isabel ventured to lengthen some enquiry about what she was engaged on into anything like an attempt to converse with the proscribed girl, the old man never failed to repress the momentary feeling by a frown, which was fully understood, and instantly attended to.

It was after a day thus wearisomely passed, that Elinor gladly sought the shelter of her own little chamber, where alone, as it appeared to her, she dared even think of freedom. The day had been boisterous, and Betsy, who was now permanently employed in the house, in the place of another female who had left at Christmas, had, unknown to any one, lighted a fire in the room, an indulgence which the thrifty habits of Mrs. Dorcas did not permit on ordinary occasions.

"You did look so cold and miserable, Miss Elinor," she observed, "every time I came in and out of the parlour to-night, sitting out at the other side of that great table, as if you didn't belong to the family, that my heart quite ached to see you, and I thought, at any rate, you should have a bit of comfort to yourself before you went to bed, and so now you can read as long as you like, when you've locked the door after me."

Simple as was this act of thoughtful kindness, Elinor felt deeply grateful to the poor girl, though she gently chided her for running the risk of making Dorcas angry with her, should she discover what she would call her extravagance.

"Oh, there's no fear of her finding out anything to-night," returned the girl, with a confident smile, "for you know it's New Year's eve, Miss; and though we couldn't keep it up in the kitchen much, when all was so dull and gloomy in the parlour, Mrs. Docras treated us all with plenty of cake and hot elder wine after supper; and as she did not forget to take her share, and put rather more than the share of brandy in it, as well as in Kitty's, why, they've both got more good-natured than ever I

saw them, and are sitting quite cosey by a fire big enough to
roast a sheep, now that the old woman's got master off to bed,
so there's no fear of her coming up to look after your fire. I had
a good mind to steal a glass out of her tankard of wine, and
bring it up to you," continued the girl laughing, "but I was
afraid you would be offended."

Elinor gravely thanked her, but assured her she had judged
quite right in abstaining from so doing, both on her own account
and hers (Elinor's); and Betsy, who was evidently anxious to
get back to the enjoyments of the kitchen fire-side, having
fulfilled her mission of kindness, bade the former good night,
and left her.

It was the first moment of comfort Elinor had known that day
when, after fastening the door, she drew a volume from her small
store, and her seat by the bright little fire; but alas, the book
soon lost its powers to interest.

It had been given her by Edward, and as a New Year's gift
too, only a short twelve months before.

Her name, written by his hand, the date, and the wish for her
future happiness, expressed in terms of affection unconscious of
its own nature, and therefore seeking no disguise, met her eye
on the very first leaf, and banished all inclination to read.

She laid the book on the table, and leaning her head on her
hand, sat ruminating on the past and the future—the past how
inexplicable to her, now that circumstances induced her cir-
cumstantially to review it—the future so hopeless, dark, and uncertain, as to defy her every effort to pierce its mysteries.

The wind, which had been so boisterous all day, had sunk into
perfect quietness, and the faint sounds of suppressed merriment,
which from time to time reached Elinor's ear from the kitchen,
alone broke the stillness of the night, until the striking of the
hour of midnight by the old-fashioned house clock which stood
on the landing place close to her door, reminded her that another
year was added to those which had glided away in such comparative calmness and felicity.

The bells of the neighbouring village church at the same
moment struck into a musical, but to Elinor's ear, most melancholy peal, and overcome with a thousand vague thoughts, reflections, and apprehensions, she burst into tears.

For nearly an hour she sat listening to those sounds, and
reflected to how many they were the harbingers of pleasure and
delight, as they had once seemed to her, who could now hear in
them only the knell of departed happiness.

Last year, what a bright and joyous circle had encompassed Mr. Copeland's blazing hearth at this hour, vying with each other in enhancing the enjoyments of the season by the liveliest sallies of youthful mirth and gaiety.

It seemed as if she could at that moment hear the boisterous "huzza," with which Walter Copeland had greeted the first sound of the bells, and feel the pressure of the warm kiss (a brotherly one she then thought it) with which he enforced his wish that she might enjoy a happy new year, and many of them.

Yet even at that moment it now occurred to her Edward had felt a prophetic indication of the sorrows that awaited him.

How well she recollected that he joined not with heart and soul, as he had on former occasions, in the frolics and gaieties of the time.

Even Isabel had complained of his inattention and want of spirit in the dance; and Walter, with his usual bluntness and vivacity, had alternately scolded and rallied him, until some casual observation awakened him, as he thought, to the true cause of Edward's depression, or what he called his lumpishness.

"You are fretting, like a good and dutiful son as you are, Ned," he observed, "that your mother is sitting lonely at home. I wish to Heaven she would have yielded to our persuasions, and joined our party. It's a poor heart, indeed, they say, that never rejoices; and surely once in a year she might relax her rule of never visiting anywhere. By the bye, Edward, I wonder what made her form such a whimsical resolution, and keep it for so many years."

"It is easily explained," returned Edward, gravely, "neither my mother's circumstances nor health would allow of her receiving company, and she will not therefore incur obligations she cannot return."

"Oh! but with us—" Walter was beginning, when the fiddler struck up one of his liveliest tunes, and in another minute the thoughtless youth was on the floor, bounding and capering with all the exuberant vivacity which ever distinguished him in the pursuit of pleasure. Easily and satisfactorily as Edward had replied to Walter's remarks on that occasion, it was very evident to Elinor, who unconsciously felt it influence her own good spirits, that the former was suffering from some cause of unusual depression and embarrassment, and this was still stronger confirmed, when, on the breaking up of their party at a late or rather early hour of the morning, Walter, who was determined, as he said, not to go to bed, proposed that they should all run over to the Nunnery with Edward, and wish Mrs. Hatherleigh the compliments of the season.

"We will take a bottle of wine and some cake with us," observed Walter, "and I will be the old lady's first foot, as they call it in the North, and then she will be sure to have good luck all the year through. Bless her kind heart and good temper, I have never forgotten how she comforted and doctored my bruises, when I fell out of her pear-tree, when I was a wicked urchin of ten years old, and never said a sour word to me, though she knew I had come to rob her of her fine Windsor pears, that she set such store by, and of which there were not more than a score on the tree that year. Anybody but her would have talked me to death about the sin that I had committed, and the judgment that had fallen on me, but her kindness made me more ashamed of myself than a thousand sermons, and I walked home, making a resolution all the way that I would never take so much as a single apple or pear again from anybody's orchard, and I kept my word too. So come along, we will go and salute her with a song, as she wouldn't come here to hear our

> "'Very good song and very well sung
> Jolly companions every one.'"

Grateful as Edward evidently was at the eulogy bestowed on his mother, he was much more alarmed at this proposal, which he opposed with an earnestness that even to Elinor seemed extraordinary. Walter, however, was not to be diverted from his purpose; indeed, such was his disposition, that to oppose was but to make him more strenuous in his determination.

It was a fine clear moonlight night, or rather morning, when the party, consisting of some eight or ten young people, sons and daughters of the farmers around, besides the family of Mr. Copeland, set out from the Grove on their mirthful expedition, Walter roaring at the top of his voice the burthen of one of the common songs of the country,

> "We won't go home till morning,
> We won't go home till morning.
> Till daylight does appear,"

and the rest of the lads and even some of the lasses, uniting in the chorus. Edward did not join in this uproarious mirth; he kept close to Elinor, and she could see that his cheek was paler than ever; his eye appeared bent on vacancy, and his lips firmly compressed, betraying not only the extent of his vexation, but that he was lost in thought how to prevent the frolic, for such it was to all but him, being carried to the full extent projected by Walter.

On, however, went the latter, thoughtless and reckless, leaping stiles and gates, and practising a thousand manual jokes upon his less excited and less agile companions.

"You do not seem to like this noisy excursion," observed Elinor, as Edward, muttering some apology for his inattention, turned to offer his assistance in crossing a stile.

"Like it!" he repeated, "oh no, I would give all that I can call my own in the world to prevent this intrusion on my mother to-night."

"I am afraid there is no possibility of altogether preventing it," returned Elinor; "but I think if they keep up this uproar all the way, Mrs. Hatherleigh will be so well warned of our approach, that she will be enabled to prevent any intrusion, by barring the door against such unseasonable visitors."

"You are right," returned Edward, quickly, as if that moment struck with the same idea, "yes, you are quite right;" and darting from her side, he mingled with the thoughtless throng, shouting with all his might, and seeming to emulate them in noise and uproar.

The device, however, did not succeed, at least, in the sense Elinor then understood it was intended; for when they reached the Nunnery, Mrs. Hatherleigh was waiting to receive and welcome them to her bright fire and clean swept hearth, which was soon surrounded by the merry group.

Elinor had *then* seen nothing extraordinary in this, though she had certainly thought Edward's conduct strangely inconsistent; but now that she calmly and quietly recalled all these circumstances, which were so deeply engraven on her mind, she became convinced that there was more than she then suspected in Edward's reluctance that his mother should be intruded upon.

"That man, that strange, unaccountable man, was, in all probability," thought Elinor, "even then an inhabitant of his mother's house, and if so, can I for an instant doubt who he is, or at least what tie there is, between him and Edward?"

The thought was inexpressibly painful, and under its influence Elinor rose and paced her room, from time to time looking through the window, the curtains of which were not entirely closed. Several times had she repeated this, with her thoughts so entirely absorbed as to be unconscious of what she was doing, but at the last turn her attention was suddenly arrested by something white waving immediately beneath her window. As much from the desire of shrouding herself from observation, should any one be there, as of ascertaining who it was she saw below, Elinor softly stepped back and extinguished the candle. The fire had already burnt so low as to give scarcely any light, and when she returned to the window, and glided behind the curtain, she stood there in complete obscurity. Some moments passed, however, before she could discover anything of the object that had so strongly excited her curiosity, but at last it again appeared and then she distinctly ascertained that it was some person who waved a white handkerchief as a signal. That there was but one person in the world who was likely to adopt this course, Elinor was certain, and without a moment's hesitation, except what arose from her excessive agitation, she opened the casement and leant out.

"Elinor," breathed the well-known tones of Edward Hatherleigh, though so low as would scarcely have been audible to any but the anxious ear of love.

"Edward, if you love me—if you have any pity for me—if you do not wish me to lose my senses, go away!" returned the terrified girl, bending down as low as she possibly could, so as to let her voice be heard by him, without raising it above a whisper. "You are watched, Edward," she continued, "even perhaps at this moment."

"Fear not, dear girl," returned Edward, still speaking with caution, yet evidently with more confidence. "I have taken every precaution, and I am satisfied no one is within sight or hearing. Elinor," he continued, impressively, "I have risked much to see you; do not, therefore, let unfounded alarm deprive me of this opportunity of conversing with you for a few minutes. I can easily reach your window, or if you prefer to come out, do not waste the time in objections. "Elinor," he hastily added, interrupting the remonstrance she was about to utter, "say, indeed, that you reject and discard me—that you no longer feel any interest in my fate, and I will instantly go."

Elinor had in these few instants hastily run over in her mind the probable consequences of yielding to either of his proposals, and she replied in a decisive tone. "If it is to answer any good purpose, Edward, I will hazard the attempt to join you, on condition that you wait for me at what we used to call our seat. If I do not come within half an hour, you must conclude I have been intercepted. Go now, pray go, for I am in agony every moment that you linger here."

"But if you should not come, Elinor," said he, doubtingly.

"I will come," she replied; "if you have any faith in me, believe that I will come, if it be possible.   If I do not, be assured that my attempt is discovered, and secure your safety by instant flight."

For an instant Edward still lingered; but as if suddenly recollecting himself, he observed,

" I will obey you, Elinor; but oh! remember how wretched I shall be if you fail."

Elinor closed the casement, to prevent any furthur prolongation of the conversation, which exposed them every instant to the danger of being overheard; and then for an instant she threw herself upon a chair, to recover her full recollection, and consider how she should act.

Fortunately, the chambers in which Mr. Copeland and his daughters slept were in a different direction to that of Elinor's, which looked into the garden.   There was thus little fear that by them any discovery should be made of Edward's proximity. The only persons whom Elinor had any reason to fear were the housekeeper and the other female servants, who slept in the room over her.

Of their observation, however—though she did not know it, or rather, was not sufficiently *au fait* in such matters to suspect the truth—there was little reason to be afraid.   The elder wine of which Betsy had spoken, and its accompaniments, having sent them all so comfortable to bed that there was little danger of their being awakened, even by a much louder noise than Edward's dulcet tones.

Of this Elinor was not, as we have before said, aware; and she therefore remained for some minutes listening in great trepidation to noises, as she fancied, in the apartment above, and which, to her terrified imagination, prognosticated nothing less than an immediate discovery and pursuit of Edward.

A few minutes' silent attention, however, to these formidable sounds, which recurred at regular intervals, convinced her that she had much greater reason to rejoice than to be alarmed at them, as, in fact, they only indicated the soundness of Dorcas and her companions' slumbers, or, in other words, was a complete chorus of snorers.

Without furthur hesitation, therefore, she threw on her bonnet and shawl, and cautiously opening the door, stole down by the back staircase, which led to the kitchen, thus saving her the necessity of passing Mr. Copeland's or the girls' chambers, and running the risk of awakening them.

The large log, which, in compliance with Christmas custom,

had been added to the kitchen fire, was still smouldering when
Elinor entered the room, and afforded sufficient light to enable
her to see to unbar one of the windows, through which she
could much easier find egress, than by the heavy house-door,
the bolts and locks of which she could not have removed without considerable noise.

Prosperous as she had been in her attempts hitherto, however, Elinor started and trembled at every shadow, as, after
quietly drawing to the shutter behind her, and closing the
casement so as to leave no outward appearance that any one
had passed that way, and yet afford her the means of easily re-
entering the house, she sped swiftly along the winding path
that led to the appointed spot.

Edward was there; he flew to meet her; and in the fervent
embrace that followed, and in the hurried expressions of his
love, his delight, his gratitude, Elinor for a few moments
forgot her fears and her sorrows.

But the consciousness of Edward's danger soon returned upon
her mind, and tenderly she reproached him with the risk he ran.

"It was once, Edward," she continued, "my most earnest
prayer and wish that you would come forward and vindicate
yourself from this horrible charge, but the time is now passed,
and I shudder at the thought of your falling into the hands of
your bitter enemies."

"Is it true, then, that Mr. Copeland still believes me guilty?"
said Edward, in a tone of deep dejection. "I had hoped," he
continued, as Elinor replied to his interrogation by a deep sigh,
"that time and calm reflection—even if no other testimony
should have arisen—would have suggested some doubts in my
favour. But this is not what I came to say, dearest Elinor.
When I last saw you," he proceeded, "in the anguish of
excited feelings, I bade you adieu, as I feared, for ever. I
believed then that not a hope existed of rescuing myself from
utter degradation. I do not allude to the circumstances attendant on Walter's death, Elinor, for I confess I thought then that
the truth would come to light, and that I should stand acquitted
in the eyes of all concerned in my guilt or innocence, without any
intervention on my own part. But there were other circumstances which made me despair that I should ever be able or
worthy to claim the fulfilment of that promise, which you so
nobly gave me. Elinor, I have sought you now to lay before
you, as far as I can, these circumstances, to ask you—dare you
—will you keep to your engagement, when you know all; and

if not, Elinor, there is but one alternative. I will release you from all ties and obligations, and leave you to—"

" And do you, then, think so meanly of me, Edward, " interrupted Elinor, " as to suppose that——"

A sound, resembling the shrill scream of an owl, at that moment interrupted Elinor's protestations, and made her cling closer to Edward, who looked around him with an air of bewilderment. The cry was repeated, and he hurried her away towards the heart of the wood, whispering at the same time, in an agitated tone—

" There is danger abroad, Elinor; that is a signal to me, but as yet I know not——"

" Save yourself! Oh! Edward, linger not an instant here," exclaimed the terrified Elinor. " Do not bestow a thought upon me; let me not have the misery of knowing that I have been the means of bringing you to destruction. Oh! Edward, go; pray go."

Edward, however, only clasped her still closer, as he still hurried on, carrying rather than leading his affrighted companion, until they had reached the Haunted Oak, where he paused.

" Do not be alarmed, Elinor," he observed in a low voice; "if any danger approaches, I can from this spot discover it in time to place both you and myself in safety. There is a retreat near which will defy their search."

" Do not hesitate then, but instantly seek it," exclaimed Elinor; "for me there is no danger. Leave me, then; oh, pray leave me! I will return home, and——"

At that instant a figure bounded to their feet, with a spring so sudden, that Elinor uttered an involuntary shriek of terror.

" Ah! that's done the business at once," exclaimed the figure, in a shrill voice, which seemed most strange and unnatural in Elinor's ears. " If we don't make the best of our way to cover, we shall eat our breakfasts to-morrow morning in Newton Cage, and I don't want to go there yet, for there's old scores to pay that make my flesh creep already. Come on, Master Ned, we must to earth as quick as possible, or the hounds will be at our heels."

During this speech, Edward had continued to follow the speaker, forcing Elinor on with him with a rapidity that denied her the power of utterance, almost of breath.

The strange being who had excited in her bosom such terror, continued to precede them, but in a manner as singular as had been his first appearance, for he neither walked nor ran, but

vaulted along the ground in a succession of long leaps, which
cleared every obstacle that lay in his way, though it rendered it
more difficult for those who trusted to his guidance to follow,
as he did not seem to consider it at all necessary to keep in any
direct path, or to stand for shrubs, bushes, or underwood, over
all of which he passed with a lightness and agility that few
could have pretended to emulate.

Edward, however, forced his way through all difficulties, and in
a few minutes they had reached a heap of grey stones, piled up in
shapeless disorder, and partly overgrown with weeds and nettles,
and from which might be traced in more than one direction, the
foundation of walls, which seemed to bespeak that a building of
some extent, probably a monastery, had once stood there, of
which these were all the remains.

All that had been convertible into use of the building materials
had undoubtedly been removed from the spot at probably distant
as well as recent times, and only a portion of the walls, and rude
unwieldy masses of stone, were left to encumber the desolate
spot, which, from its nature and situation, looked the ideal of
barrenness and neglect.

Over this heap the creature preceded them, descending on the
opposite side with as much quickness and alacrity as if it had
been the smooth turf he traversed, while Edward, on the
contrary, was compelled to pick his steps, and support Elinor
from stone to stone, in the attempt to follow him.

"A few moments only, a few more of exertion, Elinor, and
we are in safety," whispered Edward, still urging her forward.

"In safety here," she replied, recoiling with alarm at finding
that, having crossed the heap of ruins, they were on the edge of
a deep dell, the descent into which appeared to her utterly impracticable.

Their guide had disappeared, and Edward now stood on the
very edge of what, from its abruptness, if not its depth, might
almost be called a precipice.

"Yes, dearest girl," he replied, "trust to me, and remain
where you are for an instant."

With little apparent difficulty he lowered himself over the
edge of the descent, until he had gained a firm footing, and then
imploring Elinor not to be alarmed, but to trust to his guidance,
he lifted her cautiously down to the same spot.

"We will wait for our guide, before we attempt to enter the
place which will afford us a secure refuge," observed Edward, as
he stood with his arm round Elinor, supporting her on the nar-

row ledge of rock on which they had found a footing; "we are close to the entrance," he continued, " and I could find my way, but the steps are broken, and it would be dangerous to you in the dark; Zekiel will bring you a light in a moment."

It was well that he had given her this intimation, or Elinor might have started at the sudden flash which issued at that moment from the aperture close to the spot on which they were standing, and a start would have been dangerous in her present situation, standing as they were upon a narrow ledge of earth which seemed to be crumbling from under their feet.

She had no time, however, to reflect on her danger, of which, indeed, she was not entirely conscious, until the flash of the torch distinctly showed it to her.

Edward now entered the aperture, which was only wide enough to admit, and that with difficulty, one person at a time, and Elinor, without hesitation, followed down the steep stone steps, which were, as he had represented, so decayed and worn away, as to render them dangerous without extreme caution.

The moment they reached the bottom, Zekiel, as Edward had called him, thrust the torch into the latter's hand, and bounded up the steps again, observing—

" We must shut the nabmen out, though it arn't very likely they have tracked us here; but safe bind safe find is one of granny's sayings, and none the worse for that either."

Elinor had now time to discover that the being whose sudden appearance and strange movements had so much surprised and alarmed her, was a singular-looking lad, whose dark features were almost hidden by the profusion of black locks that hung over his face, and from the midst of which his dark eyes flashed like diamonds as he turned them with curious interest on her.

Until this moment Elinor had scarcely uttered a word, but now, as Edward, placing her arm within his, would have led her forward through a long and arched passage which faced them, she suddenly drew back, while a dreadful suspicion crossed her mind that she had been betrayed.

" Edward ! " she exclaimed, raising her eyes to his expressive features, in which, however, she could read nothing like sinister designs, " I have trusted implicitly in you hitherto, but whither is it that you would lead me? or why were you not content to seek safety here without bringing me?"

" Ah, you are right there," exclaimed the strange voice of Zekiel close behind her, " that's just what Paul Dangerfield will say to Master Ned when———"

" Silence, fool !" exclaimed Edward, with violence.

" Oh, aye, the fool is no use now," muttered the boy, sullenly, taking the torch again from Edward, and knocking it against the wall to brighten the flame. " I wonder where you'd been, though, by this time, if I hadn't kept my senses about me a little quicker than——"

" Well, well, I was hasty, good Zekiel," interrupted Edward, soothingly; " I know that I am deeply indebted to you, and you shall not find me ungrateful; but come, lead on, this lady will trust herself a little to our guidance without distrusting our intentions."

" Lady !" repeated the urchin, with a chuckling laugh, which evidently again irritated Edward, though he bit his lip and suppressed it, in obedience to Elinor's signal not to notice the boy's impertinence.

All Zekiel's activity, however, seem to have vanished with the necessity for exertion, and he plodded heavily and sullenly before them, until the passage opened into a large but low-vaulted room, which, to Elinor's surprise, was furnished with chairs, a table, two beds, and a number of other articles, bespeaking that it was used as a habitation.

" This is a sad place to bring you to, Elinor," observed Edward, " but it is the only place that I can call my home now, and that for, perhaps, only a few days, it may be only a few hours."

" Your home !" repeated Elinor, unable to restrain her horror and astonishment.

Edward sighed without replying, and Elinor gladly accepted the offer of a seat which Zekiel, with an attempt at civility that seemed unusual to him, placed for her, bringing also a large thick mat from a distant corner to put under her feet.

" It's damp and cold here to them that are not seasoned to it," he observed, in a softened tone, " and I dare not light a fire now, because the smoke would betray us, but in the night, when everybody's in bed and asleep, we'll have a jovial fire, and the place then is as snug as you'd wish it to be."

Elinor now saw that there was an aperture in the vaulted roof to let the smoke out; but she thought only of the risk Edward must run to enjoy even the comfort of a fire, and she shuddered with terror and dismay as she uttered her fears to Edward that his imaginary safety rested on a very insecure foundation.

" I should have thought so myself," he returned, with a

melancholy smile, "had I not known that it has at various times for years afforded a safe retreat to one who has had, perhaps, more reason than I have to fear discovery. Zekiel could, if there was time, tell you some anecdotes of this place which would prove to you that there is little danger of our residence being discovered; could you not, Zekiel?"

The boy to whom this was addressed, evidently with a view of conciliating him, smiled archly, displaying a set of teeth the pure white of which contrasted strongly with the darkness of his complexion, his roguish eyes at the same time twinkling with added brilliancy as he shook the thick, heavy black curls back from his brow, and looked up in Elinor's face. In a moment, however, he seemed to relapse into his former sullen mood.

"The place was well enough," he observed, "but that was when nobody knew anything about it but I and——well, you needn't frown so, Master Ned; I can tell you if Paul finds out that I've helped to bring any one here I shall get my bones broke, though I am a fool; and indeed none but a fool would have gone with you on your mad scheme to-night; and now how's the young woman to get home again without betraying us? They'll be sure to ask her a thousand questions where she's been, and——"

"Do not alarm yourself," gently interrupted Elinor, "no questions, no inducements the world could offer, would induce me to betray your secret."

"Alarm," he repeated sarcastically. "Oh, I'm not alarmed, but it's Paul Dangerfield, and Master Ned there, that——"

"Silence, you malicious being," interrupted Edward, angrily, "why should you thus take a pleasure in tormenting?"

"What have I got for all I've done to-night," returned the boy, "but been called a fool, and——"

"I did not mean it, you know I did not, Zekiel," interrupted Edward, in a soothing tone; "as to the shilling I promised you, there it is, I had forgotten it; and now, Zekiel, you will go and keep watch, will you not, that Paul does not surprise us here? You can give me the same signal as that of to-night, you know, if he should come, though there is no great fear till daybreak, I dare say."

The boy's eyes sparkled with pleasure at the sight of the coin, which he had eagerly seized, and after biting it to ascertain that it was genuine, he hastily conveyed it into his pocket, and seemed now to have lost every trace of anger or malice.

"Well, well, I'll go," he observed, "and I'll take care that Paul don't catch you, but——"

"Indeed!" exclaimed a voice which made all start; and Zekiel, with every symptom of terror, bounded at one leap across the room, and took refuge behind Elinor, who, too much alarmed to speak or move, sat trembling, with her eyes fixed on the part of the room or rather vault, from whence the voice proceeded, but which was too deep in shadow for her to be able to discover the person who spoke. In a few seconds, however, a man walked slowly forward, and fixed his frowning look upon Edward.

"This is well done in you, young man, is it not?" he observed in a voice of rage. "You have rewarded my confidence in you, have you not, by betraying my only place of shelter?"

"I have not betrayed it," returned Edward, firmly, "the secret is as safe in Elinor's bosom as it is in mine."

"Yes, I do not doubt it," replied the man, sarcastically. "You have proved how safe it is with you, by betraying it on the very first temptation, or rather no temptation at all; and do you flatter yourself that a weak girl can have more——"

"You are mistaken," interrupted Edward, hastily; "mistaken in both your assertions; I have not confided the secret to a weak girl, but one whose strength of mind and resolution would shame many—nay, the greater part of those who call themselves the stronger sex. As to the first temptation to which I so readily yielded, it was urgent necessity; we were pursued, Elinor and I, and I was compelled to take refuge here."

"But why bring *her* here?" demanded the stranger, whom Elinor had, immediately that she beheld his dark features, recognised as the person whom she had seen in Mrs. Hatherleigh's kitchen. "She could be in no danger from pursuit."

"I know not that," returned Edward, "and, in fact," he added, suddenly recollecting himself, "I was not aware what the danger exactly was against which Zekiel's signal warned me."

"I can tell you, then, that all your apprehensions are unfounded; there was no danger to you at all."

"You are wrong there, Paul," exclaimed Zekiel, coming forward, and seeming to gather courage by the comparatively calm tone in which the former uttered the last sentence. "You are quite wrong there," he repeated, "for they were all up and afoot at the Grove, for I heard their voices and saw the lights flashing through the trees, before ever I gave the signal."

ELINOR CLARE.

"'TIS ELINOR! OH! SHE IS SAVED!"

"Lights indeed!" he coolly repeated, "if you look forth now you will see them a little brighter. Your uncle's house is on fire, young woman," he continued, addressing Elinor; "I don't know whether you have had any hand in it."

Elinor started up with an exclamation. "Oh God! let me go to them! Isabel—Annie, let me fly to——"

"There is no necessity for alarm on account of the family," interrupted the stranger, "for they are all safe; I saw them collected together on the grass plot, and heard the girls' loud exclamations for their 'dear Elinor,' who they believe has perished in the flames."

"Oh, let me go to them instantly, then!" she exclaimed, turning to Edward, who had stood silent.

"I will go with her, shall I, Paul?" observed Zekiel, looking entreatingly at the person he addressed, "I should like to see a fire, and besides, there might be something to be——"

A tremendous frown, and an exclamation in a language which was incomprehensible to Elinor, interrupted Zekiel's earnest entreaty, and the latter slunk away to a far corner of the room, where he crouched down upon some straw which was spread there, more like a cur that had been beaten by its master than a human being.

Elinor, in the mean time, stood in the most painful suspense and agitation. There was something in the stranger's manner that completely appalled her, and the expression of Edward's face, as she turned to entreat of him that he would conduct her out of the place, from which she knew she could not hope to find her way without assistance, confirmed the impression of terror on her mind.

Edward's eyes were fixed on the countenance of his companion, with a look of mingled anger and apprehension.

"She *must* go home, sir," he observed, with emphasis, after a few moments' silence. "If she remains here——"

"She *must* remain here, sir," returned the other, sarcastically imitating him. "You have chosen to bring her here, and for her own sake, as well as yours, here she must remain, at least, until we can remove her to a place of greater safety."

"I—remain here—in this place—with you!" ejaculated Elinor with difficulty, yet trying to speak with calmness. "You must be jesting, sir," she added, "though it is certainly a strange time and place to choose for such an amusement. Edward," she continued, turning to the latter, "I trusted implicitly in you, when I suffered you to bring me here, and to you I look to be (as far as is consistent with your safety) conducted to my home."

"Your home! where will you find it?" sneeringly observed Dangerfield, for so henceforth we must call him.

"To my relations, then, sir," returned Elinor with emotion; "let me at least share their fate, whatever it may be."

"I wish," he replied, in a tone of petulance, "that it were in my power immediately to grant your request; Heaven knows I have no inclination to add to my troubles by detaining you here;

but I will just seriously lay the case before you, and leave it to you to decide whether you can with safety, either to you or those for whose safety you pretend to be so deeply concerned " (glancing at Edward, who had with evident difficulty restrained himself from interfering decidedly in Elinor's favour,) " return to your relatives.   From what I casually learned of the fire, which had been raging some time before I came in sight of the Grove, it had originated in your room———"

" It is impossible," interrupted Elinor, hastily, " I had extinguished the candle safely at least a quarter of an hour before I quitted the room, and the fire had burnt so nearly out that there was scarcely a spark in the stove."

" Did you lock the door of your chamber?" he demanded.

" I did," she replied; " my motive was to prevent any one by accident discovering that I was not there.   I recollect now," she quickly added, " that after I left the house I looked back, and saw a light glimmering through the curtains of Dorcas' room, but I was too agitated at the time to pay much attention to it, though I knew it was not Dorcas' habit to burn a light during the night."

" The case is plain, then," returned Dangerfield, " the fire has commenced in that room.   I understood that the old housekeeper was missing as well as you, whose name I knew from frequent repetition; and that the other female servants were with difficulty rescued from the flames.   I heard, too, one of the sisters exclaiming, amidst her lamentations for you, that if you had not locked your door she could have saved you, for when she first tried to arouse you there was no sign of flames, nothing but a suffocating smell of fire and smoke : to which some one standing by observed that, in all probability the smoke had long before overpowered you and deprived you of sense, so that, after all, you had suffered comparatively little."

The horror that Elinor felt at this recital can be better imagined than described.

There was little hope, she thought, that Dorcas had escaped as she had done, for she could not doubt that the fire had originated in the room of the former, which opened into that occupied by the other females.

The unusual indulgence which Betsy had laughingly spoken of, by which the old woman had attempted to make up for the loss of their customary mirth and frolics at this season, had no doubt deprived her of her usual prudence.   She had gone to bed, forgetting to extinguish her candle, and had thus occasioned the conflagration, in which she had lost her own life, and in all probability brought ruin on the family, to whose welfare she had for so many years devoted all her toils and thoughts.

Deep and unfeigned was Elinor's sorrow at this melancholy event, which increased, if possible, her desire to rejoin the family, and relieve them from the apprehensions which she was sure they were suffering on her account.

The calm manner in which Dangerfield had given her this account had removed for an instant her apprehensions of him, and she now again renewed her request to him to allow her to depart.

"If you or Edward," she observed, "will only assist me to reach the outside of the ruin walls, I can easily find my way through the wood.

"The ruin !" he repeated, in astonishment, looking at Edward, "which way then did you bring her here?"

"We couldn't come any other way than the Hole in the Wall, as granny calls it," observed Zekiel, hastily, as if anxious to vindicate himself for having guided the unwelcome guest thither. "How could I know," he added, with increasing confidence, "that the light I saw flashing through the trees was a house on fire; I thought it was the whole set of 'em with torches out after us, and so there was nothing to be done but to run straight ahead, and get into cover as soon as we could."

"Oh ! and so this was your work, was it ?" exclaimed Dangerfield, in a menacing tone, and darting forward, as if to seize him.

"Do not blame the boy, sir," said Edward, hastily, throwing himself between them. "It was I who prevailed on him to accompany me to keep watch while I had for the last time an interview with Elinor. A few short hours are only passed since you approved of my desire to see and explain to her, as far as possible, circumstances which I was conscious must have appeared, even to her, so singularly corroborative of the accusation."

"I have never thought so," interrupted Elinor, hastily.

Edward pressed her hand, but proceeded without otherwise replying to her, to vindicate Zekiel, whose error, he said, "was so natural, that though it must be regretted, it could not be considered blameable."

"There is no necessity, however," he continued, finding that Dangerfield yielded to his arguments, and relinquished his intention of chastising the boy, "to discuss this subject any

further now, when Elinor is suffering, I know, the greatest
impatience to be restored to her friends ; so that I am willing to
yield up my last hope of clearing, in some measure, the mystery
that seemed doomed to hang over me, for in all probability, as
you well know, I shall never———"

" Psha, let us dismiss all this whining, lovesick nonsense." interrupted Dangerfield, whose looks, however, strongly contradicted
the rough tone he thought proper to assume, for they betrayed
a sympathy with the agitation which rendered Edward's voice
tremulous, that he tried in vain to conceal. " Let us come to
the point at once," he continued. " What security have I that
Elinor will not betray this retreat ? If I could depend upon
her, I would not hesitate myself to———"

" I will bind myself by the most solemn oath that you can
dictate," interrupted Elinor, eagerly.

" ' And when they swear the most, believe them least,' "
repeated Dangerfield, sarcastically. " No, no," he added, " unless
there is some stronger motive to bind you than an oath, I dare
not trust you. But come, for this once I will be guilty of an
act of imprudence, which I dare say I shall have reason to
repent ; so make your adieus, Edward, as quickly as possible,
while I go and see that the coast is clear."

" And you won't let me go, then," observed Zekiel, with
childish disappointment of manner, " though I never saw a fire
in my life?"

Dangerfield held up his hand in a menacing manner, and the
boy crouched down again, as if fully understanding the threat.

There was little time, as had been insinuated by Dangerfield,
for much interchange of thought between Elinor and Edward
before the former returned ; but short as had been the period,
she had found an opportunity to express to her lover her surprise
and repugnance (she used no harsher term) to his companion.

A deep blush spread over Edward's pale and thoughtful
countenance, as he replied—

" Elinor, that man is my father ; yet there are moments when
I shrink from him with disgust and horror. Yet he is to be
pitied, though even I, his own son———"

He caught at this moment the keen basilisk eyes of Zekiel
fixed full on him with an expression of intense earnestness.
The boy, indeed, had risen from the ground in his eager desire to
hear more distinctly, and was leaning forward resting on one
hand, with his dark locks flung back, and his face raised to catch
the expression as well as the words Edward uttered.

"That boy is a spy upon me," whispered the latter. "I dare not say any more, Elinor, than again to entreat you to believe me guiltless. I will not so insult you as to ask you to be cautious."

"You need not," returned Elinor, with firmness; "no power or persuasion on earth, Edward, could wring from me one word that could prove injurious to you."

A long and fervent embrace was interrupted by that peculiar chuckling laugh from Zekiel which had before sounded so discordant in Elinor's ear, and with a deep blush she drew back, while Edward turned to reprove the mischievous urchin for his impertinence.

The re-entrance of Dangerfield, however, prevented his saying much on the subject.

"There seems nothing to prevent your going, if you are determined to run the risk of the reception you may meet with," observed the former; "but I would have you once more reflect seriously that you will most undoubtedly be called upon to account satisfactorily for your absence from the farm at such a time of night, and if you are not prepared with a story——"

"I shall tell no story," interrupted Elinor; "I shall merely say that I had a reason which I do not choose to reveal for——"

"Then, by Heavens! you will bitterly repent it if you act so foolishly!" exclaimed Dangerfield, with vehemence. "Nay, ask Edward if I am not right," he continued, "when I say that so sure as you answer the inquiries that will of course be made of you in that manner, so sure you will be accused of having set the farm on fire."

For a moment Elinor repelled the idea as not worthy a serious thought; but Edward's thoughtful, and, indeed, alarmed look, convinced her there was more reason for being apprehensive than she had been willing to believe.

"Mr. Copeland is no friend to you, Elinor," observed the latter, in reply to her look of consternation, "and he may perhaps eagerly seize on any circumstance which may afford him a plausible plea——"

"I see it all," interrupted Elinor, with excessive agitation; "you are indeed right; but surely no one would credit such an assertion—no one would believe me capable of such a horrible crime."

"No one that knows you as I know you, Elinor, would believe it," replied Edward, "but——"

" Aye, aye, there would be plenty who would believe it,"
interrupted Dangerfield, " if the crime were ten times more
atrocious and revolting. When you know, if ever you do, as
much of the world as I have learnt, from bitter experience, you
will be aware that there is a propensity in mankind to believe
the very worst of their fellows. Accuse any one of a crime,
ever so improbable, ever so atrocious, ever so contradictory to
his known habits, his disposition, his principles—to the practice
of his whole life—and you will find for one that is disposed to
assert his innocence, a thousand ready to proclaim his guilt and
hunt him to destruction."

The vehemence with which this was uttered so surprised
Elinor, that for a few moments she forgot her own situation,
and remained silently contemplating the glowing and expressive
features, which betrayed how deeply Dangerfield felt what he
had uttered.

She turned her speaking look upon Edward, but he saw it
not ; his eyes, filled with tears, were fixed on the excited countenance of the man whom he had avowed to be his father, and
Elinor thought she discovered that he repented of the harsh
construction he had put on the conduct of his parent.

Whether the latter saw and understood this she could form
no conjecture, for he was now, with hasty and irregular steps,
traversing the gloomy apartment, apparently unconscious of the
earnest looks that were fixed upon him, and totally absorbed in
some gloomy and corroding reflections.

The recollection, however, that every minute that she remained
rendered her absence more difficult to be accounted for, and
therefore her return more embarrassing to herself, soon banished
the diffidence Elinor felt to intrude upon his reflections, though
she nominally addressed herself to Edward when she again
ventured to express her impatience to depart.

" And what, then, have you resolved upon saying ?" demanded
Dangerfield, suddenly shaking off all his abstraction of manner,
and resuming the cold sinster expression of countenance, which
had, at first sight, appeared so repulsive to Elinor.

" I can only say," returned the latter, whose heart recoiled
with the greatest repugnance from even the attempt to form a
falsehood—" I can only allege, that being unable to sleep, I was
tempted by the fineness of the night to take a walk, and had
gone so far that I knew nothing of what had happened until I
was on my return."

Dangerfield mused for some moments, as if debating with

himself whether this account was likely to answer its intended purpose.

" You know best," he at length observed, " the characters of the people you have to deal with. It may be that such a plea will succeed, but I fear it is a weak one to rely upon. Once more, therefore, I ask you to think well what you are about, before it is too late. It will be difficult, perhaps, if not impossible, to escape from their hands, should those who you now call your friends prove your enemies, as seems to me to be but too probable. Here you are safe, so long as we remain here, and though beyond safety I have little else to offer, yet——"

" No, oh, no," interrupted Edward, who seemed to be struck with the earnestness with which his father pleaded to detain her—" No, this is not a place for Elinor to remain in, nor are my prospects at the present moment such as I could dare ask her to share. She is strong in innocence, and let her go forth boldly to meet the charge, if there is any against her. Would to Heaven that I had done so before it was too late; but no one will think of suspecting Elinor of such a crime. I was a fool to entertain the thought for a moment."

" Certainly, it was the height of folly," observed Dangerfield, with a bitter sneer, " for is it at all likely that the same persons who have accused you of a murder, of which you say you are innocent, would dare be so unjust as to attempt to affix another crime upon one who can so satisfactorily prove the falsehood of the imputation ?"

Edward's eyes, while his father uttered this, were fixed upon his countenance, as if he would have read the very bottom of his soul; but the latter seemed totally to disregard the inquisition, or, if he did see and appreciate his son's motives, he managed well to disguise it by an assumption of the utmost coldness and indifference, as he turned to Elinor and observed,

" Now, then, I am at your service, and ready to attend you."

" I will accompany you to the foot of the steps," observed Edward, taking her hand; " but do you mean to go that way, sir ?"

Dangerfield frowned significantly as he roughly replied,

" What other way would you have me go ? Have you not done enough, think you ?"

A quick flush of resentment crossed Edward's cheek; but he suppressed the reply that seemed hovering on his lips, and led Elinor forward.

It was in vain that either of them tried to utter a word at

parting. A look of anguish and a fervent pressure of the hand was all that passed, ere Edward, in obedience to Dangerfield's command, retraced his steps along the arched passage; and the latter, with an ease that showed him well accustomed to the spot, assisted Elinor up the broken and dangerous ascent, and soon placed her in safety on the firm ground, and in the open air.

Some minutes passed before she could sufficiently collect herself to express her thankfulness for his assistance, and assure him that she now felt herself quite capable of proceeding without giving him any further trouble.

Her conductor, however, did not seem disposed so soon to leave her; and Elinor was too fearful of offending him to offer more than a slight objection to the proposal he made, of seeing her through the most intricate and solitary part of the wood; he therefore continued to walk by her side, until the distant hum of voices, and the flashes of light which were occasionally visible through the leafless trees, warned her that she was fast approaching the scene of the late disaster; and forgetful, at that moment, of everything but her anxiety to ascertain that her relatives were safe, she darted forward with a quickness that left her startled companion far behind before he well comprehended her intention. She had not, however, emerged from the wood, before she felt herself seized, and forcibly retained by his powerful arm.

"Listen to me!" he exclaimed, "for a few moments before we part. The imprudence of that foolish young man has this night placed his life and mine in your hands. You may be, I hope you are, worthy of his confidence; but I warn you, that should you betray it, no human power can save you from the just reward of your perfidy. I may fall, but there are those whose eyes will never sleep till they have avenged me in your heart's blood. Recollect the fate of Walter Copeland, and tremble how you provoke—Ah! am I watched?" he suddenly ejaculated, as something was heard rustling among the dry shrubs behind him.

Before Elinor could reply, he darted away in an opposite direction, and she was left alone. For a few moments she stood fixed to the spot, not knowing what fresh danger awaited her, and undecided whether to attempt to escape by flight or endeavour to conceal herself; but her fears were quickly converted in a feeling of joy and security, when she discovered that the noise which had so alarmed her companion was occasioned by Mr. Copeland's large house-dog breaking through the bushes to join her.

"Poor Carlo!" she exclaimed, as the faithful animal evinced his pleasure at recognising her by licking her hands, uttering at the same time a low whine, which was so different from his usual joyous gratulation, that she could not but be struck with it—"Poor creature!" she continued, "do you mean to tell me that you have lost your office, and have no longer a home to guard?"

A burst of tears, at the thoughts of the desolation which had thus taken place within a short hour—for not longer had she been absent—prevented her for some moments from proceeding; but the dog ran backwards and forwards in the path, as if chiding her delay, and hastily drying her tears, she followed him.

———

CHAPTER VII.

A sound
Of far-off tumult, murmurs on mine ear,
Like ocean's chafing surge—
Behold the sky
Doth redden in the black horizon's verge.
A strong unnatural light streams o'er the dark,
And mocks the dawn of morn.

SHIEL.

LONG before Elinor had emerged from the wood, the crackling of burning timber, the suffocating smell of fire and smoke, and the tall spires of flame, that shot up above the highest trees, assured her that the disaster had not been exaggerated; but when she at length reached the open field which intervened between her late habitation and the wood, the whole awful spectacle burst at once upon her sight, and she stood in utter dismay and consternation. Not only from every window of the dwelling-house were the flames streaming, but they had communicated to the out-houses; the barns, the ricks of wheat, and barley, and hay were all involved in one tremendous sheet of fire.

Some minutes had elapsed before Elinor had discovered, among the various groups who were assembled in front of the burning edifice, unable, as it appeared, to offer any resistance to the devouring element, the unfortunate Mr. Copeland and his daughters. Isabel was leaning on her father's arm, but seeming rather to render him assistance than to require it; while Annie, seated on the grass at their feet, with her face hidden on her knees, appeared to be totally overcome with grief and terror.

Without a moment's hesitation, Elinor flew towards them, the dog heralding, as it were, her approach by its quick bark and light boundings, as it preceded her.

"Lie down, Carlo," exclaimed Isabel, petulantly, as the dog jumped up to attract her attention, and then quickly bounded back to Elinor. Isabel's eyes seemed unconsciously to follow his motions, for it was evident her thoughts were otherwise employed than in attending to his gambols, but the instant she discovered Elinor approaching, her look of intense grief vanished, and she uttered a wild shriek of pleasure, exclaiming—

"Tis Elinor! oh! she is saved! she is saved!" flew towards her, and threw her arms round her neck, while she gave way to a flood of tears.

Grateful and rejoiced as Elinor felt at this reception, she was compelled hastily to break away from the embraces of the ardent girl, for she saw that Annie, who had lifted up her head at her sister's exclamation, and stared wildly round, until her eyes encountered Elinor's, had sunk down again fainting with surprise and terror, while her father, in a state of distraction, in vain endeavoured to raise her in his trembling arms, as he looked earnestly around, to discover, as it appeared, what new evil had occasioned this increased excitement in his children.

Throwing herself beside her on the grass, Elinor raised the gentle girl's head in her arms, and tenderly entreated her to be composed.

"Oh Elinor! dear Elinor! they told me that you were lost—had perished in those frightful flames," she exclaimed, with a shudder, looking towards the house, and then averting her eyes with horror from the awful spectacle. "Oh! what I have suffered," she continued, straining Elinor to her bosom; "but you are safe, thank God you are safe! And Dorcas, too; where is she, Elinor? Did you not escape together? Is she not preserved?"

"We will hope so, dear Annie," returned Elinor, "but—"

"How, then, did you escape? And you are dressed too, while we had scarcely time to throw these light coverings over us," interrupted Isabel.

"How, indeed!" repeated Mr. Copeland, sternly, as if at that moment struck with the singularity of Elinor's appearance, dressed as she had been all day, with the addition of her bonnet and cloak. "Where were you, girl," he demanded, "when the alarm of fire was given? And how came it that you have kept out of sight till this minute, though you must have known the anxiety those poor children would suffer?"

"I could not know it, sir," returned Elinor, meekly, "for I was far from this spot when the fire commenced. The moment I knew of it," she continued, with increasing embarrassment at every word she uttered, "I hastened here as fast as terror would allow me."

"Far from this spot!" repeated Mr. Copeland, with amazement; "out at this time of night! when we all believed you in bed. What is the meaning of this? how can you explain it?"

A loud murmur ran through the crowd, who, attracted by Elinor's unexpected appearance, had surrounded them. It was evident that they had caught the tone of Mr. Copeland's suspicions, and for a moment Elinor's heart sunk with apprehension. She repeated, however, with tolerable firmness, the excuse she had previously planned, while Mr. Copeland's keen eyes were fixed upon her countenance, with a look that seemed to search her very heart.

"A probable story, is it not?" he exclaimed, looking round him, when she ceased speaking.

Only one or two voices re-echoed his observation, but Elinor read in the looks of all, that they were of the same opinion. Philip at this moment came up, to inform Mr. Copeland that a chaise-cart had been sent over from a neighbouring farm to remove the family thither, and again Elinor was compelled to listen to the astonishment which her appearance excited, and to reply to the questions which Philip's curiosity prompted.

Mr. Copeland's anxiety to remove his daughters, however, soon relieved her from the general observation, every one being ready to offer their services to the poor girls, whose situation excited general compassion. For a moment Elinor hesitated what to do; not a word had been said about her going with them; Annie had been sent on first and placed in the vehicle, which was drawn up to the gate at some distance. Isabel, and the poor shivering maid servants, who were still worse clad than her, followed, all equally anxious to quit the sad scene of their disaster, and Mr. Copeland only lingering behind, to give some directions to Philip.

"You are going too, sure, Miss Elinor, to farmer Benson's?" observed the latter, seeing Elinor still stand undecided how to act. "Miss Elinor is to go, sir, isn't she?" he added, appealing to Mr. Copeland, who had turned to follow his daughters.

"Perhaps she will prefer renewing her midnight rambles in

the wood," replied the latter, with a bitter sneer. " But come, girl," he continued, sternly motioning her to go before him, " be assured, I am not going to lose sight of you; there is a fearful reckoning yet to be settled between you and I, and depend upon it, unless you clear yourself better than it seems you can do, heavy will be the penalty."

Elinor made no reply; she would not affect not to understand him, yet she felt that this was not the moment, when he was still excited by the awful wreck before him, to assert her innocence, and she therefore proceeded in silence to take her place by Annie, who again, in broken accents, expressed her thankfulness that her dear Elinor was spared from the dreadful fate, from which they had all so narrowly escaped.

The friendly, though bustling welcome, with which the now houseless family were received by Farmer Benson and his wife, and the arrangements were made for their comfort, in some measure revived the spirits of the drooping girls, though from time to time, as the recollection of poor Dorcas rushed on their minds, a shudder of horror would betray their thoughts; but by none was the poor woman more continually lamented than by the girl Betsy, who seemed almost distracted with grief, and refused to listen to all consolation. It appeared, from the confused account of the other two maid-servants, that Betsy had been the first who had given the alarm of fire, and that she had made a desperate attempt to enter Dorcas' room by the door which communicated between the chambers, but had been driven back by the volume of smoke and flames that burst forth, and compelled them all instantly to fly for their lives by the other door which led out upon the staircase; and one of them having had the presence of mind to close this door behind them, they had been enabled to gain time to alarm the family.

From Betsy herself, however, they could learn nothing; she could give no account how she had been first awakened to the danger, or what she had observed when she had made the attempt to enter Dorcas' chamber. In fact, the terror she had suffered seemed to have affected the poor girl's understanding; and Mr. Copeland, after vainly endeavouring to elicit from her some particulars, which might enable him to judge when and how the fire originated, was compelled to yield to the desire she continued incessantly to repeat, that she might be let go home to her mother, who lived some miles from their present home.

As might be expected, Elinor's extraordinary absence, at such an hour, formed not the least interesting topic between Mr.

Copeland and his friends, the Bensons; but she fortunately was spared, for the present, the uneasiness and mortification of hearing her mysterious conduct discussed, for she had retired with Isabel and Annie to the bed-room, which had been prepared for them by Mrs. Benson.

To sleep, however, was impossible, although Isabel and her sister yielded to Elinor's persuasions, and went to bed, while she attempted to rest her weary limbs in a large easy chair by the fire-side.

" And now, Elinor, do satisfy me, what it was that caused you to leave your bed, and wander out at such a time of night?" observed Isabel, after over and over again expressing their gratitude and thankfulness for their providential escape.

" I cannot, Isabel, satisfy you," returned Elinor. " To you I acknowledge, that a far more powerful motive than mere restlessness induced me to leave the house, but more than that I cannot explain. Do not, therefore, dear girl, ask me further."

Isabel mused for some moments in silence.

" Elinor," she at length observed, with quickness, " I have penetrated your secret—you have seen Edward Hatherleigh."

It was fortunate that, from Elinor's position, Isabel could not see her countenance at this moment, or it would undoubtedly have betrayed what she was compelled to teach her lips to deny.

" You are wrong, Isabel," she replied, with as much firmness as she could assume. " Think you," she continued, " that Edward would be so mad as to return to a place where he knows—but I will not argue this point further with you. I will own to you, because I am sure I may rely on your generosity not to betray me, Isabel, may I not——"

" If you rely on my keeping any secret, where the murderer of my poor brother is concerned," exclaimed Isabel with vehemence, " you are mistaken in me, Elinor. Do not, therefore, tell me another word of——"

" We will drop the subject, Isabel," interrupted Elinor, glad to avail herself of this opportunity to do so. " Do not, dear girl," she continued, " let us add to our present misfortunes, by suffering mistrust to creep in between you and I; that my motives in leaving your father's house this night were perfectly innocent, I dare most solemnly avow, and I trust you will believe."

" And you knew nothing of the fire then, until you saw it?" said Isabel, doubtingly.

" I did not say so," returned Elinor; " on the contrary, I

freely confess that I heard of it long before I could see it, from a stranger, who had left me but a few minutes before I saw you."

"A stranger!" repeated Isabel, incredulously.

"Yes, a stranger," reiterated Elinor, "one with whom, I solemnly assure you, I had never before exchanged a sentence, though I believe I once before saw him for a few minutes."

Isabel made no further remark. It was evident that she was ashamed to express continued distrust of one whose word she had never before for an instant doubted. The subject, therefore, was dropped—most gladly, indeed, on Elinor's part; for, unused to deception or falsehood, she trembled at every word she uttered, lest she should betray more than she intended.

Sad, silent, and spiritless, were the guests, who, at a late hour on the following morning, assembled round Farmer Benson's hospitable table; but among them none were so completely miserable as Elinor Clare. The misfortunes of Mr. Copeland and his family, of course rendered them objects of general sympathy; but towards Elinor, except in the bosom of Annie, there existed no feeling but mistrust and suspicion. The result, indeed, of Mr. Copeland's conference with his friends, the Bensons, on the subject of Elinor's unaccountable absence at the time of the fire, had been, that she should as soon as possible be called upon once more to explain her mysterious conduct, and that, if she either refused or failed to give a satisfactory account, a representation of the circumstances should be made without delay to the nearest magistrate, who, there could be little doubt, would think there was sufficient cause of suspicion to grant a warrant against her.

This determination, however, was carefully concealed from Isabel and her sister, who, Mr. Copeland well knew, would shrink with horror from such an intention. Some hours, therefore, elapsed before an opportunity could be found of separating Elinor from them, without exciting suspicion in their minds; but the difficulty was at length surmounted.

It was, of course, desirable, and indeed almost indispensable, that Mr. Copeland should speedily find a temporary habitation for himself and family, as many months must necessarily elapse before his own could be rebuilt; but for some miles round there was not a place vacant that could accommodate them; and besides, Mr. Copeland wished to remain as near as possible to the spot, both that he might superintend the restoration of his residence, and attend to the business of his farm. It should here be observed, that his loss, in a pecuniary sense, was comparatively trifling, nearly the whole of his property being insured. In the predicament above mentioned, it was at length suggested by Mrs. Benson that Mrs. Hatherleigh's late residence, the Nunnery, might be made to answer their purpose. It was true that, nominally, Mrs. Hatherleigh still kept possession of it; but there was very little probability that she would ever return, and even if she did, it was strongly suspected that she would find it difficult to prove any stronger title to the place than prior occupation. It had always been a mystery how she got possession of it, and it was quite certain she paid no rent for it; nobody, indeed, that could pay rent, would have lived so many years in such a habitation; and, besides, if she did come back and claim the house, he (Mr. Copeland) would be no worse off than at present.

Such were the arguments Mr. Benson used to reconcile the latter to what he, selfish as he was, and accustomed to practise the law of might against right whenever it suited his purposes, and he had it in his power, could not help feeling in the present instance was a rather unjustifiable proceeding. But, then, to stand out against this proposition would, under the present circumstances, look as if he had an intention of quartering himself and the family on the Bensons, though he could not but know that every hour of their stay must put the good people to considerable inconvenience.

Mr. Copeland was still wavering, when a suggestion from Mrs. Benson, who, like many other clever bustling persons having been the first to propose a plan, make a point of carrying it through all objections, decided the point.

"Your daughters are too ill," she observed, "to go over and see whether the place can be made fit for Christians to live in, but Miss Elinor might go, and I wouldn't mind going with her, and seeing what we could do to make it comfortable. I never was inside the doors myself, and therefore can form no idea about it."

It was very plain to be seen that curiosity was Mrs. Benson's chief incentive in making this proposition; but Mr. Copeland instantly saw, that in adopting it he should secure the means of carrying into effect, without fear of interruption or opposition, his intentions towards Elinor.

It cannot be supposed that, in his heart, embittered as were his feelings towards Elinor, Mr. Copeland could or did believe her guilty of the horrible crime with which he meant to charge her unless she satisfactorily explained the mystery of her

ELINOR CLARE.

"I WILL DELIVER YOU INTO THE HANDS OF THE CONSTABLE."

absence at the time of the fire; but he had strong reasons, as he thought, to suspect that she had been made the tool of others. He had all along believed that she was in possession of the secret of Edward Hatherleigh's retreat, and was by some means still in secret communication with him. He had followed, and stealthily watched her, in her visit to the wood, in hopes of making some discovery, and though it so happened that he could not keep her in view sufficiently to observe her find the paper as related, yet her earnest look around her, her evident agitation even the manner in which she surveyed the woodman who crossed her path, were all seen and noted by him, and he returned to the house, more firmly convinced than ever of the justice of his suspicions. It was with the view, therefore, of terrifying her into a confession of what she knew rather than any intention of injuring her, that he now resolved upon carrying into effect, if she persisted in remaining silent, the harsh measures that had been suggested by the conversation between himself and the Bensons, and for this purpose he eagerly acceded to Mrs. Benson's proposition, that Elinor should accompany her to the Nunnery.

It was with extreme surprise, and almost equal sorrow, that the latter heard from her intended companion the purpose for which she was summoned from the room to which after breakfast she had retired with Isabel and Annie; but she knew her feeble opposition to what she could not help thinking a most unwarrantable and unjustifiable proceeding would not only be of no avail, but only subject her to galling and malicious remarks on the part of Mr. Copeland; and she, therefore, merely replied to Mrs. Benson's announcement that she was ready to attend her as soon as she pleased.

" Well, then, I'll tell the men folk that they may go on before and get the doors and windows open," replied the bustling little woman, who, to do her justice, it must be acknowledged, had no suspicion of the snare into which she was trepanning Elinor, and had, indeed, in the eagerness of this new pursuit, almost forgotten the subject altogether of Elinor's supposed delinquency and the measures that both she and her husband had joined in considering necessary.

Reflecting that many circumstances might arise to prevent Mr. Copeland's putting in practice his present intention of taking possession of the Nunnery, Elinor considered it most advisable to say nothing to Isabel or her sister as to where she was going, and she therefore left them under the impression that she was about to visit the ruins of their late habitation, a sight which they avowed neither of them had sufficient fortitude to behold or even to think of without horror.

The walk across the fields from Benson's farm to the Nunnery was a very pleasant one, and Mrs. Benson, who was never so happy as when busied, and made of consequence in other people's affairs, was in high good humour with her companion for her unlimited deference to all she proposed in the intended arrangements at the Nunnery.

" I have always said, my dear, that you have a deal more good sense, and far better behaviour than Isabel Copeland," she observed. " Now, if I had gone to give my opinion so free to her, as I've done to you, about how things should be managed, she would have drawn herself up and have given herself a thousand airs, but you—and by the bye, Elinor, now that we're quite by ourselves, let me give you a little bit of friendly advice. I don't mean to say anything at all to hurt your feelings, but you must own yourself, that for a young woman like you—a mere girl, indeed, as I may say—to get out of her bed at midnight, and go rambling, nobody knows where, or why, or wherefore, has a bad look, a very bad look, and it can hardly be wondered at that your uncle is greatly enraged about it. Well, then, the fire, it seems, began in your room, and of course there must have been some carelessness——"

" Not on my part, ma'am," interrupted Elinor, hastily; " I left no light or fire, and I am certain——"

" Well, then, how did it begin ?" demanded her pertinacious companion ; " that is the question."

" It is one I cannot answer," replied Elinor, quietly.

" But, my dear, they'll make you answer it," rejoined Mrs. Benson ; " and only think, what a dreadful thing it would be, if Mr. Copeland was to take you before the magistrate, and he was to send you to prison, on suspicion of setting fire to the house, and all because you are so obstinate, that you won't tell what it was that made you——"

" Has Mr. Copeland threatened this, ma'am ?" demanded Elinor, betraying rather by the deadly paleness which overspread her features than any alteration in her manner, the terror which had seized her.

" He hath both threatened it, and will carry it into effect,'; exclaimed the stern voice of Mr. Copeland, who, unseen by either Elinor or her companion, had been for some minutes walking on the other side of the hedge along which they were proceeding, and thought this a favourable moment to show himself.

" It is no empty threat that I hold out, girl," he continued, coming towards them through the gap which they were about to pass, and seizing Elinor roughly by the arm, " for unless you give me instantly, without prevarication or reserve, a full explanation of the circumstances, which Mrs. Benson has truly said have a most black appearance, I will deliver you at once into the hands of the constable, who is now waiting at the top of the croft; and then remember, it will be out of my power to save you—you must go through the regular course of law, and——"

" God help me then," said Elinor, pathetically, clasping her hands, and raising her beautiful eyes to Heaven, "for if I can be no otherwise cleared from the foul accusation you would bring against me, but by betraying the purpose for which I left your house last night, I must submit to suffer the penalty of guilt. I will not deceive you, sir," she continued, with emphatic earnestness, "I am innocent of everything approaching to crime, but I cannot, I dare not explain——"

"That is enough," interrupted Copeland, with suppressed rage; and forcing her onwards, without paying any attention to Mrs. Benson, who began to pour forth a torrent of common-place entreaties, "not to be so hard," "to govern his temper," &c. &c.

Elinor was scarcely conscious what was passing around her, even when she found herself surrounded by Farmer Benson, the constable, his assistant, and one or two more, whom chance, or some hint they had gotten of what was likely to happen, had drawn together.

"There is your prisoner, Thornhill," observed Mr. Copeland, dragging her forward, and putting her hand into the rough, hard grasp of the person he addressed, who seemed, however, to be very ill disposed to the ungracious task he was compelled to fulfil, and regarded the astounded and terrified girl with evident compassion.

"I be very sorry for this, miss," he observed, addressing Elinor, "but what can I do, if Mr. Copeland is resolute——"

"Nothing, nothing," said Elinor, in a faint voice; "let us go on at once, the sooner it is over the better. Where am I to go to—the prison at——"

"Lor bless your heart, no," returned the compassionate Thornhill, "you ben't a going to prison at all, I do hope you are going before Justice Russell, to see what he says to it, and I hope you'll be able to prove to he, that you've no hand in the business. If you'll only, you see," he added, in a lower voice, as if desirous of persuading her to what he considered beneficial,— "if you'll only just tell the plain truth, where you was, and what you was about when the fire broke out, why that will settle the matter at once, and you'll get discharged free."

"I cannot, I cannot," murmured Elinor, replying rather to the suggestions of her own mind than her conductor's suggestions, though he thought otherwise.

"No," she continued, with emphasis, "I will die rather than betray——"

She stopped short under the consciousness of the curious eyes that were fixed upon her.

"Oh, then there was somebody concerned in it," observed the constable. "Well, now, if you'll take my advice you won't lose a moment's time in taking care of yourself. Tell 'Squire Russell, the minute you see him, that you will 'peach against them that led you into the mischief, and——"

"I have never been concerned with anyone in committing what you call a mischief," observed Elinor, who was beginning to recover from the first shock, and resume her calmness. "If Mr. Copeland thinks to terrify me into any confession of guilt," she continued, "he is mistaken; I am as innocent as you are of any knowledge how this dreadful accident happened."

"I hope you'll be able to convince Justice Russell so," returned the constable, drily; "howsomever, here's Benson's cart waiting for us at the top of the lane, and we shall soon be at the end of our journey, and then we shall see how matters will be settled."

Elinor felt a bitter sensation of contempt and indignation at this confirmation of how deliberately she had been inveigled into the snare laid for her; but the next moment the big tears stood in her eyes, as she thought of the pain which Isabel and Annie would feel when they discovered the cruelty and indignity to which she had been subjected by their father's hard and obdurate disposition.

Elinor had lost sight entirely of Mrs. Benson and Mr. Copeland from the time she entered the vehicle which had been stationed ready for her conveyance; but that gave her little concern, for she would have scorned to make an attempt upon the pity and compassion of those whom she now thoroughly despised. Thornhill having exhausted all his logic in his attempt to persuade her to save herself by betraying those who, from Mr. Copeland's account, he believed had induced her to commit the crime with which the latter charged her, remained silent. Elinor, therefore, during the latter part of their ride, had ample time to reflect upon her situation, and the result was a more firm determination, if possible, than ever, not by a single word to betray the cause that had induced her to leave Mr. Copeland's house, and which had thus afforded him the opportunity of accusing her of a crime so revolting to her nature.

"'Squire Russell," as Thornhill emphatically called him, was not yet visible when they reached his residence, and poor Elinor had to suffer all the mortification of being exposed to the curious gaze of the servants, who having learnt from the constable's whispered communication that she was charged with having set her uncle's house on fire, and burnt the housekeeper, came on various pretexts into the justice-room, to look at the horrible monster who could be guilty of such outrageous crimes.

It would, perhaps, have been a subject for Elinor rather to smile than to weep at, could she have known the different impressions that her appearance made upon those who came thus to gratify their curiosity. With the females, especially those who were ugly, there was not a doubt of her guilt. " She had it in her very face, a sly demure-looking hussy, that looked as if she could do any artful trick," was the observation of one; while another, on the contrary, declared " that a more bolder, confidenter, brazen-faced creter they never set eyes upon,"—a declaration which was not at all softened by the prevailing opinion among the men, namely, that " it was very unlikely such a pretty, modest, gentle-looking girl could be guilty, and if she were so, it was a thousand pities."

Elinor, however, though she shrank with inherent modesty and diffidence from the curious and scrutinising glances that she was exposed to, was too proudly conscious of her own innocence, and the cruelty and injustice of the charge brought against her, to feel to its full extent the humiliation of her situation. A cold chill indeed struck upon her heart when the constable turned the key upon her, while he went to join the *lunch* to which he was invited by the footman in the servants' hall; and still more did her spirits sink, when a short time after the door was unlocked, and Mr. Copeland and his friend Benson were ushered into the room, the obsequious constable excusing his apparant neglect of his prisoner by observing that " he had kept his eye on the room all the time that he had been out of it, and would defy the devil himself to cheat him."

Not a word passed between Elinor and her persecutor. He seemed, indeed, to shrink from encountering the glance of her mild yet speaking eye; and his friend Benson betrayed, in a thousand ways, his uneasiness at the situation in which he found himself as the abettor of such a harsh proceeding, which, though he had at first agreed with Mr. Copeland as quite necessary, he had probably never contemplated as likely to be carried into effect, and certainly now heartily repented of, though Elinor's calm, reserved, and somewhat proud look and manner discouraged him from making the attempt he was inclined to, to convince her of his sympathy and good wishes, that she might, to use his own expression, " get safe through her trouble."

The approach of the great man (the justice) was at length announced by the entrance of the long, lank, lean, important-looking personage who officiated as his clerk, who proceeded, without seeming to notice any person, to seat himself in his place of office, arrange his pen, ink and paper conveniently, open and for some minutes apparently consult a large venerable-looking folio, and then taking off his spectacles, wiping and putting them on again, cast a supercilious glance around the room, and in a pompous tone demanded of Thornhill, what charge he had to bring before "his worship."

It would have made even Elinor smile with contempt, could she have been aware that this consequential personage, who by the most studied starts, contortions, and grimaces, expressed his horror and surprise at the information, which was communicated in an under tone by the constable, and enforced by sundry references to Mr. Copeland for the truth of what he advanced, had long before he entered the justice room been in full possession of all the particulars, and had canvassed over with the butler, and footman, and cook, and housemaid, and in fact all the justice's establishment, while he took his usual ample allowance of cold meat and ale in the hall, their several opinions and prejudices in favour of or against the supposed criminal. As it was, even with all the anxiety, perplexity, and humiliation which she felt from the strange situation in which she was placed, she could not but experience the greatest astonishment at the ridiculous self-conceit of the man, and his evident want of the common feelings of humanity, which would certainly have induced something like an expression of regret or compassion at seeing a young female placed in so awful a situation.

The entrance of the justice himself, however, soon banished all recollection of so insignificant a person as his clerk; and Elinor, with more confusion than she had yet felt, shrunk from the earnest gaze of the man who was to decide her fate.

Mr. Russell was, or rather had been, a gay man of fashion, who had lately been compelled, much it was believed against his inclination, to fix his permanent residence on the estate which he had scarcely ever visited since it came into his possession by his marriage with the heiress of the last owner. Elinor had never until now seen him, but many scandalous tales of his habits and pursuits had reached the Grove, which had greatly prejudiced her against him, and which sent the blood in torrents to her pale cheeks, as he fixed his keen eyes on her with a look of undisguised admiration.

"Why have you not asked that young lady to come nearer the fire, Fowler?" he observed, in a tone of reproach to his clerk, at the same time courteously placing a chair for her.

With a ludicrous grimace of alarm at his worship's supposed degradation, in thus condescending to one charged before him as a culprit, Fowler hastened to explain to the magistrate that this was the young woman charged with the capital crime.

"Impossible!" exclaimed Mr. Russell, involuntarily, as his eye caught the speaking glance of disdain which Elinor could not avoid darting at the formal, cold-hearted clerk, who seemed from his haste thus prematurely to pronounce her guilty. "It cannot be possible," repeated the justice, more mildly, as if just then recollecting his judicial capacity, "or at least, I would hope," he added, "that guilt of so heinous a nature could never find a dwelling-place in the bosom of one so young, and apparently so artless."

The burning blush which had a few moments previous suffused Elinor's cheek, faded, and left her paler than before. She cast her eyes to the ground to hide the tears that trembled in them, and could scarcely be restrained from falling, and some moments elapsed before she could recollect herself sufficiently to attend to the recital by which Mr. Copeland sought to establish her guilt.

Of course there was little to tell, though Mr. Copeland's disposition to make the most of it could not have been doubted by any one who heard him.

"In what capacity did this young person reside in your family?" demanded the magistrate.

"She is an orphan,—I have supported her since her birth," returned Copeland, with some confusion.

"Indeed! and with no claim but on your benevolence?" rejoined Mr. Russell, "is she not a relative?"

Elinor's eyes and Mr. Copeland's met at this instant, and for a brief moment he tried in vain to give utterance to the reply, which at length broke in faltering accents from his tongue. "She is my niece, the daughter of—of—my sister."

"Her uncle—her benefactor!" repeated the magistrate, "yet suspect her to be guilty of such an enormous crime; one involving, indeed, another of still deeper dye, for if she were guilty of firing the house, undoubtedly she is guilty of murdering the poor woman who has lost her life in the flames; but let us hear what explanation the young woman can give of the cause of suspicion —her absence from home. Where were you," he continued, addressing Elinor, "when the fire broke out?"

Elinor hesitated for a few moments, but at length she said calmly, and with decision—

"It is as well that I should spare you all trouble, sir, by declaring that on this subject I neither can or will give any explanation. If I would have done so before, I might have saved myself the humiliation of standing here as a criminal. Mr. Copeland, however—my uncle, I should have said, for so he has avowed himself upon his oath to be—knows, well knows, that I am innocent of the charge he brings against me, a charge only with the view of extorting from me a secret, that death itself would fail to wring from me."

"This is very extraordinary!" observed the magistrate, whose eyes had followed the expression of her animated looks at Copeland, and had beheld with surprise the mixture of confusion and bitter hatred which the old man's stern countenance betrayed.

The necessity, however, of preserving his official indifference and dignity, seemed to check the remarks, which, in his private capacity, he would not in all probability have spared, and, with extreme gravity, he proceeded to point out to Elinor the serious situation in which she would place herself by persisting and refusing an explanation.

"I acknowledge your kindness, sir," she replied, when he ceased speaking, "but I have nothing to add to what I have already said."

Mr. Russell paused, and seemed for some minutes to be debating within himself how to proceed; he then bent over the table, and remained for a considerable time in earnest conversation with his clerk.

"And do you still then persist, Mr. Copeland, in your charge against your niece?" he at last demanded, with a look and manner that was evidently intended as a remonstrance.

The person he addressed was, however, not to be so easily turned.

"Let her, as I said before, explain where she went, and for what purpose, and I will be content," he replied.

"It certainly is but reasonable," observed the magistrate, gravely; "but she evidently has strong reasons why she wishes to keep the secret. Now I think it may easily be guessed that there is some love affair which she wishes to keep concealed, or is fearful of your disapproving. Is it not so?" he continued, turning to Elinor; "come, tell the truth. Did you not go to your sweetheart and are afraid of your uncle's anger?"

"No, sir," returned Elinor, firmly, "my motive for leaving

the house was very different; but I again solemnly declare that it had not the slightest connection with the fire, which I am positive did not begin in my room, as I had been some time in darkness before I left it."

"Have you any witnesses, Mr. Copeland, as to where the fire originated?" demanded Mr. Russell.

He replied, by stating the fact that the young girl who had first discovered it was too ill from terror to give a very connected account, but he added, that from his knowledge, he could state that the fire was at first confined to the housekeeper's room, and one tenanted by—he hesitated for a moment before he added—"the young woman at the bar."

There was again a pause; Mr. Russell was evidently favourably inclined towards Elinor, and Copeland saw it, for again he urged, with more emphasis than ever, all that he considered warranted his charge against her, especially her locking her door, which, he said, "had prevented his being able to ascertain where the fire originated, as he had in vain attempted to force the door open, under the supposition that she was there."

"I will speak plainly, your worship," he continued, finding that Mr. Russell continued still apparently incredulous as to Elinor's guilt. "I will tell you, that I suspect her of being a confederate of one who has already been the means of bringing the deepest misery upon me, and last night completed, as he thought, his vengeance, by attempting to destroy me. Yes, I charge that girl," he continued, shaking his hand at Elinor with violence, "with being in league with the murderer of my poor boy; let her deny, if she dare, that she was not with him last night, that she has not known that he has been lurking in the neighbourhood for some days, and——"

"I can deny it—I do deny it, solemnly deny it," interrupted Elinor, with energy, "and as I hope for mercy here or hereafter, I declare I speak the truth."

Mr. Copeland remained silent for a minute, looking earnestly in her face, the calm and holy serenity of which certainly bore the strong impress of innocence.

"And you have not seen Edward Hatherleigh, then?" he at length observed, doubtingly.

A slight tinge of confusion crossed Elinor's expressive countenance, but it was only momentary.

"What I have said, sir, was the truth," she replied; "but I shall answer no more questions."

"Ha! I am right, then, after all!" exclaimed the old man, in a tone of exultation. "You see, sir, she dares not deny that she has seen the villain, but she tries to equivocate, by pretending not to believe that he was the murderer of my poor son."

"This is a serious affair, young woman," observed the magistrate, who had been attentively watching her countenance during Copeland's exclamation. "Are you aware," he continued, "of the situation in which you stand, that in the eye of the law you are equally guilty, and incur the same punishment as the actual murderer?"

Elinor bowed her head in assent, and Mr. Russell proceeded to put a number of questions to Mr. Copeland, acknowledging that, having been absent in London at the time, he had heard but slightly of the dreadful event Mr. Copeland spoke of, and therefore knew nothing of the attendant circumstances.

As may be supposed, Mr. Copeland's narrative was exactly such as was likely to persuade his auditor of the truth of his accusation against both Edward and Elinor, the latter of whom he represented as having been the sole means of enabling Edward to escape from justice. Mr. Russell's looks became more and more serious as the old man proceeded, and when the latter had concluded he remarked that there certainly appeared strong grounds for suspicion.

"But still, as you will have her under your own eye, Mr. Copeland," he suggested, in a low tone, "it would perhaps be advisable to let the matter rest for the present; you may be able to ascertain some stronger circumstances."

"If your worship thinks there are not circumstances strong enough to send her to prison," returned Copeland, with marked emphasis, "of course there is an end of the matter. It is you that is to decide."

Mr. Russell seemed embarrassed. Another consultation followed with his clerk; and Elinor read her fate in the decisive and consequential manner in which the latter evidently enforced what she could see was contrary to the wish, if not the conviction, of the magistrate.

Prepared as she certainly was for an unfavourable decision, it was rather a relief to her than otherwise when the magistrate announced that he should commit her to the custody of Thornhill, the constable, for three days, to be then again brought before him.

"I warn you, however," he continued, addressing Elinor, "unless you, before that time, or then, give a full and satisfactory account of your conduct, it will be my imperative duty to send you to the county gaol to abide your trial."

Elinor bowed without speaking.   She felt indeed that her case was hopeless if it depended on any account she could give; but it was something to have three days' respite from the fate that threatened her; and she retired to the seat to which the constable directed her with a calmness that strongly contrasted with Mr. Copeland's agitated manner, as he listened to some observations from Mr. Russell, who had left his magisterial chair, and was now conversing with him at a distant window.

For one moment Elinor raised her head as he passed her to leave the room; their eyes met; but though he seemed to have made up his mind to bear her resentment, he appeared unable to meet the calm reproach of her looks, and hastily turned away and hurried out of the room.

"I be sorry, Miss Ellen, I'm sure," observed Farmer Benson, approaching her with a sheepish look, "I be main sorry, that I be, that things should ha' turned out so cross; I didn't think that anything would have come of it more than just getting you to tell——"

"There is no occasion for any apologies on your part, Mr. Benson," she replied with coolness.

"Be there anything I can do for you?" he demanded, still lingering, and evidently desirous to compensate in some measure, by present attention, for the part he had taken against her.

"Nothing," she replied, "except to ask Isabel Copeland to send me a change of clothes if she should have it in her power. She, of course, will be obliged to purchase for herself and her sister, and as I too have lost all that I could call my own by this calamity, I must be compelled to depend (for the last time, I trust,) upon Mr. Copeland's charity to supply me with immediate necessaries."

"I'll do it, you may depend on it," returned the farmer. "Aye, and what's more, if they—that is to say, if Copeland won't do what's handsome by you, why I'll stand the damage out of my own pocket, and my little woman shall get you what you want."

Elinor thanked him; but she had no fear, she said, that Mr. Copeland would refuse; and the farmer, reiterating his good wishes, left her.

During this short colloquy, Mr. Russell had been speaking at the farther end of the room with the constable, and they now both approached Elinor.

"I have been desiring Thornhill to make your stay with him as comfortable as possible," he observed to her, "and I beg, therefore, you will freely make known to him your wishes."

Elinor's eyes sought the ground as she faltered her thanks.

"You had better go and take some refreshment, Thornhill, before you go," he observed, turning to the constable, who hesitated, and looked at Elinor.

"Oh! do not be afraid," rejoined Mr. Russell, "I will take care that your prisoner does not escape."

Thornhill quitted the room, casting at the same time a significant look towards Elinor, who would fain have entreated him to stay, could she have found an excuse for so doing. The clerk, however, still remained, and she felt that his presence, hateful as he appeared to her, from his formal cool-blooded assumption was still a security.

A security from what? Was not Mr. Russell a magistrate, one appointed to administer justice—to aid the oppressed, and to punish the guilty? And she who was innocent, and helpless, and oppressed, could she have anything to fear from him? Such were the thoughts that darted into Elinor's mind, as Mr. Russell turned from her to his clerk, who still remained appearently busily occupied at the table.

"What are you about there, Fowler?" at length demanded the magistrate, in a tone that was sufficently indicative of the vexation and impatience he felt at the delay of his assistant.

The clerk hastily closed the folio, which he was pretending to consult, and muttering some unintelligible apology, for what certainly needed none, took his hat, and with an obsequious bow, under which, however, Elinor could detect a saucy sneer, departed.

Involuntarily she started from her seat, at the moment he was closing the door, but Mr. Russell, with apparent surprise, gently seized her arm, and, half ashamed of her reluctance, she suffered herself to be reseated on the bench.

"I must not let you escape, you know," he observed, seating himself beside her, "though would to Heaven you had nothing more to fear than from me; your imprisonment should be light indeed."

Elinor most inarticulately reiterated her thanks, though she felt at that moment as if the utmost severity of his office would have been more welcome to her than his kindness.

"How I envy Thornhill," continued Mr. Russell, attempting to take her hand, which she instantly withdrew, "the happiness which he will be insensible to, of beholding for so many hours that lovely face; and how do I curse the ungrateful office I hold, which renders it impossible for me openly to avow myself your friend and protector."

"I have need of a protector, Heaven knows," returned the innocent girl, clasping her hands, while the big tears, which she had until now successfully restrained, broke from their confinement, and coursed each other down her fair cheek.

"Trust in me, and you shall not want one, dear Elinor," returned Mr. Russell, warmly. "I cannot, indeed, at present, do all that my heart would dictate; but, rely on it, I will not only release you from the danger that at present threatens you from this hard-hearted uncle of yours, but I will remove you entirely from his power. Confide, then, in me, dear girl, and banish that look of doubt and distress. Even your present imprisonment will be only so in name, for Thornhill understands my instructions to him, and you will only have to express your wishes to find them complied with. Smile, then, my lovely girl, and make me happy by telling me that you confide in me, and look forward with some share of the impatience I feel for those happy hours, when you shall be released from all bonds but those of love."

"Sir—Mr. Russell—I beg, sir," said Elinor, endeavouring in vain to interrupt the florid bombast of the speech, which, while it breathed nothing as she felt of true passion, alarmed her by its elaborate counterfeit. "I hope—I entreat, sir," she continued, "that you will remember that I am a friendless, persecuted girl, whom it would be the height of cruelty to trifle with, or to attempt to betray. I ask of you, sir—nay more, I will receive of you no other favour than you can conscientiously and honourably grant to any one placed in the same unhappy situation that I am."

For some moments Mr. Russell remained silently gazing on her upraised eyes, glittering like diamonds through her tears, and every feature animated by the glowing blush of conscious modesty and shame, at being compelled to make this appeal to his honour.

"By heavens!" he at length exclaimed, in a transport of admiration, "you are the sweetest creature I ever beheld, and if you look thus lovely in grief and distress, what will you be when smiles of happiness, such as I hope to be fortunate enough to inspire, shall dimple that charming face? Nay, Elinor, you must, you shall listen to me, for I feel that every hope I can indulge of future felicity depends upon you. Even now, if you will but smile upon me, and promise to be mine, I will run every risk to rescue you from your present degrading situation. Thornhill, I know, can be bribed to anything, and he and I will arrange the means by which you may escape to London; there I can secure you a retreat, where you may remain in safety, until I fly on the wings of love to you, and then in a foreign country we may defy the utmost malice of fate, and live but to make each other happy. Say you consent, dearest Elinor; before Thornhill returns, breathe only the one blessed word 'yes' in my ear, and——"

" Off, wretch !" exclaimed the indignant girl, violently resisting the attempt he made to embrace her. " If you dare lay your hand on me again," she continued, with increased vehemence, " I will proclaim to the whole house, to your own injured, insulted wife, your infamous proposal."

" Softly, softly, if you please, fair Elinor," retorted Mr. Russell, with a malicious smile, " this rhodomontade might answer very well for a young lady of unsulled innocence, and unsuspected character, but for one who has confessed that she only last night left her bed, and the protection of her uncle's house, for a midnight assignation——"

" I never said so," interrupted Elinor, with a vehemence that compelled him to pause in the midst of his taunt. " I acknowledge," she continued, " that I secretly quitted the house, but it was no improper motive drew me from thence, nor was my going premeditated; but I am wasting words, I see, in attempting to vindicate my innocence to you, sir; and yet, what must you be, if you really believe me guilty, and yet can propose to make me the companion of your future life."

" I believe you guilty of being the sweetest, loveliest, most persuasive and eloquent orator that ever attempted to bewilder man's senses," he replied, with a mixture of passion and levity, that rendered Elinor still more indignant, and she was about to reply with increased bitterness, when the door opened, and a tall, thin, lady-like female, evidently suffering from extreme ill-health, entered the room, and stood for some moments gazing in excessive surprise at Elinor, who felt ready to sink to the ground with confusion, though conscious she had not been guilty of any impropriety, but was, in fact, herself the injured person.

" To what strange circumstance am I indebted for the honour of this visit, madam?" demanded Mr. Russell, in a tone of asperity, which was evidently intended to conceal his extreme embarrassment. " The justice room," he continued, " was the last place in the world in which I should have expected to see a lady of your delicacy and feeling."

"I have no doubt of it, sir," she replied, with a significant look; "but I will spare you all trouble, either of question or conjecture, by at once acknowledging that curiosity has brought me here."

"And having satisfied it, I presume," returned Mr. Russell, preserving the same air of coolness, "you will allow me to conduct you to a more suitable place."

"Not so hasty, if you please, sir," she replied, rejecting his offered hand with extreme haughtiness. "I wish to ask that young person a question or two, with your permission."

"I am sorry to oppose any wish of yours, madam," he returned, "but, under the present circumstances, such a proceeding would be highly improper—I cannot indeed allow it."

"Oh! do not alarm yourself, sir," observed the lady, significantly, "the questions I would put are not such as you may not hear. I would merely ask you, my dear," she continued, "whether you are really the niece of farmer Copeland? What is your name, and where were you born?"

It was not without evident emotion that Elinor replied to these strange and abrupt inquiries.

"I have always been told, madam," she observed, "that I am the niece of Mr. Copeland, and that my name is Elinor Clare; but your last question I cannot answer, for I do not know the place of my birth—though, from something I once heard when a child, but have now forgotten, I know I used to think that I was not born in England."

During this reply, the lady, who, it may be readily guessed, was Mrs. Russell, continued to gaze in Elinor's face with a look of the deepest interest.

"It is strange," she at length observed, with a deep sigh; "and the very voice, too; but why should I indulge such visionary ideas? It is impossible that——"

"Visionary indeed, I suspect," observed Mr. Russell, interrupting her with a contemptuous smile; "but come, madam, let me entreat your to retire to your own apartments, unless you have a particular wish to indulge yourself with the society of the constable, &c., who will be here in a few moments."

"But this poor young creature, Mr. Russell," replied the lady, scarcely seeming to notice what he had said to her, but still continuing to regard Elinor with a wild and wistful look, as if recalling to her memory circumstances connected with the

ELINOR CLARE.

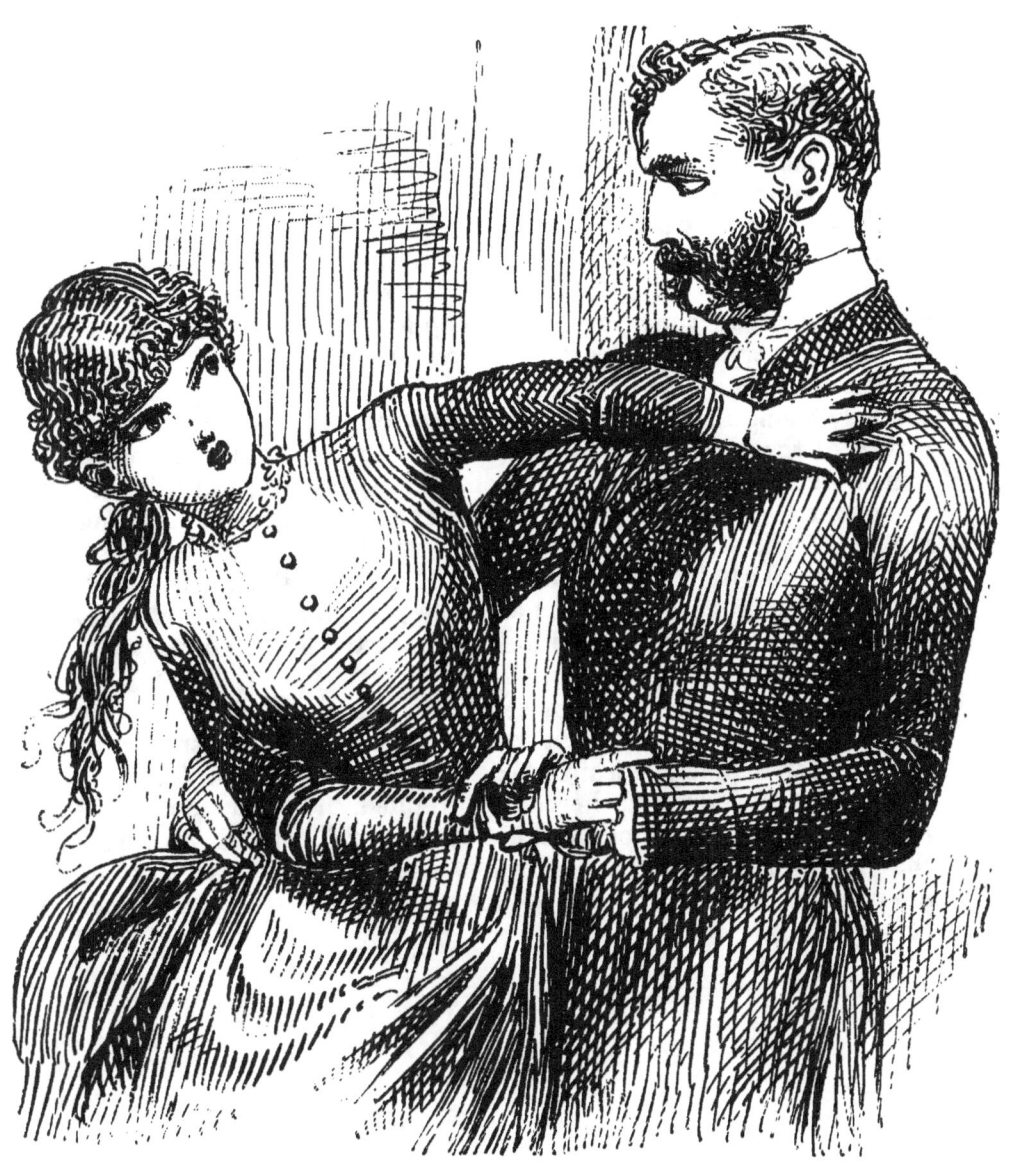

"LET ME GO INSTANTLY, OR I WILL ALARM THE HOUSE."

likeness she had discovered in the latter. "Surely," she added, "they cannot mean to charge one so young and gentle looking with a serious crime."

"It is one thing to make a charge, and another to prove it," returned Mr. Russell, with more courtesy of manner than he had hitherto shown towards her.

"But you will not send her to prison?" demanded the lady, imploringly.

"No, no, make your mind easy," he replied, "she is not going to prison; and now pray go, for I do not want it to be talked about all over the country that I allow your interference here."

The last observation seemed instantly to make an impression on the lady, and she suffered him to lead her without further delay to the door, at which, however, she stopped for an instant, to make some request to her husband, which did not reach Elinor's ear, but to which he hastily, and with seeming cordiality, replied—

"I will, you may depend upon it. Mrs. Russell," he observed, returning to Elinor, with a smile, "is anxious to be better acquainted with you, and she charged me to beg of you, as soon as you have it in your power, to come and see her."

"She is very kind—I am very grateful—I am sure," faltered Elinor, who had been at once greatly surprised and agitated by the lady's singular remarks and behaviour towards her. The return of the constable, however, prevented any further observation on either side; and Mr. Russell, in his presence, immediately re-assumed all his magisterial reserve and dignity, advising Elinor to reflect seriously in the interval which would elapse before she would be "brought up" again, on the situation in which she would be placed, should her uncle persevere in his charge, which he certainly would do unless she gave a satisfactory explanation of her conduct.

It was with some surprise that Elinor listened to his dictatorial assumption, which was so strangely at variance with the familiar manner in which Mr. Russell had but a few moments before addressed her. She replied, however, only by a respectful curtsey, and followed her conductor, Thornhill, to whom the magistrate reiterated his orders, and that he was to treat his prisoner with all the indulgence possible consistent with her safe keeping.

CHAPTER VIII.

And sayest thou that I dare not face
　The storm that bursts above my head!
The proud most keenly feel disgrace,
　And 'tis disgrace, alone, I dread.

ANON.

Then fare thee well, my own dear love,
　This world has now for us
No greater grief, no pain above,
　The pain of parting thus,
　　Dear love!
The pain of parting thus!

MOORE.

OCCUPIED more by what she had recently heard and seen, than her present situation, Elinor accompanied the constable without bestowing a thought or conjecture whither he was conducting her. Two or three times he made an attempt at conversation by some common-place observation, but Elinor's mind was too deeply employed to allow her to answer, except by a monosyllable; and more than half offended, and muttering something about "pride," and "no occasion for it," he gave up the attempt, and amused himself by whistling and cutting at the bushes as he passed them with the switch he carried in his hand, eyeing his companion askance from time to time, with a look that betrayed that he would, had he dared, have made her feel the weight of his authority, much more than was at present the case.

Totally unconscious, however, of having given him any offence, Elinor continued to walk on by his side, absorbed in deep reflection on the strangeness of Mrs. Russell's address to her, and forming in her own mind a thousand romantic conjectures confirmatory of that suspicion which had so long inhabited her bosom, namely, that Mr. Copeland's account of her birth and relationship to himself was totally false. From this reverie she was suddenly aroused by the accents of a voice she had heard before, inquiring how far it was to the nearest village, and looking up she beheld Paul Dangerfield, attired in the garb of a decent countryman, a large stick over his shoulder, with a bundle tied up in a handkerchief suspended on it, and altogether having the appearance of one who had travelled some distance.

One glance Elinor caught of his expressive eye, and that was sufficient to warn her not to appear to know him. She turned away with assumed indifference, while her companion the constable was replying to his question, and putting others to him in return, which had for their object the ascertaining whence the stranger came who knew so little of this part of the country as to make such an inquiry, and whither he was going, as the road he was in was a considerable distance from the highway, and led, to use Thornhill's own expression, " nowhere," meaning to say only to the adjacent hamlets and villages, and not to any post-town.

The answer to these questions was given in a broad Somerset-shire dialect, which was nearly unintelligible to the inquisitive constable, and would have persuaded Elinor that she was mistaken in the person, had she not ventured again to look at him, and read in the assumed simplicity of his looks an expression of derision of the consequential person before him, which confirmed her that it was Dangerfield.

Not until this moment did she perceive that the double portion of " refreshment " he had imbibed at Mr. Russell's had taken a very considerable effect upon the constable, and at any other time, perhaps, she would have been diverted at his ludicrous assumption of authority, and the awkward attempt he made to impress the simple countryman, as he thought him, with a proper sense of his importance; but at the present moment she had no impression but of vague terror and alarm at Dangerfield's sudden appearance and disguise. She could not help trembling at the thought that Edward was not far distant, and the fear that, if he was acquainted with her situation, he would make some rash and desperate attempt to rescue her, so completely banished all self-possession, that it was not till she had walked some yards that she became capable of comprehending that Dangerfield had, in seeming compliance with the constable's advice, turned back with them, and was now walking by the side of the latter, intending, as it appeared, to take his advice and finish his day's journey at the Bold Huntsman, on the common towards which they were now proceeding.

" It's a ten thousand chances as you wouldn't ha' got a bed if you'd gone on," observed the self-satisfied constable, " and as to ale, Lord love you, there's none like that at the Huntsman—no, not for ten miles round."

" Why, then, dang it I'se in luck to ha' met wi' ye," returned the supposed countryman, " vor I'se desput vond o' a drop good yale."

For some minutes the conversation was confined to this topic, and Elinor in vain listened to catch, if she could, some clue to Dangerfield's appearance and disguise.

An inquiry at length, made with apparent indifference and simplicity by the pretended countryman, whether the young woman (meaning herself) was his companion's sister or wife, led to a full and particular account of the occurrences of the preceding night—the fire, the accusation against Elinor, her examination before the magistrate, and finally her being committed to his safe keeping for three days, to give her time, as he said, to tell the truth.

"And it wouldn't be every one, I can tell you," he concluded' "that would get that favour shown 'em, nor more would she, if she'd been an old ugly woman, instead of a good-looking young 'un."

The pretended countryman, who had listened to the foregoing recital with all the marks and exclamations of ignorant wonder. grinned knowingly at this last remark.

"Eh! what, the justice likes a pretty maid, do he?" he observed.

Mr. Constable nodded his head, and winked significantly.

"It ain't for me to say nought about my betters," he replied, "'specially his worship Squire Russell, who's a gentleman, every inch of him, but a nod's as good as a wink to a blind horse, and I reckon I can see as far into a milestone as here and there one; howsomever, I says nothing, because it's nothing to me, but if she do go to gaol at last, it will be her own fault, and not his worship's, that's all."

Dangerfield now seemed to have learned all he wanted, and he suffered the loquacious and self-sufficient constable to talk on without replying to him, or even seeming to attend to him. Once or twice Elinor's eyes and his met, and it was evident he intended to convey to her a look of encouragement; but what good, as she thought to herself, could his interference do her, since she had made up her mind that no apprehension of the consequences — no consideration, indeed, on earth — should tempt her to avoid meeting the charge and asserting her innocence.

The Bold Huntsman, the house which Elinor now learned for the first time was to be her residence for the assigned three days of captivity, was a large old-fashioned farm house, the occupier of which followed the two-fold employments of gamekeeper to Mr. Russell, and alehouse, or as he called it, "Inn Keeper" for himself; the latter business, however, being under the sole control and management of his wife, with whom, it appeared, both Mr. Russell and his subordinate, the constable, were especial favourites, her first greeting to the party who now entered the house being pretty equally divided between welcoming the latter and inquiring with solicitude after the former; her eyes, however, being the whole time turned on Elinor with a mixture of surprise and scrutiny, which the constable soon hastened to relieve, as it appeared, by taking her aside, and communicating the particulars of her (Elinor's) situation.

It was during this conference that Dangerfield found time and opportunity to address a few words to the latter, indicative of his motives for being there.

"You see I judged rightly," be observed, "and you are placed precisely in the situation I predicted you would be."

Elinor bowed her head without speaking, and he rejoined,

"You have as yet carried it off bravely; but it would be too much to expect that, if that fellow Copeland should perservere in his malice, you could maintain your resolution of continuing silent. Make up your mind, therefore, to profit by the opportunity, which I will soon contrive, for your escape, which Edward and I have come to the conclusion is the only means, not merely of securing our safety, but of removing you from the misery which must be your lot should you remain a dependent on Copeland."

"And for what should I exchange that dependence?" returned Elinor, fixing her piercing eye full on his face, with an expression of distrust that he could not misunderstand.

"You will have an asylum with one whom you have ever professed to regard and respect," he hastily replied. "Mrs. Hatherleigh will be happy in gaining such a companion to enliven her solitude."

"Mrs. Hatherleigh!" Elinor's heart leaped at the sound, and the prospects which were thus suggested to her imagination; but she quickly recollected herself, and shook her head despondingly.

"That would be indeed acknowledging all that the worst malice of my worst enemies could accuse me of," she replied, with a melancholy smile. "No, Edward never could wish me to act so basely; and, as regards himself, I'm sure he knows me too well to believe for a moment that I would sacrifice his safety for any selfish consideration. Return then to him, and tell him to rely with confidence both on my firmness and on my being eventually cleared from this foul charge, of which he knows my innocence as well as I know it myself."

Dangerfield was about evidently to remonstrate; but Thornhill having concluded his communication to the landlady at this moment, returned to his charge.

" The missus will have a fire lighted for you in the parlour, in a minute or two, miss," he observed, " and then you'll give your own orders as to what you'll eat or drink; and remember," he added, in a whisper, " it won't do to be too sparing, for the good of the house. It isn't everybody as would like to 'commodate you, all things considered. The squire, you know, pays for all," he added, with a significant tone.

Elinor knew not how to reply to this. She was most desirous, for her own part, to avoid incurring obligations to Mr. Russell, yet she knew not well how to object to what, perhaps, after all, was a mere matter of course. Without making any remark, therefore, she took the seat to which he pointed, while he retired to a distant part of the room with Dangerfield, who had resumed all his pretended clownishness and stupidity.

It is probable that, had the constable been a little more sober, or the landlady less anxious to hear his prolix narrative, the earnest conversation between Elinor and Dangerfield would not have passed either unsuspected or uninterrupted; as it was, it was not entirely unobserved, for Thornhill, as soon as he was seated, and had given an order for some ale, remarked,

" So you've been having some talk with the young woman, eh? Well, and what was it all about?"

" Oh, I can make nought of her," returned the pretended countryman, with an assumed grin of contempt; " she be too proud and uppish for I. I tho't I'd be a bit civil, and cheer her up a bit; but her turned up her nose, and talked so larned, that I was glad to gi' it up, thof I could ha' as good as her any day in the week, in my own place."

The constable replied by a loud laugh; and Elinor, who could not help hearing all that passed, and felt more disgust than admiration of Dangerfield's successful personation of a feigned character, which she thought he was carrying much farther than was necessary, was heartily glad to be relieved from society so little suited to her, and left to her own reflections in the room to which she was conducted by the landlady, the constable having first taken a cursory survey of it, for the purpose, as it appeared, of ascertaining that it presented no opportunities for his prisoner to escape.

It was some time, so glad was she to be alone, before Elinor thought even of the place to which she had been introduced; but when she did so, the prison-like appearance of the only window, guarded by heavy iron bars, and looking into a small stone yard, surrounded by lofty walls on every side, struck a chill to her heart.

It was evidently a place fitted up for the purpose of temporary confinement; and she sighed heavily, as her eye glanced around the bare walls, and over the scanty furniture, and thought, if this were an indulgence, what must be the wretched place to which in all probability she would be consigned, when she quitted it! Of herself or her own fate, however, Elinor thought far less than she did of the dangerous situation of Edward Hatherleigh, and the mysterious conduct and character of the man whom with his own lips he had acknowledged to be his father, and yet had spoken of with doubt, as scarcely comprehending his conduct or motives; thus proving, as she considered, that he had only recently become acquainted with his existence, or, at least, had had no personal knowledge of him.

What could be this man's situation in life, and what the circumstances which compelled him to seek security in such a place as that she had last night visited, were conjectures to which she in vain tried to give a rational solution; but these were comparatively of little moment to the uneasiness and anxiety which the conviction it gave her, that Edward's connection with this mysterious personage increased tenfold the danger of his falling into the power of Mr. Copeland.

"And he is at the mercy, too, of that strange, wild-looking being whom he calls Zekiel," she thought to herself, "whom he is evidently obliged to humour like a child, and who might, in one of his outbreaks of temper, such as he last night displayed, wreak his malice, by betraying the secret of Edward's retreat, if the latter was indeed mad enough to remain in such a dangerous neighbourhood. And then, again, what could Dangerfield's eventual object be in offering her, as he had implied, the means of escape from her present enthralment? Could it really be that he considered her in danger, and was anxious, for Edward's sake, to save her? or was it that he doubted her having resolution and fortitude to preserve the secret with which she had so unfortunately become acquainted? If it were the latter motive, she felt, proudly felt, that he greatly wronged her.

Hour after hour passed away in this uncertainty. She could hear the distant sounds of carousal, but the voices were too indistinct to convey the information she wanted. The gloom of evening, and at length the darkness of night, were only relieved by the glimmering of the fire, which was now fast decaying; and Elinor, yielding to the weariness and exhaustion attendant on so many hours' exertion of mind and body, laid her head on the table, and sank into a deep sleep, which lasted until she was aroused by the entrance of the landlady with candles and the necessary preparations for laying the cloth for supper, which she proceeded to do without at all consulting Elinor's pleasure, remarking only, that she was sure the latter must be quite tired of sitting so long alone, and apologising for having neglected to bring up candles, and make up the fire, which was gone very low.

Elinor answered without knowing what she said, for her eyes were fixed on the supper-table, which was evidently intended for more than one person; and she at length ventured timidly to ask if there was company coming to sup in that room: if so, she should be glad to go to her bed-room, as she was very unfit for company.

The woman smiled significantly, as, pointing to what Elinor had considered a chest of drawers, she replied,

"That is the only bed I can give you here, my dear, for you mustn't leave this room. And as to company, why, Mr. Thornhill, you see, has ordered supper here, and he's the master; you know we can't say him nay."

Poor Elinor's discomfort was sadly increased by this discovery, for she had looked forward to bed-time as certain of bringing a change from her present gloomy abode; but she was still more annoyed at finding that she had it not in her power to exclude at all times the coarse, ignorant Thornhill, who soon after entered, at the same time with the supper, and with an assumption of great consequence took his seat at the table.

" You wouldn't give no orders, miss," he observed, helping himself to some veal cutlets and ham, "so I was forced to do it for you; for Squire Russell would not like it, I know, if we didn't do honour to his generosity; and he told me to spare no expense."

"I leave it all to you, Mr. Thornhill," returned Elinor, suppressing her disgust at the freedom of his manners; "for myself, I assure you, I never eat suppers, and should be, perhaps, little inclined to do so now, even if it were my common custom."

" Well, just as you like, miss," he replied; "there's no force;

only it's a pity so much good victuals shouldn't have more respect paid to it."

Elinor remained silent, and kept her seat to the fire, until the constable, having satisfied his appetite, laid down his knife and fork, observing that he didn't envy the king his supper.

"I wish, howsomever, that I'd had somebody to help me with it, for the squire will have just the same to pay as if it was all eat."

"You had better send some to your companion, then," observed Elinor, who thought this a good opportunity of trying to learn what she was so desirous of knowing, namely, whether Dangerfield had departed.

"My companion!" repeated the constable, contemptuously; "I hope you don't call such fellows as he my companion—a poor, ignorant, dirty, shabby fellow, that I thought to do a kindness to, in bringing him to a decent house; and after swilling ale for two or three hours, he's gone off, and left me to pay the piper. Catch me doing a kind action again. Three quarts of eightpenny ale, and I can't put that down in the squire's bill."

Elinor was at once surprised, mortified, and rejoiced, at hearing this; surprised and mortified that one bearing such near affinity to Edward Hatherleigh could so degrade himself; and rejoiced at his departure, from the hope that he had ceased to indulge any project as regarded her, and would hasten to remove with Edward from a vicinity where he must know they were in constant danger.

"The fellow marched off so sly, too; I'm sure he was up to more than he seemed, for there was a gipsy chap came into the kitchen, to show us some conjuring tricks, and tumbling, and standing on his head, and the like o' that; and I noticed the country-fellow could talk to him in his own tongue. I wouldn't be sworn they wasn't old acquaintances; for the boy contrived to keep us all staring at him. I do believe the fellow deals with the devil. Howsomever, as I was a saying, while we was all taken up with his cunning tricks, the t'other steals out, without saying with your leave or by your leave; and presently I finds he's off, nobody knows where."

"And what became of the gipsy boy?" demanded Elinor, who had listened with breathless interest to this recital, having instantly recognised Zekiel in the description given.

"Oh, I left him fast asleep in the chimney-corner," he replied. "And that's well thought;—he may as well have a bit o' this supper; the poor devil looks as lank as a greyhound; and he's a merry one, too, and sings like a nightingale."

"Not here! Oh don't, pray, bring him here!" eagerly exclaimed Elinor, who dreaded the consequences of this apparently half-witted being recognising her in her present situation.

"Lord love you!" observed the constable, who looked surprised at her earnestness, "you needn't be frightened—the boy's harmless enough, and he'd serve to pass away the time for an hour or so; but, if you have any particular objection——"

"Oh, no," replied Elinor, striving to speak with indifference, though she trembled with agitation, "only that my spirits are not in a fit state——and, besides," she added, recollecting herself, "I suspect Mr. Russell would not be well pleased, were he to know that——"

"I don't see that he need know anything about it," interrupted the constable, peevishly; "howsomever, I don't want to compel you to anything you don't like. And, now I think of it, I suppose you'll be glad to get to bed, as you was up all night!"

Elinor replied in the affirmative.

"Well, then," he rejoined, "I'll send the missus to you. I s'pose you know you're to sleep here; and recollect that I shall be close to that door all night, so that you musn't hope that you can take an advantage of being accommodated here, instead of being sent to gaol."

"If you mean to insinuate that I should be likely to attempt to escape, sir, you are mistaken, and your caution is needless," returned Elinor, angrily; "for I can assure you, were you to leave the door open, I would not go until cleared from the imputation of guilt."

"It may be so—I can't gainsay it," he replied, with an incredulous sneer, that increased Elinor's vexation and mortification. "Howsomever, safe bind safe find, you know. I somehow have my thoughts that the fellow that went off in such a strange manner wasn't altogether what he seemed to be; and how do I know that that artful young imp that's now in the kitchen—— Why, how pale you're turned, all in a minute, young woman! I do really believe that I've hit the right nail on the head. I'll go and see what account he can give of himself; and if I don't make him remember, if he thinks to come any of his tricks on me."

The door closed behind him as he rushed out with this intention; and Elinor sank into a chair, in a state of alarm and suspense, which almost deprived her of reflection.

It was not the mere vague suspicion of the constable, however, which had produced this; but the fact was, that at the very moment he had expressed his distrust of the gipsy boy, Elinor had discovered the brilliant, snake-like eyes of the latter delibe-rately surveying her, Thornhill, and the whole interior of the room, through the interstices of the iron bars which guarded the window.

How he had got there she paused not to think; it was sufficient that she was convinced he was there; for she not only saw the glance of his eye, but beheld him smile, so as to show his pearly teeth (which so strongly contrasted with the dark-ness of his complexion) when convinced that she had discovered him, while he still remained unseen by the constable.

The instant, however, that Thornhill arose from the table, Elinor lost sight of the gipsy boy; and as the former did not return to the room, but sent the landlady to prepare the bed, &c., she had no opportunity of ascertaining what had been the result of his inquiries.

To retire to bed, however, in the uncertainty she felt as to any attempts that might be made to induce her to leave her prison, was impossible; and accordingly, Elinor declined the landlady's assistance, and allowed her to take the candle away, observing, that as she should not undress, she could lie down without the assistance of the light.

Contrary to what she intended, or even thought of, this ob-servation seemed to give great offence to the woman, who, observing that people that was squeamish might, and in all probability would, be glad of a worse bed than that they turned up their noses at, abruptly quitted the room, leaving Elinor to her own reflections and observations.

It was in vain, however, that she sat scarcely breathing, so intense was her expectation, and never for an instant removing her eyes from the window—all remained still and silent; and at length, yielding to exhausted nature, she threw herself on the bed, and fell into a deep sleep, from which she did not awake until the sound of voices, and of people moving about in the adjoining room, convinced her that the morning was advanced.

During the whole of this day Elinor was left almost entirely alone. Her meals were brought regularly; and two or three times the door was unlocked, and the constable looked in, as if to convince himself that his prisoner was safe. But he seemed in no humour for conversation, probably half ashamed and repent-ant for his excess of the preceding day; and Elinor did not attempt to break the silence, much as she longed to hear the result of the investigation which he had threatened, the preceding night, into Zekiel's character and conduct.

During these long, solitary, and wearisome hours, she had opportunity calmly to review the past, and weigh the consequences which were likely to result; and from this mental review, she became more satisfied than ever, that, from the present inquiry into her conduct she had nothing to fear as concerned her personal safety, though she could not but feel more acutely than ever the misfortune of being compelled to be silent when it depended only on her explanation to clear herself from the accusation brought against her.

Night closed without a single incident having occurred to break the monotony of her confinement. The landlady, who was the only person who waited on her, appeared scrupulously attentive to her comfort; and the fare placed before her (she having declined to give any orders, leaving it to Mr. Thornhill, as she said, to send in what he pleased,) was far more delicate and expensive than she wished or expected. Yet there was a superciliousness, and an evident wish to avoid speaking more than was absolutely necessary, in the landlady's manner, that Elinor could not but feel mortified and vexed at, though subjects of more importance soon banished the reflection from her thoughts.

With the darkness returned her recollection; or rather, was renewed more strongly the impression of terror she had felt at the intrusion of Zekiel on the preceding night. During the day, she had tried in vain to discover how he could have got into the small square place, to which there was apparently no entrance but by a door from the room in which she was confined, and which was kept locked, except for a few minutes, when the landlady opened it, to give the room, as she said, a little air. Over one of the walls, therefore, he must have come; and Elinor, in spite of what she had seen of his extraordinary habits, and surprising agility, shuddered as she contemplated the supposed danger he had run. Would he return? and for what purpose had he come? were questions that continually recurred to her mind, as the hour drew nigh at which she had previously beheld him; but all recollection of the gipsy boy was quickly banished, when, hearing the door behind her hastily unlocked she turned and beheld Mr. Russell ushered in by the constable.

" You may go, Thornhill," observed the former, " I will call when I want you; or, stay—send or bring in a bottle of wine and some biscuits—the poor thing looks quite sinking. I am afraid——"

"I hav'n't been able to persuade her to take a drop of anything, your worship," began Thornhill; but Mr. Russell quickly interrupted him.

"Do, pray, dismiss that title, my good fellow," he observed; "I am not sitting in judgment now; though I shall ever be thankful," he added, turning to Elinor, "that fortune placed me in that capacity, odious as it is to me in general, since it has afforded me the opportunity, I trust, of being of service to you."

"And to every one innocently accused, I hope, sir," returned the trembling Elinor, with more of composure and calmness in her manner than she felt in her heart, which was fluttering with indefinable alarm and anticipation of evil.

"Yes, the innocent certainly are always under the protection of justice," returned Mr. Russell, evidently disconcerted at the gravity and emphasis of her reply; "but now"—and he seated himself familiarly by her side—"tell me candidly all the particulars of your situation, and what has really given rise to this cruel, and, I am convinced, unfounded accusation against you."

"It is as unfounded as cruel, sir," returned Elinor, thrown off her guard by the seeming kindness and interest of his question. The difficulty, however, of becoming the heroine of her own tale, restrained her from proceeding; and with her eyes cast down and cheeks deeply glowing at the recollections that rushed upon her mind, she remained silent, scarcely conscious that Mr. Russell's eyes were fixed on her face with an expression of the most ardent admiration.

"You are unwilling, I see," he at length observed, "to recount the mischief your beauty has occasioned. Well, I will spare your modesty the recital, and tell you that I have heard the whole particulars; and really I cannot be surprised that the fear of losing you should have driven young Hatherleigh—that is his name, I believe—to the madness of getting rid of his more fortunate rival. But tell me—can it be possible, that you really loved this——"

"Edward Hatherleigh had no rival, sir, in my affection," interrupted Elinor, with emphasis; "he knew he had not—he well knew that no temptation on earth could have induced me to listen to the addresses of Walter Copeland; and, therefore, if I had not a thousand other securities for his innocence of the foul crime that is laid to his charge, it would be to me a sufficient proof that the motive never existed which his enemies have chosen to allege prompted him to the murder. No, Edward knew my heart; and he never, never distrusted me. He pitied Walter too much to feel the slightest symptom of hatred towards him. No, as surely as I am innocent—and that I am Heaven above knows!—so surely is he so too."

Mr. Russell looked perfectly astonished at this simple and candid declaration, to which he knew not how to reply. It was impossible, indeed, for him not to see and to respect the perfect innocence and artlessness of this avowal; while, at the same time, he felt that these qualities considerably increased the difficulties;—for how could he hope to succeed with one who thus openly and fervently avowed her affection for another? He was, however, too little accustomed to combat his inclinations, and had been, unfortunately, too successful in most of his attempts, to be easily discouraged, though he felt, perhaps, more confusion and embarrassment at the present moment than he had ever done before in addressing a female.

To his first attempt, which was with great appearance of gravity and friendly interest, to prove to her that Edward was unworthy of the enviable distinction of being beloved by her, Elinor quietly and gently replied, with a smile,

"You must pardon my saying, sir, that I, who have known him from childhood, must be rather better qualified to judge in this case than you, who yourself avow never even heard of him till to-day."

"But, even if he be all that you represent, my dear girl," returned Mr. Russell, with increasing animation, "his circumstances in life render it the height of folly for you to encourage his addresses. Oh, no, dear Elinor," he continued, "your beautiful face and form were never intended to be buried in such obscurity. You, who ought to be—and shall be, if you will only listen to me, and smile on me—the admiration of thousands——Hear me patiently, dear girl," he hastily added, seeing her about indignantly to interrupt him. "I have the misfortune to be, as you know, married—married to a woman whom it is impossible I can love. We have, indeed, for some time, contemplated a separation; and——"

"Why do you address this to me, sir?" interrupted Elinor, insisting on making herself heard, and hoping to prevent his offering any farther insult to her, by at once effectually repulsing him. "Recollect, Mr. Russell," she continued, "your situation and mine; and do not degrade yourself by insulting one who is unfortunately unprotected, and in your power."

"Insult you, dearest girl?" he returned; "far be it from my thoughts to do so; I am only pointing out to you that it is impossible for me to do all that my heart dictates. I cannot marry you, dear Elinor; but you shall be my wife in all but the name. Every luxury and indulgence that my fortune can procure you shall——"

A burst of indignation from Elinor prevented his proceeding. In every term that insulted innocence and modesty could suggest, she expressed her abhorrence of him and his proposal, and insisted on his immediately leaving her.

"You can have no right, sir," she concluded, "to intrude yourself here, although your situation may give you the power. Be assured, however, that every instant that you remain in my sight, increases my detestation of you, and your infamous offers."

Mr. Russell seemed at first a little piqued at the strong terms in which she expressed her resentment, though he showed no disposition to obey her bidding by quitting the room. A few moments, however, banished the frown from his brow; and he commenced anew, with all the eloquence he could call to his aid, to place before her the advantages that would result from accepting his offer, and the different consequences which must attend a rejection of them.

"I offer you, on the one hand," he observed, "liberty, affluence—everything that money and affection can command. I will instantly leave this place with you, and convey you where you will be treated with all the respect and distinction you deserve; while, if you remain here, what will be your portion? —contempt, calumny—perhaps a long imprisonment and a disgraceful trial, even if you can reckon with certainty on being eventually cleared. Then, what is to become of you? You cannot remain dependent on Copeland, even if he were willing, which is very unlikely, and——Nay, do not look so scornfully upon me, Elinor; by Heavens, I cannot bear it, nor I will not! You must, you shall be mine! I will force you to be happy, in spite of yourself!"

"Happy!" repeated Elinor, with disdain; "happy with you, a disgraced, dishonoured, despised wretch!—never! I would die first! Unhand me, sir," she continued, as he threw his arms around her waist, and attempted to draw her towards him. "Let me go instantly, or I will alarm the house, and expose you to the infamy you merit."

Mr. Russell laughed deridingly.

ELINOR CLARE.

EDWARD, GUARDED BY FOUR RUFFIANLY-LOOKING MEN, ENTERED THE ROOM.

"You know little of me, if you think I have not laid my plans better than to be foiled by the affected coyness of a silly girl," he replied. "All your violence, therefore, I assure you, will be thrown away; for every one in this house is devoted to me, and have too much confidence in my honourable intentions towards you to take notice of any attempt you make to persuade them to the contrary."

Elinor felt her heart sink at this assertion. Could it be really possible that she was so completely in the power of this un-principled man as he insinuated. She endeavoured, however, to conceal her terror as much as possible, and replied with coolness,

"I will not believe you so base, sir, even as you strive to make yourself appear. But I entreat you to consider what would be the consequences to yourself, should it be known even that you took advantage of my helpless situation to endeavour to ruin me. Friendless as I appear, I am not so utterly desolate as—as——"

The words died on her tremulous lips; and yet there was a flush, as if of some new-born hope, passed across her speaking countenance, that did not escape her companion's earnest gaze.

"What is the meaning of that sudden pause and look, lovely girl?" he demanded. "Do you at last relent, and——"

Again Elinor vehemently repulsed the effort he made to embrace her; but Mr. Russell had been gradually making up his mind that he would not submit to have his purpose baffled by any resistance a weak and unprotected girl could offer, a determination which was both accelerated and strengthened by the repeated glasses of wine which he had taken, and which he had in vain endeavoured to persuade Elinor to taste.

That, therefore, which in the first instance had borne the semblance of only gentle constraint, became now absolute rude force; and Elinor in vain struggled to free herself from his arms.

"Say—swear that you will be mine," he exclaimed; "that you will leave this place with me, and become the companion of my future——"

"Never!" shrieked Elinor. "Wretch! monster! release me this instant! Oh, God! help—help!"

Her cry was not unheeded, for at that instant a violent blow demolished several panes of glass in the window, and the next an attack was heard at the door leading from the yard, by some unseen assailant, who, though unable as it seemed to force an entrance by the former, on account of the strong iron bars, was evidently much more likely to succeed in the latter attempt.

At the very first sound of an approach in this quarter, where of course he had considered intrusion impossible, Mr. Russell, his eyes glaring with rage and disappointment, released Elinor, and apparently resolved to defend himself against the unknown and unlooked for intruder; but a moment's recollection suggested to him that it would be wiser to retreat, if possible, while there was a probability that his person and purpose there remained unknown.

That it was an attempt to rescue Elinor, not from him but from her present confinement and its prospective consequences, and which had been probably accelerated by her cries for assistance, was the only rational means of accounting for the presence of the intruder, whoever he or they might be, in that apparently inaccessible spot. If, therefore, he made good his own retreat before they entered, he might reckon with certainty on their being secured by the persons about the house, with whose aid and testimony in his favour he might defy all that Elinor might assert respecting him and the motives of his visit.

Actuated by these considerations, therefore, he hastily unlocked the door by which he had entered from the house (the key of which he had put in his pocket when he dismissed Thornhill) and precipitately retreated; while Elinor, whose terror was now transferred to another object, flew first after him to the door, which she bolted on the inside, and then to the window, and in tones of the most piercing agony called upon Edward (for it was indeed he) to escape while there was yet time and opportunity.

"He is gone, Edward; he will not dare, after this, to renew his infamous conduct," she exclaimed; "for he will fear again an interposition which he will not be able to comprehend if you escape. For heaven's sake, then—for my sake, fly, while you have the power!"

"Take her advice, Master Ned," hastily uttered a voice which Elinor knew was Zekiel's; "for my part, here goes; for I shan't stay to be caught."

There was just light enough for Elinor to see the boy ascending the high wall by means of a rope, which was suspended from the top; and her anxiety to behold Edward secure the same means of, as she supposed, safety, increased to the most frantic agony, and rendered her totally incapable of comprehending or even listening to one word that he uttered, as she heard two or three persons at the door through which Mr. Russell had passed, violently shaking it, and demanding instant admittance.

"Bring an axe—chop the door down," exclaimed a rough voice, the speaker making at the same time the most violent attempts to force the door inwards.

Elinor could not speak—she could only raise her hands in breathless, imploring agony to Edward, who still lingered irresolutely.

The silent expression of her despair, however, as she sank on her knees, which was fully revealed to him by the strong light within the room, apparently decided him.

"I go, Elinor," he whispered; "fear not for me—in a few instants I shall be in safety."

Elinor started up with an intensity that scarcely suffered her to breathe. She strained her sight to watch him in his daring attempt; he gained the dangerous height—the dangling rope was drawn up after him, to aid, as she supposed, his descent on the outside—for a moment she distinctly saw his tall figure erect on the top of the wall—he lowered himself, disappeared; and Elinor, no longer able to contend against the variety of emotions that were struggling in her bosom, fell senseless on the floor.

CHAPTER IX.

Then, take me with him too!
I must not be held back! Unhand me, villains!
Keep me not from his arms,—to the same dungeon,
To the same grave,—they bear him from my sight!
Let loose thy dreadful grasp! living or dead—
Thy hand hath clench'd me with a demon's power,
And stopp'd my circling blood.—Oh, sir, have mercy!
                                        SHIEL.

THE confused chattering and exclamations of half a dozen strange voices, and the sight of as many faces, all with looks of wonder and curiosity surrounding her, failed for some time to recall to Elinor's mind any distinct image of what had befallen her when she became again restored to life and consciousness. For some moments she continued to stare wildly around, without replying to or even seeming to hear the eager questions which poured in upon her from all quarters; but the sight of the broken window, and the now open door, leading into the small enclosure where she had so recently beheld the being most dear to her on earth, revived in her bosom recollections which their words had failed to do, and with a gesture of pious thankfulness she articulated,

"Heaven be praised for this mercy!"

The entrance of the mistress of the house, whose countenance expressed a mixture of rage, fear, and exultation, interrupted the eager interrogation as to what mercy she alluded, and what danger it was that had occasioned her to faint, which was uttered at once by two or three of the bystanders.

" What is the use of asking her any questions? You may be sure she won't tell anything; and very nat'ral too," she added, as her eye met Elinor's expressive glance of reproach. "It arn't no fault of the poor girl's," she continued, in a lower voice, pretending to address herself exclusively to one person, who was most officious in the group, but in reality, speaking purposely to conciliate Elinor; " for you know," she added, in the same tone, "a bird would get out of its cage, if it could. However, it's all over now; so you'd better all of you go, for Thornhill will be in a passion with me, if he comes back and finds you here. Don't frighten yourself," she continued, speaking to Elinor, with a significant look, " I will stay with you for the present."

The disappointed people, who expected to hear from Elinor a full explanation of the alarm, which still remained a mystery to them, reluctantly withdrew; and the artful landlady, having closed the door upon them, returned to Elinor, who was now sitting by the table opposite the window, on which her eyes were fixed with intentness, as she recalled to her mind all the particulars of the late event, and continued inwardly to offer up her thankfulness for Edward's escape as well as her own.

Suddenly, however, an alarming doubt intruded to check her gratitude. Russell and his underling, the constable, were absent—probably they were at that moment even in pursuit of Edward; and again her fancied security vanished, and was succeeded by all the horrors of suspense and uncertainty.

" You had better take a glass of this wine, child," observed the landlady, who had seated herself opposite to her, and was attentively watching Elinor's countenance. " Oh, you needn't scruple about it," she continued, as the latter put back the offered glass with a strong though silent expression of dissent; " there's nobody will come back to claim it," she added significantly; " for *he's* had enough to frighten him out of his wild tricks for some time to come. Don't be foolish, then, but take what will do you good; and I will take this other glass, for I'm sure I've almost as much need of it as you, I've been so flustered and frightened."

Though very reluctant to be indebted to such a source, Elinor felt too strongly how greatly she needed it, to refuse longer the offered restorative.

" There, that's right—you will soon get over it now," observed her companion. " I'm sure, I little thought, when I see that party come in, that he would go such lengths; though I know he's a wild devil and can't bear contradiction. However, I don't want to take his part; only, I would advise you, for your own sake, to be silent about his coming here; because you can't do him much harm, and he may do you a good deal, if you make an enemy of him."

Elinor's expressive features strongly betokened the contempt with which she heard this cunning attempt to secure her silence, and she could not but feel some slight satisfaction that she had it in her power at once to revenge herself on the infamous Russell and his passive tool, the landlady, by exciting their fears of exposure.

"There are others beside myself," she coolly replied, "who can bear witness to the infamous conduct which you seem inclined to treat so slightly."

"Others!" repeated her companion. "Was there any one who dares come forward, or whose oath would be taken in such a case?"

Before Elinor could frame an answer to this malicious remark, a confused sound, as of many voices and feet, was heard in the house, and the landlady started to her feet.

"I shouldn't wonder but they've caught him, after all," she exclaimed; and without paying the least regard to Elinor's agitation, she hastened from the room, leaving the latter in the most painful and pitiable state of suspense and anxiety.

Hours had passed away; the night, indeed, was far advanced, and still Elinor was alone and wretched. From time to time, the busy hum of voices penetrated even to her gloomy solitude, but still she remained in suspense and anxiety. At one moment she imagined that Edward had been intercepted and taken; but the next, the belief that, if it had been so, the very desire of triumphing over her would have induced some of those whom she could not but consider as her enemies, to have visited her, if *only* to triumph over her, banished this thought, and led her to conjecture some other cause for the neglect with which she was treated.

At last the door opened; and the landlady, with some confused apology for her long absence, proceeded to make up the bed in which Elinor had rested the preceding night.

"You needn't be afraid," she observed, turning a scrutinizing look towards the latter, who kept her seat by the almost expiring fire without speaking. "You needn't be under any alarm, I say," repeated the woman significantly, "for, thank goodness, I've got the place to myself again, at last, and I'll take care I'll keep it so. I'm sure, I wouldn't go through again what we suffered this night, no, not for five pound."

"I should think not," returned Elinor, with emphasis; "I should think that no money would recompense a person who thinks rightly, and wishes to sustain a fair character, for the disgrace which has been brought upon you by that man's conduct."

The woman's eyes (which had at the first sound of her voice been raised to Elinor's face with a look of intense curiosity) sought the ground before the latter had completed the sentence.

"I wasn't talking altogether about Mr. Russell," she at length observed, seeming to have gained confidence by reflection; "because, after all, I don't believe he meant any harm. And, besides, if he did, it's best to keep that to ourselves. A decent young woman won't get any credit by making herself a talk all over the country; and after all's said and done, what good will come of making a fuss about it?"

Elinor remained silent. She saw plainly that the woman was endeavouring (probably by Russell's instructions) to ascertain whether it was her intention to make public his conduct towards her; and she resolved, therefore, though nothing could be farther from her thoughts than to make herself, as the woman had said, the talk of the country on such a subject; yet she determined to punish both him and his abettors, and in that light she could not but view the landlady, by leaving them in doubt as to her intentions.

"You can bolt both the doors inside," observed the woman, finding she did not speak; "and then you're sure you can't be interrupted. As to the broken window, I can't do anything to it to-night, so you must put up with it as it is."

Elinor coolly replied, that it was of little consequence. "So that I am secure from intrusion," she emphatically observed, "I am content in all other respects."

The woman muttered something which Elinor did not understand; nor was she very desirous of so doing, as, from the expression of her eye, she was convinced it was nothing very pleasant. And then she quitted the room, observing, as she shut the door, that she should be heartily glad to be quit of so much trouble; but, thank goodness! another day and night would end it.

All Elinor's forced composure vanished, as soon as the door was finally closed upon her for the night, and she had secured herself from intrusion by bolting the inside; and throwing herself on the bed as she was—in her clothes—she gave free vent to the tears which a sense of her forlorn condition excited, until nature was exhausted, and she fell into a disturbed and uneasy sleep, which lasted till morning.

The next day and night passed over, without any event occurring to disturb the monotony of her gloomy prison. The landlady waited upon her at stated times; but she had resumed her former taciturnity, and Elinor felt too much contempt and dislike of her to attempt to break the silence. Twice during the day Thornhill looked in, as if to ascertain that his prisoner was safe; but he, too, seemed to shun all communication, though Elinor fancied there was an expression of malicious triumph in his countenance, which she was at a loss to comprehend the meaning of, though it considerably increased the uneasiness she felt.

A change of clothes was brought her in the course of the day, from, as she supposed, Isabel; but not a line expressive of sympathy or concern for her situation accompanied this, the only mark of attention she had received from those whom she had been accustomed to consider as her only relatives and friends; and bitter were the tears that Elinor shed over this disappointment.

At breakfast, on this her last day's residence in her gloomy abode, the landlady informed her that Thornhill would be with her at ten o'clock, to accompany her to Mr. Russell's.

" You had better, therefore," added the woman, with emphasis, " make up your mind what to say and how to act, for, depend upon it, it's in your power to make a great friend of him, whereas, if you make him an enemy——"

" I neither want his friendship nor fear his enmity," observed Elinor, calmly. " I trust to the justice of my cause to place me beyond the reach of either."

" Then I can only say, you'll be lucky if you get off without a better friend in court," returned the woman, affecting to laugh contemptuously, yet evidently disconcerted. " However," she continued, after a pause of consideration, " you know your own affairs best; only, I hope you won't bring me forward, because I am sure I know nothing at all about the matter."

" Then, of course, you cannot have anything to fear," replied Elinor, coolly.

The woman darted a look of malice at her, but Elinor's apparent composure remained unshaken, and she left the room.

It was evidently Thornhill's policy to pretend to know nothing of what had passed on the occaison of Mr. Russell's visit to his prisoner ; and he, therefore, spoke little, and that on indifferent subjects, to the latter, while on their road to the magistrate's. A few moments, however, before they entered the house, he turned round to her, and, with apparent nonchalance, observed,

"I wouldn't, if I was you, take any notice about a certain party's visiting you; because, you know, it's going a little out of the usual course, and he wouldn't like it to be known to everybody."

"I dare say not," was Elinor's contemptuous and laconic reply ; but, unsatisfactory as it was, the constable did not think proper to make a second attempt to ascertain her determination ; but, after a rather awkward silence of some moments, resumed all his bustling official *dignity*, and ushered her into the justice-room, which, to her great surprise, she found nearly filled with people.

To say that Elinor was perfectly composed, in such a novel and trying situation, would be wrong. She could not be insensible that every eye was turned on her, and that, in the loud buzz that ensued, every tongue was employed either in descanting on her appearance, or discussing the probability of her guilt or innocence of the charge against her. Mechanically she took the first seat which she saw was vacant ; and it was not till she had been some time seated, and had argued herself into courage to look up and face the assemblage of gazers with which the room was crowded, that she discovered, exactly opposite to her, her accuser, Mr. Copeland, and by his side—yes, it was Isabel, unkind, cruel Isabel—who had come there, not to sympathize in Elinor's sorrow—not to support her by her presence, or aid her by her counsel—but to behold with apathy her shameful degradation, and strengthen the general impression of her guilt, by showing publicly that she shunned her.

Such was Elinor's first impression, as her eyes rested on Isabel, who, with her head averted, was speaking to her father. A second glance, however, altered her opinion—Isabel turned her looks upon Elinor, and never did looks more strongly depict excessive grief and dejection. Her face, too, was as colourless and fixed as marble ; and Elinor saw plainly, as she thought, that she was only restrained from flying to her by the authority of her father—that stern old man, whose every feature seemed to swell with vindictive triumph, as he turned his withering glance upon the innocent object of his persecution.

"Can it be possible." thought Elinor, "that he really believes me guilty? or is it that he glories in the opportunity of at last wreaking on me his long-cherished hatred? Poor Isabel! how I wronged her! she is suffering more than I; for I can read, in that anguished look, the contention between her obedience to her father and her affection to me."

Alas! little did Elinor divine the true cause of Isabel's excessive agitation; little did she suspect that pity and affection for her whom she had so long loved as a sister, was vainly struggling in her bosom with the vindictive pleasure she experienced at an event, which, she well knew, must crush her (Elinor) to the earth. But we must not anticipate.

The entrance of the magistrate was announced to Elinor, just as she had ceased to remember, for the first time for many hours, that such a person existed.

"Here is Mr. Russell," whispered the constable, who had stood close by her, from her first entrance into the room. Elinor trembled, but it was rather with indignation than fear, as she saw the great man, with a look of calm importance, return the humble bows that met him on every side.

"How little do they know the creature they are worshipping!" thought Elinor, turning away her eyes in disgust, while he proceeded to his seat. In a few moments, the name of Mr. Copeland was called, and the old man stepped boldly forward. Elinor glanced at Isabel, but she had hidden her face in her hands, evidently overcome by her feelings. The name of Elinor Clare sounding through the room, recalled the latter's thoughts to herself; and, with a firm step and composed air, she walked forward to the place assigned her at the bottom of the table.

Contrary to all that she anticipated, the very first words that Mr. Copeland uttered, evinced a disposition to abandon the charge against her. But he was not long allowed to proceed, for a noise was heard outside the room, the door was thrown suddenly open, and a voice was heard, as if struggling with some one who wished to keep the person back.

"I must, I will speak, I will tell the truth. Miss Elinor is innocent; it was me that did all, wicked wretch that I am.—She is innocent!—she is innocent!"

And in an instant, Betsy, the simple girl whose partiality towards Elinor has been before mentioned, rushed forward, and threw herself on her knees beside the latter, who scarcely recognised, in the pale, ghastly being she now beheld, the fresh, ruddy sturdy girl, to whose kindness she had been so often indebted.

"Who are you, girl, and what brings you here?" demanded

the magistrate, as Elinor, whose surprise had not got the better of her humanity, raised poor Betsy from the floor, and whispered to her, to recollect where she was, and compose herself.

"I will, I will," returned the poor girl, who, though almost fainting with agitation, had evidently imbibed a sufficient fear of "his worship," to render her anxious to answer his question with due haste and perspicuity.

It was not, however, without considerable prolixity and wanderings from the question, and amidst plentiful floods of tears and expressions of penitence, which poor Betsy's appearance fully corroborated, that the whole truth was elicited from her, and Elinor's innocence established beyond a doubt.

Dorcas had, it appeared, broken up the party in the kitchen at the Grove rather arbitrarily, just when they were in the height of their enjoyment. This had given rise to some murmuring among the servants, and it appeared that the two females with whom Betsy slept, suggested to the latter, that, she being the lightest and most active, should steal into the housekeeper's room, so soon as they should be certain of her being asleep, and bring away the keys of the pantry and cellar, which were always placed on a chair by the bedside; and then they could easily get down stairs, and rouse the men-folk, and have two or three hours' more mirth and jollity.

"I was as willing as them, at first," continued poor Betsy, sobbing, " but we waited a goodish bit before Dorcas began to snore, when we knew she was asleep, and then my heart failed me, and I wanted them to give it up, but the girls wouldn't, and they called me a coward and a spoil-sport, and said they'd tell the chaps in the morning that it was all my fault; and so I took the candle, and went into Dorcas' room, in a pet. She was fast asleep, and I went round the bed, and took the keys; but just at that minute she moved, and I was so frightened, that I stumbled and dropped the candle. It went out, as I thought, and I ran in a fright into the other room, and told the girls.

"We all kept still, listening whether Dorcas was waked," continued the girl, gasping for breath, at the remembrance of what she was describing, " and Sarah the dairy-maid, was just calling me a fool for being so easily frightened and putting out the light, so that they should be obliged to finish dressing in the dark—for we had all been in bed and got up again—when I happened to cast my eyes towards the door into Dorcas' room, and I saw the bright light shining under it and through the keyhole—and oh! good God forgive me! I knew the place must be on fire, and I rushed into the room, but I could see nothing but flames and smoke and—"

"That is enough," interrupted Mr. Russell, who evidently commiserated the poor girl whose self-condemnation rendered her truly an object of pity. "You are satisfied, now, I trust, Mr. Copeland," he added, addressing the latter.

"I am, your worship," replied the old man, stiffly.

"I am happy to be able thus satisfactorily to discharge you, Miss Clare," began the magistrate, with the most bland and winning politeness; but Elinor waited not to hear the conclusion of the sentence, she turned almost unconsciously to herself, with an air of disdain from his congratulations, and devoted all her attention to soothing the poor girl, who continued in broken accents to entreat that she would forgive the uneasiness and suffering she had brought upon her, by not telling the truth at first, as to the fire.

"But the two girls both charged me to hold my tongue, or we should all three be sent to prison," she observed, "and so I never said a word, even to my mother, till this morning. She told me that you had been took up, and that Squire Russell was going to send you to the county gaol, and when I jumped out of bed, and—but is it true, Miss Elinor," (and she lowered her voice to a whisper) "that poor Mr. Edward was taken, trying to get you away from——"

Elinor turned deadly pale, as she faintly articulated the question.

"Who told you so?" but she heard not the girl's answer, for her eye at that moment encountered Copeland's glance. She turned from him to Isabel, and there her worst fears were confirmed; Edward was in the power of his inveterate foes. Isabel turned away her head, to avoid her keen, inquiring look; and there was in the old man's face an expression of triumphant revenge, that could not be mistaken.

"Hadn't you better be getting home, miss?" observed Thornhill, to whom Mr. Russell had been whispering his instructions, of which this observation was undoubtedly the result.

"Home? God help me!" exclaimed Elinor, wildly looking round; "but why are all these people waiting here," she continued, "they have homes to go to? Oh, God! can it be that——merciful Heaven, preserve my senses!"

"Thou shalt come home wi' me, lassie," exclaimed a rough, old countryman, who seemed struck with compassion at her wild looks and manners. "It's but a homely place I can take thee to, but I'll warrant my ould dame will make thee welcome; and thou shalt share wi' us till summut better turns up."

Elinor's looks spoke the thanks her tongue refused to utter; she tried, but in vain, to command her voice; and then, putting one of her fair, soft hands into the brown, horny one of the rustic, she burst into tears.

There were several voices now loud in consolation and kind offers, as they surrounded the poor girl; but Elinor suddenly recollected herself, and hastily dried her tears.

"I am weak where I should be most strong," she observed. "Am I right," she continued, looking up in the face of Farmer Benson, who was one of the foremost in proffering assistance and consolation,—"are you not waiting here—is not the magistrate sitting in expectation of——"

"Yes, yes; I know what you mean," replied Benson, compassionately. "Poor fellow! I be main sorry for him."

"Aye, and so be I." "And so be I," echoed half a dozen voices.

"Then, you don't think him guilty?" observed one, standing behind Elinor,—the effect of which was instantaneously to rouse her from the death-like stupor into which she was sinking at this dreadful confirmation of her worst apprehensions.

It was Dangerfield who spoke, and who, as she now hastily turned, imperceptibly to the others, but palpably to her, conveyed a look and gesture of encouragement.

"Guilty!" returned the clodpole to whom his question was addressed, "why, that's what nobody he e can say but his worship; but if you were to ax me whether I believes that young Hatherleigh killed Walty Copeland, I should say I never could believe it."

"Nor I," "Nor I," echoed a dozen voices.

Dangerfield smiled.

"And yet I dare say there's not one among you would lend a helping hand to get the poor fellow out of the scrape," he replied, with pretended indifference, but with a searching look that would have convinced anybody possessing discrimination, that he meant much more than his words seemed to imply.

"Why, the law, you know, master,—the law musn't be broke," returned one of his rustic auditors, looking earnestly at him, as if to discover who the person was who dared speak thus boldly in the very presence of justice.

"Not if it's contrary to justice?" returned Dangerfield, emphatically. "At any rate," he continued, "if I knew a man was innocent, and saw that he was likely to be made a victim to malice, I would never be the person to stand in his way, if I saw an opportunity for him to get off."

" Noa, nor I either," observed the old man who had before addressed Elinor. "I'd rather lend him a helping hand instead."

Elinor raised her eyes to the man's face with a look of gratitude, as he spoke. She had scarcely looked at him when he made his friendly offer to her; but now something induced her more closely to scan his features, and she became instantly convinced that he was not what he seemed—a plain, unsophisticated countryman. The knowledge of Dangerfield's previous disguise assisted her conjectures on the subject; she glanced her eyes anxiously around, and in the several dark faces and large black eyes that met her view she became convinced she beheld the companions of the man whose mysterious conduct excited at once her surprise and terror.

It was indeed wonderful to her, when she could regain sufficient composure to reflect upon it, how Dangerfield could have the boldness thus to face Thornhill, whom he had so lately imposed upon; but Elinor did not at this moment reflect, that she had previously seen the former in what might be called his real and undisguised character, and was therefore much more likely to detect him than the constable, even had the latter been more remarkable than he was for quickness of apprehension or intelligence.

In the present instance, the alteration in his appearance was so great, that probably no person but one so deeply interested as Elinor could have recognised him. The first time she had beheld him he had appeared in a light so doubtful, that it would have been difficult for her to have assigned him his proper place in society. He had resembled, in fact, more the imaginary picture she had conceived of the chief of banditti, than anything in real life. In the second instance, his disguise was such as she thought none but one like Thornhill could have failed to penetrate; but, at the present moment, he appeared as what his looks, his manners, and his features well corroborated, a respectable country tradesman, or small farmer.

No one, however, seemed to know him; and Elinor thought even that there was something of suspicion in the looks of some of the persons who had been drawn together to listen to his remarks. The fact was, however, that their whispers and doubtful glances were excited rather by the boldness of the stranger's observations than any suspicion as regarded himself;

for, though not one among them could have, if called upon, name him, or say in what part of the country he resided, there were several who could have vouched for having occasionally met with him either at the markets or fairs in the neighbourhood; and one or two could have spoken to his having made purchases of them which he had liberally paid for, and, *therefore*, must be a man of respectability.

All this, however, of course, Elinor knew nothing about; nor was she, indeed, at the present moment, very capable of seriously reflecting on the subject. She could not but believe that the presence of Dangerfield, and those whom she was convinced were his associates, boded some attempt on their part in favour of Edward; and she trembled at every look she saw cast towards them, lest it might lead to a discovery that would thwart their plans.

Whatever was his intention, however, in thus sounding, as it were, the sentiments of his auditors respecting Edward, he did not pursue it farther; and gradually the group that had collected around Elinor dispersed, and she was left sitting with Betsy on the bench, to which she had led the latter to recover herself.

"Don't you, for goodness' sake, Miss Elinor, listen to that old man that offered to take you home with him," whispered the girl, as soon as she found they were by themselves. "I know him well, he is one of the gipsies. I've seen him scores and scores of times, when I and our children used to be in the wood. And there's another,—and there's another," she continued, as her eyes wandered from one to the other of the tall, athletic forms that glided about among the crowd, and who were easily distinguished, not only by their features and complexions, but the agility and suppleness of their motions, which were strongly contrasted with the heavy, plodding, awkward movements of the rustics by whom they were surrounded.

Elinor had listened with breathless interest to Betsy's information. It only, indeed, confirmed what she had before suspected that in the person of Dangerfield she beheld the far-famed gipsy chief, whose mysterious existence and wonderful exploits had so often formed the subject of discussion and amusement at their winter fire-side at the Grove. But, though she was not surprised at thus discovering the truth of her suspicions, it did not diminish the bitter feeling of shame and anguish, which wrung her very heart, at knowing that henceforth Edward's fate was irrevocably united with these wretched, degraded outcasts of society.

"And me, too, they would draw me into their toils," she mentally exclaimed, while a burning blush of pride suffused her before pallid cheek. "And yet, what am I now?" she continued, unconsciously expressing her thoughts in a voice of anguish, that reached the ears of her attentive companion; "what am I but, like themselves, homeless, houseless, and a beggar, without the means even of purchasing the next meal, or a roof to shelter me for a single night?"

"But you wouldn't go with the gipsies, Miss Elinor?" exclaimed the simple Betsy, looking up in her face with an expression of horror. "My grandmother says they're not Christians, and that they eat human flesh, and——"

Betsy's farther exposition of the evil doings of the gipsies was interrupted by the appearance of an uncommon bustle. Every one seemed pressing towards the door; and then, having satisfied their curiosity, as hastily returned, to secure as near a station as possible to the long table, at the head of which the magistrate presided.

"Come this way with me, young woman," observed Thornhill, who had been in earnest conference with Mr. Russell, and now returned to the side of Elinor.

For an instant the tone of authority in which he spoke prevailed, and Elinor was about to follow him the way to which he pointed, which was in an opposite direction to that by which strangers were admitted to the justice-room; but she suddenly recollected herself, and sat down again.

"You can have no right to control me now, Mr. Thornhill," she observed; "and I choose to remain here."

The constable looked disappointed.

"His worship, Mr. Russell," he observed, "wished to spare your being hurt; but, howsomever, if you're obstinate, you must take your own way; only, I can tell you, you'll do no good, neither to yourself or anybody else, by stopping here."

Elinor made no reply—she did not even hear the conclusion of his observation—for her eyes were strained with agonising earnestness on the countenance of Edward Hatherleigh, who, fettered as a malefactor, and guarded by four ruffianly-looking men, at this moment entered the room.

It was not in human nature not to feel and to look dejected under such circumstances. The very sight of so many eager and curious eyes, all fixed upon him, and all desirous, as it appeared to him, to find him guilty of the crime attributed to him, was sufficient to depress an ordinary spirit; yet, serious,

ELINOR CLARE.

"YOU ARE A FALSE-SWEARING OLD VAGABOND!"

and it might be melancholy, as he looked, Edward still retained the lofty dignity of conscious innocence; and Elinor, agonised as her heart was at the sight of him she loved in so painful a situation, felt, nevertheless, a proud satisfaction in the certainty that he was suffering guiltlessly.

From the position in which she was placed, it was a considerable time before Edward was conscious that she was present, and beheld the indignity to which he was subjected; but when his eyes, which had been wandering round the room, in search, as it appeared, of some friendly face from which to derive consolation, at last rested on her for whose sake more than his own he was grieved at that moment, a burning crimson succeeded to the before pale hue of his cheek, and he lost for a moment the self-possession and calmness of look and manner which distinguished him at his first entrance.

The first interrogation, however, uttered by the magistrate, restored him to a full recollection of the circumstances in which he was placed; and he replied with a firmness and calm demeanour, that was never shaken during the remainder of his examination.

Far different was the deportment of Mr. Russell; in his bosom, jealous rage at the interchange of ardent feeling which he had observed between the lovers, struggled with fear and anxiety as to what would be the result, should Edward consider it prudent or necessary to bring forward the subject of the attempt to rescue Elinor, which had led to his own capture.

To deny point blank the accusation, and to pretend to treat it as a conspiracy between Elinor and Edward to blacken his character and impeach the even course of his justice, was Mr. Russell's firm resolve; yet the fear, which he could not entirely divest himself of, that even this might be insufficient to disprove the charge, should it be made, gave to his manner an air of indecision and hesitation, which most of those present attributed to a very different cause than the real one, believing it sprang from a leaning towards the prisoner, and a belief in his innocence.

It would be useless to recapitulate the evidence by which Mr. Copeland sought to establish the guilt of Edward, since there were no additional particulars to those with which the reader is already familiar. It was very evident, however, that time and reflection had not diminished in the slightest degree the inveterate feelings which Mr. Copeland entertained towards the supposed murderer of his son; but it was a matter of joyful surprise to Elinor, that Mr. Russell absolutely refused to listen to what he (Copeland) called proofs of guilt, but which were, in reality, only his own overstrained inferences from what he had considered evidence.

"I cannot listen to this, sir; this is not evidence," was the continual interruption Mr. Russell gave to his narrative; and at length, most reluctantly, the old man was compelled to acknowledge that he had no more to say.

"But here is my daughter, sir," he observed with sudden exultation; "she will tell you——"

"We will let her speak for herself, if you please, Mr. Copeland," observed the magistrate.

Isabel came forward, and Elinor's heart sank at the first

glance at her determined countenance; for she saw that Edward would find no mercy at her hands. Little, however, did the former suspect that she herself had been instrumental in producing the change that had taken place in Isabel's looks as well as sentiments; yet such was the fact. From the moment that Isabel had learned that Edward was taken, and heard her father's exulting anticipation of the fate that awaited him, her heart had relented towards the object of her former vindictiveness. The tears, the lamentations, and the certainty that her sister expressed of his innocence, all combined to render her doubtful and unhappy at having gone so far in her accusation against the friend of her youth—the playfellow of her childhood. A thousand traits of kindness, of humanity, and generosity, on the part of Edward, forced themselves on her recollection, and combined to make her fear that she had accused him unjustly, and repent that she had acted so rashly. At this time she knew not that Edward's capture was at all connected with Elinor, whose real situation Mr. Copeland and the Bensons had concerted to keep secret from the sisters, until her guilt or innocence was finally established. They were, therefore, persuaded that Elinor was gone to Newton, to purchase furniture, &c., to make the Nunnery, their intended residence, habitable; and as it was well understood that Edward had been taken at the Huntsman, on the common, which was in a totally different direction, not a suspicion entered the minds of either sister that Elinor was in any way concerned in it.

Determining in his own mind to abandon the charge against Elinor, now that his ardent wish was realised of getting Edward into his power, or at least within the reach of his fierce revenge, Mr. Copeland felt it no longer necessary to keep Isabel in ignorance of the proceedings he had adopted towards the former; and on their way to Mr. Russell's, whither they were going, as Isabel supposed, for the sole purpose of giving evidence against Edward, the old man communicated to her that she would behold Elinor also a prisoner.

" Do not be so frightened, girl," he continued, " she is sure to be discharged; and she richly deserves all she has suffered, for leaguing with that villain against me. Neither do I acquit her of being the cause of the fire, perhaps not intentionally; but I'll never believe but that her leaving the house to meet the villain was the occasion of it. I do not, however, care for that, now I have got him safe; and it will be sufficient punishment to her, to see him brought to the——"

"Oh, do not talk so, father," interrupted the shuddering Isabel, whose imagination at that instant presented to her a scene of horror from which she shrunk with dismay.

"Well, well, we shall see," returned the obdurate old man; "but mark me, Isabel, no flinching from the truth. My eternal curse would attend you, I would disown you as my child, would spurn you, hate and detest you for ever, if, through any wavering on your part, the wretch—the monster who has robbed me of my son, should escape my vengeance!"

Isabel's pale cheek became still paler at this denunciation; but she was too well acquainted with her father's disposition, to venture to remonstrate, or even to suffer a word to drop that could lead him to suppose she repented of her former hasty condemnation of one whom she was now more than half inclined to believe she had unjustly accused.

It was this struggle in her mind, added to her real sorrow and shame at the cruelty and indignity with which Elinor had been treated, that had occasioned the alteration in Isabel's looks which had been already noticed, as having been observed by the former, when first she beheld her in the justice-room.

Isabel's first impulse, when she beheld Elinor, was to fly to her, and attempt, by the expression of her sympathy, to console her for all she had suffered; but her father's stern command restrained her.

"Let her be, girl!" he exclaimed, "she has deserved all she has met with, and she shall be humbled still lower, before I will forgive her, if ever I do."

Disposed thus to feel kindly towards Elinor, Isabel rejoiced with unfeigned pleasure at the total acquittal of the latter from all suspicion, by Betsy's candid confession respecting the origin of the fire. Mr. Copeland's feelings, however, did not appear to be in the smallest degree softened by the discovery, and Isabel's ardent feelings were still kept in check by his severity.

"Do not tell me of her innocence," he harshly replied to Isabel's pleadings in favour of Elinor. "Has she not from beginning to end been the cause of all the misery I have suffered? And even now, look at her conduct; though, certainly, I ought rather to thank than condemn her in the last instance, for, but for his mad and desperate attempt to rescue her, the murderer might be still at liberty. Oh, yes, certainly so, for I owe some obligation to her!"

The blood, which had rushed in torrents to Isabel's cheek, retreated again, and left her paler than before, as, in reply to her earnest questions, her father stated, what he believed to be the fact, namely, that Edward had, in making a desperate attack to rescue Elinor from confinement, been discovered and taken.

All the evil feelings which the evident preference of the latter for Elinor, to the exclusion of what she (Isabel) considered her superior claims, had engendered in her bosom, again took full possession of her. She felt as if she could, without remorse, at that moment sacrifice them both to her offended pride and jealousy; and this feeling was increased to madness, when Edward soon after entered the room, and she beheld the interchange of looks between him and Elinor; then all kindly feelings towards the former instantly vanished. Scarcely had Edward deigned to bestow a cold glance upon her, while the moment he discovered Elinor, a flush of emotion had lighted up his features, and he had for some time appeared unconscious that any one was present but her.

"Yes, he scorns me!" repeated Isabel to herself, with all the vehemence of jealous rage; "he does not even think it worth his while to bespeak my forbearance, or remind me of our former friendship, by a single glance or look; and he may take the consequences. I would not save him if a single word could do it."

Such were the reflections that embittered Isabel's testimony against him whom she had so long fancied she loved. Edward did not bear it unmoved; surprise and sorrow at her evident inveteracy, was at times very visible in his countenance, and once or twice he smiled contemptuously at her over-strained eagerness to prove his guilt, by relating her own impressions rather than what had actually occurred. Still, however, he could not but see that her recital of her having seen him in the wood near the spot where the body was found, and his eagerness to avoid her, produced a strong impression against him; and it prepared him for the result, which Mr. Russell with apparent reluctance announced, namely, that he (Edward) must be committed to take his trial for the murder of Walter Copeland.

"As to the other charge," continued the magistrate, "that of being concerned with Elinor Clare in setting fire to Mr Copeland's house, that is, of course, now set at rest, by the voluntary declaration of the young woman who was, it appears, the unfortunate cause of the disaster."

Edward's countenance lighted up at this observation. Again he glanced round at Elinor, and the sight of Betsy, who was still sitting by the latter, endeavouring in her simple way to console her, fully explained to him the whole of the affair.

"Thank God for this!" he softly murmured, as, at the suggestion of the men who were now to convey him to the prison, he was turning from the table at the foot of which he had been standing.

The agony of Elinor's feelings, which had hitherto manifested itself only in the convulsive swelling of her bosom, and the anguished expression of her features, now broke through all the restraints of custom and timidity, and rushing towards Mr. Russell, who was addressing Copeland in a low voice across the table, she threw herself on her knees before him.

"He is innocent!" she shrieked, in broken accents. "Have mercy! oh, have mercy! Do not——"

"Not for me, Elinor," exclaimed Edward, wildly; and breaking, in spite of all opposition, from the men, who would have held him, he flew to her, and raised her from the ground. "I ask no favour," he continued, fixing his piercing eye on Mr. Russell, "I demand only justice."

"You do not impugn that which you have received at my hands?" demanded Mr. Russell, hastily; but immediately recollecting himself he haughtily added,

"Your case is now in other hands, Edward Hatherleigh. Officers, do your duty," and at the same moment hastily quitted the room by the side door near which he was seated.

There was a momentary pause; the men who had rushed towards Edward with eagerness when reminded by the magistrate, found themselves frustrated in their intention of immediately seizing upon him, by the interposition of a great number of the persons present, both male and female.

"Let 'em be for a few minutes,"—"Poor things, let 'em be," —"Keep back, let 'em speak to one another afore they're parted," were the exclamations that resounded on all sides, bewildering the men, who, totally unused to opposition in their offices, knew not how to act, and suffered themselves to be overcome by the torrent.

Mr. Copeland, with Isabel hanging upon his arm, as if totally overcome with the exertion she had made, was hastening to quit the room by the opposite door to that at which the magistrate had departed. At the sound, however, of the opposition that arose to Edward's immediate removal, he instantly turned back, but he was directly assailed by a group of women, who, in no measured terms, assailed him with all the vituperations that language could supply.

"You are a false-swearing old vagabond," exclaimed one

beldam, sticking her skinny hands in her sides, and thrusting her withered face close to his, with an air of the most determined opposition. "The curse of curses light upon all, I say," she continued, looking at Isabel, who shrunk in undisguised alarm, "that try to part true lovers. May they never——"

"Who are you, woman? and what do you mean by this?" exclaimed Mr. Copeland, furiously. But at this instant, and before he could execute his intention of forcing his way through the band of female furies who opposed his progress, in order to enforce the authority of the officers in the instant removal of their prisoner, a loud yell arose from the interior of the room; the candles, which the darkness of the room and the decline of daylight had rendered necessary for the last half hour, were suddenly extinguished, and a scene of confusion ensued, which words would vainly attempt to describe.

Overcome with terror, Isabel clung shrieking round her father's neck, so as effectually to prevent his interposition, and embarrass his every faculty. The men in whose charge the prisoner had been left, were driven to the further extremity of the room, and there, unable to distinguish friends from foes, their cries for assistance, and charges to the bystanders to assist in the king's name, were overpowered by the yells, the cries, the almost supernatural noises, which at once drowned their voices and confused their senses, so that they knew not how to act.

For a minute or two after the first commencement of this tumult, Edward continued to hold the nearly insensible Elinor in his arms, straining her to his bosom with all the fervour inspired by the consideration that this might be the last time that his arms should embrace her; but he was quickly recalled to other recollections, by the voice of Dangerfield, or, rather we should say, his father.

"Fly, boy, while there is yet time," he exclaimed. "Nay, do not hesitate, follow Zekiel, who is here to conduct you; your life and mine depend upon this moment."

"And Elinor——" said Edward, hastily.

"Leave her to me," returned the father, I will take care of her. Elinor," he continued, forcibly drawing her from Edward's arms, "rouse yourself, girl, and tell him to go, while he has yet——"

"Oh, yes, yes, yes; fly Edward—for my sake, go!" ejaculated Elinor, thrusting him from her, and seeming to have regained all her energy at the prospect of his escape.

Edward still hesitated, but the din around him grew still

louder. Zekiel, who, unseen, had crept close to him, seized his hand, and at the very instant the lights were extinguished, he found himself drawn towards the door, through which he was thrust rather than led, by half a dozen eager hands, who had all been eagerly watching this eventful moment, and now rushed after him into the open air.

For some minutes Elinor remained totally unconscious of her own situation, supported by Dangerfield, and every sense absorbed in one overpowering sensation, that of terror lest Edward should be pursued and re-taken; but she was at length recalled to self-recollection, by a hasty communication, part of which only she overheard, or at least was able to comprehend, between Dangerfield and one of his companions.

"The boy is safe," she heard the latter say; "had you not better follow, and leave me to give the signal to our people, to draw off as fast as they can?"

"Elinor, what is your intention?" exclaimed Dangerfield. "You have found me a friend in need, trust in me still, and share the fate of Edward. I will conduct you——"

A loud crash at the door through which Mr. Russell had retired, interrupted his speech, and made Elinor, from the mere instinct of terror, cling closely to the only person from whom in that riotous assemblage she could claim protection.

"They will be upon us in another minute—the window, make for the window!" exclaimed the same rough voice which had before addressed Dangerfield.

In an instant the window close to which they were standing was thrown up, half a dozen dark forms leaped through it, hurrying the half unconscious and terrified Elinor with them; and then one of the most robust and active among them, at a few hasty words from Dangerfield, caught her up in his arms and exclaiming, "Make yourself satisfied, lady, I will carry you as safe and as easy as if you were seated on a side saddle on the best-going nag that ever was taught his paces, if you will but keep still, and throw your weight as much as you can on my shoulder," commenced running with his companions, at a rate of speed which showed he felt but little incumbrance from his burthen.

The whole transaction had been so sudden, and terror and surprise had so completely deprived Elinor of all reflection, and, indeed, almost of consciousness, that she had not power either to remonstrate or object to the proceedings which had thus placed her entirely in the power and at the mercy of the strange people by whom she was now surrounded. When, however, she recovered her recollection, she entreated the man who carried her, to allow her to walk.

"I am sufficiently recovered now," she observed, "to be able to keep up with you; and I will give you my word——"

"We shall be at our journey's end in ten minutes," interrupted the man, who had relaxed his pace for a few moments, to listen to her. "But come, we shan't be many minutes behind the best of them, if you put your best leg foremost; if you don't, you know, I must carry you again; for our chief is gone on to prepare the women for your coming, and he will be all on thorns, I know, till I bring you in."

The speed which Elinor was compelled to use, to satisfy and keep up with her conductor, left her neither power nor opportunity to make any inquiries of him, or in the slightest degree satisfy her curiosity and anxiety as to where he was leading her.

The steepness of the hill which they were now ascending, however, compelled them both to pause when they had reached the top, to recover their breath; and Elinor then ventured to take advantage of the opportunity to inquire how much further they had to go.

"Look down there, to the left," observed her blunt, unpolished companion; "you will see the light of the fire that's cooking our suppers; I can almost fancy I smell it up here, so savoury it is. Come, let's be jogging; for my mouth waters, and I'm sure I've earned it to-night."

In silence Elinor obeyed this intimation; she had, indeed, seen enough to enlighten her fully as to the situation in which she was placed by her tacit compliance with Dangerfield's proposition, for the fire to which her companion had pointed arose from a regular gipsies' encampment, and left her not a doubt as to the sort of life to which she was about to be introduced.

So steep, indeed, was the hill from the brow of which she contemplated the scene, that she seemed to look down perpendicularly on the top of the tents, and could discern not only the poor, miserable-looking cattle that were grazing about within reach of the light of the fire, but could also see the reflection of its red flames on the countenances of a large group of half-naked children, who, extending their length on the grass, seemed impatiently waiting the conclusion of the cookery, about which two or three aged and withered crones were employed, whose very looks would, in Elinor's best days, have been an antidote to appetite, but at the present moment inspired her with complete horror and aversion.

"And with such as these am I to be doomed to associate ?" was the reflection that forced itself upon her mind, as she began, with her companion's assistance, to descend the steep and winding path which led to the spot which, she understood, was to be the conclusion of her toilsome journey.

The nature of the path which she was now treading, rendered it impossible, after the first few yards, to catch a second glimpse of the encampment, until she arrived at the bottom, when a sudden turn brought them full in front of the fire; and the loud barking of the dogs, which sprung forth to meet them, and which was quickly changed into the whining of joy, as they recognised her companion, brought forward all who had remained there to congratulate their arrival ; and in an instant Elinor was nearly stunned by the shrill voices and eager vociferations of five or six decrepid beldames, who surrounded them, demanding intelligence of the business he (Reuben they called him) had been upon ; and inquiring, before he could give an answer, where the others were, and why they did not come in to their supper, which had long been ready for them.

"Is not Paul come, then?" he demanded, looking eagerly towards one of the tents, which, somewhat better in appearance, and somewhat more capacious than the others, was also distinguished from them by being closed.

"Yes, he is come, and the youth and Zekiel," replied one of the women, in a low tone, pointing at the same time to the tent, to indicate that the persons he spoke of were there. "But you know," she continued, "Paul likes not to be questioned ; and as to Zekiel, the froward little imp told us that we might look to see none of our people to-night, but might find them all to-morrow morning, either in the cage or the stocks at Newton."

Reuben shrugged his shoulders.

"I think we stand a fair chance of being all kid by the heels," he replied, in an under tone, "if we're not soon moving. What said Paul? did he give no orders ? no——"

The person of whom he spoke raised at this moment the canvas that closed his tent, and walked forward ; he had already got rid of the habiliments in which Elinor had so recently beheld him, and now appeared precisely as when she had first been surprised by his appearance in Mrs. Hatherleigh's kitchen.

"This is not exactly such a place as I could have wished to welcome you to," he observed, stepping forward, and courteously taking her hand; "but here you are, at least, safe from insult, and among friends."

He led her towards the tent as he spoke, and in a few moments Elinor was once more in the arms of Edward.

To repeat the broken expressions of mingled grief and joy—of rejoicing for present safety, and terror and fear of future danger, which was all that for some minutes either could give utterance to—would be impossible. They were alone, for Dangerfield had quitted the tent the moment Elinor entered it; and yet the affrighted girl looked around her from time to time with a feeling of alarm she could not control, and which seemed to wring Edward's heart with anguish.

"Oh, Elinor," he exclaimed, "what misery I have brought upon you! to what wretched scenes have I been the means of introducing you! Can you forgive me? Can you still love one who is so unworthy of you? That man—my father—oh, how my heart revolts to call him so! he has assured me that by your own choice you came hither. He tells me that Mr. Copeland has utterly deserted you, and that, wretched as this alternative is——"

"He told you true, Edward, that I am utterly friendless, homeless——" Elinor burst into tears; she could not complete the picture she would have drawn of her situation; and she felt that, however repugnant to her feelings her present shelter might be, she had no right to be ungrateful to those who had, with such risk, trouble, and exertion, brought her thither.

For some moments Edward hid his face with his hands, sympathising, as it appeared, too deeply in her sorrow to control it; but at length he roused himself, observing with animation,

"And yet, dear girl, hope whispers me not to despair. I am young, and strong, and willing to work; and I *will* work. I will think nothing too difficult or too humble, that will enable me to free you from this degradation. We can be happy, Elinor, in poverty, can we not, dearest girl, if free from disgrace?"

Elinor's heart, as well as her soft voice, responded "Yes" to this question, while the deep crimson of her cheeks betrayed the modesty of maiden innocence, fearing lest her ready acquiescence might be misinterpreted, and yet feeling that it would be ill-timed and ungenerous, in the present circumstances, to raise objections and give utterance to scruples that could not be indulged.

"Oh, yes, we shall be happy yet," repeated Edward, with all the animation of youthful and sanguine hope.

Elinor sighed; she tried to reply in the same strain, but her lips refused to give utterance to what she could not feel.

Happy! with an accusation of murder hanging over his head, which, by a strange fatality, every circumstance seemed to corroborate, and of which even the last desperate attempt to escape would of course appear as a confirmation, oh, how could she feel, how could she hope to be happy? She had been taught, indeed, to believe that Heaven makes innocence its peculiar care; and her own naturally pious and trusting disposition induced her to believe the axiom. Yet, when she looked around her—when she thought of the past, and contemplated the present—how could she, how dare she indulge hope for the future?

Edward's countenance caught the impression of her sadness.

"Your looks reproach me, Elinor," he observed, in a melancholy tone, "for daring to rejoice in thus securing my own happiness at the expense of all that the world thinks valuable—all that habit and education have taught you to consider indispensable; but——"

A violent uproar outside the tent suddenly interrupted the vindication of his disinterestedness which Edward was about to attempt. Elinor's cheek changed to the hue of death, and her lover, though he attempted to remove her terror by assuring her that it was nothing but the noise occasioned by some of the "gang," who had been absent, and were now returning, was evidently discomposed, and anxious to listen to what was passing.

In a few moments, however, all suspense was put an end to by the re-appearance of Dangerfield.

"There has been the devil to pay, yonder," he coarsely observed; "one of our people has got dangerously hurt by a blow from that villain, Russell. They have brought the poor fellow off, however; and he will be here in the tents in a few minutes. But I rather suspect, from the confused account I have got, that the rascally Justice has got scent of us; and, if that is the case, it will be too great a risk for you, Edward, to remain here."

"Oh, no, no," eagerly exclaimed Elinor; "not for the world! Do not delay a moment! for, if you once fall into the power of that man again——"

"And you, Elinor, then, will accompany me?" interrupted Edward.

"That is impossible," exclaimed Dangerfield, hastily. "Look at her, does she look fit to sustain a flight of some miles, in the darkness of the night, and through rugged paths and places where there are no paths? No, no; Elinor is too considerate—too discreet, to wish, I am sure, to peril your safety by becoming an impediment to your flight. Besides, there is no occasion for it; with me she is safe. Mr. Russell has no power to remove her from my protection, unless, indeed, she prefers his."

Elinor's expressive countenance betrayed the shame and vexation she felt at this sarcastic observation; and Edward, with a look of anger and reproach, observed,

"This is neither a time nor subject, sir, for jesting; yet it is impossible you can seriously mean to imply a doubt that Elinor would reject with scorn——"

"Stop, stop, young man—you are rather too hasty in your conclusions," interrupted Dangerfield. "I assure you I was never further from jesting in my life than in the remark I made, which was merely to point out the necessity of Elinor's being decisive and resolute in resisting any attempt that may be made to induce her to return to the *friends*, I suppose I must call them, that she has renounced. I am aware," he continued, "that in my present situation, I can offer her but little beyond safety and freedom; but——"

"Elinor's mind is made up to share my fate," exclaimed Edward, hastily, and appealing to her by a look, to which she instantly replied with firmness,

"It is."

"Then you will urge him to go as quickly as possible, and trust to me to restore you to each other," returned Dangerfield, hastily; "or, I fear, his fate will be to return to the prison from which he has been with such difficulty rescued."

Elinor tried to speak, to implore Edward to go instantly; but terror at the threatened danger in which he stood deprived her of the power of uttering what her heart dictated, and she could only in broken accents implore him not to lose another moment, but confide in her resolution, and consult only his own safety.

"If you do not," exclaimed Dangerfield, fiercely, "I must consult mine and my people's; they have already hazarded too much for one——"

"Say no more, sir; I am at your disposal," interrupted Edward, in a tone of anguish. "Elinor," he added, straining her to his bosom, "again fate separates us; the next time——"

A sudden and peculiar cry, or wail of distress, at this moment arose from numerous voices outside the tent. Dangerfield rushed out; and Edward, in obedience to Elinor's agonised entreaty, followed.

Left thus to herself, and to all the horrors of suspense and alarm not only for Edward, but at her own strange and melancholy situation, Elinor remained for a considerable period motionless, in the attitude in which the former had left her, just within the entrance of the tent. The sounds of grief and lamentation, which had evidently called Dangerfield forth so hastily, had ceased, as it appeared, at his presence; and only a low busy hum of voices, at some little distance, as it seemed to Elinor, broke the stillness of night.

Gradually she recovered sufficiently to look about her, and note the appearance of the place she was in; but the result was only a still deeper conviction of the wretchedness and misery of the fate which she had now, as she believed, irrevocably doomed herself to. An old brass lamp, which gave a flickering and unsteady light, was suspended by an iron chain to the top of the fragile habitation, and served to make the squalid appearance of all that surrounded her but too visible. A low, broken stool was the only article resembling a seat; while a rough board, placed on four supporters driven into the earth, formed at once an apology for a table and a shelf or cupboard, sustaining sundry articles of coarse and mutilated earthenware, a knife and fork or two, a few metal spoons, and coffee-pot, all arranged in a manner that seemed to say that, humble as they were, they were thought of no little value by their possessor.

The only remaining article of furniture that presented itself to Elinor's view was the bed, if such it could be called, the heap of rags, which, spread upon the bare earth, occupied nearly a third part of the tent, and was attempted to be made as decent in appearance as possible, an old patchwork counterpane being smoothly spread over it, and a piece of crimson stuff pinned to the canvas walls and roof of the apartment, so as to form a sort of curtain, extending nearly half the length of the resting-place.

Little did Elinor think while she noted with aching heart these, to her, miserable, scanty, and insufficient accommodations that they were such as might be envied by most of the singular beings among whom her present lot was cast, being such as could only be appropriated to the dignity of their chief, one of whose privileges it was to have a separate tent, and to be served with his meals, if it so pleased him, alone.

The inventory of this splendid abode of royalty was, as may be supposed, soon completed; and Elinor, at once desirous to shun an interview with Dangerfield by himself and to ascertain the extent of the evil which had caused those singular and melancholy sounds, that seemed still to dwell on her ear, as if still uttered, though in such low and subdued accents as scarcely to be audible, ventured to lift the canvas opening of the tent, and look out.

Not a living creature, however, was visible. There were, in all, five tents, irregularly placed, and of different dimensions. Of those nearest to Elinor, one or two were closed; and the others, though open, had neither light, nor any other visible sign of being inhabited. But there was one placed at some distance, and apparently much longer than the others, from which strong gleams of light were issuing at every crack or rent that time had made; and from which, she soon ascertained, proceeded those low, and now, as she stood in the silence and obscurity of night, to her, awful sounds.

It was a far better and more elevated feeling than mere curiosity that led Elinor, after a pause of some minutes, to subdue all selfish cares and feelings, and venture across the open space to the tent in question. She paused, however, in alarm and suspense, as she drew near, at discovering that a group of men were collected around the entrance, a part of which was unclosed; and the light from within falling full upon the countenances of those nearest to her, disclosed the strong impression of pity, terror, and grief, with which they contemplated the scene that was passing within.

A few moments' observation convinced Elinor that their attention was too deeply absorbed to allow them to notice her approach; and, besides, she reflected, " Why should I fear or shun those among whom I have sought shelter and protection?" Without further delay, therefore, she stole softly round to the back of the tent, where a convenient fissure afforded her (unseen herself) a full view of the scene within.

A fine, tall, athletic young man was extended on a miserable bed on the ground, the deep olive tint of his arms and neck, which were bare, contrasting strongly with the ghastly paleness of his face; his glazed eyeballs were strained upwards, and his manly features convulsed with the agony of approaching dissolution. Bending over him, on the opposite side to Elinor, was the Gipsy Chief: he had been, it appeared, performing the operation of bleeding the wounded man, and was now carefully bandaging the arm, while his eyes from time to time were turned with earnestness on the sufferer, as if seeking in his countenance to learn the effect of the remedy; while around, some kneeling, others sitting on the ground, but all with the strongest expression of solicitude and sorrow depicted on their expressive features, were at least a dozen women, most of them young and well looking, but one or two bearing the marks of extreme age, and equally remarkable for their ugliness and forbidding looks.

On all alike, however, old and young, was impressed the same character of tenderness and feeling towards their suffering companion, whose every look was watched, and motion solicitously aided, while, whenever a groan of pain escaped from his pale lips, it was re-echoed in a suppressed tone as if unable to control their sympathy, though fearful of disturbing the object of it.

Towards Dangerfield, Elinor observed, their behaviour was that of the deepest respect and reliance on his knowledge. Every suggestion he made was instantly attended to—every hand eagerly stretched forth to assist him when he arose from his kneeling posture; and all seemed to vie with each other in anxiety to receive the commands he was apparently giving as to the treatment of the patient.

A large torch stuck in the ground, which had thrown its flaring light over every object, and had thus enabled the attentive Elinor to make these observations, was removed, and a single candle lighted in its place; and Dangerfield, and all the women, except one or two whom he had apparently appointed to the office of watchers by the bed-side, quitted the tent.

So absorbed had Elinor been in the contemplation of this interesting scene, that until the moment she saw him disappear, she thought not of herself or her own situation. The probability that he would return to the tent in which he had left her, and be surprised if not angry at her absence, at this moment occurred to her; but Elinor, in spite of the proof of his kindly feelings which she had just witnessed—in spite of the respect which his presence seemed to inspire, experienced an irrepressible dislike to a solitary interview with the man. There was an expression in his eyes, a levity in his tone and manners, whenever he addressed her, that, unwilling as she felt, to acknowledge it even to herself, considering him as the parent of Edward, disgusted and alarmed her.

She had little time, however, at the present moment, to reflect or hesitate; for, by the light of the torch, which was now fastened in front of one of the tents, between the spot where she now stood in concealment and that which she had quitted, she beheld him crossing the open place towards the latter.

ELINOR CLARE.

THE OLD GIPSY HELD A LOOKING-GLASS BEFORE ELINOR.

"The women," thought Elinor, as she glanced her eyes towards the group, who, unconscious of her being near them, were huddled together, in low tones discussing, as it would seem, the late melancholy event, "the women, ignorant and repulsive as they seem, are evidently sensitive and kind-hearted; with them I should be safe."

Acting upon this impulse, she hastily advanced from her hiding-place towards them, but so light was her step, and so absorbed were they in the subject that engaged their attention, that they heard her not, until, gently laying her hand upon the shoulder of a young and prepossessing looking woman she observed,

"The poor young man whom you have just left, will recover, I hope."

For an instant the woman seemed struck with alarm, as she gazed on Elinor's features; but she quickly recovered herself, and replied, in a melancholy tone,

"We all hope so, but it is in an evil hour he has met his hurt. Last year, on this day, he was cast into prison. 'Twas a false charge, and he broke his bonds; but he could not forget it. And to day, when Eunic, his mother, would had him 'bide in the tents, he would not be staid, because he hoped to have revenge on the unjust man that sent him there. But see how his evil planet has prevailed; from that man did he receive the blow that will too surely make his mother childless, and his wife a desolate mourner."

"He was deserted, betrayed," observed one of the women, in a sullen tone. "Had your father and brothers done their duty, and seconded him like men, they would have killed the wretch."

"Yes, and have been food for crows, their bones whitening on a gibbet, for the murder," screamed an old woman, interposing between the speakers, with every mark of the most violent excitement. "And why should my husband and sons take up the grudge of the Kennedies, who, it is well known, were never friends to me or mine? Hav'n't they——"

"Silence, woman! what is all this?" exclaimed the Gipsy Chief, who had approached the contending parties unobserved, and now stepped in between them with an assumption of authority and dignity that was well suited to have the effect he intended. "Is this a time," he continued, "when the angel of death is hovering over our tents, ready to seize his victim—is this a time, I say, to be raising your voices in brawls? Go, go, and pray that the powers of darkness may be defeated; for well you know their malice is at work to rob us of one of our bravest and our best. Elinor," he continued, stepping forward to her, and taking her hand with an air of protection, and without expressing any surprise or vexation at seeing her there, "Elinor, this scene is not suited, I am sure, to compose your hurried spirits; let me lead you to where you will find the rest and quietness you so much need."

Elinor was about to reply, that she had rather remain where she was; but the sound of a shrill whistle, which seemed to be in the air above them, but in reality came from some person planted on the brow of the hill which Elinor had descended, and which, it may be recollected, rose almost perpendicularly from the spot on which the gipsies' camp was placed, at once interrupted her speech, and withdrew the chief's attention from her.

With a bitter execration he sprang towards the spot where the men, still silent and gloomy, were gathered together.

"The devils are upon us," he exclaimed, as they one and all turned with alacrity to meet him. "How they can have discovered us, or tracked us hither, I know not. What is to be done? Shall we stand out, or——"

"Fight till we die!" exclaimed two or three ferocious voices with savage eagerness.

"There is no time to strike our tents, and disperse," observed another, in a doubtful tone; "or else, perhaps, we might get off."

"What, and leave Lemuel behind us?" hastily exclaimed two or three of the women, who had hurried to join in the conference. "Would you desert the poor fellow in his dying moments, and leave him to be dragged off to gaol, as you know he would be?"

"No, no, no!" was tumultuously re-echoed on all sides.

"No," repeated Dangerfield, "we will try, first, what fair speeches will do with them; and if they won't take them, why, let them come to blows as soon as they like; I warrant we'll be a match for them."

A loud huzza broke responsively from the crowd, but it was suddenly checked by an expressive gesture of the chief, who pointed to the tent which contained the dying man.

"Now," continued he, addressing the men, "away to the top of the hill, and await my coming. Keep them in parley, if they are there before me; at all events, do not let them come a step beyond the old lime-kiln: keep them at bay there, if you can do no better; but I shall be there as soon as you, so away!"

The men waited not for a second command, but flourishing the heavy bludgeons, which appeared their only weapon, they rushed towards the path, and were instantly lost in the obscurity of the night.

For an instant after their departure, Dangerfield stood with his keen eye intently fixed on Elinor, whose countenance betrayed the agitation and alarm she felt at these indications of violence. He was evidently revolving in his mind some measure with which she was connected. "Minna," he at length exclaimed, turning suddenly to a woman whom Elinor had noticed in the tent as possessing a singularly repellant countenance, "Minna, a word with you in private."

The woman bowed her head in acquiescence, and followed him, till they were at a sufficient distance to render their conversation inaudible to those whom they had quitted.

"Paul is not used to talk when he should fight," observed one of the women, with a sarcastic laugh.

"How long has Minna been such a favourite?" demanded another.

"Oh, there's some mischief afloat," returned a third, "or Minna would not be chosen."

The meaning glance which the last speaker turned upon Elinor was not unobserved by the latter, who though she could form no conjecture on the subject, felt considerably disturbed at the belief that she was the subject of the directions which, it appeared, Dangerfield was giving to Minna, whose eyes were from time to time turned upon her, as she nodded assent to what he was saying.

A repetition of the shrill whistle from the top of the hill interrupted, as it appeared, his directions; he sprang hastily away from the woman, and was in an instant out of sight.

"Come with me, lady, if you please," observed Minna, returning to the spot where Elinor still stood. "Come," she repeated, laying her hand on the arm of the latter, in a persuasive manner, "I have much to say to you, and there is no time to be lost."

"Whither would you lead me?" demanded Elinor, who liked neither the woman's looks nor her manners, and would fain have remained with the collected group, from whose presence she seemed to derive protection.

"Oh, not far," she replied; "only to our Chief's tent. You are not afraid to trust yourself with me, are you?" she hastily added, as Elinor involuntarily drew back.

"No, not afraid," returned the latter, making an effort to disguise her reluctance; "but I would rather stay here in the open air, the tent is so close."

"Well, you can come back here in a few minutes," observed Minna; "but you *must* come—I must obey my orders."

Elinor looked round her. She would fain have resisted this command, but there was no expression in the countenances of the other women, except surprise at her hesitation; and she reluctantly followed Minna.

"I will tell you what is required of you," observed the latter, as soon as they entered the tent. "Our Chief is fearful that our

people may be overpowered, and that he may be compelled to let
the rascally justice and his men search our tents. In that case,
you are aware, Paul says, that you will be sure to fall into the
hands of Russell again, if he should discover you ; for, of course,
we sha'n't be able to oppose it."

"What, then, am I to do ?" exclaimed Elinor, in alarm.

"Why," she replied, "if you will let me, I will disguise you
so that your own mother shouldn't know you if she was to see
you."

The sound of the word "mother" struck so forcibly upon
Eliner's ear, that, unable to utter a word, or even reflect for a
moment on any other subject than her desolate situation, possessing not one single relation in the world, she burst into tears.

"What a simpleton you are, girl !" exclaimed Minna, contemptuously. "What harm can it do you, to appear as one of
us for an hour or two ?"

With some difficulty Elinor explained that her agitation arose
from a different cause, and expressed her readiness to adopt any
disguise Minna might think proper ; and the latter, observing
that she was glad to find she (Elinor) was above such nonsensical
scruples, hastened to fetch the necessary articles of dress, which
were in another tent.

In a few minutes she returned, and Elinor was quickly arrayed
in a snow-white bedgown and petticoat, a gay flowered handkerchief covering her bosom, and another of the most brilliant colours
and showy pattern being arranged so as to cover the back of her
head, and come round her neck in the most fanciful manner. A
bright scarlet cloak was hung jauntily on her shoulders, thus
completing the metamorphose, from her before neat and unpretending appearance, to a gay, showy damsel, whose occupation it
would have been impossible for any one to mistake.

The disguise, however, was, it appeared, not yet complete; for
Minna, taking a bottle from her pocket, poured some of its contents into a basin, and observed,

"There, a little of that to your hands and face, will give a
complexion worth all the pale ones in the world. Do not be
afraid of it, it will wash off again ; though it's my belief, when
you see your face, you will find it such an improvement, that you'll
never want to get rid of it."

Elinor cared little at that moment about improvement of her
beauty, but, prepared as she was for the change, she could scarcely
forbear starting when the old gipsy took down from one corner
of the tent a piece of broken looking-glass, and held it before

her, so completely was her appearance altered by the deep brown hue which the liquid had given her—a hue, however, which was well suited to her large oriental eyes, and, indeed, the whole style of her features.

"Now, then, you're to be my daughter, and deaf and dumb, if they *do* come," observed Minna. "Keep close to me, and take no notice, let who will speak to you; point to me, as if to 'tell them to ask me to answer their questions; and I'll be bound I'll carry you through."

Elinor, however, was far from being so confident herself, and she only replied, that she hoped there would be no occasion, after all, for the precautions they had taken.

"Well, well, we shall see," returned Minna; "and now, then, if you will, we'll go back to our women; they'll be proud of you, I'm sure. I wish, indeed, you were my daughter in earnest, for you'd make my fortune."

"Heaven forbid!" thought Elinor, to whom the woman's present familiarity was more repulsive even than had been her former sullen manner. She followed her, however, in silence, and was received by the women with a thousand expressions of wonder and admiration, which were soon, however, broken off, to return to the subject they had been discussing when Minna and Elinor joined them, namely, their wonder and alarm at not hearing anything of the chief and his men.

While they were yet speaking, however, a confused noise was heard on the brow of the hill, which was instantly declared to proceed from the party returning.

"There's strangers with them, then," observed one, who had been listening silently and intently for some moments.

"Now," exclaimed Minna, addressing Elinor, "sit down by me, and feign not to notice anything you see or hear."

Elinor did as she desired. Three or four of the women seated themselves in the same manner, one of whom put an infant into the lap of the former, observing, "that will serve for an excuse for your not getting up and——"

Before she could finish the sentence, five or six of the men belonging to the gang rushed towards them.

"They are coming! they are coming!" they exclaimed, "where is the stranger?"

"She is safe enough," returned Minna, "if you will keep quiet."

"Who is that?" demanded one of the men, looking earnestly at Elinor.

" Cannot you guess ?" was the laconic reply.

" Zarah Kennedy, is it not?" demanded he, " how she has grown !   But when did she come ? and why has she left——"

" There, go along with you," interposed Minna, with a laugh ; " this is not a time to be asking questions."

" What is to be done with Lemuel ?" exclaimed several voices, in alarm, as if that moment recollecting the danger that might result to the wounded man from a visit of the authorities whom he had so determinedly resisted.

" Not a hair of his head shall be touched," returned one of the men.   " Mind, you are all prepared to swear that he hasn't been out of his bed these three days past, and got his hurt in a skir mish at Rosedale Fair, the day before we came here.   Neither the justice nor his men have been able to fix on any of our party yet, though they tried hard to swear to me; but you must all stick to it hard and fast, that we hav'n't been away from the tents all day, and were going over to Somerton feast now."

" That will do,"—" That will do," repeated two or three of the women, clapping their hands, as if glorying in the ingenuity of this invention.

Alarmed and agitated as Elinor was, the thought involuntarily rushed into her mind, " How habituated must these people be to fraud and deception, when they can thus readily invent and agree to maintain a tale in which there is not one particle of truth .   And yet it is to them," she continued, " that I am now trusting for protection and support."

Striving in vain to suppress the conviction that she had done wrong in suffering herself to be thus, as it were, thrown on the protection of Dangerfield ; trembling alike at the dangers that threatened her should she again fall into the power of Russell and those which she feared awaited her if she remained undis covered, and continued an inmate of the gipsy camp, an associate of the lawless people whose wild and coarse manners and unre strained habits at once terrified and disgusted her, Elinor remained apparently occupied with the baby, which she was tenderly hushing on her bosom, but in reality a prey to the most distracting cares and terrors.

The flash of numerous lights, and the confused buzz of many voices, as well as a sort of watchword that passed in a suppressed tone from one to the other of her companions, warned Elinor that the expected party were approaching.   She ventured to glance towards them, and beheld a large posse of people, some of whom wore the livery of Mr. Russell; many were countrymen assembled in haste for the occasion, and the rest were composed of farmers and tradesmen, among whom Elinor recognised Benson, and two or three others whom she knew. The dreaded Mr. Russell did not appear, and Elinor seemed to draw her breath more freely.

Tossing the torches about, with which they were plentifully furnished, and seeming to consider themselves in perfect security, the party advanced nearly into the centre of the open spot around which the tents of the gipsies were scattered; but there they halted, and conferred together, as if unresolved what course to pursue, and Elinor, who sat in the shade, at the distance of a few yards only from them, could observe that, in spite of their bold demeanour, frequent suspicious glances were thrown on every side, as if the intruders did not feel themselves quite at ease in their position, and were apprehensive of some covert danger.

The men of the gipsy tribe who were in the camp were all collected in sullen silence near the tent which contained their wounded companion; most of the women were huddled together with Elinor, near the smouldering embers of the fire over which was still suspended the pot containing their evening's meal, which all had as yet been too much occupied to think of tasting.

From time to time Elinor could discern a malicious smile dimpling the cheeks of the two or three young women who sat nearest to her; but no one spoke, with the exception of one wrinkled and decrepid old sybil, who kept hovering about the fire picking up bits of sticks to put under the pot, and endeavouring with her feeble breath to rekindle the flame; while every now and then she paused to mutter curses upon the intruders, whom she designated by every opprobrious epithet her memory could supply.

For a time no one seemed inclined to notice her; then one or two laughed at her impotent revilings; and at length one, bolder than the rest, replied to her, by inquiring in a jeering tone, what was the matter with her.

"Have we put ye out o' temper, Goody," he continued, "by coming at supper time? I'll warrant me there's something good, now, in yon pot; I should like to taste it."

"Would I might have the pouring of the hot broth down thy throat," returned the old woman; "thou shouldn't want another meal, I'll be bound."

The man laughed.

"There's an old saying," he observed, "that them that feeds

with the devil, had need of a long spoon, and I've a notion that if I was to sup wi' you—Ha! what's this?" He suddenly interrupted his observation, stooping, and gathering up from the ground a few scattered feathers. " So, so," he continued, " you live bravely here; fowls for supper, eh? I'd give sixpence, now, if I was sure my old speckled hen was safe upon her roost at home."

" I'll tell ye, if ye'll cross my hand with the silver," observed an arch-looking woman, springing up from the ground where she had been seated, near Elinor. " But first, let's look," and she dexterously whisked away the feathers, and threw them into the fire, which the efforts of the old woman had just kindled into a flame.

" That was cunningly done, mistress," observed the countryman, angrily; " but, dang me, if it shall save your bacon, if old Tibbie is gone when I get home; for I can almost swear—Ha! here's the justice come, at last," he continued; " and when we've settled the other business I shall make bold to tell him——"

" Do, do, do," exclaimed the old woman who had first spoken, in a violent rage; "try if you can't persuade him to send us all to gaol, before you know whether your old hen is gone or not. The curse of famine light upon you, I say : may you never——"

" What is all this, woman?" exclaimed the well-known voice of the magistrate, who, unseen by Elinor or her companions, had come close up to them, having entered the camp by a different path, the steep road down the hill not being practicable for his horse.

Not only the old woman, but all the others of the party, shrunk into silence at the sight of the justice, whose power many of them had but too well experienced on different occasions; but among them all, none felt such trepidation as Elinor. For some minutes she dared not raise her eyes from the ground; while terror rendered indistinct to her ear all that was passing around her, and left her only the overwhelming consciousness that she was within a few paces, and immediately in the presence, of the person she most dreaded and detested on earth.

In a short time, however, she became aware that another person was present, in whose actions she was deeply interested. It was the voice of Dangerfield that she heard, and apparently addressing Mr. Russell with boldness and confidence.

" Now, sir," she heard him say, " I have, you, see, fulfilled my engagement; I have guided you here in safety ; and you are at liberty to make the most minute search you please, if you are

not satisfied that you are mistaken as to our people having any
concern in the affair you speak of."

"I am not, then," returned Mr. Russell, "I assure you; for
I can even now imagine I see many of the faces who were
engaged in that outrageous violation of the laws. But, let us
examine the tents first," he continued; "we will talk of other
matters afterwards. Here, boy, hold my horse; and, mind, no
tricks with it, d'ye hear?"

The boy whom he addressed sprang forward to obey him;
but what was Elinor's surprise and alarm when she recognised
in the latter Zekiel, whom she had believed far distant, with
Edward, to whom, she understood, he was to act as a guide.

Could it be possible that the latter was so mad—so rash, as
to be still lingering in the neighbourhood, where he was in such
imminent danger of being discovered?

Forgetful almost of her own peril, her eyes followed every
movement of Zekiel's, in hopes that he would approach near
enough, and that she should find an opportunity of making the
inquiry of him which she so longed yet dreaded to have answered;
but the boy heeded her not, his attention was divided between
the noble animal which had been entrusted to his care, and its
master, who had now moved off, accompanied by Dangerfield,
and two or three of the stoutest of his (Russell's) attendants, to
commence the important search.

Tent after tent was entered, but not a living creature was
found within them, except some sleeping children, whose loud cries
at the unusual disturbance of their slumbers occasioned numerous
angry remarks from the women upon the shamefulness of their
being treated so. Even the men joined in "curses not loud but
deep," against the intruders; and to Elinor, who was not aware
of the peculiar fondness and indulgence with which a gipsy
regards his offspring, it was no small matter of surprise to see
how strongly the men were excited at what appeared to her of
comparatively little importance.

Elinor had by this time recovered in a great measure from the
panic which had seized her at the first appearance of Russell.
She had stood the ordeal of being gazed at and even spoken
to by two or three to whom she was well known in her real
character, without suspicion seeming to have been excited in
their minds that she was other than she now appeared; even
her old acquaintance, Farmer Benson, had singled her out,
to address with some uncouth attempt at gallantry, without,
evidently, the slightest suspicion of her disguise; but Elinor

remembered her lesson, and kept silent, without appearing to hear or comprehend him, and the watchful Minna instantly came to her assistance.

"Ah, it's no use," she observed, "your trying to beguile that poor innocent with your lies and glosing speeches, she cannot hear them. You may as well talk to yonder rock; nay, better, for that has an echo, and can repeat your words, if it don't answer you; and that's more than she can."

"What! is the girl deaf?" demanded Benson, with surprise.

"Deaf! aye, and dumb too," replied Minna, sharply,

"Poor soul, poor soul!" returned the farmer, "that's a sore affliction indeed. Is she your daughter, mistress?"

Minna boldly replied in the affirmative; and Benson, after fumbling in his pockets for some time, during which his eyes remained fixed on the object of his compassion, threw a sixpence into her lap, and walked away to his companions.

"This is a good beginning," muttered Minna, picking up the coin from Elinor's lap, and unceremoniously conveying it to her own pocket. "Did you ever see that man before?" she whispered to Elinor, as she bent over her, and affected to be busy with the child the latter still held in her arms.

Elinor, of course, replied in the affirmative.

"You must tell me, to-morrow, where he lives," returned Minna, "it sha'n't be the last bit o' silver I have out of his pocket."

The near approach of Russell, who had now minutely inspected every tent but that containing the wounded man, recalled the attention not only of Elinor, but her companions, to his proceedings.

"If it be as you say," he observed, as he passed close to the feet of Elinor, "I will go in with you alone. I have no wish to be harsh towards you or your companions; but a great wrong has been committed, not only in favouring the escape of a suspected murderer, but in carrying off a young female from her friends; and I am determined to search the matter to the bottom. There is a girl, who was present at the time, ready to swear that she saw several of your tribe in the room in disguise, and that she heard one of them offer the protection of his house to the young woman in question.

"Why was not the girl brought hither, sir, to see if she could point out any one, sir?" demanded Dangerfield, with confidence.

"Because she has been seized with fits, in consequence of

terror and agitation, and is not in a proper state," returned the magistrate; "but come, let me proceed to see this sick man that you speak of, and then——"

He passed on, to the infinite relief of the trembling Elinor, and entered the tent of Lemuel.

The gipsy men, who had kept as far back and as much in the shade as possible during the previous proceedings, now came anxiously forward, planting themselves close to the canvas opening to the tent, and evidently listening with the most earnest anxiety to what was passing within. In a few moments, Elinor, who was intently watching every motion, saw a hurried communication pass from one to the other through the whole group; and in an instant, six or seven of them rushed into the tent.

"Something's wrong, there's foul play going on!" exclaimed one of Russell's men, who had been left standing in the centre, as if keeping watch upon the motions of the inhabitants of the camp. He had scarcely uttered the words before Mr. Russell came hastily out of the tent, together with Dangerfield, who was violently remonstrating with him.

"You would not, surely, disturb the man in his dying moments," exclaimed the latter, as he came nearer to Elinor, "even if he was the person you say; but I tell you, sir, you are mistaken—ask any of the people where——"

"I shall ask nothing," returned the magistrate, peremptorily, "I will trust my own senses. That is the man who was the ringleader, and whose desperate assault upon me I repaid by the blow from which it appears he is now suffering. I demand, therefore, that he is given up as my prisoner, or——"

"What!" exclaimed one of the women, who had followed him from the bed-side of the wounded man, with the strongest anxiety depicted in her countenance, and now thrusting herself between him and the Gipsy Chief, so as to face Mr. Russell, "What! have you not had your revenge? What more do you want? Is it not the law, an eye for an eye, a——"

"Silence, woman! interrupted Russell, with vehemence. "Thornhill, do your duty; take the man into custody that lies in yonder tent; and you, my friends," addressing the rest of his own party, "aid and assist, if necessary; I call upon you in the king's name."

It was evident, by this appeal, that Mr. Russell had discovered already that there was some wavering on the part of his friends; and, in truth there were three or four among them, more wary than the rest, who began to think the service they had engaged in one of considerably more danger than honour. They had noticed the manner in which the gipsy men kept aloof, and the signals that passed between them, and began to apprehend that they should meet with more serious resistance than they had calculated upon.

Mr. Russell's energetic appeal, however, was not to be entirely disregarded; some half dozen of his party instantly came forward to obey his commands; but, as if this was the appointed signal for which they had waited, the whole tribe of the gipsies instantly rushed upon them on different sides, at once preventing their approach to the tent in which their intended victim was lying, and preventing their retreat by either of the paths by which they had entered the camp.

Elinor shrank with terror as she heard the savage cry, resembling the famed war-whoop of the Indians, and beheld the fierce expression of the gipsies' features, as they bent their dark and glowing eyes upon their enemies, with an air of defiance that could not be mistaken, had not their upraised bludgeons and the sounds they uttered plainly spoken their intentions to resist to the utmost the execution of the magistrate's orders.

"What is the meaning of this?" exclaimed Russell, in a voice which had lost none of its firmness or tone of command, though he was evidently taken by surprise, and was totally unprepared for those open indications of rebellion against his mandates. "Do you mean, fellows, to resist the law?"

"Yes, if the law is not also justice," exclaimed a voice, which Elinor instantly recognised as Paul Dangerfield's. "Look you, Mr. Russell," he continued: "when I met you, you were expressing to some of my people your suspicions that we concealed in our tents two persons who had by some strange means escaped from your power. I told you then, as I tell you now, that had those persons claimed protection from us, no threats or temptation would induce us to give them up; but I told you, too, that they were not in our camp, and that, to prove it, if you would give me your word of honour to depart peaceably, as soon as you were convinced that your search was fruitless, I would engage both to guide you to our encampment and to give you free admission to every part of it, in order to convince you of the injustice of your suspicions. I have kept my word; you see that the persons you seek are not here; and I now demand that you keep yours."

"And who are you, fellow," demanded Mr. Russell, haughtily, "that dare thus attempt to make conditions with me? But I

am wasting time," he abruptly added, "in parleying thus."
"Come on, my friends, follow me, and——"

He was hastily proceeding towards the tent of Lemuel, but
his intent was instantly arrested by the upraised bludgeons of at
least a dozen determined opponents, who, with Dangerfield at
their head, threw themselves before him in the path.

'You pass not one step this way, Mr. Russell," exclaimed the
chief, in a threatening tone. "Do not tempt my patience too
far, but retire while the road is still open to you; should you
linger much longer, you may find——"

"Villain!—reptile!" interrupted Russell, with furious rage,
"dare you threaten me? Stand back, or take the consequences!"

The quick flash and loud report of a pistol instantaneously
followed this warning; but Dangerfield's keen eye had warned him
of the approaching danger; and a dexterous blow from the heavy
bludgeon, which appeared to be the only weapon of the gipsy,
at once disarmed his opponent, and rendered him powerless to
repeat the attack.

"The fellow has broken my arm!" exclaimed Russell, writh-
ing with pain, yet appearing no way daunted; while the mischance
which had befallen their leader seemed to have the effect of
additionally enraging his followers, who, uttering oaths and
execrations of vengeance against the whole tribe, commenced an
indiscrimnate attack, striking alike at men and women; while
the shrieks of the latter, and the furious yells of the former at
the unmanly conduct of their adversaries, gave to the whole the
appearance rather of a conflict between fierce barbarians than an
attempt to enforce the laws in a civilised country.

Two or three times Elinor made an attempt to rise from the
ground, but was forcibly held down by her nearest companion,
the old woman, who, while she seemed the most determined and
energetic in encouraging her tribe in their defence against the
justice and his satellites, kept a most vigilant eye upon every
movement of the helpless girl who was the real cause of the
warfare.

"Sit still, girl," exclaimed the old virago, grasping Elinor's
arm with her bony hand, with a force and violence which the
latter felt it would be vain to attempt to resist; "sit still, I tell
you there's been mischief enough on your head already. Woe
be to the hour your pale face came among us! many a brave
fellow shall rue it, many a gyve fetter free limbs, and many a
mother have cause to curse your name."

" Let me go, then, from among you," returned Elinor, gaining spirit and courage from these undeserved reproaches. " If I give myself up to the magistrate," she continued, " it will at once put an end——"

" Ha, indeed !" interrupted the amazon, with a sneer, " are you a gem of such price ? Well, then, we will keep you ; we shall have need of a rich prize, to pay the smart of cracked skulls and broken bones. If you speak to betray who you are," she hastily added, as she saw that the countrymen, having gained an advantage over the gipsies, were pressing towards the spot where she, Elinor, and two or three other females of the tribe were congregated, " if you utter but one word," she repeated, " I will brain you against that tree ! They shall never take you alive !"

Elinor trembled almost as much with indignation as terror at this threat. She turned her eyes away with disgust from the fiendish visage of the old woman, towards whom a half-intoxicated, savage-looking countryman now rushed, exclaiming, as he furiously flourished a hedge-stake over his head,

" Down wi' 'em, all, the devil's imps—the thieving old hags. Down wi' 'em, I say ! We'll teach 'em to set themselves up against the law !"

" Aye, do strike, do, you unmanly coward !" screamed the old woman, " do strike a woman who has seen four of your generations spring up and die away, like the worthless insects that are born in the morning upon the stagnant pool, and, when evening comes, strew its surface with their carcases ! Do strike, and may my curse, and the curse of the Great Spirit, wither your arm, and make it cling useless to thy side !"

" Hear how the hell-cat bans," exclaimed the man, who, however, had suspended his intended attack, and betrayed evident signs that his fear of the supposed power of the sybil was, at least, equal to the hatred he felt against her race.

" Why don't 'e give in, then, like Christians, and go to gaol, as you desarve ?" he observed, but his eye at that moment caught the outline of Elinor's face, which she had raised upon hearing his voice, which she recognised as that of a man who had been a farm-servant to her uncle for some years. The recognition seemed to be mutual.

" I'm blest if it ben't she herself !" he exclaimed, rushing towards her ; but the old woman instantly threw herself upon Elinor, clasping her in her arms so as almost to stifle the poor girl, while she uttered the most terrific screams for assistance.

"My child! my daughter!" she exclaimed, "the villain would murder my child!"

To this was added some words, which were unintelligible to Elinor, but which had the effect of instantly drawing to the assistance of the speaker all who were within reach of their sound.

Elinor's perceptions of what passed subsequently to this appeal were not very clear; for she was hemmed in and nearly suffocated by the females, who seemed to have very little regard for the inconvenience she suffered but were evidently most determinately and obstinately bent on preventing her falling into the hands of the opposite party. She saw, however, that the countryman was struck down to the earth by a mere comparative stripling, who rushed suddenly upon him, and then the next minute she was caught up and borne rapidly away, while the well-known voice of Edward Hatherleigh whispered in her ear,

"Elinor, do not be frightened, all will yet be well. Let me place you in safety, and I care not."

CHAPTER X.

Upon that boundless plain below,
　The setting sun's last rays were shed,
And gave a mild and sober glow
　Where all were still, asleep or dead;
Vast ruins in the midst were spread,
　Pillars and pediments sublime,
Where the grey moss had form'd a bed,
　And cloth'd the crumbling spoils of time.

CRABBE.

THE sound of the distant contest—the threats and execrations of one party, and the triumphant shouts of the other—rang in Elinor's ears long after she had quitted the scene of strife and violence. But she thought little of what was passing there, little of what might be the issue of such a conflict, except as it would probably influence the fate of the hapless, persecuted, and, as she firmly believed, innocent youth whose pale cheek and restless eye spoke volumes of suffering.

Silently yet ever and anon pausing and listening anxiously to the sounds borne by the passing gale, Edward hurried on his unresisting companion through the deep recesses of the adjoining wood, turning from time to time a look of earnest inquiry upon

ELINOR CLARE.

THE WILD BOY BOUNDED OVER THE TOPS OF THE BUSHES.

her agitated features, and sometimes uttering a few words intended to soothe her anxiety and inspire hopes that she would speedily be in safety.

Elinor's strength, however, was nearly exhausted. It was in vain she tried to disguise it even from herself, and to urge herself on by a recollection of all the motives that should impel her forward. The fear only of exposing her companion to danger was sufficient for a time to support her efforts, but the demands of nature became every moment more imperious and resistless; and, sinking down from his supporting arm, she at length exclaimed :

"Edward, I can go no further; consult your own safety, and leave me to chance. I am so ill that I cannot proceed; but I am not likely to be discovered here by any one unfriendly to me; and a few hours' rest will restore my strength, and——"

"And where, then, are you to go, Elinor? or what is to become of you?" returned Edward, mournfully. "You cannot exist upon the air; and to attempt to return to those who have treated you so cruelly, would only expose you to worse indignities, perhaps even to dangers which I shudder to think of. And think you, then, that, to purchase safety to myself, I would desert you? No!——not if even the riches of the whole world were added to the gift! Our fate is bound up together. Wretched, indeed, is the lot I have to offer you; but if we can only escape the present danger——if we could but reach some distant spot, where we could remain unnoticed and unknown—— I am willing to toil, Elinor; and strength and ability would grow with exertion; and oh! how happy could I be with you, in the lowliest cot that——"

A rustling in the bushes beneath which he had seated Elinor, and was now supporting her, with his arm encircling her waist, suspended his speech, and occasioned him to look hastily and fearfully around; while Elinor, uttering a faint exclamation of terror, pressed closer to him.

Not long, however, were they left in suspense as to the source of this interruption of their temporary rest and security; for the next moment, the uncouth form of the wild and half-witted boy bounded over the tops of the bushes, without even bending them, and after two or three strange antics, twirling round upon one heel, stood silently before them, gazing into Edward's face, and evidently waiting for the interrogations of the latter.

"Why have you come hither? and where did you leave your people?" demanded Edward, hastily.

"You might say our people, Master Ned," returned the lad, with a malicious grin; "but when you get in fine company you're ashamed of us."

Edward muttered something which was unintelligible to Elinor, but which the boy appeared to understand well enough.

"I don't think I've much occasion to be afraid of that, for one while to come," he replied; "for I reckon he'll be fast enough by the heels, in —— Prison, before to-morrow's sun goes down."

"Where, then, did you leave him?" demanded Edward, whose countenance betrayed the deepest sorrow and vexation at this information.

"Where?" returned Zekiel, "why, flying like a fox, with a whole pack at his heels, and no earth to run to. It's no use for him to try to double, with such a keen one as Master Russell; for he's got scent of all his old holes, and stopped him out. I made way to the oak, as soon as I saw which way the game lay, for I thought he'd make for that; but he wasn't there, and I guess he'll cut right across the country; that is, if they don't run him down. Gemini! how I did laugh, when I see 'em all in full cry, over hedges and ditches, tumbling over one another, and the Justice crying out that he'd give ten pounds to the man that first laid hold of the rascal. He'd be a strong fellow that could hold him, I reckon; but there's too many for one. And then they've got their cursed dogs, some of 'em: one of 'em got hold of me by the leg, but I whipped little Jacky here (showing the knife which was suspended by a cord round his neck, and concealed in the folds of his coarse brown shirt), and I soon sent it up to the horn in his throat: he won't bark, nor bite either, again, I warrant me."

"But, how did you escape?" demanded Edward, while Elinor turned away, shuddering at the fierce and ferocious spirit which gleamed in the boy's eyes, as he surveyed with evident satisfaction the instrument of his vengeance on the dog.

"She's afraid of the knife, I suppose," observed Zekiel, half muttering to himself, as he returned the weapon to its hiding place; "and yet I've seen her brave enough sometimes, when other ones of her complexion would squall and scream and faint."

"How did you get off undiscovered, I say, Zekiel?" repeated Edward; "and what has become of the women and Lemuel and——"

"Oh, you must ask them when you see them, Master Ned," he replied, with great indifference. "I didn't stay to concern myself, when I see you make off one way, and Paul another; though I don't think he would have given in so soon, only he found you were gone; for I heard him cursing all cowards, when he darted right over me, as I lay hid in the dry ditch; and then came the others helter-skelter after him, and I expected I should be trampled to death; for one or two came right in, one upon the other; but, lucky for me, they fell right upon the dead mastiff; and so, while they were feeling about to find out what it could be, he crawled softly away, and scrambled back again; and there was our people scampering off for dear life the other way; but I did not stop to ask questions, but made away for the oak, as fast as my legs could take me ; but he wasn't there that I expected to see, and you know I've no great liking to that spot ever since——Well, I'm not going to say anything about it," he added, after a brief pause; "so you need not shake your head, and look so awful."

Elinor turned her quick eyes with a piercing look of inquiry on Edward's face, at this observation. For an instant he seemed to shrink from her gaze with embarrassment, to avoid that inquiry, with what might have been deemed by an observer conscious guilt; but the next moment, his usual calm confidence returned ; and though he sighed heavily, he returned Elinor's long, searching look with one that said, "I am innocent, Elinor; you dare not, cannot believe me guilty."

Elinor did not : she had never, for a moment, suffered such a thought to dwell in her mind. Yet she felt a momentary pang of extreme anguish at the implication the boy's words conveyed.

Edward's thoughts evidently dwelt but for a moment on this painful subject; he returned almost instantly to his questions to Zekiel, as to the probable movements and final destination of the tribe; to all which, however, the boy returned the most wavering and evasive answers, until, thoroughly provoked, Edward started on his feet, threatening him with chastisement on the spot, if he did not return a plain and straightforward reply to what he was asked.

"Gemini ! one would think you were Paul himself, you're so grand and so positive," observed the lad, shifting his position suddenly to the side of Elinor, with a view, evidently, of ensuring her interference to save him from the threatened punishment. "I suppose, however," he continued, with the same taunting sneer that had before provoked the wrath of Hatherleigh; "I suppose, I say, that if Paul does dance on the woodie, or is sent across the herring-pond, you think they'll choose you in his place; but you are mistaken, I can tell you ; they won't have one that forgets his duty, and runs off with a girl, when he should stay and fight his enemies."

"I deserve this, perhaps, from them," murmured Edward ; "yet, Heaven forbid that such a fate should befall him ! What could I have done, had I stayed ?"

He threw himself on the grass, and covered his face with his hands, evidently overwhelmed with the most painful feelings. The expression of Zekiel's countenance instantly changed. He stood for a moment or two regarding him with obvious uneasiness ; and then, in a compassionate tone, observed,

"What's the use of grieving about things that may never happen? Paul's old enough, and cunning enough, to take care of himself; and I've seen him get out of worse scrapes than this. I shouldn't wonder now, if he's safe with the lady—you know who I mean,"

"My mother!" exclaimed Edward, starting up, as if only that moment reminded of her existence. "Oh, how shall I look her in the face? how acknowledge that I deserted him in the moment of danger, whom I should have watched over and protected with——"

The boy broke out into one of his most unnatural and discordant fits of laughter.

"Ha! ha! ha!" he exclaimed, while his voice seemed to ring and echo through the deep recesses of the wood. "Ha! ha! ha!—you watch over Paul?—you protect the chief?—the lamb watch over the ravenous wolf?—the dove protect the kite?"

Again he laughed and danced about with the strangest contortions of derision and mockery, until at length recalled to seriousness by the sound of a distant halloo, followed by the discharge of a pistol.

"There's some of them," he whispered, coming close to Edward, and looking in his face with a strong expression of alarm.

"Yes, and your folly has betrayed us," returned the latter; "your noise will guide them to this spot, and it will be impossible, now the sun is risen, to conceal ourselves."

The boy looked round him in anxious reflection.

"Come this way," he at length observed; "there is a place hard by that at noonday will be as dark as Erebus; I have hidden there even from Paul himself, when he threatened me; and if his eyes couldn't pierce it, you need fear no other; only, don't betray my hiding-place to him; for if you do——"

"No, no, fear not; lead on, my good lad, lead on," interrupted Hatherleigh, with extreme impatience. "Elinor, for my sake, for your own, bear up a little longer."

Elinor needed not, however, this exhortation. The impending danger had roused her to renewed exertion; and she followed, without hesitation, her conductors, along the narrow and difficult path which led to the proposed place of safety.

It was, indeed, a den dark as the depths of midnight, and so overgrown at its entrance with brambles, nettles and bindweed, that it was with extreme difficulty a way could be made for Elinor and Edward to enter; and then the place was so low and small, that they were compelled to sit in a most constrained and painful position.

"There," observed Zekiel, when they were fairly seated, and were beginning to think how the boy would be able to dispose his ungainly form in the small space that remained unoccupied, "there, now you keep quiet, and trust to me; I'll lead them a dance far enough to tire them, I'll warrant me; only, don't move till you hear me call."

Before Hatherleigh had time to utter a word of either remonstrance or advice, the lad darted away; and in a few minutes the wood rang with the loud, shrill, and discordant noises to which he gave utterance to mislead the supposed pursuers.

The necessity for silence, the warmth and closeness of the place, and the previous fatigue and excitement she had suffered, combined soon to lull Elinor, in spite of the insecurity of her present situation, into a happy oblivion of all her toils and troubles, with her head reclining on Edward's shoulder, his arm encircling her waist, in that perfect confidence in his honour and the purity of his motives and intentions, which only the innocent and pure can feel towards those whom they love, and by whom they are beloved. Elinor resigned herself to the repose she so much needed; and suppressing almost his very breath, lest he should disturb her gentle sleep, Edward continued to support her, even long after the lapse of time, and the utter silence that reigned around, had convinced him that the necessity for concealment had passed away.

At length she awoke, and her first expressions were those of terror and surprise; for she had been dreaming that she was restored to the happy thoughtlessness of childhood, and was once more partaking of its pleasures with her young companions.

"And Walter was there too," she observed. "Oh, how plainly I saw him, with his arm linked in yours, just as he used to be when he was in good humour, and when——"

A slight shudder shook Edward's frame at these words, and was plainly perceptible to his companion, though, from the darkness with which they were surrounded she could not see the expression of his face. The effect, however, was to make her pause; and Hatherleigh, as if to prevent her continuing the subject, observed,

"I have been thinking, dear Elinor, all the time you have slept, as to what course it will be best for us to take; and I have concluded that, however abhorrent and repulsive to our feelings and habits, there is no better plan than to make the best of our way to the rendezvous where I am sure of meeting the scattered party, who, though they will take different routes, are sure, or at least the greater number of them, to meet there on a certain day, to receive orders for their future destination. They are a singular people, Elinor," he continued, finding she did not speak: " so long as they are trusted and confided in, or believe themselves so to be, they will be faithful through every temptation and peril.; but if you betray mistrust of them ; if you attempt. after having once engaged them in your interest, to act independently of them, or pursue your own measures without confiding in or consulting them, they will sacrifice you without remorse or pity ; the honour of the tribe is concerned in revenging the fancied insult; and woe be to the unhappy wretches, whatsoever or whosoever they be, they are sure, sooner or later, to be their victims."

" But I have been told," observed Elinor, timidly, " that those who once become members of their community, can never quit it ; never renounce their vagrant habits, or return to society again."

" That is but too true," returned Hatherleigh, in a tone of deep melancholy; " and bitter, indeed, has been the lot of those who, perchance in an honr of thoughtless revelry, lured by their seeming generosity and freedom from all restraint, or, it might be, to serve some temporary purpose, in which their lawless and reckless habits might make them useful ; bitter, I repeat, has been the lot of those who have thus unconsciously made themselves slaves to laws and customs hateful and repulsive to every right principle and feeling. But there is a great difference, Elinor, in enrolling yourself a member of their community, and claiming hospitality in your distress, or their protection against your enemies. Both will they freely afford ; and that, too, without hope or prospect of reward ; though, mark you, should fortune afterwards favour you, they will expect and demand of you as a right payment of their former services. But unless you have specifically consented to become a member, and have been enrolled with certain ceremonies, they have no further claim upon you, nor will attempt to enforce any. It will be in your power, therefore, dear Elinor, to quit, at any favourable moment or opportunity——"

" And yours, too, Edward ?" interrupted Elinor, hastily, and evidently with extreme anxiety.

" Certainly—I hope so, Elinor," he replied, after a slight hesitation.

" You only *hope* so, Edward !" she returned, in a tone that betrayed her alarm and anguish. " Do you mean to say, then, that you will bind yourself, or have bound yourself by those bonds of which you speak with such horror and aversion, and from which you express your desire to keep me free ?"

" I have not, Elinor," he replied, " nor will I voluntarily do so ; but there are ties, circumstances——"

A sound which denoted the approach of Zekiel, at this moment interrupted that which Elinor had begun to hope would lead to some explanation of his real situation, and the mystery of his father's (for in such relationship she no longer doubted Paul Dangerfield stood to him) connection with the gipsies.

" Thank Heaven !" he exclaimed, " that sound assures me that we may leave our concealment in safety. Zekiel is froward and malicious in speech, but he may be safely relied on where serious services are required of him."

" Heaven grant that we shall not long need such services !" sighed Elinor, as, with his assistance, she crept through the tangled brake, climbed the steep bank, and stood once more on the verdant sod and in the open daylight.

Contrary to Zekiel's custom, he did not appear for many minutes after he had made himself heard ; and when he did come forward, instead of, as usual, bounding and leaping to their feet, his gait was slow and lagging, and the expression of his countenance, as he came near, sullen and lowering.

" Something has happened to displease him," observed Hatherleigh. " How now, Zekiel ! what ails thee, boy ? what is the matter ?"

" Matter enough," replied Zekiel, " I didn't wish any harm to Paul, though his words were often sharp and his hand heavy. And, besides, though my mother was not a lady, but a true Egyptian, there be those that say——"

" Never mind what any one says," interrupted Hatherleigh, impatiently ; " tell us what has happened to Paul."

" Happened !" returned the boy, with a sullen leer ; " you can't guess, I daresay, what is likely to happen to a poor devil, when everybody runs away, and leaves him to be hunted down by a dozen bloodhounds, and without a fair start, too. If he'd had a fair start, he'd have beat 'em ; and not have been, as I saw him but a little while agone, thrown into a cart, more like carrion for the dogs than living human flesh and blood, and his poor wrists fastened behind with shackles, and his legs loaded with irons, and his face covered with blood ; and every dirty coward that did not dare look at him when he was free, having a blow at him, and———"

"Oh, God ! and he has endured all this, while I have been meanly crouching here, consulting my own safety !" exclaimed Edward, in agony

"Aye, and you call yourself a man, too !" observed Zekiel, tauntingly. "I'm but a boy, but I stuck to him to the last, and kept by the side of the cart till it stopped at the prison-doors, and I'd have gone in with him, too, in spite of their whips, only that he told me himself to be off, and find you out, and to tell you———but what's the use of telling you ? you hav'n't got a bit of Paul's spirit in you."

"I will prove that by breaking every bone in your body, if you do not deliver every word of his message," exclaimed Edward, rushing furiously towards him.

"You must catch me first, though," observed the boy, bounding away to an almost incredible distance; and then stopping, he commenced the most provoking grimaces, mocking and mowing more like an ape than a reasonable creature.

"We must leave this humour to exhaust itself," observed Hatherleigh, turning to Elinor ; "I am ashamed that I should for a moment forget my temper towards one whom nature seems to have created in one of her most perverse and malignant moods. Come, Elinor," he continued aloud, "let us quit this spot ; the only one who could give us any directions to guide our future conduct refuses to do so. We must, therefore, trust to chance."

"You'd better not trust to anybody but me ; and so Paul said," observed Zekiel, coming slowly forward.

"Did he ?" returned Edward, " well, then, I am ready to follow Paul's directions."

"Then you must, first of all, get rid of she," observed the boy, grinning maliciously, and nodding his head at Elinor ; "Paul says it is she who has brought all the mischief upon us, and you'll never do any good till———"

"He did not say it, he dare not say it," interrupted Hatherleigh, with vehemence. "It is contrary to every principle, every maxim even of the lawless tribe to which he belongs, to desert the friendless and oppressed. I will never believe that he directed, that he wished———"

"Who said anything about deserting her ?" interrupted Zekiel, laughing openly at the burst of passion he had elicited from Edward. "I only said that you were to leave her ; and so you are, and to go straight to Oakleigh, and see the person Paul spoke to you of. And then, according to what happens there, you are to go to the great town, or cross the ditch beyond Dover, to you know where; and you're not to trouble yourself about what's going on in this part of the country, till you hear from Paul, or see him; and he says, may be you'll see him before you either expect or wish it."

Edward, who had listened to these instructions with a look of consternation, now turned to see what effect they had had upon Elinor. That she had heard the mandate that was to separate them, perhaps for ever, without anguish and regret, it would be unnatural to suppose; but painful as it was to her feelings, and she was convinced to Edward's also, she felt that it was both his duty and his interest to obey commands dictated by a parent at such a moment. She, therefore, by a strong effort, suppressed all expression of regret.

" Fear nothing for me, Edward," she observed, in a plaintive voice; " the same almighty power that has hitherto preserved me, will still watch over me. I feel, indeed, more confident at this moment than ever, that I have, in reality, nothing to fear; and that, if I were to go boldly this moment, and give myself up to the law, and demand that the charges against me should be put to the proof——"

" You must not think of it, Elinor," interrupted Hatherleigh, hastily. " At this moment of excitement, everything, the most trivial circumstances, would be misinterpreted, and wrested into confirmation of the guilt your enemies charge you with. Copeland is bent on your destruction and mine. Heaven and himself only know what are his motives, or whether they shall eventually succeed or fail; but I entreat, I implore, Elinor, that you do not throw yourself into his power, from a mad confidence that innocence and truth must always prevail. But why do I talk so? I must, I will see you in safety, before I leave you. It is a more sacred duty than——"

" I thought you said, just now, that you were willing to be guided by Paul's words?" interrupted Zekiel, who had stood a silent auditor of Elinor's calm determination, and of the passionate outbreak of her lover's feelings.

" And what, then, did he say of me, my good lad?" demanded the former, before Edward could utter a word.

" He said that you will be safer with the women than with a headstrong, wild young fellow," returned Zekiel, looking askance at Hatherleigh; " and so, if you can be content to bear hardships and scanty fare, till better times come round, I am to take you to where, if they don't receive you with welcome—there can't be very warm welcome where poverty keeps a cold hearth—but, at any rate, they will neither frown upon you nor shut the door in your face."

"There, you hear, he has been provident even for me," observed Elinor to Hatherleigh, who had listened doubtingly, and with marks of evident dissatisfaction, to the boy's exposition of Dangerfield's orders and commands.

"And how am I to know that this is true?" he demanded, looking searchingly into Zekiel's face.

"Do you think that I dare lie to Paul, when he is in affliction and trouble; and, may be, his days numbered, and the last words spoken that may sound from his lips in my ear?" demanded the boy, with a solemn, reproachful look. "No, Master Ned, you may deceive him, and refuse to obey him, because you are a gentleman, and the son of a lady, and scorn to own——"

"No more of this, Zekiel, my good boy; I am sorry I offended you by my expression of distrust, but you cannot comprehend all my feelings, you cannot know the misery——"

"I should be sorry if I could," interrupted the boy, with an arch leer, which gave to his before serious countenance such a rougish look as to force a smile even from Elinor. "And so," he continued, nodding, "as I don't want to go to your school to learn to make long faces, and sigh and be miserable, I'll just go yonder and cut a good hazel rod, against the next time I want to go fishing in the Mere; and then, when you've done all your hugging and crying, may be the young woman 'll come after me, and you'll take your nearest road to Oakleigh. I'll be bound, if she puts her best foot forward, she and me will be at the end of our journey first."

He bounded towards the spot he had pointed out, without seeming to have any other object in view than the gratification of his childish fancy for a fishing-rod.

"We must be brief, dear Elinor, in our adieus," observed Hatherleigh, with a melancholy smile, "for I know the urchin's humour well. The moment he has attained his present object he will become froward and impatient of a moment's delay, and you may find some difficulty, perhaps, in inducing him to proceed with you."

"Let us part, then, at once, Edward," returned Elinor, leave-taking cannot soften the pangs of absence. We know each other's hearts, and——"

"We do, I trust and hope we do," returned Hatherleigh, hastily; "yet, oh Elinor, forgive me, if I confess that at this moment doubts and fears will intrude, that you may not always regard me in the same light. What right can a wretched creature as I am, without friends or fortune—an outcast, hunted from society——"

"And what, then, am I?" interrupted Elinor, "or what can you say of yourself that is not equally applicable to me? What are my prospects, Edward, that they should raise a doubt in your bosom? No, no; the fear, if any, should be on my side. A young man, possessing talents, activity, and perseverance, may reasonably hope to rise superior to circumstances, and obtain consideration and independence in the world; but a female, destitute of friends, her character——but I am foolish to give way to such thoughts," she exclaimed, dashing away the tears that had forced their way from her eyes, and were rolling down her cheeks, and forcing a smile, "I intended only to convince you how impossible it is that I should ever feel otherwise than I do now to you. No, Edward, believe me, my heart is incapable of change. Trust, then, in me, as I do in you, with the fullest, firmest confidence; and believe, too, as I do, that we are both destined to a brighter fate than that which now presses so heavily. Farewell, dear friend! farewell!"

"Dearest, dearest Elinor!" was all that Hatherleigh could answer, as he strained her in a long and close embrace, and pressed his glowing lips to hers in one fond kiss of the purest affection.

Elinor did not at first resist this impulse of passion; but at length, with gentle force, she released herself from his arms; and again murmuring "Farewell!" left him standing as if rooted to the spot, and proceeded to join Zekiel, who had just completed his wish, and was surveying the long, taper, hazel rod he had cut with looks of the greatest satisfaction, and appearing totally regardless of what had been passing so near him, of the anguish which was still heaving Elinor's bosom, hard as she struggled to conceal it, or the still more passionate and expressive despair that kept Hatherleigh still fixed to the spot on which she had left him, his arms stretched out towards her, as if silently imploring her to return.

The boy replied to Elinor's half timid observation that she was ready to go as soon as he pleased, by raising his eyes to her's with a vacant stare; and then, without uttering a word, he proceeded leisurely onwards, without turning even a look towards Hatherleigh, who remained gazing after Elinor until the winding of the path shut her from his sight.

For nearly an hour Elinor continued to follow her strange, eccentric guide, without his making a single attempt to interrupt her melancholy thoughts by a single remark or question. They had left the wood far behind them; but Zekiel still chose the most by and unfrequented paths, and from time to time paused in his hurried progress to cast an anxious look around, as if to ascertain that they were not watched. Elinor, too, observed that, while assuming an air of unconcern and simplicity, he narrowly examined the countenances of the few persons they encountered; and more than once, when he saw that he and his companion were regarded with considerable curiosity by the rustics, who, as they passed to their respective employments, bade them good-morrow, he, almost immediately that they were out of sight, changed the direction in which they were going; sometimes compelling Elinor, to her no small inconvenience and discomfort, to scramble through a hedge, and cross two or three ploughed fields; and, in one instance, even to wade a brook nearly up to her knees, merely observing, by way of apology,

"It's better to do this than find yon fellow coming behind you, and slipping the darbies on you, before you know where you are."

Elinor could not contradict this. She scarcely, indeed, comprehended it; but she knew, from the expression of Zekiel's countenance, that he apprehended danger; and ill as she thought of his temper and disposition, she had seen enough of his shrewdness and discernment to be satisfied that it was perfectly safe to trust herself implicitly to his discretion.

Willing, however, and anxious as she was not to thwart or embarrass him by unnecessary interference with his plans, she felt, after an hour or two's exertions, that her strength was fast failing, and that it would be impossible for her much longer to continue her present exertions.

Hitherto she had contented herself with merely assenting to what he had proposed, but she now felt it absolutely necessary that she should ascertain something as to the final end of their journey, though she dreaded speaking to him, lest it should call forth either an insolent reply or produce a sullen fit, in which perhaps he would leave her.

"Are you not almost tired, Zekiel?" she at length ventured to observe.

"Tired?" he replied, looking round at her with his keen black eyes, "I should have been tired enough, hours ago, to have crept under the first hedge I came to, and fallen fast asleep; but I've got you to look after, and I mustn't think about being tired till you are safe."

"And how long do you think that will be?" replied Elinor. "I mean," she added, as she saw his sneering smile, "how much further have we to go before we reach our destination? I am very tired, I assure you."

"Ah, you need not tell me that," he replied, indifferently; "but I cannot help you. Hark! what is that?"

He bent his ear to the ground, in the attitude of listening. Elinor scarcely drew her breath; yet she was unable to detect any sound which could give occasion for the vigilance he displayed.

The boy's sense of hearing proved, however, much more acute than hers.

"Come this way," he whispered; "they may be friends or they may be foes. We shall see."

Elinor followed him almost mechanically; for she felt at that moment so wearied, not only with her own exertions, but of his continual alarms, and what appeared to her unnecessary caution, that she could have been content almost to resign herself into the hands of her worst enemies, rather than continue longer in the state of anxiety and uncertainty she was at present suffering. She followed, however, into the field to which he led the way; and imitated his example, by crouching down behind the hedge, while the tread of horses' feet became every moment louder and louder. Presently they came quite close, and she heard voices conversing loudly; but instead of proceeding at the rapid pace at which they came up, they stopped, just as they arrived at the precise spot at which she and her companion were hidden on the opposite side of the hedge.

"Well, I am completely thrown out now," observed one of the horsemen; "and yet I could have sworn I caught sight of a petticoat just as we rose the hill. I do not see where they could have disappeared."

"You may depend upon it, we have got completely out of the direction we should have taken," returned another. "I am certain the fellow said the second lane on the right after we passed the wooden bridge; and you have taken the left hand. I am certain we are going wrong; and then we shall be too late for dinner, and commit an unpardonable offence in the eyes of——"

"Not a living soul have we met for this last half hour in

this cursed, uncivilized place," rejoined the first speaker. "I would give five shillings now to any one that could guide us to the Hermitage."

Before Elinor had well heard the words, or could suspect what was about to happen, Zekiel had bounded over the hedge; and the first thing she heard was his offer to the gentlemen to assume the office of conductor to the place mentioned.

"And who the devil are you? and where did you come from?" demanded the person whose liberal offer had tempted the boy to forsake for the moment his trust.

Zekiel made some reply, which Elinor did not distinctly understand; and then she heard the other observe to his companion,

"We had better take his offer, Fred, let him be who or what he may."

"And he will leave me here, to perish," thought Elinor, in agony; "and this is he whom Edward said I might safely confide in.'"

Zekiel, however, had proceeded but a few steps, it appeared, before the recollection of the trust he had deserted recurred to him.

"My sister must go with us," he observed, suddenly stopping. "Elinor, come; it won't be much out of our way; and, may be, the good gentlemen——"

"Are you sure there's only your sister?" said one of the gentlemen, in a suspicious tone. "You're not going to bring your whole gang down upon us, I hope."

"Bless your honour, it's only my poor sister, that's as tired as a dog, and so was resting for awhile under the hedge," returned the boy, in a canting tone. "Come, Ellen," he continued, stretching over the gate, and giving Elinor a significant look; "come, put your best foot foremost, and, maybe, the gentlemen will give you something for yourself."

Most unwillingly and reluctantly Elinor arose; but the moment she reached the gate she repented that she had done so, for her appearance instantly excited in both the strangers the most evident astonishment.

"Zounds, Fred!" exclaimed the elder of the two gentlemen, "here is a girl beats your black-eyed beauty all to nothing. Here's shape and make for you! And what features! did you ever see anything more purely Grecian than that nose and mouth and chin? A perfect Venus, with all the modesty and dignity of a Diana or a Juno! Hold up your head, my pretty dear, and don't blush so unmercifully at hearing your own praise. Now, I'll be bound you've heard a hundred times, from your dark-skinned, cunning-eyed lovers, that you are the prettiest girl in your tribe, and yet——"

"That girl is no gipsy," interrupted his companion, who had been intently gazing at Elinor during the *badinage*, which had brought the blood in crimson torrents to her cheeks. "Look at those ivory hands, and compare them with the colour of her face, and you will see that the complexion she wears is not that which nature gave her."

"By Jove, I believe you are right," returned the other. "Here's an adventure! Faith, I'll try whether the colour will stand," and he threw himself off his horse, evidently with the intention of appproaching Elinor, who was still on the other side of the gate, determined not to cross until they removed from the spot.

"Come, my dear," he observed, stretching out his hand, "let me assist you. I'll be bound you need not be ashamed to show your ankles. If they are but half as handsome as your face and person, you are the most bewitching creature——"

"My sister is not used to be talked to by gentlemen," observed Zekiel, bounding over the gate, and placing himself between the speaker and Elinor, who had retreated a few paces back in alarm at the stranger's free looks and manners.

"*Your sister*, you young vagabond!" exclaimed the latter; "she is no more your sister than she is mine. If you were a few years older than you are, I should suspect those raven locks and sloe-black eyes had beguiled her fancy, and that she was some noble lady, and you a second Johnny Faa. Do you know the tale, boy, how one of your tribe——"

"I could sing you the ballad, if we had time, and you would give me sixpence," returned Zekiel, with a roguish smile; "and I will sing it, too, if your honour likes, to all the fair ladies and noble gentlemen at the Hermitage, after dinner. It will not be the first time I have pleased them, and had a shower of silver for my pains. Only that the slaveys there are such devils, and the dogs——"

"That is well put in, Sir Stanley," observed the other gentleman. "The boy very properly reminds you that we are expected to dinner at the Hermitage, and that there are fair ladies there, who would frown not a little if *they* knew you were detained from their presence by the charms of a——"

"Of an angel, Fred," interrupted Sir Stanley. "Do but

ELINOR CLARE.

HE THREW HIMSELF FROM HIS HORSE, AND ADVANCED TOWARDS HER.

look at the lovely trembler, and tell me if ever you saw such beauty and grace, even in those paltry weeds. What would she look if she were clothed in a dress becoming her person?"

"You forget that 'beauty is, when unadorned, adorned the most,'" returned the other, smiling. "The maxim's somewhat stale; but I have heard you apply it with great effect in reference to certain dairy-maids and cottage-girls in the neighbourhood of the Hermitage."

"Dairy-maids! cottage-girls!" repeated Sir Stanley; "mention them not—the animals! Look at this creature—she moves a goddess, and she looks a queen!—But, after all, Fred, and to lay aside all rhodomontade, and speak plain sense——"

" Which you never did in your life," interpolated quickly the gentleman called Fred.

" Be it so," replied Sir Stanley, with much more gravity than he usually assumed: " I ask you, then, as a man of sense and discernment, and all that, are you not convinced that there is some mystery about this girl? You say yourself that she is not a gipsy."

" No doubt she is a princess in disguise," returned the other, sneeringly. " Most probably she is under the power of some vile enchanter, and you are the knight destined to free her, and marry her for your pains, Sir Stantley de Grey; and the fair—— how do you call yourself, maiden? Elinor, is it not? Well, that is a name that has often figured in the pages of romance; and, of course, it will be sufficiently attractive in those of true history: but, as I have no ambition to play second part, Sir Stanley, suppose I accept the offer of the boy to be my escourt to the Hermitage, and leave you and the maiden to——"

" No, no, I will not be left here!" exclaimed Elinor, almost shrieking, and seizing the boy's arm with the strong grasp of extreme terror. " Zekiel," she continued, " remember your promise to *him*, remember the charge you received to conduct me to a place of safety; remember what will be required at your hands, if he—you know who I mean—should again be restored to his place at the head of your tribe. How will you answer him when he demands of you——"

" I should not answer him at all," interrupted the boy, sullenly; " it won't do to answer Paul. But that is always the way, when a poor boy could earn a few shillings, though he's been fasting for hours and hours, and his feet are cut to pieces with the stones," (holding up his naked feet, and showing them, indeed, lacerated and bleeding, from his recent exertions) " and his flesh is torn from his bones with the brambles, and the bloodhounds are tracking his steps, and the prison is opening its great iron jaws to swallow him up. Oh, no, he must not think of himself; he must not try to earn an honest shilling, to get a bit of bread with; he must not hope to rest his weary limbs for an hour or two, to have a meal's victuals comfortable, like Christians, or else he's threatened and baited and——"

" I do not threaten or bait you, Zekiel," replied Elinor, who saw no end to his complaints; " on the contrary, I shall be glad if you can benefit yourself, without deserting the confidence placed in you. If you can give me any directions how I am to proceed," she added, in a low voice, " or if you think I can remain here in safety till your return, I am quite willing that you should go and get the promised reward, but——"

"Pshaw! you're a fool," he whispered, coming close to her, and leering at the two gentlemen, who were now conferring together. "Don't you know," he added, "that we're not a quarter of a mile from the Hermitage? I could run there in two minutes and a half. And they could see the chimneys now, if they were only to stand up in their stirrups, and look to the left behind yon ashen tree. You see how easy I can get the five shillings; for I'll take care to have it before they know they're so near."

"And then, perhaps, you will get the horsewhip over your back, when they find how you've cheated them," returned Elinor, who, independent of all other objections, by no means relished the probability of being considered as a party to such a barefaced trick.

"Oh, let me alone for that," he replied, with a cunning laugh; "I'll give 'em leave to lay it on as hard as they like, if they catch me within reach of the lash. Besides, five shillings will buy a plaster for worse wounds than they will make; so don't be afraid, but come on. I would tell you to stop here, only that would be losing time. And there's another thing, too; may be that tall chap might take it in his head to come back; and I dont think you would like to——"

"Oh, no," interrupted Elinor, hastily; "I will run no risk of that; persuade them to move on a few paces, and I will follow you directly."

Zekiel approached Sir Stanley, who was leaning over the gate, with his back to them, talking earnestly to his companion.

"If your honour will mount your horse," he observed, "I will run before you, every step, to the Hermitage."

"And your sister, as you call her?" returned Sir Stanley, looking round at Elinor, who stood timidly at some distance, turning away her face from his ardent gaze.

"Oh, she will follow us, and tell the ladies at the Hermitage their fortunes," replied the boy, confidently; "that is, if they'll cross her hand with a bit of silver."

"I will cross it with gold, if she will tell mine," observed Sir Stanley. "Come, my boy, take my horse by the bridle, and go on leisurely with my friend there, till I overtake you. I've a mind to try your sister's skill in fortune-telling. If she be a true gipsy, and not an impostor, she will be able to tell me whether——"

"No, no, that will not do," observed Zekiel, in a decisive tone. "She is young and shy; and though she can read the fate of young maidens, she——"

"Nay, nay, Sir Stanley, this will not do," observed the companion of the latter, who had seemed during the whole dialogue to regard Elinor with as much compassion as curiosity. "You say yourself," he continued, in a voice that was evidently not intended to reach the ears of either Zekiel or Elinor; "you are convinced, you say, that the girl is not what she pretends. Do not, then, run the risk of insulting or wounding the feelings of——"

"The companion of a vagabond gipsy-boy," interrupted Sir Stanley, sneeringly. "Pshaw! Fred, the feelings of a girl who has quitted, most probably, a decent home, to lead a vagrant life, sleeping under hedges and in ditches, must be very sensitive and refined, no doubt. But, I am not going to insult the little would-be gipsy. I am only determined to know her true history before we part; and if I can by fair means persuade her to exchange her present situation for one more becoming her youth and beauty——Zounds, don't look at me with those grave eyes. Do you think me capable of——"

"And you, doubtless, mean to consult Lady Agnes respecting your protegé, if she consents so to become," observed his companion, with a sarcastic smile.

"Consult," returned Sir Stanley, pettishly, vaulting over the gate, and then into his saddle, without bestowing another look upon Elinor, who had heard all that passed, and breathed a secret thanksgiving in her heart to the young man whose interference had rescued her from all apprehension.

"Am I to go with your honour?" demanded Zekiel, who seemed apprehensive that, after all, his services would be dispensed with.

"Certainly, my lad," returned the younger gentleman; "and your sister, if she be your sister, can follow. I can, perhaps, make interest with some ladies at the Hermitage in her favour. At the least, I will take care that both shall have a good dinner, if we arrive in dinner-time."

"There is no fear of that," observed Zekiel, with an arch smile, as he placed himself at the head of the horses, "the bell hasn't rung yet."

"The bell, are we so near, then?" demanded the gentleman.

"You wouldn't find it in an hour," returned the roguish lad, "if I were not to show you the way," and making a sign to

Elinor to follow, he moved swiftly forward, the two gentlemen following at a footpace.

Elinor's apprehensions were subdued but not entirely removed; she crossed the gate, and took the same direction, but so slowly and only just within sight, and was thus unable to hear what was passing between the gentlemen and their guide, though she could see him from time to time turning up his face to the horsemen, as if either replying to or expostulating with them. At length the lane branched off in two different directions; and here, as she rightly supposed, the boy considered it a favourable opportunity to secure his gratuity, as, from the direction in which he had pointed out to her the chimneys of the Hermitage, she knew they were almost close to it.

As she expected, his demand for the money before he had completed his engagement, seemed to excite the gentlemen's anger; and she could distinctly discern that Sir Stanley once raised his whip, as threatening the urchin; but the next minute, one of those discordant bursts of mirth, which resembled shrieks rather than laughter, proclaimed the boy's triumph; and at the same instant the well-known sound of the dinner-bell at the Hermitage rendered all further direction or explanation unnecessary, and revealed the trick Zekiel had played upon them. The younger gentleman instantly rode forward in the direction that he now discovered would take him to the back of the residence of which they had been so long in search; but Sir Stanley still lingered; though, contrary to Elinor's expectations, instead of bestowing chastisement on the boy for the advantage he had taken, he burst into a long and loud fit of laughter at the strange antics by which the former endeavoured to express his satisfaction at his acquirement.

Suddenly, however, he seemed to recollect himself; and almost at the same moment that Zekiel bounded to the side of Elinor, he presented himself at the other.

" You are not going to give us the slip," he observed, "now you are so near. You must come and tell the ladies I spoke of their fortune, and we will see if we cannot better yours."

" I cannot, indeed, I cannot," returned Elinor, who anticipated nothing less than instant discovery by the inhabitants of the Hermitage, who would undoubtedly, she thought, ere this, have become acquainted with events which had happened within the distance of twenty miles; for not more, she knew, was the space between Mr. Copeland's late farm and the beautiful and splendid residence so inaptly denominated the Hermitage.

Zekiel, however, did not seem to comprehend, or, at least, share in her fears, for his looks expressed the strongest dissatisfaction at her refusal.

"I wonder what you'll be good for," he muttered, in her ear, "if you can't earn money when it's offered in an honest way. What is there to tell a parcel of girls, but that they shall have husbands, and lots of money, and everything else that their hearts can wish for? Look here," and he showed her the palm of his own long, skinny hand, "this is the line of life, and that is riches, and this shows how many husbands they will have, and these are all crosses in life; but you must not say too much about them, for they don't like to hear of anything but good fortune. And, mind, don't forget these little branching lines mean children. You can soon guess, from their faces, whether they wish to have them, and promise accordingly; and, mind, you must dash in a little about rivals and jealous lovers; but let the women always get the better of everybody. There, you can't do wrong now, if you're careful. I only wish our Miriam or Abigail were here, and had your chance, it would be a bright day for them."

Vexed and irresolute, yet determined, let what would happen, that she would not attempt to practise the lesson of deception he considered so easy, Elinor remained for a moment silent, thinking by what means she should try to prevail on the wilful and mercenary lad to be content with what he had gained so easily.

"Come, let me add a few instructions to those you have received," observed Sir Stanley, who had fallen a little behind with his horse, and rode up to her side. "You will, no doubt," he continued, with something of anxiety in his countenance, which she knew not how to interpret; "you will, I say, undoubtedly, be desirous of preserving the character you have assumed; and I will take care it shall be profitable to you. I, of course, know you are no gipsy, though I cannot divine your motives for the disguise. Cannot you send that boy away for a few minutes?" he added, in a low tone; "you would find it to your advantage to confide in me."

"I have nothing to confide, sir; no secrets but such as Zekiel may and must hear," returned Elinor, for the first time putting her arm within that of the boy, with an air of confidence in his protection, but in reality to prevent that which she most dreaded, that he should be tempted by Sir Stanley to leave her.

The wide stare of astonishment with which the latter listened to her words and regarded her dignified manner, recalled to her recollection how much she was departing from the character she wished to preserve; and with part real and part assumed embarrassment, she added, with a humble curtsy,

"Zekiel and I are very much obliged to your honour, are we not, Zekiel? but, if you please, we will go on now, for we have a long way to travel, and——"

"Who told you so, pray, mistress?" interrupted Zekiel, angrily, and shaking her arm from his with violence. "If you know better than I do, you had better set up for yourself. If we've got a long way to travel, the more need have we of rest and food; and where shall we find it like we shall in a gentleman's kitchen, when the master orders it?"

"I am not the master, my good lad," observed Sir Stanley; "but——"

"No, but you hope to be, some day," returned the boy, quickly; "and you will be, too, if you do not mar your own fortune; though there's one that you little dream of whispering, it may be, even at this minute, tales in a lady's ear that will serve his own suit more than yours."

Sir Stanley's countenance expressed the deepest amazement; and even Elinor gazed upon the boy, whose animated features, at that moment, so little resembled the vacant, half-idiotic look he usually wore, that she could scarcely believe it could be the same.

"And where did you learn all this, pray?" demanded the gentleman, after a long pause of astonishment. "Come, I cannot, now, consent to part with you, any more than your sister, without an explanation of the mystery."

"Mystery!" repeated the boy, "what mystery? I am a true Egyptian born, whatever she be; and it is well known that we possess the art of reading——"

"Pshaw! this is all cant and nonsense," interrupted Sir Stanley; "you cannot persuade me that you have acquired the knowledge you appear to possess by any supernatural means; but I will reward you handsomely, if you will tell me candidly what you do know, and——"

"Ask the lady of the Hermitage when she frowns or smiles upon you—it may be that she will smile, for women often do so when they mean most mischief—but ask her, I say, when you are next alone with her, what was the tale that was whispered in her ear in the long chestnut walk, when she and one who calls himself your friend lingered so long that you were fain to leave her mother and seek her."

"That is true, by Heavens!   And did he then dare——"

"Ha! ha! ha! trust a rival in love with a secret—trust a cat with the cream—trust a monkey with a nut, and fancy he won't crack it," shouted the boy, with one of his hideous laughs. "But may be it was not true that he told her; and if it was, do not be afraid; you have but to vow, protest, and swear you adore her beyond all worldly blessings, and she will believe you; for a woman in love will believe anything rather than that her lover is false.   Yes, yes, you will be the master of the Hermitage, if you play your cards right; and then I hope you'll not forget Zekiel, and you won't let the slaveys in the stable come out with their long whips, or set the dogs on to bite his heels."

"That I certainly will not, my boy," returned Sir Stanley; "but come, now, I know you love money, look here, I will give you all this handful of silver if you will tell me the whole truth how you came possessed of the information you have given me."

The boy looked with a longing eye at the money, and for a few moments seemed inclined to accept it; but suddenly his countenance changed, as if from the effect of recollection; and turning away with a sullen air, he replied,

"What is the use of asking me how I know it?   It is a gift to our people to know what no one else can know."

"The fellow is a greater fool than rogue," muttered Sir Stanley, seeming perplexed how to deal with him.   "You do not suppose, boy," he continued, "that you can persuade me into believing in your mummery?   You will find it much more to your interest to deal honestly with me, I assure you."

"And so I will, if you'll pay me for it," returned Zekiel, bluntly; "and I'll serve you all I can, too, and Elinor here shall tell the lady of the Hermitage that you are the true lover, and all the rest are false, and——"

"I will undertake nothing of the sort," interrupted Elinor, decidedly.   "It is no use to attempt to carry on any deception by my means, sir," she continued, "for I candidly avow I am not a gipsy, nor have I ever practised gipsy arts or habits."

"There, it is all out now," exclaimed Zekiel, almost shrieking, and darting the most fiery glances of indignation at her. "Well, it's all your own doing, and you may take the consequences.   I shall away, and tell them how you've served me."

And before she could utter a single word of remonstrance he

bounded off, at a rate that defied all pursuit or hope of overtaking him.

For a moment or two Elinor stood in silent consternation, gazing after him, until the look of Sir Stanley recalled her recollection; and, suppressing as far as possible her feelings, she coolly observed,

"It is of little consequence, the desertion of such a wayward being," and with a slight curtsy was turning away, when Stanley interrupted her.

"You are quite right, my dear girl; the loss of such a companion must rather be an advantage to one who might command the attention of princes. Do not bestow a moment's thought upon him, but suffer me to——"

"Pardon me, sir, I shall continue my journey no further than to the next village," interrupted Elinor. "I am not a stranger," she continued, "in this part of the country; and, strange as my appearance and situation may seem to you, I have friends and connections who——"

"I have no doubt of your having friends wherever you choose to command them," he observed, "but be assured that you will find in me the best friend you ever met in your life. I am only puzzled," he continued, looking round, "as to where to bestow you for the present. You must not go to the Hermitage; for if Lady Agnes were to see you——"

"Then I am determined I will go nowhere else," interrupted Elinor, with quickness; "unless, indeed, you give me your word of honour that you will proceed on your journey, and not attempt to follow or molest me in any way."

He looked at her for a minute or two, in evident astonishment.

"You are a strange, unaccountable creature," he at length observed; "but I suppose you must have your own way. But, tell me now, seriously, do you really mean to renounce your frolic; for such I suppose I must consider your being in this masquerading habit, or——Why do you look so dismally? Surely it cannot be possible that a girl of your manners, and with such a person, can be reduced to the necessity of becoming the companion of the miserable, strolling vagrant tribe of whom it is plain your associate was a regular member."

"It matters little what my situation is, or my fate may be," returned Elinor, in a tremulous voice; "you cannot assist me; and, therefore, once more I entreat that you will allow me to depart without further interruptinn."

"If I could be certain of seeing you again," he replied, "if I could be sure that, at no very distant time, you would listen to what I have to propose, without all this evident excitement, I would consent to your going; but as it is, I cannot—will not part with you."

"Then I go to the Hermitage," replied Elinor, calmly. "Nay, sir, do not compel me to expose you," she continued, seeing that he was disposed to prevent her putting her resolution in practice. "Recollect what you have at stake; for, depend on it, the Lady Agnes of whom you speak will never pardon——"

"I care not for a thousand Lady Agneses," he exclaimed, throwing himself from his horse, and advancing towards her. Elinor, however, fled from him with the utmost precipitation in the direction of the Hermitage; but she had not run more than fifty yards before, turning the corner of the lane, she found herself in the presence of a party of ladies and gentlemen, who all stood still, and stared first at her and then at her pursuer, with evident astonishment and surprise.

The first impulse of Sir Stanley was evidently to retreat, and avoid the observation of the party; but second consideration probably suggested to him that it was useless to attempt this; and accordingly, putting on an air of easy, smiling *nonchalance*, he advanced towards them and Elinor, who had instantly stopped, but remained in a state of the most painful embarrassment, uncertain how to proceed, and ashamed to ask the protection of which she stood in so much need.

"So, young woman, I have caught you at last," observed her pursuer, advancing towards her, and attempting to lay hold of her arm, which she eluded by wheeling round, and placing herself behind one of the ladies, a remarkably plain, prim, precise, middle-aged woman, with nothing very attractive in her countenance, to invite the preference which Elinor seemed tacitly to have shown in choosing her as the barrier between her (Elinor) and Sir Stanley.

"You must know, ladies," continued the latter, "that I met with this truant female, for such I am convinced she is, and from very respectable friends, too, under very peculiar and suspicious circumstances. The youth who was with her has managed to escape; but I have been, with your aid, more successful with the girl."

"Whom you pursued, no doubt, with a view of restoring her to respectability, Sir Stanley," observed the lady behind whom Elinor had taken refuge.

"Certainly, madam," he replied. "I could have had no other

motive; and I trust I have taken the most effectual means in introducing her to the notice of Mrs. Clifford, to whom, if she pleases, I will resign all my pretensions."

He passed on as he spoke, and approached a tall, pale, languid-looking female, who had been surveying Elinor with looks of no pleasant import, and who now turned away with extreme disdain from the inquiries Sir Stanley appeared to address to her.

"And pray who are you, and what are you doing here, in this ridiculous garb?" demanded the lady whom he had designated as Mrs. Clifford.

Elinor, to whom these inquiries were addressed in the very harshest tones of a very harsh voice, shrank back abashed, and cast her eyes to the ground, as the piercing ones of the lady surveyed her from head to foot.

"Why do you not speak, girl?" continued Mrs. Clifford. "Who are you?—who do you belong to?"

"I wish I could answer your questions, madam," replied Elinor, with difficulty suppressing her tears, "I wish I could say who I am, or who I belong to; for, then, perhaps, I need not appear in such a garb."

"Indeed!" returned the lady, in the same sarcastic tone; "then what, pray, may be your suppositions as to your actual situation and quality? I suppose you have formed some conjectures on the subject. You imagine yourself, perhaps, to be some poor, persecuted——"

"Persecuted enough, God knows!" interrupted Elinor, clasping her hands, and speaking with an energy that seemed to startle the lady. "But I beg your pardon, madam," continued the weeping girl, "I do not wish to intrude; I can now, I trust, go on my way, without fear."

"And what had you to be afraid of before?" demanded Mrs. Clifford: "not, I hope, of that gentleman?" looking at Sir Stanley, who (although he tried to appear very indifferent, and to be wholly engrossed in attending to the other ladies and endeavouring to soften the scornful and sullen demeanour of the tall, fair-haired lady, who was, in fact, Lady Agnes, the heiress and lady of the Hermitage, as Zekiel had called her,) was, nevertheless, uneasily watching the event of Mrs. Clifford's interrogations.

"I would rather not say anything about the gentleman," returned Elinor, with embarrassment: "it is not for such as I to question his intentions."

"It is pretty plain you had a strong suspicion that they were not for your good, or you would not have been flying from them, like a frightened hare," observed Mrs. Clifford, in a lower voice, and with a look that somewhat reassured the trembling and embarrassed Elinor, who fancied she traced in it indications of a kinder spirit than her tone and manner conveyed an impression of.

"You are a gipsy, are you not, child?" demanded another, a very young lady, who had been evidently impatiently watching the terminatian of Mrs. Clifford's questions, and now took advantage of a moment's cessation, during which that lady seemed to be reflecting on some subject.

Elinor hesitated how to reply; and the young lady immediately added, almost in a whisper,

"Oh, you need not mind owning it to me : if you like to come to me this evening, at dusk, there is my card : ask for my maid, and she will——"

"What, are you going to be charitable, as well as Sir Stanley, Lady Frances?" interrupted Mrs. Clifford, with a sneer, which proved that she was sufficiently aware what the young lady's motives were. "But, beware of imposition," she continued, altering her tone: "remember, none but a true-born, double-dyed Egyptian can tell you the secrets you are longing to know; and this girl is, I am sure, not——"

"La ! you don't think she is an imposter, do you?" interrupted the lady, with evident vexation. "Sir Stanley says that she told his fortune; and he whispered something in Lady Agnes's ear that made her start and blush: so I am sure it must have been true. Now, didn't you tell him something, young woman?"

"Not one word, madam," returned Elinor, mildly.

"And you can't tell fortunes, then?" rejoined the young lady, in a tone of extreme disappointment.

"I cannot, indeed," replied Elinor, scarcely able to suppress a smile, albeit she was in no smiling mood.

"How provoking !" exclaimed the young lady. "Come, Mrs. Clifford, shall we go? See, they are all going on ; and, of course, it's no use loitering here any longer. The first bell has rung, you know ; and we shall not have ten minutes time to dress."

"Go on, then, my dear, and commence your toilet," observed Mrs. Clifford, quietly ; "I will follow you."

Lady Frances tripped lightly away to join her party, leaving Mrs Clifford with Elinor.

" That silly girl would have paid you handsomely, had you only promised her success to all her wishes; why did you not accept her invitation?" demanded the lady.

" Because I cannot practise deception, madam," returned Elinor, modestly.

" Pshaw! then you are not fit to live in the world," observed Mrs. Clifford, a kind expression beaming in her eye, which strongly contradicted the harsh expression of her voice and words.

" I believe I am not, indeed, madam," returned Elinor, sighing deeply; " for, I am sure hitherto——"

" But how comes it," observed Mrs. Clifford, harshly interrupting her, " that you who profess to despise deception should be appearing in a false character? You own you are not what your dress would imply you to be; though, indeed, it is of little consequence whether you own it or not, for any one must be a fool to take you for a gipsy. I have no time, however, now to listen to the tale, whether true or false, by which you can, no doubt, make it appear that you have good and sufficient reasons for assuming such a disgraceful disguise; however, if you choose to appoint where I can see you to-morrow morning, as early as you like——Why do you change countenance so? Is there anything to startle you in my proposing to assist you?"

" No, madam, it was not that," returned the trembling and timid Elinor.

" Then, what was it?" demanded Mrs. Clifford, earnestly.

" I was thinking only," returned the former, raising her tearful eyes to the lady's; " I was startled only at the thought, how many hours were to be passed between this time and to-morrow; and where are they to be passed."

" Where? have you not, then, the same home you had last night?" demanded the lady.

" I have no home, madam," returned Elinor, impressively; " the people with whom I was associated are all scattered and dispersed, I know not whither; and——"

" Good Heavens!" ejaculated Mrs. Clifford, recoiling back a few paces, with seeming horror; " do you mean to acknowledge, then, that you have really been the companion of vagabonds; a partaker in the coarse, lawless habits of wretches who are notoriously restrained by neither law nor principle? Answer me, girl, directly. Have you really been herding with a gang of gipsies?"

" Misfortune has compelled me, madam, for a short time, to

be indebted to such people for shelter and protection," observed Elinor, "but I have adopted neither their habits nor their——"

" What am I to do with her, after this admission ?" observed Mrs. Clifford, as if speaking her thoughts aloud; "Burchall will never condescend to be so degraded as to be made the companion of a gipsy; without her assistance I am afraid we can do nothing. There, there is the dinner bell; and I, who am always scolding others for want of punctuality, shall now be the last at table. And do you really know nobody, girl, that will give you a night's lodging, if they are well paid for it?"

" I may, perhaps, find some cottager, madam," returned Elinor, doubtfully; "but my appearance——" and she looked despondingly at the paltry and tawdry rags which had been substituted for her own neat dress.

" Aye, your appearance, indeed," observed Mrs. Clifford; " I am afraid you would stand a sorry chance of being admitted into any decent habitation; at all events, it must not be left to chance, so come with me. I can but go home at once," she murmured, as she hastily led the way to the Hermitage.

The porter and his wife at the rustic lodge, and the various servants whom they met with on their way across the spacious lawn, alike testified by their looks their astonishment at the appearance of the visitor whom Mrs. Clifford was thus introducing to the splendid residence of their master; but not one of them ventured to express further than by looks their surprise, until on the very threshold of the mansion they encountered Mrs. Clifford's own maid, Mrs. Burchall, a little, short, plump, consequential-looking woman, arrayed in all the colours of the rainbow, and presenting in her appearance the strongest contrast to her mistress, who was unusually thin and tall, and attired with almost Quaker-like simplicity and neatness.

" Oh dear, madam," commenced the *soubrette*, fanning herself violently with the perfumed handkerchief she held conspicuously displayed in her hand, and panting between every word for breath; "oh dear, madam, what a fright I've had about you when the dinner-bell rung; and I never knew such a thing as you not to be dressed, ma'am; and that saucy Mr. Thomas, Mr. Montague's man, telling me you was gone a gipsying; and I knowing what a set of thieves and murderers the gipsies are, ever since I was over persuaded to trust one of the gang with a golden guinea to cross my hand, and then——"

" We will hear that story another time, Burchall," interrupted Mrs. Clifford; "at present there is none to spare. Take this

young woman to your room, and see what you can manage in
the way of dressing her a little more decently and suitably."

"Me, madam!" ejaculated Mrs. Burchall, "my room!
Lord, madam, you can never, to be sure, mean that such a
creature——"

"Never mind, Mrs. Burchall, she can go to mine; and you
will go to Lady Harwell, and tell her I cannot dine with her to
day—that particular——"

"Oh dear, no. Pray, ma'am, don't be angry; I will do
whatever you like; and if you think she can be trusted, I can
just show her the way, and leave her there, while I run back to
help you ma'am; and, after all, you'll be ready before——"

"There, never mind all that; I shall make but little alteration in my dress," observed Mrs. Clifford, hastily; "but stop,
one word with you Burchall," and she led the bustling waiting-
maid aside, and addressed a few words with peculiar energy
and severity of look and manner.

What they were, Elinor, of course, did not hear; but she
guessed their purport, from the effect they seemed to have upon
Mrs. Burchall's manner, as with a much lowered tone, though
still with a look of suspicion and reluctance, she desired Elinor
to follow her up the back stairs.

"There, sit down, young woman," she uttered, pointing to
the chair nearest the door. "I'm sure I don't know what I am
to do with you: as to my lady's clothes, that is quite out of the
question for such as you; and as to mine, though I know my
lady will make me amends, yet it is not pleasant to give one's
nice clothes, that one has taken care of, to be——"

"I hope and beg you will not put yourself to any inconvenience
on my account," observed Elinor, a rising blush betraying the
humiliation she felt at the manner of the upstart menial.

Mrs. Burchall opened her unmeaning light eyes with a wide
stare of astonishment.

"Inconvenience!" she repeated. "I fancy, young woman, you
would think it something rather more than inconvenience, if you
was in my place, to have a person that you know nothing about
brought in, all of a nonplush, as I may say——and then there's
my lady obliged to dress her own blessed self; and she knows no
more about propriety than a child unborn. I'm sure I shouldn't
wonder if she was to make herself quite a laughing-stock."

"It is your taste, then, that arranges Mrs. Clifford's dress!"
observed Elinor, something of her natural archness breaking
through the cloud of melancholy that had so long obscured it.

"Taste!" repeated Mrs. Burchall, tossing her head, "I'm sorry to say Mrs. Clifford knows nothing of taste : she's the most ignorant woman, in that respect, that ever I did see.   Now I don't suppose, if I was to go down upon my bare knees to her, she'd wear a feather or an artificial flower; no, nor a pink nor a yaller ribbon; though, as I often tell her, there's them that's a deal older and worse looking than her, that are dressed like young gals, and nobody thinks nothing about it."

"I dare say," replied Elinor, looking at her with a smile, as the thought struck her what a complete exemplification of what she asserted was her own dumpling figure and coarse face, bedecked with such childish and paltry finery.

For some minutes Mrs. Burchall continued in silence to look over the well-filled drawers which contained, as it appeared, the greater part of her wardrobe, from time to time putting aside some article, and then again, with a wise shake of her head, returning it to its place, with a look which Elinor easily interpreted to mean, that it was by far too good for the required purpose.   At last, however, the necessary selection was made; but Elinor with dismay looked at the large-patterned, gay-flowered gown, the cap decked with scarlet ribbons, the bonnet, by way of contrast, lined and trimmed with yellow, and a shawl which combined all the colours of all the preceding articles, with numerous additions.

"There, I think you'll be smarter now than ever you was or expected to be in your life; so do, for goodness' sake, get off those paltry rags, that we may surprise Mrs. Clifford when she comes."

Elinor knew not how to frame an objection to what she considered was intended in kindness; but most reluctantly she commenced the task of disrobing, Mrs. Burchall, who seemed to become every moment more disposed to be gracious, and play the part of a patroness, looking on with visible impatience to behold the effect of the metamorphose she contemplated.

"Merciful! what a load of hair!" she exclaimed, as Elinor, removing the coloured shawl which had been twisted round her head into a fantastic but not unbecoming turban, shook down her glossy and luxuriant tresses, which fell nearly to her feet.

"Yes, it will prevent the necessity of my depriving you of your cap," returned Elinor, smiling; "I have never been accustomed to wear anything but my own hair, and——"

"Oh, well, then, I'm sure it is quite time you did so," returned the waiting-maid, pertly; "for, I'm sure it is not at

ELINOR CLARE.

"I SHOULD ADVISE YOU TO CUT ALL THAT OFF!" SAID MRS. BURCHALL.

all becoming a decent young woman in your station of life, even if you're not a gipsy, as Mrs. Clifford says, to be flaunting with your hair dressed like a lady."

"I do not wish any such thing," returned Elinor, meekly.

"Well, then, I should advise you to cut off all that long hair, or best part of it, at least, and tuck the rest of it up under a modest cap, that will make you look like a Christian," observed Mrs. Burchall, producing at the same time a pair of scissors, with which she seemed inclined at once to put her proposal into execution.

"A *modest* cap I should have no objection to," observed

Elinor, retreating at the same time, to avoid the threatened infliction.

"And pray, then, do you mean to say that my things are not modest?" exclaimed Mrs. Burchall, in a violent rage.

Before Elinor could utter a word to deprecate her violence, the door opened, and Mrs. Clifford, attired with a neatness that rendered even her plainness becoming, looked in.

"There, Burchall," she observed, without noticing the violent excitement of the person in question, "I have just come to show myself, that you may not say I disgrace you; but what is the matter?" she continued, glancing at the obnoxious articles, which were lying in a heap, and then at Elinor's dishevelled locks and bare shoulders. "Why, Burchall, you have done nothing all this time. And what is all this trumpery for? Did not I tell you to look among my clothes and see what you could make suit the girl?"

"Suit!" muttered Mrs. Burchall. "I'm sure, if it isn't presumption to dress such people up in such people's clothes, I know nothing. As to trumpery, things that cost me——"

"Too much to be thrown away, my good Burchall," interrupted Mrs. Clifford, with a smile at Elinor; "so put it all away, and I dare say this poor girl will be quite as well content with one of my sober brown or grey dresses; and as to caps, I'm sure she wants no other covering or ornament than that nature has given her."

"The goodness gracious keep us!" exclaimed Mrs. Burchall, elevating her hands as her mistress disappeared. "Well, I've heard of people being bewitched; and I think if my lady isn't ——but come, ma'am, as it seems you are to be made a lady of, you had better come with me to Mrs. Clifford's wardrobe, and choose what you'll be pleased to wear."

"I am quite willing to leave that choice to you, ma'am," returned Elinor, who, with her usual good nature, felt really vexed that she had been the cause of wounding the prejudices—feelings they could not be called—of her companion.

Mrs. Burchall, however, was too much offended to be so easily appeased; and it was not without considerable difficulty that Elinor succeeded in convincing her that she was abundantly content with the very worst gown that could be selected from Mrs. Clifford's stock, a plain white shawl, and a coarse straw bonnet, which was designated by the lady's maid her mistress's garden bonnet.

"Well, you certainly look a little more decent now," observed

Mrs. Burchall, surveying Elinor with something like satisfaction at what she considered the result of her own cleverness, though, in reality, it had been in direct opposition to her wishes. In a few minutes, however, a fresh source of dissatisfaction arose in her mind.

"I wonder what my lady meant was to be done with you, after you were dressed," she observed. "She could not mean, I suppose, that you were to stay here till she comes; because she knows very well that we of the second table dine as soon as the dessert comes on theirs; and so she can't think I can stop here with you."

"I do not wish it," returned Elinor, quite unconsciously; "I can, if you please, remain here; for I do not think it is Mrs. Clifford's intention that I should leave without seeing her."

"No, indeed; that's quite out of the question, to suppose that I should leave a person like you in persession of my room," observed Mrs. Burchall; "I've got things of value, I assure you, young woman; and my trinklets alone, though my lady sets no store by them, and calls them rubbish, cost me a matter of——Lord bless me, if that isn't my lady's bell ! whatever can she want now, just as I'm going to my dinner ! I declare, everything seems turned topsy-turvy in this house, to-day."

Forgetful, in her haste to obey her lady's summons, of her distrust of leaving Elinor with her valuable things and trinklets, the consequential little woman bustled out of the room; and the former, for the first time, had the opportunity to reflect upon the new turn her affairs had taken, and the probable consequences of the situation in which she was placed. The result of these reflections was, after a long struggle with herself, the determination to confide implicitly to Mrs. Clifford the whole particulars of her melancholy story.

CHAPTER XI.

We wander there, we wander here,—
We eye the rose upon the brier,
Unmindful that the thorn is near
        Among the leaves,
And tho' the puny wound appear,
        Short while it grieves.

                      BURNS.

A CONSIDERABLE time had passed before Mrs. Burchall returned; and when she did so, a great change had taken place in her manners towards Elinor. Her ill humour, indeed, appeared by no means diminished; but instead of, as before, seeming anxious to talk, and not at all scrupulous as to how what she did say would be relished by her companion, she was now silent and reserved, and assumed what to Elinor, after her former contemptuous treatment, appeared rather a mockery than true respect.

"My lady desired me to inform you, ma'am, that your dinner is served up in her own dressing-room; and that you will be pleased to stay there till she is at leisure to talk to you. She thought it wouldn't be pleasant to you to be exposed to the questions and curiosity of a parcel of gossiping servants at our table."

"I am sure I am greatly indebted for such a mark of kind and delicate consideration," replied Elinor, affecting not to see the air of mock respect with which this was delivered.

Mrs. Burchall's cocked-up nose was elevated still higher, and her puckered face drawn into still closer wrinkles; she looked earnestly at Elinor for some moments, as if to read in her countenance whether the latter was serious or not, and then finding she still preserved the same unruffled demeanour, she bounced out of the room, observing,

"If you want your dinner, ma'am, you'd better come at once; for I've got something else to do, I assure you, than to be waiting your pleasure."

Without making any reply to this ungracious remark, Elinor followed to the neat and airy dressing-room, in which the absence of all finery and pretension marked as strongly the contrast of disposition as did the persons of the mistress and the maid. The plain, comfortable meal, to which Elinor did all the justice that might have been expected from her long abstinence, was scarcely concluded, before Mrs. Clifford entered the room. For several moments she stood gazing at Elinor, with a look of perplexed amazement, as if she had totally forgotten who she was, or how she had come thither.

"It can never be the work of chance," she uttered, in a tremulous tone; "it is her very self, such as she was when——tell me, child, truly—what is your name?—who are your parents?"

"My name, madam, I believe, is Elinor Clare; and I believe, also, that I am an orphan; but I know nothing with certainty, for there has always been so much mystery and contradiction in the accounts I have received from the relations by whom I was reared——'

"Relations you have, then; tell me, who are they? where do they live? in what station of life are they?" demanded Mrs. Clifford, rapidly.

"I will willingly tell *you* all, madam," returned Elinor, with humility; "but," and she looked expressively at Mrs. Burchall, who was listening, with strong expressions of dissatisfaction and incredulity imprinted on her countenance.

"I understand," said Mrs. Clifford, impatiently. "You may go, Burchall; I will ring, if I want you."

Mrs. Burchall quitted the room, not, however, without bestowing a most malignant glance, which, though unseen by her mistress, did not escape the observation of Elinor.

"Now, then, child, explain what is the mystery you speak of, and what are your reasons for doubting that a true account has been given you of your parents," observed Mrs. Clifford, seating herself opposite to Elinor, into whose face she gazed as if she would have read her heart.

As briefly as possible, and without any attempt to varnish or disguise a single fact, Elinor proceeded to recount the whole history of her life, as far as the memory went, suppressing nothing of the unaccountable reluctance and dislike Mr. Copeland had ever shown to speak of her parents, his occasional coldness and reserve to herself since she had grown up, and his stern discouragement of the warm affection shown to her by Isabel and Annie, her supposed cousins. To all this Mrs. Clifford listened with deep interest, and without interrupting the detail, except by once asking from what part of the country Mr. Copeland had originally come, or where was his birth-place, questions which Elinor declared her inability to answer, he having always preserved the strictest silence on the subject, and repulsed with the greatest asperity any attempts on the part of his family to draw from him the circumstances of his early life.

One particular, however, he had accidentally betrayed, which Elinor's memory had retained; and that was, that he had been at some part of his life a traveller in foreign lands. Mrs. Clifford's expressive eyes seemed to dart fire, as she eagerly exclaimed,

"Did he not say where? with whom? how he came to be in that situation?" she demanded.

Elinor replied in the negative. It had been only when in conversation some question had been started respecting the customs of different nations, she replied, that he had betrayed how intimate his acquaintance was with many foreign parts; so much so, that Mrs. Hatherleigh had observed, "You have resided, then, or travelled much on the continent, in your younger days, Mr. Copeland?"

"And who was this Mrs. Hatherleigh, my dear?" demanded Mrs. Clifford. "Probably, if I could see her——"

Elinor shook her head mournfully.

"Well, never mind, proceed with your story," returned the lady. "I am anxious to know, as this man seems, with all his cold and hard nature, to have done his duty towards you, so far as supporting and educating you, how it is that I have found you in this destitute state."

Elinor's countenance betrayed the distressing feelings that this observation had excited; but she had already resolved to conceal nothing from her benefactress, and she proceeded to relate the dreadful occurrence of Walter Copeland's death, with all its strange, mysterious circumstances; the fire, and all that had ensued to involve her in suspicion, and in some measure excuse the harshness and severity of Mr. Copeland towards her.

"Yet, I am innocent, madam," she exclaimed, raising her streaming eyes to the deeply searching ones of Mrs. Clifford, which were fixed upon her with a look of mingled amazement and horror, which her tongue refused to express; "I am innocent of having even in thought injured Mr. Copeland, and far less poor Walter, whom I would have given my life to save."

"Innocent, child!" repeated Mrs. Clifford, shuddering; "yes, from my soul I believe you; but I fear, greatly fear, that you have been made the dupe of wicked designing people. This Edward Hatherleigh, I am sorry to say, appears——"

"Oh, no, no, do not, do not condemn him!" exclaimed Elinor, eagerly. "Oh, if you could see him, could hear him speak, you would say, as I do, that it is impossible, utterly impossible that he could commit an act so foul, so base, so treacherous."

Mrs. Clifford shook her head.

"If I were as young and credulous as you, child," she replied, " I should, no doubt, believe in his innocence, even against the evidence of my own senses; but I hope, I most earnestly hope, for your sake and his own, that he is, like you, the guiltless victim of appearances. Go on, my poor girl; tell me how you have contrived as yet to escape from these threatened dangers; and we must then try to devise the means by which you may eventually, I trust, be rescued entirely."

For some moments Elinor's grateful emotions prevented her uttering a word, she could only press Mrs. Clifford's hands between hers, while her streaming tears bore testimony to the excess of her feelings.

"They are her very hands, too," observed the lady, shudder-ing, and hastily withdrawing; "I could fancy that the time that has passed has been obliterated, and that it is herself holding me with that cold and trembling grasp which I have never forgotten, while she—but these are all phantasies of the brain, she is dead and gone, and——Go on, child, go on, do not look at me with those eyes; at some future time, perhaps, I may explain. And yet, why should I? It is nothing in which you are interested. There, what were you saying? this man, this Hatherleigh, I think——"

Elinor resumed her story; and Mrs. Clifford, collecting herself, listened with attention to the end.

"And you have really been an associate with—have been sheltered by these gipsies," she observed; "and you have been left alone, to the protection of this young man—this Edward Hatherleigh, for I know not how long a time, and yet you are still pure and innocent," she observed, looking fixedly at Elinor.

The blood mantled in a rich glow, not only the face, but the neck and bosom of the fair girl; but she did not avoid the searching gaze, as she meekly replied,

"I have never voluntarily, madam, committed an action for which I ought to blush; but your suspicion is——"

"No, no, child, I do not suspect you," interrupted Mrs. Cliff ford, hastily; "I was thinking only of those who, without hal your temptations, have forfeited self respect—have become—— but no matter, we must think now only of your situation—of the means of redeeming you from the danger, the imputations which——"

A gentle knock was at this moment heard at the door of the chamber, and a soft voice exclaimed,

"May I come in, aunt, for a moment?"

Mrs. Clifford rose hastily, evidently vexed at the interruption; but before she could reply to the intruder, or reach the door to prevent her entrance, it was opened, and the fair, unmeaning face of Lady Agnes looked doubtingly in.

"Oh dear, she is here, then," she observed, her eyes lighting up with pleasure; and hastily entering, without further ceremony, she closed the door after her.

"Now, dear aunt, you know how doatingly fond I am of a secret," she observed, coaxingly, throwing her arms round Mrs. Clifford's neck, while her eyes were intently examining Elinor, who had respectfully risen from her seat and remained standing.

"I am sorry I cannot gratify you, then, Lady Agnes," returned Mrs. Clifford, gravely; "I have long since ceased to have secrets of my own, and am very unwilling to become the depository of those of others; but when I am entrusted, I cannot betray them, even to one so prudent and discreet as you."

"Oh, but I half know it already, aunt," replied Lady Agnes; "for everybody is talking about it all over the house; and Sir Stanley himself told me——but, oh dear, I forgot; but don't think, aunt, that I have forgiven the wretch. He is an ungrateful, deceitful monster; and I have desired him never to speak to me, or think of me again; so you need not suppose, aunt, that——"

"I wish it were as easy to persuade *you* never to think of him again," observed Mrs. Clifford, sharply; "but now, my dear, do leave me, for I have more important business to settle than your quarrels with Sir Stanley, of which I can easily forsee the termination."

"Can you, indeed?" said Lady Agnes, looking at her with a silly smile. "Then you do think, aunt, that——"

"We will postpone my thoughts on the subject to some more fitting opportunity, if you please, niece," returned Mrs. Clifford; "for the present, I am busily engaged."

Lady Agnes pouted, and looked offended, but Mrs. Clifford affected not to see it; and the young lady was compelled to quit the room, not, however, without another survey of Elinor, towards who, in spite of her affectation of childishness and innocence, her looks betrayed no very pleasant feelings.

"The silly moth, in spite of all warnings, will flutter round the flame till it is burnt," observed Mrs. Clifford, with an air of vexation, when she was gone; "but come, it is of no use to dwell on evils that are irretrievable—fools will be fools, and knaves will profit by their folly as long as the world stands. Tell me now, child, where is this Copeland's residence?—where can I write to, or, if it be not too far, see him, without delay?"

Elinor named the farm-house of Burton as the place where she had last beheld her *soi-disant* uncle, and described its situation; but the distance was too far to either go or send that night; and Mrs. Clifford's thoughts were next turned towards the means of providing her *protégée* with a safe temporary shelter.

"It will not do for you to remain here, even if I could conveniently accommodate you," she observed, "for I dare say that silly girl spoke truth when she said that everybody was talking of you; and although I, who have only been here a few days, had heard nothing of the circumstances you have related, it is probable they have made noise enough in the country to lead to a discovery which may be anything but pleasant to all parties concerned."

Elinor could only reply with truth by confirming this conjecture. She was indeed startled by the conviction that rushed upon her mind at this moment, that Mrs. Clifford might be involved in most serious consequences by knowingly harbouring one accused of such heinous crimes as she was. All her new-born hopes—her confidence of eventually clearing her innocence from all imputation, and triumphing over her enemies —faded at once; and with extreme earnestness she besought her protectress to let her go, and trust to Providence for her further safety.

"In my desire to avoid a present evil," she observed, "I had almost forgotten a far greater one; but I am now strong again, and refreshed, and able to continue my journey, and——"

"And where, then, do you propose to go? and what is your final aim?" demanded Mrs. Clifford, earnestly.

"I have thought, if I could, that I would endeavour to reach London," returned Elinor. "I remember hearing the man who is called the Gipsy Chief remark to Edward—to his son, that it was in great cities only perfect security from observation could be found; and that there, too, only could the poor and unfriended hope to extricate themselves from and surmount their misfortunes."

"And his son—this extraordinary and persecuted young man, no doubt, intends also to seek this asylum for virtue in distress," observed Mrs. Clifford, satirically.

Elinor felt keenly the insinuation conveyed in these words, but she felt too much real respect and gratitude towards the lady to utter anything like resentment; and she therefore only gravely replied,

"I believe not, madam; I have already, I think, mentioned that, by his father's orders, delivered through the boy who was my companion until I had the good fortune to meet you, Edward was directed to a place which he called Oakleigh, though that I believe is not the real name of the place."

"Perhaps not," returned Mrs. Clifford, seeming, however, hardly to know what she uttered, and totally to have forgotten the remark which had called for this explanation. "I am thinking, however, child," she continued, "that perhaps your plan of going to London is the best that can be pursued, at present; though not exactly in the romantic style you propose."

She rang the bell, and Mrs. Burchall, who evidently was near at hand, expecting the summons, immediately entered.

"Send Pritchard to me," observed the lady, laconically.

"Pritchard, madam!" returned the maid, with a stare, as if she doubted the evidence of her own hearing.

"Yes, Pritchard; there, go at once, you need not return."

Mrs. Burchall saw at once that it would not do to hesitate; and she departed on her errand, though evidently strongly inclined to murmur and hesitate.

In a few minutes the person Mrs. Clifford had sent for knocked at the room-door, and at her invitation a hearty, hale, well-looking old man entered the room, with a respectful bow, and a look of strong surprise directed towards Elinor, to inquire his lady's commands.

"Pritchard, have you any objection to go to London for a week or two?"

"Certainly not, madam, anything you may please to command," returned the man, heartily.

"Aye, but you must go directly, within an hour, at the furthest," rejoined the lady. "Can you be ready by that time?"

"To be sure, madam; I can tie up a change in a handkerchief in five minutes," he replied. "But how be I to go? The London mail passes the lodge in half an hour; but perhaps that will be too soon."

"No, not for me, I have very few directions to give," returned Mrs. Clifford. " They are merely to see this young person in safety to Hertford Street; tell Mrs. Hargrave to make her as comfortable as she can, till she hears further from me; and if Sir Stanley Egerton, or any one else, comes there to inquire for her, not to suffer them to see her, or even acknowledge that she is there, if she can by any means avoid it."

" I understand, madam," replied the old man, bowing; "and be I to stay in Hertford Street, too, for if I be, leave me alone to deal with Sir Stanley, or any other of the gay chaps? They won't come twice, I know, if I answer them."

" You may do as you please about that, Pritchard," returned the lady; "though, upon second thoughts, I believe it would be best that you should not be seen in the affair. You can sleep there, you know; but, perhaps it would be as well that you should not be seen in the day time. You will hear from me, however, in a day or two; and then we can settle all that. Now go and get ready; and if you are asked any questions, either by Burchall or any one in the house, say that it is my desire that you do not answer them."

Pritchard bowed, and hurried away.

" I have not time to tell the good man the whole particulars; though, perhaps, he ought to know the extent of your danger," observed Mrs. Clifford, when he quitted the room. "And yet, perhaps it is better that he thould not know it; since, if anything should unfortunately occur, his ignorance of your real situation will acquit him of all responsibility."

Elinor sighed heavily. It was not only a mortifying, but a dreadful reflection, that she could not make a single person her friend without exposing them to danger; but she felt it was not her place to suggest this to one who was evidently quite as conscious of it as she was herself, and yet was generously determined not to be deterred by it from doing her utmost to serve her.

The time Pritchard was absent was occupied by Mrs. Clifford in writing a note to Mrs. Hargrave, who, she explained to Elinor, when she delivered it to her care, was her (Mrs. Clifford's) housekeeper in town.

" There, do not speak," she observed, preventing the expressions of gratitude which Elinor's full heart prompted. " We have no time to waste. There is some money, though I do not know that you will need it; for Pritchard will pay all expenses. Now I have only one condition to make, and that is, that, let what will happen, you take no step without consulting Pritchard and his sister, Mrs. Hargrave; they are plain people; but, remember, plain sense will carry you through difficulties which——Oh, here is Pritchard; and you have not a moment to spare. Go, then; and God prosper you!"

She closed the door upon them before Elinor or her new companion could utter a word; but to the latter this seemed no subject for surprise; he was apparently too well acquainted with his mistress's eccentric modes of acting; and making a sign to Elinor to follow him, he proceeded, as quietly as possible, down the back stairs, and through the servants' hall, to a side entrance, through which they passed, apparently unnoticed.

"We must go quick now, or else we shall miss the mail," observed the old man; "and, after all, may be there won't be two places vacant, perhaps none at all; and then I wonder what I'm to do; I forgot to ask madam. And, indeed, she always does everything in such a hurry, that it's a thing impossible to have one's wits about one."

Elinor knew not how to reply to this supposed difficulty. She saw, or fancied she saw, that the old man, with all his apparent readiness to obey his lady's commands, was by no means pleased at having to undertake so sudden a journey; and she sighed heavily at being thus compelled to incur obligations without a prospect of being able to repay them.

"What dost sigh for, young woman?" demanded the old man, in a good-humoured tone, and turning round to let her come up with him. "I hope it ar'n't for leaving that good-for-nought Sir Stanley behind. What, I s'pose he pretended to sweetheart you, did he, and talk a parcel of his fine deceitful flummery to you, as he does to every young girl who'll be foolish enough to listen to him? Aye, aye, a pretty life Lady Agnes will have with him; and yet, I'll be bound, she'll be foolish enough to have him, in spite of all she sees or hears. But I hope you don't think nothing about him; because what could he mean to a poor girl like you, but just to ruin you, as he's done scores of others? I think it is a very kind thing of Madam Clifford to send you out of his way: and you ought to pray upon your bended knees for her."

"That I am well aware of," replied Elinor, warmly, "though not on the account you think; for I never saw Sir Stanley in my life till within these few hours, and therefore could be in no danger from him."

Pritchard was about to make some reply, expressive,

apparently, of his incredulity of this assertion; but, much to Elinor's satisfaction, the sound of wheels approaching gave another turn to his thoughts; and exclaiming, "Odd's bobs, but here's the mail coming, as hard as it can rattle; we must run, girl, or we shall be too late to meet it at the lodge," he set off at a pace that precluded all attempts to continue the conversation.

The coach stopped; and, much to Elinor's satisfaction, two places were vacant. It was, however, with extreme chagrin that Pritchard found there was only one inside; and that, "of course," the coachman observed, "must be for the lady."

Elinor, indeed, would willingly have forgone her privilege, to have accommodated the old man; and she even insisted that she should be far better in the open air than in the close coach; but, after an apparent struggle, between the selfish desire of a comfortable berth in a corner, which, he observed, he had hoped to get, and his consciousness not only of impropriety, but that his lady would not approve of such an arrangement, the former gave way, and he mounted to a seat behind the coachman, depositing his bundle in the lap of Elinor, whom he first saw seated in the coach, and desiring her to take care, and not let it fall under her feet, if she fell asleep, as "the shirt frill" would be "tumbled all to pieces."

"The old gentleman means to cut a dash in London, my dear," observed the pert, lisping voice of a young man who sat opposite to her, as soon as the coach was in motion.

Elinor did not reply. She felt annoyed by being intruded upon just at that moment, when she hoped to enjoy uninterrupted communion with her own thoughts; for the night was too dark for her to discern more than the outlines of the persons of her companions, and she was thus prevented from feeling the timidity and embarrassment which are the natural attendants of an inexperienced traveller. The stranger, however, seemed not at all repulsed by her silence, but proceeded to ask her several questions, in a style of familiarity which he seemed to think betokened his great superiority. To some of these Elinor returned mere monosyllables—yes or no; while to others she remained entirely silent, half-angry and half-astonished that any stranger should be so presumingly importunate. But if she was surprised at his conduct, she was not less so at that of a person who, muffled up in a large coat, and with his hat drawn over his eyes, leant back in the corner beside the impertinent questioner, and, at every word he uttered, testified his anger and impatience by some half-suppressed exclamation or sudden change of position. The other passenger was a female, who either was or affected to be asleep.

" Have you ever been in London before, my dear ?" demanded the pertinacious babbler.

" No, sir," returned Elinor.

" Nor your father either ?" he added.

For a moment she was startled at the apparent folly and incomprehensibility of the question, but the next it suggested itself to her mind that Pritchard was the person to whom he applied the title of her father, and between a sigh and a smile she replied,

" Net that I know of."

The stranger in the corner seemed in his emotions to partake of the equivocal nature of her reply; for he gave way to a laugh, which ended in a deep sigh.

That laugh and that sigh, however, were alike startling to Elinor; she could not but believe that they were no strangers to her, and almost did she feel disappointed that the silence of the coxcomb who had called forth these demonstrations of feeling prevented any further necessity for them.

Whether the young man whose curiosity had been so troublesome was for the first time apprised that it was so, or whether the muffled stranger's singular manners had roused a suspicion in his mind that he was not a very pleasant or companionable neighbour, Elinor could not judge; but certain it was, something acted as a restraint upon his heretofore ungovernable tongue; he sunk into utter silence, and drawing a fur travelling cap close down over his face, leaned back, and soon gave unequivocal and no very pleasant evidence that he was asleep.

A long silence ensued; and at length Elinor, becoming satisfied that her suspicions must have been unfounded, yielded to the fatigue she felt; and, closing her eyes, and leaning back in the easiest posture she could assume, she tried to forget the world, and all the troubles which had befallen, and still probably awaited her, in her communion with it. Gradually all sights and sounds faded into indistinctness. She still felt the whirling of the carriage along the smooth road, but its motion rather lulled than disturbed her ; and she was just on the point of attaining the enviable state of forgetfulness she so much coveted, when she was aroused by a low sound that seemed close to her ears, and which she soon discovered was occasioned by a conversation carried on in whispers between the muffled-up stranger and the female who sat by her side, and whom she had hitherto supposed to be strangers to each other.

Forgetful for the moment of the impropriety of listening to that which was evidently not intended for her ears, and anxious only to ascertain whether there was any foundation for the suspicion she had entertained, she cautiously removed the shawl in which she had enveloped her head; but the movement, silent as it was, did not escape the notice of her companions; and, except that a deep sigh from the man was re-echoed by the female, no sound from that time which indicated any correspondence between them met her ear.

Elinor's attention, however, was now thoroughly aroused by the seeming mystery, and all thoughts of slumber were banished, though she tried again to resume the appearance of it; but either her dissembling was bad, or they had exhausted the subject on which they were desirous of exchanging thoughts, for she could not discover that a single word passed between them.

The coach stopped to change horses, and everybody was roused and on the alert; but again Elinor's hopes of making a discovery were baffled. The moment the motion of the horses ceased, the muffled stranger, who had been leaning his head, for some minutes previous, through the window opposite to the side on which she sat, opened the door, which he must have held ready unclosed for that purpose, and leaped out, without waiting for the formality of letting down the steps, or the approach of the waiters and chambermaids, who were seen in the distance with lights, to inquire if any lady or gentleman would please to alight, ten minutes were allowed, etc., etc. The female traveller merely made a motion of dissent with her hand when the question was put to her; and before Elinor could answer the same question addressed to her, Pritchard, who was already on the ground, approached and prevented her, by demanding if she would like to take a glass of ale, or a drop of brandy and a biscuit, adding,

"Thou'lt have a long way to go before thou gets anything, my girl."

Elinor declined the offer, and the coach-door was closed, leaving her and the female passenger to their silent meditations.

A hundred times did Elinor attempt, during this short ten minutes, to utter something which should break the freezing reserve of her fellow-passenger, but in vain; she knew not what unaccustomed timidity and embarrassment restrained her, but she could not bring out a word.

The female, on her part, seemed equally restrained and reserved in her deportment; and, except that once or twice she gave utterance to a low and evidently half-suppressed sigh, neither sound nor motion would have betrayed her proximity.

The passengers returned; but Elinor felt considerably disappointed when she found that the young man who had so excited her curiosity did not resume his seat in the coach, having arranged, it appeared, with Pritchard, to exchange places with him, much to the satisfaction, as it seemed, of the latter. Another person, too, a plain, farmer-like man, was added to those who occupied the inside of the coach; and Elinor, losing all hope of satisfying her half-formed suspicions as to her female fellow traveller for at least some hours, till the day should break, endeavoured to imitate the example of her companions, and compose herself to a short repose. At length so far her object was attained, that she had become alike oblivious of her present situation and the circumstances that had led to it. The rolling of the wheels was still faintly heard, and the rocking motion of the coach so far felt as to prevent her falling into a sound sleep; but even this temporary suspension of thought and care was soon broken up; the coach suddenly stopped, the door was banged open, the steps let down with a crash, and the coachman exclaimed,

" Now, ma'am, if you please;" and before Elinor was well aware what was intended or what was passing, the strange female had alighted, and was gone.

" Was the young man gone, too ?" was the first thought that occurred to her mind, as soon as she became collected; and that thought continued to occupy her, to the exclusion of all others, until the day breaking occasioned a general movement among her fellow-passengers, and something like an attempt at conversation, Mr. Pritchard beginning to wonder how long it would be before he should get his breakfast, etc., etc., and the last new comer re-echoing his hope that it wouldn't be long first. The young man who had at first annoyed Elinor by his impertinence now joined in; but the latter in vain listened for a word that could lead her to suppose that any of them knew anything or thought anything about their late companion, or he whom she hoped rather than expected was still near enough to be called their companion.

The desired moment at last arrived; the coach stopped, and

ELINOR CLARE.

"AND IS THAT, TOO, ONE OF THE FAMILY?"

she eagerly accepted Pritchard's invitation to alight to breakfast.
But in vain she cast her eyes around, as soon as she was on
the ground, in search of the muffled passenger; no such person
was to be seen; and she now became more than ever convinced
that her suspicions were right, and that they had quitted the coach
together, to avoid the recognition which otherwise must have taken
place.

Yes, it was Edward Hatherleigh and his mother, she was now
assured of it, with whom she had travelled so many miles,
without exchanging a single word — they to whom her every

thought had once been known, and to whom she believed she was equally an object of interest. A thousand circumstances now occurred to her recollection, to prove that she was right in her conjectures. How could she ever be so foolish as to doubt? or, even doubting, how could she be so backward as to suffer them to depart without satisfying herself? From henceforward Elinor's journey was devoid of all interest. She cared nothing about its termination—cared not what became of her,—Edward had renounced her and had proved that he was indifferent to her fate; his mother had evidently considered her unworthy of even being spoken to: and what, then, was there in the world worth caring about?

CHAPTER XII.

Indifference now, with icy fetters, binds
  This soul, which once with wild emotion beat,—
This soul, that still in friendship's haven finds,
  From fate's rude storms, a calm and sure retreat.
ANON.

MR. PRITCHARD'S long experience in travelling prevented Elinor's feeling many of the annoyances and inconveniences which the uninitiated are apt to encounter, on their first introduction to the metropolis. In a few minutes after their arrival at the inn where the coach stopped, they were comfortably seated in a hackney-coach, and, without let or hindrance, were set down at the door of Mrs. Clifford's town residence, in Hertford Street, May Fair.

Though perfectly aware of Mrs. Clifford's rank in life, and expecting, of course, that she lived in a style befitting it, Elinor was by no means prepared for the evidences of luxury and grandeur which met her eyes at every step, after she had passed the threshold of the mansion. The lady's own plainness of appearance and unpretendingness of manner were, indeed, so completely at variance with all that the former now beheld, that she could scarcely believe that there was not some mistake; and it was not until she heard it repeated from her companion's lips, that she was now in Mrs. Clifford's town-house, that she could believe it possible that this was merely one of the residences of an ordinary, plainly-dressed, unfashionable-looking, single female, of at least forty-five. But Elinor's thoughts soon became more interested by the mode of her reception, and the persons who were to be, as she understood, for some time, at least, her companions and protectors, than by any of the magnificence with which she was surrounded.

Mrs. Hargrave, the sister of Mr. Pritchard, was a short, fat, active woman, whose bustling disposition and habits of industrious occupation seemed to defy the ravages of time and the infirmities of age; which had, nevertheless, blanched her locks, and deeply furrowed her brow. At the very first glance, Elinor felt disposed to like her; and the impression was further confirmed by the extreme solicitude with which she, after the first expression of surprise at so unexpectedly beholding her brother, three weeks and five days, as she particularly observed, before the regular time, inquired respecting the health and spirits of her mistress.

"She is much as usual," returned Pritchard; "sometimes, I think, a little more fanciful than ever; and so, perhaps, you'l think, when you've heard all."

Elinor's cheeks glowed at the allusion which his looks, even more than his words, conveyed to her situation, and Mrs. Clifford's generous interest in her behalf; but she felt somewhat comforted in the conviction that, whatever the housekeeper and her brother might think on the subject, it was certain they could not know the particulars of her history, and therefore could not even suspect the real extent to which their mistress's bounty had been carried.

The "all," however, that Mr. Pritchard had alluded to as having to communicate, seemed less to interest Mrs. Hargrave than that which personally concerned her mistress; and having by repeated questions, which he at last began to answer rather testily, ascertained that Mrs. Clifford ate, drank, slept, and took her usual exercise, as she had been accustomed to do, she turned her attention to Elinor, observing, that the poor child looked sadly jaded and fatigued, and, she dare say, did not look worse than she felt.

The significant shake of Mr. Pritchard's head brought tears into Elinor's eyes, and redoubled the earnestness with which Mrs. Hargrave gazed upon her. The old lady took off her spectacles, wiped them, and then put them on again; and shifted from her own easy chair, to one nearer to the object of her curiosity. A natural glow rushed into Elinor's cheeks, and she cast down her eyes in timid confusion, at the intenseness of this survey.

"Mercy on me, if the dead could come to life again!" murmured Mrs. Hargrave. "And I not to see it before! My poor lady, this must have been a surprise to her, to be sure. But, what a fool I am! Twenty years are past, and *she* is resting quietly in her grave; though——"

"What are you talking about, Peggy?" demanded Pritchard with amazement depicted in his broad, round, good-humoured face. "You are getting as fanciful as my lady herself, I think: what wonderful discoveries have you been making now?"

"None, none, none," returned his sister, in a tone of extreme agitation; "but I knew it could not escape Mrs. Clifford's keen eyes, and I do not wonder——but you have not told me yet, David," she added, in a low tone, "who this young lady is, not even her name."

"Young lady!" repeated the old man, looking up in surprise, and with a slight sarcastic expression. "Why, really then, Peggy, you must ask her herself all particulars, for—nay, stop; I forgot, I have a bit of a note here from my mistress to you, that—my stupid head, how could I forget it? but it's not to be wondered at, sent off at a minute's warning, and stuck up half the night, on the top of a coach, where I was afraid to fall asleep, lest I should tumble off my perch."

"Mercy! to forget a letter from my mistress!" observed the housekeeper, in a tone that showed she considered the omission an offence of the deepest dye, though she was too impatient to become mistress of the contents of the note to waste time in scolding at its delay.

It was in vain, however, that the spectacles were wiped and re-wiped, and that she held the writing in two or three different lights. It was plain that she could make out but little of its contents; and that what she could understand, had served doubly to stimulate her anxiety to become mistress of the rest.

"Dearee me!" she at length impatiently exclaimed; "I never saw Mrs. Clifford write such a cramp hand before. I can make out only that the young person's name is Elinor Clare. Clare, I never heard the name before. What part of the country was you born in, my dear?"

Elinor replied with that embarrassment which any inquiries respecting her birth never failed to produce, that she was not quite certain; she had reason to believe that she was born in a foreign country, but——

The spectacles were again taken off; not this time, however, to be wiped, but impatiently pushed away, together with the letter, still only half read, while Mrs. Hargrave returned to a perusal of Elinor's countenance, muttering at the same time,

"I would swear it was her very voice. Abroad, too: and she, they said, died abroad. But that can't be; twenty years must——do, my dear child, forgive my anxious questions," she continued, collecting herself; "tell me, is your father and mother living? Where did Mrs. Clifford—or how came she first to——"

"I rather think, Peggy," interrupted Pritchard, significantly, "that my lady wishes no questions to be asked; and I dare say they're not very pleasant ones to the young woman to answer. I never saw you so inquisitive before."

"Inquisitive!" repeated Mrs. Hargrave. "Lord! Davy Pritchard, how can you talk so? If you'd any eyes in your head you would see as well as me——but, perhaps you know all about it," she added, half offended; "and if so——"

"I know nothing at all, I tell you," returned Pritchard, vehemently; "nor do I want to know nothing. My maxim is, to obey my mistress's orders, without asking questions; and if she *have* tantrums in her head, that's not my business, nor your's either, I take it."

Mrs. Hargrave made no reply to this; she had returned to the attempt of deciphering Mrs. Clifford's letter; and having at length, as it seemed, made it out somewhat more to her satisfaction, again turned to gaze upon Elinor, in apparent deep abstraction.

"Had you not better see about giving orders for the young woman's room to be got ready? And, I take it, she'll want a change of clothes, Peggy," observed Pritchard. "I suppose you've found out, by this time, from the letter pretty well how she's sitivated."

"Ah dear, I am very remiss, to be sure," returned the old lady, rousing herself, and ringing the bell, which was immediately answered by a female domestic, to whom orders were given to light a fire, and make other preparations for the reception of Elinor, in one of the chambers, which the housekeeper designated as the Primrose room.

Pritchard laid down the knife and fork with which he was busily engaged on a cold sirloin of beef, to stare at his sister.

"Are you gone out of your senses, Peggy?" he observed. "You never can have rightly understood my lady's letter, or

she does not explain properly who the young woman is that
you're going to put in———"

"It's my maxim as well as yours, Davy Pritchard, to obey
Mrs. Clifford's orders, without questioning their propriety,"
returned his sister, with marked emphasis.

Pritchard uttered a low whistle, indicative of surprise; and
then, for the first time betraying any particular interest in his
late fellow-traveller, he turned himself round to survey diligently
Elinor's features.

"Well, don't you see now, David, the likeness?" demanded
Mrs. Hargrave, who had watched attentively the effect this
investigation had produced.

"Yes, but it's all chance, it must be chance," he returned, in
a dissatisfied tone. "You know, as well as me, that there can
be nothing in it; for she had not a relation in the world; and
the child was born dead; that, you know, I ascertained."

"Yes, I know you were satisfied at the time it was so,"
replied Mrs. Hargrave, with a sigh; "but you know, too, that
Mrs. Clifford has had doubts, and that———"

"Pshaw! stuff! I tell you there was no doubt. Didn't I see
the words myself on the tombstone, and copy them out because
they were French and I did not understand them? and did not
I get them translated before I sent them to my mistress, and
they meant the mother and her child—the full-blown rose and
and unopened bud? Pshaw! you've heard them a hundred times,
and now to pretend to doubt; I tell you it's all casualty. I've
seen as strong likenesses before, where there was no relationship,
and so it is now. I am only very sorry that it's happened to
come in Mrs. Clifford's way, to put fantastic notions in her head
again, that she had almost forgot."

Mrs. Hargrave was silent, but she was evidently by no means
convinced; and Elinor, as may be readily conceived, was in a
state of agitation, doubt, perplexity, hope, and fear, which
Pritchard's positive decision was far from allaying. Right glad,
indeed, did she feel when, having finished his hearty meal, the
old man rose, and declared his intention of going to his own bed,
to have what he called "a comfortable snooze," to make up for
his last night's privation.

Mrs. Hargrave, however, though evidently still preserving the
same interest towards her, did not seem inclined to enter into
any explanation, although Elinor was sufficiently unreserved on
all questions respecting her birth and early life, as far as her
recollection, and what she had been told, would allow her to

answer. On late events she was, of course, silent; for it was plain that Mrs. Clifford had been so; and what she had not chosen to speak of, Elinor did not feel herself called upon to reveal.

"Copeland—Copeland," repeated the old woman, when Elinor mentioned the name of her *soi-disant* uncle. "I do not recollect ever to have heard of such a person; and yet somehow——and his wife, you say, my dear, she is dead; but did you never hear who or what she was, or where she came from?"

"I have always understood," replied Elinor, "that Mr. Copeland and she were of the same family; were, in fact, first cousins, and, I suppose, of the same name."

"And she is dead, you say?"

Elinor assented.

"There is no hope, then, from that quarter," observed Mrs. Hargrave, reflectively; "had she been living, a sight of her would have been sufficient; for no time could have altered her so that I should not have known her. Can you describe her, my dear?"

Elinor did describe an exceedingly fair, light-haired, and light-eyed woman.

"What," she continued, "people in general consider very handsome, but in reality had no claims to be thought so, beyond a fair complexion and a showy figure."

"But tell me, my child," interposed Mrs. Hargrave, "had she not some distinguishing mark, by which——"

"Yes," returned Elinor, eagerly; "a large brown mole on her left cheek greatly disfigured——"

"It was she, her own very self," interrupted Mrs. Hargrave, triumphantly. "Will my brother say now that it is all casualty and chance, and talk of tantrums? Did you tell Mrs. Clifford all this, my child?"

Elinor replied in the negative; she had been too short a time with Mrs. Clifford, and the latter had been too much occupied with more pressing matters.

"But Mrs. Clifford intends to see Mr. Copeland," she continued; "and then, no doubt, he will be compelled to explain——"

"Heaven grant it!" exclaimed Mrs. Hargrave, emphatically. "It will be the means of restoring, I hope, peace to one who little deserved to suffer what she has done, and——but we'll hear all in good time, my child. It is not proper that I should speak of my mistress's secrets, or betray what she has thought proper to conceal."

Elinor's mind was busied with a thousand conjectures; but she felt that it was her duty to respect the delicacy which prevented Mrs. Hargrave from giving a full explanation of her strange mysterious hints, and, therefore, refrained from asking a single question, trusting that the time was not far distant, when she might hope to receive a full elucidation from the lips of Mrs. Clifford herself.

"Could it but once be proved," she reflected, "that I owed neither duty or gratitude to this man (Mr. Copeland), how would my heart be relieved! And yet I never did him harm, that I should wish this load of seeming obligation removed, and far less should I wish those ties broken which bind me to his children. No, even should all my suspicion prove correct—should it become as plain as it is now obscure, that I in reality, instead of being indebted to him, have to complain of the injuries he has done me, still Isabel and Annie Copeland will be as dear to me as sisters, and for their sakes I would pardon and forget every wrong I have suffered from their parents."

A week of suspense, conjecture, and uncertainty, passed away; yet it must be confessed that, anxious and earnest as Elinor felt on her own account, she thought far less and seldomer of what immediately concerned herself than of others. Mrs. Hatherleigh—Edward, where were they? and what had she done to deserve the treatment she had met with from them? Could they be so unjust as to distrust her?—to believe that any circumstances would so change her nature, as to render her deserving of distrust? The thought occupied her night and day; she would have given all her newborn hopes—all the comfort she enjoyed, or hoped to enjoy—every advantage, in fact, she possessed, or hoped to possess, to hear from their lips an explanation of their conduct, and to be able to vindicate herself, if they suspected her. And yet there were moments when natural pride prevailed over these feelings of affection and tenderness—when she felt that to those who suspected her without reason, it would be degrading herself to seek to vindicate herself.

"In the midst of suspicion, of accusation, of what appeared to the whole world overwhelming proof of guilt," she observed to herself, "I yet firmly believe—I do believe in Edward's entire innocence; yet I am condemned by him, without a shadow of proof against me—I am abandoned, merely because I have found a friend to whom they think it will be my interest to sacrifice them. Be it so; they may abandon me, but I shall ever remain the same. They may find others to supply my place in their hearts, but none will ever be to me as they have been."

During this long and tedious week, Elinor had confined herself entirely to the apartment which Mrs. Hargrave had assigned for her use. The old lady had, indeed, with evident pride in the magnificence of the establishment of which she was the ruler, prevailed on her once to visit the principal apartments; and had pointed out to her, not only the richness and splendour, but the rarity of much of the furniture and decorations.

Mrs. Clifford's father, she observed, had passed a great part of his life in India, and most of these articles had been brought from that country.

"Has Mrs. Clifford been married?" inquired Elinor. The housekeeper looked very grave, as she replied, "No."

"And was she an only child?" inquired Elinor, not from mere motives of curiosity, but merely because at that moment it occurred to her, that, with none of near kin to share so much luxury and wealth, how valueless it must appear!

"She was the only child by Mr. Clifford's second marriage," returned the housekeeper.

"Oh, yes, I recollect now," observed Elinor, "Lady Agnes calls her aunt; of course, therefore——"

"Lady Agnes is the child of Mr. Clifford's eldest daughter," returned Mrs. Hargrave; "but, of course, she is only half-sister to my mistress. It was my Mrs. Clifford's mother who brought the large fortune into the family. I will show you her picture, in my mistress's bed-room, presently."

The picture was shown, but it possessed nothing very interesting in Elinor's eyes; for there was nothing peculiar in it to distinguish it from any other common-place portrait of a rather well-looking but very insipid countenanced female. Mrs. Hargrave, however, did not forget to point out that the immense number of jewels with which every part of the person and dress were decorated, were all, to use her own expression, "drawn from the life," and were of inestimable value.

"They are all, too, still in the possession of my mistress," she observed, "and, perhaps, some day I may have the pleasure of showing them to you."

Elinor thanked her, with a smile; but she did not tell her what she was at that moment thinking—how little jewels could add to real beauty—for her eyes were at that moment fixed on a small half-length portrait of a young female, which hung near that of the stately dame whose decorations excited so much pride and admiration in the good housekeeper's mind. The young lady in question was clothed in a plain white dress, without a single ornament but those nature had bestowed on her; yet Elinor's eyes were rivetted to the face, which was one of the loveliest she had ever beheld.

"And is that, too, one of the family?" she asked.

"She was, and she was not," was the equivocal answer, given in a hurried tone. "Some day, perhaps, you may hear more about her; but that is as my mistress chooses. It is not for servants to talk of the secrets of families."

Elinor was silent; she felt that it would have been wrong for her to have asked another question; but she stole, as she followed Mrs. Hargrave, another look at the lovely portrait, which seemed to follow her with its sweet intelligent eyes.

"It can never be that that is a representation of her whom I am said so strongly to resemble?" she thought to herself, as she returned to her chamber. The next moment she blushed at her own vanity; and then again, the moment she was alone, she found herself at the looking-glass, comparing the colour of the eyes, the hair, the features, one by one, and feeling more and more convinced that it was, indeed, the original of that sweet portraiture whom she was said to resemble.

Who was she? and what was her history? There was a secret connected with it which Mrs. Hargrave had considered it improper to divulge. Mrs. Clifford's agitation, too; her broken exclamations on the occasion of their first meeting, returned with redoubled force to Elinor's recollection; and for hours after she was left alone, her thoughts remained engrossed solely by that one subject.

"Do you want anything more to night, my dear child?" inquired Mrs. Hargrave, who regularly waited upon Elinor herself, in spite of all her remonstrances, and never addressed her but in terms of the most respectful kindness. "I have got a bad cold," continued the old lady, "and so I am going to nurse myself, and go to bed early. David is gone to the play. I tell him he has grown quite a rake; but I only mention it, though, that you may not be surprised or alarmed, if you hear them stirring about below stairs later than usual. And now I'll wish you a very good night; it's a long time since I have been so poorly as to go to bed before my usual time; but I always recommend bed and a basin of gruel to others for a cold, and I should be a very bad physician to shrink from following my own prescriptions.

Elinor expressed with warmth and sincerity her hopes that she would find the remedy effective; and the old lady, again bidding her good night, departed.

Elinor took up a book. It was yet much to early to think of repose, even had not her mind been too much excited to bar the possibility of her finding it. But it was in vain she tried to interest herself in the pages of fiction, her thoughts still reverted to her own strange and eventful history; and still, though upon such slight grounds, as almost to bring a blush into her face at her own weakness, did she in idea connect with that history the image of the young female whose portrait had so excited her interest and her curiosity.

One by one, the sound of doors shutting, and the silence that succeeded, told her that the servants (of whom she understood there were a large number, though the mistress was absent,) were retired to their respective rooms. Pritchard, whose interference, though she knew not why, she feared more than that of any one else, was, she knew, absent: Mrs. Hargrave would not, of course, again quit her chamber; and, in short, there was nothing to prevent Elinor's indulging the inclination she felt to steal unobserved to Mrs. Clifford's apartment, and contemplate undisturbed the features which had so deeply interested her. Shading the candle with her hand, she lightly crossed the gallery, and entered the chamber in which hung the valued portrait; but, at the very moment she softly closed the door after her, lest, if by accident any one still remained up, her light might be observed, she was startled by a loud knocking at the street-door, which was, she heard, immediately opened.

"It is Mr. Pritchard returned," she thought to herself, after a moment's reflection. "Well, there is no fear of his coming here, I dare say; and I can but wait quietly till he goes to his room, I am sure to hear his heavy foot pass; and then I can hide the light, so that he shall not see it."

Many minutes passed, however, and she heard nothing of the heavy step, to the sound of which she had become accustomed, from its regularly passing her apartment night and morning. Once or twice a faint murmur of voices from below reached her ear, but she paid little attention to anything but the lovely semblance of those sweet and innocent features which seemed to smile upon her, and before which she stood, as it were, entranced. Suddenly a light footstep was heard, the door of the chamber opened. Elinor hastily blew out the slender wax taper she held in her hand; but the precaution was useless. Two persons entered the room; and to her extreme astonishment, she beheld Mrs. Clifford, and her attendant, Mrs. Burchall, the latter carrying a candle, the light of which fell full on the pale face of the embarrassed occupant of the chamber.

"Merciful Heaven!" exclaimed Mrs. Clifford, sinking on a chair, while Mrs. Burchall uttered a succession of screams, which soon had the effect of rousing the sleeping inmates of the house; and Elinor in vain attempted to prevent them, by trying to explain the cause of her being there.

Whatever might have been the source of the agitation the lady had at first betrayed, it was plain Elinor's voice and expressions of sorrow at having alarmed her had soon the effect of restoring her self-possession, though her looks still betrayed agitation and astonishment.

"You have completely defeated my intention of remaining here quietly till the morning," she observed to Elinor; "and you, Burchall, ought to have known better than to make such a disturbance, because a simple girl chooses to wander about the house at midnight, instead of being in her bed. But go to Hargrave—the noise, of course, has reached her—and tell her I positively forbid her to get up. I will come to her presently, for it is useless to think of sleeping here to-night. And, do you hear, Burchall, send all those gaping, frightened maids to bed again directly."

She closed the door as she finished speaking; and then, reseating herself in the chair which was exactly opposite the portrait, she took Elinor's cold and trembling hand, and drew her close to her.

"Now tell me the truth," she said, pointing with the other hand to the picture, "what do you know of that portrait?"

"Nothing, madam," returned Elinor, earnestly. "Mrs. Hargrave brought me here, this afternoon, to show me another," pointing to the one over the fire-place; "and I then saw this, which——"

"You know resembles yourself," observed Mrs. Clifford, seeing that she hesitated. "So far you are correct; but do you know nothing of the history of her whose likeness you behold there? Tell me, have you not been sent to me by some one who is aware——Elinor, if your name be Elinor, do not fear to speak the truth to me. Oh, that she whom I loved with more than a sister's love," and she fixed her eyes again on the portrait, "that she had spoken but the truth!—that she had but done mo justice, and trusted to the love I bore her, instead of making me the victim of a cruel, heartless deception!—instead of leaving me to the scorn of the world! *That* I have never forgiven her. All else might be pardoned—would have been pardoned. Yes, my heart might have broken in the effort; but I would have looked smilingly on their happiness, and none but they should have known that I was despised and rejected."

Tears stole down Elinor's cheeks, as she listened to this involuntary ebullition of passion, from one whose generally cold and austere manners would have indicated her utter freedom from the sensitive feelings which now shook her whole frame to agony. But Mrs. Clifford saw not the sympathy she had excited, her eyes were still fixed on the picture; and she had sunk into a reverie, in which the past only was contemplated, the present obliterated from her thoughts.

A slight involuntary motion on the part of Elinor, whose hand she still held in hers, recalled Mrs. Clifford to recollection; and she turned her penetrating eyes full on the face of the former.

" Well, child," she observed, trying to resume her usual cold tone of conscious superiority, "you have not yet fully explained your motives for being here, at this unseasonable hour of the night. Was it really only the desire of again contemplating a resemblance which is certainly attractive enough to make you vain? I do not want you, Mrs. Burchall; I thought you understood me sufficiently, to prevent your returning until you were sent for."

Mrs. Burchall started at the angry tone in which this was uttered.

" I only came to tell you, ma'am, that Mrs. Hargrave is so sorry that——"

" I know all about that," interrupted Mrs. Clifford; "now go and see if you can get some chocolate made, and send it up; and tell Robert to go round to the stables, and desire the carriage to be here in two hours, instead of six o'clock. The sooner we are on the road, the better."

Mrs. Burchall was sufficiently acquainted with her mistress's temper not to offer a word of remonstrance, though her looks betrayed her dissatisfaction of this new arrangement; and once more Elinor was left alone with Mrs. Clifford.

" I almost forget what you said, child," observed the latter, drawing her hand across her brow; "but I think you still disavow that you are in any way connected with the original of that portrait?"

"I could almost be bold enough to say, that I wish I were, madam," returned Elinor, warmly, "since it is plain I should then have a claim upon your affection, instead of being the mere object of your bounty."

"Affection!" repeated Mrs. Clifford, with bitterness, "girl, you know not what you say. But I am convinced, now," she added, "that you are indeed ignorant of the circumstances which have poisoned my existence. You could not talk of affection from me—you could not have the hardihood to look me in the face—Pshaw! what folly is this, to be led away by an imaginary likeness! You have disclaimed all knowledge, all connection with her—with Anna Warwick; tell me, did you never hear that name?"

"Never, madam, I assure you," returned Elinor, with firmness.

"I forgot—probably she bore another name," continued Mrs. Clifford, with a sneer. "You may have heard of her, perhaps, as Mrs. Blandford."

"My mother's name, madam," returned Elinor, mildly, "I have already told you I have always understood to have been Copeland before her marriage; and I have been taught to call myself Elinor Clare. It is, therefore, very unlikely I should know anything of the names you mention."

"You are right, child, and I am wrong," observed Mrs. Clifford, rising from her seat, and walking across the chamber, as if to shake off the effects of the violent agitation which for a time had seemed totally to have changed her nature. In a few minutes she returned to Elinor, with seeming calmness.

"I ought to have told you, long before this, child, that circumstances render it necessary that you should leave this place. I am about to depart immediately, for perhaps, a long sojourn in foreign countries. Do you object to accompany me?"

"Object, madam!" repeated Elinor, "oh, I shall be but too happy, too honoured—oh, can it be possible that you indeed——"

"There, we will not waste time in useless raptures," interrupted Mrs. Clifford. "You have not much preparation to make, of course; but you had better now go to your room. Stay, here is Burchall with chocolate; you will take some, for it will be many hours before we breakfast."

Elinor's raptures, as her benefactress had called her surprise and gratitude at the favour intended her, had now given place to painful and melancholy reflection. She was then going to quit England, without seeing Edward Hatherleigh—without the slightest knowledge of his fate—with the certainty that a heavy charge was impending over him, from which it might be impossible for him to clear himself. How could she know that even at this moment he was safe? and, even if for the present he escaped the rancorous and determined persecution of Mr. Copeland——

A faint shudder shook her whole frame, and involuntarily a low exclamation of terror broke from her lips, as her imagination presented to her Edward in prison, sinking beneath the anguish of unmerited ignominy, and perhaps even worse, oh, far worse!

"What is the matter with you, child?" demanded Mrs Clifford, whose thoughtful eyes had been fixed on her countenance and had seen the alteration that had taken place.

Tears almost choked Elinor's voice, as she replied, that she was thinking of friends whom she should perhaps never behold again.

"Friends!" repeated Mrs. Clifford, sharply; "I thought that you professed to be friendless. I do not mean to hurt your feelings; but who do you, or will you leave behind you, deserving that name? Not, certainly, your uncle or his daughters, if he be your uncle."

"You have seen him, then, madam?" observed Elinor, her looks expressing surprise and curiosity.

"No, I have not seen him, Elinor," she replied; "he refused, harshly and insolently, to see *me*. I was foolish enough," she continued, "to avow to his daughter my desire to learn some particulars respecting you. He was ill, or, at least, it was said, too ill to see strangers. I thought it was possible I might gain some information from his daughter—Isabel, I think you called her; but she was either too guarded to betray what she knew, or she really knew nothing about you."

"The last was the truth," observed Elinor. "Isabel is anything but guarded—anything but cautious."

"It may be so," returned Mrs. Clifford; "but, at any rate, she was conscious that there was something to conceal, and conscious, too, that her father was guilty of cruelty and injustice, when she repeated to me his determination of pursuing you. Yes, child, it is as well, perhaps, that you should know the little cause you have to regret quitting England, since the fact is, you cannot remain in it without being exposed to the greatest danger from the malice of that man. I have promised to protect you, and I will keep my word. As yet, I believe and hope that your place of refuge is undiscovered; and before to-morrow night, you will, I trust, be beyond the reach of pursuit.

Elinor could only reply to this by tears—tears of gratitude for the disinterested benevolence which thus snatched her from impending danger, and of agony at the unmerited persecution which she endured from those to whom only, as it appeared, she had a right to look for protection. Yet, not for herself alone were Elinor's tears shed. If Mr. Copeland was thus implacable towards her, who he must know to be innocent, what must be his feelings and intentions towards one whom he certainly believed guilty?

"Oh, that Edward, too, could fly beyond the reach of his power!" she fervently ejaculated to herself, as she entered, for the last time, the apartment which she had been allowed to call her own, "that some powerful and beneficent hand could be stretched forth to save him, or some kind interposition of Providence would bring the truth to light, and enable him to establish his innocence!"

Few as were the preparations necessary for her departure, Elinor had scarcely completed them before Mrs. Burchall knocked at the door to say that Mrs. Clifford waited for her; and suppressing, as far as possible, all traces of agitation, lest it might be construed into an ungrateful reluctance to comply with the wishes of her benefactress, she followed the ungracious and supercilious waiting-maid to the apartment of her mistress.

Mrs. Clifford was now cool, composed; and, in short, appeared quite a different person to what Elinor had recently beheld her. She glanced her eyes over the figure of the latter, and then observed,

"You are but poorly provided for travelling, or a sea-voyage. Burchall, have you not a cloak to wrap round her?"

"Dear me, ma'am, everything in the world is packed," returned Mrs. Burchall; "and it would take an hour to get at them. I'm sure, for one that's been used to all weathers, as you may say, I should think a large shawl like that——"

"I did not ask for your opinion," interrupted Mrs. Clifford; "but, no matter, she can have this—the pelisse and shawl will e sufficient for me."

Mrs. Burchall commenced a very warm remonstrance against her mistress exposing herself to the cold morning air, she that was always so delicate; but the lady paid no attention to it; and Elinor, though with reluctance, proceeded to envelope herself in the cloak, which completely covered her from head to foot.

ELINOR CLARE.

"WAS THE WRONG MERELY IMAGINARY?" DEMANDED MRS. CLIFFORD.

"Throw this veil over your bonnet, and gather it close about your face, child," observed Mrs. Clifford, taking the article in question from her own head; while Mrs. Burchall, unobserved except by Elinor, held up her hands and raised her eyes in anger and astonishment at what she, no doubt, considered the very foolish and unbecoming condescension of her mistress.

"Aye, that will do," observed Mrs. Clifford, looking at Elinor with satisfaction; "I do not think it possible, now, that you should be recognised, even if we should be so unlucky as to meet with any one that—— Do not alarm yourself, my good girl; and, above all, do not betray to my servants——"

Mrs. Burchall, who had gone into the adjoining room, at this moment returned ; and Mrs. Clifford suddenly stopped.

"Are we all ready now, Burchall ?" she demanded.

The waiting-maid replied in the affirmative ; and Mrs. Clifford, taking the arm of the trembling Elinor, led her down stairs.

It was not until this moment that the latter felt fully impressed with the danger of her situation. Under the protection of Mrs. Clifford, she had fancied that she must be safe ; but when the latter seemed to think disguise and concealment necessary, a full sense of the perils which surrounded her forced itself upon her mind, and made her shrink with terror from even quitting the house which had afforded her its friendly asylum.

The morning was cold and damp, and the grey light was scarcely sufficient to afford a distinct view of surrounding objects, yet Elinor, as she stood on the steps of the mansion, while Mrs. Clifford seated herself in the carriage, cast a fearful look around her, as if dreading that she might be even now intercepted.   Not a living creature, however, appeared in sight ; and in another moment she would have been seated securely by the side of her protectress, but Mrs. Burchall discovered that a valuable parcel, which should have been put in the seat of the carriage, had been left out ; and at her petulant, " You must wait a bit, if you please," she again shrank back under the portico ; and in an instant after, a man, who must have been hidden in the shadow of some of the neighbouring houses, walked hastily past, and threw an inquiring glance into the carriage.

" Who is that ?—the watchman ?" demanded Mrs. Clifford, leaning from the window of the coach, to look after him, and speaking in an uneasy and doubtful tone of voice, which sufficiently betrayed her suspicions.

Elinor's first emotions were those of terror and affright. Unable to move, or to comprehend what was said to her, she stood fixed as a statue, expecting that the man would return and seize upon her as his prisoner ; but as he still went on, and she could hear the sound of his retreating footsteps, she ventured to cast a look in the direction he had taken ; and then another not less agitating and afflictive thought rushed into her mind.   The large rough coat, with many capes, the height, the light active gait, and, in short, the *toute-ensemble* of the whole figure, so strongly resembled that of her mysterious fellow-traveller in the mail-coach, that she could scarcely doubt that it was the same person. And now more than ever was she convinced that it was Edward Hatherleigh himself; and that she should again behold him without being able to utter one word of explanation, without even saying farewell, or assuring him that though her prospects were changed, her heart remained, and ever would remain the same, was a grief exceeding for the moment all others.

"Do you hear, Miss What's-your-name ?" exclaimed the sharp shrill voice of Mrs. Burchall in her ear; " my mistress is waiting for you."

Elinor started, and took her seat by the side of Mrs. Clifford, who seized an opportunity to whisper, while Mrs. Burchall was giving some directions to one of the servants,

"You need not alarm yourself, Elinor; if the man's object had been what you feared, he would not have delayed for an instant."

Elinor was silent. She dared not confess the truth, that it was less fear than regret and disappointment that agitated her; for she remembered how strong had appeared Mrs. Clifford's prejudice against Edward; and she feared again to hear from her lips observations so painful, and, she was convinced, so unjust.

The carriage rattled on through the now quiet and deserted streets of the metropolis. From time to time Elinor cast a hasty and inquiring glance, as some solitary being was seen loitering along the pavement, but none resembled him she sought,—

"Except," her heart whispered, " that he too is, perhaps, like those wretched-looking beings, houseless, friendless, and compelled to shrink from the face of day."

The sun broke gloriously from the thick mantle of clouds that had obscured its majesty. The travellers were just crossing Westminster Bridge, and Mrs. Clifford leaned from the carriage-window, to look back at the lovely effect of its golden rays lighting up with splendour the noble towers of the abbey.

"This is a good omen for our journey, I trust, Elinor," she observed; " a few moments ago, all looked cold and gloomy and desolate, and now see how changed the scene appears! And so it will be with many, I trust, whose prospects now look cheerless and clouded, but who still struggle on, in spite of fate, determined to keep the right path."

"Heaven grant it!—Heaven in its mercy grant it!" responded Elinor, fervently. But she thought not at that moment of herself—she paused not to reflect to whom Mrs. Clifford considered the observation applicable. There was one only present to her mind to whom it could be applied; need it be said that it was Edward Hatherleigh for whom that ardent prayer was uttered?

CHAPTER XIII.

"Look not mournfully into the past. It comes not back again. Wisely improve the present. It is thine. Go forth to meet the shadowy Future without fear, and with a manly heart."

ANON.

MONTHS had rolled away without a single incident to renew in Elinor's mind the sense of danger which had pursued her, until the waves rolling between her and the white cliffs of her native land seemed to place an insuperable barrier to the pursuit of her implacable enemy, Mr. Copeland.

It was not, indeed, until she herself felt that her *protégée* was removed beyond fear of pursuit that Mrs. Clifford revealed to Elinor the circumstances which had combined to induce her (Mrs. Clifford) to take the sudden and decisive resolution of quitting England. Not only, it appeared, had Mr. Copeland avowed his determination to show no mercy to Elinor, if he discovered her retreat, but he had insolently and unwarrantably threatened punishment to all who should shelter her.

"I saw," observed Mrs. Clifford, "that, although his daughter spoke with the bitterest acrimony of your obstinate adherence to the supposed murderer of her brother, she was yet desirous of preventing your falling into the hands of her father, and anxious to soften as much as possible the threats he held out to all that had or should espouse your case.

"'Yet I cannot but, for your sake,' she observed, 'caution you, madam, that my father is most inveterate and violent on this subject. You know best, I dare say, whether he has it in his power to do all he threatens; but, at any rate, I am convinced he will spare no means to get Elinor into his power, as the only means of discovering the retreat of that wretch——' Do not look so indignant, child; I am only repeating her words; and whatever your own opinion——"

"My conviction !" exclaimed Elinor, vehemently, " Edward is innocent—as innocent as I am myself; and she knows it—she ought to know it—she does know it, but that she is blinded by passion and prejudice. And if her vindictive wishes, and those of her father, were to be accomplished; were Edward to fall into their power—to become, as many others have done, the victim of circumstances; were he, I say, to be condemned on the evidence that they have so anxiously accumulated against him, none would so bitterly rue it as Isabel. Oh yes, well I know and feel that, when too late, she would give the whole world to recal what she had done."

" She loves him, then, and he has slighted her ?" exclaimed Mrs. Clifford, in a deep tone, and grasping Elinor's arm with a force that was absolulely painful. " Yes, and he has dissembled; and, while he pretended love to her, he has breathed his secret vows of passion in your ear, and laughed at the fool he has made. I do not blame her, she has fair cause for revenge ; and though she may afterwards repent——"

" You are mistaken, indeed, madam," interrupted Elinor, half frightened at Mrs. Clifford's vehemence, and yet feeling that she had thus unconsciously become possessed of the secret of her life; "you are mistaken, indeed. Edward was incapable of deception. We grew up together from children ; he was to all of us as a beloved brother; and he thought of us—of me, and Isabel, and Annie, as sisters. Walter, poor Walter, was more than a brother to him; for never did a brother so indulge the wayward temper, so mildly counsel and guide, one who was superior to him in age and bodily strength, but far, far his inferior in the gifts of mind and heart. Walter, nurtured in indulgence, was impetuous, headstrong, and (I must speak the truth) selfish. Edward, the child of misfortune from his birth, was mild, reflective, and, if it were possible to be so, to a fault disinterested and indulgent to the wishes of others."

" Yes, till they crossed his love," interrupted Mrs. Clifford, looking earnestly in Elinor's blushing face. " If I read aright, that was the test before which friendship and affection all withered away."

" It was the cause that, for a brief time, dissevered the ties between them," returned Elinor, in a low and melancholy tone. " Walter imagined himself injured, and——"

" Was the wrong merely imaginary ?" demanded Mrs. Clifford, hastily.

" Yes," replied Elinor, firmly; " for I was not a puppet, who was to have no voice in the affair. Walter scarcely knew his own wishes, until he discovered that Edward and I were mutually attached. I can solemnly assert, that never had he uttered a word to me which he might not with equal propriety have addressed to his sisters, until the suspicion of Edward's preference aroused his passions; and even had it been otherwise, he would have had no right to complain, for in the words of an old song, of which he was very fond, I might have said,

> "' My heart's my own, my hand is free,
> And so shall be my choice.'

I never, never misled him," she continued, with increased emotion, "from the first moment that he opened his heart to me, I told him that I never could think of him but as a brother; and the persecution I afterwards underwent on the subject did not alter my sentiments or my behaviour towards him."

"And this Isabel—this rejected fair one—whose black eyes seemed to dart fire, as she spoke of the wretch, as she termed him, how did she bear the discovery that you were preferred to her?"

"Isabel too strongly resembled her brother to bear any disappointment with patience," returned Elinor, calmly; "but she was also too proud even to confess her disappointment. It was only by her actions, by the violence of her indignation against Edward, by the bitterness with which she has urged on the persecution against him, that she has betrayed herself; but, as I have said, her revenge, should it ever be consummated, will recoil on her own head, and she will weep tears of blood for the victim of her unjust and blind passion."

Mrs. Clifford's lip quivered, and her features appeared almost convulsed.

"You are right, child, you are right," she uttered, "such will ever be the feelings of those who pursue revenge against the conviction of their heart and reason. Such have been my feelings for years, Elinor. Nay, do not start," she added, with a faint smile, "I have not hunted my faithless lover to death; but—but—no matter, some day you may know the story; and then, perhaps, you will hate me for my resemblance to your unjust and ungovernable Isabel."

"I do not hate her," returned Elinor, warmly. "Oh, no! Heaven forbid that I should feel anything towards her but pity and affection; and to you, madam, what can I ever feel but——"

"Not pity at any rate," interrupted Mrs. Clifford, with a forced smile; "but come, let us speak of this young man—this Edward Hatherleigh, who, it seems, was fortunate enough to be beloved by both you and the black-eyed Isabel."

"Rather say unfortunate, madam," returned Elinor, with a sigh; "since from that circumstance has arisen the greater part of the evils that have befallen him. Had not Isabel loved him, she would never have persecuted him; and without her to inflame and direct his suspicions, Mr. Copeland would, I am certain, never have fixed upon Edward Hatherleigh as the murderer of his son. Oh, how often, even now, am I tempted to doubt the reality of all that has passed, and think it a frightful dream, from which I shall some time awaken."

"And you know not, I think you have told me, what has become of the young man, or what course he intended to pursue at the time you parted with him?" observed Mrs. Clifford.

"I do not think he knew at that time himself," returned Elinor. "He appears to be completely under the dominion and guidance of the mysterious being whom he calls his father; and it was his desire and command, conveyed through the means of that strange lad whom you beheld with me, that he quitted me, leaving me to his guidance."

"A strange guide, indeed," observed Mrs. Clifford; "but now tell me candidly, Elinor, have you never seen or heard from young Hatherleigh since?"

Elinor looked, as she felt, astonished at the question; but she replied with sincerity, by detailing her suspicions of his having been her fellow-traveller by the mail-coach that had taken her to London, as well as her belief that she had beheld him on the morning of her departure from thence.

"You are right, child, I dare say," exclaimed Mrs. Clifford, who had listened to her with earnest attention. "And now I will tell you—for your openness deserves equal candour from me—that I, too, saw and conversed with him, an hour or two previous to your departure from the Hermitage. Perhaps I did not then do him full justice for his disinterestedness; but I will relate what then occurred, as well as what I have since learned respecting him. I had scarcely left you with Burchall, on that day when you were so strangely introduced to my notice, when I was informed, by one of my own servants, that there was a young man in the hall, who insisted upon seeing you; and that Sir Stanley Egerton, who had accidentally heard the demand, had taken upon himself to speak to the stranger, and ask questions which had been so unceremoniously repulsed on the part of the stranger, as to be likely to lead to a quarrel."

"'The people are all whispering, ma'am, that the man is one of a desperate gang of gipsies that have been committing shocking offences in the neighbourhood,' observed the servant; 'for my part, I think he looks too much of the gentleman; but as they say, they can disguise themselves in all manner of shapes.'

"I waited not to hear any more," continued Mrs. Clifford; "for I was struck with the probability that I had brought danger upon the household by my imprudence in so hastily following the impulse of my feelings towards you; and I, therefore, ran to the scene of contention, and there, indeed, beheld a tall young man, whose appearance certainly was, as Thomas had asserted, very superior to the tribe to which it was said he belonged; though his olive complexion and glowing black eyes, which were darting fire at Sir Stanley at the moment I entered the hall, might have excused the supposition.

" 'Who are you that question my right?' he fiercely demanded. 'Does she authorise you to refuse me? Let me see her, and hear it from her own mouth, and I will instantly go; but without that you shall tear me piecemeal before I will move.'

" 'There is no occasion for all this violence, young man,' I observed, hastily interposing. 'Pray, Sir Stanley,' I continued, 'go to Lady Agnes, and prevent the alarm she will feel should it reach her that you are——'

"He vanished before I could finish the sentence, for he well knew what I intended to convey by it; and I then, opening the door of one of the parlours, invited the young man to enter, and explain his business to me.

"The coolness and firmness which, I own to you, I assumed rather than felt, for I acknowledge I was rather alarmed at first, they had, however, I say, their due effect; and before the door was well closed that separated us from the host of curious servants, the fire had all faded from his eye, and he looked the very personation of melancholy and despair.

" 'Are you a friend of the young person you demand to see?' I asked.

" 'Yes, madam; almost, I may say, her only friend,' he replied, with emotion: 'unless, indeed——'

"He paused, and looked earnestly in my face.

" 'I understand you,' I observed: 'unless I will be her friend.'

"He bowed; and that, too, in a manner that convinced me that the promise his face and person held out was not deceptive, but that he had indeed been used to the gentler courtesies of life.

" 'I will tell you, then, that I am fully disposed to be so;

that I am determined, indeed, to protect her from every danger. I have heard her story, or, at least, so much of it as accounts for her present destitute situation; and my resolution is taken to save her, if it be possible. If, therefore, you are really her friend, you will not, I think, attempt to withdraw her from my protection, to plunge her again into——'

"'Heaven forbid!' he fervently exclaimed. 'Oh, no, madam, to you I willingly resign her; for, though I know you not even by name——'

"'My name is Clifford,' I replied, observing he hesitated; 'and for my character,' I continued, 'I do not wish you to take it from my own lips. If, however, you are not perfectly satisfied that the young woman will be in safe keeping, at least as safe as any you can entrust her to——'

"'Do not mock me, madam,' he observed, in a tone that went to my heart, determined as I was to suspect and distrust him. 'It has been my misfortune, not my fault,' he continued, his face crimsoning as he spoke, 'that I have been the means of bringing upon her innocent head evils that, had she not been what she is, would have overwhelmed her quite, or have tempted her to have done what almost any other woman would—to have deserted and given me up to my fate.'

"'The women are much obliged to you for your opinion of them, young man,' I observed; 'but let me now suggest to you, that henceforth it *will* be your fault, if you involve her in further evils. I will tell you candidly,' I continued, 'that I cannot consent to her maintaining any correspondence with you, until you are cleared from the dreadful imputation that now lies upon your name. I do not wish her to renounce you, nor do I call upon you for any sacrifice that I am sure, if you love and respect her, you will not be willing to make; but, while she is under my protection, she can—she must not have communication with——'

"'A proscribed felon—that is the term you hesitate to utter, madam, is it not?' he exclaimed, his eyes darting fire, and his whole frame shaking with the violence of his emotion.

"'You are too hasty, young man,' I replied, gravely—'the term would be only applicable were you proved guilty of the crime imputed to you. I hope and trust that you are innocent.'

"He hid his face with his hands, and burst into tears.

"I confess to you, Elinor, I was at a loss how to interpret these tears. Were they those of compunction for his guilt? Could it be possible that one so young, so apparently gifted, had been guilty of so barbarous and treacherous a crime?

"I do not know whether he read in my silence and evident uneasiness these thoughts, but he presently raised his head, and shook off his tears.

"'Do not judge me wrongfully, madam, that I am thus affected by the voice of kindness. With the exception of my mother and Elinor, there is not, perhaps, another human being besides yourself who does not believe me guilty. Yet I *am* innocent,' and he raised himself proudly, as if to look defiance to all who should dare assert the contrary—'I am innocent of having even in thought injured any mortal being. It would have been easy,' he continued, in an earnest tone, 'for me to have proved that I was far distant from the spot at the time of the fatal deed; but in so doing I must have involved the safety of another, and I preferred to suffer myself.'

"'But there is a duty to yourself, as well as those who love you,' I observed, 'that should induce you to——'

"'Do not try to shake my resolution, madam. It is taken; and I must abide the consequences. Tell me now, what is it you require as the price of your protection to Elinor?'

"'Only that you shall refrain from all communication with her until the mystery is cleared up, and you are pronounced innocent,' I replied.

"'That may be never,' he murmured; 'but what you ask is but reasonable,' he continued, aloud. "Promise me only that you will not attempt to shake her affection for me—that you will not seek to influence her in favour of any other, and I will solemnly swear——'

"'I require no oaths,' I observed; 'give me only your simple promise, as I give you mine that I will religiously observe your conditions, and I will trust to your keeping mine.'

"'I do promise, then,' he replied; 'and Elinor shall be a stranger to me, until even you shall acknowledge that I may claim her without bringing disgrace upon her.'

"'Be it so,' I replied; 'but, remember also, that there must be no equivocation—no indirect means employed of evading the strictness of our treaty. Your mother——'

"'My mother,' he interrupted, his face glowing with proud resentment, 'would scorn to seek an intercourse where her son is forbidden and despised.'

"'Not despised,' I replied, for I was really sorry," observed Mrs. Clifford, "to be compelled to inflict so severe a wound upon his self-love—'not despised, young man. It is prudence only, and a regard for the interests of the young person to whom I have promised my protection, that induces me to exact this sacrifice. The time will come, I hope, when you will both thank me for my precaution, and acknowledge that I was right.'

"He bowed his head in acquiescence," she continued, "but I could see that his pride was bitterly wounded; and I was very glad to put an end to the interview, having first made him an offer of pecuniary assistance, which I was, I confess, not at all surprised at his refusing; for there was altogether an air of romantic independence about him that made it but consistent that he should spurn the offer of money. I could not but think, however, that there was a sad struggle between his spirit and his necessities, when he rejected it; and I did not like that he should leave me without having anything to remember me for but what must give him pain; I therefore called him back after he had bade me farewell.

"'You are too resentful against me, young man,' I observed, 'to gratify me by showing that you can consider me as a friend, and accepting the only means by which I can at present prove that I am guided by friendly motives towards you; but you have a mother, whom, from all I have heard, you love. Can you in conscience reject that which will enable you to add to her comforts, which, I fear, are at present but very few? I do not offer you this as a gift to humble you,' I added, as I saw he wavered, 'but as a loan, which I shall expect you will repay, whenever fortune favours you so far that you can spare it without inconvenience,'

"'On these terms, then, madam, I accept it,' he replied. 'For my mother's sake,' he added, in a tone of deep dejection, 'I have already stooped much lower than I do now, in receiving what is offered in such a spirit.'

"I will tell you candidly, Elinor," added Mrs. Clifford, "that I doubled the sum I at first intended to offer; and it was to me a proof of his sincerity and proper feeling, that he expressed no surprise at the sum, which to you I may say was not a trifling one. He merely remarked, with glistening eyes,

"'This will, I trust, enable me to provide for my mother more than present comforts; and, perhaps, eventually, not only to repay you, madam, but to prove to you that I am not wholly undeserving your kindness.'

"I have nothing more to add, Elinor," concluded Mrs. Clifford. "We parted; and, I confess, on my side, and I hope on his, with better feelings than we met."

Elinor had listened with breathless attention, and with various emotions. There was nothing to complain of in Mrs. Clifford's conduct. On the contrary, she had acted generously, nobly, by one who to most would have appeared an object of suspicion and condemnation, rather than of compassion, and, in some measure, respect; and yet she felt that she (Mrs. Clifford) had not done him full justice. She had seemingly regarded him as a foolish, romantic boy, who was to be pitied rather than respected. In Elinor's eyes he was the most injured and exalted of human beings; and yet even she did not know how great were the sacrifices he had made to what he considered his duty.

"But you have seen him since, have you not, madam?" she demanded, suddenly recollecting herself.

"Yes; it was he who induced me to take this sudden journey," replied Mrs. Clifford. "You look astonished; it is nevertheless true. I have already told you of my bootless visit to Mr. Copeland. The threats he held out, not only against you, but all who harboured you, vexed and irritated, but did not make me uneasy. I was foolish enough to think that my character and situation in life was a sufficient protection for myself; and as to you, I thought it scarcely within the pale of probability that it should be discovered where you had found an asylum. But I was speedily awakened from this imaginary security. On the very evening of the day that I had seen Isabel Copeland, a note was delivered to me, to the effect that a person who wished to give some important information was waiting to see me in the great avenue of the park. The concluding words were, as nearly as I can recollect—

"'Mrs. Clifford will know who the person is who dares not append his name to this, lest it should fall into hands less friendly than hers, who has already proved her confidence in the writer, and will not, he trusts, hesitate to add this additional proof, by trusting herself to a few minutes of conference.'

"I was not long," she observed, "before I fixed upon young Hatherleigh as the writer, and instantly decided on giving him the required meeting. To 'make assurance doubly sure,' however, I inquired of the servant who delivered the letter to me what sort of person it was who brought it.

"'It was a wretched-looking boy, who looks hardly like a human being, madam,' was the reply. 'But though he pretends to be a fool,' he continued, 'he has got plenty of cunning, and can keep a secret as close as a lawyer. The servants, who are always in mischief, and glad to lay hold of anything for fun, got him into the hall, and gave him plenty to eat and drink; and there I left him, playing as many antics as a monkey. But though he'd do anything to oblige them, they could not get a word out of him, either as to where or who he came from, whether he expected an answer, or, if he got it, where he was to take it.'

" 'A prudent messenger, indeed,' I replied, 'and ought to be rewarded accordingly; but, really, I am infinitely obliged by the interest that it appears is taken in my affairs. If, however, the good folks below have finished their interrogations, I shall be glad to ask the messenger a few questions myself.'

" In consequence of this, in a few minutes, as I expected from the description, the boy—who was your companion, Elinor, when I first beheld you, and whom I recollected you called Zekiel—was ushered into the room. I will tell the truth. When I had formerly seen him, on the occasion alluded to, I had been so entirely occupied with you, that I paid little attention to your companion, whom, indeed, I only saw for a brief minute. You, who know him well, of course, therefore, will not be surprised at my saying that I was completely startled at his wild, unearthly appearance, though I attempted to disguise it and assume an air of indifference.

" 'Well Zekiel,' I observed, 'where is the person who sent me this letter?'

" He looked earnestly at me, with his cunning black eyes, and then laughed.

" 'What a fool he must be that wrote the letter,' he observed, ' if he wanted you to know that and did not put it down.'

" 'You will not tell me, then?' I observed.

" He shook his head, and then turned away, to examine the furniture of the apartment, glancing over everything with a look of mingled surprise and contempt.

" 'Did you ever see any place so handsome before, Zekiel?' I demanded, anxious to hear his opinion.

" 'Yes, a great deal handsomer,' he replied with earnestness.

" 'Where?' I inquired.

" 'The fields,' he replied, 'when the grass is green beneath your feet, and the heaven blue above, and the flowers blooming in the hedges; and the woods and forests, too, when the trees are thick with leaves and blossoms, and birds are singing in their branches, and squirrels hopping from spray to spray, and the golden sun darting down here and there upon the green moss, and making the old brown trunks shine like copper, and sometimes bits of blue sky showing overhead, and white clouds flying along—oh, you that are shut up in these rooms, looking all day at such dull things as these, know nothing of what is grand and beautiful! You lie in your beds, with curtains round you, and all as dark as the grave, and call it rest; but come and lie one night in our tents, where you can look up and see the beautiful moon riding among billowy clouds, like a noble ship among the white waves, or sitting in the clear dark spangled sky, like a queen upon her throne, and the stars waiting upon her like her handmaids. Come and see all this, I say, and you'll never again call such dreary places as this handsome.'

"'But these sentiments are not your own, boy,' I replied, 'you have been taught this lesson.'

"'We are all taught it,' he returned, seriously; 'we begin to learn it as soon as, we are born, we suck it in with our mother's milk, and as Paul Dangerfield says, even if we live to the full age of man, and that is threescore and ten, though there's some of our people live many years longer than that——"

"'And who is Paul Dangerfield, pray?' I interrupted.

"He smiled contemptuously.

"'You'd be a wiser woman than I take you to be,' he replied, 'if you knew that; but I'll tell you what he is not. He is not one of your fine gentlemen, frightening poor simple girls to death, and chasing them away from their friends, like some you know; and he's one, too, that never cringes and bows to the rich and treads upon the neck of the poor. No, no, with all his faults, Paul is not one of those. It would be well for many if he had more power to do what is right; but if they won't let him—if they will hunt and harry him, all as one as if he were a monster or a wild beast, why, then, let them stand clear; for Paul is one that will not take an injury quietly. He will have his revenge; and in that, more than anything else, he proves himself a true Egyptian; though there are those among the tribe who whisper that, although he is their Chief, he has not a drop of the old ancient blood in his veins.'

"'So, then,' I observed, 'after all, this redoubted Paul is only the Chief of a gang of gipsies.'

"He darted a malignant look at me; and I confess for a moment I repented my folly in having provoked him.

"'Only!' he repeated softly, his countenance relaxing into an expression of pity and contempt. 'Do you know, now,' he added, 'that the person you speak of is greater than the king of England on his throne? for the king can't take a man's life away, let him have done him ever so much mischief; but woe be to the man that injures Paul, for there is not a man in the tribe that has not a knife at his command.'

"I shuddered," continued Mrs. Clifford, "as I heard this ferocious and lawless declaration, the truth of which was attested by the gleaming eyes and wild gestures of the strange being who was led, by his desire, to exalt the power of his master, into thus betraying him. The thought, I confess, darted involuntarily into my mind, that it was perhaps in revenge for some insult or injury and at his bidding and suggestion, if not actually by his hand, that young Copeland had fallen.

"I concealed, however, these thoughts from the boy, who was now, with childish curiosity, and seeming total forgetfulness of the subject on which he had made such a startling admission, examining a fan of feathers, which he had taken up from the couch on which I was sitting.

"'Man never made such colours as these,' he observed; 'and yet I never saw any bird with plumage like this.'

"'No,' I replied; 'the birds from which these were taken were natives of countries many thousand miles from here.'

"'Aye,' he observed, nodding his head, thoughtfully, 'perhaps of the country from which our people came, many, many years ago, and where they were great and rich and powerful, and had kings and princes and nobles among them, of their own blood; and of the noblest of that blood was my mother, as I have been told, though Paul scorned to call her his wife, and said that I ——no matter, I ought not to talk about this to you, though, when he treats me like a dog, the blood boils in my veins, and I wish that she were alive, and I as strong as him, to make him do her justice.'

"'But he is already married, is he not?' I demanded.

"'They say so,' he replied, with a sneering smile; 'but that pale-faced, weak woman was never fit to be the wife of a Chief. How she could bring him such a son, I cannot think; for quiet and mild as he seems, there is not one in the tribe of more spirit and courage—aye, nor one that will face toil and hardship better, than Edward——by Ashtaroth, and 'tis himself, the prince of darkness, I believe, that has made me do it, I have forgotten, all this time, that Edward is waiting your answer to his letter.'

"'Go to him, then, and tell him that I will meet him as he desires, in half an hour,' I replied.

"'And then, perhaps, you will tell him that I have been talking to you,' observed the boy, with an apprehensive look; 'and he will think that I have been betraying——'

"'You have betrayed nothing, Zekiel,' I replied; 'and be assured, I shall tell him nothing.'

"He was bounding away, apparently happy and satisfied at this declaration, when suddenly he seemed to recollect himself, and returned.

"'Will you not give me something,' he observed, 'for bringing the letter? They promised to give me some money below; but I know their tricks—they are a bad set, and I don't want to go among them again. I told them I was hungry and thirsty, and they put mustard in the soup, and pepper and salt in the beer they gave me; and then laughed to see me make faces at it. May they live to want it worse than I do; for I know, when I get back, I shall have a good meal.'

"'And if you do not find it ready for you, my boy, there is that will purchase one,' I observed.

"The boy looked with sparkling eyes at the handful of silver.

"'I wish I knew what I could do to please you,' he observed. 'How I should like to be always near you, and to run of your errands! and I would fetch you flowers, such as you never saw in your fine gardens:—and I know, too, where there's a plover's nest; but if I were to bring you anything without I had a letter, they would drive me away.'

"'I will give you this; and when you wish to see me, they will admit you at all times,' I observed, giving him a card, with my name written by myself; for the boy's evident gratitude had interested me in his behalf, in spite of the strange wildness of his manners, and some not very amiable traits of disposition and temper he had betrayed.

"This gift, while it astonished, seemed to delight him even more than the money; and having first carefully secured them both in his bosom, he bade me farewell; and before I could have imagined that he had even reached the bottom of the stairs, I beheld him, from the window, flying across the lawn, with the swiftness almost of a hare.

"You are all impatience I see, Elinor, to hear whether I kept my appointment with Hatherleigh. I did so; but our interview was of very short duration, and I was not inclined to prolong it, I assure you, when he told me that, at the greatest risk possible to himself, he had come to tell me that Mr. Copeland, who pretended in the morning to be too ill to see me, or even to admit me to his chamber to converse with him, which I had been, waving all ceremonies, desirous of doing, had, within two hours of my leaving his house, departed from it, no one knew whither;

VINCENT RAISED HIS HEAD AS ELINOR APPROACHED.

but that it was believed by those from whom Hatherleigh had his information, that he had discovered some clue to your retreat, and was gone to take measures accordingly. The young man's object, therefore, in seeing me was to implore me instantly to remove you; and, if it were not in my power to effect this, to authorise him to do so.

"'Do not think, madam," he observed, "that I wish to break the terms of our agreement; if I were so dishonourably inclined, I should have departed for London without seeing or consulting with you. All I would point out is, that I am going thither immediately; and that as I am convinced Elinor's safety is hazarded by her remaining where she is——"

" ' Do you know where she is ?' I demanded.

" I could not see his face, for it was too dark; but there was evident confusion in his voice, as he replied,

" ' I acknowledge I do, madam; though, believe me, I have never even seen her since she entered the house.'

" ' Nor sought to do so ?' I retorted, quickly.

" ' It was not stipulated that I should not look upon her,' he replied, with evident resentment; 'though I should have taken, and did take, every precaution to prevent her recognising me.'

" I would not, of course," continued Mrs. Clifford, " vex him unnecessarily, by expressing any doubt of this; but I at once declined any interference on his part with you.

" ' I will go to London myself,' I observed, 'it will be only hastening my journey a day or two, for I intended going thither; and on my way I can finally decide what is to be done with the poor girl.'

" ' And I shall not, then, know whither she is removed,' he replied, with evident discontent.

" ' It is impossible for me to tell you now,' I returned, 'what I shall do; but it is most likely I shall leave England for a short time. I have long contemplated a few months' tour on the continent of Europe, and have been only deterred from the want of a suitable companion. This want she will supply; and I shall be at once benefiting myself, and securing her safety.'

" He was silent for a moment.

" ' I cannot, I dare not object,' he at length replied, in a melancholy tone; ' but I feel that it is signing the death-warrant to all my hopes, to consent. What shall I have to struggle for —to cheer and support me, when she is gone ? While she is near me I can know, if only by her countenance, whether she still thinks of me, and is faithful to her promises; but when I shall be ignorant even what country she inhabits——'

" ' You need not be,' I observed, ' or of anything that relates to her welfare. If you will let me know where I can write to you, at stated periods, I will promise to do so.'

" He started, and caught both my hands in his, and pressed them so fervently to his lips, that I was not quite sure, Elinor, that I was not, after all going to rival you. You smile. Ah ! well you may. It is a ridiculous idea, is it not, that I should ever have dreamt of love ?"

" Oh, no, I did not mean that," exclaimed Elinor, warmly; " there are none who know you, as I do, but must love you."

" Yes, as you do," replied Mrs. Clifford, with a sarcastic

expression, which was most painful to Elinor, who fancied it implied a doubt of her sincerity.

" What is the matter, child ?" demanded the lady, rousing suddenly from the abstraction of thought into which she had fallen. " Oh, I forgot, I had not finished speaking of your lover; and yet, I believe, I had little or nothing more to tell. He expressed more gratitude for the promised favour than ever he had done for those which most men value more than all besides. Twenty times over, I believe, he repeated the address to which I was to write, lest I should forget it before I reached home, and could commit it to paper."

" But you did not forget it—and you do write—and you know he is safe? Oh, dear, dear madam, what a load you have taken from my heart !" exclaimed Elinor, bursting into tears of gratitude and joy.

" I have written, Elinor," returned Mrs. Clifford, gravely; " and, of course, as I have heard nothing in return, I conclude my letters were safely received. Had they not been so, I should suppose they would have been returned to me."

The manner in which this was uttered was at once a damp upon the pleasure Elinor had felt at thinking that Edward had enjoyed the satisfaction of knowing, not only how she was situated, but that she still remained faithful to her engagements to him; for that, she thought, Mrs. Clifford must be well aware of, and, of course, would not withhold from him.

A few moments' reflection, however, suggested to Elinor what she thought a very rational and satisfactory explanation of the change Mrs. Clifford's manner had undergone. Mrs. Clifford was proud, very proud, Elinor sometimes thought her; though it was plain that, in many instances, her kind heart and excellent understanding triumphed over this besetting infirmity of nature.

" She would, no doubt, have considered it a degradation," thought Elinor, " to have entered into a regular correspondence with one so much beneath her, and Edward is, therefore, forbidden to write; while Mrs. Clifford, perhaps, confines herself so strictly to the terms of her promise, that he knows nothing of me, except that I am still alive, and the inhabitant of such or such a town or village."

At the time this conversation took place, Mrs. Clifford and Elinor were residing at a beautiful and romantic chateau, near the little village of San Domenico, between Terracina and Naples; it was a spacious, but simple and unornamented dwelling, of which the chief recommendation was the unpretending comfort of the apartments and the loveliness of the scenery around. The chateau was almost surrounded with woods, which formed a complete amphitheatre, open only in the front, where a green lawn of never-fading verdure swept down to the edge of the blue waters of the lake. To the left, at the distance of little more than half a mile, lay the village, with its church and spire; while behind, the mountains thickly covered with trees almost to their very summits, overshadowed the scene.

Mrs. Clifford had decided on passing the winter (it was now the commencement of autumn) in this comfortable retreat; and Elinor, to whom all places had been hitherto alike but that which she was forbidden to visit, and to which her thoughts were much oftener given than to the actual scene around her, was now beginning to feel more at home than she had previously done when they had been flitting from place to place. Besides, these woods, with their wild romantic walks, trodden rather than cut through in all directions, resembled so strongly that in which she had sported away the happiest days of her life, that she could scarcely sometimes help thinking that she was, indeed, restored to the scenes of her childhood; and would startle at an unexpected and equivocal sound, and look around, almost fancying she should meet the piercing black eyes of Isabel, the (once) laughing blue ones of Annie, or the serious, thoughtful and more dubitable ones of Edward Hatherleigh, varying in colour with the passing emotion of the moment, from the lightest brown dye of the hazel, to the brightest and deepest and most intense black. Of Walter she never thought; or if she in vain tried to drive the recollection of him from her mind, it failed not to banish all pleasant retrospection.

CHAPTER XIV.

And the ice of despair
Chill'd the wild throb of care,
And he sate in mute agony still,—
Till the night-stars shone through the cloudless air,
And the pale moonbeam slept on the hill.

ANON.

WINTER—the mild winter of the climate of Naples, not the blood-freezing, sluggish, foggy, cheerless winter of the northern nations —had set in; and Mrs. Clifford, rather in emulation, as it seemed, of the comforts to which she had been accustomed to resort, to defeat the inclemency of the season in her native land, had gathered together in the principal apartment of the chateau everything that could remind her of home. A bright fire sparkled and crackled on the hearth, a thick carpet of the most brilliant hues covered the floor, and curtains of rich damask hung in ample folds around the windows. Mrs. Clifford, seated on a couch, her feet resting on an elegant footstool, was employed in netting, an occupation to which she often seemed resolutely to confine herself, as an antidote to her naturally wandering and restless disposition, which, if indulged, or at least not combated against, would, as she often acknowledged, have poisoned every enjoyment. Elinor was reading aloud one of the last newly received publications from London; and everything, in short, around them, bore the stamp of perfect freedom from care and anxiety—from all the fiends that so often transform this paradise of a world into a pandemonium; and yet neither Elinor nor Mrs. Clifford was at that moment happy. We will not pretend to judge what occupied the mind of the latter, and made her look so melancholy. Elinor was thinking of the enjoyments of the same season at home—of the talk and preparations for the convivialities of Christmas—of the anxiety with which the first approaches of frost were watched by the lads, in the hope that the great pond would soon be strong enough to bear their weight —of the peals of laughter that would attend the first essay of some unexperienced novices in the science of making long runs and cutting figures on the ice—of the pleasant, refreshing feeling of the keen, frosty air, on a bright, moonlight night, when, having danced and sung till they were tired, and the elders thought it time to break up, it would be suddenly proposed that the whole party should escort, or, as they termed it, send some one of their companions, who had the longest and most solitary way to go; and out they would all sally, unheeding the remonstrances and predictions of taking cold from the old people, who had, as they all agreed, done just the same as themselves in their youth, and were only wise and prudent now, because they could not afford to be gay and thoughtless any longer.

From these scattered reminiscences Elinor's mind gradually became fixed upon the sad events of the last winter, which had for ever broken all their enjoyments. One by one she reviewed every incident of the eventful tragedy which had so changed her prospects in life; and, for at least the thousandth time, a deep sigh broke from her bosom, at the uncertainty, which to her seemed never to be removed, as to the fate of those who had been

the principal actors in that scene. The book she had been reading remained unclosed upon her knees; but she saw not a line or
letter of it, her eyes were turned to the open window near which
she sat, though they saw nothing beyond it; for they were fixed
upon vacancy, her spirit was wandering in far distant scenes. But
suddenly she started! A man, whose approach she had not
noted, stood within a few feet of her, and fixed his large dark
eyes with a look of meaning on her face.

Elinor did not scream, but she was breathless with alarm: yet
there was nothing in the man's looks or appearance to distinguish
him from the common peasantry of the neighbourhood; and his
aim might be merely to ask some favour, which they had all
learned to know was much more likely to be granted, when they
could get an audience of the signora herself, than if they applied
to the servants of the establishment, though the greater part of
them were their own country people. The thought, however,
had scarcely entered her mind, before its fallacy was proved.
Mrs. Clifford raised her eyes from her netting, and, in a startled
tone of voice, exclaimed,

"Who is that man? What does he want?"—but before the
sentence was finished, he had vanished; and Elinor, who rose
hastily to look after him, beheld him rush into the thickest part
of the wood that skirted the lawn to the right of the chateau, in
a direction from which there was no egress, but only pathways
for pleasure, leading all to the same point—a small boat-house
at the edge of the lake.

"What could this mean? and why do you look so terrified,
Elinor?" demanded Mrs. Clifford, "the man could have had no
evil intention, or he would not so openly have showed himself,
or have been so easily scared away by the mere sound of my
voice. Ring the bell, child, and let us inquire whether anything
is known about him. Perhaps he is a stranger whom Vincent
has employed about the grounds, and was led here by curiosity,
not expecting to see or be seen by us."

Elinor obeyed, though she spoke not a word, either in contradiction or confirmation of this supposition.

Vincent, however, who was the principal gardener, any more
than the other servants, who were all questioned, could give no
explanation or clue to the man's appearance, or offer any reasonable supposition as to who he could be.

"He did not enter by the regular way, that is certain,"
observed Vincent, "since I have been all day employed on the
flower-beds in the front of the house, and must have seen him if

he had passed. It is my opinion, that he was some saucy lazarone, who had been on the lake, and landed, thinking, perhaps, to pilfer something; or, may be, did not know the chateau was now inhabited, seeing it has been empty for more than two years before our lady—whom God preserve!—took it; and so, as I was saying, it may be that he came, thinking to get a shelter for the night for his lazy bones, and, I'll be bound, was frightened enough when he found he had been trespassing on a noble lady's grounds."

Mrs. Clifford affected to be satisfied with this explanation, since she saw it was in vain to hope for a more reasonable one; but, though she said nothing to Elinor that could lead to any suspicion as to what was her own thoughts on the subject, it was plain to the former that she was far from easy, and that somehow or other she connected that uneasiness with her—Elinor.

"Yet, she never saw him," thought the latter, as her mind reverted to the object of her suspicion. "If, therefore, by any possibility, it could be him, she could not suspect it."

And why did Elinor hesitate to name the person to Mrs. Clifford—almost to herself, whom she believed she had seen? It was because she hated to acknowledge, even in thought, that Paul Dangerfield was connected with Edward Hatherleigh; and she knew that the moment she mentioned the former, the name of the latter would be on Mrs. Clifford's lips, perhaps accompanied with a thousand injurious suspicions respecting him.

Mrs. Clifford *was* suspicious; perhaps her intercourse with the world justified her in being so, at least to herself; but to Elinor it was one of the worst traits in her disposition, that she would frequently seize on a slight clue to unravel a long tissue of imaginings, which, after all, perhaps, proved to have no more real substance than the slight, cobweb-like films which stretch across the garden-path in the morning, and vanish at the first ray the sun casts upon them.

The name of Paul Dangerfield would, in all probability, have conjured up a host of fearful recollections in Mrs. Clifford's mind. It did, indeed, banish all her recently acquired feeling of peace and security from Elinor's own bosom. The fastenings of the windows were examined and made secure; the thick damask curtains were drawn close, even before the last ray of daylight had faded; more wood was thrown upon the fire; numerous wax lights shed brilliance and splendour around; and yet Elinor could not feel herself secure; she started at every sound, and listened with intenseness, whenever the murmur of voices in the servants' apartments rose somewhat beyond their usual pitch, fancying that she should hear the deep full tones of Dangerfield.

"After all, there is no security like that of a town," she unconsciously uttered aloud.

Mrs. Clifford looked up at her with surprise. She had been, for a long time, lost in one of those fits of abstraction which were habitual to her, and appeared for a moment to have forgotten the temporary cause of alarm.

"What sort of security do you mean, child?" she at length demanded; "or what sort of danger do you apprehend here? If that man was a thief, as I suppose you think he was, he must be a bold one, indeed, if he should return now, when he must be aware that his person is known, his intentions suspected, and, of course, guarded against."

Elinor did not reply, for she feared to say that she entertained no such apprehensions as those Mrs. Clifford suggested, lest she should be called upon to state what she really did fear.

The evening passed away gloomily and comfortless, and yet Elinor, almost unconsciously to herself, prolonged to the last possible moment her stay in the drawing-room. She knew that it was Mrs. Clifford's habit generally to remain an hour or so after the whole household had retired to bed, with the exception of her maid, Mrs. Burchall, who awaited her mistress in her dressing-room. For the first time Elinor showed a disposition to trespass on this hour of solitary indulgence, if such it could be called. In vain Mrs. Clifford looked at the timepiece, and then, drawing her watch from her bosom, wound it up with an observation, that she believed they were both somewhat slow. In vain she became silent, yawned, and at length began to pace the room with evident symptoms of impatience. Elinor still lingered. She felt an equal repugnance to leave Mrs. Clifford alone, and to be alone herself. And yet, if it were Paul Dangerfield, what danger could she apprehend to the former? what, indeed, to herself? for, cold and stern as his manner had ever been towards her, he had, in the pressing moments of necessity, proved himself a staunch friend.

Eleven o'clock sounded from the spire of the neighbouring church; and Mrs. Clifford, no longer able to conceal her surprise and impatience at Elinor's pertinacity in affecting to be still busily engaged with a protfolio of prints, which had remained open before her for the last two hours, now observed, in a more petulant tone than was usual to her,

"You intend, I suppose, Elinor, to keep watch to-night against this formidable being whom your imagination, it seems, has converted into a robber, or, I should not wonder, a midnight murderer? If so, I had better leave you undisturbed possession of——"

"Oh, no, dear madam, I am going to bed immediately," exclaimed Elinor, starting up with evident affright, at the idea of being left alone in that room. "I only thought——I only wished," she added, with hesitation and timidity, "not to leave you alone here."

"Go, you silly girl," replied Mrs. Clifford, "I have no fears; and if there was any real danger, what protection do you think your presence would be to me?"

Elinor could no longer frame an excuse for staying; yet, even after she had bade adieu for the night, and closed the door, she hesitated to proceed to her chamber, without avowing to Mrs. Clifford the real source of her terrors. The thought, however, which had at first restrained her, that she might in some way compromise Edward Hatherleigh, again prevented her. As if anxious to avoid further temptation to do what she might have cause afterwards to repent of, she glided swiftly away towards the stairs which led to her apartment.

The servants had all retired nearly an hour before, and as perfect a stillness reigned through the house as if she had been the sole inhabitant of it. Elinor shrank from the sound of her own footsteps, light as they were; and as she crossed the large hall, looked suspiciously around, in the fear that she should behold some unwelcome intruder. Neither sight nor sound, however, impeded her progress; and she was soon safe in the sanctuary of her own room.

"Safe!" she repeated to herself, as the thought occurred to her, after she had secured the door with bolt and lock. "Safe! where could I be safe, if that man should meditate evil against me? And yet, why should I fear him? Be his crimes what they may towards others, to me he has ever proved a friend."

But though thus striving to reason herself into composure, Elinor could not divest herself of suspicion that some evil was intended. Cautiously she surveyed every nook and corner, not only of her bed-chamber, but the dressing-room which opened into it; and then, convinced at last that no one was hidden, and that it was impossible for any one to enter without using a violence which must alarm the household, and bring them to her aid, she approached her toilet, to make the necessary preparations for bed. At the moment, however, that she set down the night candle, which had hitherto assisted in her search, her eye rested on a note, without superscription, yet properly folded and sealed. All the fears and terrors, which had begun to subside, again resumed their dominion over her mind. That the note was intended for her she could not doubt; yet how it had been conveyed thither was the question that agitated her more than even her anticipation of its contents, though that induced the exclamation from her lips,

"All my fancied security, my peace, my comfort, are gone for ever!"

For some moments she remained immoveable, with the paper in her hand, which she trembled as much to open as would a criminal the fatal mandate which he dreads conveys the irrevocable sentence of death. "It may be that it contains news of Edward," rushed into her mind, and the seal was broken.

The note contained but a few sentences; and so much effort had evidently been used to disguise the hand, that it was some time before she could fully decipher the characters. But at length she read that which, while it confirmed her presentiments that some evil would arise to her from the vicinity of the Gipsy Chief, re-assured her with the conviction that some friendly eye watched over her, who would, if possible, defeat the intended mischief.

"Be on your guard," commenced the writer, "nor suffer yourself, under any pretext, however plausible or specious, to be deluded into leaving your home, without proper protection. The friend who sends this is watching over your safety, but is as yet too little acquainted with the particulars to give you more than this general caution. Do not leave your home *alone*, let *who* will solicit you so to do."

Again and again Elinor read this mysterious scroll, which, from the absence of all name or address, might, as she thought, have been as applicable to Mrs. Clifford, or to any one else, as to her, had she not been previously warned of danger by the appearance of the Gipsy Chief. And yet what danger? and who could it be that felt so interested in her safety, as to have run the risks they must have done to place the note in that situation?

They had, perhaps, bribed some one of the domestics; but if that was the case, how little dependence could be placed on the latter, and how unsafe it must be to trust to their fidelity.

For the first time, a suspicion of old Vincent glanced upon

her mind. He had, it was true, being apparently the most alarmed at the appearance, and the most indefatigable in trying to trace the stranger who had trespassed upon his mistress' privacy. But, then, it had seemed, at the time, that it was almost impossible for any one to have been in the grounds without his knowledge; and it was also so easy for him to have entered her dressing-room, as he had been, during the day, removing some flowers and plants from the garden to the balcony into which the windows of both her apartments opened.

There was one consoling circumstance, however, which tended to quiet her immediate apprehensions; and that was, that the danger, whatever it might be, was evidently, as yet, remote, and there appeared not the slightest reason to suppose that any evil was meditated towards Mrs. Clifford. Unwilling as Elinor had been to acknowledge it to herself, her chief fear had been that something was meditated against Mrs. Clifford. Paul Danger-field was—she had learned the unwelcome truth from lips which never uttered a falsehood—the father of Edward Hatherleigh; and irreconcilable as the fact appeared with all that she knew of Mrs. Hatherleigh—with the character of Mrs. Hatherleigh's son—Paul Dangerfield was a villain—a robber—a murderer!

Often and often had Elinor, in moments of calm review of the past, when there could exist nothing to warp her judgment, nothing to lead her to false conclusions on the subject; often had she reviewed the horrible circumstances of Walter Copeland's murder, and as often had she most unwillingly come to the conclusion that in that act Paul Dangerfield was deeply implicated, and that for the sake of plunder alone could the atrocious deed have been committed.

That Edward was innocent of all participation in that deed, she was equally, nay, far more certain; but she recalled to her memory the looks of more than coldness, of aversion, with which she had seen him regard the man whom he was compelled to acknowledge as his parent; and the conviction forced itself upon her, that Edward himself was conscious that his father was capable of any enormity that would gratify his passions or advance his interest. What, then, more likely than that he had fixed upon Mrs. Clifford as a victim? She was known to be very rich; and from her ready liberality in all cases, might be presumed to have always plenty of money in the house. The display of plate, too, in common use, was such as probably was seldom seen in private life, and in such a retired spot; while, although the establishment of servants was large considering the style of living, there were not near so many men in the household as would have been considered necessary, had there been a gentleman at the head of affairs.

Naturally fearless and unsuspicious, no thought of insecurity had ever seemed to enter Mrs. Clifford's mind ; and still less would these causes for apprehension have occurred to Elinor, had it not been that she had formerly witnessed the lawlessness and daring spirit of the tribe of which Paul Dangerfield appeared to be the head.

It was evident, however, that this frindly warning pointed at no danger of this kind, but at some personal evil to herself; and this relieved her from her worst apprehensions ; for all evils would be to her comparatively light, that did not involve the safety of her benefactress ; while, to have known that she had been the remote cause of injury to her (Mrs. Clifford) would have been in her estimation the heaviest misfortune that could have befallen her.

The night passed away quietly, though it was a sleepless one to Elinor, whose mind was distracted by a thousand conjectures as to the source of the danger that threatened her, and the motives of the person who had taken this strange method of warning her against it. The only probable (and that to cool reflection would scarcely have appeared probable) cause of fear that she could assign to herself was, that Mr. Copeland had discovered her present retreat ; and that, knowing that it would be impossible openly to seize upon her as a sacrifice to his bitter spirit of revenge, he had laid his plans to trepan her into his power, and to convey her to England. But, then, whose was the friendly hand that had conveyed to her this warning of her danger? and how was it that Dangerfield, who was, far more than she herself, interested in keeping out of the way of all those connected with the melancholy event which had exposed her to so much peril ; how could it be that he was now hovering about the very spot where, if she was right in her supposition, he had the most cause for alarm ? Again and again she relit her taper to examine the note, in hopes of tracing, by some inadvertence of the writer, characters which were known to her, and would reveal the source from which it came; and again and again did she revolve every circumstance connected with the receipt of it, before she came to the final resolution to conceal all from Mrs. Clifford, and trust to her own precaution to avoid the threatened evil.

This determination, however, she resolved should not prevent her making the attempt to learn who had placed the note on her table; and accordingly, as soon as the bright beams of the sun assured her that Vincent, who was remarkable for his early rising and industry, would be at his post, she dressed herself, and descended to the garden.

The old man was, as she expected, already at his work; but as she approached him, he raised his head to greet her with such an open and unembarrassed smile, that her heart reproached her for having for a moment doubted him.

"Ah, signorina," he observed, "you are coming to make my roses look pale by the colour of your cheeks; but yet, now I look at you again, I must own there is more of the lily than usual in your complexion, this morning: I am afraid you have rested ill."

"You are right, Vincent," returned Elinor. "Cannot you guess the cause?" and she fixed her eyes earnestly on his face.

"Me! Holy St. Dominic, no, how should I?" he replied, with visible amazement. "Stay—surely the signorina has not been frightening herself about that varlet that came——Ah, I see I am right! but, dear me, I couldn't have believed it. I always thought you were so brave. There now, when, three or four weeks ago, there was the foolish talk among the servants about banditti having been met with up in the mountains, and some of them (the servants, I mean,) were afraid to go even to the village after sunset, lest they should meet the robbers, neither you nor my lady seemed to give any heed to it, but went your ways, and took your walks, just the same as if you had never heard the idle tale."

"Yes, because we considered it an idle tale," she replied, struck with a new idea from his observation. "And yet, Vincent, perhaps, though we were unconscious of it, we were braving real danger at that time. I can scarcely now, upon reflection, think but that there was some foundation for the report; and you know you told me yourself, that, three or four winters ago, yon ruined fortress, whose black outline is already becoming visible, now that the leaves are dropping from the trees——"

"Yes, yes," interrupted the old man, "I have good reason to remember the time when the brigands made that their dwelling-place, and sallied out at pleasure upon the surrounding country. Holy Maria! how I have trembled when I have heard their shrill whistle among the rocks! and then, perhaps, another answering from the other side of the lake! And how could I know, when I was trudging along in the dark, but some of the band were lurking in ambush, ready to spring on me?

"And then, if they were disappointed in their expectations of booty, they made nothing of sticking a stiletto in your throat; or, at the best, carrying you off to their den, and keeping you there, and ill-using you, and threatening every hour to hang or shoot you, till your friends sent a ransom for you, whatever they fixed upon : sometimes it was money, and sometimes it was wine and provisions, according to who they got hold of; so that, at last, not a soul dared stir out of their houses after dark. And it was not always houses, either, that would protect you.

"There, signorina, you see that farm-house on the rise of the hill, that looks as if it was peeping over the spire of the church, though it's a good long mile beyond it. Well, that was inhabited at that time by a man who was well to do in the world, and who had saved a pretty portion to give his daughter; and a nice, modest, brisk, young girl she was, and well-looking too.

"Well, there was a young tradesman in Naples that had seen her when she paid a holiday visit to the city ; and, to make short of my story, the match was made up between them, and it was settled that he should come over and keep the wedding at her father's house, and receive her portion at the same time; and then the bride was to go back with him the next day to his home.

"Well they were married, and a fine show it was ; and everybody that could go did go to share the good things at Andrea Martini's, that was the father's name. There was dancing and singing, and merry-making of all sorts; and nobody thought about the brigands, except those who had a long way to go home; for the rascals had never been known to come near the houses, or attack any but single travellers, or, at most, two together.

"I own myself, I was shaking in my shoes, when I thought of the way I had to go ; for I lived here then, to take care of the chateau, and I knew none of my companions had to come further than the village. However, I tried to drown my fears in Andrea's good wine; but I need not have been afraid—the brigands had got other fish to fry than such a poor trout as I, as the song says; for just after we had all taken leave of the bride and bridegroom, and were still within sight and hearing of what passed in the house, that whistle was heard; and it seemed this time as if the devils—Heaven preserve us !—were all round us, though we saw none of them. Holy Maria ! there were some twenty or more of us, reckoning the women, all bound for the village, and some two or three stout fellows too among us; but you never saw a flock of sheep, when the wolf suddenly rushes among them, more frightened than we were; for we did not know which way to run, whether to go back to the house, or fly towards the village.

"It seemed we were beset; and there we cowered all together, the women clinging round their husbands and sweethearts, and only kept from shrieking their hearts out by the fear of betraying to the brigands whereabouts we were; for we were descending the woody path yonder that you and the signora have so often traversed, and the shade of the trees as we hoped concealed us; though, if we had our senses about us, we should have known there was little chance of our being hidden from the wretches, for we had been all laughing and talking and singing up to the minute that we heard the devilish whistle. Excuse me, signora, for swearing; but I can't help it, when I think of the vagabonds.

"Well, presently all was silent; and I for one began to think they had either missed us, or had gone on the route after the father of the bridegroom, and two or three friends, who had taken the high road to Naples, an hour or two before, being afraid to remain till after dark. But just as I was thinking so, there rose such a shriek from the house where we had left them but a few minutes before so happy and so envied, because we believed them safe from the dangers with which our path was beset. A second —a third shriek followed. I looked towards the house, and saw lights flying, as it were, from room to room, as if in pursuit of some one.

"'The brigands!—the brigands!' I exclaimed, 'the villains have dared to attack the house!'

"'Yes, and we shall be the next,' replied one of my neighbours. Before I could speak another word, away flew the whole of my party down the hill, towards the village; and I was fain to follow, for what could I do by myself?'

"The cowards!" exclaimed Elinor, indignantly, "to desert thus their friends in necessity!—but go on, Vincent, I am impatient to know how it ended."

"Ha, very sadly, indeed," returned the old man, shaking his head mournfully. "Well, as I was telling you, signorina, we made to the village in breathless haste, and there we called up everybody to consult what was to be done. Some proposed one thing, and some another; but before we could come to a conclusion, in rushed the poor bridegroom among us; and never shall I forget his looks. His face was whiter than the sleeves of my shirt, saving your presence; and his eyes looked like two red hot coals, with rings of lead round them. He tried to speak; but he could only make a hoarse and rattling noise in his throat, and threw his arms up towards the old fortress, while his body shook as if he had an ague fit upon him.

" Our village doctor was there among the rest, and he poured something down his throat, which had the effect, after a minute or two, of bringing him to himself, and restoring his speech; and then, oh, what a tale he had to tell! A gang of eight or ten ruffians, all armed to the teeth, had rushed into the house, the door of which had, in the carelessness of the moment, been left open and unguarded.

" The bride had just retired, with her young companions, to her chamber; and the bridegroom was drinking his parting glass for the night with her father, when the wretches burst in upon them. The poor young man was seized by two of them, and pistols held to his head; while the father was commanded by the chief of the gang to produce the money which the next morning was to have been paid as the bride's portion. But this was not the worst. While part of the gang were thus occupied, the others had rushed up stairs; and what must have been the feelings of the father and the husband as they heard the shrieks of the poor young creatures, who, a few minutes before, had been so innocent and so happy! It would have been more merciful, as the wretched young man said to us, when he was telling the story, if they had blown his brains out at once with their pistols; but there he was, pinioned down where he sat, by two great brawny fellows, with a grasp like a blacksmith's vice. At last, the fellows came down stairs again; but, Holy Virgin! what should he see, but his own beautiful bride, stretched out like a corpse, between two of them!

" ' Carry her off!' said the wretch who was their leader; she'll come to, when she gets into the open air; and if she don't, Ulrica will find means to bring her round at home.' Well, signora, would you believe it: the villains carried her off before the face of the young husband and her poor father.

" ' Now, if you want her back again,' said the chief of the brigands, with a laugh like a fiend; ' you must send up three hundred livres, before noon to-morrow, and she shall be delivered up to your messenger. I will wait for him myself, beside the great stone cross where the priest had his throat cut, for playing false and trying to betray some good fellows like us. But, beware! let his fate be a warning to you. We are men of honour, and we expect you to act honourably. If you stir beyond the village, where, I suppose, you must go to raise the

ELINOR CLARE.

DANGERFIELD, MRS. CLIFFORD, AND ELINOR

money, as you all say you have no more here, I shall know that you intend to betray us; and, by the bones of St. Dominic, you never see your lady-bride again!"

"What could the poor young man do? The moment he was released he flew to us; and oh, if you'd seen him on his knees, imploring us to raise the ransom between us, and swearing by all the holy saints and martyrs, to sell all he had in Naples, when he should get back there, to repay us. Some people's hearts are made of stone. Mine was a small mite towards the sum, but I gave it readily; and so did two or three more who were poor as I. But the rich, who could have done it easily, held out. He was a stranger; and how did they know when the service was done, whether he would keep his word? Besides, they could none of them tell how soon they might want ransom themselves. And, then, there were other reasons whispered among them why they should not send the money. And, in short, what with one scruple and another, it was within half an hour of noon before the money was collected. It was thought best that the poor fellow himself should not go to carry the ransom; and the father was not able, for he seemed to be death-struck; but it required all the persuasions and power of our priest to detain him, and suffer two old men, who had been up the mountain once or twice before on similar errands, to depart with the ransom.

"Well, you may be sure, we were all anxiety till the poor girl came back; and many of us, and I among the rest, went as far as we dare do up the mountain, to meet her; because, as we said, may be she hasn't got over the fright enough to be able to walk home. Every minute seemed an hour to us; and what must have been the feelings of the poor fellow at home? At last they came. She was walking between the men, quite quiet, and, as we thought, composed, though she never spoke a word in answer to us, when we all rushed to welcome her back; and her eye looked dreadfully wild.

"For my own part, I saw in a minute that there was something horrible yet behind; and, one by one, everybody began to feel the same; so that, by the time we had reached Andrea Martini's house, where pretty well all the village were collected to witness the joyful meeting of the bride and the bridegroom, we were more like a funeral procession than anything else. The husband was at the door, to receive her. It seemed as if his shaking limbs would not bear him any further. He stretched out his arms to her, and looked in her face with such a searching glance, that her eyes dropped to the ground; and she put him gently aside, as she murmured,

" 'Let me go to my father.'

"Poor Andrea! he cried like a child, when she threw her arms round his neck, and laid her head on his bosom; but when her husband would have claimed his turn, she whispered,

" 'Let me go to my own room for a few moments, beloved of my heart: I shall then be more worthy of your caresses.'

"Well, the husband thought, and many thought, that she was going to offer up prayers and thanksgivings to her saint for her restoration; but I had my misgivings—there was something so desperately calm in her manner. However, she went to her room, and we heard her lock her door; for we were all so silent, you might have heard a pin fall. Old Andrea, her father, was the only one that seemed not to be uneasy. He thought only of the pleasure of seeing his child again; and began to talk of selling his farm, to pay the friends who had advanced her ransom, and the portion he had promised with her, and then going to live for his few remaining years with his daughter and son-in-law in Naples.

" All the while he was talking, the young husband sat with his eyes fixed on the staircase, impatient to see his wife return; and, at last, even Andrea himself began to think her prayers unreasonably long.

" ' Go to her, my son,' he at length exclaimed, ' you have the authority of a husband, now, to demand admittance; and tell her we are waiting for her to take her place at the table, and welcome our friends, though it is but a scanty repast we can give them; for the villains loaded themselves, last night, from our stores, and I'll be bound are feasting their ungodly carcases to-day at our expense.'

" The young man did not wait twice telling, signorina, he flew up stairs, and we heard him knocking gently at the door, and calling upon his Therese to admit him. No answer. He shook the door more violently: and I, and one or two more, crept softly up one or two stairs, in fearful expectation of the result.

" I won't keep you in suspense, signorita; the end was, that he burst the slight door open with his foot, one minute of awful silence followed, and then I, and those who like me, had anticipated evil, could no longer contain ourselves, but hastily followed to the room.

" There she lay, the blooming bride of yesterday, prostrate on her face before the image of St. Therese, her name-saint and patroness ! It might have been thought that she was humbling herself in prayer; but the streams of blood that were flowing in every direction told the fatal tale too plainly. The husband was not looking at her, he did not seem even to notice her, so busily was he engaged in reading a paper, which shook in his trembling grasp, like the leaves of an aspen-tree shaken by the wind. What were its contents we never knew; for, the moment he had read it, he crushed the paper in his hand, and, snatching the dagger he had drawn from the bleeding bosom of the self-murdered girl, he rushed out of the house; but we could readily guess, signorina, that it contained the history, written by herself, of the wrongs and disgrace which the poor Therese

had suffered, during that night of horror, in the abode of devils
to which she had been taken, and which had made life insupportable to her.

"Well, the end of my sad story is, that Therese and her father
now lie, side by side, under a green mound in yonder churchyard."

"And what became of the unfortunate husband?" demanded
Elinor, whose tears had denoted her sympathy with these victims
of vice and brutality.

"I cannot answer that question," returned old Vincent; "all
that I know is, that he led on the soldiers who were sent from
Naples to exterminate the brigands, and it was said that he
himself acted as executioner upon the two that were taken. The
rest of the gang, unfortunately, got scent of the expedition
against them, and made their escape. Since that," continued
the old man, "strange stories have been told about him, that he
had turned brigand himself, or, at least, that he was leading a
wild life in the mountains. Certain it is, that he deserted his
home, and never was seen in the city where he was bred and
born, after he had laid the poor girl and her father in the grave.
But, dear me, I have made you look melancholy, signorina, with
my long story."

Elinor did indeed, feel melancholy; and, as the old man
resumed his work, with seeming forgetfulness of all he had been
saying, and a desire to make up for the time he had lost, she
turned to gaze on the ruined fortress, which had now acquired
so deep an interest in her eyes.

Hitherto, tales of brigands and their deeds had appeared to
her rather like the pages of romance, than matters of real fact;
but now she was living on the very spot which had witnessed
their cruel and daring exploits, and her fancy pictured their dark
forms and ferocious countenances peopling the now still and silent
woods, or lying in ambush, ready to spring upon the unwary
traveller, and drag him to their den.

From these reflections, however, her mind soon reverted to
her own more immediate cause for alarm; and as she recalled to
her mind the wild and predatory life which Dangerfield had led
since she had known him, his places of concealment, and aptitude
at disguising and changing his appearance at will, she could not
help thinking that this was a scene exactly fitted for him, and
that he would be capable of emulating even the deeds of his
predecessors in the gloomy building upon which her eyes were
fixed with almost a conviction that there was his present abode.

"I must not forget my resolution," she thought to herself,

suddenly pausing in her walk, and turning round to ascertain that she was still within sight and hearing of the house, or, at least, of old Vincent. At this moment, her eye rested on a man who was assiduously employed in lopping away the superfluous branches of a hedge, a few feet beyond the bed of flowers at which the old gardener was at work. The man's back was towards her; and he appeared so totally occupied with his work, as never to turn his head in the direction in which she was. Yet she could not help fancying that the form, the dress was the same as that she had seen, and believed to be the Gipsy Chief; and for an instant she stood motionless with terror and surprise.

"Yet, what occasion can I have to fear him?" she again reflected. "Is it not far more probable that his errand to me is friendly, and that it is to him I am indebted for the warning I have received? At least, whatever may be his intentions, I am safe while I am here, where a single cry would bring the whole household to my assistance. I will satisfy myself, therefore, whether it be him or no."

Stopping again, as she passed Vincent, to speak a few words, she sauntered leisurely on, assuming a confidence and indifference she was far from feeling. Before, however, she could approach near enough to ascertain whether her suspicions were correct, the man appearing to have finished that part of his task, walked slowly on to another and more distant part of the hedge, and again commenced his work.

The manner and action were so natural, and apparently unstudied, that it was scarcely possible to suspect that it was design; and Elinor's first impulse was still to continue her walk until she should come up with him, and be satisfied; but suddenly the warning she had received struck upon her mind. She looked back—Vincent was already at a considerable distance from her. Might not this movement of the supposed labourer be a feint to draw her further from the house, and, of course from the reach of assistance, if any violence was premeditated against her?

The instant the thought darted into her mind, she turned back with precipitation; and again a suspicion crossed her, that Vincent, in spite of the tale he had just related with so much pathos, was treacherous.

"At all events," she thought, "he must know who the man is whom he employs," and, disguising as well as she could the agitation she felt, she again approached the old man.

"That seems but a new hand at his trade, yonder," she observed, looking towards the stranger, who appeared totally absorbed in his employment.

"Why, yes; I suspect he has been used to lighter labour than what he has now undertaken," returned the old man, with a look so unembarrassed, that Elinor was instantly convinced she wronged him.

"Is he a countryman of yours, Vincent?" she demanded, carelessly.

"Bless you! no, signorina," he replied, with evident amazement. "It is the Englishman of whom I spoke to my mistress, when he was lying ill in the village; she sent him, you know, money and wine and a doctor, and he got well; and so he would come here, and help me for a little while, till he gets strong enough to begin his journey home."

"And who or what is he?" inquired Elinor, who recollected Vincent's having applied to Mrs. Clifford under the circumstances he had now mentioned.

The lady's charity, however, was rather of a passive than an active nature; and she considered that she had done quite sufficient, when she sent such assistance as money could readily procure, without putting herself to any inconvenience. The man was said to have been travelling in some menial capacity with an English family, and had been discharged, as he said, on account of his incapacity (from ill health) to the duties of his situation. He had lingered, it seemed, till the little money he had was spent; and, according even to his own account of himself, had been for some time leading a vagrant sort of life, which he wished now to amend by getting home as soon as he could. Knowing that Mrs. Clifford had liberally supplied the means for so doing, and that the man had got well, Elinor had felt no further interest in the matter, and had, indeed, ceased to think at all of the circumstance, until now reminded of it. To her question Vincent could only reply by telling her what the man had said himself, which amounted to nothing more than that already related.

That it did not strike Vincent that this was the man whose sudden appearance at the window had occasioned so much alarm and conjecture, was accounted for by Elinor from the circumstance of his having been working, it seemed, for more than a week, in the garden, and being well known to the servants; although it had never happened to reach Elinor's ear, and he had, probably designedly, never before chanced to cross her path.

Convinced now beyond all doubt that she was not mistaken, she returned to her room to reflect on what course see should take, to ascertain his intentions ; but the more she thought on the subject, the more she became convinced that they could not be such as she ought to encourage by silence; and she, therefore, at length came to the resolution of making Mrs. Clifford acquainted with all that had occurred, and all that she conjectured. With this intent she descended to the breakfast-room ; but, after waiting long beyond the usual time, Mrs. Burchall at last entered, with constrained civility, to inform her that her mistress was very unwell, and would not rise till late in the day.

For the present, therefore, the intended communication was necessarily delayed, and Elinor passed a solitary morning in her own room, afraid to take even her customary exercise, lest she should again encounter the mysterious being whom, although she had never experienced any evil at his hands towards herself, she could not help dreading as the worst of enemies.

At dinner Mrs. Clifford was present, but so evidently indisposed and disinclined to enter into conversation, that Elinor was discouraged from speaking on the subject which occupied her thoughts ; and again she was compelled to pass an uneasy night, fearing she knew not what, and blaming herself she knew not why, except that she had not in the first instance—namely, at the moment the stranger appeared at the window—acted with her usual openness, and declared to Mrs. Clifford her suspicions that she knew who he was.

On the second day the indisposition of the latter was so much increased, as to confine her entirely to her chamber. There Elinor visited her after breakfast, and read to her for more than an hour ; but she was evidently so abstracted in thought, as to pay little attention ; and afraid of exciting her, and increasing the nervous affection which she complained of, Elinor again deferred her intended communication.

Day after day passed on in this manner. Mrs. Clifford remained confined to her chamber, a decided hypochondriac ; and the only mitigation Elinor received of her secret uneasiness, arose from Vincent's assurances—at an interview which she contrived should take place, without suspicion of her motives, at the very window where she had first been disconcerted by the appearance of Dangerfield—that the cause of her anxiety had quitted the neighbourhood.

" I was not sorry to tell the truth," observed the old man,

with a sagacious nod; "when he bade me good bye; for he was very little use in the matter of hard work, which was all I wanted of him, for his hands were as white and as soft as a lady's; and I could not help often thinking that the history he gave of himself was altogether false, and that he was not what he pretended to be."

"And what, then, do you think he was, Vincent?" demanded Elinor, anxious to hear whether any conjectures had been formed which approached the truth.

The old man shook his head. "It is hard to say," he replied, "for he was very deep; and though he spoke our tongue better than any foreigner I ever heard, whenever he was asked a question he did not wish to answer he would always pretend not to understand it. That, you know, signora, did not look like an honest man. But some say one thing, and some another; and it's even been whispered that he belonged to the very gang that was driven from the mountains, as I told you; for it was well known that there were men of all nations among them, even Jews and gipsies; and that, you know, signorina, is not improbable, because it is well known that they are a vagabondizing sort of people, that have neither home or nation. However, let that be as it may, I am glad he is gone; for this was not a fit place for him."

"But are you sure he is gone?" demanded Elinor.

"Sure!" he replied, "yes, certain, signorina; he borrowed a mule in the village, which has been duly sent back from the appointed place, though there were many who laughed at Ginotti, who lent it him, and told him he would never see the beast again."

Elinor was, however, far from feeling perfectly assured of the fact; and though several days passed over without any event calculated to renew her alarm, she still preserved her caution, and confined herself to the house, or its immediate vicinity

CHAPTER XV.

The good old law—the simple plan,
That they should take who have the power,
And they should keep who can.   ANON.

THE indisposition, or, rather, the fit of melancholy—for it was evident the disease was rather mental than bodily—which had so long kept Mrs. Clifford confined to her room, at length abated; and Elinor, with true and heartfelt joy, beheld her return to her former occupations and habits, which, though not of the most active kind, were certainly far more conducive to her health than yielding herself up, as she had latterly done, to lassitude and ennui. It was not, however, without considerable trepidation, that Elinor accompanied her in one or two short rambles beyond the confines of their own garden and grounds. The caution she had received was ever present to her memory; and Mrs. Clifford remarked with surprise that she who on former occasions was always anxious to extend their walks, and appeared never weary of admiring and pointing out the beauties of the scenery, was now the first to propose returning, and seemed to be not only indifferent, but too pre-occupied to attend even to the observations which were sometimes made by the former, when she discovered any new point of view.

"What can be the matter with you, child? and why do you keep looking around you, and peering behind every bush, as if you feared that some one should start up to intercept you?" she observed, one evening, when, tempted by the calm, clear atmosphere, and delighted with the rich autumnal tints that had succeeded to the verdant green of summer, she had, in spite of Elinor's very strong indications of disinclination and reluctance, ascended a considerable distance the woody path which led up the side of the mountain, in the direction of the ruined fortress which had been, according to Vincent's tale, the haunt of the banditti.

Elinor did not immediately reply, her attention was at that moment engrossed by an indistinct sound, which she fancied was that of human voices in earnest conference; and Mrs. Clifford, evidently angry at her silence, turned from her, and quickened her steps up the laborious ascent.

Again the sound was borne by the breeze to Elinor's ear; and now convinced that she was not mistaken, and forgetting that it was possible that the persons towards whom they were quickly aproaching might be, like herself and her companion, merely harmless wayfarers, she flew to Mrs. Clifford's side, and in the breathless accents of terror entreated her to return immediately.

"You are at perfect liberty to return or go on, as it pleases you," replied Mrs. Clifford, in an offended tone; "but unless some reason is given me why I should not do so, I shall certainly continue my walk. You can accompany me or not, as you please; but as I am so far on the way, I have made up my mind to reach the frowning ruin which crowns this hill, and which I have hitherto only contemplated at a distance, though I am convinced it must command a finer view of the country than I have yet .seen."

"I will tell you all—everything, the moment we are in safety," returned the terrified Elinor; "only, pray listen to my prayers to return."

"Tell me all!—in safety!" repeated Mrs. Clifford, suddenly stopping, and turning round. "What is the meaning of this? —what danger threatens us?—and why have you had any concealment from me, if you knew that——"

"Hush!—hark!" ejaculated Elinor, raising her finger in an attitude of attention, as at that moment a voice of the sweetest melody was heard chaunting a wild but pleasing air, the burthen of which was taken up by three or four rougher, but still harmonious tones.

"Well, what is there to be feared from persons so harmlessly employed?" demanded Mrs. Clifford, during a momentary pause of the melody. "They are, most probably, a party of wood-cutters enjoying their evening meal before they return home; or, perhaps, persons who, like ourselves, have been tempted to ascend the mountain by the fineness of the weather and the beauty of the prospects; and, bye the bye, I dare say it is the party whose boat we saw on the lake, this morning. Do, pray, lay aside these childish fancies; or, if there is any real cause for the alarm you seem to feel, condescend to let me be a sharer in the secret."

Elinor, however, was incapable at that moment of speaking— she had recognized in that voice, and in the strain also, sounds which she well remembered to have heard before; and her thoughts were in a tumult of mingled hope, fear, and joy. Yes, it was Edward Hatherleigh who was singing; and it was a song in which she and her then dear companions, Walter Copeland and his sisters, had borne their parts.

"Surely, where Edward is, there can be no danger to me,"

she reflected, as she hastily followed Mrs. Clifford, who was already considerably in advance of her, having evidently made up her mind to ascertain who the persons were who were thus "making the woods vocal."

Another winding of the narrow and rugged path was passed, and she and her companion were in sight of the singers, who were seated on the green sward beneath the outer mouldering wall of the ruin, with which their wild and picturesque appearance strangely harmonised.

There were five persons in the group, and the cups and flagon, with the scattered remains of provision that were spread on the grass, denoted that they had been, as Mrs. Clifford had conjectured, taking their evening meal in the open air; but even the latter herself, unsuspicious of danger as she had up to this moment proved herself, paused when she beheld them, and would from her looks have gladly retreated unnoticed. It was very plain indeed, that they were not of a class that were likely to be drawn to such a retired and remote spot by mere admiration of the beauties of nature; and equally certain it was, that they were not, as Mrs. Clifford had first conjectured, peasants who had been pursuing their hardy toil in the neighbouring woods. There was a strange, motley mixture of dresses and appearance among them; for while one or two were attired in handsome suits of the fashion of the country, others were in the coarsest garbs of the peasantry; and one, who was lying on the grass, leaning on his elbow, was literally barefoot, and in rags that fluttered in the breeze, and gave to his whole appearance an air of the most abject misery.

This was the songster whose clear and sweet voice again rose on the air, and would have fascinated even Elinor into silently listening, had she not at that moment discovered who he was.

It was Zekiel—the strange, half-maniac, gipsy lad, and not, as she had at first believed, Edward Hatherleigh; though, so strong was the resemblance between their voices, that she could scarcely believe the evidence of her senses, that he whom she sought was not there.

The instant she became convinced of this, all her previous terrors returned with redoubled force; and grasping Mrs. Clifford's arm, she whispered, in low breathless accents, " They are gipsies—we are lost for——" Before she could finish the sentence, Zekiel bounded to her feet; but he had not time to utter a word, before a fierce voice, behind the terrified girl and her scarcely less terrified companion, exclaimed,

" Back, fellow, how dare you thus intrude ?   Back ; you know your place better !"

A slight shriek escaped from Elinor's lips. She could no longer doubt the reality of her suspicions, for it was Dangerfield himself who uttered these words, and who now stood silently regarding her and Mrs. Clifford with a look of evident satisfaction.

" I can scarcely credit the reality of my good fortune," he observed, with a smile, " that I should behold you here, ladies ; but, pray, let me conduct you into my abode. Do not let the rough appearance of my people alarm you. I assure you they will be as anxious as myself to do the honours of the place to such guests. Unfortunately, we have no females with us, to give you a proper welcome ; but you must take the will for the deed, and excuse the roughness of our accommodations."

" I do not know who or what you are, sir," exclaimed Mrs. Clifford, evidently divided between fear and astonishment ; " but I assure you we had no intention to intrude upon you or your companions. You will allow us, therefore, to depart——" and she made an attempt to pass him, as he stood in the path, his bold, dark eyes fixed upon them, as if exulting in their terror.

" Elinor Clare will tell you who I am, madam," he replied, with a meaning smile ; " and she will tell you, too, that I am not used to have my attentions rejected. You *must* not depart, after so long a walk, without resting yourself, and partaking of such refreshments as I can offer you."

" Elinor !" repeated Mrs. Clifford, without regarding the latter part of his speech ; but the expression of astonishment and reproach to which she was about to give utterance died upon her lips, when she beheld Elinor's pallid and alarmed countenance ; and she only added, in a low voice, " This, then, was the secret of your reluctance to come hither ; but why was I not warned in time ?"

" Come, madam, let me lead you forward," observed Dangerfield, taking her hand with studied politeness, but, at the same time, with a look and manner that evidently was intended to convey to her his determination not to be refused. Bewildered and confounded, Mrs. Clifford grasped Elinor's arm, and proceeded some paces towards what had once been the principal entrance to the tower, but suddenly recollecting herself, she paused upon the threshold.

" We may as well understand each other at once, sir," she observed. " I do not think I run any great risk of offending you, by observing that I suppose your aim is money. If you will name what sum, I will at once agree to your terms, without putting you to any further trouble."

"You are very kind and accommodating, madam," he replied, "but my views extend, perhaps, further than you imagine; and it may require a little more time than you suspect to explain them. I must again, therefore, entreat you to enter my residence. Elinor will tell you," he added, sarcastically, "that I am much more accustomed to command than entreat; and if I do not do so in the present instance, I trust you will attribute it to my respect to you, and not to my not possessing the fullest means of enforcing obedience."

Convinced that it was useless longer to delay, where it was plain he had determined she should comply, Mrs. Clifford suffered herself to be led forward, across what had once been the court-yard of the building, and through the great hall, now roofless, and nearly choked with heaps of rubbish and weeds and nettles, into an inner apartment, which though miserably ruinous, dark, and dilapidated, was somewhat more tenantable. A long rough board supported by two large stones, formed a substitute for a table; around which were placed several rude wooden stools. A quantity of straw heaped in one corner, and two or three coarse rugs and blankets thrown carelessly on it, denoted that the apartment served the double purpose of a sleeping and a sitting-room. A fire of wood was crackling in the large fire-place, and various domestic utensils were scattered in confusion about the room.

Dangerfield motioned his visitors to be seated; and Zekiel, at his signal, placed on the board two candles, a bottle of wine, glasses, and some biscuits.

"I am fortunate in having this store in reserve," he observed, as he handed a glass to Mrs. Clifford; "but I had a presentiment that I should be honoured with a visit from those to whom such coarse viands as are our daily fare would not be palatable."

"You were prepared, no doubt, for this visit, sir, as you are pleased to call it," returned Mrs. Clifford, glancing with disdain at Elinor, who, scarcely conscious what she was doing, had taken the seat to which Dangerfield pointed on the opposite side of the table. "I beg, however, that you will dispense with all further affectation of ceremony, and tell me what it is you require of me. It is, in fact," she continued, rising with dignity, and waving her hand in rejection of the wine, which he still continued to press upon her acceptance; "it is quite ridiculous, this pretence of respect, from one whose aim is undoubtedly to plunder me. That I have been led purposely into this snare, I cannot doubt, though the means adopted were a seeming opposition to my wishes."

"Not by me!—oh, do not think that I have acted treacherously towards you!" exclaimed Elinor, in agony. "I would have died, rather than have betrayed you!"

"You knew these people were here," returned Mrs. Clifford; "and if you did not actually urge me forward, you were silent when you should have spoken: but all this is useless. It matters not how I was brought here: I wish only to know on what terms I shall be allowed to return."

"If you will allow me a few moments' conference with you, madam, we will settle those terms," returned Dangerfield; "and, perhaps you will then be inclined to allow that I am not quite so unconscionable a person as you suspect me to be. Elinor, your old friend Zekiel will show you some of the beauties and conveniences of our residence, while I explain to Mrs. Clifford——"

"You know me, then," interrupted Mrs. Clifford; "and, as I suspected, this is a premeditated plan to entrap me."

"Not as far as you are concerned, I assure you, on my honour," he replied, impressively; "though I will not deceive you, 'my poverty, and not my will,' may compel me to take advantage of the circumstance—but I will explain this. Elinor, Zekiel waits for you."

"No, no, no," exclaimed Elinor, flying to the side of Mrs. Clifford, and clasping her arm with breathless terror, "no, I will not leave her!"

Dangerfield smiled contemptuously.

"This is the extreme of folly," he replied, "when you know that I have it in my power to enforce instant obedience. What do you know of me, girl, or of my actions," he added, with a dark frown, "that you should show this reluctance and terror, either for yourself or your friend?"

"I know that mystery and concealment almost always imply guilt," returned Elinor, assuming a courage she did not feel; "and I know, too, that, from the first moment I beheld you up to the present, your actions have been those of a desperate, lawless man, who——"

"It will not be much to your advantage, I suspect," he coolly interrupted, "to recall the circumstances of our first introduction to each other. Recollect, girl," he continued, with that dark and stern expression of countenance which had so often before

made Elinor recoil from him with horror, "recollect *who* was
the cause of the lawless and desperate actions with which you
now dare to reproach me.   Do you owe me no gratitude, no
confidence?   Have you any right to taunt me with mystery and
concealment—you who are even now——but I am wasting time,"
he interrupted, "which might be much better employed.   Mrs.
Clifford, I am sure, will not object to favour me with a few
moments' conversation, in spite of the character you have chosen
to give me.   She will feel herself, I dare say, quite as safe
without your very valiant protection."

"Go, Elinor," observed Mrs. Clifford, in a tone of kindness,
which showed that her confidence in her integrity, which had
been momentarily shaken, was again restored.   "Go, child—
it is useless to dispute with those who have it in their power to
command.   Do not let him lead you far away from this spot,"
she added, in a hasty whisper, as Dangerfield turned away to
give some instructions to Zekiel.

Elinor grasped both her hands, with an agony she could not
control; but she felt, as Mrs. Clifford had said, that it was
useless to resist; and, with trembling limbs, she obeyed Zekiel's
signal to follow him.

"You little thought to see Paul and I, did you, when you
came out this morning?" observed the boy, turning round, with
one of his most malicious smiles, as soon as they were out of
hearing; "and you as little think that there is a chance of your
seeing somebody else, if you are not foolish, and cross Paul in
what he's doing, all for your sake."

"For my sake!" repeated Elinor, bitterly; "but who is it
you meant I should see, Zekiel?" she added, recollecting herself,
and speaking in that soothing and familiar tone which she knew,
by experience, had great influence with the boy, accustomed as
he was only to the harsh manners and commands of Dangerfield.

Zekiel, however, had probably been enjoined silence; for he
put his finger on his lip, and shook his head archly.

"You know who you would best like to see," he whispered—
"that is, if you are not altered by being made a grand lady."

"I am not a grand lady Zekiel," she replied, with a deep sigh,
as the remembrance of Mrs. Clifford's recent suspicions and harsh
observations rushed upon her mind—"I am only, like yourself,
a poor dependent on the bounty, and subservient to the will of
others.   But, is it indeed possible that Edward is here, companion
of——"

"Hush!—walls have ears!" interrupted Zekiel.   "I did not
say he was here.   I said you might see somebody, but I did not

mention *him*. You cannot say I did. But, come on: we can talk better when we are in the open air. I hate these prison-walls."

"It is indeed a gloomy abode," returned Elinor, looking round her, shuddering; "but I must not go farther, Zekiel. I cannot desert my friend," and she looked towards the heavy door of the apartment she had just quitted.

"Desert her!" he replied, with a meaning smile. "Do you, then, think that she is any safer for your remaining here?"

"I hope there is no fear of her safety, Zekiel," she returned, with trembling earnestness.

"Fear!" he repeated, "is she not with Paul? You know Paul; and you ought to know whether there is any reason to fear him."

Elinor's anxiety and alarm were increased rather than relieved by this evasive answer.

"At any rate, I will remain where I am, Zekiel," she observed, seating herself on a stone bench, which occupied a recess in the wall, from which she could command a view of the door already mentioned.

Zekiel looked displeased and dissatisfied.

"You must do as you like, of course," he observed, seating himself by her side; "but if you think you can do any more good here than where I was going to take you, I can tell you that you are mistaken."

Elinor, however, paid little attention to what he said; her thoughts were now solely occupied by the situation of Mrs. Clifford; and she sat with her eyes fixed on the door, listening intently for any sound that might indicate what was passing in the room, which she now bitterly repented she had been induced to quit.

While she was thus occupied, Zekiel sat silently watching her, with a look of mingled derision and surprise. Suddenly a thought seemed to strike him; and, drawing quite close to her, he whispered,

"What a brave girl you are, to have no fears for yourself! and yet, I can tell you, you are but a fool, after all."

"You know, then, that danger threatens me," exclaimed Elinor, quickly.

"You may call it danger, perhaps," he replied, with a mysterious smile; "that's as it may turn out; only that I don't think Paul would have taken so much pains and trouble to get you here for nothing."

ELINOR CLARE.

EDWARD CAUGHT UP ELINOR IN HIS ARMS.

"*Me!*—how do you know he wished to get *me* here?" demanded Elinor, in surprise. "What interest could he have in——"

"And yet, that note," she suddenly thought to herself, "was a caution only to me. It spoke not of any danger to Mrs. Clifford."

Her reflections were suddenly interrupted by the entrance of a female, who, apparently unconscious that the room was pre-occupied, entered from a small door, which Elinor had not before observed, and was proceeding straight towards the entrance of the other apartment, when Zekiel started from his seat, and intercepted her.

"You cannot go in, Paul is engaged," he observed.

"Engaged," she repeated, with surprise, "who, then——" but before she could finish the sentence, Elinor had recognised the voice and person of Mrs. Hatherleigh; and, uttering an exclamation of unfeigned delight, she flew to her, and clasped her in her arms.

"Elinor, my dear child!" she exclaimed, in faltering accents, "you have not, then, learned to despise me. But why are you here?" she added, seeming suddenly to recollect herself, "by what strange fatality——"

"Paul brought her here," interrupted Zekiel, hastily, "and what he does, you know, must be right. You must not ask her any questions, either; and so, do go away, and don't say you have seen her, or I shall be blamed."

"I will take all the blame on myself," replied Mrs. Hatherleigh; "but tell me, Elinor, did you come here voluntarily, knowing whom you should meet, or——"

"No, no," exclaimed Elinor, eagerly; "but I care not for myself—I have no fears but for my friend, my kind benefactress, Mrs. Clifford, who——"

The door of the inner apartment was at this moment thrown open, and Dangerfield hastily entered. At sight of Mrs. Hatherleigh, his countenance suddenly changed, from a look of triumph and exultation, to a dark and deadly frown.

"What is the meaning of this, madam?" he exclaimed, "how often am I to repeat, that I will not allow any interference with my plans?"

"Your plans!" she repeated, in a tone of despondency, shaking her head. "Ah! how often have I repeated, that your plans would bring ruin on yourself, and all connected with you! The time will come, that you will confess that I am right, that——"

"You are quite a prophetess," he replied, with a sneering smile; "a true Cassandra, always dealing out death and destruction to——"

"I speak the truth," she interrupted, with vehemence. "Look at what you have already done, by——"

"We will postpone, if you please, a recapitulation of my good deeds," he scornfully replied; "at present, I have matter of more moment to attend to. Your friend," he continued, addressing Elinor, "awaits you."

Elinor flew hastily towards the door of the room in which she had left Mrs. Clifford, but the melancholy look of Mrs.

Hatherleigh arrested her purpose; and, reproaching herself, for her thoughtlessness and inattention to her former friend, she returned, and held out her hand, to bid her farewell.

Dangerfield, however, interposed.

"There need be no leave-takings between you," he observed, with that air of supercilious scorn which so often deformed his otherwise handsome features. "You will meet often enough to get heartily tired, perhaps, of each other's society, ere long."

"I hope not," exclaimed Mrs. Hatherleigh, fervently; "much as I value Elinor's society, I would willingly forswear——"

"You would do many foolish and ridiculous things, were you left to yourself, no doubt," interrupted Dangerfield rudely; "but I will thank you to forbear, at present, these sentimental effusions; or, if you cannot bridle your tongue, it will be necessary, henceforward, that you confine yourself to your own —apartment, I was going to say; but I see the smile of derision on your lips; and as I acknowledge that your accommodations are not quite consistent with your merits——"

"Spare your sarcasms on that subject, sir," interrupted Mrs. Hatherleigh, mournfully; "or, at least, reserve them till I give you cause by complaining; though you are the last," she added, raising her eyes to his with a look of deep meaning; "who should reproach me with my demerits. Go, Elinor, my dear child. Heaven grant, when we meet again, it may be——"

Elinor did not hear the conclusion of the sentence; for Dangerfield, who had advanced with alacrity to open the door for her, contrived to close it upon her and himself, the moment she had passed the threshold; and she found herself alone with him.

Where was Mrs. Clifford? The question rose to her lips, but she was unable to give it utterance; for as she turned to Dangerfield, the expression of his features chilled her very blood; and, but that he caught her arm, she would have sunk to the earth.

"You think I have deceived you," he coolly observed; "and, I dare say, are in imagination supposing all manner of dreadful things have happened to your friend. You are mistaken; she is, at this moment, quietly pursuing her way homewards."

"Without me!" exclaimed Elinor. "Oh, no—do not tell me so; she would not have deserted me—she would not have left me here to——"

"To what?" he demanded, as she paused, "what are the dangers you apprehend from me? or what occasion have I ever given you for this excessive alarm?"

"Why have you wished to get me into your power?" demanded Elinor, summoning up courage to reply to his questions—"why——"

"I will answer you in a few words," he returned. "I have your interest at heart; but circumstances compel me to act with seeming mystery. You look incredulous. Do you not believe that I speak the truth?"

"Can it be for my interest, to separate me from the only friend—the only friend, at least, who has power to protect me?" she replied. "But I do not believe," she added, with increasing spirit, "that Mrs. Clifford has quitted this place; I know her too well. She would die, rather than tamely yield me up to the evils from which she once rescued me, at such sacrifices that——"

"If you will come this way, I will convince you that my word is to be taken," he replied coolly.

Elinor passively followed him to the green platform in front of the principal entrance, which, from its elevated situation, commanded a view of the whole of the winding road into the valley beneath.

"There is your friend, and the guide whom I have deputed to see her safe to her own habitation," he observed. "Will you now be satisfied that I speak the truth?"

"Thank God, she is safe!" ejaculated Elinor, as she watched the retreating form of her benefactress, who was with rapid steps descending the rugged path, accompanied by a female wearing the peasant garb of the country.

Dangerfield did not interrupt her for some minutes; and she continued to gaze, until the distance between them was increased so that she could scarcely discern the forms on which her eyes were fixed with such intense anxiety.

"And now, sir, will you be pleased to tell me why I am detained here?" she demanded, endeavouring to assume a calmness to which her faltering accents gave a strong denial.

"I will tell you, then, candidly," he replied, "that you are a hostage for your friend's complying with certain conditions I have proposed to her, and to which she has agreed. But that is not all. Chance, or, rather, your good fortune, has thrown into my hands the means, if I mistake not, of rendering you a great service—of, in fact, restoring you to your proper place in society, and clearing up the mystery in which, if I understand aright, you have been involved from your birth. I am told—you will correct me, if I am wrong—that you have never believed the tale that Copeland, as he called himself, has told you of your origin, and the circumstances which threw you a helpless dependent on his bounty."

"I have certainly doubted that he stood in the relationship to me which he pretended," returned Elinor, in extreme surprise; "and I have confided, upon more than one occasion, those doubts to Mrs. Hatherleigh, who has perhaps also told you that his conduct was such towards me, on many occasions, as to warrant my suspicions."

"It matters little," he observed, coolly, "how I became possessed of my information, so that you acknowledge it be correct. But we will, if you please, re-enter our abode: the air is getting chill; and it will be at least two or three hours before my messenger returns from Mrs. Clifford."

The confidence which Elinor had begun to feel towards her singular companion was again shaken by this mention of Mrs. Clifford, and the recollection of the unworthy advantage which, she could not doubt, he had taken of her having been thus thrown into his power. As she re-entered the grim and frowning walls, a cold chill struck upon her heart. She thought of the scenes of violence and misery which it had witnessed; and as she looked at her dark and mysterious conductor, she shuddered to think that he, perhaps, had been an actor in them.

The room which they had left empty was now tenanted by a motley group of both sexes; some of whom, seated at the table, were engaged in noisy conversation; while others, surrounding the ample fire-place, in which a large fire was now burning on the hearth, were silently watching the flame, which reflected its redness upon their dark countenances.

Elinor's anxious eyes glanced from face to face—she was desirous of discovering whether any of them were known to her as belonging to the tribe of which she had formerly beheld Dangerfield the acknowledged Chief; but, though the same characteristic style of features, the same mixture of tawdry finery, with squalid wretchedness of attire, prevailed among them as had distinguished the gipsies with whom she had been casually associated in England, there were no faces here whom she could recognise, with the exception of Zekiel, who, as usual, was now with his peculiar look of servile assiduity, watching, as it appeared, the eyes of Dangerfield for directions. To some question which the latter addressed to him in a whisper, he replied in the negative.

"And the lady?" observed Dangerfield, loud enough for Elinor to hear.

"She is gone to the tower, I guess, to look out for him," replied Zekiel.

Dangerfield's dark countenance betrayed his displeasure.

"She had better not attempt to thwart me," he observed. "Run, boy, to the south wing—it is there he will enter; and take care to give me the signal, before he can see her."

Zekiel was out of sight before the words were well uttered; and, turning to Elinor, Dangerfield courteously invited her to be seated on a bench which was placed at the side of the room, at some distance from the rest of the party.

"You will, perhaps, think it strange that I should invite you to remain here, amidst this noisy assembly," he observed, "when I have such ample room at my command. But the fact is, that I believe, with the opinion you have conceived of me, you will feel yourself safer here than with me alone."

Elinor did not reply. She felt, indeed, that he had judged rightly; but she did not wish to exasperate him by openly avowing the dread she felt of him.

"There are none here," he observed, after a few moments' silence, "who understand our language. We may, therefore, converse freely, without fear of being comprehended."

This, however, was no subject of gratulation to Elinor; for, little as the appearance of those around her was calculated to inspire confidence, she would have felt some hope that an appeal to them for protection, should she require it, would not have been made in vain, had they been of her own country, and speaking her own language. From the looks of eager curiosity which they, from time to time, turned towards her and her singular companion, she shrunk with irrepressible aversion and disgust; for they conveyed, on the part of the men, an expression of licentious freedom which it was impossible to mistake, while the eyes of the women, if they conveyed anything beyond mere curiosity and surprise, expressed only undisguised scorn and contempt. A remark or two, however, which were addressed in a laughing tone to the Chief by some of the latter sex, were immediately repressed by the stern frown with which he replied to them; and by degrees, seeming to understand the reserve of his looks and manners, they withdrew apparently their observation entirely from him and his companion, and devoted their attention entirely to their own affairs.

"This is not altogether so agreeable a party as that to which you were first introduced under my guidance," observed Dangerfield, who seemed to possess the power of reading her thoughts in her countenance; "neither," he continued, "are these dreary walls so pleasant as our light and airy tents, in the green woods and forests of our native land. But it is the truest wisdom, to accommodate ourselves to circumstances; and I beg of you to practise it for a little while, and not look as if you expected a mine to spring beneath, and bring down ruin and destruction upon you."

"You best know, sir, whether I have or have not cause for the uneasiness I feel," replied Elinor.

"There is none," he returned, hastily, "if you are willing to submit to my guidance, and accede to my plans."

"And if I do not?" observed Elinor, quickly.

"Then you must take the consequences," he replied, "it will be you, not I, who will suffer. Do not suppose," he continued, after a moment or two of silence, "that I am such a fool or hypocrite as to pretend that I have only your interest at heart. I have long dismissed from my vocabulary the romantic impracticable word, disinterestedness, and boldly acknowledge that I am always prepared to take advantage of any circumstances that may conduce to my own welfare; but, in the present instance, I shall be serving you, as well as myself. And, now, not to keep you any longer in suspense, I will candidly tell you that my object in detaining you here is to bring about a union between you and——"

"He is coming, I saw him leaping from rock to rock, in the direction of the ruined chapel, which he is so fond of," exclaimed Zekiel, bounding into the room. "If you make haste, you may meet him; for——"

"There cannot be a fitter place for our interview," interrupted Dangerfield. "Zekiel, remain here until I return. Stay, boy, it will, perhaps, be better that you follow slowly with Elinor."

"To the chapel?" demanded Zekiel, with visible discontent.

"Yes, to the chapel!" repeated the Chief, sternly. "What objection can you have to that? Pshaw! you are a fool, a stupid obstinate fool!" he exclaimed, with vehemence, as Zekiel looked down to the ground, with a sullen dogged look, which showed that he had some strong motive for departing from that unlimited and unquestioning obedience in which he was generally so consistent towards Paul, as he always called him. "I cannot stay to argue with you," continued the latter, in a threatening accent, "will you come, or——"

"Well, I will come," interrupted Zekiel, with a vehemence that strongly resembled Dangerfield's own manner.

The Chief uttered something which was unintelligible to Elinor, but which the boy seemed perfectly to understand, for he crouched, as though he already felt the chastisement which was, no doubt, threatened; and the moment his master had quitted the apartment, he turned to the former with that peculiar look of malice she had seen his features assume on former occasions, when he was thwarted.

"I'll play him a trick for it, when he little expects it," he observed, "but come, we must set off, for I'm not going through the dark passage and gloomy halls at this time of night, when nothing but a blind bat or a blinking owl could find its way. Besides," he continued, with an arch smile of sudden recollection, "I should run the risk of breaking your delicate neck over some of the heaps of stones that lie in the way, or you might fall into some of the vaults that gape with their open mouths to swallow up those who are not aware of them; and then, what a pretty tale I should have to tell Master Ned."

"It is Edward, then, whom he has gone to meet?" exclaimed Elinor, who, though she had suspected the truth, had, till this moment, fluctuated between doubt and fear.

"Yes—ha! how the colour has come back to your cheeks, at hearing his name," returned the boy. "Well, I suppose, by the time we get there round the ruins, he will be as anxious to see you, as you are to see him."

Elinor did not reply. She scarcely, indeed, noticed the boy's sly insinuation, for her thoughts were in a tumult of fear, alarm, and apprehension for the consequences of the anticipated meeting; and it was not until Zekiel had twice repeated his summons, that she arose from her seat, to follow where he should conduct her.

"And yet," she reflected, "why should I fear, if Edward is there? he will protect me. Yes, if he is not changed, to him I may confidently look for safety and support."

Zekiel's exhortation to her, to make haste, or he should suffer for it, as they had a long way to go round, interrupted her reflections; and, with trembling steps, she followed him through the spacious ruined hall by which she had first entered. The moon was shining clear but cold, as she emerged into the open air; and she paused for a moment to gaze upon the calm and quiet scene beneath. To the right, gloomy and deserted, lay the farm-house, which had been the scene of old Vincent's tragical story, the remembrance of which thrilled her with horror, as she recollected that she stood upon the very spot which had echoed with the cries of the miserable victim of avarice and cruelty.

The way which Zekiel had chosen to conduct her around the ruined outer wall of the fortress was not only a long, but, from the heaps of rubbish which they were compelled either to cross, or make a wide circuit to avoid, a tedious one; and Elinor had full time to collect her scattered thoughts, and attain, at least, an appearance of calmness, before she came in sight of the chapel; which, though gloomy, and dilapidated by the hand of all-destroying time, was the most perfect and picturesque part of the building she had yet seen. It stood in the shade of the more lofty building, which prevented the moon's rays reaching it; but a faint light streamed through its narrow-pointed windows, gilding the branches of an immense cork-tree, which hung over its roof, and extended its wide-spreading arms, as if to protect the sacred edifice.

All Zekiel's usual levity and recklessness of manner seemed to desert him, as they approached the building. He trod as lightly as though he feared the very echoes of his own footsteps, and startled at the rustling sound which arose from Elinor's dress sweeping along the ground among the showers of leaves which the autumnal blasts had strewed there.

As he came nearer the walls, he paused for a moment, to listen.

" If they are not there, I will not go in," he murmured, in a faltering voice; but, at that moment, the deep tones of Danger-field were heard, speaking as if under the influence of violent excitement; and, no longer hesitating, or bestowing a thought on her recreant guide, Elinor rushed forward and entered the building.

For a moment she doubted if it were indeed Edward whom she beheld, so striking was the alteration which his person had undergone during the time that had elapsed since she last beheld him. He was then but a slender stripling, though giving promise of that manly grace and activity which a free life and unrestrained exercise had since confirmed. He was now nearly a head taller, and his gait and motions were those of manhood in its prime. His dark hair clustered in thick curls around his manly brow; and the striking and picturesque costume of the country, which he had adopted, gave added interest and dignity to his appearance. He was speaking in an impassioned voice, in reply to Dangerfield, when Elinor glided into the porch; her light foot-steps were unheard; and she paused for a moment, almost doubting whether those full, manly tones could be his.

"It is too true," he observed, "I have, indeed, suffered myself to be guided and directed by your counsels, even till they have brought me to the very verge of destruction; but I have never swerved from one principle—that of doing always what my conscience told me to be right, when I have been allowed the choice. In the present case, the happiness, the reputation of one whom I regard more than my life is at stake; and I boldly tell you that I will not be made the instrument of your schemes, be they what they may. If Elinor be here as you assert———"

"She is here," interrupted Dangerfield, who had descried the light drapery of the trembling girl fluttering in the night-breeze, as she stood a few paces within the porch, in an attitude of eager attention, and now advanced to lead her in.

Edward's eyes were fixed upon her with a look of mournful interest and anxiety; and he uttered not a word of welcome or of pleasure, though he fervently pressed the cold and trembling hand which Dangerfield placed within his grasp.

"I will leave you, for a few moments, together," observed the latter; "and, in so doing," he added, nodding significantly at Edward, "adduce, I suspect, a stronger argument in favour of my scheme than anything I could say. Zekiel—what ho, Zekiel? —where are you, boy?" he added, in a voice that seemed to imply his belief that he had triumphed.

The voice of Zekiel answered from without, and Dangerfield quitted the building.

"Elinor," exclaimed Edward, the moment he was gone, "you have been betrayed hither. I need not, I do not ask you how; but sure I am, that never would you voluntarily have sought me under such circumstances. But you will believe, dear girl, that I am innocent of all participation in this treachery—that I am sorrowing more to see you than———"

"I do believe it—I knew it, Edward," interrupted Elinor, with earnestness; "but, surely, with you I am safe! That bold, bad man, whom I tremble to name or to look at, will not dare to oppose you in your firm decision to do that which is right."

"Do you know what it is he proposes, Elinor?" he demanded, looking fondly but mournfully in her face, as he encircled her slender waist with his arm.

Elinor's cheek glowed with the deepest crimson, as she replied,

"Yes, he has told me that it is his wish to unite our fates beyond the power of man to separate, Edward," she continued, in a more decided tone of voice. "I have no reserves from you—my heart remains the same still attached to you; and to be your wife would——"

"I must not think of it—I dare not trust myself to think of it," interrupted Edward, passionately. "Oh, Elinor, it is a temptation that shakes all my resolution."

She gently disengaged herself from his fervent embrace.

"Do not wrong yourself, Edward. You are incapable, I am sure you are, of taking any advantage of my present situation. I cannot," she continued, hastily preventing his reply, "I cannot, of course, form any idea of this man's motives for the course he has taken, or what he can have in wishing to unite us under our present circumstances; but——"

"I will tell you, then, dearest girl," he interrupted, "all that I know on the subject. He has acquired, by what means I am unable even to guess, some knowledge respecting your birth and connections. He believes that he has it in his power to substantiate your claims to a considerable fortune, and—I blush while I own it—he wishes to secure a great part of it to himself, which he thinks he should do if you were to become my wife."

"But why not, then, dismissing all these stratagems, which must expose him to certain danger?" observed Elinor, "why not take the straightforward course—establish my rights, and trust to the gratitude I must feel towards him, and—why should I hesitate to say it?—my love for you? Does he think that money would change my heart? Ought he not to know that, if I were at this moment independent——"

She paused, blushing and confused at the warmth with which she was expressing herself, and the looks of passionate love with which Edward regarded her.

"I could believe all this, Elinor," he at length replied, "and perhaps he, vitiated and sophisticated as his heart is, by constant intercourse with the worst and basest part of mankind, even he, I say, might believe it of you, if he thought that you would be independent; if he did not know that riches would bring with them friends, connections, who would consider it their duty to oppose—like your present protectress, Mrs. Clifford—all intercourse with one so degraded, so poor, so destitute of every recommendation, as Edward Hatherleigh. Even you, Elinor," he continued, in a melancholy tone, "even you would feel that a new situation in life had brought with it new duties. You would feel that you owed a deference to the opinion of your friends—the opinion of the world; and I, Elinor, what should I be? How should I despise and hate myself, if it were otherwise, if I could take advantage of your attachment to me—if I could descend to become a mean dependant on your generosity, despised and pointed at by the whole world?"

"Let me, then, remain as I am," observed Elinor, warmly. "Let me return to Mrs. Clifford, and trust to fortune, or rather to that good Providence which has hitherto preserved us both from the perils that at one time threatened to overwhelm us——"

"Would it were in my power instantly to restore you to your home !" exclaimed Edward, passionately. "Would that I could extricate both you and myself from the meshes in which that bold, bad man, as you have justly styled him, and whom I blush to call my father, has entangled us ! But of this be assured, Elinor, I will not be made the tool of his base intentions. I will protect you with my life——"

"But why not seize this moment to escape together?" interrupted Elinor, eagerly ; "he has left us, it appears, and——"

"Yes, he has left us," reiterated Edward; "but do not suppose that we are not guarded and watched. I know well for what purpose he has gone. There is a priest, a disgrace to his name and holy calling, who is associated with him and the wretches of whom he is the Chief. It is to summons the priest he has gone, to perform the ceremony of marriage, to which he believes neither you nor I will dare persist in refusing our consent; but, were I ten thousand times more desirous of calling you mine, Elinor, I would not——"

"But if we are both resolute, Edward," she exclaimed, looking anxiously in his face, "what can he do? He dares not detain me here long, because, whatever may be the tale with which he has deceived Mrs. Clifford into leaving me behind her——"

"Mrs. Clifford !" exclaimed Edward, with extreme surprise and agitation; "does she, then, know that you are here? Speak, dearest, tell me all, for you have awakened hopes——"

In a few words Elinor related the manner in which Mrs. Clifford and herself had fallen into Dangerfield's power; adding, that, from the speed with which the former was proceeding towards her own residence when she had last beheld her, she was convinced that she had some important object in view.

"I will own to you," she continued, "that I was inclined to believe that *he* had no other motive for detaining me but to extort from her a sum of money for my release ; and though I was not without terrors and apprehensions, yet as I felt that I might confidently rely on her, let his terms be ever so exorbitant, I looked forward with hope to a speedy return to my home and——"

"You are right," returned Edward, vehemently; "he has thus made doubly sure of profiting by you. Had I not unfortunately kept my engagement by coming here to-day, nothing would have been said of this second plot, and you would have been allowed to return with the messenger who should bring the price of your freedom and——"

"But you said that the discovery that Mrs. Clifford knew of my being here, opened new hopes to you," interrupted Elinor, eagerly.

"Yes, if we could but gain time," he replied, looking wildly around him; "if we could secrete ourselves but for a few hours, until the time is past that has been appointed for the performance of the contract between Mrs. Clifford and him. Yes, that will do," he continued, "he will not dare to stay to abide the means that she will undoubtedly take to recover you. He and his gang will be compelled to make a hasty retreat from this neighbourhood, and——Elinor, will you dare trust yourself to follow me, whithersoever I shall lead you? will you not be terrified at——"

"At nothing, with you for my guide," she replied, with energy. "Lead on, then, if you know of any means——"

"One moment, then," he replied, catching up one of the torches which were stuck into the crevices of the ruined altar.

Elinor's heart beat with the most intense anxiety, as she watched him retire behind a projecting buttress at the further end of the chapel. A heap of rubbish, which had fallen from the roof, concealed him for a few moments from her view; but he quickly re-appeared, and flew rather than ran towards her.

"Now, then, Elinor," he exclaimed, "not a moment is to be lost. Confide in me; and if, as I believe, the secret is mine, and mine only, we are saved."

Elinor uttered not a word, but she clung to his arm with perfect confidence, as he led her to the spot he had so recently quitted. A stone, which differed in no respect from the flooring of the chapel, which still remained in tolerable preservation, except where it was covered by the ruins which had fallen from above, was raised from its prostrate situation, and leaned against the wall, disclosing beneath a dark chasm, which looked like a spacious repository for the dead. It seemed not very deep; for with very little difficulty, Edward lowered her, so that she could stand on the firm earth beneath; and, then, jumping into what appeared to her excited imagination a yawning grave, he drew down the stone over their heads, and extinguishing the torch, they were left in total darkness.

A horrible feeling of suffocation—an appalling dread that they should never be released from that dark tomb, for a moment overcame Elinor's fortitude. She gasped for breath, as the heavy stone closed over them. It evidently required an exertion of almost supernatural strength on Edward's part to prevent it, from its weight, falling with a sudden crash, that must have alarmed those who were in all probability on the watch outside the chapel, and revealed the means by which the fugitives had been enabled to escape.

And how, then, would it be possible for him to raise it again, and allow them to return from the other world, as it seemed, to the "realms of cheerful day?" was the apprehension that seized upon her mind, as she clung to Edward's arm for support, in this dreary abode.

"Be not alarmed, dearest Elinor," he whispered, "there is nothing in reality to terrify you, in so far as I have already penetrated into this subterraneous region."

"It does not end here, then?" exclaimed Elinor, in breathless accents, "we can go on? We shall not be doomed to remain in this horrid place, buried as it were alive, till——"

"No, we will proceed immediately," he replied, "if you are capable of the exertion."

Elinor replied only by a pressure of his arm; and he led her forward in the darkness, until they reached a low door, which yielded immediately to his strength. A current of fresh air gave instant relief to the oppressive sensations which had so overpowered Elinor, and she stepped forward with confidence into the large, vacant space, which was comparative freedom to the narrow, dreary, and tomb-like spot they had quitted.

"We will secure this door, before we proceed farther," observed Edward; "and then, even if the passage should be known by which we have effected our escape, there will be obstacles in the way of their following us which may delay them until we have succeeded in finding the means of eventual escape."

Elinor's spirits, which had risen at finding herself freed from the intolerable confinement of the first entrance to this subterraneous region, again sank at Edward's expression of uncertainty; but she carefully suppressed any expression of alarm and trepidation during the time that he was employed in forcing the rusty bolts which secured the door into their sockets. The noise that occasioned, however, reverberating through what appeared a long range of dreary vaults, greatly increased her terror; and she urged her companion to proceed, without farther delay, lest the sound should have reached the ears of those who probably by this time had entered the chapel, and, if so, were, as she supposed, now immediately above them.

Edward, however, assured her she was mistaken—the range of vaults ran in an opposite direction, crossing, as he believed, under the south wing of the building.

"I own I have very little knowledge whither they lead," he observed, "for I have only visited them once, and that within the last few days; and then I had not time properly to examine them. It seems, however, but reasonable to conclude, that there must be some outlet other than that by which we entered, and it is that which we must now endeavour to find. If I had dared retain the torch, it would have materially assisted our search; but it might also have betrayed us if, as I suspect from the rush of air, some part of the arched roof has fallen in the way we are now pursuing. The south wing," he continued, "is the most uninhabitable and ruinous part of the edifice; and is, therefore, seldom visited by those who have found a refuge in the other parts. Still, as I could not be aware where the reflection of a light from beneath might fall, it would have been dangerous to hazard it; and now, dearest Elinor, I have only to entreat you to keep up your spirits, and follow me closely. There can be no danger to apprehend, except, perhaps, a stumble over some of the rubbish that may have fallen from above; and from that I will take care to guard you, by proceeding with all possible caution."

For nearly ten minutes they continued to progress slowly and silently onwards, until at length the welcome sight of the moonbeams, streaming through "a rent which time had made," verified Edward's anticipations, and relieved the oppression which had arisen from the state of total darkness in which they had hitherto journeyed on. Hastily, yet still with cautious footsteps, they approached the spot which was thus favoured with the light of heaven. The chasm, or, rather, it might have been with more propriety called, a fissure—between two stones in the arched roof, was too high above them, and of too limited an extent, to allow them to see anything except the clear, blue sky, and the moon shining with unclouded splendour, over their heads; but from that he was enabled to decide that his first conjecture was right, and that the vaulted passage led directly under the southern wing, which was roofless, and exposed to "all the airs of heaven."

Leaning on his arm, Elinor stood in silence, inhaling the pure air, and gazing on the lovely lamp of night; but she was soon recalled from these pleasurable feelings, by the anxious expression of Edward's countenance, as he gazed forward into the gloom, which seemed deepened by the strong but circumscribed light in which they were standing.

"I am considering, dearest, which way it will be most advisable to pursue," he murmured, in reply to the question which her eyes only asked, so fearful was she of uttering a sound which might betray them should any one be near to hear. "There are two passages," he continued, in the same low tone, "the one to the right, the other in a contrary direction. That, if I am right as to the position in which we now stand, can end only in the inaccessible precipice on which the south-western part of the edifice, now completely in ruins, formerly stood; and I fear there is scarcely any probability that there can be any egress thence. This," he continued, pointing in the contrary direction, "must either——"

A slight noise—so slight, indeed, that Elinor scarcely knew whether it was not the echo of her own footstep, as she moved a pace forward, to endeavour to gain a more distinct view of the passage to which he had directed her attention—at this moment arrested Edward's words. He drew her closer to him, and stood, with his eyes intently fixed on the range of vaulted arches to the right. Again the noise was heard, and now more distinctly than before. It was the hollow echo of a man's voice; and Edward, believing that some one was approaching to intercept them, caught up Elinor in his arms, and dashed desperately and reckless of all impediment, along the opposite passage. For a considerable distance—until, indeed, he was compelled to stop from absolute exhaustion—Edward continued this hurried flight; and then, though obliged by strong necessity to set down his precious burthen, he continued to press her to his panting bosom, as if to be assured that he had her still in safety. Elinor could not speak; her every faculty was strained, in listening whether their fancied pursuers were approaching; but no sound reached their ear, except their own quick breathings, and the audible throbbings of their own hearts; and again Edward's hopes of

ELINOR CLARE.

EDWARD'S WATCHFULNESS NEVER FOR A MOMENT RELAXED.

eventually escaping revived, and he strove to reassure and cheer the spirits of his trembling companion.

"We cannot have much further to go, dearest," he whispered, "if there is any outlet by this passage; and there certainly must be, or to what purpose has it been constructed? Even now I fancy I feel the freshness of the evening breeze. Yes, and that—surely that is a ray of moonlight again, blessing us with a promise of liberty!"

Elinor's eyes were anxiously strained to discover the friendly harbinger of freedom of which he spoke; and at length the little star-like ray was discernible.

"Let us not lose a moment," she murmured, "I am strong, quite strong, now."

Edward pressed her fervently to his heart; and again they proceeded, the light becoming more and more distinct at every step they took. At last they reached the termination of the vaulted passage: and, then, to their unspeakable dismay and disappointment, discovered that there was no visible outlet, or means of quitting their dreary prison, the light which had guided them being admitted through a small grated aperture, in what seemed the solid wall which terminated the passage. For a moment or two Edward stood silent and confounded, his eyes turned upwards to the aperture, which was so high as to be apparently beyond his reach. Suddenly a thought seemed to strike him, and he proceeded narrowly to examine the wall, which was to appearance composed of solid smooth stones. Inch by inch he cautiously examined the apparently impracticable barrier, in hopes of finding the means of obtaining a footing which would enable him to look through the aperture, and ascertain what lay beyond; but, though he was disappointed in this, he at length made another discovery, which he was instanly convinced was of more consequence; for he found that one large stone, nearly half way from the ground to the ceiling, was moveable; and convinced that he had now discovered the secret, he applied himself with unremitting perseverance to effect their release. A dagger, which, until then, Elinor had not observed, he carried, and which, at first sight, made her shudder, as the bright moonbeams glanced on its polished surface, supplied the only means of removing the stone, which for a long time resisted all his efforts. At length, however, it gave way; and with transport Elinor beheld a passage large enough to admit her without difficulty into a recess, or natural cave, the mouth of which, partly overgrown with shrubs, admitted the clear light of the moon, while the soft moss beneath her feet, and the fragrant though chilly evening breeze, assured her of the welcome fact, that they were at last beyond the confines of the fortress.

Elinor's first care was to assist Edward to replace the stone, which, she now found, regularly fitted in with a groove, and was further secured by a strong iron bar on the side they now were, so as to prevent all immediate apprehensions of being followed thither by the way they came. Most fortunate it had been for them, that this fastening had been left unsecured, or to a certainty they would never have been able to enter their present place of retreat.

Cautioning Elinor still to remain silent, Edward proceeded to the entrance of the cave, or cell, to reconnoitre whereabouts they were placed; but the instant after he returned to her, with evident marks of haste and trepidation: and before he had well seated himself on the broken stone bench, which was the only mark that the cave had an inhabitant, the light of a torch was reflected on the shrubs and overhanging branches of the trees in front, and then again receded.

Elinor sunk on the ground, in speechless terror, and Edward, as he bent over her, softly whispered,

"We are in the very face of our enemies, Elinor, and nothing can be done, but to remain immoveable until they have relinquished their search, and withdrawn from the spot altogether, which they must inevitably do at daybreak, since it is not probable but that Mrs. Clifford, finding herself deceived as to your return, will take the proper measures, by giving information of the outrage; and a party of soldiers will, as is usual in all such cases, be sent hither."

"But if they should enter here?" murmured Elinor, half rising, and pointing with extreme terror to the mouth of the cave.

"There is no fear of that," he replied. "This place is called the Hermit's Cell; and strange tales are told of one who did penance here for years for some heinous crime. There is no accessible path to it from below; for we are on the very face of the rock, around the feet of which the person who bore that torch was winding towards a distant part of the ruins, doubtless with the belief that we must be secreted in some of its numerous recesses. Be assured, that they would as soon think of climbing to the eagle's nest on the opposite pinnacle to look for us, as to direct their search hither. Even I," he continued, "have often turned my eyes upwards, as I crossed the vale beneath, and wondered by what means the hermit, if there were such a person, could have reached his aerial abode."

"But if that passage by which we entered should be known?" observed Elinor.

"Even then we have little to fear: for before they could force an entrance——"

Elinor shuddered at the expressive action with which he grasped his dagger; but the light of the torch was again seen flashing at the entrance, and Edward's fervent pressure of her hand again enforced silence. Hour after hour passed tediously away; at times their solitude was disturbed by the distant sound of voices and various indefinable noises, which betokened that the inhabitants of the fortress were still in a state of commotion. Edward's watchfulness never for a moment relaxed—he did not even attempt to raise Elinor from her lowly seat on the earth which she had taken, evidently lest she should embarrass him, if an attack were made either way upon their place of retreat; but at length, quite exhausted, a deep sleep overpowered her.

CHAPTER XVI.

Then he pronounc'd adieu! and yet would stay,
Till, chidden—sooth'd—entreated—forc'd away,
He would of coldness, though indulg'd, complain,
And oft retire and oft return again;
When, if his teazing vex'd her gentle mind,
The grief assumed compell'd her to be kind;
For he would proof of plighted kindness crave,
That she resented first, and then—forgave,
And to his grief and penance yielded more
Than his presumption had requir'd before.

                                 CRABBE.

NEARLY thirty years before the period at which those events commenced which we have already narrated, a gay wedding party were assembled in the drawing-room of Mr. Dewarden, a London merchant, of some eminence in his profession, and of greater reputation for probity, integrity, and benevolence. He had himself risen from small beginnings to the possession of a handsome fortune; and, far from seeking to ennoble himself by an ambitious connection, he considered that he could not do better than to bestow the hand of his only daughter, and the reversion of his wealth, on a most deserving and industrious young man, who, originally a clerk in the house, had recently been made a junior partner.

Felicia Dewarden was at this time just seventeen, extremely pretty and pleasing in person and manners, and possessing a sweetness of disposition that made her the idol of all around her. By her father she was perfectly adored. Her mother had died young; and the father, who saw in his child the image of his regretted wife renewed, had for her sake resisted every temptation to form a second marriage. Felicia's wishes and will had been his law; and, contrary to what is the general result of unlimited indulgence, she had never shown a disposition to abuse her power. When, therefore, her father first hinted to her that he should prefer to see her the wife of Lionel Moreton, his thriving, active, and well-conducted partner, than to bestow her on any of the fashionable foplings who fluttered around her, she betrayed no reluctance, but merely playfully demanded whether it were possible that one so grave and serious as Mr. Moreton could have any preference for such a silly, thoughtless girl as herself.

"He does not consider you silly or thoughtless, my dear," replied the fond parent, " neither is he naturally so grave and serious as you seem to think; but he is modest and unobtrusive; and unless he receives a little more encouragement from you——"

"Mercy upon me, dear papa! you would not have me go a wooing to the bashful gentleman, would you?" interrupted the lively girl.

"Do you then really like him, Felicia?" demanded the gratified father.

"Like him," she replied, "the man is well enough. Some of my female friends say he is very handsome; and certainly, for a middle-aged gentleman——"

"Middle-aged, dear Felicia? Moreton is not more than thirty," exclaimed Mr. Dewarden.

"Thirty! dear me!—I declare I thought he must be fifty, so very serious and reasonable and circumspect," returned the rattling girl.

"You would not wish your husband to be other than circumspect and reasonable, I hope, my child," observed her father, gravely.

"Oh no, dear papa; only I should like him all the better, if he were to smile a little oftener, and——"

"He will smile soon enough, if you smile upon him, Felicia."

"Do you think so?—Well, then, I will try my influence, this very day. Seriously, dear papa—you know I have no will but yours; but I should not like, in your anxiety to secure me a good husband, that Mr. Moreton should—should——there, settle it all your own way," and she threw her white arms around her father's neck, and kissed him. " I am sure, whatever you do will be for the best for your own Felicia; and as I am not one of those daughters who think it necessary to have a violent aversion for the man their father recommends—-not but what I think," she continued, disengaging herself from his embrace, and assuming a very important air, "that it will be quite time enough to think of marrying me, two or three years hence. I am very happy and comfortable as I am; and, if Mr. Moreton is the docile, obedient, and modest man he pretends to be, he will be quite contented to live upon my gracious promise, and let me enjoy my liberty for the time I have mentioned."

"But I shall not, Felicia," returned her father. "Life is uncertain, at all times; and I am fast going down the hill. I am nearly sixty, my child; and I have lately had some warnings that ——Do not weep, my Felicia; but tell me that you will be, as you have always been, good and obedient. It is my most ardent wish to see you shielded from all probable danger, as the wife of a worthy man. Besides, my dear girl, you will in reality enjoy more liberty——"

"Not another word, dear papa," interrupted Felicia, smiling through her tears. "I will marry Mr. Moreton to-morrow, if he asks me."

"I do not wish to be precipitate, dearest; but——"

Felicia flew out of the room, for she heard the well-known footstep of Mr. Moreton ascending the stairs, and she wished to avoid meeting him at that moment.

Exactly one month from the period of this conversation, Felicia Dewarden became the bride of Lionel Moreton; and from the gay party which were, as before said, assembled to grace the nuptials in the drawing-room of the rich merchant, at his suburban villa, the bridegroom was suddenly summoned by the unwelcome intelligence, that a person who said his business admitted of no delay, and intimately concerned Mr. Moreton himself, was waiting to see him below.

"I should not have ventured to call you, sir," observed the servant who had delivered the message, and now preceded him down stairs, "only that the young man seemed so much agitated, and I fancied that——"

"Agitated !" repeated Moreton to himself, "surely there can be no ill news? That bill on the Portuguese house—I've always been doubtful. Or can it be that the underwriters refuse——"

The servant opened the door of the little parlour before the sentence was concluded; and Moreton beheld, instead of one of the clerks of the establishment in the city, as he had anticipated, a fashionably-dressed, good-looking, dark young man, to whose person he was a perfect stranger.

"Your business, sir, if you please," said Moreton, in a hurried tone, very different from his usual calm, deliberate manner. "It is rather an awkward time——"

"I am aware, Lionel, that it is not pleasant to be intruded upon in the hour of felicity by those less fortunate than yourself," returned the stranger, hastily; "but, I assure you, I was not aware of this being your wedding-day. The answers returned to me by the clerks at your house in London were so evasive, that I knew not what to think. By mere accident, I discovered that you were here, and——"

"Lionel!" repeated Moreton, who till that moment had been unable to give utterance to the surprise he felt, "it cannot be that you are the child——"

"Of your father, or my mother played him false," returned the young man, in a tone of levity that suited little with Moreton's feelings at that moment. "Yes," continued the former, more seriously, "I am the brother to whom your heart has often been poured out in terms of kindness and affection that your present coldness sadly belies. But think not I come to trespass upon you on the plea of relationship. Thank Heaven, I am not yet so destitute, but that——"

"Oliver, my brother, how can you so mistake my feelings?" interrupted Moreton, seizing his hand with cordiality. "I am glad, heartily glad to see you; but I am so little used to meet with events out of the common routine of my hitherto every-day life, that two such events as my unexpected marriage to one so —so, in short, superior to all that I had hoped or dared aspire to, and the arrival of a brother whom I have never before seen, and who——"

"Falls as much short of your expectations, as your bride exceeds them," interrupted the young man, with an air of ill-concealed superiority, as he glanced at his own handsome and striking figure in the mirror opposite, and then at the comparatively plain and unpretending person of his brother.

Lionel Moreton's age at this time did not much exceed thirty, as Mr. Dewarden had said in recommending him to his daughter; but habits of constant application to business, years of close confinement to a desk in a close counting-house in a close lane in the city, and the numerous anxieties attendant upon his efforts to raise himself from a state of dependence, had made him look at least ten years older. His features were regularly handsome, and his figure good; but there was an air of unnatural gravity on the one, and a rusticity about the other, which rendered them much less attractive than they might have been. His dress, too, though on this occasion much more carefully attended to than was usual with him, was not of the very newest fashion. The white waistcoat, though of the richest silk, was of a fashion of at least twelve months past; his blue coat and black unmentionables, of the same date; and the awkwardness which ever arises from the consciousness of being unusually fine, made him appear to still less advantage. Altogether, certainly, the balance of good looks was greatly in favour of his brother Oliver, who was an active, animated young man, still in his minority; and perhaps at that precise moment Lionel felt the fact with some little uneasiness, at the thought of presenting him to his bride.

A short silence followed Oliver's last remark, and he arose as if to go.

"I shall, of course, see you as soon as you can spare time from——"

"See me!" interrupted Moreton. "You are not going? you surely do not think that I am going to part with you, the very minute I behold you for the first time? No, I must introduce you to Mr. Dewarden—to my father-in-law that is now—and my wife. How sorry I am that we are going down to Brighton for a week; but such is the fashion, and the females must be indulged, you know; though I can very ill spare the time, and everything will be at sixes and sevens till my return."

"What an insensible being," thought Oliver, "regretting a pleasurable excursion with his bride."

He did not, however, give expression to this thought, but made some slight excuse for his appearance, which, he said, was not suitable to a wedding-party.

Lionel, however, overruled this; and, with all the natural warmth of his kind heart, which sometimes broke through the coldness of his manners and deportment, hurried him up stairs, and presented him to Mr. Dewarden and Felicia as his brother, unexpectedly arrived from Italy, where he had resided from infancy.

Of Lionel Moreton's connections or family Mr. Dewarden or his daughter knew but little. The former recollected, now that the fact was thus strongly brought forward, that Moreton had told him, in the early part of their connection, that he had not a single relative in existence, except a half brother on his father's side, whom he had never seen. His father, he said, had, in consequence of some misfortunes in business, gone abroad, while he (Lionel) was a boy at school, leaving him dependent on a distant relation of his mother; who, at a proper time, had taken him into his counting-house, from whence, at his death, Lionel had been transferred to that of Mr. Dewarden.

Of the nature of those misfortunes which had compelled the

elder Moreton to become an exile from his native land Mr. Dewarden knew nothing; for the son had betrayed an emotion so uncommon in merely slightly alluding to them, that the kind-hearted merchant avoided a single question on the subject. He learned, however, that Mr. Moreton had in some measure re-trieved himself by an advantageous marriage with a native of the country in which he resided until his death, which took place about the time that the son and Mr. Dewarden became acquainted. Lionel, it appeared, had received the intimation of his father's death from the widow, who at the same time bespoke his kindness and affection for her young son, who, she hinted, might at no very distant period personally claim it from him.

From that time to the present Mr. Dewarden had never renewed the subject between himself and his *protégé*. He valued Moreton for himself alone; and that had been his reply to Felicia when, on the contemplation of her approaching nuptials, she had once somewhat sportively demanded of her father whether her intended bridegroom had no friends to consult—no relatives to whom she would henceforward have to pay her duty.

It was, therefore, an agreeable surprise to her, when her new brother-in-law was introduced, to behold such a fashionable and distinguished-looking a personage standing in so near a relation-ship to her plain and unpretending spouse; while, on the young man's part, there appeared an equal degree of surprise and admiration of his brother's choice.

There was little time, however, for the expression of anything beyond common compliments. The bridal party departed for Brighton; and Oliver, the new-found brother, was left to pass the interval of their absence with Mr. Dewarden, who was but too happy in being enabled to show the respect he felt for his son-in-law, by extreme kindness to his relative.

Lionel and his bride returned to find Oliver an established favourite with the old gentleman, who had in his favour departed from all his usual cautious habits towards strangers, and received with implicit credence all that he chose to assert respecting the cause of his present destitute condition; for destitute he was, in the fullest sense of the word, in spite of his dashing and fashion-able appearance.

To establish him in a way to provide for himself, and advance his future fortunes, became now the joint care of Mr. Dewarden and Lionel; but it was not so easy a task as it might have been supposed; for it was soon discovered that neither his habits, his taste, nor his education, fitted him for commercial pursuits.

Week after week, month after month, passed, and he was still alternately the guest of Mr. Dewarden or of his brother, and the idle attendant and promoter of every pleasure, in which his lovely and thoughtless sister-in-law engaged.

Moreton had, immediately after his marriage, returned to the active, business-like habits, which had been the basis of his prosperity, and which now constituted the chief happiness of his life. Not that he was indifferent to his youthful wife; on the contrary, he loved her with a fervour that was perhaps but the more intense from its being restrained in its expression. He rejoiced in everything that could give her pleasure, though he himself could not partake of it; and in secret felt glad that Oliver, who was so much better fitted to be an attendant on ladies, was at leisure to accompany Felicia, and promote all her little schemes of amusement. In the kindness and rectitude of his heart, Lionel Moreton had insisted that nearly the whole of Felicia's fortune should be settled on herself, and left at her own control; but, disinterested as he was in all that concerned her, he could not but be startled when, in a few months after their marriage, he discovered that the very handsome income she received was quite inadequate to her expenses, and that he was called on to pay bills which to him, moderate and economical as he was in all his own indulgences, seemed enormous. Still he could not bear to cheek her, or even to remonstrate. She was so young and gay and thoughtless, that it was excusable; and it was a fault that, no doubt, time would amend; he would himself retrench. And then he thought of Oliver—Oliver, who was still leading an idle life, and whose expenses, too, he—good easy man—was called upon to supply, and that with no sparing hand. Most reluctantly, indeed, as it appeared, did Oliver submit to these obligations; aud never did he cease talking of doing something to relieve himself from the necessity of submitting to them; but still the time passed on, without anything being done, and still he remained the constant companion of Felicia, the petted favourite of the whole house, and the especial friend of Mr. Dewarden, who seemed to regard him as a second son.

But suddenly the face of affairs changed. Felicia became indisposed, melancholy and averse to all the gaieties in which she had so long delighted. Her husband saw nothing in this but the natural consequences of her situation; for she was announced to be in the way "that ladies wish to be who love their lords," but it was singular, that Oliver, too, lost his spirits.

Sometimes he would absent himself for days, and then return, apparently more miserable and dispirited than he had left them ; and then Felicia, who had perhaps regained in some measure her health and spirits in his absence, would again take to her room, and give herself up to overpowering melancholy.

Little did the guiltless, the unsuspicious father and husband suspect that these were the struggles of a guilty passion—the last faint efforts of expiring virtue to shun the ruin to which they were both advancing. Yet so it was. From the first moment of Felicia's introduction to the brother of her husband, she had been struck with the superiority of the gay animated youth over the comparatively plain plodding man whom she had made the master of her fate. Habits of constant intercourse confirmed this impression, and tended but to alienate the more her heart from her husband, to exaggerate his defects, and lessen her appreciation of his good qualities ; while Oliver's sparkling manners, his various accomplishments, and his constant attention to her, and eagerness to contribute in any manner to her comfort or her pleasure, were enhanced in her eyes by the seeming indifference and cold reserve of Lionel's disposition.

On the part of Oliver, the impression in favour of Felicia was not, perhaps, decided at first. He had been accustomed to female society of a much higher order than that into which he had now fallen ; but it was dangerous to be constantly with one so lovely, so ingenuous, and, above all, so incapable of concealing the feelings with which she regarded him. Oliver felt that he was in danger ; he tried to withdraw himself—he tried to remember the obligations he was under to his brother ; but he read the hopeless despondency which his absence occasioned in Felicia's eyes, and again he forgot all his good resolutions.

As yet, however, the consciousness of their mutual guilty attachment to each other was confined to their own bosoms. It had never been breathed in words ; and the infatuated Felicia fondly imagined that she could still live on in this silent intercourse without incurring further guilt. But let no woman so deceive herself. *Il n'y a que le premier pas qui coute;*—the first step forward made, and she is hurried irresistibly to the bottom of the precipice.

She became a mother. As yet Felicia was comparatively guiltless ; and, with that new tie on her affections, might— ought to have revived the slumbering dominion of virtue. Alas for the frailty of human nature ! With the first kiss that she beheld Oliver bestow on her boy—the first pressure of his hand in congratulation of her recovery, vanished all her good impulses —all the resolutions she had formed to look upon him only as the brother of her husband.

Lionel Moreton was at this time unfortunately absent. Some unforeseen difficulties had arisen in business transactions with a foreign house, that compelled him to go to Lisbon for, as he supposed, only a few weeks. His residence there was unavoidably protracted to months; and, before his return, Felicia and his unworthy brother had broken through all restraints, and sunk as low in guilt as their worst enemies could imagine them.

By Mr. Dewarden alone, of all their intimate connections, was the degrading secret unsuspected. How could a father suspect his child, and such a child as Felicia had been to him? but the fatal truth at length burst upon him, like a clap of thunder in a bright and cloudless summer-day.

As in most such cases, the faithless and guilty wife had been compelled to make a confident of her own maid; and, as ever follows, where selfish, ignorant, and low-minded persons become possessed of such power as a secret of that kind throws into their hands, her demands became so exorbitant, her insolence so intolerable, and her familiarities so disgusting, that Felicia's endurance became exhausted; and, in spite of prudence, she resolved no longer to bear the bondage, but to get rid of her.

Mrs. Perkins, however, as she was called, was too cunning not to see through her mistress' affected anxiety for her welfare, which motive alone, Felicia pretended, induced her to press her to accept an advantageous opportunity that offered of going abroad with a family, where, as the latter pointed out, she would have much higher wages, lighter duties, and the advantage of seeing a great deal more of the world than she had yet done.

With dissembled rage Mrs. Perkins listened to the proposal; she could not deny that the situation was exactly such as she had long wished for; nor did she hesitate to take advantage of the means which her mistress' strong recommendation supplied to secure it; but the motive—the motive was ever present to her mind, and she resolved bitterly to revenge it. With well affected reluctance she parted with Felicia, receiving, or, rather, extorting up to the last moment, most valuable and expensive presents; and then, the instant she had quitted her presence, hastened to Mr. Dewarden, to whom, with dissembled tears and penitence for having so long concealed it, she revealed the fatal secret of his daughter's guilt, alleging, as her motive for quitting her mistress, that she could not bear the thought of facing poor Mr. Moreton, and seeing the misery and disgrace which would be brought upon him by the discovery which must take place, of his wife's dishonour and his brother's ingratitude.

"Not," she continued, finding the poor old man continued silent, as, indeed, he was from necessity, not being able to utter a word, "not that, in my humble opinion, Mr. Oliver Moreton is half so much to blame as my mistress; because young men will be young men; and, of course, if they see that ladies——"

"Wretch!—monster!—liar!" interrupted the excited father. "Do you dare to say that my innocent, spotless daughter has been the seducer of the villain who——but I believe your whole story is false. You are belying them both; and I will have you punished—punished! Oh, what punishment can be enough for such——where are your proofs?—where are your proofs? Do you think I will believe the bare word of such a creature as you, against the evidence of a whole life such as my Felicia's has been?"

"If you go there, you will find them together now," returned Mrs. Perkins, with a smile of malice.

"And why not?" demanded the old man, vehemently; "may not a brother visit his sister in innocence, without exciting such horrible suspicions?—without——"

"He may write such notes as these, too, in innocence," she tauntingly replied; "and his sister may answer him in this manner."

The old man eagerly clutched in his trembling hands the written records of infamy which the treacherous woman held out for his inspection, and which she had long since secreted, for the very purpose to which she now appropriated them. The first on which his eye rested was written by Oliver; and as he read its withering contents, the muttered sounds, "Villain!—cursed, ungrateful monster!" reached the gratified ears of Mrs. Perkins; but when, crushing the hated scrawl in his hand, he eagerly opened another, in the well-known, beautiful writing of his daughter, the effect appalled even the heartless and malicious fiend who was intently watching the termination of his incredulity. Twice he read it, or, rather, attempted to read it; for the manner in which he passed his withered hand across his eyes, told that his very sight was blasted by the characters which thus, beyond a hope of denial, confirmed the dishonour of his daughter. The colour which agitation had before heightened on his cheek, faded into ghastly paleness; the eyes, which had just lightened with doubt and anger, lost all expression, and became fixed on vacancy; and the papers dropped unheeded from his nerveless hand.

Mrs. Perkins began a whining apology for having been compelled, as she said, to be the bearer of bad news; but she had scarcely uttered a sentence, before Mr. Dewarden fell senseless at her feet. With that quickness and cunning which never deserted her, she first secured the evidences of guilt which had occasioned this lamentable sight, and then quietly and deliberately left the house, merely observing to the servant who let her out, that she was afraid the old gentleman was not well, and recommending that they should send to let Mrs. Moreton know it.

"I hav'n't a moment's time to spare," she observed, "for the carriages are ordered for twelve, and now it's past eleven; so that I must run every step to be in time, or else I would call on Mrs. Moreton myself, and tell her how poorly her papa seems."

From that shock Mr. Dewarden never recovered. He lingered for some days, and regained just sufficient recollection to reproach Felicia with her guilt, and to alter the will he had made, and leave the whole of his property to Lionel Moreton. From his death-bed the unhappy daughter was banished; but, painful and heart-rending as this was to her, who, though she was a guilty wife, had never ceased to be an affectionate daughter, it was comparatively light to the evil that still impended over her head.

How her father had become possessed of the fatal secret she knew not; for, anxious to conceal their own neglect, in not having immediately attended to Mrs. Perkins' intimation that their master was unwell, the servants had avoided mentioning that person's visit to him, and had merely related that, not finding him ring the bell, as was usual, for his luncheon, they had entered the room, and found him lying senseless upon the floor. It was natural, therefore, for her to conclude that the same means which had revealed her guilt to him, would betray her to her husband, who was hourly expected to arrive. To meet his reproach was impossible—even Oliver confessed it to be so; and there was but one resource—instant flight.

Before even the cold remains of her beloved father were in the grave to which she had prematurely hurried him, Felicia and Oliver had fled together; and when Lionel Moreton returned, full of joyful anticipations, it was to find his home deserted, and the man who had been more than a father to him a corpse. He stayed but to see him laid in his last home; and then, having gained, as he believed, a clue to the route the fugitives had taken he again quitted his native land, in pursuit of them. Not that he contemplated revenge against them. He knew that their crime would bring its own punishment; and in the hands of that Great Being to whom only vengeance belongs, he was content to leave them. But Felicia had taken her child—his child with her. All Oliver's persuasions, all his representations of the folly —the worse than folly of such a step, had been useless. The child, she said, was her's as well as Lionel's—she nurtured him at her own bosom; and, until he was of an age to exchange a mother's for a father's care, she would keep him.

A brief letter which she had left behind, addressed to her injured husband, contained the same assurance; but this, of course, did not satisfy the anxious and unhappy father. He was bent upon reclaiming his child from such hands; and believing, from some information that he had received, that the infatuated pair had sailed for America, he embarked, on the very morning after the funeral of Mr. Dewarden, in another vessel bound to the same part.

That vessel, however, never arrived. It was supposed to have foundered at sea, and none escaped to tell its fate; and, at the end of two years, Mr. Oliver Moreton, of whom nothing had been known with certainty during the interval, reappeared as the representative of his brother in a double sense—both as his next heir, and the husband of his widow. The young Lionel had died, as it was supposed, in his infancy, and there were none to dispute Oliver's claims.

CHAPTER XVII.

Proud minds and guilty, whom their crimes oppress,
Fly to new crimes for comfort and redress.
So found our fallen youth a short relief
In wine, the opiate guilt applies to grief.
From fleeting mirth that o'er the bottle lives,
From the false joy its inspiration gives,
And from associates pleas'd to find a friend
With powers to lead them, gladden, and defend—
In all those scenes where transient ease is found
For minds whom sins oppress and sorrows wound.
CRABBE.

THOSE two quick fleeting years had been to Felicia and her companion an age of misery, doubt, and despair. The passion

for the indulgence of which they had broken through all laws,
"both human and divine," still survived in her bosom, but only
to add to her wretchedness; for too soon she became convinced
that Oliver's heart was incapable of true affection. Even had
it been otherwise, was she an object to inspire it—she who had
led him into the depths of disgrace—for whose sake he was
compelled to renounce every friend, and to hide even his very
existence in strange scenes, and under a borrowed name? Her
beauty, too, faded, her health was broken, and that vivacity and
indescribable *naiveté* of manner which had rendered her so
enchanting, exchanged for continual tears, suspicion, and vain
sorrow for the past.

Oliver's was not a disposition to soothe or sustain her, or even
to bear with common patience the evils which he had certainly
brought upon her, but of which he now most unjustly sought to
throw the whole blame upon the partner of his crime. The
sudden death of Mr. Dewarden, and the subsequent melancholy
loss of his brother, pressed at times heavily on his mind, and
produced transient fits of penitence and remorse; but these he
soon learned to drown in dissipation; and before they had been
twelve months together, Felicia had the additional misery of
beholding the man for whom she had given up the world, her
honour, her reputation—all that should be dear to woman—a
desperate, reckless profligate. Seldom now did he visit the
home which she possessed no power—which she studied not to
endear to him; and when he did return to it, for a few days at a
time, it was only to recruit himself from the effects of a long
debauch, or to tear from her the means to renew his excesses.
At the gaming-table, or amid all the scenes of revelry and vice
to which his associates there introduced him, was his youth, his
health, and her fortune wasted; and Felicia, terrified at his
violence, and not unfrequently a sufferer even from personal ill
usage, in the fits of madness which were produced by constant
excesses, saw with terror, but without daring to oppose him, the
time fast approaching which would leave her and her children
(for she had now another boy—a pledge of her disgrace) without
the means even of support. And he to whom she still clung, in
spite of all his vices and ill usage, with that fondness which
seems inherent in woman's heart towards the object of their
early love—what was to become of him, when the means which
now supplied him were exhausted? In vain, in the short calm
that sometimes succeeded to long and riotous indulgence, she
ventured to point this out to him, and, at the same time, to

ELINOR CLARE.

FELICIA AND HER CHILD.

suggest that something ought to be done, at least, for Lionel—
the rightful and lawful heir of his brother—to rescue him from
the evils that impended over their head. How her husband had
disposed of his property, or what arrangements he had made in
behalf of his son, she knew not, nor had any means of ascertaining; but she felt certain, from Mr. Moreton's naturally prudent
habits, that he would not leave to uncertainty and chance a
matter of so much moment. On this point, however, she was
mistaken. The suddenness of the events which had overwhelmed
the miserable husband and father had driven him entirely out of
his natural course. He had been solely occupied with the
desire to get possession of his child — the only wreck of his

domestic happiness which he could hope yet to save ; and, leaving all his affairs in the hands of a friend of undoubted probity and intelligence, he quitted England without making any provision for the chance that had, it seemed, befallen him.

To Felicia's remonstrances on this point, Oliver, at first, listened with impatience.

" There is time enough yet," was his general reply. At other times he would become angry, and reproach her with bitterness for her evident preference of his brother's child to his.

" And you would wish him to live in luxury—to be brought up as the heir to a fortune, and be taught to despise even yourself," he would remark, " while my boy is to inherit nothing but his parents' disgrace and poverty. No, I will see the brat perish piecemeal before my eyes with hunger, before I will consent to it. He shall share our fate, be it for good or be it for bad ; so let me hear no more whining and puling about the boy whom you ought never to look at, and I never *do* look at, without wishing him in his grave, that I might not for ever have before my eyes the image of his wronged father."

" And would you, then, prove your remorse for one crime, by committing another and more deliberate one ?" was the question that hovered on Felicia's lips ; but she now feared her wretched partner too much, to hazard provoking him to violence ; and the subject was dropped.

Poverty was already staring them in the face in all its horrors ; and Oliver, compelled in a great measure to relinquish his vicious pursuits, and the associates who encouraged them, by the want of means to continue them, was now perforce a more constant resident in the humble cottage to which the fallen Felicia and her children had been obliged to retire. But she gained little happiness by this change : for his temper had become so morose, and his frequent fits of passion so vehement, that she trembled even to speak to him.

To increase her misery, and as if in punishment of the unjust preference shown to him over the injured child of Lionel Moreton, Edward, her second child, was seized with a lingering illness that left no hopes of his recovery. This circumstance, which she dreaded would but the more alienate Oliver's heart from her, and break the last tie that bound their fates together, to her great surprise appeared to have a contrary effect. His manner became softened ; and even, at times, glimpses of his former tenderness towards her took the place of the habitual indifference, and even worse than indifference, which he had so long betrayed towards her. He shared her privations without murmuring, and even sometimes exerted himself to lessen the toils which she was compelled to endure, and to which she, brought up in every luxury and indulgence, was so little fitted.

Again was Felicia comparatively happy. The loss of his love had been in her estimation the worst of all evils, and that restored would give her courage to face every difficulty.

The boy died; and it was while yet weeping over his cold remains together, that Oliver ventured to pour into her ears the villanous scheme which his mind had been employed in concocting, while he appeared only attentive to the sufferings of the child, and anxious to soothe the sorrows of the mother.

"Had it been the other boy, Felicia," he whispered, as she lay with her head upon his shoulder, " I should now be able to place you, my poor girl, again in affluence : and, as my wife, enable you to defy the frowns and censures of the world ; but we are fated to misery ; and I—I have the additional sting of feeling that I have brought it all upon you."

Felicia's heart bounded at this unusual tenderness; and for a moment she forgot even the recent calamity, as she murmured,

" Oh, no, no, dearest, never, never have I reproached you. It is, as you say, our hard fate to——"

" But see you not how the worst evil of that fate might have been avoided?" he interrupted, with an impatience that was little accordant with the mild and chastened tone which had drawn from her the endearing expression of her still devoted love. " Poverty, Felicia," he continued, as she raised herself suddenly from his arms, and gazed upon him with a look of earnest inquiry ; " poverty, my dearest love, however we may talk of it, and affect to bear it with fortitude—poverty is the bitterest curse that can befall poor human nature. Even now we feel its pressure; but what shall we do, when the small sum which you have so providentially hoarded shall be gone, and——"

" I will bear all patiently, Oliver, I will work for you— I——"

" Pshaw ! you must do more, and yet less, Felicia," he again impatiently interrupted. " To prove your love for me, you must give up the treasured rights of that boy, which I know you secretly, in your heart and——I will be plain with you, Felicia, and tell you that on your compliance with my schemes depends our future happiness. Say that you consent, and I will make you my wife—my honoured, treasured wife. Refuse, and I quit you for ever ; for I will never live to see you reduced to the humiliating necessity which you seem to contemplate with so much calmness, but which maddens my brain to think of."

"What is it you mean, Oliver? Think you that I shall shrink from anything that can make you happy?" returned the trembling Felicia, whose heart, however, foreboded, while she uttered the words, that some sacrifice would be required of her which would involve her still more deeply in guilt. And so it proved.

Calmly, but with a determination of look and manner which showed that any remonstrance from her would be useless, he proceeded to unfold his scheme. His brother, he said, he had recently ascertained, had left no will; his son Lionel, therefore, was indisputably the heir to his property, which was now more than doubled by Mr. Dewarden's unconditional bequest of all his wealth.

"But if that boy," continued Oliver, "were removed," glancing at the sleeping and unconscious child, " I, as the only relative of Lionel Moreton, have an undisputed right to take possession of the whole."

"Removed!" repeated Felicia, her blanched lips trembling with horror.

"Yes! What, woman?—you do not think I mean to commit murder, do you? I am not yet come to that !" he exclaimed with vehemence.

"Oh, no, dear Oliver, do not be angry," returned Felicia, rejoiced to find her first most dreadful fear thus unfounded. "Proceed, pray proceed."

Oliver proceeded to unfold his scheme. There were none in the place where they were now living who knew anything about them or their children. Edward, the deceased boy, was only a year younger than the heir of Lionel Moreton; he was also remarkably tall and stoutly made for his age; while Lionel was slight, and only of moderate height. Nobody who had not previously known the children, but would readily believe that the one who now lay dead before them was the eldest of the two; and, accordingly, he proposed that he should be buried as Lionel, the son of Lionel and Felicia Moreton. He would then place the real heir at nurse as his own child; and, to finish the whole to her satisfaction, he would go with her immediately to London, procure a licence, and thus legally make those one whose hearts had been so long united.

"With this double security, my Felicia," he continued, "none can dispute my claim; and it will, in fact, be no injustice to your child, who will eventually, of course, inherit his father's wealth. *That* I will take upon myself to secure."

Can it be wondered that she who had already yielded so much to him, did not now oppose a plan which she yet knew, in her conscience, was wrong?

The scheme answered; a few days' tuition taught the innocent boy to call himself Edward, a name which he ever afterwards retained, and soon forgot that he had ever borne another. All that they possessed was turned into money; and, having found a person willing to take charge of the child, whom the mother was led to believe she should reclaim, the moment they were firmly settled in their expected possessions, Felicia and Oliver returned to London, and were as soon as possible married.

Oliver had now cast off all shame or desire of concealment; and, heedless of the feelings of disgust and horror of those who had known the circumstances already narrated, he appeared suddenly among his brother's former friends, demanded that which he called his rights, and, after a short and ineffectual attempt at opposition by the agent of the late Lionel Moreton, succeeded.

Once more Felicia was rich—rich beyond what she had ever been led to expect; for the united wealth of Mr. Dewarden and his partner and son-in-law had increased under the skilful management of the agent, and was now a princely fortune. She was a wife, too—the legal wife of the man to be united to whom had once seemed a happiness surpassing all worldly enjoyments; and yet she was miserable. No longer than while it was necessary for his purposes, did Oliver Moreton preserve the appearance of love and tenderness which had made her a passive tool in his hands, to rob the rightful heir of his brother, and plant himself in his place. Her anxious wish to reclaim her child from the care of strangers was at first temporised with, and then treated with bitter scorn.

" It is too soon, madam," he observed, " while the news of our marriage is still ringing in the ears of our friends, to bring home a heir. The child can, of course, only appear as an illegitimate pledge of our love; and it would be rather awkward for you to receive congratulations as a bride and a mother at the same time. Besides, we may have other children to claim your tenderness, and——"

" Never, never, Oliver !" she returned, with vehemence. " I am your wife now, it is true, in form, as I was once in heart; but your cruel, your cool-blooded indifference to the child whom

I have sacrificed for your sake, has extinguished all affection for you in my heart.   I hate you," and she burst into tears, "hate you almost as much as I hate myself!   Henceforward I am but in form your wife !"

" Be it so, madam," he replied, with provoking coolness. " Fear not that I shall attempt to shake your resolution.   Enjoy, if you please, all the *honour* and advantage which your position as my wife confers upon you; and fear not that I shall exact from you any unpleasant proofs of your duty and obedience, except that of keeping your boy, whose very sight is hateful to me, at a distance."

Months had passed away, and Felicia, in complete retirement at the villa in the suburbs of London which had once been her father's, was left to reflect how little the enjoyments which now surrounded her could compensate for the continual gnawings and reproaches of conscience.   She pined for her child, whom she was not allowed to see, and to whom she could only testify her affection by presents such as she considered were certain to ensure him kindness and good treatment; but Oliver turned a deaf ear to her entreaties, when she saw him, which was but seldom.   He had again found *friends*—associates who were willing to assist him to spend his wealth, and administer to his passions; and he thought little of Felicia, or only thought of her as a clog upon his freedom which he wished removed.

Months, as has been already said, had passed, when she was one evening startled by his sudden and unexpected return home at a late hour, after having departed in the morning with the avowed intention of passing a week or two at Cheltenham, whither he had been persuaded to go by some of the pseudo-fashionables with whom he had become acquainted.

Felicia was, at the very moment that the violent ring at the gate startled her, planning in her mind whether it would not be possible for her to take advantage of his absence, to pay a stolen visit to her boy, who was at a village in Devonshire; and was considering how she should conceal it from him, whose violence she still trembled at.   What then was her astonishment when, instead of as usual proceeding to his own room, he knocked at the door of her chamber!

"I wish to have a few moments' conversation with you, Felicia," he observed, in a tone which, though he tried to disguise it, was evidently hurried and agitated.

The tone—the name which he had so long ceased to address her by, vibrated through her heart.

OR, THE HAUNTED OAK.

" Good heavens ! what has happened, Oliver ?" she exclaimed jumping out of bed. " You are ill, or——"

" No, no, I am well enough," he replied; " do not alarm yourself. I have only been thinking," he continued, throwing himself into an arm-chair, evidently unable to support his tottering frame, " I have been reflecting that it is very selfish of me to be leaving you here so much alone; and therefore I have given my friends Lechmere and Dawlish the slip, and am determined to take you with me for a tour. And we will go and see our boy, too; I know you are dying to see him. But, mind, I can't wait. You know how impatient I am, when my mind is made up to anything; and so you must be ready to be off by daybreak. And let your maid pack up all your clothes and gewgaws; for I do not know how long I may be tempted to be absent. I shall to go to bed myself; so say at once, do you consent to my scheme ? and will you be ready at the time ?"

" Can this be real, or am I dreaming ?" thought Felicia; but she knew too well her husband's disposition, to utter anything but an implicit assent to his proposition, and he hastily quitted the room.

She was not, however, deceived by his assumption of kindness to her, or his pretended regret for his neglect of her child. Too well did she remember the dissimulation which he had practised on a former occasion, and the consequences to which it had led; and, during the whole time that she was occupied in preparing for the intended journey, her mind was occupied in vainly conjecturing what purpose he could have to serve in this sudden change.

Oliver was in the mean time busily occupied in his arrangements. Felicia heard his voice and his step continually, denoting how actively he was employed, and how deep an interest he took in facilitating his departure.

" Am I to go with you, madam ?" demanded her maid, who was assisting her in packing.

Felicia started at the question, which was uttered in a doubtful tone, as if the woman expected an answer in the negative.

" Certainly—I suppose so—of course—I should think so— why——"

" Oh, only because I understand, ma'am, that Mr. Moreton is paying all the servants' wages and three months' extra, on condition they're all off before he goes ; and he's given them all written characters, and reference to some friend in London ; and as they all seem to think that there's something wrong, and as it would be a great detriment to me, perhaps, to be taken away nobody knows where, and after all——"

Felicia's pale cheek flushed. Even her very servants anticipated that disgrace and ruin were about to overwhelm them.

"I do not wish in the least to constrain you," she replied, with assumed calmness. "You had better at once speak to Mr. Moreton. For my own part, I——"

"Oh, yes, ma'am; we all very well know that you have nothing to do with it," replied the woman, pertly. "The more's the pity, that a lady like you should suffer yourself to be——"

"I want no comments, if you please," interrupted Felicia, haughtily; "you had better go at once to Mr. Moreton."

"I never was with a lady before, that hadn't the power of keeping or dismissing her own maid, as she chose," muttered the woman; "but this comes of——"

The door closed, and rendered the remainder of the sentence unintelligible.

"God help me!" exclaimed the mortified and agitated Felicia. "Already am I beginning to be deserted and insulted; and what will be my fate if, as I suspect, the short reign of prosperity, which alone has commanded attention and respect, is passing away?"

Too truly did her fears prognosticate the ruin that impended over her; but we must not anticipate.

The woman returned; she was evidently angry and excited; but Felicia disdained to ask her a single question, and she proceeded in silence to finish the preparations for the departure of her mistress.

"Now, ma'am," she at length observed, turning to the latter, "is there anything else I can do for you? You have been a good mistress to me, that I shall always say, come what will; and I am only sorry that——"

"You are, then, discharged?" interrupted Felicia, whose heart sank at the prospect of being thus left entirely alone with the man whom she had learned so to distrust.

"Discharged! oh, yes," returned the woman insolently, "it wouldn't suit me, of course, to be dragged nobody knows where, at a moment's notice. I am only sorry—I that have lived in the best of families——"

"If you have anything to complain of that I can remedy," interrupted Felicia, who feared further insult; "I——"

"Oh, no, ma'am," she hastily replied, "I hav'n't a word to

say against you; but I've told Mr. Moreton his own; and when next he forms an establishment, I hope——"

"That is quite enough; he will profit by your advice, no doubt," observed Felicia, coolly; "for my own part, I have no need of either that or any further assistance. You had better go at once, and commence preparations for your departure."

The woman obeyed; for there was an air of command in Felicia's manner when excited, which did not admit of dispute; but with her vanished all attempts at self-control, and bitterly did she weep and lament her fallen state, until the voice of Oliver, giving what appeared to be some final directions as he approached her chamber, aroused her to the necessity of dissembling her feelings.

"All is ready, Felicia," he observed. "You, I hope, are prepared."

"Prepared for everything," she murmured, in a faltering voice.

He looked searchingly in her face.

"What is the meaning of this?" he demanded, in an angry tone. "Have you not told me, that the absence of your child and my constant engagements from home rendered your life miserable? And now that I propose to devote myself entirely to you, and to restore your child to you——"

"Do that, Oliver, in spirit and in truth, promise me that such is your intention, and I will follow you, without a murmur, to the farthermost ends of the earth," she exclaimed.

"Foolish woman! why should you think I intend to deceive you?" he replied. "No, I assure you, from the bottom of my heart, that it is my firm determination that your boy and you shall never be separated. But, come, take a cup of chocolate; it will be long, perhaps, before we shall stop for refreshment."

Felicia obeyed in silence; she exerted herself to appear calm and composed, though she was convinced that a hidden meaning lurked in his words, and gave a sinister expression to his eyes, which evidently dared not encounter her piercing looks. They departed, and her suspicions received further confirmation by her discovering that the carriage was heavily laden; so much so, that it was palpable her husband had taken care to secure everything of value that was portable in this way. Her uneasiness was further increased by observing that the only servants retained by him were his own valet and groom, whom she especially disliked for their general conduct. The former he left in possession of the house and furniture, under what arrangements or directions she knew not; the latter accompanied them as coachman, and, from his familiar and confidential manner with his master, seemed to be in full possession of his views and projects.

Felicia knew nothing of the road they travelled; and, for the first two or three hours, Moreton avoided all questions on her part by taking a place on the coachbox beside his confidant, with whom he continued in earnest conversation.

At length, however, he alighted, and entered the carriage; and though the morning was hot and stifling, drew up the blinds, as if desirous of concealment.

"You must not be surprised, Felicia," he observed, after a few minutes' silence, "at finding yourself presently in London, which, I dare say, you thought you had left miles behind. It was my first intention to have gone on straight to our destination—I mean to the place where your child is; but some circumstances have induced me, since we set out, to change my plans. And we are now, as I said, going to town, where it will perhaps be necessary that we remain two or three days. Do not interrupt me with questions, my dear; but listen to what I have to say. Events have occurred, which I will hereafter explain to you, that will prevent for some time our return to the home we have quitted, and may perhaps render it necessary for me to quit England. I have hitherto, Felicia, found you rise above difficulties, and bear with most admirable patience what would overwhelm women of weaker minds. May I now rely upon *you?* I own with shame—I own it, that I have done you great injustice, Felicia, and have made a most ungrateful return for your constant and untiring affection; but you will not now desert me? I am sure you will not!"

Felicia's tears fell fast.

Her heart distrusted his penitence, and dreaded the explanation of his mysterious conduct; yet, with that weakness which had ever marked her conduct towards him, she replied, that she was as ready as ever to follow his fortunes, and be guided by his will.

"One—only one condition," she falteringly added; " my boy, my Lionel——"

"Perish the name of Lionel !" he exclaimed, with violence. "Forgive me, Felicia," he added, as he saw the effect this sudden burst of passion had upon her; "you know not, nor can I explain, the reason I have to curse that name. Forget it for ever. Your child is mine—he shall be mine, and share my fate; but he is Edward, remember, and must remain so. Never let the name of Lionel be recalled. Would I could forget it for ever!"

A deep and shuddering sigh from Felicia responded to this wish.

She felt, however, that, after his declaration of his intentions towards her child, it was needless to say more on the subject; and both of them remained in silent and painful meditation until the rattling of the carriage over stones revealed to her that they were entering the metropolis.

"You will not meet with very elegant accommodations where I intend stopping for a day or two," observed Oliver; "but I know you do not mind a temporary inconvenience for my sake."

Prepared as she thus was, Felicia, however, could scarcely conceal her surprise, when, on the carriage stopping, she was handed from it into the dark and dirty passage of a mean-looking house, in a narrow and obscure street, and was received by a young and rather good-looking woman, whose soiled and shabby finery was quite consistent with the appearance of the room, or parlour, as she called it, to which she introduced her guest, with numerous apologies for its " untidiness," &c.

" But, why didn't you let me know, Tom Humphreys, a little afore, as the lady was coming, and I'd have got the place ready for her ?"

" I couldn't tell you what I didn't know, Sarah," was the reply; " but Mrs. Moreton will excuse all deficiencies."

The Tom Humphreys who was thus addressed, and who so readily took upon himself to answer for Mrs. Moreton, was the groom who had driven the carriage, and who, to Felicia's infinite surprise and dismay, had with saucy familiarity followed her and Oliver into the room.

The latter avoided Felicia's eyes, which were turned on him with a look of reproachful inquiry, while he assured Mrs. Humphreys, as it appeared the young woman was called, that there was no necessity for apologies.

" Come, Tom," he continued, " we have no time to lose. Let us get the things out of the carriage; there will be time enough to talk afterwards."

Felicia sunk on the chair which Mrs. Humphreys set for her. Never in all her reverses of fortune had she felt so degraded, so hopeless, so despairing, as at this moment; for how disgraceful must, she thought, be the circumstances which thus compelled

Oliver to seek an asylum with the lowest of his servants, and make him stoop to a familiar association with them !

Mrs. Humphreys, however, left her little time for silent observation or reflection on what was passing around her, for she kept up an incessant bustle and chatter in her attempts to render herself agreeable, and excuse and remedy the disorder apparent in her domestic arrangements.

"But the truth is," she observed, "I was raking last night; for I went to the play; though I musn't tell Tom so, for he's dreadful jealous, and don't like me to stir out if he can help it. But, lor', what's the use of expecting young people to be always moped up, and see nothing? I gives in a good deal to his whims—but the more a woman studies a man, the more she may; and I think a woman's no friend to her *sect*, that don't stand up for her own rights."

Felicia made no reply.

She shrunk, indeed, with disgust from her new associate's offensive familiarity; and Mrs. Humphreys, seeming at length to comprehend in some measure the motive of her silence, became as sulky and silent as she had before been garrulous.

The luggage was removed from the carriage, Oliver Moreton —the so lately proud and fashionable Oliver Moreton—himself assisting with alacrity in the task; and then taking the seat offered him in Mrs. Humphrey's parlour with as much apparent ease and alacrity as if he had been in his own splendidly furnished drawing-room, or that which had so recently been his own; and conversing with such seeming interest with Mrs. Humphreys, as completely to restore that lady's good humour and good opinion of himself, which she evinced by numerous little coquettish airs and affectations, which increased Felicia's dislike of her.

The second day of the latter's residence in this abode, so ill suited to her habits, manners, and inclinations, passed over without Oliver's evincing any intentions of quitting it.

During the day Humphreys was his constant companion, Felicia confining herself, except at meals, to her little close and ill-furnished chamber; where, without any means to divert her thoughts, the window looking out upon the smoke-dried tiles of a workshop or manufactory of some sort, she sat for hours undisturbed, endeavouring to fathom the mystery in which her husband's actions were involved, or assign some cause for their sudden fall, as it appeared, from their "high estate."

Each night Oliver and his *friend* went out together; and, during the day, Felicia repeatedly heard strange voices of men

with whom her husband seemed to have business.   But all her conjectures failed in divining what was passing, until Oliver himself
revealed it on the third morning of their residence there.

"You have been wondering, I dare say, Felicia, what I have
been about, and what detains me so long in this miserable
abode, which, you may be sure, is quite as unpleasant to me as
to you.   I will tell you, then, candidly, that circumstances render
it necessary that I should convert all our superfluities into
money.   You know, I dare say, that I brought away all our
plate—everything, in fact, that was at once valuable and
portable; and I have been engaged, with Tom's help, in selling
them to the best advantage.   The task was one of some difficulty; but it was less so in London than in any other place,
and that it was that induced me to come here.   And now, I
assure you, I am as anxious to quit as you can possibly be, but
I am compelled to dissemble for a little while.   I have made
this fellow Tom useful to me; but I know he is a consummate
rascal, and would not hesitate to betray me, if he could gain a
greater advantage than he thinks he shall by my remaining here,
and being completely at his mercy.   It will require, therefore,
some adroitness for us to get away without leaving him any
means of tracing us; and for that reason, Felicia, I have been
compelled to dispose of everything except a mere change of
necessaries."

Felicia started.

It was a sad blow to hear that even the last remnants of her
late luxurious life were gone; but Oliver affected not to see her
agitation, and continued to observe that it would be necessary
for her to affect to be more reconciled to her residence there—to
keep downstairs during the day; and then, when he saw a
proper opportunity, and Humphreys and his wife were engaged,
they could walk out of the house together and leave no clue for
them to follow.

"And what dreadful circumstance can have happened to
render this concealment necessary, Oliver?" demanded Felicia,
who could no longer bury the fears and terrors that assailed her
in her own bosom.

"You will know soon enough, Felicia," was his evasive
reply.   "Of this be assured—your part in the danger is not
less than mine."

CHAPTER XVIII.

Oh ! could I feel as once I felt,
Or be what I have been ;
Or could I weep as once I wept,
O'er many a vanish'd scene :
As springs, in deserts found, seem sweet,
All brackish though they be,
So, in the wither'd waste of life,
Those tears would seem to me.

ANON.

THE plan Oliver had suggested for their departure succeeded without any difficulty; and he and Felicia, with no more luggage than each could carry in their hand, were seated, within a few minutes, in one of the night coaches, to Bristol, and probably already on their road before they were missed by the Humphreyses.

"I have not taken the direct route," he observed, "because I am not certain that I might not have mentioned that I intended going to Exeter; and, of course, I should be traced, if I went direct thither. But make your mind easy, Felicia: I am as anxious and impatient to see your boy safe in your possession as you possibly can be, and will not delay a moment longer than is necessary."

Felicia did not doubt this: she was only doubtful that he had any good motive for his intentions towards the child. But she was compelled to suppress all doubts and fears, for well she knew that the expression of them would avail nothing.

Three days after they left London, Felicia had the happiness of straining to her bosom her wronged and neglected child. Fortunately the woman to whom she had confided him had strictly done her duty by him; and the gratified mother received him from her hands improved in health and stature, and in temper and disposition unaltered.

Oliver absented himself until the first emotions of the interview were past; and then, having handsomely rewarded the nurse, who parted with tears from her young charge, he hurried the mother and child into the post-chaise that was waiting for them, and in a few hours they were on board a vessel bound to a port in Sicily, near which, as Oliver had often told Felicia, his happy days of childhood had been passed.

It was then, and only then, when they were out of sight of land, and he felt that he had no longer anything to fear from either the obstinacy, as he would have called it, or any sudden impulse of contrition on the part of Felicia, that Oliver revealed to her the cause of his flight.

Lionel, his injured brother, was still living; nay, more—he was actually in England. How he had escaped from the wreck, or where he had been so long hidden, he said he knew not; but the fact was beyond doubt. He had himself seen a letter from him, addressed to his friend and former agent, announcing that he was then at Dover, where he had been detained two days by a trifling accident; but that, on the morrow, he should be in London.

"The letter," continued Oliver, "concluded with denouncing vengeance against you, Felicia, and me. He had, it seemed, received correct intelligence as to our marriage and other circumstances, and expressed his conviction that the laws would afford him ample revenge on both of us. You, for having contracted an unlawful marriage while he was still living; and me——but I need not go on, Felicia; you see at once the danger that threatened both of us, and that there was no prospect of saving ourselves but by the means I have adopted. We are now safe, my love; and as I have taken care to secure a tolerably large sum, in this cheap and delightful country, we shall be able to live happily."

"On the fruits of robbery," thought Felicia, though she dared not say so; but it was impossible for her not to feel that Oliver's last act had been an added injury to his brother, since not a shilling had he brought away that did not belong to the wronged Lionel.

And she—she, too, was loaded with additional infamy; and her boy—the son of her injured husband, how could she look in his innocent face, without the bitterest remorse for the injury she had inflicted on him, by robbing him, not only of the fortune to which he was rightfully heir, but the kind-hearted and affectionate father to whom he would have been so deservedly dear?

Oliver's dissembled tenderness towards herself, and kindness towards her boy, gradually, however, had its usual effect on the weak-minded Felicia. He was again the lover who had ensnared her youthful heart; and, in the new scenes and enjoyments to which he introduced her, she drowned, as far as possible, the memory of the past.

In a moment of weakness and folly she had been induced, by the artful suggestions of Oliver, that she would at some time or another, betray him and the secret of the boy's birth to the latter, she had uttered the most solemn oath that heart could frame or tongue could utter, that never from her lips should any mortal learn the deception that had been practised; and thus considering that the young Lionel's (or Edward, as he was now called) fate was fixed beyond the power of recall, she tried to forget the injury she had done him, or, at least, to retrieve it as far as possible by the utmost tenderness and attention to him.

During the three years that were passed by the fugitives in the vicinity of Naples, where they had finally settled, after some months of wandering amid the beautiful and romantic scenes of Italy, Oliver Moreton never forgot the line of conduct he had adopted towards Felicia, and which he had found by experience was the best calculated to keep her firm to his interest.

She was still his dear Felicia—the only woman whom he ever had or could love; and the foolish woman believed him. Yet she could not blind herself to the fact, that the life of dissipation which he was, even now, leading could not fail eventually to reduce them again to poverty, though he tried to persuade her that her mildly expressed fears were groundless, and from time to time promised, with seeming penitence, to reform.

But Oliver was a gambler—a desperate, reckless gambler; and, even if he were ever sincere in his professions to her, the gaming-table presented to him attractions which it was impossible for one so devoid of all firmness and true principle to resist. The dreadful consequences of this propensity at length burst suddenly upon the hapless Felicia.

She had been waiting hour after hour for his return from the haunts in which he passed his evenings, when she was terrified by his rushing in, his dress torn, his hair hanging in wild disorder, and blood streaming profusely from a wound in his arm.

The tale was soon told of his mischance. An Englishman of rank had been plundered unfairly at the faro-table: he had resisted payment; an attempt had been made to take the money by force. Swords had been drawn, and the Englishman killed. Oliver (who, *of course*, had been of the side of the aggrieved party, his countryman) had been wounded, and with difficult escaped with his life.

ELINOR CLARE.

THE GENTLEMAN STARTED FROM HIS SEAT.

"But this is not the worst, Felicia," he continued, after she had bandaged the wound, which was comparatively slight, and stopped the bleeding, "this is not the worst, my dear love. I shall be obliged to fly from this place; for the innocent will be confounded with the guilty, and even now the sbirri (officers of justice) are in pursuit of all who were present; and even if I should eventually be cleared, I shall have to suffer a long imprisonment in their loathsome prison."

"Oh, fly, then!—fly before it be too late!" exclaimed the terrified Felicia. "We will return to England—anywhere rather than——"

"No, no, my Felicia—you must remain here with your child,

until I can reach a place of safety; when I will send for you. Let me have what money you can spare, and I ———"

Felicia waited to hear no more: she *forced* upon him nearly every shilling she had in the world; and, with an assurance that she should hear from him as soon as it was possible, he departed.

Months had passed away, and Felicia knew not what had become of Oliver. As he had predicted, their house was, in a few hours after his departure, visited by the officers of justice; but, after a close search, and Felicia's assurance that she knew not whither he had fled, they departed, and she was left to count, hour after hour, day after day, and at length month after month, in the vain hope and expectation of receiving his promised summons to join him.

A very short time dissipated the trifle he had left in her possession, and she was compelled to give up the establishment she could no longer maintain, and seek shelter with her child, in a humble cottage, the residence of an aged couple, the parents of her female servant. But even here she could not live without money; the old people were miserably poor; and though they would willingly have shared their wretched pittance with the unfortunate stranger in a foreign land, and her beautiful and sweet-tempered child, Felicia would have died rather than have diminished their scanty allowance.

One by one, all the clothes, trinkets, &c., which she had purchased since her arrival in Italy, were disposed of by the old woman, to procure food, which she shared with her humble protectors; but even this fund was at last exhausted; and Felicia one night retired to her hard and coarse bed, without having tasted food during the day, and with the agony of seeing her child smiling through his stifling tears over the piece of black bread and the herb pottage which the old people had given him, and which he in vain pressed his poor mother to eat of, with the assurance that it was "very good—very good indeed."

That whole night was passed by the wretched Felicia in tears; but, towards morning, nature was exhausted, and she slept soundly; while Edward, as he was called, crept softly from her side, in obedience to old Nanine's summons, to share their coarse and scanty breakfast.

"I am going to the city, Edward," observed the old woman, when they had finished. "Will you go with me? we may perhaps bring mamma home a nice breakfast."

This was a sufficient inducement, even if the boy had not

wished to see the fine sights of which Nanine so often talked to him; and without hesitation he accompanied her, chattering away as they went along, with all the animation of childhood, alive only to present gratification, and heedless alike of the past or the future.

Nanine led him to a large hotel, which she knew was the residence of an English gentleman who was famed for his charity; and there, with the boy in her hand, she told the story of the mother and child's destitution, and the " wicked" father's desertion; enlarging, with all the eloquence she possessed, on the beauty and goodness of the signora Inglese, and the blessed temper and cleverness of the boy, who, she declared, was a little angel, and the only comfort of his poor mother.

The gentleman heard her with a smile of benevolence.

" And you are an Englishman, then, my brave boy?" he observed, in his native tongue. The conference between him and Nanine had been carried on in Italian.

Edward's fine dark eyes lighted up with joy at hearing his own language, which, except from his mother's lips, seldom met his ear. He made his best bow.

" Well, and what is your name, my little man, and your mother's ?" demanded the gentleman, looking at him with extreme interest.

" Edward Moreton, sir; and my mother's is Felicia Moreton; and my father's——"

The gentleman started from his seat with a cry of anguish. " Do not name him, the villain !" he exclaimed; " wretched, wretched Felicia, this, then, is thy deserved fate, to be left to perish in a strange land, by the monster who——but I forget myself; I will——Take that child away, woman," he continued, addressing Nanine, to whom the boy had fled in alarm at the stranger's emotion; " take him away, I say; the sight of him is too much for me. Yet, stay, they must not perish; there, there is money," and he flung a heavy purse to the old woman. " Go, and relieve her wants."

Neither Nanine nor the child could, of course, comprehend the meaning of this scene; but the old woman knew that Moreton was universally execrated by all as the murderer of his countryman in the affray which had driven him from his home, and she considered herself very sagacious in guessing that the charitable English gentleman was a friend or relation of the murdered man, and that had caused his apparent horror at hearing the name of Moreton.

" You must not tell your poor mamma what the gentleman said, my dear child," she observed, as soon as they left the house; "for she cannot bear to hear your father spoken ill of, and it will do no good to tell her. It will only grieve her, and make her worse, you know."

It was a heavy task to Edward to conceal anything from his mother; but Nanine's injunctions prevailed; and, before they reached home, he promised that he would be silent.

They were just quitting the city, where Nanine had already expended some of the money in necessaries for the poor lady, as she called her, when they were overtaken by one of the servants of the hotel of the English gentleman.

"Holy Virgin! how I have run up one street and down another, to find you," he exclaimed. " Signor Inglese has sent me to demand your name and residence. What, in the name of all the saints, have you being doing to his excellency to put him in such a way ?"

Nanine replied she had done nothing—she had only been pleading the cause of a poor countrywoman of the English signor, who was left destitute in a foreign land; and she finished by giving a clear and explicit direction to her humble cottage, which was a mile and a half distant from the city.

Edward and the exulting Nanine returned home at once, to gladden Felicia's heart with the hope that she had raised for her a friend to herself and child, and to humiliate her with the conviction that she had at last fallen so low as to be indebted to charity for her preservation from the horrors of starvation.

" And my boy, young as he is, feels it, too," she thought to herself, as she watched the unusually grave and thoughtful looks of the child, and the colour which suffused his cheeks, while replying to her question as to what the gentleman had said to him.

" He only asked me my name, and yours, mother," he replied, " and I told him; and he asked me nothing else."

" He knew, perhaps," thought the unhappy woman, "that disgrace was connected with that name; otherwise he would have been anxious to hear something of the history of those for whom his benevolence was demanded."

All that day Nanine was busily employed in cleaning and setting off her poor little hut to the best advantage; for she had a strong presentiment, as she told her aged partner, that the English signor, when he got over his first surprise, would be coming to see the poor lady whose situation she had so pathetically represented to him.

Night, however, put an end to these hopes, and threw the inhabitants of the cottage into the greatest consternation and perplexity. A letter and parcel, brought by an English servant in livery, guided by Nanine's countryman, to whom she had described her residence, was delivered to Mrs. Moreton, whose cheek became deadly pale the moment her eye rested on the superscription. She looked anxiously in the face of the messenger, who was an elderly man, and her lips quivered as she attempted to utter the name of Reynolds.

"Yes, madam," he replied, in a tone of pity, "it is Reynolds, who is sorry—most truly sorry to see you in this situation. But open the letter, pray, ma'am; and see what my noble-hearted master proposes. Little, I am sure, did I think, when I listened to that old woman's story this morning, and took the boy in to him, that I was going to give him what I may say is almost his death-blow."

"It was then my—my— his——" The words died on her lips, and Felicia fell back in strong convulsions which for many hours held her on the verge of death.

Reynolds remained with her. He had been her father's servant, and had loved her in infancy as his own child; and bitterly had he lamented the disgrace and ruin she had brought upon herself and her father's unsullied name. When Lionel Moreton so unexpectedly returned home, Reynolds had sought him out, and his services had been immediately accepted; and he had now accompanied his desponding master to Italy, in search of health, little, as he said, expecting that he was there to meet with such a shock as the discovery of his lost and ruined wife.

Felicia recovered her recollection only to feel more poignantly than ever the misery the indulgence of her unbridled passions had brought upon her.

Moreton—Lionel Moreton—her noble, forgiving husband, had written to her with his own hand; had not only offered her a refuge from poverty and disgrace, but had entreated her, by the respect she owed her father's memory, not to reject the proposal made to her.

This was, that she should immediately return to England, where, under an assumed name, and in the character of a widow, she might pass the remainder of her days in peace, and devote her time to the education of her child, who he hoped would resemble his unhappy father in nothing but the graces of his person.

"How blind!—how deceived!" thought Felicia, as she turned her tearful eyes on the countenance of the boy. "He is his own very image! That open, yet thoughtful brow is his. Oh, that I dare tell him that he has a right to claim him, as his father!"

Strongly was the wretched and perturbed Felicia tempted to confess to Reynolds, from whom she had no other reserves, the secret of the imposition that had been practised upon her husband and the wrong that had been done his child; but the remembrance of the oath she had sworn—the bitter imprecations she had uttered, should she ever reveal the secret, closed her lips, whenever she would have spoken.

She had a secret presentiment, too, that, some time or other Oliver and she might again meet; and the dread of his reproaches —of the revenge which he might take upon her, contributed to keep her silent on this subject; though, to have revealed it would, as she felt convinced, go far to restore her long-suffering and deeply injured husband to happiness.

Under the guidance and protection of Reynolds, who acted implicitly by Mr. Moreton's directions, she returned to England with her child; and, through the agency of the gentleman who has been before spoken of as Lionel's confidential friend, was eventually settled in the long-deserted habitation called the Nunnery, where, under the name of Mrs. Hatherleigh, which had been her mother's maiden name, she hoped to pass the remainder of her life in quietness and obscurity.

A yearly sum—much more than sufficient to meet her now moderate wishes and expenses—was settled upon her by Mr. Moreton, free from all restraint, except one, that she never again voluntarily held intercourse with Oliver Moreton.

In this peaceful asylum, year after year glided away, undisturbed by anything but her reminiscences of the past, and a fearful thought that, some time or other, he who had been the bane of her life would again intrude to change the now calm current of her life.

To Edward, whose innocent questions respecting his father, and his imperfectly retained impressions of his early life, frequently pained and embarrassed her, she had acknowledged that her character of a widow was assumed, and that circumstances compelled her to preserve a mystery which was as repugnant to her feelings as it could be to his; but further questions she forbade, and the agony which he saw they inflicted soon taught him to be silent.

To say that Felicia, or Mrs. Hatherleigh, as she was now called, had forgotten the man who had been the bane of her life, or even that she had ceased to feel any interest in his fate, would be untrue. Many, many sleepless hours did she pass, recalling to herself the circumstances of their last parting, and trying to conjecture what had become of him—whether he was living or dead; and (her weakness must be confessed) if he were still living, whether she should ever again behold him. Such an event was to be dreaded. It would bring with it certain ruin to herself and to her child; for well she knew that a strict watch was kept upon her actions by the agent of her injured husband through whom she received the means of support for herself and her son.

If she could but have known—have been certain that Oliver was dead, she would then have been released from the oath she had taken to conceal the real birth of her child; and oh, with what pride and satisfaction should she restore to the arms of his father the son who was so worthy of him—who was the true heir not only of his fortunes, but his virtues. She had sworn only never to reveal the truth while he (Oliver) lived; and if he were dead——

"Oh that I should ever wish his death!" was her frequent exclamation to herself, as these thoughts passed through her mind; "and yet, when I look at my noble boy, and think what may be his fate, should I be taken from him before he is old enough to win his way through the world——And even if I live, how hard for him it will be—nameless, unfriended, unconnected—he that ought to be rich, to have the protection of——Oh yes, I ought—I do wish that I could know with certainty that Oliver is dead!"

Every year that added to Edward's age increased this feeling. "How easily do we admit the thing we wish were true!" Mrs. Hatherleigh had almost persuaded herself that it was impossible that Oliver should still be living, and she remain in ignorance of it. She was wavering and resolving, and wavering again, whether she should not seek an interview with Mr. Saville, the agent of Lionel Moreton, and reveal to him the cruel deception that had been practised so long towards him, when every hope was at once dashed to the earth—every intention rendered nugatory, by the sudden appearance of the very man on whose death she had at last brought herself confidently to rely.

Edward Hatherleigh, as he was called, and had been taught to call himself until time had banished from his memory that he had in early childhood borne another name, had after the unfortunate discovery which had taken place of his and Elinor Clare's mutual attachment, found his time hang heavy on his hands. He could no longer take the deep interest he had done in books. He had no pleasure in society; for with none could his mind claim kindred, but those whom he was now forbidden to call his friends.

Mr. Copeland's had been a second home to him; and from that he was ignominiously expelled. The girls shunned him; and Walter looked daggers at him, whenever they accidentally met; while from all intercourse, except by stealth, and that "few and far between," with his most loved and prized—the gentle, dove-eyed Elinor, he was jealously excluded, by the watchfulness of those who took an interest in keeping them apart.

Edward's habitual melancholy and thoughtfulness deepened into the deepest gloom; and in the hours of solitude in which he nourished the feelings that preyed upon his heart, not a few nor the least painful of his thoughts were given to meditation on the mystery that hung over his birth, his mother's actual situation, and his own future prospects.

He had one day indulged to even a greater extent than usual the morbid feelings which sprung from this review of his apparently hopeless situation; and, in accordance with those feelings, had wandered away, without aim or purpose, many miles from his home, which had now become as hateful and distasteful in his sight as it had once been congenial. Even the landscape—the sweet charms of

> ————hill and dale—
> The forest sanctuary or sunny vale,

which once would have called forth such admiration, were disregarded. He saw nothing in the world but wretchedness and discomfort. He quarrelled with himself—with every one; with those who had interposed to check the current of that true love which

> ————conceives no paradise but such as Eden was,
> With two hearts beating in it.

But, most of all, he quarrelled with himself for having suffered his mother's foolish fondness; it might be that suspicions of a worst motive crept into his mind; but, if so, he resolutely smothered them in their birth, as all will do who love a mother, and determined to believe it foolish fondness only, that had kept him so long a supine, worthless being, incapable, as Mr. Copeland had truly said, of getting his own living, much more of providing for a wife.

> " Thou might'st have earn'd thy bread as thousands earn it;
>   Or, if that seem'd too humble, tried by commerce,
>   Or other civic means, to mend thy fortunes."

he repeated aloud, as he stood on the edge of a steep, rocky descent, so abrupt that it might almost have been called a precipice.

The passage had struck him in one of his favourite poets as applicable in full force to himself, and he now repeated it with heartfelt energy.

" You are not so far advanced in life, young man, but that you may practise the lessons that you preach, if you are in earnest," said a voice so close to him, that he started as if a supernatural being had risen out of the earth to address him.

The person who spoke, however, was a man clad in very coarse and apparently travel-worn garments, and who, as Edward after-wards discovered, had been, unseen by him, resting himself and taking his humble meal at the foot of a large tree, a few yards distant from the spot which he himself had paused upon to utter his soliloquy.

Unused to be addressed by strangers, abundantly conscious of the awkward and ridiculous position in which he stood, and unsuspicious as he naturally was, yet marvellously inclined to suspect the respectability of the person who thus familiarly entered into his most private thoughts, Edward stood for a minute or two absolutely bewildered and unable to reply.

" Excuse me, if I am intrusive, sir," observed the stranger, with a much more courteous tone and aspect than he had at first assumed. " I was so struck with the forcible expression of your thoughts—thoughts such as I once myself cherished, that——"

" They are such as every one must cherish, I should think, who wishes to render himself independent of the changes of this wearisome world," returned Edward, timidly, as the stranger paused, seemingly absorbed in the contemplation of the latter's speaking and expressive countenance.

" And do you already find the world so wearisome?" he demanded, with a look that savoured (it seemed to Edward) rather of ridicule than sympathy; and the natural spirit of the youth instantly rebelled against what he considered a gratuitous piece of impertinence on the part of the stranger.

" I do not know," he observer, " that it would be of any

particular service, either to you or me, to explain my feelings on the subject. I wish you good day, sir," and he was turning away, with considerable dignity in his looks and manners.

The man, however, was evidently not disposed so easily to part with him. He sprang to his side, observing,

"I beg your pardon, if I have offended you; but as to the service I am capable of rendering you, you are perhaps a little too hasty. Do you remember the fable of the lion and the mouse?"

"I do not see how it can apply to us, who are perfect strangers to each other; and likely, I suspect, to remain so," returned Edward, coldly.

"Indeed! It may be your wish to remain so," observed the stranger, "but my suspicions are of a very contrary tendency. It is my suspicion that we are not strangers to each other; but, on the contrary, acquaintances of very old standing. If I am wrong, you will easily correct the mistake, by telling me your name."

"My name!" Edward's heart beat thick; and he looked in the man's face, with an agitated earnestness that met no correspondent reflection there. The stranger met his searching gaze with a calm imperturbable smile. "My name!" again repeated Edward, in a faltering voice. "It can be of little consequence to you, I should think; but I have no motive for concealment. It is Edward Hatherleigh."

"That is the name you are known by here," replied the stranger. "Cannot your recollection carry you back to the time when you bore a different appellation? Has your mother never mentioned to you the name of Moreton? Has she never spoken to you of one bearing that name, long an exile, and perhaps deservedly so; but still a wife—a son——"

He paused, as if overcome with emotion. A tide of recollections seemed to rush at once into Edward's mind. The name of Moreton, uttered in that voice, had recalled to his memory the long-forgotten days of his childhood; and yet his heart revolted from the thought, that that man, with his dark, sinister-looking countenance—that reckless, daring expression of eye and voice—and that indescribable look and manner, which nothing but a long intercourse with vice of the lowest and most abandoned description can imprint in such legible characters on the whole person—could be his father—the father whose idea he had so often tried to recall to his memory, and whose existence had seemed a mystery which he dared not attempt to penetrate.

Now, however, all seemed explained; and he wondered no longer at his mother's unwillingness to speak of one whom she must have felt was a disgrace to her.

A few faltering questions from Edward's lips set the matter at rest. The young man could no longer hope; for the stranger boldly avowed himself to be Oliver Moreton, and his (Edward's) father.

"I do not wonder at your reluctance to believe this fact," observed the former, in a sarcastic tone, and with a look of keen reproach in his deep, fierce eyes. "It is mortifying, no doubt, to one brought up in luxury, and taught, no doubt, to think highly of himself, to find a father in such a one as I—a poor, destitute being, despised——"

"Oh, no, no," exclaimed Edward, "do not say so. Heaven forbid that I should despise my father for his poverty! or ever even think of him with any other feelings than regret for his sake, and sorrow—bitter sorrow that I have——"

"I do not want anything of you, boy," interrupted his (supposed) father, abruptly. "Do not mistake my motive in coming hither, or suppose that, because I am meanly clad, I am so mean in spirit as to seek my wife and child, to rob them of the little that is justly their own, and which I confess I have no right to share."

Ah! how little did Edward know the heart of the man who thus cunningly appealed to his generosity, while affecting to disclaim all right to it!

During the years that Oliver Moreton had been separated from Felicia, all that had been good—if there had ever been good in his character—had been effaced and obliterated by the vicious life he had led, the companions with whom he had associated. He had learned to laugh at—to despise the terms honour, generosity, and disinterestedness, or to regard those who were deluded by such unreal shadows as fools destined to be the dupes and prey of wiser men. Oliver Moreton saw in a moment what he considered the weakness of Edward's character, and he determined to profit by it accordingly.

Long and deeply interesting to the latter were the communications that followed this unexpected discovery. Oliver, having first, by his deep cunning, ascertained from the unsuspecting youth, that Felicia had been faithful to her engagements to him, and that her son was in total ignorance of all that the former wished concealed, affected the utmost frankness in speaking of the errors of his youthful days; and without acknowledging any of the greater crimes which had stained his life, and brought misery and disgrace upon all connected with him, proceeded to tell a varnished tale, which at once bespoke pity and compassion for him in the bosom of the sensitive Edward, and accounted for his long estrangement from his native land, and those who rendered it, as he said, dear to him.

That he still retained some of his power over the weak-minded Felicia, he considered proved by her having forborne ever to mention him to her son; and it was, therefore, with very little dread of a discovery on her part, that he determined to accompany Edward to her abode. He had been, as he said, for some days in search of it; for though he had received vague intelligence, he said, that she resided in that part of the country, he knew not that she had assumed a borrowed name, and that circumstance had baffled his inquiries.

Had he told the truth, he would have acknowledged that he had been for days prowling about the habitation of his destined victims, seeking in vain an opportunity of making himself known to Mrs. Hatherleigh, lest, in the excitation of the moment, she might reveal how little claim he had in reality to the characters he meant to assume of husband and father.

Hour after hour he had watched Edward from his secret lairs, without a fit opportunity occurring of sounding him upon those events of his life of which he wished to ascertain his knowledge. The time at last came when he at least expected it; for he had been on a distant journey, and was now on his way back to the purlieus of the Nunnery, when he encountered him in the manner narrated.

A thousand painful thoughts agitated Edward's mind, as he slowly paced by the side of his pretended parent, on their way homewards. What could be the mode of life which the latter now pursued, and which he ambiguously spoke of as the only one suited to a lost and desperate man—one who had forfeited for ever his place in society, and yet retained so much of his lofty spirit as to scorn to stoop to common means to prolong a miserable existence?

" It is too late for me to learn the arts of thrift," he observed, " or bend my stubborn mind to those petty pursuits by which men make fortunes; and I find too many charms in freedom, to renounce my ' free, unhoused condition' for all the goods of fortune, if it must be acquired by the systematic slavery, which men dignify with the name of industry."

" What can he possibly do; or how can he possibly get a

living?" were the plain and homely questions which, in spite of all he could do to drive them from his mind, continually suggested themselves to Edward, as from time to time he glanced at the threadworn and neglected habiliments of his companion, and contrasted them with his lofty assertions of independence.

Not even the coarse meal of brown bread and hard cheese, which he was eating with such gusto when he first descried him, as to continue the occupation long after he had addressed him, even till the last crumb was consumed—not even that could be procured by one who avowed himself destitute of all funds, without first working for it, or (Edward blushed up to the very eyes at the bare thought) of begging for it.

There was certainly a third way of explaining the mystery; but from that Edward's heart recoiled with horror. His father could not be a robber—a common thief; and yet, it must be confessed that he was just such a personage in appearance as, had he possessed enough of the world's gear and the world's caution, he might have thought it necessary to have avoided.

Not more than a mile or two of the tedious distance which lay between them and the Nunnery had been travelled over by those who were now wending their way towards it with such different feelings, before the mystery which had so tormented poor Edward's mind was explained—rather sooner, possibly, than he who had given rise to it intended.

In his way to the spot on which he had encountered his *soi-disant* father, the former had passed the newly-formed camp of a gang of gipsies.

They were far beneath him, in one those "bosky dells," which are so peculiarly suited to their purposes of shelter and concealment, and near enough to the high road and the habitations of civilised man as to afford them other conveniences.

Edward had stopped a few minutes to observe them; the men occupied in fixing their ragged tents—the women, some of them tending the meal, which they were preparing in the primitive manner which Cowper picturesquely describes—

> A kettle slung
> Between two poles upon a stick transversed;

while others, seated on the smooth, green turf, were either playing with the children—of whom a whole troop were scattered about —or quietly watching the labours of their companions. All looked healthy, happy, and contented; and Edward, as unseen he gazed down upon them, and heard their cheerful voices and bursts of laughter, had almost envied them their seeming freedom from care.

They (he and Oliver Moreton) were in silence pursuing their way along the same path which the latter had travelled in the morning, and were within a few yards of the spot from whence he had looked down upon the gipsies, when a dog, with a fierce yell, suddenly sprung upon them.

But, before either of the travellers could prepare for defence, the surly notes of defiance were changed for a delighted whine and all the indescribable noises by which the faithful canine race denote their pleasure at the sudden recognition of the friend from whom they have been long parted.

"Down, Cato! down! Be quiet, can't you, fool!" exclaimed Edward's companion, removing thus all doubts in the mind of the former as to the sagacity of the animal, who he thought at first had been mistaken in the idenity of the person he was thus caressing. In another moment, one who appeared scarcely less rejoiced than the dog, and little more rational in his mode of expressing it, bounded forward, exclaiming,

"It is him! it is Paul himself! The poor beast was never wrong in his life: he told me, as plain as dog could speak, that his master was come. But I will be the first to carry the good news. I shall get a dainty bit from old Minna; for she has been prophesying, these two hours, that the Chief was near; and I and Cato were the only ones that believed her, and kept watch. Come, Cato, come; and Minna, mayhap, will give you a bit, too."

Away bounded the boy (it was Zekiel who uttered thus wildly his gratulations) but the dog still refused to quit his master; and Oliver Moreton (who must henceforth be recognised by the name he had chosen to assume of Paul Dangerfield) having with some difficulty freed himself from the animal's boisterous caresses, turned to see what effect this discovery had upon his companion.

To say that Edward was struck dumb, as it were, with amazement—that he was mortified, humiliated, crushed, as it seemed, by a mighty blow to the very earth, would be but imperfectly to describe the feelings which rivetted him to the spot, a breathless, speechless statue of flesh and blood.

"There is no time now for explanation," observed the Gipsy Chief; "remember, for your life, not to know me by any other name than that by which I am known to my people: I am Paul Dangerfield, and you——"

Before he could finish the sentence, he was surrounded by a dozen wild-looking forms, who, however, suppressed the noisy exclamations of their joy the moment they beheld Edward, on whom they all turned their curious and suspicious glances.

Paul, as he was called, and as he called himself, led two or three of the men a little way aside. What explanation he chose to give them Edward knew not; but it sent all the blood, which had before seemed frozen in his veins, in warm currents of shame to his cheeks, at the belief that the chief of this band of vagrants was securing their civility and good offices towards him by acknowledging their affinity.

CHAPTER XIX.

Now I will believe
That there are unicorns ; that in Arabia
There is one tree, the phœnix throne—one phœnix
At this hour reigning there. * * I'll believe both ;
And what else doth want credit, come to me,
And I'll be sworn 'tis true.

SHAKSPEARE.

MANY hours—hours of misery—was Edward compelled to pass among that wild crew, in obedience to the dictates of one whose behests he dared not dispute.

Dangerfield assured him that it would be dangerous for him to quit them too suddenly, under the present circumstances.

"They are obedient to my orders, and would risk their lives to do my bidding," he observed, " while they believe me faithful to them, and that I have no separate interests—none but those with which theirs are identified ; but they are jealous and suspicious to excess; and were I to leave them abruptly, after some weeks of absence——"

"Not for me—not for my sake," returned the shuddering Edward, in whose eyes the gipsy life had lost all its attractions, since he had been an eye-witness of the coarse manners, the stormy passions, the scanty and miserable accommodations of the vagrant tribe. But that which shocked him most—which filled him, in fact, with horror and despair, was the conviction that was forced upon his mind by the broken sentences that from time to time reached his ear, in the heat of narration to the

Chief of what had passed during his absence—the conviction that, in the wild and lawless set around him, he beheld men whose lives were devoted to systematic plunder—who shrunk not from any crime, not even from murder, so that it could enable them to secure the gold which would buy the means of indulging their passions.

And *he*—*he* listened with an approving air to the tales they poured into his ear. He—Paul Dangerfield—Oliver Moreton—his father—yes, call him by whatever name convenience might prompt, still that title remained—his father was the promoter, the encourager, the counsellor to whom they looked for aid, advice, assistance in their nefarious schemes. Possibly he, too, sometimes personally mingled in similar scenes of fraud and violence to those to which he listened with such complacency; now checking the narrator, but only for some act of rashness or imprudence which had evidently exposed him or his companions to the danger of detection ; and then, when a defeat was recorded, pointing out, with fierce and glistening eye, the course that he should have adopted to secure success.

Suddenly he stopped, in the midst of a violent declamation, in which he had forgotten the usual caution of clothing his thoughts and meaning in language that must have been in a great measure unintelligible to any but the initiated. He caught Edward's meaning eye fixed full upon him with an expression of undisguised horror, while his pale cheek bore testimony to the feelings which shook his whole frame.

The looks of the men, with whom Dangerfield had been so eagerly conversing as to have forgotten even the presence of one from whom it was necessary to conceal all that had passed—their looks instantly followed the direction of the eyes of their Chief, and in an instant Edward was seized by the throat by one of the ruffians, while, with loud curses and vociferations, the greater part of the gang surrounded him, threatening him with instant death for having dared to thrust himself into their secrets.

It was in vain that Dangerfield raised his voice in commands and entreaties to let the boy go; in vain he exerted his almost Herculean force to drag him from their hands. There were too many to contend with ; and they were too much infuriated with the liquor they had drunk, and the conviction that they had betrayed themselves into his power, to listen ; and all Edward's troubles would have been speedily finished, but for the sudden interposition of the women of the gang, who, shrieking like a set

ELINOR CLARE.

"SILENCE, WITCH!" EXCLAIMED DANGERFIELD, FURIOUSLY.

of furies or wild Indians, fell upon the men, armed with the glowing brands which they had plucked from the fire, or whatever other "weapon of offence" they could seize upon, and fairly drove them away, at the very moment that Edward's sight and senses had all so completely deserted him, that, the moment he was relieved from the grasp of his ferocious assailants, he fell apparently lifeless to the earth.

When he recovered his recollection, he was stretched on a miserable heap of straw and rags, which served the office of a bed, in one of the tents. Two or three women, with pity in their dark and lustrous eyes, were kneeling around him, and administering such simple restoratives as their limited knowledge and means allowed; and the most unaffected joy was expressed, both in their faces and their words, when he recovered sufficiently to look around and thank them.

The storm of tongues still, however, raged fiercely without; and Edward raised himself hastily on his lowly couch to listen, as he heard the now well-known voice of Dangerfield, raised to the utmost pitch of its deep and powerful tones, to enforce silence.

"You demand who the boy is, and why I have brought him hither, to peril your lives," he exclaimed. "Fools! are you in more danger, if he were treacherous, than I am—I who, as you well know, have hazarded my life for spoils, which you have all shared with me to the uttermost farthing? When have I ever proved myself deficient in caution, in prudence, in any of those qualities for which you chose me to be your head, and swore— all of you swore, unlimited obedience to my will? And why now should you doubt me, and take upon yourselves to judge and punish an imaginary crime? The boy was frightened—his looks, you say, betrayed his alarm. Be it so. That was no evidence of his intention to betray us. He could not—dare not do it. I have a security for his faith stronger than any bond, more inviolable than the most solemn oath. He is my long-lost, newly-found son; and I will answer for him with my life, if, indeed, your violence has not rendered unnecessary any pledge for his silence on what he has seen or heard. I know not, at this moment, whether even he be living; but——"

"Oh, yes, yes," exclaimed several female voices, "the poor youth is alive: he will recover, and——"

A loud huzza from the lips of every one present interrupted the speakers; and, a moment after, Dangerfield entered the tent in which he was lying, followed by those who were now as friendly disposed and as anxious to prove their kindly feelings towards the son of their Chief, as they had before been brutal and ferocious—Edward could not refuse to pronounce a general pardon to those who so warmly professed their penitence for the consequences of "the mistake" into which they had fallen; but he saw that Dangerfield's eyes were on him; and he felt, too, how little the expression of those eyes agreed with the sentiments he had so recently uttered. Dangerfield read his heart, and knew that the men were not mistaken—that his countenance had truly expressed the feelings of that heart—horror, disgust, abhorrence of the crimes which he had heard boasted of—the deeds which were yet comtemplated.

The Chief had now resumed all his authority—the people

more than their usual submission to his mandates; for they were anxious to prove their sorrow for the late outbreak.

"It is time to seek rest," he observed, "I cannot enjoy our proposed merry-making while my son is suffering; and you, I should think, feel as little disposed to mirth. To-morrow night will, I trust, be more propitious; and we will sleep now, that we may be able to keep awake for a full carouse then."

Another loud huzza was the token of acquiescence to his will; and, in a few minutes, Dangerfield was left alone with Edward in the tent, which, it seemed, was given up to their convenience. The Chief walked to the entrance of the tattered canvas, which was scarcely raised high enough from the ground to permit him to stand upright. He stood there in silence a few moments, as if to see that his commands were not eluded, and then returned to Edward, who, shaken as he had been, both in body and in mind, by the recent events, was already risen from his sorry bed, and awaiting anxiously the expected signal to prepare for the continuance of their journey to the Nunnery, which had been so painfully interrupted.

"You must not quit this place to-night," observed Dangerfield in a low but decisive tone. "The storm has passed over for the present, but the clouds yet linger in the horizon. A single spark would re-illume the fire, which is smothered, but not extinguished, and bring down destruction on both our heads. If they were to discover that you were gone——"

"But, my mother—my poor mother!" interrupted Edward; "already I know that she is suffering agonies from my long absence; and should I not return to-night——"

"Pshaw! your mother knows that young men will be young men," returned Dangerfield, with a smile: "she will only think that some rosy-cheeked damsel has tempted you to forget the hours, and play the truant."

Edward looked as he felt—displeased at this ill-timed attempt at raillery. From the lips of a father it appeared to come with peculiar ill grace; and Dangerfield seemed to comprehend his feelings, and feel abashed at the silent rebuke which his looks conveyed; for he hastily added,

"However, you may set your mind at rest about your mother; for I will bear your excuses to her myself."

"You!" uttered Edward, in a tone of alarm and surprise.

"Yes, I," he replied. "Can you wonder that, after so many years of painful absence—painful, I trust, alike to her as me—I should be anxious to see her?"

Edward's heart throbbed with anguish. Would this man tell her all? Would he tell her that he was the leader of a gang of thieves—murderers? for in no other light could he (Edward) now regard the fierce and dissolute tribe from whose violence he had so narrowly escaped with his life.

"I know what occupies your thoughts," observed Dangerfield, whose keen eyes had been fastened on his face. "Believe me, however," he added, with that hateful, sarcastic smile which so often deformed his handsome features, "believe me, I know your mother's heart and disposition better than you do. There is no fear of her sinking under the affliction which is so appalling to your gentlemanly feelings. She knows me well enough to know that it has ever been my ruling axiom, that 'tis

Better rule in hell than serve in heaven;

and, depend upon it, she will be but little surprised at discovering the *honourable* situation which I hold in the world."

Edward's heart sickened with disgust at this, which he considered a foul libel on his mother. Had it been any other than his father who uttered it, how deeply—how fiercely would he have resented it; but as it was, he buried the painful thoughts in his own bosom, and remained silent.

"But, why may I not accompany you, sir?" he at length demanded, with earnestness. "The way from hence is tedious and intricate; and you say you are unacquainted with the country. Years of trouble and sickness, too, have rendered my mother weak and timid; and your abrupt appearance, whatever may be her feelings towards the husband of her youth——"

A dark cloud stole over Dangerfield's countenance, and his piercing eye seemed to dart lightnings, as he turned fiercely round on Edward.

"What do you mean, boy?—what do you know of the husband of her youth?" he demanded. "But I forget myself," he added, in a milder tone, as he read the unequivocal astonishment which the looks of his companion betrayed; "my mind is bewildered, I believe, so many contending thoughts are battling there. Of this be assured, however: you must not quit this tent to-night. I leave you with my people as a hostage of my faith, their belief in which your imprudence to-night has shaken. If you were to leave with me, we should both be sacrificed to their jealous suspicions. In my hands you may safely trust the task both of accounting for your absence, and gradually revealing my existence to your mother, without too much alarming her sensitive feelings."

There was a latent sneer in the conclusion of this sentence, which again went to Edward's heart. How could it be possible that this heartless man could love or be beloved by his kind and gentle mother? Alas; little did he know the weakness and inconsistency of woman's heart—little did he think how often their fondest affections are bestowed on those most opposite to them in disposition—in principle—in all that should constitute the bond of sympathy.

Dangerfield departed. He had parried Edward's observations on the difficulty, in that lone and thinly inhabited country, of finding the habitation of Mrs. Hatherleigh, by alleging that Zekiel, whose searching eyes and inquisitive disposition nothing could escape or evade, had already explored the route to the ancient building, and, though unsuspecting who were its inhabitants, had sought and received charity from the hands of Mrs. Hatherleigh.

"He, therefore, will be my guide; and to him will I trust for an introduction which shall prepare Felicia for my appearance, without too suddenly alarming her."

Felicia!—how did Edward's heart ache, at hearing his mother thus familiarly named by one——

"But he is my father," he ejaculated to himself; "and I must try to stifle these feelings, which so rebel against him."

Dangerfield had quitted the tent, to commence at once, as Edward supposed, his toilsome journey; but, in a few minutes, he returned, accompanied by an old woman, whom he called Minna.

"I leave him under your charge, Minna," he observed; "remember, I hold you responsible for his safety. I am going now on business of importance to us all; see that he be not disturbed until I return; and, hark ye——"

The remainder was whispered softly in her ear; but Minna responded to it in a way that showed the instructions, whatever they might be, were not disagreeable to her, though she affected to undertake the task with reluctance.

"Aye, aye," she muttered, "when there's aught to do that others shrink from, then Minna's called upon. Minna is alone trustworthy—Minna——Well, well; I shall do your bidding, though it cost me my night's sleep. Many a sleepless night have I had before for your sake; and what has been my reward? When you are joyous and happy, you forget that old Minna——"

"Silence, witch!" exclaimed Dangerfield, furiously: "if you will not obey me, say so at once; and I will seek in the tents of the sleepers some one more tractable and more faithful."

Minna regarded him with a look of deep reproach.

"Not more faithful," she uttered, with a deep sigh; "for I have been ever true to you, though you have been false to me and mine. But, hush! this is no time to speak of that."

She laid her skinny finger on her withered and pale lips, as if to enforce silence; and then, on tiptoe, approached the miserable couch on which Edward had again thrown himself down, partly from the feeling of extreme weakness, and partly because he loathed and wished to avoid, as much as possible, the sight of him with whose destiny his own, he feared, was now bound up for ever.

"He's a fine lad, and a bonny one," muttered Minna, bending over him; "but so was the child of my——"

Dangerfield seized her roughly by her shoulder, and forced her to the entrance of the tent, uttering at the same time some expressions in a language which Edward did not comprehend, but which, from the expression of his face, as he stood in the full light of the great glaring torch which was stuck in the ground just within side, he could readily understand were threats and denunciations of vengeance against the old woman, who replied in the same language, in a tone of hoarse and deep reproach.

In a few moments, however, the feud seemed to pass away. Dangerfield uttered what appeared to be his parting directions; and Minna, re-entering the tent, crouched herself in a corner on the ground, where, except that the fitful light, in its flickerings from time to time revealed the steadfast gaze of her snake-like, brilliant eyes fixed on him whom she supposed to be quietly sleeping, she might have been taken rather for a motley heap of rags of all textures and colours, than a living being.

Sick at heart, and scarcely caring what should become of him, it was long, after he thus saw himself committed to the surveillance of this ancient crone, before Edward raised his head, or looked about him; but when at length he did so, he became conscious of the malignant gaze with which those basilisk eyes were fixed upon him. He closed his heavy and wearied eyelids, and opened them again; and still there was the same parchment-like face, and the same expression in the fixed eyes.

Edward chided himself for weakness; but to lie there, with that Hecate-like gaze fixed on him, was impossible. He thought of the fascinating power that is attributed to the eyes of the rattle-snake, and fancied that he was under the same influence.

"I must go out into the open air," he observed, rising, "this place is too close for me."

The old woman rose, too, and approached close to him.

" Did you not hear Paul say you must not quit the tent till he returns? Be advised—there is danger in disobeying him," she whispered, in accents that sounded friendly in his ear. " Besides," she added, "I shall suffer, if any harm should happen to you. He told me that my life should answer for yours : for my sake, then, be advised."

When was ever Edward's heart insensible to the tone of kindness? He returned to his wretched bed. The old woman again crouched in her corner; and, still conscious that her keen and oppressive gaze was fixed upon him, he no longer anticipated danger from it, but yielded to the exhaustion which his recent exertions and excitement had induced, and slept.

The chill and grey light of morning had succeeded to the shades of night, the torch was extinguished, and the frail and temporary canvas abode which had been his shelter and resting-place looked more wretched and comfortless than ever, when Edward awoke and looked around him. Hours had passed away; yet, there still crouched the old woman, in her undeviating and unnatural, as it seemed to him, position, her chin resting on her knees, her eyes still bright and sleepless, and still fixed on him.

For a moment Edward was bewildered, and unable to recollect the circumstances that had brought him there. His head throbbed to distraction, every limb ached and trembled, and a parching thirst announced the fever that was rioting in his veins.

The old woman arose at the first sound of his voice.

" The morning is come, and he is not arrived," she observed, with a look of mysterious import. " The birds of night are all winging their flight to their hidden nests ; and the beasts of the forest, that fear mankind, are creeping to their dens ; and yet he comes not."

" I would he were come," returned Edward, " that I might be released from this irksome confinement."

" And if he comes not quickly, you may be glad of such a shelter, if it will save you from——"

The sentence was yet unfinished on her lips, when a light form sprung into the middle of the tent, and the old woman hailed him with a shrill cry of satisfaction.

" It is Zekiel ! You are safe, my child," she exclaimed, "and he——" but the inquiry was answered by the appearance of Dangerfield himself, in the narrow opening of the tent.

He beckoned the old woman forth, and they walked away together.

Edward was again constrained to bridle his impatience; but it was not now very severely tried, for in a few minutes, Dangerfield returned, alone.

"Well, sir," observed the latter, "I trust your apprehensions of danger are by this time pretty well quieted. You have found you could sleep as safely, if not as softly, in a gipsy's tent, as in——"

"I have not feared for or thought of myself," interrupted Edward. "My mother——"

"Your mother is quite well," observed Dangerfield, abruptly; "and, like a woman of sense and experience, as she is, quite disposed to make the best of what cannot be avoided. I beg, therefore, that no squeamish scruples on your part may make her unhappy. She tells me," he added, in a somewhat softer tone, "that you have been exemplary in your conduct towards her. I trust, therefore, that you will continue to act so, without questioning either her motives or mine. You can depart now, as soon as you please; but, be careful that you do not reveal to any one where you have passed the night; and, above all, remember that a single incautious word on your part, as to what you may have heard or seen here, will, to a certainty, cost both you and me our lives. Circumstances, which it matters little to speak of now, have placed me in a situation from which it is impossible for me to disengage myself. I must, therefore, make the best of it; and, I trust, it will not be my son who will add bitterness to a fate so little enviable."

"But is there no hope of your being able, at some time," began Edward, but he was instantly silenced by Dangerfield's significant gesture.

"This is not a time or place to speak of hopes for the future," he observed, "we are content to live for the present only, and leave to chance——But come, I expected you would be all anxiety to return home. Perhaps you would rather rest for the day. If so, you can; for there will be none left in the tents in another hour, except an old woman or two to take care of them, until night. You had better stay with them, and let them nurse you, till you feel strong enough to commence your walk; for your pale face yet shows that——"

"Oh, no, I am well and strong enough," interrupted Edward, hastily. "I wish not to——But you, whither do you go?" he added, in a tone of the deepest interest.

"Not with you," replied Dangerfield, "that would be an indulgence I dare not yet allow myself; I have already been absent from the tribe for some weeks. Perhaps that absence would have been still further prolonged, had I known exactly where their rendezvous was to be; but, as I have accidentally encountered them, I must for some time take my chance with them. You will see me, however, soon—sooner, perhaps, than you may wish."

Edward departed unnoticed, as it seemed to him, and uncared for by the few persons who were straggling among the tents, and whose idle and lounging, indifferent manner formed a striking contrast to their wild and furious excitement on the preceding night.

During his hurried walk homewards, the young man's mind was a chaos of contending emotions. The mystery was indeed explained that had rendered his mother so unwilling to speak of the events of her early life, and had kept her lips entirely closed respecting his father. Never, indeed, had Edward heard her utter a single allusion to that person. And how could he now wonder at it?—how could he be surprised that she should shrink from the recollection of the man who claimed that title? He himself, anxious as he was to feel something like affection and respect for him—to shut his eyes to his faults, and attribute them all to that "stern ruler of mankind," necessity—even he shrunk with involuntary hatred and disgust from acknowledging as a parent the Gipsy Chief. And by what strange fatality could his mother—his gentle, delicate, and, as far as he had an opportunity of observing her conduct, his right and noble-minded mother—how could she have been induced to link her fate with one so opposite? Again and again he recalled to his mind the coarse language, the fierce and sinister looks, the sensual and unprincipled sentiments, which had betrayed the character of Dangerfield in their recent intercourse; and still more decided grew his loathing towards the man whom, by the laws of nature, he should have been compelled to obey and honour.

Mrs. Hatherleigh's looks spoke a volume, when she admitted him. Shame, agony, and remorse were depicted in the glance of her eye; and when she fell upon his neck, and strained him to her bosom, uttering in broken accents her joy at seeing him again, Edward felt that it was impossible for him to add to the bitterness of her feelings, by uttering a single question or remark on what had passed.

By degrees, however, this reserve in some measure passed away. Mrs. Hatherleigh was evidently anxious to learn what had passed; and, by degrees, Edward became sufficiently calm and collected to speak to her without reserve of the misery he felt at discovering his father in a situation so dangerous and degraded.

"I do not ask you, my dear mother," he observed, "what were the circumstances which led to his estrangement from you and drove him to such a desperate way of life; for certain I am that you have not been to blame; but I would pray of you, if you have still any influence left with him—if you have the power, by any sacrifice to withdraw him from this horrible life ——Oh God! I would work for him day and night—what would I not do, to restore him to society, to——"

"My dear, dear boy, do not so humiliate me—do not make your wretched mother feel how utterly worthless she is of your love and duty! Oh, if you did but know——"

"I wish to know nothing that is painful to you to tell me," returned Edward, warmly. "Sure I am, that you have been more unfortunate than guilty—more sinned against than sinning. And I—to whom you have ever been the best, the kindest of mothers—I should be the last in the world to utter a word of complaint against you. I own I have received a severe shock; for although, from your silence, and the distress I have seen you suffer at any casual allusion to my father, I guessed that he had not been altogether deserving of you, still I thought——but no matter," and he dashed away the tear that glittered on his burning cheek, "no matter, he is my father; and if the whole world despise him, I will defend him; I will try—yes, I will try to love him."

Mrs. Hatherliegh hid her face with her hands, to conceal her shame—her agonies. Never had she felt more strongly tempted than at this moment, to reveal to her injured son the whole truth, and trust to his affection for her, not only for forgiveness, but for his intercession with his wronged and deceived parent— the bereaved, the long-suffering Lionel Moreton. But the image of the desperate, reckless man who had so recently re- minded her of her solemn engagement—the recollection of those awful words by which she had bound herself to silence, rushed upon her mind, and once more sealed her lips.

A long and wretched day was that which ensued. The mother shrunk from encountering her son's eyes: and the son, for the first time, was constrained and reserved towards his mother.

As the evening closed in, he became conscious that she was busied in some unusual domestic preparations, and at length he ventured to say,

"Do you expect any one here to-night, mother?"

"Yes, *he* will be here at nightfall," she replied, in faltering accents. "It is natural, you know, Edward, that one who has long been destitute of the comforts of a home, and compelled to associate with those whom in his heart he abhors, is it not natural, that he should be desirous of passing as much of his time as he can with—with——"

"Natural!" repeated Edward, as she paused and hesitated. "Oh yes, most natural. Would that it were in our power to detain him here for ever! And surely, if the life he leads be so abhorrent to him—if he is really desirous of quitting his wretched associates, he will——"

"Hush! he comes!" interrupted Mrs. Hatherleigh, as a low, soft, prolonged whistle was heard echoing among the old buildings of the Nunnery. "That is the signal of his approach," she continued. "How often have I heard it in happier days, when my heart has danced at the sound! And last night, when I heard it again and again repeated, to prepare me for his appearance, oh, Edward, it sounded like a voice from the grave, prophesying the destruction of my quiet home—of all I have learned to value and enjoy as my portion in this world—the knell of all my hopes, of your love, of——But I must not let him see me thus; I will leave you to receive him; and oh, Edward, for my sake be cautious. Let him not suspect that I have prejudiced you against him—that I——Oh, you know what I would say. Go to him, and welcome him hither."

Without waiting his reply, she quitted the room; and Edward, trying to suppress the emotions he felt at this involuntary admission on her part of his father's utter worthlessness, proceeded to admit him.

Dangerfield (for so it will be best, for perspicuity's sake, henceforth to call him) appeared to far better advantage than when Edward had before beheld him, though his dress was of the fashion of a different country, and his large flapped hat increased rather than concealed the bandit-like cast of his features, which was further heightened by the immense black whiskers which met under his throat, and were fully exposed by the snow-white collar which was turned down over his dark dress.

Singular and *outré* as was this habit, Edward could not but

see that it was eminently calculated to render the form and
features of the wearer most striking and impressive; but it was
with pain he looked upon it as a proof how completely the
former was severed from the ties and forms of society, whose
very outward appearance he seemed to scorn and set at nought.

Few words passed between Edward and him previous to Mrs.
Hatherleigh's return to the room. A mere formal inquiry how
he got home, and whether he felt any ill effects from the occurrences of the preceding night, was coldly uttered by Dangerfield;
while Edward in vain attempted to obey his mother's injunctions
by teaching his tongue to belie his heart, and uttering a warm
and cordial welcome to one from whom that heart recoiled. He
shuddered as he beheld his mother locked for a moment in the
apparently warm embrace of the man who he felt to be unworthy
of her, and whose familiarity seemed, like the poisonous touch
of the toad, to defile all it lighted upon.

"He is her husband!—he is my father!" he repeated over and
over again to himself; but the words had no magic in them to
reconcile him to the being so opposite to the idea he had often
conceived of him who had borne those sacred titles.

Some hours passed in Dangerfield's society tended only to
confirm Edward's impressions to his disadvantage. There were
moments, indeed, when the latter felt that he (Dangerfield)
might, to one less prejudiced than himself, appear a pleasant
companion; that his boldness and recklessness of manner might
be considered as proofs of frankness and openness of disposition;
and that the utter contempt in which he professed to hold mankind in general—who were but the tools, he said, which a wise
man would use as best he could to advance his own interest—
was only the bitterness of one who felt that he had been ill used
by the world. But Edward was proof against all his sophistry
—all his arts; and when his words needed any comment, he
read it in his face—that face which was

"An index to a volume of black thoughts—
Of dark, designing, and of treacherous deeds."

The first interview of Edward with Dangerfield, and the
commencement of the visits of the latter to the Nunnery,
occurred some weeks before the event which gave so dark a
tinge to the future life of Edward, and of her whom he valued
dearer than life—the orphaned Elinor Clare. That event, it
need scarcely be said, was the mysterious death of Walter
Copeland. For some time previous to that period, Paul
Dangerfield had become nearly a constant resident at the

Nunnery, though his presence there was carefully concealed from every one who chanced casually to visit that retired and solitary spot.

During the day, indeed, he seldom or ever quitted the concealed chamber which had been fitted up for his use, passing most of his time in bed, to recruit the fatigues, or, rather, the riotous revelry in which, as Edward too truly suspected, he passed most of his midnight hours in the society of the gipsies, who had now removed their camp to the wood comparatively a short distance from the Nunnery.

From the time Edward had been first a constrained visitor to the tents of these singular and lawless people, he had diligently shunned all probability of meeting with or being recognised by the tribe.

To Zekiel, indeed, he was well known; for Zekiel, from whom Dangerfield seemed to have no reserve, and whom he entrusted on all occasions, although he treated him with the most cruel, and, as Edward conceived, most unnecessary severity—Zekiel was the constant messenger from the gipsies' camp to the Nunnery, whenever anything required to be communicated to the Chief, or the presence of the latter was required out of the usual time he allotted for his visits.

From Zekiel, who sometimes passed hours basking on Mrs. Hatherleigh's warm kitchen-hearth, and feasting on what were dainties to him, though the plainest food that could be set before him—from him Edward learned many circumstances that confirmed, or, rather, strengthened the feelings of horror with which he regarded the man whom he believed to be the author of his being.

To boast of Paul's bravery—Paul's cunning—his talent at overreaching and cheating—the disguises that he could assume —the hairbreadth escapes he had experienced—and the dangers that he had faced with impunity, were Zekiel's favourite themes.

He had been taught to consider Paul's character as the very perfection—the beau ideal of what a gipsy ought to be, whose "hand is against every man, and every man's hand against his," and he believed that he was exalting the character of his hero in Edward's eyes, by every additional trait he recited of those qualities which had raised him (Dangerfield) to the station which appeared to the poor, ignorant, half-savage lad, the highest and most enviable on the earth—that of Chief of the most considerable tribe of gipsies in England.

"But he must still be in danger of being taken for some of these exploits, if he were discovered," observed Edward, one evening, when Mrs. Hatherleigh had been longer absent from the kitchen than usual (nothing was said in her presence) and Zekiel had been warmed into more than usual talkativeness by a second cup of spiced and sugared ale.

"Danger!" he repeated, with a contemptuous smile. "Yes, but does the deer, when he has escaped from the hounds, think about danger, when he has got again into the green pastures, and mingles with the herd? No, to be sure; he frisks about as merry as any of them. Yes, to be sure, Paul's always in danger; and that's what I've come here to-night to him to tell 'ware hawks; for there's bills up on the walls at West Hartley, offering fifty pounds reward for him, though they don't know his name; and as to describing him, bah! they might as well attempt to describe that smoke that is going up the chimney, twisting and turning into a thousand shapes. But then, as our people say, he is known to belong to the tribe; and there's a sharp justice here, that has an old grudge against our people; and if he should get hold——"

"But what is the crime with which he is charged?" interrupted Edward, impatiently.

"Crime!" repeated the boy, with a stare of astonishment. "Who?—Paul?—crime did you say?" he again repeated, as if beginning to be conscious that he had acted unwisely in being so communicative.

"Yes," returned Edward, with assumed carelessness; "that is what those who know no better call it; but your people, who are wiser——"

The boy burst into an exulting laugh.

"Ha! ha! ha! you say true; our people are wiser," he observed. "But you want to know what Paul did. Well, I'll tell you. You know the night that he went over to West Hartley Fair with some of our people?"

Edward assented, though he knew nothing about it. Dangerfield had, two or three times since his introduction to the Nunnery, been away, apparently on some long excursion; but Edward had avoided even asking a single question, lest he might be supposed to feel an interest in actions which his heart, his reason, and his principles, alike condemned.

"Well," continued the boy, "he went over to the fair; and as he was well dressed, and pretended to be a horse-dealer (and so he is, when he can catch them) why he got into a parlour, &c

they call it, at one of the grand inns, where some of the Don
farmers were drinking and playing at cards, and joined in.   Let
Paul alone for that : he never gets into a game that he don't
have everything his own way ; and so he went on, sweeping the
money off the table, and the farmers swearing he must deal
with the devil, or have his luck, and his own too; until at last
a 'cute old fellow, that had said but little, but watched Paul
narrowly, clapped his hand upon Paul's, just as he'd palmed a
card, and swore he'd chop his wrist off, if he didn't produce the
card, own he was a cheat, and give all he had won up to the
proper owners.   Do you think Paul would stand this?   No, to be
sure.   In half a minute, bang went the table, over cards and
candles and all.   The old man was down on his back; and Paul
catching the knife out of his hand that he'd threatened him with
laid about him till he got outside the door; and then half a
dozen of our people, that were on the look out, came up, and
favoured his getting clear off."

"And this is what they are searching for him now for ?"
observed Edward.

"Yes, two or three of the yokels got smartish cuts with the
knife ; for Paul don't stand for trifles," replied Zekiel ; "and
so they say it's felony ; and if they can lay hold of him, they'll
make him dance in the air to the one-stringed music.   But they
know little of Paul.   The tree is not planted yet that is to
make his gibbet ; nor the hemp sown that must be reaped for
his halter."

Edward shuddered at the horrid images that were thus
conjured up to his mental sight; but he knew that to have
expressed his feelings to the boy, would only have drawn upon
himself ridicule for his supposed pusillanimity ; and he, therefore, hastened away to arouse Dangerfield with the intelligence
that Zekiel wanted him upon especial business.

It was very evident that, however the Chief might affect, in
the presence of his people, to despise and make light of the
danger that threatened him, he was in reality very seriously
impressed with the chance of his retreat being discovered.

What tale he told to Mrs. Hatherleigh in excuse for himself
Edward knew not; but even she did not hesitate to tell to the
latter her fears and terrors of his impending fate.   He now
entirely confined himself to the long-uninhabited apartments of
the Nunnery ; even Zekiel was kept away, lest his footsteps
should be dogged, and the asylum of Dangerfield discovered;
and the only communication that was kept up between the

gipsies and their Chief was through Edward, who most
reluctantly was compelled to yield his scruples to his supposed
father's entreaties and his mother's tears, and become the
messenger between them.

But, though he thus became more familiarised to their wild
habits, and often saw much to admire in their warm affections,
their fidelity to each other, their generosity and absence of all
selfishness in their regard to the interests of the tribe, their
passionate attachment to their wives and children, and their
readiness to hazard everything, and make any sacrifice for him
to whom they looked up as their head, he still shrunk with
abhorrence from them; for, beyond the pale of their own community, they seemed not to possess one feeling of human nature.

Mankind were to them all lawful prey; and from nothing
did they seem to shrink in their attempts to ensnare or to run
them down.

A fortnight passed away, and then a circumstance occurred
which, for a short time, afforded Edward a welcome relief.
Little could he foresee that the very event which he so congratulated himself upon should be the means of producing to
him the most acute and prolonged misery.

The yearly sum which Mrs. Hatherleigh received from her
injured husband for her support was paid through the hands of
a banker, at the nearest post town to the Nunnery.

This agent was, as she believed, totally ignorant of her history:
she had, therefore, hitherto felt no reluctance to wait upon him
herself for her half-yearly payment; but now, so intimidating is
the consciousness of guilt, she feared to meet his eye, lest he
should know the restriction under which she received it, namely,
that she should never renew her intercourse with Oliver Moreton
—the *soi-disant* Paul Dangerfield; and knowing it, should
suspect that she had broken the compact. Poverty, disgrace,
utter destitution would be the consequences of such a discovery;
and she brooded over the probability, or, rather, the possibility,
until she became so terrified at the trial that she fancied awaited
her, as to be unable to undertake the journey.

The want of the money was most pressing; for—with shame
be it told—Dangerfield's habits of indulgence were such as to
be a heavy tax upon her limited means. *He* became impatient
for the supply which it was the very depth of meanness and
baseness for him to touch; and, at his suggestion, it was at
length resolved that Edward, furnished with proper authority
from his mother, should go over to the town to receive it.

ELINOR CLARE.

"THERE ARE SPIES ABROAD, AND YOU HAVE ENEMIES."

It was like a respite for a day to a criminal condemned to death, for Edward to leave behind him, even for a few hours, the scenes which had become hateful to him, since his evil genius, in the shape of Dangerfield, had intruded to blast his hopes of fair fame, and wither, with his hateful presence, the sweets that had once surrounded his quiet, domestic hearth.

Never since he had become conscious of his disgraceful connection with the Gipsy Chief had Edward dared to seek an interview with Elinor Clare. He could not think of her without distraction.

Little as he before thought himself entitled to her pure and modest affection, how could he now dare to hope—to wish that she should still continue to distinguish him with her preference? Yet he longed once again to see her—to hear her sweet voice reproach him for his absence—to convince her that he should never cease to love and to regret her, and then to take leave of her for ever.

"But no," he reflected, "I cannot—I dare not expose my mother to her scorn and contempt. I dare not tell her that she has given me a father whose very name is a disgrace and reproach to me. Oh, how Walter would exult, could he know the utter extinction of all my pride—all my hopes! And yet I wrong him; he might rejoice that a bar is for ever placed between Elinor and myself; but he would pity me. And his upstart, insolent, purse-proud father, would he, too, pity me? Oh, they shall never know it. Elinor may think me fickle, false, anything but the truth, that I am sunk beneath her regard."

Such were his thoughts, as he journeyed onwards towards the town at which he was to receive his mother's money. From many points in the high road he could catch either a full or a partial view of the Grove—the residence of the Copelands, and of her who formed its principal ornament; and often did he linger and forget his errand, to gaze on the seemingly peaceful and happy retreat.

Edward's visits to the "thronged haunts of man" (for such by comparison appeared to him the country town of Newton Regis) had been "few and far between." Five years had passed since he, then a mere stripling, had accompanied his mother thither on the same errand on which he now came alone; and there was much to attract and divert his attention from dwelling on the griefs and mortifications which had occupied his mind on his solitary route.

Yet, every now and then, when he met the curious and inquisitive gaze which is so freely bestowed on strangers in a country-town, a sudden flush would suffuse his fine features at the thought that he alone, perhaps, could claim no kindred here —that he alone would become, the instant they should know him rightly, as the son of a vagrant, a common robber, the object of contempt and suspicion.

The persons at the bank, to whom he made known his business, and delivered his testimonials, received him with great civility; but yet he thought there was something of suspicion and hesitation in their answer to him.

Mr. Ashurst, their principal partner, was in London; and they had received no instructions respecting the payment of Mrs. Hatherleigh's money. They had rather, indeed, a suspicion that there was some obstacle in the way of its immediate payment; but Mr. Ashurst would arrive by the mail at four o'clock the next morning; and he (Edward) could see him at office hours, ten till three; and then, of course, the business would be settled.

Edward was, therefore, compelled to return to the inn, and engage a bed for the night. It had been his mother's suggestion that he should do so, without foreseeing the difficulty that had arisen, but merely that she considered the distance too great for him to attempt to return the same night.

The sneering smile, however, with which Dangerfield had listened to this proof of maternal tenderness had decided Edward to return the same night, merely to disprove the charge of effeminacy and self-indulgence which the former, though not in express words, was frequently in the habit of insinuating against him.

Now, however, he was compelled to remain; and he did so with the less repugnance, because he knew his mother would not be rendered uneasy by his absence. His tea, "the cup that cheers and not inebriates," was soon dispatched. There was nothing very attractive in gazing from the window of the little parlour, to which he had been shown, into a stable yard; and, taking his hat, he walked out to try if he could find some relief from the thoughts that preyed upon his mind, in the novelty of the busy town.

For some time, the shops, with their (to him) showy and attractive appearance, claimed his attention; but he soon began to tire of looking at them, and was thinking of returning to the inn, when he was induced to stop, by observing a group of people reading a printed bill, which was stuck on the door of the town-house, or county court of justice. In an instant what he had heard from Zekiel rushed upon his mind, as he saw at the head of it " Fifty Pounds Reward," and the colour faded from his cheeks, as he proceeded to read a description of Dangerfield's person, as charged with an attempt to murder.

After describing his dress, which appeared to have been that of a grazier or horse-dealer, the bill went on to state that it was strongly suspected he was one of a gang of gipsies, who had been recently guilty of many atrocious acts, especially horse-stealing, in one of the northern counties; for which two of their members had been convicted and transported, and the tribe compelled to separate, and scatter themselves.

That the man for whom the reward was now offered was believed to be their head or leader, and well known to many persons by the name of Gipsy Paul, or Dangerfield.

Edward's cheek grew pale, and his head dizzy. How could he hope that his wretched father could long escape the fate that impended over him? He listened eagerly to the comments that were made by the persons who were reading the bill.

"Some do say that one of the farmers that he stabbed be dead," observed one old man, "but whether he be or no, it's hanging matter, if they take him, for it comes under the cuttin' and maiming act, that's what they call the black act."

"Aye, and he was a black villain that did it, for I saw him in the fair, pretending to chaffer for a horse; and I couldn't help thinking then what a hang-gallows look he'd got."

"Pooh, if it was Gipsy Paul," returned a young sprightly woman, "he's as good-looking a chap as you'd wish to see of a summer's day, and such a dancer! I saw him dance everybody down at Newton wake. And he's as generous as a prince, too; and they say he is a prince, or a chief, or something, among his own people. But I don't believe it was him that did this; for I was over to West Hartley myself that day; and though I saw a good many of the gipsies there—for I knew them all, because they used to camp not half a mile from our place, and civil neighbours, and quiet enough they were——"

"Yes, I suppose they used to tell your fortune," interrupted the old man, "and promise you a pack of rubbish to turn your head; but, for my part, I'd have them all hung up in a string at once, and clear the country of the vagabonds."

The crowd separated with a laugh; and Edward was left standing alone before the bill, which appeared to him like the sentence of death already pronounced against the wretched Dangerfield.

That night was a night of misery. A thousand improbable and impossible wishes and projects passed through Edward's mind; and with extreme impatience he awaited the hour which was to dismiss him to his home, that he might urge with all possible energy the necessity of Dangerfield's at once quitting that part of the country, where it appeared he was so well known as to be in hourly danger of being recognised.

Again he was doomed to disappointment. Mr. Ashurst had not

come by the mail : but it was expected he would post it, the clerk said; and as it was certain he would arrive in the course of the day, Edward was urgently pressed to remain until he did come. Another day was thus wasted, and Mr. Ashurst did not at last arrive until long after " office hours." Edward was, therefore, compelled to remain another night; and then, when at last he was admitted to the principal, Mr. Ashurst, after asking a number of questions, under which Edward writhed as if under the torments of the Inquisition, at last observed, that he was very sorry to disappoint Mrs. Hatherleigh, but he had received instructions, while in London, to suspend payment of the money until she gave a satisfactory reply to some questions put to her in the sealed paper which he now delivered to Edward.

On what terms, or from whom, his mother received her annuity, Edward had never heard; but he could scarcely doubt now that some stipulation respecting Dangerfield was connected with it; and that although delicacy prevented Mr. Ashurst's asking him the direct question, the intention was to ascertain whether he knew anything of his worthless father.

Edward had, in the first instance, alleged that his mother's inability to wait on Mr. Athurst herself, arose from indisposition; and this was not, in strictness, departing from the truth, for the many conflicts and the excitement she had of late undergone, had materially shaken Mrs. Hatherleigh's health, and rendered her very unfit to meet any further agitation.

Mr. Ashurst, however, kindly observed, that there was no necessity for his seeing Mrs. Hatherleigh.

" I am instructed," he observed, " that it will be sufficient for the lady to give a plain and decisive answer to the questions proposed in that paper. If she *can* do so," he added, laying a great stress on the word can, " I will pay you immediately, or whoever she may appoint to receive the money."

Edward dared not raise his eyes to Mr. Ashurst's while he was speaking; but, immediately upon leaving the office, he set out on his return at a rate little suited, rapid as it was, to his impatience to be at home.

During Edward's absence all had been alarm and consternation at the Grove, which he had fancied the abode of peace and comfort, from the circumstances narrated at the commencement of this history—the mysterious disappearance and consequent discovery of the murder of Walter Copeland. Little did Edward think, when he entered the confines of the wood, across the borders of which a short cut led to the Nunnery, that the lifeless remains of his former companion and friend were at that moment lying within its precincts.

He had proceeded but a little distance, when sundry short barks and a whine expressive of pleasure, from his dog, which had been his sole companion in his journey, announced that some one was near whom the animal recognised; and a moment afterwards Zekiel made his appearance from the covert of some neighbouring bushes.

"What are you doing, boy? and where is Dangerfield?" demanded Edward, who was startled at the lad's unusual silent and mysterious manner.

"Hush! don't say a word here; but get home as fast as you can. There's mischief abroad," whispered Zekiel. "Aye, and some that you know are concerned in it; but take my advice, don't you make any stir; if you do, it will be the worse for all. Hark! there's some of our people now. Don't speak to them, don't see them, if you can help it. I can't tell you what I mean now, but it will be the worse for you, and others beside you."

The boy darted away as he spoke; and Edward, with a heavy presentiment of approaching evil, pursued his hurried way through the wood.

The circumstances of his meeting with Elinor on that eventful night, of his having been seen by Isabel Copeland within a few minutes of her discovery of Walter's murdered remains, and all that followed, have been already detailed; but it must be mentioned, that he had, but a few minutes before his meeting with Elinor, encountered a young female of the gipsy tribe, who had always evinced a particular interest towards him, and who now delivered to him, though in still more mysterious terms, the caution he had previously received from Zekiel.

"Do not look to the right or left," she observed, "there are spies abroad, and you have enemies. Go on without delay, and seek the shelter of brick walls and closed doors; and if you hear or see aught before you reach them, shut your eyes and your ears, for there is as much danger in knowing too much as knowing too little."

Edward broke impatiently away from her. Everything seemed to conspire to mystify and bewilder him; and, to add to his perplexity, he soon after encountered Elinor, as has been related.

CHAPTER XX.

Oh! a prison is something infamous indeed! There is within its walls a vermin which defiles everything.—Did you find a little bird there, there would be slime on its wing. Should you gather a beautiful flower there, its odour would prove fœtid.

VICTOR HUGO.

THE intelligence with which Edward returned to the Nunnery excited general consternation there; but still he, though the bearer of it, only in part understood the cause of it.

The peril in which Dangerfield stood, indeed, and the urgent necessity there was of the latter immediately quitting the neighbourhood, was readily enough comprehended; but it was sometime before Edward could understand how he could expedite that object, or what connection his (Dangerfield's) departure could have with the receipt of his mother's money.

A blush of shame for the meanness of the latter crimsoned his cheek, when he at length discovered that the sum in question was to be appropriated to secure Dangerfield's escape to France or Italy; but little did he think that that money could only be obtained by his mother's perjury. The sealed paper which he had received from Mr. Ashurst, and delivered to his mother, required of her a plain and decisive answer to the questions. "Had she seen or heard from, or was she in any, way directly or indirectly, in communication with Oliver Moreton?"

There had been, on the first reading these interrogations, a violent struggle in Mrs. Hatherleigh's mind, between her conscience and her inclination; and it had ended, as most such struggles will do, where passion is allowed to usurp the place of principle, in a determination to sacrifice the dictates of the former on the altar of expediency. With a trembling hand she wrote a decisive negative to the questions asked; adding to it, at the suggestion of Dangerfield himself, a few words indicative of surprise that, after so many years, it should be deemed necessary to revive a subject that she had hoped would never again have been mentioned. She concluded this deceptive epistle by observing that her present precarious state of health rendered the immediate receipt of the money of material importance to her; and that she hoped, therefore, her present unqualified denial would be sufficient to remove all obstacles.

The moment Dangerfield got possession of this document, he determined to prevent all possibility of its being recalled by the weak woman over whom he had been obliged to exert his utmost influence to prevail on her to write it.

It was to be the last time, he assured her, that she should be called upon to falsify her conscience, or even to submit to the degradation of receiving money on such terms. Fallen as he now appeared to her, he had still resources, could he quit with safety the wild and lawless band with whom he had in desperation connected himself, at a time when he believed himself forgotten and deserted by the only being on earth for whom he wished to live, or who could make life bearable to him. If he could disentangle himself from the gipsies, they would once more leave England and their cares behind them, and pass the remainder of their lives together, in the quiet retreat which had descended to him from a relative of his mother; who, as has been mentioned, was a native of Italy, and belonged, as Felicia knew, to a wealthy family. Often as her hopes had been deceived—often as she had proved the falsehood and hollowness of his professions, the credulous woman again believed—again trusted him.

"Edward must depart with me before daybreak," he observed the moment that he got possession of the paper. "Not a moment must be lost; for I will own to you, that I know the danger is greater than even you suspect of my being looked for here. Shall I tell you the truth?—it is the agents of—of Lionel whom I dread more than those concerned in this affair, which, after all, was not half so serious as it is represented. Still it will be made the means of satisfying the revengeful feelings of ——but I will say no more, Felicia, on this painful theme. You must prepare Edward to accompany me; and I will, on the way, give him instructions how to act, to keep the tribe from suspecting that I intend to desert them; for then nothing could save me. While they believe me faithful to them, no temptation on earth would induce them to betray me : they will protect me, in fact, to their own certain ruin. But go, my love, and prepare Edward; and, above all, be careful to conceal from him the cause of the delay in receiving the money. If he were to suspect——"

" Ah ! if he were to suspect," repeated Mrs. Hatherleigh, as she hastily quitted the room, " if he were to suspect that he is to be made the instrument of falsehood—of fraud, how would his noble nature shudder and recoil ?"

It was not without considerable surprise that Edward heard

that he was to depart so soon; but his mother's agitation and tears seconded her assurance, that the life of *his father* depended on him; and Dangerfield's affected reluctance to implicate him in his fate, and the mysterious hints of the part he was to take in rescuing him from the impending danger, not only silenced all his scruples, but rendered Edward forgetful of everything but his extreme anxiety to commence their journey. Even his recent interview with Elinor in the wood, which had at the moment so surprised and alarmed him, was forgotten; until every circumstance was in an instant recalled by her unexpected appearance, as has been narrated, for the purpose of warning him of the suspicions that had fallen upon him respecting the death of Walter Copeland.

The manner—the look of Dangerfield, on that occasion, struck terror and anguish to his heart. He would have dared all consequences to himself, to have remained and faced the proposed investigation into his conduct; but his supposed father's look filled him with horror. He knew that he had been many nights absent from the Nunnery; he knew, too, how little appeared in his eyes the sacrifice of human life, if it stood in the way of his designs; and as he gazed upon his dark features, and marked the look with which he listened to Elinor's recital, involuntarily the horrid thought forced itself upon him, that he (Dangerfield) was the murderer of Walter Copeland.

"Yet, he is my father!" he exclaimed, in despair; "and shall I then vindicate my own innocence, at the expence of his life? No, guilty as he is—abhorrent as he is, even in my sight, let me not forget that he is my father. Rather, ten thousand times rather, let me bear the imputation of the crime he has committed than incur the misery, the guilt of parricide, by delivering him up to the punishment he so justly deserves!"

It was under this impression that Edward quitted the Nunnery; and in so doing confirmed, in the sight of his enemies, the imputation of his guilt.

It was believed by Mrs. Hatherleigh, and, indeed, by Edward himself, when he quitted his house on that eventful night, that Dangerfield was to accompany him to the town in which the banker resided; and, the moment he received the money, Edward was to deliver it to him, in order to enable him to depart immediately for the nearest seaport, from whence he was to embark, as soon as he could procure a passage. But he soon discovered that this was not the real plan of his companion. Under the pretext that it would be dangerous for him to enter a place in which he was well known, and where every wall was placarded with descriptions of his person, and the offer of reward for his apprehension, he proposed that he should remain at an obscure, road-side public-house, about three miles before they reached the town. It was in vain that Edward suggested that it would be more politic to pass at once through the town, as that way he must go to procure any conveyance, and allow him (Edward) to follow him with the money to some spot that he should appoint. Dangerfield was resolute to pursue his own plan; and, leaving him at the "Bold Foresters," which was the sign of the house he had chosen, the young man went forward to execute the remainder of his commission.

It is not to be supposed that Dangerfield had neglected to enforce upon him the necessity of his being silent, should the banker think fit to ask him any questions; but the utmost that the former could obtain from Edward, was the assurance that he should at once tell Mr. Ashurst, that he declined answering any inquiries on the subject.

"I cannot utter a falsehood," was his reply. "No, not even to save you, could I utter that which I know to be untrue. If, therefore, he should ask me any questions about you, I can only tell him that the subject is one on which I do not wish to speak —on which I *will not* speak; and if he has the feelings of a man, he will not even wish the son to utter a word that can criminate his father."

"The fool! the romantic, headstrong fool!" muttered Dangerfield, as he watched his departure from the window of the public-house at which he was to await his return. "Little does he suspect who *the father* really is whom he so evidently despises, and yet whom he is so disinterestedly solicitous to preserve."

Fortunately, as Edward thought, Mr. Ashurst did not put a single question to him on the subject he so dreaded to hear started. He read Mrs. Hatherleigh's note twice; and then, without further remark, paid the sum demanded: and by a cool "Good day, sir," to Edward, intimated that their intercourse, at least for the present, was concluded.

"He knows my fatal connection with that man, and despises me," thought Edward, as he hurried back to where he had left Dangerfield. What was his surprise—his grief—his indignation, to find the latter engaged in a carouse with three or four persons, whom at a single glance he knew to be gipsies.

"My evil fortune has thrown them in my way," he whispered to Edward. "They do not belong to our party; but circumstances have driven them to join us for a short time. I dare not attempt to leave them at present, but must accompany them to the camp whither they are now on their way,"

"But I—surely I need not go there?" observed Edward, in a tone that sufficiently betrayed his reluctance.

"You would not desert me until you know that I am, certainly, on the road to my final destination?" he replied. "Your mother expects you to accompany me for, at least, one day's journey; would you wish, then, to return to her with the unsatisfactory intelligence that you have left me here?"

Edward yielded without another word; he felt that it would indeed be unsatisfactory to himself as well as his mother, thus to return; and having delivered the money, which he eagerly asked for, and answered his inquiries, he seated himself in a distant corner of the room.

It was but little that he could understand of the conversation that was passing between Dangerfield and his companions; but that little was sufficient to increase, if possible, his horror and disgust towards the former, who, evidently disregarding entirely the effect his conduct would have upon Edward, abandoned himself to mirth and enjoyment, swallowing down glass after glass of spirits, and inviting from time to time the latter to join him in drinking toasts which made the young man shudder with horror. The remonstrances which he ventured to give utterance to repeatedly, were either treated with contempt, or met with a fierce frown of defiance; and convinced at last that it was useless to expostulate with him, Edward threw himself along a bench, and, completely overcome with fatigue, and the total loss of the previous night's rest, at length slept soundly.

Some hours had passed before he awoke; and when he did so, the noise and jollity which had reigned around him had ceased, a single candle was burning on a table at some distance, and a decent, farmer-looking man was quietly reading a newspaper by it.

Edward started to his feet, and looked anxiously round him: while the man, who appeared not till then to have known that he was in the room, observed,

"You have had a sound nap, young man; I hope you vagabonds, that went out as I came in, did not take advantage of it to rob you. I doubt they were upon no good errand."

Edward confusedly replied that he had little to be robbed of; and at the same moment the landlord, entering with some beer for his customer, exclaimed,

"Zounds! what, ben't you gone with your comrades? I tho't the house wur clear of the gang; for, I tell you the honest truth, I don't want to harbour any such——"

Edward waited not to hear the conclusion of this mortifying speech, but instantly rushed out of the room and the house.

The night was very dark, and he stood for some moments in the road, doubtful what course to take, when suddenly he received a smart slap on the shoulder, and Zekiel's eldritch laugh sounded in his ear.

"Come on," he observed; "it's a fine thing to be a pampered baby, that wants a guide to lead him a few miles through a straight road that a blind horse might travel, and never stumble or run his nose into a bush. But, come, do put your best leg foremost; or you will lose your supper, and so shall I: and such a supper! Oh! Paul has the spirit of a king, when he does treat!"

"Where, then, is Paul?" demanded Edward, whose heart sunk still lower at hearing the purpose to which the money was applied which his unfortunate mother had given up for so different a purpose.

"Where is Paul!" repeated the boy; "where should he be, but with his friends? and he has sent me to bring you to him."

"Would I had died before I had ever seen him, or knew the claim he had upon my obedience!" thought Edward, as he followed the lad, who set off at a pace which the latter had considerable difficulty to keep up with.

It was past midnight before they reached the place where the gipsies had now pitched their tents; but the revelry in which they were engaged was still at its height, though, to Edward's great surprise, he learned that this was only their resting-place for the night, and that at daybreak they were to resume their route for some distant part of the country. What had been their motives for decamping from their former quarters he knew not; but in the intervals of noisy mirth which sometimes occurred it was plain that some recent events had rendered it necessary for them to do so. Dark hints were given and looks exchanged, which Edward could not but connect in his mind with the recent tragical event—the death of Walter Copeland; and he shuddered with horror at the thought, that he was now seated amidst, and in apparent fellowship with, those who had been witnesses of, and probably participators in that deed. By degrees he learned, too, that Dangerfield and his companions had been driven from the house where they had left Edward by some apprehension that the landlord suspected who the former was, and had sent intelligence that he was there, to the town; and, it appeared that, in their alarm, and more than half intoxicated state, they had quitted, without recollecting, until some time after, that they had left the former behind them.

"And what now do you intend, sir?" demanded Edward, when Dangerfield had concluded this explanation. "My mother——"

"Your mother knows you will not return for some time," interrupted Dangerfield, hastily. "It is time, young man," he added, sternly, "that you should think of shaking off your dependence on your mother. You are old enough, now, to be making your own way in the world. I know what you are about to say; but do not interfere with my plans. Be assured that, however I may wander from what you think the right path, I have nothing but your benefit in view."

Edward's heart strongly rebelled against this assertion. He felt that, had this man possessed one spark of true parental feeling, he would have carefully avoided bringing him, his son, into contact with the degraded people with whom he was himself associated. Neither could he believe that his mother knew of, or was reconciled to, his remaining among them, even for a brief season; but Dangerfield's sneering remark respecting his dependence on his mother had wounded him to the heart; and he resolved that, let what would be his fate, he would return no more to the Nunnery to incur again such a reproof.

The sun had scarcely risen above the tree-tops, before the gipsies were in motion, removing their frail habitations, and packing them, and their scanty stock of domestic utensils, upon the backs of their few animals; and making other preparations which convinced Edward that they contemplated a long and weary march before they again pitched their tents. Dangerfield remained an idle, but evidently not an unconcerned spectator; addressing, from time to time, words of encouragement to the women, and of kindness to the children, which were apparently intended to conciliate the men, some of whom seemed discontented and sullen at some arrangement that had been made which did not entirely meet their approbation. What this was he did not long remain in doubt. One of the children brought to Paul, as they all called him, a bunch of berries, the fruit of the thorn which were already beginning to ripen.

"I fear," observed the latter, "that, if old wives' signs of the seasons are to be trusted, we shall have a severe winter."

" And what matters it to you?" observed one of the men:
" the bird of passage flies to another clime, and heeds not his
mates, who are left to starve and shiver in their native groves.
You, in the sunny skies under which you say you were born, will
care little whether we are cowering beneath the wintry blast, or,
it may be, perishing like the silly sheep, beneath the snow-wreath;
while you like the careless shepherd——"

" You wrong me, Gordon," he replied. " Long before the
winter whitens the earth, I shall be again with you. Have I not
told you the purpose which leads me thither ?"

" We shall see—we shall see," returned the man, waving his
hand, as if to prevent further discussion.

In a few minutes the brief arrangements of the tribe were
completed; and Dangerfield, having bidden them all separately
farewell, left the spot, accompanied only by Edward; who,
wretched as were his prospects, felt his heart lightened as he
lost sight of the dusky tribe.

" Now, then, for London, Edward," observed Dangerfield, as
soon as the last sound of their footsteps ceased to be audible.
" That, my lad, is the only place to see and to enjoy life. That,
too," he added, in a graver tone, as he marked the startled and
surprised look which his levity had called forth—" that is the
only place where I still possess some interest that may benefit you,
and enable you to get forward in life."

Edward bowed his head in silence. He wished—he tried to
express his gratitude for the only mark of kindness or interest
he had ever received from *his father*; but suspicion and distrust
of its reality prevailed; and, after a few moments' silence, he
ventured to utter an inquiry on the subject nearest his heart—
his mother.

" What will become of her, left thus solitary and alone
during——"

Dangerfield hastily interrupted him.

" Do not trouble yourself on that head," he observed. " You
do not suppose that I am going to desert her ? Your looks, I
see, still express doubt and dissatisfaction. Well, then, I will
remove it, if possible, by telling you that she will join us in
London. Zekiel is now gone off to her, the bearer of my intentions and wishes."

" And she will be deprived, then, of her quiet, peaceful retreat,
and once more launched out into that stormy world which it had
been her comfort to think she had for ever renounced," exclaimed
Edward, scarcely conscious that he was giving utterance

aloud to thoughts that could not fail to give offence to his companion.

"And you attribute this to my influence—my fatal influence?" observed Dangerfield, sneeringly.

"To what other cause can I attribute it, sir, than to your unfortunate situation?" returned Edward, with spirit, galled by the tone of unfeeling sarcasm which the former, on all occasions, assumed towards him.

"Well, then, you do me too much honour in this instance, I assure you," resumed Dangerfield, "for it is you who are answerable for the crime of driving your mother from her most happy and quiet abode. Think you that she could remain there while the very ruins around her are echoing with the voices of those who are searching for her son, to drag him to prison as a murderer? Yes, you may look as horrified and indignant as you please, but such is the fact. The whole neighbourhood is out in search of you, as the undoubted murderer of your friend and rival; and even now——"

"I will go instantly to Mr. Copeland myself," exclaimed Edward, frantically, "I will demand that the charge against me shall be fully investigated. I will——"

"You will get yourself committed, to remain until the assizes —some four or five months, I believe," interrupted Dangerfield. "a whole dreary winter, in chains, and a cell——"

"What, before the crime is proved?" exclaimed Edward, incredulously; "that, surely, cannot be justice?"

"You will find it law, though," returned Dangerfield, "the law of this *free* land. But this is not called punishment. Oh, no, it is only holding you in safe custody until your trial; and surely it is just and right that the innocent should thus suffer, rather than the guilty be allowed a chance of escape. But we will suppose you willing to bear all this—suppose that the consciousness of innocence will make fetters of iron light as wreaths of roses, and turn the cold, stony walls of a dungeon into the gilded hangings of a palace, what have you to hope for at the end? How are you, who have been shut up from all communion with man, to be able to collect proofs of your innocence, to rebut the mass of evidence which will be brought to establish your guilt? Trust me, young man, conscious innocence (and I know you *are* innocent) will avail you but little against the smallest link in that chain of damning circumstances which your enemies will have accumulated against you. Many a good fellow has died the death of a dog, and his bones whitened on a gibbet, condemned only by the ingenuity of the hounds of the law, who can wrest the most trivial circumstance from its proper place and bearing, and make it stand out a hideous and incontrovertible proof of a guilt which was never dreamt of, perhaps, by the unfortunate wretch who has fallen into their hands, and is doomed to be hurled to destruction."

There was but little of this speech which fell connectedly on Edward's ear. Fetters—dungeons—a gibbet; could these horrible images really be held out in perspective to him? could he thus be threatened with punishment who had committed no crime?

It was too true. Dangerfield still went on speaking; and every word that he uttered was either a prophecy of the consequences that were to result from Edward's obstinacy, should he persist in acting from his own mistaken impulses, or the means that he was to adopt to escape being apprehended and immured in a prison. Edward heard him in silence; it seemed as if his very mind was paralysed, and his fate yielded up into the hands of his companion, on whom it depended to rescue him from the horrors which he with such seeming truth and candour depicted.

Dangerfield departed for London, though not so soon as he had intended; for circumstances which Edward did not comprehend rendered it prudent to remain concealed for a time; and in that time the latter was made acquainted with all the hiding places which had for years been known to the gang, who made them serviceable in various ways during their periodical sojourn in this part of the country. Often was he left alone for hours in one or other of these gloomy, subterranean abodes, while Dangerfield was absent, he knew not on what errands; and then the horror he had conceived of a prison seemed all realised, and he sunk into a state of gloomy apathy, which threatened the destruction of his reason.

At last they quitted the country; and Edward once more had the satisfaction of being re-united to the mother whose tenderness and affection had so indissolubly linked him in the bonds of filial love. Happily, he was yet in ignorance of that mother's crimes. He saw—too clearly saw her weakness, her infatuation, as regarded Dangerfield; but he was his father! and he tried to shut his eyes to his real character, and think of him as he had been when, as he (Edward) supposed, he had won his mother's virgin heart and hand

It would be painful and needless to follow, in all their sickening

THEY STARTED WHEN THEY BEHELD PAUL DANGERFIELD.

details, the scenes that followed this re-union of the mother, the son, and the man who assumed the character of her husband and his father.

Dangerfield, despairing of again imposing on his injured and unhappy brother by a repetition of the falsehood of which Edward had been made the innocent messenger, had resolved to make what he called a *grand coup;* and again Edward was fixed upon to be made the unconscious instrument of torture.

Let no one say that Dangerfield is such a monster as the world ne'er saw. No hatred is so deadly as that which the injurer feels towards the injured; and every fresh crime that the *soi-disant* Paul Dangerfield perpetrated against his brother, became to him a source of triumph.   What business had Lionel still to be rich—to be respected—to be blessed in the enjoyment of a pure conscience, a "heart void of guile, and hands that worked no shame," when he—*he* was a miserable, degraded, skulking, despised wretch, who "dared not look back, and trembled to look forward !"

Lionel Moreton was at this time in London.   A very trifling exercise of Dangerfield's wily craft put him in possession of all the necessary information to perfect his plan ; and long practice enabled him so nearly to copy the fine, business-like hand of the former, that it would have been difficult for any eye but his own to detect the difference.

But the difficulty to be got over was Edward's suspicions ; and Dangerfield knew that he did regard him with suspicion— that he doubted and distrusted him, even when he did not deserve it.   He was obliged, therefore, gradually, and with the wily pace of a serpent, to approach towards his destined victim. He began by affecting to place confidence in Edward—by assuming extreme regret for the situation in which his *folly* (such were the terms he used) had placed those whose interests were dearer to him than his own.   And then he pretended to devise means of escaping from the pressure of that fiend, poverty, which already began to lay its cold and chilling hand upon them.   A part of his family history was then confided to *his son ;* and Edward learned, as he believed, the secret of his mother's reluctance to speak of the history of her early life ; for he heard that she had been engaged to marry the brother of his fath..t, but had preferred poverty with the latter, to the brilliant fortune which her match with the former would have conferred upon her.

"Neither her father or my brother ever forgave our having disappointed their plans," continued the plausible deceiver, " and we were left destitute to struggle through the world, while Lionel my brother became the possessor of an immense fortune, which he still enjoys.   Never from that time to the present have we met ; and never, in all my sufferings and reverses, have I humbled myself to ask from him the slightest favour.   But that which I could not do for myself, I must now stoop to for the sake of those who are dearer than self.   I have written to him —I have painted to him the misery of seeing my wife——but I will not tell you what I have said of you, though I confess that it is for you I have the strongest hopes ; but we shall see.   Do not, however, mention a word of this to your mother. I would not have her agitated, perhaps disappointed—cruelly disappointed; for it may be that Lionel still retains undiminished the hatred which once led him to pursue me in every vindictive way that hatred could suggest; to blast my name—my prospects, by calumnies. No matter, he cannot now say any evil that I do not deserve; but it is to him I owe it all."

A day or two elapsed without the subject being renewed; but, at the end of that time, Dangerfield sought an opportunity of again speaking to Edward in private.

"The die is cast," he observed, "and all my hopes of benefiting you through my unrelenting brother are at an end. I am glad—most truly glad, now, that the subject was not mentioned to your mother. Read this."

He put into Edward's hand a letter signed Lionel Moreton. It was cold, heartless, and unfeeling. It declined all further communication with Mr. Oliver Moreton or his family; and warned him that, for the future, any application from that source would be returned unread. The enclosed, it concluded, was the last that would ever be bestowed by Lionel Moreton.

Edward's cheek flushed with pride, as he read this insulting and pompous epistle. How could he wonder that his mother had been unable to love such a man? and yet how could she have bestowed her affections on the one whom it was his misfortune to call his father?

"Do not you feel some anxiety to see the enclosure?" demanded the latter, with a smile.

Edward shook his head. "No money," he observed, "could compensate for such a letter as this."

"And yet it will prove very serviceable," returned Dangerfield, putting into his hand a cheque for five hundred pounds.

The sum was certainly startling, after reading the letter, as Dangerfield remarked.

"Nevertheless," he added, "to one who is now in possession of as many thousands a year, which should have been your mother's, and which he gained by nursing and fostering the rage and resentment of a doting, half-childish, old man, as her father was at the time he disinherited her, it is but a trifle."

So thought Edward upon hearing this statement; and much as he wished it had been in his power to provide for his mother without any reference to this unfeeling and purse-proud relative, he still felt that his mother had no right to feel humiliated by accepting so small a part of what ought to have been all her own

" We will say nothing about the money till we have got it," observed Dangerfield, " and, by the bye, Edward, it will be better that you should go and receive it. It is not impossible that Lionel, with all his coldness may yet relent, if he were to see you ; and for your mother's sake it would be your duty to conciliate him, if it were in your power."

" But is it likely that he will be at the banking-house upon which this cheque——"

" Yes, very likely," hastily interrupted Dangerfield. " He will guess that the money will be immediately applied for ; and curiosity, if nothing else——You still look dissatisfied—give me back the paper. I will go myself: though, if we meet——"

Edward professed his perfect willingness to go. How could he doubt that this representation was true to the letter? and yet every word was false, and the cheque a forgery.

Strong in innocence, he proceeded to the banking-house, the cheque was presented, crossed, and the money paid ; and Edward returned home in safety to the exulting demon who had thus again made him his instrument.

Dangerfield, however, concealed his joy ; he affected to be greatly disappointed that his expectations were not verified, as to Lionel's requiring to see the person who should present the cheque ; and, after a long conversation on the subject of the cold and bitter nature of his brother, he at length brought Edward round to his own expressed opinion, that it would be best to conceal from his mother the whole transaction, since it could only agitate her by recalling past events to mind.

" Leave me to account for the possession of the money," observed Dangerfield. " She knows that I have still resources untried ; or, at least, she believes so."

That very night, the greater part of that ill-gotten sum was sacrificed at one of the low gaming-tables to which Dangerfield devoted the most of his time ; and, the very next day, he announced to his wretched wife, as he called her, the fact that his brother had discovered his residence in London, and was again in full pursuit of him.

" It is no use to hope that we can as yet quit England," he observed. " His emissaries would be sure to intercept us, at whatever port we might try to embark from; and to remain here is equally unsafe. I have received, too, an intimation that I must speedily return to the tribe—that is a command I dare not disobey ; and you will be safer there with me than here."

The wretched Felicia yielded to her fate ; and Edward, to her tears and pathetic implorings, that he would not desert her. Had she told the whole truth, she would have acknowledged that a stronger motive than that of merely wishing to have him near to protect her, influenced her nearly frantic entreaties that he would accompany her. Dangerfield had with the malice of a fiend hinted to her that, if Edward now deserted him, he should no longer regard him but in the light of an enemy; and too well did she know what would be the consequence of that enmity.

All her influence, therefore—her prayers and persuasions, were exerted to keep Edward with her, to prevent his discontent at his hatred of the idle and dependent life he was leading, breaking forth.

"What can you do, my dear boy, without friends, without character, and without money?" and " Wait—only wait till this cloud has passed away; and rely upon *his* assurances that, in another land, you will be freed from the shackles that bind you here," were the constant arguments that she used, and of which he could not deny the truth; though they served but poorly to allay the feelings that were burning in his bosom—the ardent desire to free himself and her from their miserable dependence on one whom he every day found fresh cause to dislike and distrust.

In sullen despair, he learned Dangerfield's intention to rejoin the vagrant tribe in the country; but the latter for once condescended to explain, or pretend to explain, his motives.

"Were I to attempt to leave England," he observed, "secretly or without their consent, my life would pay the forfeit of my offence against their laws. I am absent now from them only on leave, and because they consider it necessary for my safety that I should be so; but the time is come that I must show myself among them, or be considered a traitor to their cause. I trust, however, that I shall be able to reconcile them to my leaving England, having first appointed some one to take my place among them. I cannot explain to you why it is necessary that your mother should accompany me, but so it must be. For you there is no constraint; though I should think, it would be a satisfaction to you to be near her, under circumstances that may require both protection and consolation: I allude to the fate that may await me, if my proposition to the tribe should be rejected, and it should be suspected that I mean to desert them. Should it be so, no power on earth can save me from their revenge. You do not know them as I do. Abject and degraded as they appear, the mightiest potentate on earth is not more absolute in his decrees of death against offenders, or more certain of its execution, than they are.   If I were now to leave them, there is no part of the world in which, sooner or later, their vengeance would not overtake me.

Edward yielded to this representation, and accompanied his mother, Dangerfield preceding them by some hours only.   Little did he suspect that the anxiety of the latter to leave London himself, and to induce them to do so, was occasioned by his fears that his infamous forgery upon his brother would be discovered by Edward, and that in the end it might perhaps be the means of revealing the deception that had been so long practised, and restoring to the injured Lionel Moreton his son.

The events that followed Edward's return to the neighbourhood of the Grove, and in which Elinor bore so prominent a part, have been already related.

Fortunately for Mrs. Hatherleigh, she knew nothing of these transactions.   A lingering feeling, perhaps, of affection towards her, or some other motive, had induced Dangerfield to provide somewhat better for her comforts than could have been done in the miserable tents of the gipsies, with whom he was, however, content to dwell; while she was lodged in a solitary cottage, at some distance, the occupant of which, a deaf and almost childish old woman, was too glad of the additional comfort such a tenant brought her, to be scrupulous or curious as to her affairs.

It was to this place, which they had, from its vicinity to the Haunted Oak, agreed to call Oakleigh, that Edward proceeded to meet his mother, after parting with Elinor, leaving her to the guidance of Zekiel; and which, as the reader already knows, happily guided her to the protection of Mrs. Clifford.

On his arrival at the cottage, he found, to his surprise, that his mother, though still in ignorance of what had happened, or that Dangerfield was (as he had learned from Zekiel) in prison, had received a hasty communication from the former; in which she was directed to go immediately to London, and specifying a house there, where she was to leave directions for him where he should find her when he followed, which would be most likely in a few days.

Edward almost doubted his senses, when he beheld this confident prediction, and remembered what Zekiel had told him; but it was verified, for within a week the Gipsy Chief presented himself at the obscure lodging which the mother and son were inhabiting in the suburbs of the metropolis.   Of the particulars of his escape he was silent; but Zekiel, whom he had brought with him, though now metamorphosed, from the ragged and abject gipsy boy, to a decently clothed and foreign-looking lad, was too proud of the part he had taken in it, not to boast to Edward of it, the moment they were alone together. He it was, it appeared, who had climbed the prison-wall, which was considered inaccessible, and had conveyed files and ropes, and all that was necessary to enable the captive to get free.

"And he did get free, and he threw his arms round my neck, and cried! Think of that—Paul cried, Master Ned! and he said that we would never part again; and so I'm to go with him across the wide sea, where we need never be afraid; for he's got a castle there, and a troop under his command. that would frighten the king himself."

Edward smiled at this assertion, which he thought originated in the boy's own flighty imagination, and his propensity to exalt Dangerfield's power; but when, after many months of wandering and vicissitude, he stood in that ruined but yet formidable fortress on the mountain in a foreign land, and beheld the numerous and fierce band over which Dangerfield ruled with a sway not less absolute than he had done over the comparatively insignificant tribe of gipsies in England, he remembered the boy's words, and was compelled to acknowledge to himself that Zekiel had formed a much truer estimate of the Chief's power than he had done.

Nothing but his mother's threats, that she would instantly reveal the secret of his birth, had saved Edward from being compelled to embrace the same wretched course of life to which his supposed father was devoted; but to that threat Dangerfield was compelled to yield; and from the time the wandering and predatory band, with whom the latter had been connected for years before his last visit to England in search of her whom he had so heartlessly abandoned, returned to their ancient quarters in the fortress, Edward was suffered to follow his own inclinations, and remain a kind of prisoner at large, being allowed to wander at will about the country, on condition that he previously made known the route he should take, and related the occurrences of the day when he returned, Dangerfield cunningly thinking that from the latter he might often derive information which might be useful for his purpose, without Edward's being aware of it.

Such, indeed, was the case when, on his return from one of his excursions, the latter mentioned that he had discovered that the beautiful villa on the banks of the lake, the white chimneys of which they could discern above the green trees which shaded it from the hill on which stood the fortress, was inhabited by an English family, a fact which he had learned from an old fisherman on the lake, to whom he had been useful in disentangling his nets from some bushes in which they had caught.

The fisherman, however, though he spoke highly of the generosity of the family, whose table he often supplied, did not know their names; but Dangerfield had heard enough to excite his curiosity, or perhaps some worse feeling; and the result of his inquiries was the discovery of Elinor and her protectress, and the consequent realisation of a scheme which had occupied him from that time night and day.

CHAPTER XXL

Come, now again thy woes impart,
  Tell all thy sorrows, all thy sin;
We cannot heal the throbbing heart,
  Till we discern the wounds within.
Compunction weeps our guilt away,
  The sinner's safety is his pain,
Such pangs for our offences pay,
  And these severer griefs are gain.

CRABBE.

WE must now return to the period at which we broke off to take this retrospect of past events. We left Edward and Elinor in the hermit's cell, on the face of the rock above which frowned the ruined fortress which contained their enemies, or, at least, those whom they feared as such; while far beneath them lay the valley, which could they once reach, Elinor, if not her companion, would once more be in safety.

Towards morning, however, she had lost all recollection of the dangers of her situation in sleep, the natural consequence of complete exhaustion both of bodily and mental power. Edward's reflections during these hours of darkness and silence were most bitter and contending.

He felt that the barrier which fate had placed between Elinor and himself was now stronger than ever; he trembled, too, for his mother, who would now be left solely to the mercy of Dangerfield, who would, perhaps, revenge upon her *his* desertion; and he trembled too, for the latter, who, wretch as he was,

Edward could never forget was his father. And yet he did not repent of what he had done; for he had—he hoped he had saved Elinor, and should restore her with honour to her friends.

"No, rather let the whole world perish," he thought, as he gazed upon her pale, marble-like face, as it rested on his knee, the first faint light of the grey morn giving to it a still more quiet and statue-like hue; "sooner every evil that can befall me fall upon my devoted head, than that this pure, innocent being should be doomed to become the companion of such wretches as those —to become the victim of that man, of whose tale I believe not one word. And if it were true——"

Elinor awoke, she looked up wildly and doubtfully in his face; and then, suddenly recollecting her situation, she clasped her hands in fervent, though silent prayer.

"I am here, and with you, Edward," she whispered, "and why should I fear?"

Edward could not reply, his confidence, at that moment, was less than hers; for there were other interests contending in his mind. He concealed, however, as far as possible, his feelings from her; and after a few moments' silence, observed, in a low tone,

"It will soon be sunrise now, dearest; and then I shall be able better to judge whether there is a possibility of our getting from hence unobserved."

"Heaven grant it!" whispered Elinor, and, folding her arms on her bosom, she remained quietly though anxiously watching for the wished-for moment. The sun, at length, rose gloriously, illumining with its golden rays the whole valley beneath.

Edward arose, and cautiously looked from his retreat. Not a living soul was within sight; and, to his extreme joy, he discovered that a narrow path, or ledge of rock, though scarce wider than a sheep track, led from the cell in a winding direction though still descending to a spot where it seemed lost amidst the luxuriant growth of mountain shrubs and flowers.

For himself he had no fear. He had often, in his solitary rambles, in mere wantonness, surmounted worse dangers; but he trembled at the thought of Elinor's encountering the peril; and when, drawing her softly to his side, he pointed it out to her as their only chance of escape, the shuddering look with which she drew back went to his heart. In a few moments, however, she recovered her resolution.

"There is no other way, Edward," she observed; "and, if you do not fear——"

"There is no real danger, dearest; that path has been traversed, and in safety, innumerable times, depend upon it," he replied. "Were it not that our time is precious, I would descend, and return to you, to convince you there is only one caution—steadily to look on the path before you, and avoid glancing into the depth below."

"Then, I am ready: do not doubt my resolution, or my steadiness," returned Elinor, in a cheerful tone; "lead on."

Edward's heart throbbed, and his breath became thick, as he proceeded; but he dared not either turn his head or speak to her, so rapid was their descent, until they reached the little green platform of rock; and then, as he caught her in his arms, most fervently did he utter his thanksgivings that she was safe. From this spot their way was comparatively easy, though it compelled them to take a great circuit, in order to avoid getting in sight of the inhabited part of the fortress; and when they at length emerged from the wood which clothed the lower parts of the mountain, into the open valley, Edward was vexed and disappointed at finding they were still nearly a mile from the direct road leading to Mrs. Clifford's residence. They were now, however, he considered, in comparative safety; and Elinor yielded to his persuasions, to enter the first cottage they came to, where a piece of silver procured them the refreshment of some brown bread and a bowl of warm milk, all that the house afforded. With renewed strength and renewed spirits on the part of Elinor, they resumed their journey; but, with every step that lessened the distance to Mrs. Clifford's residence, Edward's heart sunk lower and lower. How could he bear to appear before her, and acknowledge he was the son of a man so loaded with crime, and from whom she herself had so recently received such insult and injury? And upon what plea, or for what purpose, should he see her at all? Oh, no; he would accompany Elinor only so far that he could behold her enter the house; and then ——then where should he go?—friendless, without money, where could he go?

"No matter," he muttered to himself; "Elinor shall not know——" But Elinor did know—her importunate tears and pleadings wrung from him the secret; and vainly he resisted her persuasions to see Mrs. Clifford—only to see, and then—— Elinor could not add the word "depart," but her tears and prayers prevailed, and he suffered her to lead him to the presence of her benefactress.

The old porter was the only servant in the way when they

entered; and his surprise and consternation seemed so great, that he could only point to the breakfast-room when Elinor inquired where Mrs. Clifford was. Forgetful at the moment of everything but her anxiety to behold her friend, she hastily opened the door with one hand, and drew Edward forward with the other; but the latter started back, and so did Elinor; for, seated in earnest conversation, they beheld—Paul Dangerfield.

It would be useless to attempt to describe the astonishment and confusion which, for some moments, prevailed. Mrs. Clifford, forgetting all her usual coldness of manner, wept her welcome on Elinor's neck; who, clasping her arms around her, could only return her kindness by uttering in broken accents,

"My mother!—my more than mother!"

"Would I were your mother!" returned Mrs. Clifford; "but —but——Oh, let me not think of it! you are—will be my child!"

"Your grateful, grateful child!" whispered Elinor.

Mrs. Clifford suddenly recollected herself.

"We are forgetting that we are not alone," she observed, returning to her seat.

Dangerfield's eyes had beamed fire at Edward when the latter first appeared at the door of the room; but he speedily repressed all outward indication of resentment; and, in the cool, sarcastic tone which was so peculiar to him, he observed,

"We meet again, young man, you see; though you imagined, no doubt, that you had escaped my power."

"I had no such thoughts, sir, or intentions," returned Edward. "To restore Elinor to her only friend, and to save you and myself from disgrace——"

"Romantic fool!" muttered Dangerfield between his closed teeth. "Disgrace to me, who have braved all that the world calls so; to me there is no disgrace but that of failing in my plans—of being foiled by such a self-willed, headstrong boy as you! Silence, sir, and do not interfere!—henceforth I command you!" he added, seeing that Mrs. Clifford had recovered from the first violence of her emotion, and was now sufficiently collected to attend to what was passing.

"I have redeemed my pledge, madam," observed Dangerfield, addressing her. "The young lady has returned to your protection; and I trust she will assure you that she has received no wrong or insult while under mine."

"Oh, no, no—all has ended well——" happily, Elinor would have added, but the word died on her lips; for at that moment her eye rested on Edward's despairing countenance, and she felt how impossible it was that she could feel happy while he was wretched.

"You have, sir, redeemed your pledge," returned Mrs. Clifford; "and I am bound to acknowledge it by fulfilling my engagement to you."

She arose, and opened a small cabinet in the room; and a burning blush rushed into Edward's cheek, as he beheld her draw from its recesses a heavy purse of gold.

"For my sake—oh, for my sake, do not take it! It is the first favour I ever asked of you," he exclaimed, seizing Dangerfield's arm, with an imploring look and gesture.

"It would cost rather too dear to indulge you in it," returned the latter, with a sneering laugh, as he shook him off, and advanced to receive the money.

Mrs. Clifford watched with evident interest every movement of Edward's expressive countenance, which forcibly pourtrayed the indignation—the shame—the sorrow with which he beheld his father, after cursorily surveying the contents of the purse, to assure himself of its value, deliberately place it in his pouch.

"This affair, then, is settled between us, madam," he observed, with the air of a man who has received a just debt, rather than that of one who had commisted an atrocious robbery. "It will be for you and that young lady," he continued, "to decide on the terms I have offered, and on which I pledge my honour to bring forward the evidence of her birth."

"Your honour!" repeated Mrs. Clifford, in a cool, calm tone. "And you, young man," she added, turning to Edward, and fixing her penetrating eye on his face, "are you, too, a willing partner in the honourable compact your father proposes as the price of Elinor's——"

"Elinor will herself reply to that question, madam," returned Edward, his countenance brightening with the consciousness of innocence. "To her," he continued, "I appeal——"

"I will have neither appeals nor explanations!" furiously interrupted Dangerfield. "It is for you, madam, and your ward there, to decide whether my secret is worth the price I affix to it; and the answer must be given before I leave this room."

"For myself I answer it is not; nor would I ever sanction its being given," returned Mrs. Clifford, in a tone of firm decision; "but I have no real authority in the case; it is in Elinor's hands, and she alone can decide it."

"No, madam," interrupted Edward, turning from the look of distress and perplexity which Elinor cast towards him; "no, it is I who must—who will decide here. Think you so meanly of me, as to suppose that I will be made the passive instrument to bring disgrace and dishonour to one whom I——"

"Silence, villain! on the authority of a father I command you; silence!" interrupted Dangerfield, with vehemence, his eyes glowing like coals of fire, and half drawing from his belt the short dagger with which he was always armed. Before he could effect this purpose, his arm was arrested by the firm yet phrenzied grasp of some one behind; and the next moment the haggard form of Mrs. Hatherleigh presented itself to his astonished gaze.

"Would you again commit murder, Oliver Moreton?" she exclaimed, as Edward rushed forward, to shield her from the vengeance which the fierce and scowling look of the former betrayed he meditated, while he struggled to free his arm from her grasp; but he had now Edward's vigorous strength to contend against, though the latter was still restrained by the belief that it was a parent with whom he contended.

"Mother! father!" he exclaimed, in a tone of agonized remonstrance. It was the first time that he had ever addressed to him that sacred title; and for a moment the word seemed to shake the fierce and determined purpose of him to whom it was addressed.

"Father!" repeated Mrs. Hatherleigh, wildly; "oh, no, no; not to him does that title belong—not to that wretch, without one touch of pity; he is not your father. No, though my soul perish eternally, I will speak the truth, and rescue you, my child—my injured child, from the monster that would destroy you. Edward—Lionel let me call you, for that is your true name—that man is not your father; he is your uncle, the villain who destroyed—ruined——"

She fell on the floor in strong convulsions; and her son, who had succeeded in disarming Dangerfield, and now left him to the care of the servants, who had crowded into the room on hearing the shrieks of Elinor, and the cries of their mistress for assistance, flew to her, and knelt by her side, addressing her by every endearing epithet, and imploring the assistance of Elinor and Mrs. Clifford to restore her.

"Let us remove her from this scene," observed Mrs. Clifford to him; "if she recovers her recollection it will be advisable that——"

"Stop, madam, one moment, if you please," observed Danger-

field, who seemed suddenly to have recovered his calmness: like
one who, having heard the worst, resolves to meet it with fortitude; "stop, if you please, and listen to me. You will remember
that, in entering this house, I threw myself upon your honour.
I came to you a voluntary hostage of that girl," pointing to
Elinor. " She is here, and I demand that I be allowed to
depart as I came, free from all conditions. With my family
affairs you have no right to interfere, and——"

" You may spare all words, sir," interrupted Mrs. Clifford,
with dignity, " you are free to go. Accompany this man to the
outer gate of the lawn," she continued, to the servants, " and
when he has passed it return to him this weapon."

The servant took the dagger, which Edward had thrown to
the further end of the room, and, without bestowing another look
on the foiled and discomforted Gipsy Chief, followed Edward and
Elinor, who had already conveyed the still insensible Mrs.
Hatherleigh into the adjoining room.

Many hours passed before that wretched woman became conscious of her situation. Mrs. Clifford had procured the best
medical attendance that the neighbourhood afforded; but the
doctor's looks, even more than his words, declared that there was
little hope of her ever awaking from the death-like stupor which
had succeeded to the violence of the fits which had shaken her
already worn-out frame.

During those hours of suspense, how many conflicting thoughts,
hopes, and wishes agitated the mind of her son ! She had been
conveyed to bed; and there Mrs. Clifford and Elinor remained,
in close attendance upon her, until she sank into that death-like
state; when, convinced that she could be no longer benefited by
their attentions, and the former leaving strict orders to be called,
if the slightest change should become visible, returned to the
room in which Edward, or rather, Lionel (for henceforth he
resumed his true designation) still remained.

In Mrs. Clifford's estimation, every obstacle to her free
communication, and the full indulgence of her liberal feelings
towards him, were removed by the declaration of Mrs. Hatherleigh, that he was not the son of the depraved—the debased
Dangerfield. But though she could not doubt that fact (who
could have doubted it, that had seen the agony—the intense
agony which had wrung the declaration from the erring, the
sinful, the wretched, yet wronged and injured mother ?) yet there
was still so much of mystery—so much to be explained and
accounted for, that she felt as if she were in a dream. And what

were Elinor's feelings? To say that she did not deeply regret and deplore the situation of her early friend—of the "dear Mrs. Hatherleigh," who had been the deposit of all her early joys, and the sharer of her childish sorrows—to say even that she did not pity the wretched man whose hopes she had beheld all crumbled into dust, and his deep-laid plans utterly frustrated, would be to belie her gentle nature.

> She had a tear for all the ills
> That fresh is heir to; and would have poured balm
> Even into th' wounds—the fest'ring wounds
> That vice had made.

Yet still one proud thought, one radiant beam of joy shed its brilliant light o'er all the darkness. Edward—Lionel she must now call him; but never would the first name, which had been for years the dearest to her heart—never could it be forgotten —but he was not the son of that man—he was freed from his control; and she trusted would now be cleared from every imputation. As yet, however, she knew nothing of his history; and Lionel himself, it seemed, knew little more. All he could tell Mrs. Clifford and Elinor was, that he knew Lionel Moreton, the brother of the man who called himself Dangerfield—but who, as they had heard, was Oliver Moreton—was a man of fortune; and then he related the circumstance of the cheque for five hundred pounds which he had received at the banking-house, and Dangerfield's artful remarks on the possibility of its being the means of introducing him (Edward) to his wealthy relative. But in this Elinor saw sufficient for heartfelt rejoicing. Edward —Lionel (again she forgot the name) would be rich after all; his wanderings, and the privations which he must have suffered would be at an end; and why should she have a wish beyond that? Yet still there was an undefined—an (unacknowledged to herself) source of uneasiness in her bosom. She was still the child of mystery, for Dangerfield had carried away with him the secret, if he did possess it, of her birth and parentage.

Mrs. Clifford, however, seemed to have forgotten it; for she made no allusion to what had passed; and Elinor tried to forget it, too, and all that related to herself, in her joy and satisfaction on Lionel's account.

During the time some necessary refreshment was being taken, Elinor gave a full explanation of the events of the preceding night; and Mrs. Clifford then related that Dangerfield had, immediately after Elinor's departure from the room, boldly avowed that money was his object in detaining them there; and had proposed that Mrs. Clifford should return home with all speed and that, on sending up a certain sum, Elinor, who was to be detained as hostage, was to be released.

"Judge of my surprise," continued Mrs. Clifford, "when, on the return of my messenger, I beheld, instead of Elinor, the Chief of the band of robbers himself. He was in a violent state of excitement; and I then learned that you and his son, as he called him, had unaccountably disappeared together.

"'I knew,' he continued, 'that you would not believe this tale, and would consider I had wilfully detained her, if I sent back this message, even though I have not touched the money, nor will not do so, until you are convinced that she is safe. Nay, more: I will, if you are not afraid to trust me within your walls, remain here until she comes; for come here I am convinced they will, though I cannot trace the way they have taken. I rely, of course, madam, upon your honour, that you will not take any advantage of my thus placing myself in your power; and that, when the terms between us are fulfilled, you will suffer me to depart free.'

"How could I refuse my consent to this stipulation? There was, in spite of his villany, and the base advantage he had taken of me and Elinor, an appearance of frankness, a courtesey of manner, and altogether something so superior, that I confess I was interested, and wished to learn from him whether it were not possible he could be rescued from a life so hazardous and so disgraceful. I admitted him with the same confidence and candour that he appeared disposed to practise towards me. But I soon learned, from his replies to my questions, that he had some deeper views, both with regard to Elinor, and in coming thus boldly to me, than he at first avowed. The last, I soon ascertained, was done to prevent my giving immediate information of the outrage, and seeking assistance to recover Elinor by force; while of the former, his conduct and intentions towards her, he gradually revealed the source, and proposed the conditions, which I naturally and indignantly rejected. I need not say what they were, Elinor; and as you yourself and Mr. Moreton (Elinor started at the name so strange to her ears) evidently acted on the same principle as myself, I trust you will not blame me; though, as matters are likely to turn out," she added, with a smile, "perhaps we could all have afforded to act on a less rigid principle of honour"

The conversation was interrupted by the information from the sick chamber, that the lady had spoken, and moved; and Mrs.

ELINOR CLARE.

"HE HAS FASTED SO LONG!"

Clifford and Elinor immediately hastened thither. Lionel would fain have accompanied them; but it was judged prudent that, for the present, he should keep away, lest the sight of him should agitate her.

The first question, however, of the sufferer was for her son.

"Where is he, Elinor? Does he despise his wretched mother too much to——"

"Oh, no, he is most anxious to see you, to assure you of his affection, his duty——"

"Duty to me!" she replied. "Oh, Elinor, he knows not yet what a wretch—a very wretch I am. Duty—affection to me! oh, no, no! I deserve only his hatred—his execration!   But let me see him, Elinor, that I may repeat the black history of the wrongs he has suffered, and his father—my—my injured husband."

Elinor would fain have persuaded her to delay her intention; but Mrs. Clifford, who, from knowing less of her, perhaps, had less pity towards her, interfered.

"It is right and just, certainly, that you should, without delay, put your son in possession of such facts as will be necessary, if I mistake not, to enable him to substantiate his claim.   I will send him to you; and, Elinor, you will then come to me; it will be best that the young man should hear alone——"

"Oh, no, no, remain with me, Elinor.   Do no leave me with him," exclaimed the sufferer.   "And you, madam, it will be necessary that Edward—that my son should have witnesses to the dying declaration of his mother.   How else will it be possible for Lionel—for his father to believe the black tale of guilt?"

Mrs. Clifford sat down; and Mrs. Burchall, who was in the adjoining dressing-room, was desired to request Mr. Moreton's presence in his mother's chamber.   Lionel was in a moment at her bedside; but he beheld with anguish the agony that distorted her pallid countenance, as she raised her hands to him in an imploring attitude.

"I have sent for you, my son," she at length gained strength to utter, "that I may reveal, for your sake, the particulars of the heartless imposition that has been for so many years practised on you and your father.   I——"

"Not if it is thus to agitate you, dearest mother, not if I was to gain a kingdom—the whole world, would I listen," interrupted her son, in impassioned accents.

"It is an act of justice, Mr. Moreton," observed Mrs. Clifford, solemnly, "not only to you, but to your father, that all should be explained at once.   Delays are dangerous, and——"

"You are right," interrupted Mrs. Moreton (we will no longer call her by the assumed name of Hatherleigh), "you are prefectly right; I ought not —I will not delay; for it may be that a few days, perhaps a few hours may deprive me of the means of doing justice.   Raise me, Elinor—dear Elinor, and you, my son, assist her to support me."

Raised in the bed, and supported on either side by those who too deeply compassionated her sufferings to regard her with any other feeling than tenderness, the wretched woman commenced the history of her life; while Mrs. Clifford, seated at the table, and screened from her observation, prepared to note down in writing every important fact that she might deem necessary to the substantiation of Lionel's claims.

To attempt to describe the feelings which agitated her auditors would be useless and vain, at the detail of those circumstances which have been already narrated. Lionel's anguish, at times, rose beyond controul; and it was in vain that he tried to repress his exclamations of horror and resentment at the conduct of the monster Oliver, or of astonishment at his mother's infatuation—that infatuation which had kept her, even to the last few hours, a willing victim of poverty, disgrace, and every evil that could result from a connection with one so utterly lost, desperate, and depraved as the Gipsy Chief.

"And he still lives!" he uttered, speaking aloud his thoughts, rather than addressing any one, "lives, perhaps, to plot fresh mischief against those he has so deeply injured!"

"His power of plotting or of executing mischief will soon be ended," observed Mrs. Clifford, rising. "From the moment he quitted the house, I considered myself released from all observance of forbearance towards him, and immediately dispatched an express for assistance to apprehend him, and break up the horde of wretches who are at his command——"

"Oh, no, no!" shrieked Mrs. Moreton, "save, save him! Lionel, my son, save him! If he is taken he will die by the hands of the public executioner—he will——"

"He will meet the reward he justly merits," interrupted Mrs. Clifford, "and you, madam—you on the verge of the grave to which he has conducted you—you whom he has robbed of all that could make life desirable—whose very soul he has perilled," she added, in a voice so solemn that her hearers shuddered, "plead not for his escape from the justice which has, at length, I trust, overtaken him. How many are there yet living, perhaps," she added, with animation, "to whom his life, should he escape, may be the source of misery!"

Mrs. Moreton did not answer; but as she held her son in her agonised embrace, she still continued, in faint accents, to murmur entreaties for mercy towards him from whom she had received none—who had ruined her without remorse—had beheld her, through years of misery, without compassion—and had, at length, as Mrs. Clifford had truely, though, perhaps, somewhat harshly said, brought her to the brink of the grave.

"I can be of no further service here, Mr. Moreton," observed the latter, "but I will speak with you, if you please, a few words."

Lionel followed her into the dressing-room.

"Your mother is evidently dying," she observed. "Nay, start not; how could you wish her life prolonged—a life of such suffering—such anguish as she must now endure, and which every hour that she beholds you must increase. I have requested to speak to you, to urge you to propose to her that she should, without delay, admit the visit of a clergyman. The parish priest of the nearest village is, I believe, a good and pious man; shall I send to him, to request his assistance?"

"Anything you think or propose must be right and proper, madam," returned Lionel, "but surely, surely, I hope and trust, my poor mother's situation is not so desperate; she may recover, and——"

"She may," returned Mrs. Clifford, though in a tone and with a look that strongly evinced her conviction of the improbability of his wishes being realized. "But, even if she should recover, Mr. Moreton, it can do no harm that her mind should be thoroughly awakened to a proper sense of her situation. Pardon me for speaking so frankly; but it appears to me that even now your mother feels less compunction for the crimes she has committed, than sorrow for their consequences to herself and others. Had this wretch—this monster in human shape—this Dangerfield, I will still call him by that name, for it would be a disgrace to the honourable one you are henceforward to bear, that he should again ever be called by it—if, I say, he had been prosperous in the world, and he had retained even the semblance of that affection he once professed to her, never would you have heard one word of her repentance or her history, never would you have been restored to your rights, or your father compensated (as I trust he will be by your restoration) for the injuries he has suffered at her hands, and those of his unnatural brother. It is right, therefore, that she should be made to feel all this— that she should be taught to "lay no flattering unction to her soul," by believing that the late justice towards you and your father, which circumstances have wrested from her, rather than——"

"Oh, do not—do not thus harshly condemn my poor mother!" exclaimed Lionel, with deep emotion. "Could you but know her gentle disposition—her kind-heartedness—her——"

"I am willing to concede all this," returned Mrs. Clifford, hastily, "but I will not plead with you against your mother. Heaven forbid that I should seek to lower your estimation of her! I am sorry I have said so much; but you, I am sure, will see it in its right light.   If I were not interested for her—if I were not anxious for more than even her temporal benefit, I should not press the subject."

In terms of the most heartfelt gratitude, Lionel professed his entire satisfaction in all Mrs. Clifford proposed; and a messenger was despatched to the village, to request the attendance of the priest.

Many hours, however, elapsed before the reverend man was enabled to obey the summons; and then it may be questioned whether the intelligence of which he was the bearer was not the means of imparting more consolation to the invalid than all his advice and counsel.

Apologising for not having attended to Mrs. Clifford's summons, and totally unconscious how deeply the person to whom he was called was interested in the subject, he proceeded to state that he was absent from home when the messenger of the former arrived, having accompanied the party of villagers and soldiers who had gone up to the fortress on the mountain to seize on the band of robbers who had found shelter there.   In doing so, he said, he had been actuated by the hope that his presence would have the effect of moderating the violent exasperation of the villagers against the bandits, and preventing, perhaps, bloodshed on both sides.

"A worthy mission for a minister of peace!" observed Mrs. Clifford, in reply; "and was I hope, successful?"

"It proved that there was no opportunity for my services, madam," he replied; "for, after the most diligent investigation it was discovered that the fortress was entirely deserted.   Its late occupants, having no doubt received intelligence of the intended attack, have most probably decamped in all directions; and as the purpose is fully answered in breaking up the horde, and taking precautions that they shall not again find a refuge there, our people have relinquished all further measures."

"And he has escaped!" murmured the dying woman; "and I have not the misery of knowing that I have been the means of betraying him to his destruction!"

Mrs. Clifford's frown, and Elinor's distressed look, betrayed the dissatisfaction with which this declaration was heard by them both, though, perhaps, not from exactly the same motives; the former being actuated solely by surprise and sorrow at the obstinacy, as it appeared to her, with which the unfortunate woman still clung to the wretch to whom she owed all her sufferings; while to Elinor the escape of Dangerfield seemed but the prelude of further evils and machinations against his nephew.

They quitted the room together, leaving the priest alone with the dying woman, who, it must be mentioned, had been educated in the Catholic faith, though she had for many years ceased to attend its rites, or practise its injunctions; but they were soon recalled to witness the declaration, which she wished again, and in the most solemn manner, to attest with her last dying breath as to the imposition that had been practised on her husband, and the reality of Lionel's birth.

That this duty had been enforced upon her by the priest, to prevent the possibility of doubt or dispute hereafter, was most probable; but the effort was fatal. Scarcely had she affixed, with trembling hand, the name—the long-disused and disgraced name of Felicia Moreton, to the written memorial of her shame before she was again seized with convulsions, from which she only recovered to bestow one agonised look on her injured son, and utter one heart-rending prayer for mercy where alone she could hope to find it, and then closed her eyes for ever in death.

Deeply and affectionately did Lionel Moreton deplore the loss of his mother, who, great as her faults had been, and especially towards him, had nevertheless so endeared herself to him, by the sweetness of her temper and gentleness of her manners—the years of utter seclusion which she had devoted so entirely to him, seeming to have no other end or object in the world but his happiness and instruction—all, in fact, that he had known of her except in relation to the one great error of her life, the reality of which he could even now scarcely believe—that he could not but mourn her death with the most fervent regret, and look forward with apprehension to a meeting with his father, from whom he feared he could not hope to meet the same tenderness and affection, while he could not but expect to hear from his lips the bitterest condemnation of her who had been the source of all their misfortunes.

But there was another source of uneasiness, which Lionel, who communicated freely with Elinor on those already stated, concealed with assiduous care from her, and which dwelt with yet greater force on his mind; and that was the light in which this new-found parent would regard his attachment to her.

He who had hitherto been considered her inferior—who had actually been, by those who considered themselves her friends and guardians, forbidden all correspondence with her—would now, if his claims were admitted—and how could they be disputed?—be placed far above her in the estimation of worldly minds; and such he had been taught to believe, even by his mother's history, was the mind of Lionel Moreton—of his father.

There were moments, indeed, in which the charge which still, of course, hung over him, as the suspected murderer of Walter Copeland, recurred to his recollection with such force as to check all hopes of his ever enjoying the advantages which must accrue from his being the acknowledged heir of the wealthy and respected Mr. Moreton.

But when do the truly innocent despair? Lionel had never done so. Even as the supposed son of the hated, proscribed, despised Gipsy Chief, he had firmly believed that his guiltlessness would eventually be proved; and now, with such advantages was it probable that he could fall a victim to such an unfounded accusation? No, there was only one thing he feared; and that was that his father might not regard Elinor, or an alliance with her, in the same light that he did; for, without her, what were all the riches of the world to him?

On Elinor's part there were none of these fears or apprehensions. Too disinterested, and too sincerely anxious for Lionel's happiness, to suffer a thought of self to intrude, she would have rejoiced, without a single drawback on her satisfaction, in his amended prospects, but for the fear that they might yet be all dashed to the ground, should Mr. Copeland still persevere in his unfounded charge against him as the murderer of his son.

Yet Lionel did not himself seem to have any fears on that head.

He spoke openly, and without reserve, of his intention to return to England, so soon as he should have performed the last duties to his mother's remains; and in this resolution Mrs. Clifford seemed cordially to acquiesce, considering it most advisable, she said, that he should enforce by his presence the wondrous tale he had to relate to his father, rather than trust to a cold narration of facts by letter.

CHAPTER XXII.

Musing on the roaring ocean
  Which divides my love and me;
Wearying Heaven in warm devotion,
  For his weal where'er he be,
Hope and fear's alternate billow
  Yielding late to Nature's law;
Whispering spirits round my pillow
  Talk of him that's far awa.

                                        BURNS.

IT was the evening of the day on which had taken place the funeral obsequies of the unfortunate and guilty, though still regretted Mrs. Moreton; and, as may be supposed, the spirits of the party who were assembled round the fire in the drawing-room of the villa for, perhaps, the last time, were sadly depressed. Yet, of the three, Elinor who affected most calmness and composure, suffered the most.

The morrow was appointed for Lionel Moreton's departure for England; and, much and disinterestedly as Elinor rejoiced in the circumstances that led him thither, the sad presentiment that she should never again behold him took full possession of her mind,

————turning her joy to bitters.

The gloomy ceremony in which she had so recently taken a part, and the uncertainty of her own fate, destined, as it now appeared, to remain wrapped in impenetrable mystery, were circumstances in themselves quite sufficient to account for the extreme despondency of Elinor's feelings; but, added to this, the weather was unusually cold, comfortless, and lowering; and her confinement for many days, without her usual out-of-door exercise, had contributed to increase that nervous excitement which she attributed to an ominous foreboding of evil. Yet she was the only one who seemed inclined to talk.

The fact was, she could not bear her own thoughts; and she was anxious to stifle them, by leading her companions to utter theirs. All her efforts, however, failed. Mrs. Clifford sat, with her eyes fixed on the fire, silent and abstracted; and Lionel's voice faltered, and seemed choked, whenever he tried to reply to her.

Elinor felt her assumed calmness gradually giving way as the hour approached for their formal separation; for it had been previously arranged that Lionel should depart at day-break; and, as Mrs. Clifford's habits would detain her in bed hours after that time, Elinor knew that the at-all-times unpleasant, but now most melancholy, ceremony, of taking leave of each other, was at hand.

There had been, from the first moment of his unexpected introduction to her house, an evident wish on the part of Mrs. Clifford to discourage all particular intercourse between Lionel and Elinor; and, consequently, they had never met but in her presence.

Lionel most probably both thought and expected that this restraint might now for this one instance be dispensed with, and that he might be allowed, now that he was about to leave her for an indefinite time, a free communication with Elinor, since there were many themes interesting to themselves which could not be discussed in the presence of a third person.

But whatever were or had been Mrs. Clifford's motive for the course she had adopted, it still apparently remained in full force, and the lovers beheld with silent dismay the near approach of the hour which was to behold their separation, without having had an opportunity of uttering one word of those thoughts and feelings with which their full hearts were fraught.

A look from Lionel conveyed to Elinor volumes of meaning. She felt the tears rush to her eyes; and, unwilling to betray the emotion, she rose from her seat; and, making some confused and indistinct observation about the weather, walked to the nearest window, and, unclosing the thick curtain, stood silently looking out upon the now obscure and indistinct landscape.

Some question which Mrs. Clifford at that moment put to Lionel, originated a conversation which, if it engrossed not all his attention, detained him in his seat; but, after some minutes of silence on the part of Elinor, a sudden though half suppressed exclamation of surprise and alarm induced him to rush abruptly to her side. Before he could demand what had alarmed her, she laid her trembling hand upon his arm, and whispered,

"Hush! do not speak, or come forward; but look cautiously towards those laurel-bushes, there to the right. Tell me, do you not perceive something creeping along under them?"

"Yes, it is a dog, or perhaps a sheep that has strayed into the garden," he replied. "You are nervous, my dear girl; and your fancy magnifies——"

"It is a human being, Lionel," she interrupted, in a voice

that faltered with terror; "and one that comes on no good intent or he would not be thus cautiously approaching the house. See now he is stationary, and raises himself to his full height, to reconnoitre whether——"

" It is Zekiel!" exclaimed Lionel, stepping suddenly forward, and letting the thick folds of the curtain fall behind him and Elinor, so that they stood in perfect darkness, to watch the motion of the mysterious being he had named. The movement, however, slight and instantaneous as it had been, had evidently been observed by the intruder, who instantly crouched down again, and remained so motionless and concealed under the leafy boughs of the evergreens, that, after gazing intently for many minutes on the spot, Elinor uttered her conviction that he was gone.

" No, no, he is not gone," whispered Lionel. " I know his movements too well. He will remain there, perfectly immoveable for hours, if he thinks he is watched. But what can be his purpose? If I were sure that he is alone——"

Elinor grasped his hand, which was already on the fastening of the window, from which he could step out upon the lawn.

" Do not—oh do not hazard it !" she exclaimed. " Remember the character you have yourself drawn of these people—of their deadly spirit. If you were to go out, a pistol perhaps might——"

" Not from Zekiel," he interrupted, " the boy, with all his strange vagaries and wildness, is most truly attached to me. I have never offended him; and, if he comes hither from his own free will, it would be, I am convinced, rather to do me good than harm. It may be, however, that he is merely the tool of another; and, if so, his obedience to that man's commands and instructions is so implicit—so blind, I may say, that——"

" But, how is it to be ascertained whether he comes on a friendly errand? not by exposing yourself rashly to danger," again remonstrated Elinor.

Mrs. Clifford had, by this time, comprehended the cause of their earnest discussion ; and her entreaties, amounting indeed to command, were immediately added to Elinor's, that he should not tempt danger.

" Remain where you are," she observed, " while I go quietly to place some of the servants where they may afford their assistance instantly, if required."

Lionel's arm was round Elinor's waist, and he felt the beating of her heart; but neither uttered a word during the few brief minutes Mrs. Clifford was absent.

"Now, then," observed the latter, when she returned, "we will, at least, be convinced whether it be the boy or not. There can be no design against me, of that I am well convinced; and, therefore, I am the fittest person to unravel the mystery."

Before they had time to move from their concealment, or utter a word to prevent her, she had unclosed another window, and was upon the lawn. Lionel would have rushed after her, but Elinor clung to him with such wild entreaties, that he was compelled to pause to remonstrate with her.

"Hark, she is speaking to him!" exclaimed Elinor; and at that moment Mrs. Clifford's voice was indeed heard.

"Zekiel, my boy," she demanded, "why do you thus keep aloof from your friends? There are none here but those who will be glad to see you and assist you. Come forward, then: you know you may rely upon my word. That card I gave you —have you forgotten that I told you if you showed it at any time——"

The boy uttered one of those startling, unearthly sounds which with him denoted excess of joy; and in another moment he was at her feet.

"Come," she continued, "let me lead you to those who will be glad to see you; but where is your companion?"

"My companion?" returned the boy, in a mournful tone: "who is my companion? I have none now—they have all deserted me. Even Paul has left me to perish in a strange land; and yet——I will tell you a secret; I am his son—his only son. I heard what the pale-faced woman——"

"Come within doors, Zekiel, and you shall tell me all," returned Mrs. Clifford, gently leading him forward through the window, which she immediately closed behind her, although scarcely doubting his assertion that he was alone. Lionel and Elinor advanced towards him, but he shrunk with some appearance of alarm from the former, whose altered appearance and deep suit of black, made him look upon him as a stranger. The moment, however, Lionel spoke, the boy recognised him; and again and again he shrieked with joy, as he bounded towards him, unable, as it appeared, to utter an articulate sound, from the excess of his delight.

"Well, you are a gentleman now; and yet you do not scorn me," at length he observed, "and you will give me food, will you not? Oh, how many days have passed since I tasted bread! and now I am so—so faint with fasting, and my head turns round, and I——"

Lionel caught him in his arms, to prevent his falling to the ground, and seated him on a couch ; while Mrs. Clifford poured out a glass of wine, and Elinor flew to obtain some more substantial refreshment, at the intimation of the former, without bringing any of the servants into the room.

Miserable, indeed, was the change which had taken place in the appearance of the poor boy, and which, now that the first animation of his joy had subsided, became every instant more and more apparent. His large dark eyes had lost all their brilliancy, and seemed sunk deep into his head ; his olive complexion was faded into a leaden white ; his long, lank locks were wet with the heavy mist ; and his features and whole form seemed shrunken, and pinched with cold and famine.

Mrs. Clifford gently restrained the mistaken kindness of Elinor and Lionel, which would have ministered without restraint to the ravenous hunger which he betrayed, the moment the wine had reanimated him, and he beheld the food with which the former had loaded herself.

"He has fasted so long," observed the lady, "that it is necessary to be cautious, or you will oppress nature instead of restoring it."

Zekiel looked up in her face, with something of his native archness, though the half-smile seemed but to make the extreme wanness of his countenance, and the death-like hue of his lips and cheeks, more ghastly.

"That may be good doctoring for such as you," he observed, "that have queasy stomachs, and never was used to go for days without victuals, and then fill yourselves with anything that came in your way, as I have done. No, no, food will never harm me, though I have been like, this time, to die for want of it. And yet," he continued, suddenly letting the hand fall which was conveying the bread and meat to his mouth, "and yet it was not altogether hunger. Oh, no, I could bear that. Many a day have I lived upon hips and haws and blackberries, and have been obliged to break the ice in the ponds to get a drink of water, that has almost froze in my throat, I have been so cold ; and then have carried to our people all I have got by fair means or foul, without touching it. But then I was sure of meeting with welcome, and of having my place at the warm fire, and my part in the warm supper that I helped to provide ; and when I went to sleep, I knew I should see the same faces round me in the morning, and hear them bid me good speed when I left them again. But here to be left, without one living soul to care for ;

and the great sea, that I could never hope to cross, between me and my own people; and to think that Paul, too, should drive me from him, and threaten to shoot me like a dog, if I followed him—oh, it was this—it was this——"

He burst into a violent fit of tears, and then hid his face with his long, thin hands, as if ashamed of the emotion he had betrayed; while the food, which but a short time before he had appeared so voracious for, remained unnoticed and neglected.

It is needless to say how deep was the sympathy with which this outbreak of natural feeling was listened to by all present.

"Well, but you are among friends now, Zekiel, who will not let you again want," observed Mrs. Clifford, "and in good time you shall cross the great sea, and visit again the scenes you regret."

The boy's sunken eyes lighted up with a beam of their former fire.

"And perhaps I shall find Paul again with our people," he observed. "Oh, how rejoiced they will be to see him! And perhaps, after all, he may own me for his son; and then, who knows but one day I may be Chief, now that——"

He stopped suddenly short, and looked at Lionel; and then, with a look of deep mystery and importance, added,

"I know all; for the lady told everything, in her rage and terror, when she believed that he had put you and her (looking at Elinor) out of the way. She would not believe that you had escaped, but that he had murdered you; and, oh what bitter things she told him in her wrath! And I was sorry to see him smile; for he was ever most deadly when he smiled; and I wished her no harm, though she had taken my dead mothers' place, so granny used to tell me. But granny was wrong; for the lady was not his wife, she told him so, before me and my mother was——"

"We will not speak of these things now, Zekiel," observed Mrs. Clifford, who saw the pained expression of Lionel's face. "You must go now to rest, if you have eaten enough; and to-morrow we will talk."

Zekiel, thus reminded, returned with seemingly renewed appetite to the viands that had been placed before him; and Mrs. Clifford turned from the painful sight of the avidity with which he swallowed the food, to consult apart with Lionel as to how the unfortunate lad should be disposed of.

It was at first the wish and proposal of the latter, that Zekiel should accompany him to England; but to this Mrs. Clifford thought there were many objections. In the first place, the boy's weak state, his wild appearance and manners, which there was no time to modify, if it could be done ; and, lastly, the difficulty Lionel would have to dispose of him safely in London, should the latter find any obstacle to the fulfilment of his hopes and expectations.

It was, therefore, finally resolved, that Zekiel should remain under the protection of Mrs. Clifford for the present; but as it was not altogether advisable to have him in the house, it was proposed that he should be placed under the care of Vincent the gardener, who occupied a small cottage or lodge on the grounds.

It was amusing and yet painful to see the effect which the intelligence produced on the boy, that he was to leave his present comfortable abode, and especially Lionel, whom he still persisted in calling Master Ned.

" Why cannot I stay where you are ?" he demanded, with the most perfect unconsciousness. " There, I can sleep in yon corner; and I will not stir or make a noise. You shall not know I am there, I will be so quiet."

Mrs. Clifford, however, undertook the task of persuading him quietly to submit. She had, by the mixture of command and gentleness in her manners, acquired a greater authority over him than any one else, Paul Dangerfield always excepted, for to him was in imagination even now everything referred, " What would Paul say ? What would Paul think ?" being his constant exclamations.

" You must forget Paul now, Zekiel," observed Elinor, who saw the painful effect this constant repetition of the name had upon Lionel.

It would be impossible to describe the look of scorn, contempt, and resentment, with which this observation was received.

" Forget Paul !" he repeated, " forget the Chief, and my father, too ! He is my father, and I am his son. Do you know that, girl ? I wish he heard you tell me to forget him."

Elinor shrunk in dismay from his vehemence ; but the return of Mrs. Clifford, who had been consulting with Vincent, and the promise of a new suit of clothes in the morning, pacified the boy; who, however, could not be persuaded to follow the old man to his new abode, unless Lionel accompanied him thither ; and it was concluded upon, that it was best to conceal from him the intended departure of the latter on the morrow for England, lest he should become totally refractory.

"And now, my dear Elinor," observed Mrs. Clifford, when they had left the room, "your adieus to your friend must be short. It is already past our usual time of retiring to rest; and I have yet much to say to him, which will be best said in your absence."

"I will go immediately, if you please, madam," returned Elinor, her heart swelling almost to bursting, in the attempt to conceal her agitation. "There is no real use in the painful ceremony of bidding farewell, and you can say all that is proper for me."

"But do you think he will be satisfied with what I may say, Elinor?" returned Mrs. Clifford, smiling. "No, no, that he will not, depend upon it. I must leave to your own good sense and decision the task of dismissing him, or, rather, yourself, as speedily, and with as little pain to both sides, as possible."

Elinor felt that this was indeed a task; but Mrs. Clifford imposed it, and she resolved to go through with it cheerfully. The moment, therefore, Lionel returned, she started up, and holding out both her hands, observed,

"I have been waiting to tell you how warmly and sincerely I wish you a speedy and safe voyage, and a prosperous termination to all your anxieties. God bless you, Lionel!"

"Elinor——" Lionel could not articulate another word, so excessive was his surprise and agitation; and, before he had recovered himself, Elinor had withdrawn her hands from his ardent pressure, and was gone. It is needless to say that her composure lasted no longer than the eyes of Mrs. Clifford were on her, and that, in the solitude of her chamber, she gave free way to her regret—her sorrow—her despair, that she should ever again behold him.

Whatever was the subject of Mrs. Clifford's long conference with Lionel, it affected not the previous arangement that had been made. Elinor heard his voice speaking in tones of comparative cheerfulness, as he retired to his chamber, to the servant who was appointed by Mrs. Clifford to attend him on his journey; and, on the following morning at daybreak, the sound of the carriage wheels announced to her that he was gone—gone even without another look or word; for her chamber window was at the back of the house, and she could not even indulge in a stolen glance. At breakfast, her swollen eyes and tremulous voice betrayed how the night had passed; but she exerted herself to appear calm and cheerful; and Mrs. Clifford favoured the effort by appearing not to notice the signs of her grief.

"We have got the worst of our task still to get through, Elinor," observed the lady, when they had finished their morning's meal.

Elinor started.

"I mean, my dear, the task of reconciling Zekiel to the absence of his friend," added Mrs. Clifford.

Elinor would gladly have being excused from being present at the scene that she expected would take place; but Mrs. Clifford seemed to think her assistance necessary, and she remained. It was late in the day, however, before Zekiel made his appearance; for Vincent had purposely detained him until the clothes which had been promised him were procured; and he entered, full of vanity and exultation at the improvement in his own appearance.

"What would Paul say? Paul would not scorn to own me, now," he observed, and then, with extreme anxiety, he inquired how long it would be before Mrs. Clifford would send him across the sea to his own people, where he should soon find Paul again.

"We are all going together, in a short time, Zekiel," she replied. "Your friend Mr. Moreton—Master Ned, as you call him—is already gone; and we shall follow as soon as you are strong enough."

The poor boy's countenance instantly lost all its animation, and he stood the picture of despair at this announcement; but his eyes suddenly turned on Elinor, and he seemed instantly to read in her countenance what was passing in her heart.

"And he would not take you with him, either?" he observed. "Well, never mind, if he forgets us, because he is a rich gentleman's son, as his mother said he was, I——"

Elinor could bear it no longer, and she rushed out of the room, to prevent a display of agitation of which she was ashamed.

Mrs. Clifford's soothings, however, and the command she had acquired over him, soon pacified the boy's regrets; and, though no persuasions could induce him to refrain from continually talking of Lionel, whenever he saw Elinor, it was with more moderation and less implied distrust of the former's intentions. All the domestic comforts and attentions he enjoyed, however, could not prevent Zekiel's pining for his native home; and though evidently impressed with the deepest gratitude to Mrs. Clifford, no persuasions could induce him to promise that he would not resume his wandering and vagrant life, or return to his old haunts.

ELINOR CLARE.

"THEY ARE GOING TO RIDE IN THE PARK, I SUPPOSE."

"But there will be danger in your so doing, Zekiel," observed Elinor, with whom the boy often held long and confidential communion in the garden, where he spent most of his time, now that the weather was again mild and genial.

"Danger of what?" he demanded, with surprise.

"If you return to the neighbourhood where I first saw you," she replied, "and should be recognised as one of the party who——"

"I know what you mean," he replied, with a sagacious nod ; "but, let them catch me, if they can.   Besides, I did nothing," he added, "and they cannot hang people that are innocent."

"Innocence is not always a protection," returned Elinor, with deep sigh.

"I know what you mean," he observed significantly. "Well, but no harm came to him; he got off, you know."

"Yes, but will no harm come to him?" repeated Elinor, almost unconscious that she was speaking her thoughts aloud.

"No, what should?" replied the boy; "he is a gentleman's son now; and, as Paul says, there is one law for the rich, and another for the poor."

"But he *was* innocent—you know he was, Zekiel," she exclaimed, with energy.

"Know it," he replied, thrown apparently quite off his guard, "to be sure I do; he was miles and miles away that night."

Elinor scarcely breathed, so intense was her emotion.

"And Paul Dangerfield—the Chief, where was he, Zekiel?" she demanded, assuming a tone of indifference, to conceal her purpose.

"Ah, if he had been there, it wouldn't have happened," returned the boy, in a tone of regret, "but he was away with his leman—the pale-faced lady, and our people were mad that night; but it was his own fault, for he should not have come bearding the lion in his den; and so Dirk told him, when he struck him that heavy blow."

"Dirk?—who was he?" demanded Elinor, but the eagerness of her tone betrayed her, and excited the boy's suspicions.

"What do you ask for?" he demanded, fiercely. "You would not betray Dirk, would you? If I thought you would ——Paul always said women were not to be trusted; and now I have been foolish enough to let her wheedle me into——"

"No, no, Zekiel; I am to be trusted. I will never betray what you have entrusted me with to your disadvantage," exclaimed Elinor, who was terrified at the wild expression of his eyes. "If I asked you questions, it was only for the satisfaction of knowing that Paul had no share in that murder."

"Paul!" he repeated, disdainfully. "No, no, Paul would have scorned to have fell upon him, three or four at once, after they had got his gun away; which was quite enough, as the Chief told them, to keep him from doing any mischief. But they were all mad with whisky; and, besides, what business was it of his, if they had committed a robbery, as he called it? Everybody robs, as Paul says. The rich rob the poor; for the earth, and all its fruits, and the birds and beasts that are on it, were made for every man's use alike; and so, if one cannot get his share freely and fairly, he has a right to take it, either by fraud or force, whenever he can."

Elinor dared not attempt to argue with or contradict the principles which had been so firmly implanted in Zekiel's bosom, both by precept and example, as it appeared. She, therefore, suffered him to go on, unmolested by a single observation, repeating all that he had learned by heart and by rote from Paul and the lawless band of which he had been so long the worthy Chief; and then, by an adroit question or two, she led him into a more particular and circumstantial detail of the murder of Walter Copeland.

That rash and ill-fated young man had, it appeared, on his return from his day's excursion, met with a party of the gipsies, who had been drinking, probably with the money of which they had robbed the poor cottager, Ralph Harrowby. He had threatened them—warned them, that if he caught them in the slightest trespass, he would make them suffer; and had finally sworn that he would persecute them, in every possible way, unless they restored poor Ralph's money.

"But they would have let him go, I do believe, even after all that," continued Zekiel; "for some of the women were with us, and they begged hard for the handsome and gay young man, who was never hard-hearted to them, and had often footed it away with our girls, and treated them too at the fairs round about

"But, unluckily, Dirk came up; and he had an old grudge against Farmer Copeland, and all of his race and name. I knew there would be mischief, the moment I saw Dirk's eyes; for they were as red and as fierce as a wolf's, as soon as he saw who it was. Young Copeland did not see him come up behind him, and in a minute the gun that had kept the others off—for he had set his back against a tree, and threatened to shoot the first that came near him—the Haunted Oak it was, you know it— well, in a moment the gun was twisted out of his hand. Dirk is as strong as a giant.

"I did not stay to see what followed," resumed Zekiel; "for I ran off, to try to bring the Chief in time to prevent mischief. But I heard Dirk ask him how he dared to come and beard the lion in his den; and then I heard a crash, and the women shrieked and I guessed all was over."

Elinor shuddered with horror; and even Zekiel seemed, from the unusually grave and thoughtful expression of his countenance, to recall with sorrow towards its victim this deed of violence and blood.

" And did the Chief come? and what said he?" demanded Elinor, when she had a little recovered.

" Oh, yes, he came the moment he heard my signal outside the old walls; and furiously angry he was, even before he found out who the murdered man was, but when he found that out, he was ten times worse; and it was a hard matter to keep his hands off Dirk. I don't know what story it was Dirk told him at last; but, as I said before, it seemed that he had an old grudge against Farmer Copeland, and all belonging to him; and it's the law of our tribe, to take revenge when and where they can get it; and so the Chief was obliged to be pacified, though he told them it would be the breaking up of our station there for one while; and so it was in the end, though not just then."

" And was this Dirk a gipsy born, Zekiel?" demanded Elinor, in whose mind a thousand wild and vague conjectures and suppositions were floating.

Zekiel shook his head.

" No," he replied, " I believe not. He was born in these parts; and I fancy yon old ruin on the hill was his nest, till something happened that made it too hot to hold him. And then he came to our country, and found out Paul; for they were old cronies, and had played Romanee before together."

" Romanee?" repeated Elinor, inquiringly.

" Yes, that is a name we sometimes call ourselves by," returned Zekiel; " and a clever fellow, too, is Dirk, only so savage. I used to think that, if ever Paul was afraid of mortal man, it was Dirk."

" And was he with your party now up in the ruin?" inquired Elinor.

Zekiel looked cunningly in her face, as he replied,

" Why should you want to know that?"

Elinor replied, with as much indifference as she could assume, that she had no particular reason; and he then added,

" Well, then, he was there; and, I dare say, has gone with Paul to England; for where one is, the other is sure to be not far off."

Convinced she had now learned all that could be learned of an affair which had cost her so many hours of misery, Elinor dropped the subject, unable to devise any means by which she could make her knowledge available to Lionel, though she felt it was to him of the greatest importance.

Of his own accord, however, the boy repeatedly renewed the subject. It seemed as if a faint glimmering of the injustice he had done Lionel, in so long keeping secret his knowledge of the murder, had at length broken upon his benighted mind; but with that struggled his habitual obedience to Dangerfield, both as the chief of the tribe and as his father; and to this was added his long-practised fidelity to those whom he called his own people, his allegiance to whom, in either good or bad, no arguments could bring him to think he ought to break.

Elinor did not spare either arguments or persuasions to induce him to promise that he would make known to Lionel what he had told her, but in vain.

"No," he would reply, "if I were to tell him, he would never rest till he had brought Dirk to the gallows; for often and often have I heard him swear vengeance against the murderers of young Copeland; and he hated Dirk, beside, for many other things. And then what, think you, would Paul say to me? or how could I ever look him, or one of the tribe, in the face? though they would take care I should not do it a second time. Why, even my own old granny would help to cut my throat, if she knew that I had turned traitor."

"Heaven forbid, then, that I should tempt you into such danger!" returned Elinor, with emotion; "but still, Zekiel, I cannot think that if Mr. Moreton's life and character were again put in jeopardy——"

"He won't be, I tell you," rejoined the boy, positively. "He is a gentleman's son now, and nobody will dare to accuse him. But if he should be in danger, Paul would soon find means to rescue him, as he did before; and I would help him, for I would not see a hair of his head hurt, no, not for all the money in the world."

There was but little consolation in this assurance; but it was not for Elinor to explain to the poor, half-witted lad, that the very person on whose powerful aid he seemed to rely with so much confidence, should it be required, was, in fact, Lionel's bitterest enemy, and the very person whose machinations she feared, might bring the dreaded evil on the head of the former.

From the period of his departure, Mrs. Clifford had seldom even mentioned Lionel's name; and when she did so, it was with a degree of reserve that discouraged Elinor from pursuing the subject. Yet, even if it had not been so, she would have considered it, of course, an infringement of her promise to Zekiel of secrecy, to have spoken even to her of the communication he had made respecting the murder of Walter Copeland. To her own bosom, therefore, she was compelled to confine her knowledge of these important circumstances; and heavily, indeed, did it press upon her mind, as day after day passed on, without any intelligence from England; and she considered that Lionel might even now be in the power of his most deadly enemies.

Not even Zekiel, therefore, felt more rejoiced than she did when Mrs. Clifford at length announced her intention of returning to England, and preparations were commenced for their departure.

CHAPTER XXIII.

The gentle bird builds in the humble bower tree,
On the top of the grove loves the foolish bird to be,
And the hawk takes the high one, and lets the low one flee,
And so goes the maiden who has pride in her ee.

ANON.

THE escape of the supposed murderer of his son, at the very moment when he was exulting in the supposed certainty of having him in his power, was a dreadful shock to Mr. Copeland. Blind to everything but his own prejudices on the subject, and his fierce desire to revenge his loss, he considered the manner and means by which Edward Hatherleigh—had been rescued from the power of the law as an additional and conclusive evidence of his guilt, and his rage and disappointment were proportionably violent. Even Isabel trembled at the fierce curses and denunciations of vengeance which he uttered against the once cherished idol of her affections, and in secret prayed that Heaven would avert them; while Annie fled from hearing them, and still openly (except to her father to whom she dared not speak on the subject) pleaded the cause of him whom she firmly believed to be innocent.

Isabel's own secret convictions had, indeed, undergone a great change, from the moment she heard the decision which would have consigned Lionel to a prison, had it not been for the interposition of those who had proved themselves, she knew not why, his staunch friends. It appeared to her at that moment as if his actual doom was sealed, and that she beheld him already sentenced to a painful and disgraceful death. It seemed as if a film had dropped from her eyes, and his innocence, whom she had so striven to prove guilty, was at once clearly established.

"No, he could not do it," she repeated hastily to herself. "It is impossible. Strong as appear the proofs against him, he must be innocent."

With these impressions, it need scarcely be said that Isabel secretly rejoiced in the escape of him whom she felt she had unjustly condemned, though that pride and obstinacy of disposition which she inherited, as it seemed, from her father, prevented her acknowledging it even to her sister.

The circumstances of Lionel's rescue were, indeed, to most unprejudiced persons, and to some who were previously inclined to believe him guilty, a strong evidence in favour of his innocence; for why, as it was argued, should the gipsies, with whom he had no connection, and who could scarcely even have known him by sight—why should they have run such risks and encountered such danger, to rescue him, if it were not that they well knew his innocence and their own guilt?

"I have said it from the first and I still maintain it," Philip, Mr. Copeland's man, would observe, "young Hatherleigh had no more to do with it than I had. It were the cursed gipsies, and none else; and the only good I ever knew of 'em in my life, was their saving the poor fellow from suffering for their bad deeds."

Gradually this impression gained ground with all who were not, like Copeland, blinded by their own passions and obstinacy; and whenever, during the ensuing winter, the sad circumstances of young Copeland's murder formed the subject of conversation at the domestic firesides in the neighbourhood, it was always coupled with expressions of sorrow and regret for the poor youth who had been driven from his home, and had so narrowly escaped a worse fate, from the unjust suspicions of those who ought to have known him better.

But though Isabel's heart and conscience were relieved by the certainty that he whom she had so virulently joined in persecuting, even almost to death, had entirely escaped, there was a thorn that yet rankled and festered in her bosom; the more so, that she was compelled to dissemble and hide it: and this was her suspicions—her almost certainty, that Elinor and her lover were together.

The circumstance of Elinor's disappearance had, indeed, given rise to a thousand strange conjectures; but it was little suspected, even by Isabel, how deeply was felt by Mr. Copeland her having escaped from his power.

Unconscious, now that Elinor's innocence was, as she believed, proved even to her father's satisfaction, why she should refrain from speaking of her beloved cousin, and lamenting her absence, Annie once ventured to inquire of the old man whether he could form any supposition as to what had become of Elinor; but the violence with which her question was answered effectually terrified her from ever renewing it.

" What has become of her ?" he exclaimed. " Would that I knew ! would that I could behold her a corpse at my feet ! Yes, if she were in her grave, I might then———"

He paused suddenly, as he beheld the strong expression of horror and surprise in Annie's face.

" Why do you ask me such questions, child ?" he resumed, in a softened tone. " I wish to know nothing—to hear nothing of the girl. It would have been a good thing for all of us, if we had never known her."

" Never known her ?" repeated Annie to herself, " what a strange expression ! How could he help knowing the daughter of his own sister ? But if they all forget her, I never shall. Dear, dear Elinor ! oh, how I wish I knew where you were, and could see you once more ! or that I could but know you were in safety ! I should then be satisfied."

Annie's last wish was very soon after realised by the visit of Mrs. Clifford, for the purpose of ascertaining Mr. Copeland's present feelings and intentions towards his supposed niece.

Before, however, Mrs. Clifford reached the Nunnery, at which place Mr. Copeland and his family were now residing, a rumour of her name, quality, and the purpose for which she was coming, had flown before her, by means of Philip, who happened to be at Farmer Burton's, to which she had been directed by Elinor, when the lady arrived there. Anxious to be the first to communicate what he considered good news—namely, that Miss Elinor, was, after all, safe under the protection of a lady of quality—the honest fellow instantly mounted his horse, which was standing at the door, and leaving Mrs. Clifford in the midst of her inquiries, and Mrs. Burton of her long stories about poor Ellen, as she called her, he galloped away for dear life, as he said, to the Nunnery, that his master and the young folks might be prepared for the lady's coming.

Mr. Copeland's stern face contracted into a still more austere and repulsive expression, at the commencement of Philip's joyous exclamations, that he had heard something that he knew would please them respecting Miss Elinor; but as he proceeded to speak of Mrs. Clifford, and describe her " grand carriage and liveries," which were "all coming to the Nunnery," the dark frown gave way to a look of excessive perturbation, his lips and cheeks became blanched, and the cold perspiration stood on his forehead.

"You are ill, dear father," exclaimed Isabel, flying to his side.

"Yes, I am ill—very ill, my child," he returned, in a tremulous voice; "and I shall be still worse, if I am to have the wounds which are not yet closed cruelly ripped open by this proud woman's questions. I am very ill, indeed," he added, leaning back in his chair, and seeming to be on the point of fainting.

There was one certain way of avoiding the trial of his fortitude which he seemed so much to dread, and that expedient was obviously suggested by his present situation. In short, he yielded instantly to Isabel's proposal, that he should retire to bed, and decline to see Mrs. Clifford on the plea of illness.

"I'm danged if I don't believe old master is afeard the lady will ax him more questions than he'd like to answer about that poor girl," observed Philip, when he returned to the kitchen, after assisting Mr. Copeland to his room.

"Aye, aye, there wor always some secret that nobody could make out about her," replied an old man who had lived off and on, as he termed it, for many years at the Grove; "and if so be as she really was the old man's niece, as they said she was, why then I must tell the truth, though it's of them that's dead and gone. But you know as well as I, Phil, that she never wor looked upon by Mrs. Copeland; and though the young uns treated her as if she was their own flesh and blood, neither father nor mother ever seemed to have a bit of love for her."

"That's true enough," returned Philip, "but then, if she wasn't no relation, who was she, or why should they keep her?"

As this was a point neither could settle, they were obliged to come to the wise conclusion, that she certainly must belong to somebody, and it was most natural to think that she belonged to those who had brought her up. But then, as Philip said, why was Mr. Copeland so unwilling to answer the questions of the lady, who had come so far to ask them?

Mr. Copeland was unwilling; and Isabel was deputed, not only to get rid of Mrs. Clifford, but to give her such answers as should prevent her coming again. How well she succeeded has been already related.

Mr. Copeland remained very unwell for several days; but, at

the end of that time, to the great astonishment and dismay of his daughters, announced his intention of setting out on a journey which would occupy him for some days—it might be weeks. In vain Isabel remonstrated and Annie wept. He had reasons, he said, for what he did. It was for their good he acted ; and hereafter, perhaps, they would acknowledge so: but he must not —would not be questioned. And accordingly, for the first time during their recollection, the father quitted his children, to go they knew not whither, or for what purpose.

It was most singular, too, that this occurred just at the time when every preparation was completed for the rebuilding of their house, which was thus necessarily suspended until his return. Not long, however, was the suspense of the poor girls protracted, though the time seemed to them an age.

At the expiration of a fortnight Mr. Copeland returned; and returned better, apparently, in health and spirits, than he had been since the melancholy event which had given so severe a shock to both. And yet the hardest trial, at least that which appeared so to Isabel and Annie, yet remained behind. Their father had finally resolved on quitting for ever that part of the country. He had in vain, he said, struggled to subdue the feelings of horror and disgust with which he beheld every scene and every person who could remind him of the loss he had sustained there; and his absence had been occasioned by his wish to find some place suitable to his views and pursuits, where he should not be constantly reminded of his poor boy.

"Fortune has so far smiled on me, my children," he continued, " that it is no longer necessary I should make any great exertions to be enabled to leave you tolerably well provided for. I, therefore, considered that, at my time of life, and when I have lost my right hand, as I may say, in my poor Walter, it would be folly to burthen myself with the cares and anxieties of a large farm, such as the Grove. I came, therefore, to the determination to sell the land; and as I knew the steward of Sir William Langford had long wished to add it to Sir William's estate, I have been to him in London, and concluded the sale of it."

" And where, then, are we to live, dear father ?" was Isabel's earnest question.

" Where you will, I hope, be happier and more contented than you ever could expect to be in this hateful place," he replied. " But I shall not name the spot where our intended abode is fixed; neither do I wish you to mention one word of my intentions, either to the servants, or those who call themselves our friends. You need not look so serious, Isabel. Though I wish to leave this place secretly, and so that no trace shall remain by which, at any future time, we may be troubled with acquaintances whom I want to forget altogether, yet I have done nothing that I need run away for. I owe no man, as you well know, a farthing; and I have certainly a right to do as I please, as to going or staying."

The tone in which these last observations were made effectually silenced all remarks or objections on the part of either Isabel or her sister; though it certainly occurred to both, that there was some stronger reason than their father wished to avow, for his sudden and extraordinary decision.

"And we shall never—never again, perhaps, see the places where we have been so happy!" observed Annie, when they retired for the night; "and we shall go to a strange place where nobody knows or cares for us."

" And yet all those who most cared for us, and who made the place pleasant to us, are gone; and why should we fret at going too?" returned Isabel, whose countenance, however, betrayed that she contemplated the proposed removal with no great satisfaction.

" Why, indeed," returned Annie, with a deep sigh, "poor Elinor, how would she be surprised, if she were to know it."

Isabel's countenance darkened, and Annie did not dare to continue the theme; but the latter little suspected the dissatisfied feelings and harassing suspicions which were connected in her sister's mind with the proscribed name of Elinor.

Annie had seen nothing in her father's agitation, his consequent illness, and his desire to avoid Mrs. Clifford, but that which he alleged as the cause—namely, the revival of a subject it was his daily and hourly study to forget. She could never herself speak of Walter, or the sad consequences which had ensued from his premature and unhappy death, without tears.

No one ever ventured to make the slightest allusion to it in her father's presence : and how, then, could she wonder at his reluctance to be questioned by a stranger, especially as what he must say, if he spoke according to that which she believed was his sincere conviction, however wrong, could not be favourable to Elinor.

" No," mentally exclaimed the pure and single-hearted girl, " he felt he could not in his conscience acquit her of all blame in that sad affair, and yet he wished not to injure her."

To Isabel, however, her father's conduct appeared in a very

different light; and, anxious as she was to believe the best of one whom she had so much cause to love as her indulgent parent, she could not but suspect that there was some hidden and not very honourable motive for her father's excessive agitation, at the announcement of Mrs. Clifford's intended visit, and his desire to shun the inquiries which he understood she purposed to make respecting Elinor.

Warmly had Isabel combated and attempted to refute the suspicions which Elinor herself had more than once given utterance to, that she had no real claim to the title she bore of niece to one who treated her with such undeviating coldness, while his parental tenderness to his own offspring was so striking; but now those suspicions re-occured to her (Isabel's) mind with the greatest force; and, although she could find no clue to unravel the mystery, she could not help repeating to herself, continually,

"Elinor was right; and, whatever were the circumstances under which she became dependent on my father, he fears an inquiry into them. And who can this Mrs. Clifford be, whose very name made him tremble?" she thought. "Never shall I forget the look or the tone with which he repeated her name, when Philip mentioned it; or the breathless anxiety with which he listened to his description of the lady. No, Mrs. Clifford was no stranger to him, though I never before heard her mentioned; and yet she evidently did not know him, at least by name; though, had they met, perhaps she would have recognised him.

The sudden resolution of her father to quit that part of the country, his anxiety to conceal even from her and her sister his intended place of abode, and the secrecy and mystery in which he appeared desirous of enveloping this intended change—all were invariably connected, in Isabel's mind, with Elinor.

"My mother was right," she thought, "when she has declared, as I have heard her, in her fits of passion, which then appeared to me so unjust, that Elinor, whom we were all so fond of, was born to be a curse to us, and that bitterly would my father repent the hour that he brought her into his house to share with his children. She has indeed brought a curse upon us; and Heaven grant the worst does not yet remain behind!"

Within a few days of Mr. Copeland's return to the Nunnery, Isabel and her sister departed from it in a coach to London, where they were to await his coming, to conduct them to the new habitation he had taken, of the situation of which they were even yet kept in ignorance. To their friends, Mrs. Burton and her husband, and a few others, as well as to the servants at the

Nunnery, he represented that he had received an invitation for the two girls to pass some months with a relative; and hateful as they felt this deception to be towards those to whose kindness they had been so deeply indebted in their late afflictions, they were compelled to obey their father's instructions, and take leave as if only for a short time of those whom they knew they were quitting for ever.

It cannnot be supposed that the prospect of seeing London, of which they had heard and read such wonderful accounts, was without its charms to two girls yet in their teens. Neither could they feel any very great regret at quitting scenes where they had lost, as Isabel observed, everybody who had made them pleasant to them; and yet the sisters wept bitterly when their father handed them into the stage-coach.

They were not going, as they felt they ought to have gone, openly, with their father to protect them; but by stealth, as it were, unaccompanied, and, from their inexperience, fearing a thousand dangers and obstacles on their journey. Fortunately, however, in this respect they were mistaken; and except the little embarrassments which generally fall to the lot of unpractised and timid travellers, they met with nothing on their road to annoy them.

The instructions and directions, too, which their father had written down for their guidance on their arrival, were so plain and clear, that, with little trouble or exertion on their own parts, they were safely set down from the hackney-coach which had been called for them by the stage-coachman, at the door of a neat house in Kensington, where their father had taken apartments for them for a month, and where they were received with the utmost civility by the mistress of the house, to whose care they had been especially recommended by their father until he should arrive in town.

So far all was pleasant, and much exceeding their expectations. The rooms were light, and well furnished, though their comparative smallness to the spacious apartments of their own house excited some surprise from the simple Annie; who had imagined, she said, that all houses in London must be far superior to those in the country; and who could not suppress a laugh at the little fireplace and the tiny mantle-piece in their chamber, which she said, never could be made for use, and put her in mind of that in the baby-house which Edward had made for her when——"

But there she stopped, and the sudden pause was followed by

a burst of tears, in which Isabel joined; for, at that moment, all the circumstances of those happy days to which Annie had so thoughtlessly adverted rushed upon both their minds; and they looked disconsolately around, and felt how desolate in comparison was their present situation.

"Oh, that my father had come with us!" exclaimed Annie; "we should not then feel so friendless and forsaken."

By degrees, however, this painful feeling wore away. There was so much to see from the windows of their sitting-room, which looked into the main road, that Annie declared she could never be weary of gazing at the passers-by, wondering where they could be all going, and admiring the succession of carriages of all descriptions which were passing and repassing; and even the more grave and staid Isabel found it difficult to confine herself either to a book or to work while so many demands were made upon her attention by her surprised and delighted sister.

It was now, however, the fifth day of their residence in their new home, and even Annie had begun to tire of the sameness of her amusement at the window, and to long for the hour which should restore them to the green fields, and all the outdoor employments and exercises of which she was now deprived. On this morning she was unusually silent and low-spirited; and Isabel, raising her eyes from her work, observed,

"How dull you are, Annie! I have not heard you make a single remark this morning. Have you seen nothing worth talking about or calling me to admire?"

"If I have not," returned Annie, smiling, "I do now. Do, Isabel, come and look at this gay party: they are going to ride in the park, I suppose, that Jane the servant-maid talks of. Two—three—five ladies! How well they sit their horses! and what beautiful animals! and what pretty riding-hats and habits! I should be quite ashamed of our old-fashioned ones now."

Isabel had risen and approached the window, attracted more by her sister's praise of the horses than desire to see the riders; for she was herself a capital horsewoman, and of course a great admirer of "beautiful animals."

There was, indeed, a gay group of ladies, attended by several gentlemen and their grooms; but Isabel had scarcely glanced at them, before she started back, a burning blush suffusing her cheeks, and giving additional lustre to her bright eyes.

"What is the matter?" demanded Annie, turning to her sister. "Did any one look up at you?" Annie had more than once been compelled to retreat from the observation of some passer by, whose eyes had casually encountered her sweet face, although she sat, as much as possible, concealed from view. " I did not see any one look up," she continued, still scrutinising Isabel's glowing face.

"Neither did I," returned the latter, resuming her seat at the table.

" Well, but now, Isabel, tell the truth. You did not blush without a cause—you are not so silly; and, besides why did you start from the window so ?"

Isabel smiled, and then looked grave, and then smiled again, and tried to parry her sister's inquiries; but Annie's curiosity was now thoroughly excited, and she would not rest until she forced from her an explanation.

" Do you not recollect, many months ago—when I was gayer and in better spirits than I have been since," she added, with a deep sigh, " but you must recollect the time and the circumstance of my riding off, unknown to anybody, to Newton Regis, to buy a new bonnet, because I could not have patience to wait till you and Elinor (another deep sigh) went over soberly and steadily, as I ought to have done, in the chaise-cart; and how the blood mare, which was a stranger, and had never before been ridden by a woman, ran away with me, and broke my fine bonnet, that was tied in a handkerchief to the pommel of the saddle; and would have broken my neck, too, I believe, if she had not been stopped by a stranger, who jumped from his horse, caught the reins, and——"

" Yes, I know; a gentleman—a very handsome, elegant man, you said. And then, as in duty bound, he thought fit to fall violently in love with you, as is always done, in such cases. But what has all this to do with your starting now ?"

" Well, then, one of the gentlemen who passed in that party just now—he who rode the chesnut horse, and was speaking with such animation to one of the ladies—is that same stranger."

" What, the knight of the white willow-bonnet, as Elinor gaily christened him, because he listened so courteously to your lamentations for the loss of your head-gear, and went back ever so far to look for it ?"

" Yes, and tried so gallantly to put it in shape for me; and then, when he found he could not get me out of the pouts, and make me laugh—for I was horribly vexed and mortified, and knew I should get a scolding when I reached home—then he tried all in his power to persuade me to ride back with him to Newton, and accept a bonnet of his choice."

" And then you refused; and then he insisted on seeing you home, do all that ever you could," continued Annie.

" Yes, and then I tried to weary his patience out by riding up one rough lane and down another, because I saw he was watching at a distance which road I took, after I had scolded and looked sulky, and declared I never would go home till he left me. But I don't know how it was," she concluded, " after all, he did watch me home."

" Yes, and oh ! what a dashing, elegant, expensive bonnet came, a few days after, for Miss Isabel Copeland," rejoined Annie, " by the errand-cart from Newton, and nobody could guess who had sent it, but those who were in the secret."

" But I did not wear it, Annie, you know that," observed Isabel, proudly, and with a bright blush; " nor did I ever tell you how glad I was that I resisted all temptation, and went to church in my old one, when I saw the same pair of bright eyes peeping at me from the rector's pew on the following Sunday. Aye, and for two or three Sundays afterwards," she added.

" And you were inexorable, then, and would not reply to those eloquent glances ?" observed Annie.

" Certainly not," returned Isabel, gravely. " Why should I have encouraged attentions which were unpleasant to me ?"

" Positively unpleasant ?" observed Annie, with an arch look.

" Yes," returned Isabel, almost angrily. " I quite hated the man for his persevering impudence ; and you know I consulted Elinor about the propriety of sending back the bonnet."

" Yes, to which there were only two trifling objections," replied Annie, " that, in the first place, you neither knew his name or place of abode ; and that, as Elinor said, you could not with certainty ascertain that it was he who sent it."

" It was so," assented Isabel, with a deep sigh ; " and then circumstances arose which banished it altogether from my mind; and perhaps I should never have thought of it, if I had not now accidentally beheld the same person."

" The bonnet, however, has been preserved with great care." observed Annie, with one of her archest smiles. " I must run up stairs, and have a look at it, just to admire, as you know I have done a thousand times, the taste of the donor."

In a few minutes she returned, with the bonnet on her head, looking, perhaps, even lovelier in it than she whose beauty it was intended originally to adorn.

ELINOR CLARE.

"WILL YOU DELIVER THIS TO ISABEL?"

"It is a downright shame," she observed, "that such a specimen of taste and liberality should be doomed 'to blush unseen, and waste its beauty' in a paper band-box. I wonder if I were to meet the gallant knight with it on, whether he would recognise it; and if I should stand any chance of his transferring to me those attentions which where so ungratefully received. By-the-bye, is he handsome, Isabel? How I wish I had known it was him! Is he, Isabel?"

"Yes, very — that is, I believe so," returned Isabel, who, seemingly lost in thought, sat leaning her head on her hand, and looking at Annie, whose blooming, cherub-like face peeped out from amid the folds of pale pink satin, blond lace, and artificial flowers, with irresistible beauty and *naiveté*.

"You believe so! Why, surely you can tell?" she replied. "But I shall form my own opinion, 'from actual observation,' as our old writing-master used to say, when, after watching us from the corner of his eye, that always looked one way when it seemed to be turned the other, he detected some of us making mouths at him."

"Not in that bonnet, for the world, dear Annie! pray put it away," exclaimed Isabel. "if you are going to sit there. But then you will not know him, if he should come back this way."

"Oh, but I will make you point out which is the man," returned Annie, "on pain of exhibiting the bonnet just so," and she twirled it round on her fair hand, in front of the window.

Isabel remonstrated; but Annie was in a more playful mood than she had been for many months.

"Is this him?" she demanded two or three times. "Come here, and tell me, on pain of the bonnet. Oh, no, you need not come, the man has got a humpback, and that cannot be your knight, I should think. Stop, here comes another, and I really do think—only he has got a fish-basket strapped to his saddle. That is not likely to be the man, is it, Isabel?"

"What a provoking girl you are, Annie; twice you have made me start, and run the needle in my fingers. Do, there's a dear, come from the window, and put away that foolish thing.

"Not till I have seen the knight, Isabel: this is a talisman that will be sure to bring him. Hush, not another word, for here they really come: I can see the sun shining on the scarlet liveries. Now, come and stand behind me, nobody can see you then; and just point out which is the man."

Isabel was compelled to obey, though she expressed the greatest reluctance to comply with her sister's foolish whims. There was a tremor in her voice, however, as she pointed out a very elegant and handsome young man, that suggested to Annie that her sister was not quite so indifferent as she affected to be, and the tone of levity which the former had assumed was instantly dropped.

"Well, he certainly fully answers my expectations," she observed; "and if he were a young farmer, or a tradesman, or in any way suitable to our situation in life, he would be worth thinking about, if one may judge from his open countenance and good-humoured smile; but as he evidently belongs to a class to which we have no pretensions to aspire, I think you were very right, Isabel, to discourage him at once."

"Are you serious, dear Annie?" demanded Isabel, looking at her with surprise.

"Certainly I am," she replied; "and as to the bonnet, pretty as it is, if I were in your place, I would throw it into the fire, and forget both the gift and the giver."

"No, that I shall not do," returned Isabel, "I mean I shall not destroy the bonnet," she added, hastily: "as to the giver, as you call him, he, of course, is nothing to me."

"I hope not," observed Annie, with emphasis.

Isabel, however, either did not or would not understand her sister's meaning. It was such a new thing to be lectured and dictated to by Annie—the timid, gentle, unobserving Annie, that she was completely startled, and began to think whether there could be any necessity for the caution Annie's words conveyed. The result of her self-examination was, that she was convinced her sister was quite mistaken—she really cared nothing about the man. Was it not a proof that she did not, when she had so shunned and avoided him in the country? Oh, it was quite ridiculous! It was scarcely probable that she should ever see him again, and quite certain that she should never speak to him.

The bonnet was carefully put away, and the subject dropped by seeming mutual consent. Annie relinquished her amusement at the window, and sat down steadily to work; and Isabel was thus prevented from knowing whether the stranger passed again as it was most probable he would do, if his residence was on that road.

"But, perhaps, it was only a mere chance that brought him this way," she thought, "and he may never pass again. I should like too, to know who he is, and whether he is the lover of that beautiful woman he was talking to. It may be he is her husband. Well, what is it to me? I should rather hear he was married than not; for then, of course, I should never——"

She checked herself, and blushed deeply at the train into which her thoughts were running; and she became still more vexed and confused when she discovered that Annie's eyes were fixed on her.

"Oh dear, how I wish father would come," observed the latter; "and that we were once more settled in a quiet home, away from London."

"We are quiet enough here, I think," returned Isabel,

smilingly; "for I am sure, except the noises out of doors—and they are not very troublesome—I have not heard a sound these two hours, not even of your voice. I was thinking how different our work-table now is, to when Elinor and you and I used to agree upon fining those who first broke silence, in order to get on with our work, which our laughing and chattering had so interrupted."

"Ah! those were happy days!" observed Annie, sighing; "but, tell me, Isabel—was that what you were thinking of when you blushed so, just now?"

"Blushed? I did not blush," returned Isabel, confusedly; "why should you think so? or, why should I blush?"

"Why, indeed," returned Annie, drily, "I am sure there was nothing in the recollection of those days to blush for."

Isabel felt angry and vexed.

"How disagreeable and ill-natured you grow, Annie!" she observed.

"Ill-natured?" repeated Annie, looking up from her work at her sister, her large blue eyes filled with tears. "Oh, Isabel, ill-natured to you? I may be disagreeable, but—but——"

"There, do not say another word—I am wrong, I know I am," exclaimed Isabel, throwing her arms around her sister's neck, and kissing the tears away. "You can never be ill-natured. It is only this confinement, and uncertainty as to when and where we may be settled, that makes me petulant and cross."

"I long to get out, as well as you do," returned Annie; "for I am sure we never passed so many fine days in the house in our lives; and yet I am not sorry at the restrictions my father laid upon us, not to go anywhere until he comes."

Isabel did not think proper to inquire why she was not sorry; and she endeavoured to prevent any farther allusion to the subject which was evidently uppermost in Annie's mind, by speaking of the various sights which had been promised them by their father when he should be with them to protect them, and before they finally quitted the neighbourhood of the metropolis.

A fortnight, however, of their residence there had passed, and Mr. Copeland had not arrived. A thousand uneasy conjectures and fears took possession of Isabel and Annie's minds. He had forbidden them to write, except to announce their arrival in town; and he had warned them that he should not answer their letter, lest it should be a means of tracing them. They were therefore in total ignorance as to what was passing at the Nunnery: their father might have left it, or he might be ill, or —and that was the most distressing of all their conjectures— some accident might have happened to him on the road. Annie, in spite of all her resolution to the contrary, could not keep from the window; but she had now ceased even to recollect the stranger who had appeared so formidable to her, for she was perpetually on the watch for her father, fancying that every hackney-coach that came in the direction from London must be the one that was bringing him. Isabel herself could not settle to her work, or even to a book; and she frequently paced the room for an hour or two, with folded arms, seldom however, coming near the window; for the recollection of Annie's cautions and suspicions were still present to her.

"Look here, Isabel; do look," exclaimed Annie, hastily throwing up the sash: "here is a coach coming, and luggage on the top, and it looks like my father's large portmanteau."

Isabel's head was quickly thrust out with her sister's; but it was as quickly drawn in. The mischief was done, and all Annie's cautions and circumspection were in a moment rendered nugatory, by her own act; for there was the stranger—the knight, as she deridingly called him; and he had seen the sisters, and Isabel caught the ardent flash of surprise and pleasure from his bright eyes, as he gazed upward, and bowed with an air of mingled gallantry and respect.

Annie's sweet face glowed with mingled anger and regret as she retreated from the window.

"Never mind, Isabel," she observed; "it was my fault: but who could have thought of his being there, and on foot, too, just at that minute?"

"Certainly not," returned Isabel, scarcely knowing what she did say.

"And, after all, it was not my father," added Annie, in a tone of regret.

The servant of the house entered, to lay the cloth for dinner; and both sisters were silent, for they had from the first disliked her forward obtrusive manners, and uniformly discouraged them by never entering into any conversation while she was in the room, and answering as coldly and reservedly as possible any remarks she chose to make. On this occasion she seemed more than usually disposed to talk, although she was only answered by monosyllables by Annie—Isabel, who was naturally proud and reserved, not speaking at all.

"I beg your pardon, young ladies," at length observed the servant; "but, pray, don't you come from Devonshire?"

The colour rushed into Isabel's face as she replied,

"Why do you ask?"

"Oh, nothing very partic'lar," she replied, with a significant smile; "only, as I was takin' in missus's beer for dinner, jest now, a gentleman—one of the soldier-officers, I b'lieve he is, at the Palace; for I often see him go by, and his groom wears a cockade, and——"

"We know nothing about any soldier-officers, as you call them," interrupted Isabel, angrily; "and I hope you did not reply to any questions."

"Oh, miss, I couldn't tell nothing, because I didn't know nothing," replied the woman, resentfully. "In course, I answered the gentleman civilly, when he asked me a civil question; but it's no matter to me, I'm sure."

"What did the gentleman ask, then, Jane?" inquired Annie.

"Why, miss, he only said, quite polite, like a gentleman as he is, 'Will you allow me to ask whether there is a family from Devonshire at your house?'"

"And what did you say?" demanded Annie, who, vexed as she was, could not restrain a smile at the manner in which the woman repeated the gentleman's interrogation.

"Why, in course, miss, I said no, that you had no famerly; for you were only two single young ladies; and I didn't know where you come from."

"And that was all?" observed Annie.

"Yes, in course, miss; though I b'lieve he was going to say something else, only missus called me; and, as I'm ordered never to talk to no strangers whatsumever at the door, upon no manner of purtence, and the beer boy was gone, why I shut the door."

"You acted very properly," observed Annie. "It could be nothing but impertinence that induced the person, whoever he was, to ask the question; for we know no one in London, and do not wish, especially such a person as you describe."

"They're mighty close and uppish," muttered Jane to herself, as she went down-stairs. "One would think that two young gals like them, that hav'n't seen nothing of life, and don't seem to have a friend in the world, would be ready to jump out of their skins for joy, at having such a fine, handsome gentleman inquiring after them. My last young missus wouldn't have glumped as they did, I know, if I had told her such a thing; and yet she had lots of beaus. Well, I shan't meddle or make with them again, let who will ask about 'em."

Jane's resolution, however, as it afterwards appeared, lasted no longer than till it was put to the test. On the very same evening she was accosted, while closing the parlour window-shutters, by the same gentleman.

"I have been waiting this hour to see you," he observed, in a familiar tone, squeezing at the same time a five-shilling piece into her hand. "Tell me, have you been able to ascertain about——"

"Oh, I'm sure, sir, I would do anything in the world to serve you," she replied; "but I got my nose almost snapped off, for only asking the question. Though I'm sure they know'd more about you than they would own; for the eldest one, Miss Isabel, as she's called, turned all manner of colours, and hadn't a word to say."

"Did she indeed?" exclaimed the gentleman, with seeming delight; "and they are alone you say—no father, or brother, or lover—are you sure that nobody visits them?"

"Not a mortal soul," she replied; "but they're expecting their father from the country every day."

"What time do they go out? Where do they walk?" he demanded.

"Never crosses the threshel of the door," she replied: "I b'lieve they're afeard of being run away with," she added, with a laugh. "But lor, there's missus; if I'm ketch'd——"

"Only one word more," he exclaimed; but the cunning and cautious Jane would not listen to that word: she retreated into the house, whispering hastily, as she closed the door,

"I goes to market always about eleven o'clock, and then you can tell me."

The gentleman made a sign with his finger that he understood her, and departed.

And this gentleman, who thus condescended to hold conversation with—to bribe and to make an assignation with a low, ignorant servant-girl, was an honourable, the son of a peer, and an officer of high rank in the army. And what was the object he had in view?—the sequel will show.

True to his appointment, Colonel Evelyn passed down the High Street precisely at eleven. He passed a reconnoitring glance upwards at the window where he had for an instant beheld Isabel, but no one was visible; and he uttered not a few impatient execrations during the half-hour that he had to wait for his worthy ally, Jane's appearance. She came, however, at last; and he walked leisurely on until she overtook him.

Jane was, in her own opinion—and she had been confirmed in it by the compliments of the butcher's boy, and the baker's man, and half a dozen others of the same genus—a beauty. She had taken extraordinary pains to set herself off on this occasion; and she did not, therefore, feel very well pleased, when the colonel interrupted the simpering apology she was beginning to make, by abruptly asking after the young ladies.

The half-sullen manner in which she replied at first surprised him; but he was too much a man of the world not to speedily discover how he had offended, and a few common-place compliments soon restored his companion to good humour. All the information, however, which she could give him respecting the sisters—their motive for coming to London, or what were their intentions, amounted to very little; and there was nothing very flattering to his hopes in the remarks—which she repeated, as nearly as she could, *verbatim*—which had been made in reply to her communication respecting him.

" It appears very plainly to me," he thought to himself "that the younger sister is my enemy—like all younger sisters, I suppose, jealous; and it is equally certain, too, I think, that the old man is reduced in circumstances—perhaps——"

" And now, my dear, what is your name? I must know your name; I am sure it's a pretty one by your looks," he continued, aloud.

" Oh dear, that's all flattery, I'm sure," simpered the maid of all-work. " My name's Jane, sir."

" Jane! Ah, I thought so; pretty and innocent, like yourself. But now tell me, my dear Jane, will you undertake to deliver this letter for me to Isabel, and bring me an answer some time this evening? I will wait anywhere, any time that you say you can come."

Jane, however, protested that she dared not do it. She should lose her place and her character, if she was found out; for her " missus " was so partic'lar, as nothing could be like it; and there was no trusting but that Miss Isabel, who was as proud as a duchess, wouldn't go and inform against her.

A piece of gold dexterously slipped into her hand, and a few entreaties, vanquished all her objections; and she promised to deliver the letter, when Isabel should be alone. As to the answer, she couldn't make no promises; because, may be, the young lady wouldn't answer it at all. But she would be at the same place to-morrow morning, and then she could tell him all about it; and with this assurance he was compelled to be satisfied.

All that day, however, Jane in vain watched for an opportunity of delivering the letter. Annie was constantly present; and he had charged her to give it to Isabel alone. She ventured, however, once or twice, when Annie's head was turned, to give Isabel a significant look and nod, implying that she had something to communicate; and as the latter, though she did not reply to her signals, did not openly resent them, as she had half suspected would be the case, it emboldened her resolution to seize the first opportunity to open her commission.

Annie's remarks and seeming suspicions had raised in Isabel's mind a spirit that was likely to be fatal to her peace. Her pride was offended, that her sister should think so meanly of her as to believe it impossible that she should have excited an honourable passion in the bosom of the stranger.

How many instances had there been to her own knowledge, where females of much humbler birth, without even education, and perhaps of not very superior attractions to those which she possessed, had been raised to the highest rank—even to share the throne of monarchs; and yet Annie seemed to think it quite impossible that she could be so loved.

And even allowing the worst—allowing that the stranger entertained any dishonourable intentions towards her, was she not fully capable of protecting herself, or did Annie think she was not to be trusted? Oh, it was insufferable to be so treated; and by one, too, who had hitherto always seemed to feel her own inferiority—who had always seemed to think whatever sister Isabel said and did was

Wisest, virtuousest, discreetest, best.

If it had been Elinor who said all this to her, she should not have wondered; for Elinor was always such a paragon of prudence. The remembrance of Elinor brought with it a train of reflections by no means calculated to soothe Isabel's wounded pride. Elinor was now, through Mrs. Clifford's means, to be introduced into a sphere of life to which *she* could never aspire.

"Oh no, a young farmer or a tradesman must be the utmost limit of my hopes," she repeated to herself, with bitterness. "So Annie says; and, of course, she is a better judge of my pretensions than I am myself. No man beyond that rank can possibly think of me with any but dishonourable views."

Totally unconscious that anything she had said could have given rise to unpleasant feelings in her sister's mind, Annie attributed her evident restlessness and irritability to the uneasiness she felt at their father's protracted absence. How little did she suspect that Isabel had already made the first step to ruin, by receiving the letter of Colonel Evelyn! The cunning and crafty Jane had at last found the opportunity she was on the watch for. Isabel went upstairs to bed an hour earlier than usual: she had a bad headache, that most convenient of all feminine excuses; and Annie staid up, to finish a book in which she was greatly interested. In a few minutes the wily Jane knocked gently at the chamber-door, and was admitted.

"Now, miss, I hope to goodness you won't be angry with me for what I've done, because I'm sure I'd no thought of harm at the time, no more than the child unborn; but since I consented, my mind has misgived me, and I've been so oneasy; for, says I to myself, if the young lady was to be angry, and was to go for to tell missus, it would be the ruin of me, for I should be most likely turned away without a character; and that to a poor servant, that's got nothing else to depend upon for her bread——"

"What is it you have done, Jane?" demanded Isabel, who both looked and felt alarmed at this preface; "and how am I concerned in it?" she added, with a hesitation that showed she was in some measure conscious whereunto this mighty preparation tended.

"Promise me, then, you won't tell no living soul," returned Jane, producing the letter from her pocket, but still retaining it.

"Well, well, I do promise," replied Isabel. "I should be sorry to injure any one who meant no harm; but if that letter is from——if it is for me, I must not take it—I will not take it, indeed, Jane; and so I beg you will return it to the person who gave it you."

"Oh no, miss, I can't do that," observed Jane, "for I promised and swore I would leave it with you, even if you put it in the fire the next minute—as you can do, in course, if you please, though I'm sure I wouldn't take upon myself to advise you one way nor t'other. Oh, gemini! there's missus missed me already out of the kitchen! I can't stay another minute," and, throwing the letter on the toilette, she ran hastily out of the room.

For some minutes Isabel held the letter in her hand unopened. She examined the hand-writing—the impression on the seal;

and then she half resolved to adopt the maid's suggestion, and burn it without reading it.

"But then, he will not know that I have done so; she will tell him that she gave it me. No, I will inclose it in a blank cover, and return it to him. And yet, why should I be afraid to read the contents? It will be more decisive if I then return it."

The seal was broken, and Isabel read.

"I have just returned from Newton Regis, my dear Miss Copeland, led thither by hopes which were doomed to be disappointed; for you were gone, and I could gain no intelligence of you. Judge, then, what rapture I felt at obtaining a glimpse of your lovely face, which has never been absent from my mind's eye since first I beheld you. Yet you still cruelly shun me. You will not give me an opportunity of proving how deep, how serious is my regard for you. From the answers I received to my inquiries respecting you, after our first meeting, I was compelled to believe, most unwillingly and reluctantly, yet still to believe that your heart was given to another; and under that impression I forbore all attempts to gain a second interview, and tried to forget you, but in vain. I have now the rapturous hope that you are free—that you may be mine—mine only, and for ever. Isabel, will you not grant me an interview? If it be only to deny me, let me hear it from your own lips. Tell me, at least, that you pity, if you cannot love; and I will try to bear it with composure. No, I will not so dissemble. I cannot bear to think that you will reject me. I fear, too, that I shall excite your displeasure by the means I have taken to get this conveyed to you; but what will not a desperate man do? The manner in which your sister withdrew from the window yesterday, convinced me that it would be useless to attempt to gain admission under present circumstances. But why is she my enemy, Isabel? Does she doubt my love for you—my honourable intentions? Grant me only one interview, dearest girl, that I may convince you, and I will not fear her. I must see you, or I shall go mad. Write, if it be only one line, to say that you do not hate me—that you will see me in private, previous to a more formal introduction to your family; and leave me to contrive the rest.

"The girl who delivers this may be trusted, for I will take care to make it her interest to be faithful; and a short time will, I hope, remove all necessity for concealment, if my beloved Isabel does not refuse the sincere and fervent affection of her ever devoted

"FREDERICK EVELYN."

Could it be possible that Isabel could be angry with such a letter? could she have the cruelty coldly to send it back to him, or refuse his humble petition for a hearing? Oh, no, Isabel had no such intention. It was impossible to read it and doubt that he was sincere. Did he not explicitly state that his intentions were honourable—that he wished for a regular introduction to her family? and already her vain and proud heart swelled with anticipated triumph over her sister.

"Yes, she will find that Isabel's pretensions were not quite so low as she rated them," she exclaimed, "that, though a young farmer or a tradesman was considered quite as high as she could aspire to, a man of rank and fortune, as no doubt he is, does not consider her beneath him. And oh, how proud my dear father will be! He has none of Annie's lowly spirit—he will not think I aspire too high. And Elinor, too, and he who despised and rejected me——"

Isabel fell into a long train of musing on her anticipated triumphs. She was already in imagination raised to rank and affluence, with a man who adored her, handsome, elegant, and accomplished; what more could she wish?

"Isabel, dear, are you better?" inquired Annie, gliding softly to the side of the bed, and unclosing the curtains. "Oh dear, no," she continued, "you are very ill, I am sure you are, your cheeks burn so, and your eyes glisten. Let me feel your hand. Oh, how feverish! Oh, Isabel, what shall I do for you?"

"Nothing, you foolish girl, only come to bed, and let me go to sleep," returned Isabel, scarcely able to suppress a smile at her sister's misconception of the cause of her altered looks. She was feverish, it was true, but it was the feverishness of delight and overstrained expectation.

Annie, however, could not so easily dismiss the fear that Isabel was ill; and many hours had passed before she could close her eyes in sleep, so attentive was she to her every movement. This favoured Isabel's plan, for Annie slept soundly in the morning; and, stealing softly from her side, she hastily dressed herself, and repaired to the sitting-room, where, as she expected, she found Jane preparing for their breakfast.

"Shall you see that person to-day, Jane?" she inquired, with difficulty giving utterance to the words, so truly ashamed did she feel at making such a confidant.

"Why, I can't say for certain, miss; may be I might," she replied, "for most likely he'll be on the look out for me, as he was yesterday."

"Well, then, tell him, there's a good girl, tell him that I cannot comply with his request—that it is quite impossible, will you?"

"Oh, as for that, where there's a will there's a way, as the saying is; and if he's the gentleman I take him for, he'll never be satisfied with such an answer," returned Jane. "You had better write him a bit of a note; for else, perhaps, he'll not believe I give you the letter; and there's no knowing what he may do, if he's drove desput."

Isabel suffered her determination not to write to be overruled, and she hastily penned a few lines, in which she assured Mr. Evelyn that it was quite impossible that she could see him, and entreated him most earnestly to forbear writing again.

To a practised man of the world, the note, which was apparently intended to discourage his hopes, was quite sufficient to convince him that Isabel's inclinations were in his favour, and that was enough.

He was on the look out, as his worthy confederate had expressed it; and she was rewarded with, not praises for her successful execution of his commission, but with what was far more acceptable—substantial coin.

"Now, tell me, my dear," he demanded, "have you a sweetheart who——"

"Laws, what a question, to be sure," simpered Jane.

"Of course I cannot doubt the fact," returned Evelyn, "but what I mean is, have you any male friend, a cousin, or brother, or anything of that sort, who sometimes takes his tea in the kitchen? you know what I mean."

Jane laughed.

"Oh, bless you, no; missus don't allow no follerers. If she was to ketch even a woman in the kitchen, I should lose my place."

"Well, she could do no worse if she caught a man," returned the colonel; "and the loss of one is often the gain of two, you know," he continued, adopting his associate's elegant style of language. "If she turns you out, I will take you in. You shall be Isabel's maid, if you will but do as I want you to do."

Jane shook her head; she had scruples. Character was everything; and if she once lost it——

Evelyn, however, overruled all her scruples. He learned that her mistress was a regular attendant at church, and that the sisters had, every Sunday, accompanied her thither. It was the only place they had ever been to. since their residence there.

"That is the very thing," he exclaimed. "Remember, I shall take tea with you on Sunday afternoon—to morrow; and I shall trust to your eloquence, to persuade Isabel to remain at home. The headache which, you say, she invented last night, proves she can do it, if she will. But, stay; I will go in to the next bookseller's, and write a note to her, to break the ice; and then I must trust the rest to your management. At all events, I shall come. Now, do you go on, and make your purchases, my girl; I will be ready here with my note when you return."

"Well, I never——" said Jane to herself, as she walked hastily on to fulfil her errands; but the sentence proceeded no further. She glanced at the handful of silver, and ascertained it was even more than she had reckoned upon when he put it into her hand. It was deposited in a greasy leather purse, in which snugly lay his former offerings; and then she began to calculate how much longer this profitable trade might be carried on.

"It won't be my fault, if he don't see her to-morrow," she continued, "and, in course, he can't do no otherwise than behave handsome, when I shall run such a risk. And, after all, if I'm found out, and he don't make good his promises, I've got over many a worse hobble; and so who's afeard? There's more places than Mrs. Whitworth's; and she's a deal too partic'lar for me, that's certain."

It is not worth while to repeat the contents of Evelyn's note to Isabel, which, in fact, contained little more than a repetition of his former protestations of honour, affection, &c.; with the addition, that circumstances had occurred which he could not trust to a letter, which might fall into other hands, but which had rendered it imperative that he must see her, if only for a few minutes. To his messenger he referred her for an explanation of the means he intended to adopt to secure an interview; and concluding with a tolerably plain hint, that it would be of no use her refusing to see him, and would only render him desperate.

Isabel was at once angry, terrified, and yet gratified by his vehemence; she refused at first to listen to Jane, who had found an opportunity to explain to her what had been resolved upon.

"Well, miss, I can't help it, you know. I am sure I never give the gentleman no encouragement; and if he comes and makes a disturbance, why, it will be the ruin of me, and nobody else; for I'll die before I'll betray you," replied Jane, pretending to cry.

"But he cannot come, if you refuse to admit him, Jane," returned Isabel, whose resolution was already shaken, but whose natural sense of propriety still prevented her yielding.

"Ah, there's no telling what a man may do that's desput," returned Jane, "howsomever, I must stand the racket, that's certain."

Isabel wavered—deliberated; and

She who once deliberates is lost.

She persuaded herself that it would be cruel to let Jane, disagreeable as she was, suffer for her. She would see him, therefore, but only for one minute—only to tell him that she would not enter into any clandestine correspondence; and that she insisted, for the future, on his forbearing to address her, unless through those who were the most proper judges of his intentions.

Isabel had, in fact, framed a speech full of proper dignity and prudence; but when, having got rid of Annie with Mrs. Whitworth by the proposed artifice, Jane came up with a look of cunning importance, to say that "a certain person" was below, and to know whether she should ask him up stairs, or would Miss Isabel come down, the poor girl was seized with such a fit of shame and confusion, that she could neither speak nor move.

"Laws, miss, how can you be so foolish?" remonstrated Jane. "I'm sure he's as humble and as gentle as a lamb; and you need no more to be afraid of speaking to him than I am. Shall I ask him to walk up?"

"No, not for the world," exclaimed Isabel, hastily: "I am only ashamed to see him, because I am afraid he will despise me for having consented to do so at all, under such circumstances."

"What a mighty fuss about nothing, to be sure!" muttered Jane, as she followed her down stairs. "If she was a king's daughter, she couldn't make a greater bother."

All Isabel's attempt at dignity and self-possession vanished, however, the moment she beheld Evelyn. He was so full of remorse for giving her a moment's uneasiness—so humble and gentle, as his confederate Jane had said, that she could not find it in her heart to utter the reproofs for his temerity, or the imperative order to quit the house instantly, which she had meditated.

Jane took his hint to leave them together. Isabel, indeed, started up from the seat to which he had courteously led her, to prevent her; but Jane's petulant "Laws, miss, I *must* go and get my things on; or else what will missus think?" and Evelyn's eloquent look of reproach and remonstrance at her distrust, prevented her persevering.

Evelyn had thus, he confessed, unwarrantably sought an interview, to explain to her candidly his situation and prospects, and to learn from her own lips whether she would be content to share the fate and hardships of a soldier of fortune—one who had little more than his sword and his connections to depend upon for his advancement in the world.

Isabel's fabric of wealth and rank and grandeur began already to tremble; but she concealed her disappointment, and listened with growing interest to his *candid* detail, by which he sought to prove that he could not—would not live without her, and yet that it would be certain ruin to him if he were openly to marry without the consent of his father, Lord Selborne, and more especially an old aunt, to whose fortune, which was entirely at her own disposal, he expected to succeed. It was this consideration only—the consideration that he could not immediately provide for his adored Isabel in a manner becoming her merits and his own station in the world, that prevented his instantly demanding her father's consent to his becoming her acknowledged suitor; and, at no distant period—immediately, if his own wishes were consulted—her happy and grateful husband. Still, if on no other terms he could hope to be so blessed—if she demanded the sacrifice, he would renounce his family—his friends—all his prospects, to call her his.

Isabel was distressed—confused; she had not foreseen or was prepared to parry the arguments he adduced for concealment at present. She would not, either, be outdone in generosity; and in an evil hour she consented to promise solemnly to be his whenever he should claim that promise; to conceal from every one the secret of their attachment, until he considered it expedient to avow it; and, finally, to indulge him with an interview whenever it should be safe and practicable.

"And now, dearest, I will not—dare not trespass farther on your indulgence," he continued. "Not for the world would I expose you to a moment's uneasiness that I could shield you from, even at the expense of my existence. Only promise me that you will calm this agitation, and will regard me as your fond, your faithful protector for life, and I will instantly leave you, and be guided henceforth entirely by your wishes.

Isabel faintly replied to this florid and studied declamation, so

ELINOR CLARE.

"LET US BE IN SECRET UNITED."

unlike the language which would have been dictated by true and honourable affection, and he departed; Jane who—had, in fact, never been beyond ear-shot, while she hurried on her "things" in the adjoining scullery—presenting herself at the critical moment, to receive the reward of her successful negotiation.

It would have been no easy task for Isabel to have disguised from Annie the agitation she had suffered, and the abstraction of mind which was the consequence of the new position in which she was placed; but Annie was totally unsuspicious — she had ceased to think of the circumstances connected with the stranger which had at that moment given her much uneasiness; and she attributed all that appeared unusual in her sister's manners to the anxiety and suspense respecting her father, in which she herself shared, though she did not indulge it to so excessive a degree as Isabel; and she tried to soothe the latter by various suggestions as to the cause of his absence, and confident predictions that he would arrive speedily, and that they should find that all their fears and anxieties had been groundless.

Little did she suspect that Isabel now dreaded the arrival of her father—that she feared to meet his eye, from the consciousness that for the first time in her life she was acting with duplicity and deception.

On the very next evening Mr. Copeland arrived. Annie was in an ecstacy of joy; but Isabel's agitation was so excessive, that she could not rise to meet him, or utter a word.

"Isabel, my child, are *you* not glad to see me?" demanded the old man, when he had released himself from Annie's embraces.

Isabel's lips moved, but no sound was heard, and she burst into an hysterical fit of tears.

"Oh, father, she has fretted herself almost to death," exclaimed Annie, supporting her in her arms; "and the confinement to these little rooms, too, has weakened her. But she will soon get well again, now you are come; and we shall be so comfortable when we get out of this nasty London, which she does not like, any more than I do. She is longing to get into a home of our own, among the green fields. Are you not, Isabel?"

Isabel faintly uttered "Yes;" and then rather petulantly pushed Annie away, observing,

"I am well enough now: I do not know what made me so foolish."

"You want air and exercise, my child," observed her father: "I am sorry I laid such restrictions on you, but I did not expect to be——"

"Oh, but I am not," returned Annie hastily, her thoughts for a moment recurring to the stranger: "I would not have gone out for the world, while you were away."

"I knew I could depend on the prudence of my girls," observed the old man; "but still, there are so many ever on the watch to take advantage of inexperience and——"

"When do you propose leaving London, sir?" demanded Isabel, hastily, turning from Annie's serious and thoughtful look.

"Why, my dear, it cannot be said that you are in London,

now," he replied, smiling ; "you have, as yet, seen nothing of the great metropolis, and——"

"Oh, but we do not want to see any more, dear father," interrupted Annie. "We saw plenty of it as we came along in the coach—all dirty streets, and crowds of people——"

"You may speak for yourself, certainly, Annie," observed Isabel, angrily ; "but I own I should be disappointed if I were to leave London without seeing a little more of it. But we are selfishly thinking and talking only of our own feelings and concerns, without making a single inquiry of my father. You look pale and thin, dear father."

"Do I, my child? Why, yes ; I have suffered a good deal of anxiety," he replied ; "and then old habits are not to be broken up, and old neighbours to be parted with, without some suffering. I was weak enough to postpone, day after day, the final step, because I could not summon resolution ; but it is taken now, and we must abide by it, and forget, if we can, everything but our new home."

"And where is our new home, father? and when shall we go to it?" demanded Annie.

"Not a day's journey from London, my dear," he replied ; "but there are a good many arrangements to make before we can take possession, for there is everything to buy in the way of furniture : and as it can be bought much cheaper and better in London than anywhere else, we must make our purchases here before we leave, and see all packed and sent off before us. It is but a humble cottage, compared to what you have been used to," he added, "but it is prettily situated, and I trust you will be content."

"Anywhere with you, father," returned Annie, warmly ; "and, besides, what should we want with a large house, now ?"

"Isabel does not look as if she were very well satisfied," observed the old man, looking earnestly at her.

Isabel started at the observation. She protested, and with truth, that she was not thinking of their new home, as Annie called it ; for every place was now alike to her. The fact was, she was thinking, at that moment, of Evelyn, and conjecturing how he would bear the separation which so soon must take place.

Mr. Copeland did not inquire, however, what it was that had imparted such a melancholy and dissatisfied look to her countenance. He thought, probably, that she was thinking rather of the home that she had quitted, than that which awaited her ;

and, as he would rather have avoided than sought to speak of that, he gladly turned his attention entirely to Annie, whose questions, all relating to their future mode of life, did not embarrass him.

The arrival of Mr. Copeland proved rather favourable than otherwise to the correspondence between Evelyn and Isabel; for Annie's attention was so often engrossed by her father, that Isabel was comparatively freed from her observation, and Jane was no longer compelled to watch for opportunities to deliver letters or receive the answers.

As Isabel expected, the intelligence of her contemplated departure from London was received with expressions of the utmost despair; and Evelyn accused her of cruelty and insincerity, in not at once saying where she was going; and, in conclusion, he declared that he should go mad, if he did not soon have an opportunity of hearing from her own lips every particular respecting this dreadful bereavement.

It was not, however, until Isabel was on the eve of leaving London, that the interview—now as much desired by her as her lover—took place; and then Isabel only saw him by Jane's management for a few minutes. But she had by that time learned the name of the village in Surrey near which her residence was to be fixed; and Evelyn learnt with satisfaction that it was within two or three hours' ride; and that, as she would there be free, in a great measure, from restraint, and especially from the observations and suspicions of her sister, it would be in reality much easier for them to meet than while she remained nearer to him.

And they did meet again and again; for Annie's fears were all dissipated with their departure from London, and her thoughts and attention so occupied in making their new home pleasant and comfortable to her father, that Isabel was left at full liberty to follow her own inclinations.

It was a pretty and picturesque cottage which Mr. Copeland had taken for their residence; but it had long stood empty and neglected, and it required considerable alterations and improvements to make it what he and Annie wished it to be. To Isabel it was a matter of perfect indifference what was done; but her avowed dislike to work-people and bustle rendered her so petulant and impatient, that Annie was often as earnest in getting rid of her for an hour or two as Isabel was to seize the opportunity of keeping her appointments with Evelyn, whose affection seemed to increase every time he beheld her

But Isabel, though now systematically engaged in a course of deception towards her father and her sister, was still too guarded and prudent for her lover's purposes, and he became convinced that he must adopt some more bold and decided means than those afforded him by stolen interviews.

Isabel went, as usual, to their accustomed rendezvous, but Evelyn was not there; she waited long beyond the appointed hour, but he came not; and she returned miserable and dejected, unable to form any reasonable conjecture as to the cause of his absence. A second day passed in the same manner; and she began to despair that she should not again behold him. On the third he came; but all the pride and resentment which she meant to show for his neglect faded before the look of melancholy and uneasiness with which he met her.

As warm and devoted as ever were his expressions of attachment to her, and yet he attempted not to explain why he had not kept his engagement. Isabel saw plainly that something painful had occurred, and at last her entreaties wrung from him the sad truth. His regiment was ordered to a distant part of the kingdom, and he was distracted at the thoughts of leaving her. In the first impulse of his despair, he had confessed to his father his unconquerable passion, without, however, disclosing her name or residence, merely speaking of her as she was—one whose situation in life was humble, but who would do honour to a throne. But his father was inexorable; and had threatened not only to disinherit him if he followed the dictates of his heart, but to be henceforward his most bitter enemy. Fearful that he should be watched, as, indeed, his constant absences from home had already given rise to suspicion —he had for two whole days sustained the misery of not seeing her; but he could no longer bear it, and how then would it be possible for him to exist when he was separated from her by hundreds of miles? No, he could never exist under the torments he should feel. Some other, more fortunate than himself——

Isabel interrupted him by a fervent protestation of her constancy, but Evelyn was not to be convinced. He knew, if they once parted, it would be for ever; and so well he acted the part of the despairing and phrenzied lover, that Isabel's heart was melted, and with tears she demanded what she could do to prove to him the sincerity and constancy of her affections. This was the point to which Evelyn had aimed to bring her.

" Become my wife," he whispered, straining her to his bosom.

" Let us be in secret united ; and then all fears—all jealousy on my part will be at an end."

Isabel would not have hesitated a moment to pronounce the final " Yes " to this proposition, but her father—she doubted whether her father would agree to such a marriage; and without his sanction, how was it possible that it could be effected?

Cautiously Evelyn proceeded to unfold his views on the subject. Mr. Copeland could never be expected to consent; or, if he did consent, he would never keep such a secret. A thousand circumstances might occur to induce—nay, to force him to reveal it; and then what would follow?—not only his (Evelyn's) ruin as to his worldly prospects, but he should be loaded with a parent's curse; for his father was implacable, and well he knew the extent to which his revenge would carry him. There was one—one only means by which this awful consequence might be avoided; but he feared to mention it—he dreaded that she would think him cruel and selfish, in demanding such a sacrifice. Yet, if she loved as he loved——

Isabel earnestly besought an explanation; but when she learned that the proposal was to renounce her home—to leave her father and sister in ignorance of her fate, and to trust herself entirely to her lover, who, as soon as they were married, would provide a retreat for her where he could visit her in secret and from which he should bring her forth to the world as his treasured and beloved wife, the moment he could do so with safety—so soon as she heard all this, plausibly and artfully as it was revealed, her heart revolted; and with tears of bitter agony she replied,

" Never—never ! anything but that—but that ! oh, never !"

" I could not expect it—I did not," returned Evelyn, in a plaintive tone. " Oh, no, I was a wretch—a villain to think of it. No, I must submit to my unhappy fate—I must leave you, Isabel, leave you for ever; for well I know, if once we part, it will be for ever!"

Isabel was not prepared, however, for this alternative. She tried to argue with him—to prove that she was worthy of being trusted, and that her affection for him would stand the test of time and absence; but Evelyn was not to be convinced—his presentiments were not to be overcome : there was one and only one way by which he could escape the insupportable misery which must be his lot if he was parted from her, and that means he would embrace.

Isabel was terrified—she could not doubt to what means he

alluded; and the thought that she should be the cause of his death was horrible. It was not to be borne. No, she would renounce father—home—everything rather than that!

Evelyn was all rapture and gratitude; and again Isabel recoiled in affright and terror, when she found that the sacrifice must be made immediately—that she must not return even to take one parting look of her fond parent, or her kind, affectionate sister.

"I will tell you the truth, dearest Isabel," observed the deceiver. "The chaise which brought me from town is now waiting in the village, to carry me onwards on my route to Ireland: your decision, therefore, must be made at once. And of what avail would it be, best beloved of my heart, that you should return? Would it not be uselessly prolonging the pangs which it is natural you should feel at parting with your friends, though but for a time, I hope—a brief time? You can write, Isabel, from the first post-town we stop at, to assure them of your safety; and explain, as far as can be, without betraying our secret, the motives of your absence."

"But I am totally unprepared for a long journey," observed the confused and hesitating girl, glancing at her dress.

"All that objection can be easily obviated, dearest," he replied. "Everything you need or wish for can be purchased at the first large town we stop at. And there, too," he added, observing that she still looked dissatisfied, "there, unless anything happen to render it desirable to proceed farther—there can we remain until the indissoluble knot is tied which will make us one."

How could Isabel find further objections to one so fervent— so devoted? Yet still she lingered; and Evelyn was at length compelled to use gentle force to constrain her to turn her half-reluctant steps towards the village, where, as he said, the chaise awaited his coming.

Long before they reached it, however, Isabel descried the chaise drawn up in a lane a considerable distance from the high road; and something like distrust at this very striking proof of previous arrangement occurred to her.

Evelyn instantly read the expression of her eye.

"If you repent, love, of making me the happiest of mortals," he observed, "it is not yet too late to return. Heaven forbid that I should purchase my own happiness at the expense of yours!"

Isabel was ashamed to acknowledge her suspicions. In

another minute her foot was on the step on the chaise. It was indeed too late to recede. The chaise drove off, and Isabel's fate was sealed.

To attempt to describe the feelings of the bereaved parent and deserted sister would be vain. For a long time no suspicion arose in the minds of either that Isabel was gone—gone for ever.

"She has strayed so far, that she has lost herself, foolish girl," observed the old man, when the dinner-hour passed, and she came not. "Never mind, Annie; we will put her dinner by, and keep it warm. It would serve her right not to let her have any."

Annie responded in the same strain of cheerfulness. Once only had a fear intruded, but it was instantly checked.

"How foolish I must be," she thought. "It is utterly impossible that he could have traced her hither; and to suppose that he could by accident again have discovered the place of our retreat would be too ridiculous."

When, however, tea-time came, and Isabel was still absent, a thousand suspicions forced themselves on her mind, though she did not dare mention them to her father; to whom such a thought as his daughter having formed any clandestine attachment never occurred, but who was completely bewildered with alarm and anxiety.

Night came, and with the dark hours a tenfold accession of alarm and horror. Nothing could persuade the old man but that Isabel had fallen a victim in the same manner that he had lost his son. Yes, she was murdered—he knew she was murdered—nothing but death would ever keep his poor child from her father; and, at last, to divert his mind from this dreadful idea, Annie was compelled to relate to him her reasons for believing that her sister had voluntarily deserted her home.

Copeland's cheeks, which had been before blanched with horror and alarm, now flushed with rage.

"Let me but once prove that she has left me for the arms of a villain," he exclaimed, "and she is no longer my child ! Not a sigh—not a tear will I shed for her fate ! She has chosen a life of infamy—let her abide by the consequences. But it cannot be—surely it cannot be ! I cannot believe it on your assertion, Annie."

"My assertion, dear father !" exclaimed the distressed girl. "Oh, no, do not say so. I do not assert it; but I mention the circumstances only in the hope that it will induce you to dismiss the horrible idea that she is dead and——"

"The hope?" he repeated, with vehemence, "the hope did you say, girl? Ten thousand times rather would I behold her a mangled and disfigured corpse, than know that—— And yet I begin to believe it is as you suspect. Her long, solitary walks —her melancholy, which I attributed to such a different cause —the indifference which she showed to our exertions to make our home pleasant and comfortable, and which I have thought arose from her pride being mortified at the change in our way of life—oh, yes, these were all signs that her heart was corrupted!"

"Not corrupted, father," observed Annie, in a pleading tone: "estranged, but not corrupted; and she will return to us. Who can tell by what artifice——"

"Return here!" exclaimed the old man, violently, "never! never does she darken these doors again! No, if I were to see her starving—dying in the highway, I would pass her by, and bestow on her only my curse—my bitter curse! She is no longer my child. She has deserted me, and disgraced herself; and may she live to feel——"

"Oh no, father—dear father," interposed Annie; but the old man interrupted her.

"Do not utter one word in excuse for her," he sternly observed, "lest I be tempted to think that you, too, might be persuaded to desert your father."

Annie was effectually silenced by this cutting observation. Almost she repented that she had disclosed what she had remarked of her sister's conduct, although it led to his taking measures to ascertain the truth of her, and now his suspicions, which soon placed the fact beyond doubt.

The visits of the strange gentleman, at regular intervals, to the village, where he always left his horse, while he proceeded on foot to meet Isabel, had excited curiosity; and he had been followed and watched until the motive of those visits was fully ascertained. The post-chaise, too, had been seen standing in that retired and unfrequented spot; and the boy who drove it had openly avowed to some casual passer-by who had questioned him that he fancied he was stationed there on some runaway concern; but that was no business of his. He was sure the gentleman was a gentleman, every inch of him; and he reckoned he should make a good job of it.

"And so," continued the garrulous landlady of the village inn, who was riving the heart of the old man by these details of his daughter's disgrace, "and so we was all on the look out for the po-shay; and sure enough it came at last, dashing along as fast as the horses could put their feet to the ground; and we could only just catch a glimpse of a gentleman and lady. But my Letty said she could swear to the bonnet being the same that the tallest young lady at Hollybank wore last Sunday at church."

The old man uttered not another word, but returned home.

"You may go to bed, child," he observed, in answer to Annie's inquiring look; for she dared not speak when she beheld the expression of his countenance. "Yes, it is all over!" he continued, with forced composure; "and, remember, from henceforth her name is never mentioned."

Scarcely could Annie believe this confirmation of her worst fears, though she had been herself the first to suggest the cause of her sister's absence; but she dared not question her father, who rigidly kept his resolution. From that day Isabel's name was never mentioned; and but for the settled expression of grief and shame which was so visible in his countenance, and the silence, and even sometimes distrust and impatience, with which he received her affectionate attentions, Annie might have believed that he had forgotten or at least ceased to sorrow for the lost Isabel.

A hastily written and scarcely intelligible note was received from the fugitive on the third day of her absence. It was addressed to Annie; for Isabel dared not, she said, write to her father, until she could give him proofs that she had done nothing to deserve his resentment, except in not having required his sanction and consent to an union which she was sure would eventually satisfy his most fervent wishes for her welfare.

"But circumstances at present compel me, dear Annie," she concluded, "from explaining farther, or soliciting personally my father's forgiveness for the uneasiness my flight must have occasioned to him and you. I can only add, that I am as well and happy as I can be away from you."

Annie was alone when she received this, and bitter were the tears she shed over it; for her heart misgave her, that the certainty with which Isabel spoke of her marriage, and the seeming composure with which she wrote, were unreal.

Her father entered, and she put the letter into his hand.

"Is she married? and to whom?" he demanded, glancing at the hand-writing. "Your looks answer my question," he added before Annie's trembling lips could utter a word, and he threw the letter in the fire.

"You are too hasty, father," Annie at length articulated: "she assures me——"

"Not one word, but the certificate of her marriage, and a full explanation why I was not consulted, will I listen to," replied the stern old man; "and henceforth, remember, you hold no correspondence with her. Promise me, girl, that you will not reply to her letter."

"I cannot, father; for she has given no clue to her present situation."

"Another proof of her guilt," he observed; "but I have done with her—done with her for ever."

Annie could only submit in silence, and weep in secret for the lost and loved companion of her childhood, her dear sister; but time—the balm that brings relief to all sorrows—gradually restored the innocent girl to composure, though never to the cheerfulness which should have been the attendant on her guileless disposition.

CHAPTER XXIV.

Thou goest, and who shall bid thee stay?
Who check thy young heart's daring?
Who turn the eaglet from his way,
To the field of blood repairing?

ANON.

MRS. CLIFFORD and Elinor returned to England, bringing with them Zekiel, whose joy at setting foot once more on his native land broke out into a thousand wild and extravagant gestures and expressions. He appeared, however, greatly disappointed when he understood that it was Mrs. Clifford's intentions to proceed to London after a night's rest, which was rendered necessary by their having encountered rather rough weather at sea.

"What should you go to London for," he abruptly inquired, "where there is nothing but smoke and dust, and high houses like prisons, so crowded together that you can hardly breathe, or catch a glimpse of the beautiful blue sky, or ever hear a bird sing or——"

Mrs. Clifford smilingly interrupted him.

"That may be partly true," she observed; "but still there are sights in London worth looking at; and, besides, you will see Mr. Moreton there—Master Ned, as you call him."

The boy shook his head with an air of dissatisfaction, but Mrs. Clifford did not consider it necessary to argue with him; and after a long silence, he uttered a hasty "Good night," and left the room.

"The young savage is getting gradually tamed," observed Mrs. Clifford; "it is the first time, I believe, he ever considered such a ceremony necessary."

The meaning of it, however, was soon explained; for Mrs. Burchall's first exclamation, when she entered her mistress' room on the following morning, was,

"So, ma'am, that ungrateful young vagabond, after all your kindness, has walked off, without leave or license."

"What young vagabond?" demanded Mrs. Clifford hastily, "who are you talking of?"

"Oh, ma'am, the pet gipsy-boy," returned the waiting woman pertly. "I'm sure it's quite a pity to see how ladies is imposed upon by cunning people."

"Zekiel gone!" exclaimed Mrs. Clifford, in a tone of regret, and without bestowing any notice on her maid's animadversion. "Poor boy, when and how did he go? Are you sure he is really gone?"

"Oh, yes, ma'am; he slunk away as soon as ever he left you, last night. He took care, though, to carry off all the good things you had made for him; but, as I said when they told me, it was lucky he took nothing that belonged to other people."

"Your observation was uncalled for, then," observed Mrs. Clifford, angrily: "the boy possessed too much gratitude, to have done anything wrong while under my protection, however defective may have been the principles he has been taught, or the habits in which he has been reared."

Mrs. Burchall did not reply—she knew how far she dared go with her mistress; and, though in her heart she rejoiced that one of Mrs. Clifford's pets, as she expressed herself, was gone, she affected to lament that the boy had not known his interest better than to desert one who had been so kind to him.

Elinor and Mrs. Clifford did both really lament the boy's departure, especially as the sum he had in his possession was comparatively a mere trifle. There could be no doubt that he had gone in search of the gipsy tribe, to whom he had so often expressed his impatience to return, and would again resume all the wild and wandering habits from which they had hoped to reclaim him.

It was useless to hope he would return thither, however, if

they remained; and accordingly, as soon as they had breakfasted they departed for London.

Elinor had forborne speaking of Lionel; yet she thought of him, and only of him, as she approached the great city, of which, as she supposed, he was now an inhabitant. Mrs. Clifford's observations to Zekiel had certainly intimated that she expected to see him; but that did not lessen her surprise when, on entering the breakfast-room of Mrs. Clifford's mansion on the morning after their arrival, she beheld him quietly seated at the table, reading the newspaper; which was, however, instantly thrown down, as he started up to meet and welcome her.

A single glance at his expressive and animated face told her that all had succeeded to his fullest expectation; and the first words she uttered were those of congratulation.

"Yes, dearest Elinor," he replied, "I am indeed happy beyond my fondest hopes; for I can now prove to you the sincerity of my affection for you. While it remained doubtful whether my father would sanction my love for you, I was forbidden by Mrs Clifford to address you on the subject; and, cruel as seemed the interdiction, I submitted to it; but now every obstacle is removed, and I dare say to you that——"

Mrs. Clifford entered, and prevented the conclusion of the sentence.

"You are here, I trust, by permission," she observed, with significance, after the first congratulations had passed.

"Not only by permission, but by special desire," he replied, with a smile. "My father saw the note you honoured me with last night, and was anxious that I should not lose a moment in acknowledging your kindness."

Mrs. Clifford glanced with peculiar meaning at Elinor, whose glowing cheeks betrayed that she fully understood the allusion.

Never were a trio in better humour with each other, and the world in general, than that which now surrounded Mrs. Clifford's breakfast-table; and yet many tears were shed by one. That one was Elinor, who could not suppress these tributes of sympathy at Lionel's pathetic account of his first interview with his father.

"I had prepared myself," he observed, "to meet with one of naturally cold and reserved manners—perhaps even rendered sour and distrustful by the misfortunes he had met with, and the treachery with which his trusting confidence had been repaid; and I resolved gradually to unfold the tale of the imposition that had been so long practised towards him respecting his son, as

having been confided to me, not as if I had any personal interest
in it.   But the agitation he betrayed at the account I gave of
my unfortunate mother's death—the mildness and tenderness
which his every word and look evinced, completely dissipated all
my pre-formed impressions of his character.

"' You will think, perhaps, that this is a culpable weakness
in me,' he observed; 'for you knew her only as a lost, guilty,
and degraded woman.   But I think of her as she once was—the
innocent, the pure, the guileless girl, who made, as I thought,
the happiest of mankind: but proceed—pray proceed.   You told
me that she spoke of me in the hour of death—that she was
desirous of repairing one great wrong she had committed towards
me.   Alas! what reparation——but she is in her grave; and I
forgive her.   We have all need of forgiveness; the best that
live need it.'

"I recommenced my narrative where I had left off," continued
Lionel.   "I told him that it had indeed been Mrs. Moreton's
dying wish to make him the only reparation in her power; and
then I added, ' You had a son, sir.'

"' Yes, but why do you speak of that?' he hastily replied,
'you cannot restore me my boy from the grave.   He died, and
never knew his unhappy father.   Oh, if they had only left that
child with me!   And perhaps then, too, he would have lived—
my care, my attention——'

"' He does live,' I replied; ' the story of his death was false.
It was the child of Oliver Moreton who died, and who was buried
as——'

"' And who—who are you, who come to tell me this?' he
faltered.

"I could not command my voice to utter a single word.   I
tried to rise and throw myself at his feet; but I had not power.
But that which words refused to speak for me, my agitation
betrayed; and with a cry of joy he threw himself into my arms.

"It was long," continued Lionel, who had been several times
compelled to pause in narration, from the emotion which was excited by the remembrance and repetition of this eventful moment,
"long before either of us recovered sufficiently to proceed with
anything like tranquillity to the examination of the proofs of my
identity which I had brought with me.   My father wanted no
proofs: he said the voice of nature spoke in both our hearts;
and he wondered, too, how he could have been so blind as not
from the first to see that I was the son of his Felicia.

"I have little more to add.   The friend who had, indeed,

proved himself a true friend, at a time when grief and disappointment had rendered my poor father unable to act for himself, was
now sent for to share his joy; and to his cooler judgment I
submitted the dying declarations of my mother, and had the
satisfaction to hear that not a doubt could exist of their truth.
To my father I have revealed as little as possible of the horrible
life of the wretch to whom he owes all the evils that he has
suffered. To Mr. Saville, his friend, who was the agent that for
so long a period transmitted to my poor mother the sum which
enabled us to live so happily on my part and resignedly on hers,
until the serpent again stole in to poison our felicity—to him I
have candidly revealed the whole of the events that have taken
place since that time."

A cloud passed over his open brow, which betrayed that ther
still, in spite of his declaration of perfect happiness, existed
some feelings of uneasiness in his bosom at the recollection of
those events; and none could better comprehend those feelings
than his present auditors. Elinor could not speak; but her
sad and thoughtful look at him uttered volumes. Mrs. Clifford,
however, had no such motives to restrain her; and, in a tone
that showed how deeply she was interested, she demanded,

"And what does your friend advise respecting the cruel and
unfounded accusation which was brought against you, and which
still——"

Lionel's voice faltered, as he replied,

"Mr. Saville is, I think, too fearful on the subject. But
for the wretchedness it would cause my father," he continued,
"I would even now demand an investigation, which must substantiate my innocence, since I can now prove the cause of my
absence, and that I was many miles from the spot when that
cruel deed was committed."

"Would that the murderer were discovered!" observed Mrs.
Clifford. "I do not hesitate to tell you that I am convinced
that the death of that poor young man was another link in the
chain of guilt of that monster Dangerfield—I will not call him
by the name he has——"

"Oh, no, no, it was not he who did it!" exclaimed Elinor,
shuddering at the recollection of Zekiel's description of the scene
which he had witnessed.

Mrs. Clifford and Lionel both gazed upon her with the utmost
amazement.

"What can you mean, Elinor?" exclaimed the former.
"Speak, you have heard something which——"

"No, no, nothing, nothing," exclaimed Elinor. "I knew not what I said. Do not ask me."

Mrs. Clifford turned her eyes from Elinor to Lionel, and beheld astonishment and horror written in every line of his face.

"Ask of her, Mr. Moreton—demand of her what she meant by that expression," she observed. "You have a right to demand, and surely she dare not refuse *you*."

"I cannot—I dare not tell him," exclaimed Elinor. "My promise—the safety of another, who would fall a sacrifice——"

"It is Zekiel who has revealed the truth. Where is the boy? I had forgotten him," interrupted Lionel starting up. "My suspicions were right; for I always believed he knew who did the deed. Let me see him; and I will force him to confess the whole."

"Zekiel has left us," observed Mrs. Clifford, "left us on the very day we landed, to join his former associates; but Elinor cannot now refuse to tell what she has learned. It can avail nothing now, that she remains silent, when she has confessed so much."

Deeply did Elinor deplore her incautious admission, which had led to the violation of the promise she had made to Zekiel; but she consoled herself with the reflection that both Lionel and Mrs. Clifford were interested in the safety of the unfortunate boy, and that they would be cautious in the use of the information she gave them.

"Dirk!" repeated Lionel, when she mentioned the name of the murderer. "Dirk, then, was the wretch. But that is not his real name; his name is Claude Giotti."

"Claude—Giotti," slowly repeated Mrs. Clifford, "surely it cannot be! I have known that name before. But this man, you say, was a gipsy?"

"An associate of the tribe," returned Lionel; "but he had been many things before. And now a light breaks upon me. He had an old grudge, Zekiel said, against Copeland and his family. I have heard him, when half mad with intoxication, speaking of his former life, imprecate curses on one who had robbed him at once of a woman to whom he was attached, and a sum of money that would have made him independent, and saved him from the evil courses into which he had since fallen. That man, I doubt not, was Copeland."

"Aye, and it was from him that Dangerfield learned the secret of Elinor's birth," observed Mrs. Clifford. "Yes, none

ELINOR CLARE.

"I FLEW TO HER CHAMBER IN MY BRIDAL ROBES."

could tell it better than Claude Giotti, for he was one of the confederates."

Elinor started, scarcely could she believe her senses. But if she was surprised at this allusion to herself, still more was she at the tone in which Mrs. Clifford uttered it, and the bitter contempt that was portrayed on her features.

The emotion, however, quickly passed away, and the lady regained her usual cool composure of manner.

"All shall be in good time explained to you, Elinor," she observed, "at least, as far as I can explain it; and that will be enough for your advantage. But we must now think of Lionel, and the use he may put your information to. Tell me, was this man Claude one of the troop who occupied the ruined fortress at the time I visited it?"

"No, he quitted it a few days before," replied Lionel, "to return, as I understood, to England. There was a quarrel, I believe, between him and the Chief, as Dangerfield was called: but I knew not the particulars; for I never, if it were possible to avoid it, even entered that part of the ruin which the gang inhabited."

"Then he is most probably still in England," observed Mrs. Clifford; "and there is a possibility that he might be traced."

"Zekiel, if he were here," returned Lionel, "could, if he would, give us a clue to his haunts; for myself, I do not see any possible advantage to be gained, even if I were to accuse him; for the boy would, to a certainty, disavow all that he has owned to Elinor, if he were called upon to bear witness against one of his people. But if it could serve Elinor——"

"It could not *serve* her," repeated Mrs. Clifford; "for my mind is made up on the subject; and I will now tell you at once, she is the heiress of all I have to bestow! for I have no longer a doubt that she is the child of the two beings I once loved dearest on earth, George Blandford and Anna Warwick. To which of those names she has the most legitimate title I cannot say; for, if she was his wife, Captain Blandford never to me acknowledged it."

There was a bitter sting in these last words which effectually dissipated the warm gratitude with which Elinor had heard the first part of Mrs. Clifford's declaration, and the eloquent blood which rose to Lionel's cheek declared how deeply he sympathised But Mrs. Clifford's bad passions always passed away with the words in which she gave them vent; and the next instant she extended her hand to Elinor, with a look that pleaded for forgiveness; and the *amende* was received with the same frank cordiality that it was offered.

No further explanation, however, was then given or alluded to by Mrs. Clifford; and Elinor, though naturally agitated by the surprising and unexpected communication respecting her own affairs, was too deeply interested on Lionel's account not to suppress all personal anxiety while he was present; and the subject continued to be discussed, of the probability that Zekiel's information could be turned to account, and the guilty and desperate Giotti brought to punishment.

"If it be the same man I knew," observed Mrs. Clifford, "he

is remarkable for wanting two fingers of his left hand; though whether from natural deformity or accident I do not remember, or perhaps never inquired; for there was something to me so repulsive, or, as I then boldly termed it, villainous in his countenance, when, as the valet of Captain Blandford, he resided in this house, that I detested the man."

"It is the same," returned Lionel. "And truly is that countenance the indication of his mind and heart; for a more deliberate, cold-blooded villain does not exist. There are many undoubtedly among the half-civilised tribe with whom he has associated himself who are guilty of great crimes against society; but it may be truly said of them, they know not what they do. Totally uneducated, and taught from birth to consider themselves a distinct people from all the dwellers upon earth, whose hand is against every man, and every man's against them, all is to them lawful prey. Rapine, plunder, and stratagems to circumvent those whom they consider their natural enemies, is their lawful occupation; and, scarcely conscious of the light of reason, they follow the dictates of their violent passions. Yet many there are among them who possess noble and generous feelings. Their fidelity to each other, and to those who treat them with kindness and confidence, is most remarkable; their tenderness to their children, their parents—to all, in fact who are dependent on them —exemplary; and they shrink not from any sacrifice that can be productive of general good to their nation. Hospitable they are to excess, and will want themselves rather than refuse the stranger who is sunk so low as to solicit their assistance. But this Dirk—or, rather, Claude—shares not a single attribute of the gipsy's tribe, but their bad ones. He is a wretch without a heart—a mean, low, selfish wretch—one who would sell his own brother, if it would secure him the means of indulging in a brutal debauch. To the gipsies he is faithful, indeed, because he dares not be otherwise; but there are many among them who hate and distrust him; and, had it not been for that bond of union among them, which teaches them that the vilest and most despicable being on earth is he that betrays the secrets of their own tribe, I doubt not that there are many among those who witnessed the murder of poor Walter who would gladly have seen the murderer punished according to his deserts. But let me not," he continued, "thus occupy your attention with this degrading and depressing theme. I have but a short time longer to stay now; for my father will be uneasy until I return and assure him that I have obtained permission for him personally to wait on you, madam, and thank you for the kindness you have, on so many occasions, bestowed on his son—who need not I hope, repeat how deeply and gratefully he is impressed with it."

"A very flattering and graceful means of obtaining your dismission," observed Mrs. Clifford, smiling. "Come when he may, Mr. Moreton would, as your father, be welcome, even if I had not strong additional motives to respect him; but, as a formal invitation will, perhaps, be more satisfactory than this general one, tell Mr. Moreton that I shall be happy if he will dine with us to-morrow. By that time," she observed, looking with peculiar meaning at Elinor, "we shall all have recovered sufficiently from our flutterings and palpitations to be able to receive him with the attention he deserves."

Lionel had departed; and Elinor, now left alone with Mrs. Clifford, awaited, with mingled hope and fear, the communication that she doubted not that lady intended to make to her.

She was not deceived. Mrs. Clifford sat for some time, absorbed in her own reflections; and then, with more mildness and kindness of manner than was usual with her—for in manners only was she sometimes harsh—she desired Elinor to close the book she had opened to disguise her impatience, and come and sit by her.

"You are naturally anxious, my dear," she observed, "to know all that I can tell you respecting your birth; but, in so doing, I must relate some circumstances respecting a far less interesting personage—I mean myself. Stop, do not interrupt me: your heart, I have no doubt, dictates something very flattering to my merits; but stop till you hear my story out, before you compliment. You look too like your mother at this moment, for me to place implicit faith in your sincerity."

Tears filled Elinor's beautiful eyes; but she cast them down, to conceal that she was hurt, and Mrs. Clifford proceeded.

"I was not born a beauty, Elinor—of that you have proof that admits of no dispute; but I was born to that which, in the eyes of the greater part of the world, is far more desirable than beauty, which is, as I dare say you have often written in your copy-book, but skin deep—I mean that I was born heiress to a splendid fortune.

"I was the only child of my mother, who died soon after I was born; and by her will a sum which would have been a jointure for a princess devolved upon me when I should reach the mature age of twenty-five, provided I then married the person she had chosen for me. This was the son of her early friend, a Mrs. Blandford, who had died two or three years before, bequeathing to my mother's care her orphan-boy, with comparatively a slender provision.

" I say comparatively only to what I was destined to possess; for it was only a few thousands.

" If I refused him, or married another, the fortune was to pass entirely from my possession to his. There was no fear that I should refuse him; for, long before I knew of this arbitrary disposal of our affections, I had learned to love George Blandford.

" We were brought up together. My father, though thrice married, never had a son; and of his daughters, though they were beautiful, and I horribly ugly and ungainly, I was his favourite. George was his idol. Disappointed in his wishes for a son, he had adopted the boy as his own; and never did the fondest father more dote upon a boy than he did. It was his cherished wish to live to see us united; but he died while I was yet a child. And as if

———to make assurance doubly sure,
And take a bond of fate

all that he had to bequeath was left to George, on precisely the same conditions as my mother had made; and thus, if either refused to fulfil them, the other became the sole possessor of the wealth.

" I was not then so conscious as I have since become that my unfortunate face and person were antidotes to love. I was vain enough, I confess it, to believe that such compulsion on the part of my parents was unnecessary, and that George would not have needed the temptation of riches to have induced him to have chosen me.

" I could have been happy with him in a hovel; and I did not disguise from him the affection which had received my parents' sanction.

" By all and every one I was looked upon as his destined wife; and he, who I suppose had made up his mind to accept the fortune, with all its encumbrances, favoured my self-conceit, and affected to love me for that which perhaps had some title to his respect, though it could not win his affection—my mind and disposition.

" Well did he dissemble; but his heart was then disengaged, and the task was not so difficult.

" My sisters were both married, and in England; my father was no more; and readily did I yield to my *fond* lover's suggestion, that I should quit India, where I was born, and settle in that which I considered my mother-land. I came hither—yes, to this very house. His taste ornamented it. Yes, everything, even to this day, remains as he arranged they should."

Elinor glanced earnestly around her. How little did she think, when first she admired the splendour and taste which had decorated those magnificent apartments, that her father had presided in their arrangement.

Mrs. Clifford's eyes followed hers, and then she resumed her story.

" A very short time, however, had elapsed before Blandford began to show symptoms of restlessness and dissatisfaction. I had taken to be my companion a beautiful girl; I was ever an admirer of beauty in every shape, I suppose by force of contrast; and Anna Warwick was beauty itself.

" But you have seen your mother's portrait in my room, and I need not describe her. Lovely, however, as was her person, that was the least of her attractions. Mild, gentle, affectionate, highly accomplished, and of most fascinating manners, she was the admiration of all who knew her. Ever in extremes—it was my nature then to be so—I attached myself to her with a truth and ardour seldom, I believe, seen in similar circumstances; for she was entirely dependent on me.

" Her mother had died in giving her birth; and her father, a poor clergyman, had bestowed all that he had to educate her, and then departed from this vale of tears, leaving her to the mercy of the world. She was strongly recommended to me by her destitute situation, and the letter of recommendation she bore in her sweet face; and I took her to be my companion and bosom friend, in spite of the hints of many of my kind visitors, and the open advice of my sisters, who all declared that they would not have one in their house to eclipse them, as she must. If they thought so, who were handsome, what ought I to have thought, whose plainness must appear as completely a foil to her beauty?

" I was proud of being superior to such weakness, and of showing that I was so, and especially to my lover, as I believed him, who had so often complimented me on my strength of mind, and my freedom from the petty jealousies and envy that too often disgrace the female sex.

" To my great surprise, however, he did not appear so struck with my companion as I expected; he was silent and reserved whenever she was present, and never responded to my eager commendations of her when she was absent. I ought to have suspected these symptoms, for they were not natural to his disposition; but I did not. A..na was more open, or, rather, less deceptive than he was. She praised him highly, and ardently congratulated me on the happiness which awaited me in my projected marriage with such a man.

"I have said already, I believe, that Blandford became restless and dissatisfied soon after she came to reside with me. His visits were less frequent; and when he did come, his thoughts seemed always abstracted, and his spirits depressed.

"At last he confessed the truth, or what he declared to be the truth. He was dying of *ennui*, he said, wearied to death of idleness, and longing for an active life. He had never been able to find pleasure in dissipation; and, in short, it at last came out, he had determined on following his father's profession. I have omitted, I believe, to say that his father was a naval officer.

"There were yet three years before the time appointed for our marriage : before that time, in all probability, his services would no longer be required by his country, and he should settle down into a sober family-man, with the cheering reflection that his life had not been utterly useless and wasted.

"'If a cannon-ball does not take off your head,' I bluntly observed; for my anger at his obstinacy at that moment overpowered all other feelings, and I determined to show him that I thought as lightly of his proposed separation from me as he did.

"His only reply to this pettish speech was a melancholy smile, and, still more vexed, I continued,

"'Or send you home shorn of a leg or arm, or both, and perhaps divers other petty wounds and concussions, as mementos of——'

"I was interrupted by a faint groan from Miss Warwick, who was apparently uninterested in our conversation, sorting some music at the piano-forte. I did not even suspect that she had heard what had passed, and attributed to anything but the right cause her falling in a fit on the floor, before Blandford, who instantly started up to her assistance, could save her. How my eyes have been opened since !

"She was conveyed to her room; but she expressed a desire to be left alone, and I returned to my conference with Blandford. I was too proud to attempt to dissuade him from his fixed resolution; and in less than a month he was a commissioned officer on board one of his Majesty's ships, and had sailed for the Mediterranean.

"I suffered dreadfully—I do not wish to disguise the fact from you, Elinor; but I bore myself most heroically in the face of the world; and Anna Warwick was the sole depository of my grief, my sad forebodings; and deeply, though silently, did she appear to sympathise in my feelings.

"Blandford, however, returned in safety, long before the period at which I had been taught to expect him. He had distinguished himself highly in an engagement, had been made the bearer of dispatches, and, of course, was promoted. I was proud of his distinction in the eyes of the world—proud, too, of the feeling which, as I believed, made him fly to me, the instant he was dismissed from the Admiralty, to communicate his success; and (fool that I was) I was delighted to see that Anna Warwick shared in my exultation at his success.

"It is useless to dwell on all this; but I have done so, Elinor, to show you how thoroughly I was deceived. How can you wonder that I am now suspicious? that I distrust every one? that I am cold and insensible to every demonstration of affection towards myself? that I cannot believe that I was ever formed to be beloved?"

Elinor answered her only by her tears, and Mrs. Clifford resumed her story.

"Blandford returned to his duty; but peace shortly after rendered his close attendance to those duties unnecessary, and his leave of absence was often renewed. He again became a constant visitor here, and I was happy. I could not, however, be blind to the fact that Anna was changed, greatly changed; her health, her spirits, daily declined; she shunned all society; and, even when Blandford, who was always looked upon as one of the family, was here, she would, in spite of all my entreaties, keep her chamber. Yet still she professed unchanged, unalterable affection for me, and affected to rejoice in my approaching happiness.

"The day of our marriage was at length appointed; but the truth at last broke upon me. My once happy, if not ardent lover, no longer looked forward with pleasure to the event which he had so often regretted had been so long delayed. It seemed at last so even to me—it had long been plain to my real friends—that he wished to recede from his engagement. My sister at last avowed her belief that he had formed some other attachment, but that he was unwilling to relinquish the money, and sought rather to pique my pride into refusing him, than incur the penalty by declining to fulfil his engagements. My first impulse was to free him at once; but then the thought of the world's dread laugh, the triumph of my unknown rival, and the affected pity and commiseration which would be bestowed on the once envied heiress, all combined to deter me from this act of extravagant generosity, as my sisters truly styled my purpose. I wavered, and resolved, and again vacillated. Anna, to whom every thought of my heart was confided, appeared as much distressed as myself; but she declined giving me any counsel. It was so difficult to advise. She could not tell how she should act in my case; and then she would weep for the misery which she could not relieve me from. In the meantime, all the preparations for my marriage proceeded.

"I was then fond of show: and I was, when the orders were first given, proud of my handsome, gallant husband. Everything, therefore, was to be in the most magnificent style; and I could not now retract the orders that were given. It wanted but a week to the appointed day, and not a word had passed between Blandford and I which could reveal the misery both were suffering. Our altered looks, however, when we met, which was as seldom as possible, betrayed the fatal secret.

" Little did I think then, that every thought, every feeling of my heart were as well known to him as to myself. From Anna he learned all my struggles; and still gained hope, no doubt, that they would end as he wished; and that I, the poor, duped, deceived fool, should at the last, with the reckless generosity of my disposition, renounce him.

" But the day arrived; our friends assembled; the carriages were at the door to convey us to church.

"Anna alone was absent—she on whose aid and counsel I most relied.

" I flew to her chamber, dressed as I was in my bridal robes, and found her stretched on the bed in a succession of fainting fits. Her own maid and Hargrave—my poor old Hargrave—were there.

" She pulled me away when I would have thrown myself on the bed by the side of the sufferer.

" ' Go, dear madam, pray go; it is not fit you should be here,' she exclaimed.

"I was ever impatient of control, Elinor; and I would not listen to my faithful servant's persuasions. I would stay till the doctor, who had been sent for, arrived.   He came at that moment.   A whisper from Hargrave explained all ; and then he joined his entreaties to hers, that I would leave the room.

"'Do, dear lady, be persuaded,' added Hargrave, in a whisper. 'Captain Blandford is——'

"The name reached the ears of Anna, who had just revived ; and with a piercing scream, she exclaimed,

"'No, no, no ! do not deceive her ! he cannot, he dare not ! Oh, forgive me—forgive him !' and she seized my hand with a grasp that I have never forgotten ; and throwing herself from the bed, knelt at my feet.

"The whole truth instantly flashed upon my brain.   She, then, was my secret rival—she it was for whom I was despised and rejected.   I am ashamed to own, Elinor, that my rage was, at the first moment, dreadful ; but the doctor's earnest and authoritative manner recalled me to reason.

"'I must insist upon your leaving the room, the life of this young woman and that of her child is at stake.'

"Her child !   She was disgraced—ruined !   Blandford could not now marry her, now that her disgrace was made known to the world.   I was revenged ; and instantly I became calm.

"For a moment I retired to my room.   I suffered my bridesmaid to rearrange my veil ; and then, with apparent tranquillity, but with the fiercest passions boiling in my bosom, I repaired to the drawing-room, expecting to find my bridegroom there.

"But he was not there ; and on every's one's countenance was expressed consternation and uneasiness.

"Is not Blandford here ?' I inquired, with assumed levity : 'I thought I heard his voice.'

"'You did so,' replied my sister.   'He was here ; but he has pleaded illness, and has gone home again.'

"I sank down on the floor, totally overcome with this disappointment of my deep revenge ; for I had resolved to dissimulate my knowledge of his baseness, and force him either to go through the ceremony of marriage, or pay the penalty affixed to his refusal.

"When I recovered," continued Mrs. Clifford, who had paused to take breath, "I was alone with my sister and Hargrave. The wedding-party were gone, and I was left to ridicule and disgrace.

"It was more than a month before I could leave my bed ; but long before that Anna had left the house.   She had given birth to a dead child, and had departed, none knew whither, the

moment she had recovered sufficient strength.   Her maid, who
had evidently been her confidante in her long course of treachery
and deceit, had accompanied her.

"Blandford, too, was gone.   He had been recalled to active
service; and thus was I again disappointed of my cherished
revenge.   He had not renounced my hand—he had only, as it
appeared, postponed his claim.

"My friends made every exertion to trace Anna, in the hope
of discovering that she was his wife, and thus at once depriving
him of all hope of inheriting my fortune; for which I believe I
have forgotten to mention, he was my heir, if I died unmarried,
and his chance was at that time a good one.

"At last it was found out that she was living in France,
where Blandford sometimes resided with her for months together:
but that was no legal proof of their marriage.

"I was all this time labouring under a delusion.   I had
forgotten all that happened, and imagined from day to day that
Blandford was coming to claim me as his bride; and my sole
delight was to preserve everything in order for our nuptials.   It
was a harmless delusion; but I at length awakened from it—
awakened to hear that Blandford was no more.   He was drowned
I believe; but "—and she passed her hand over her forehead, to
conceal her agitation—" we will say no more of that, except that
his death made a strange revolution in my feelings; and still
more so, when I found that Anna was also in her grave.   She
had indeed truly loved him, and could not survive his loss, while
I—I——She had died, as it appeared, in giving birth to another
child; and, in the cemetery of Pere la Chaise at Paris, my
emissary copied the inscription to the memory of Anna Warwick.   It is doubtful, therefore, even now——but I will not
now pursue that theme.   I did not then know that any child
survived them; but you, Elinor, are her living image; and that
added to the other circumstances that have come to my knowledge,
leave not a doubt on my mind that you are their daughter.   Time
will, I hope, clear up the mystery to our satisfaction."

Elinor hoped so, too; but her spirits were too much depressed
to utter a word.   That she truly and sincerely pitied Mrs. Clifford cannot be doubted; but there were many points in her
narrative which left a strong impression that her own vanity
and violent passions had in a great measure led to the result
which had been so fatal to her.

The love of Blandford for Anna was so strictly natural, that
it was scarcely possible to condemn it; while Elinor secretly

inclined to the belief that it was less mercenary motives than a weak unwillingness to avow how they had deceived her, and she deceived herself, that had protracted the discovery.

There were two circumstances, however, which conveyed unmitigated sorrow to her bosom—the certainty that she was an orphan, and the fear that disgrace attended her birth; but she was not of a disposition to brood over irremediable evils:

Some natural tears she shed, but wiped them soon.

Mrs. Clifford seemingly relieved her mind of a heavy burthen, in this disclosure to Elinor; and the latter had the satisfaction of receiving from her the most undeniable proofs that, whatever feelings of resentment might yet survive in her bosom at the remembrance of the wrongs she had suffered, those feelings were not transmitted to the descendant of those by whom she had been wronged.

And when, at the hour appointed, Lionel and his father were received under Mrs. Clifford's hospitable roof, the anticipation of the latter was verified; and except those natural emotions which such an introduction could not fail to excite, at least in Elinor's bosom, all flutterings and palpitations had given place to more calm and chastened feelings.

The coldness and reserve which had, in his early days, characterised Mr. Moreton's manners, and veiled his real disposition, had long since vanished before the excitement of the different events which had marked his chequered life; and Elinor, as she watched the varied expression of his countenance —the tears of mournful recollection which could not be suppressed at thus beholding those who had administered to the comforts and witnessed the dying moments of his lost Felicia— the flush of joy and hope and pride with which he looked upon his son—and the mild and benevolent smile with which he strove to encourage her, and remove the agitation and embarrassment which it was natural she should feel under such circumstances —when she beheld all this, she could not but wonder at the strange infatuation which had blinded his unhappy wife, and rendered her so insensible to the sterling worth of his character.

Before they separated that night, every particle of reserve had vanished between those whose interests and feelings were destined henceforth to be indissolubly united. Mr. Moreton, who had so bitterly experienced the misery arising from an ill-assorted marriage—or one in which, to say the least, the heart was not consulted on that side which is, in most cases, more guided by its feelings than the dictates of reason—was most anxious for the completion of a union which certainly promised such different results.

The affection of Elinor and Lionel had been severely tried, and had stood the test. Never under any circumstances had a doubt or fear intruded of the love each bore to the other. They had loved, indeed, through "evil and through good report."

" And if such a marriage be not blessed, who dare hope for happiness on earth?" observed Mr. Moreton, as he pressed together their hands in his, and pronounced his cordial sanction to their union.

Had Elinor yielded to the wishes of Lionel, not an hour beyond what was absolutely necessary for the forms of law would have passed, before the performance of the ceremony which would unite them for ever; but it was the last time, as the former observed, smiling through her tears, that she should have a will of her own; and as Mrs. Clifford warmly asserted the propriety of her resolution, Lionel was compelled to yield, with as good a grace as he could assume, to their final decision, that the marriage should take place on that day month.

Mr. Moreton had already made such arrangements as placed his son in a state of independent affluence, far beyond what Lionel's most sanguine hopes or wishes could have anticipated; but they had both yet to learn that Mrs. Clifford's noble intentions towards Elinor constituted the latter heiress to a fortune which would, in the eyes of the world, have made her an enviable match for the highest and noblest in the land.

But for the one cloud which still hung threatening over their prospects, Elinor and Lionel would now have been the happiest of created beings; but in the mind of the former there still lingered fears connected with past events. She could not but remember that the Gipsy Chief still lived; and with undiminished will, if not power, to injure.

Lionel was yet uncleared, in the eyes of the world, from the dreadful imputation which had been cast upon him; and often in her daily visions, as well as her nightly dreams, were mingled images of terror which scarcely even his presence and apparent freedom from all uneasiness could for a short time remove.

She would, indeed, have felt much more uneasy had she known that Lionel was actually seeking that danger which she believed could only be avoided by his present situation remaining unknown to those who had pursued him with such unrelenting animosity; but it was not Lionel's disposition quietly to submit to undeserved disgrace, or to endeavour to shield himself by his new position in society from a full investigation of the foul charge which had been brought against him.

For the sake of his father's peace he had preserved and enjoined on Elinor and Mrs. Clifford entire silence as to the circumstances connected with Walter Copeland's death; but to Mr. Saville, the faithful and untiring friend of the elder Mr. Moreton, he communicated without reserve every particular of that tragical event; and while all appeared, even to Elinor, to be forgotten except by her, and when pressed by her fears she renewed the subject, the agents of Lionel, guided by Mr. Saville's instructions, were indefatigably employed in endeavouring to trace out, not only the retreat of Copeland, but of every one who could throw the least light on the subject; of the gipsies, who, according to Zekiel's account, had been many of them witnesses of the murder; of Zekiel himself; and, though last enumerated, not certainly the least important, the actual murderer, Dirk, as he was called.

All this, however, Lionel carefully concealed from Elinor and his other friends; and when, at the appointed time, he led her to the altar, it was with a brow as clear and unclouded as if

No carking care dwelt on his mind.

The ceremony was performed as privately as possible, Mr. Moreton being, however, with difficulty persuaded to yield up his own wishes, which would have led him to make an ostentatious display of the pride and gratification he felt in an event which he hoped and trusted was to secure the happiness and comfort of his latter days. But the management of Mrs. Clifford prevailed, when he had positively refused to listen to his son's remonstrances, or Elinor's gentle pleadings; and few suspected that in the modest pair who so assiduously shunned observation, and whose plain and unpretending appearance would scarcely have attracted a second glance, had it not been for the beauty of the bride and the manly grace of the bridegroom, they beheld the heirs of two splendid fortunes.

CHAPTER XXV.

Oh! sacred grief, by whom thus souls are tried,
Sent not to punish mortals, but to guide;
If thou art mine—and who shall proudly dare
To tell his Maker he has had his share?
Still let me feel for what my pangs are sent,
And be my guide, and not my punishment.

CRABBE.

Some months had winged their rapid flight since the hour which had witnessed the union of Elinor and Lionel; and the former had, in the calm and quiet happiness of her new situation, seemed almost to forget the fear that had at first perpetually recurred to make her tremble, lest by some untoward event their felicity should be interrupted.

Lionel had so far confided to her the steps he had taken as to assure her that every means he could devise to discover Mr. Copeland and his family had been fruitless. It was firmly believed in the neighbourhood of his former residence, that he had emigrated to America—an idea which he had himself originated, though none could tell why he had chosen to wrap his intentions or movements in so much mystery. If this were true, and Elinor saw no reason to doubt it, she felt that all apprehension on the score of animosity towards Lionel was at an end; and for the eventually clearing up even the shadow of a doubt, if there existed any in the minds of others, she trusted in that Providence which had protected them through so many imminent perils. But this state of blissful delusion was destined not long to last.

On the morning of Elinor's marriage Mrs. Clifford had formally resigned to her the house in May Fair, with all it contained, alleging that she had always considered it only held in trust for George Blandford or his heir; and though Elinor as yet could claim no legal right to that title, she (Mrs. Clifford) was perfectly satisfied that no one could dispute the claim of the former. There, therefore, they continued to reside, Mrs. Clifford remaining their honoured guest, and affording them the countenance and protection which their novel station in life in some measure required; though even the once supercilious and contemptuous Mrs. Burchall was compelled to acknowledge, that no one who beheld her could suspect that Mrs. Lionel

Moreton had ever been other than what she now appeared—" a lady born and bred."

"And so she was, and so she is," retorted the warm-hearted old housekeeper, Mrs. Hargrave. "Her mother was a lady in birth and education and manners, and her father the finest gentleman that ever my eyes were set upon; and, though she was for a time crushed by villany and misfortune, no one that had eyes or understanding could have doubted in her worst days that my young mistress was of good parentage, and born to better fortune than seemed then to have fallen to her lot."

To return to our story.—It had been decided that the approaching spring should be spent by the happy domestic party, including Mr. Moreton, who passed now nearly all his time in May Fair, in making a tour through the most picturesque counties of their native land, and finally decide where they should permanently fix their country residence. The time fixed for their departure was near at hand; and Elinor and Lionel, in an early ramble, stolen before Mrs. Clifford's usual hour of rising, had been anticipating the delight they should feel in the proposed excursion, when, as they were returning through the park, Elinor's eye was attracted by the appearance of a tall and graceful looking female, who was pacing hurriedly and unsteadily along the margin of the Serpentine River on the opposite side. Even at that distance she felt certain that it was Isabel Copeland she beheld; and unable to give utterance to a single word, she could only press Lionel's arm, on which she was leaning, and point to the object which had suspended all her faculties.

"Do not alarm yourself, my life," he exclaimed, beholding with terror the ghastly paleness of her countenance. "The poor woman, probably, has no such intentions as you apprehend; and if she has——Oh, if I dare leave you," he hastily added, as his anxious eye again followed the direction of her phrenzied gaze, and he beheld the wretched woman—whom, however, he still did not recognise—deliberately take off her bonnet and shawl, and deposit them on the grass at some distance from the water, thus leaving not a doubt of her intentions.

"Fly! fly! save her! save her!" gasped Elinor. "Think not of me—save her!"

And Lionel hesitated no longer: but almost literally obeyed her, flying rather than running towards the object of his anxiety, and waving his arms in an attitude of command and entreaty, while he loudly called upon her, to attract her attention, which had before seemed totally absorbed in the purpose she meditated.

ELINOR CLARE.

SHE HAD FALLEN ON HER KNEES, IMPLORING PARDON.

At the sound of his voice, Isabel — for it was indeed the wretched, ruined Isabel—raised her face, which had been before bent to the earth, and concealed by the long raven locks, which had escaped from their confinement. She had fallen on her knees, and raised her clasped hands, as if imploring pardon from that heaven towards which she dared not lift her eyes; but at the sound of Lionel's frantic cries, she started to her feet, stood for an instant in wild suspense, and then, uttering a piercing shriek, plunged into the water, which instantly closed over her. That heart-piercing shriek was re-echoed from the lips of Elinor, who distinctly beheld the tragic consummation of her fears, but she saw not what followed—she knew not that Lionel had unhesitatingly thrown off his coat, and, at the moment the miserable girl rose to the surface had dashed into the water, and borne her up until other assistance arrived, and she was conveyed to the shore.

There were plenty to proffer aid to Elinor, who had fainted; for there were many who had beheld the whole scene, though not near enough to be of service in assisting to prevent the rash act; and when she recovered, all were eager to assure her that the gentleman and the female whom he had rescued were both safe. They had seen him assisting in conveying the wretched woman to the receiving-house, which they pointed out, and every tongue was loud in praise of his humanity and courage.

Elinor scarcely heard what they said, but her eyes were strained in the direction to which they pointed; and she would have rushed thither, but that her trembling limbs refused their support; and she was compelled to remain on the seat to which she had been conveyed by some of the compassionate persons who now surrounded her. At the suggestion of a gentleman, a man was despatched to the nearest stand for a hackney-coach. Just as it arrived, Lionel himself came to her, trying to veil the anguish his countenance betrayed by assuming a tone of calmness, and assuring her that the poor young woman, the object of her anxiety, was safe and well attended to; and that they had better now go home, as they could do no more.

"But must we leave her among strangers, without a friend? Oh, Lionel, let me go to her!" whispered Elinor, as he assisted her to rise.

Lionel looked anxiously in her face.

"Do you, then, know—but it is impossible," he observed, in faltering accents.

"Oh yes, I know all," she eagerly replied. "It is Isabel; her form—her step—I knew it instantly. Do not refuse me; let me see her."

"Not now, Elinor, I cannot," he replied, "for my sake, for your own, for hers. The sight of you would——be persuaded, and trust to me. I will return to her the moment I have seen you safe at home. Do not fear, they would not suffer her to depart, even if she were able."

"It is highly necessary the gentleman should change his wet clothes as soon as possible," observed one of the bystanders; and Elinor, thus recalled to the recollection, or rather, for the first time comprehending that Lionel had been in the water, and the dangerous consequences that might result from it, now became as anxious for his going as she had been before desirous to stay; and having hastily returned his thanks to those who had assisted Elinor, and more substantially rewarded one or two whose appearance warranted the offer of money, he lifted her into the coach, and was driven rapidly away.

A few brief minutes brought them to the door of their residence; but that was time sufficient for Lionel to reveal all he knew to Elinor; and that, indeed, amounted to no more than that it *was* Isabel whom he had rescued; and that, though life was not extinct, as he was assured by those around her whom he had left employing the proper means for her recovery, he had but faint hopes.

"But if she does recover?" demanded Elinor.

"If she does, my love, I will not hinder you a moment from obeying the dictates of your own kind heart; but I must warn you, that the cause of her rash attempt is but too evident. She has no ring on her finger, and yet she is in the way to become a mother."

A crimson blush of shame for the lost Isabel for a moment dyed Elinor's pale cheek; but the next, the desire to save and to befriend her resumed its full way, and she hastened to consult with Mrs. Hargrave as to the necessary preparations to receive the unhappy girl.

All, however, was in vain. Isabel indeed recovered sufficiently to recognise Lionel and Elinor, who hastened with him to attend the death-bed of her early friend. She lived long enough to deplore with true penitence the mad attempt she had made to rush uncalled into the presence of her Creator, and to relate the cause which had driven her to desperation. The villain Evelyn was a married man; and the coldness and heartlessness with which he disclosed to her this fact, when pressed to perform his promise of making her his wife, had goaded her to madness.

"Never let my poor father, or my dear, dear Annie know how I died. I have told them I should come back to them a proud and happy wife; and see, see what I am—a murderer !—the murderer of my child—of——Oh, God, forgive me !"

The prayer for forgiveness to that Great Being who judges in mercy, and not in wrath, his erring children, were the last words that dwelt on her faltering lips; and in a few moments the pale and senseless clay was all that remained of the beautiful and proud Isabel Copeland.

Deeply and affectionately was she lamented by both Lionel

and Elinor; and when, in process of time, two lovely girls were added to the boys who had blessed the first years of their happy union, the memory of their early affection was perpetuated by the former bestowing on these sweet pledges of love the names of Isabel and Annie.

Possessed now of a clue to Mr. Copeland's retreat, Lionel hastened to impart the particulars to his indefatigable friend, Mr. Saville, who without delay determined to see the old man, and, by the force of truth alone, as he believed, force him to acknowledge his conviction of the falsehood of his former accusations. Little did he think that he had been already anticipated. On the evening of that very day that Isabel breathed her last, a strange and wild-looking youth entered, without any announcement, the room in which the now feeble though still robust old man was seated in his easy chair by the fire. He was too well dressed to admit of the idea that he came to beg; and yet the strangeness and embarrassment of his manner seemed to predicate that he required some assistance.

"Who are you? and what do you want?" demanded the old man, as the youth threw himself into a chair, apparently breathless and exhausted.

"Help for a dying man—one who never did harm to you or yours," he replied; "and would have saved the poor boy, if he had been in time. Paul is dying, Farmer Copeland—dying in yon barn" (and he pointed with his finger to an outbuilding at some little distance). "It was that villain Dirk who stabbed him; but he will swing on the gallows for it. Paul has sworn it, and he always keeps his word."

"And who is Paul? and what have I to do——"

"Oh, father, it is the gipsy boy who used to sing so sweetly," exclaimed Annie, who had entered the room, and heard the last part of his speech.

"The gipsies!" exclaimed Copeland, starting up, "have they pursued me even hither? Begone, boy—your appearance has ever brought ruin and destruction in its train."

"There was never a finger lifted against you by our people, Farmer Copeland, except by Dirk," returned the youth angrily; "and he had been your enemy in olden time—you best know why. But Paul could tell all, and you refuse to listen to him. I bore him hither three weary miles on my back, because he said he should die easy, if he had told you all; but now——"

"Paul!—Dirk!" repeated Copeland, in wild amazement, "I know not——but where is the man you speak of? I will go—"

"Oh no, dear father, not alone," exclaimed Annie, whose habitual timidity time had not yet conquered; "if the man is requiring assistance, let him be brought here—nothing can be done for him in that desolate place."

Mr. Copeland yielded, and resumed his seat; while Annie hastened to give directions to the two men who composed their household, to proceed with Zekiel (for of course he was their strange visitor) to the barn, and obey his directions.

In a few minutes the once bold and formidable Gipsy Chief was borne into the kitchen; but oh, how changed!—how fallen! His eye, indeed, still glared with the vindictive fire of evil passions; but his features were sunken, the ghastly paleness of death overspread his countenance, and the vital stream of life dyed his soiled and neglected clothing. Zekiel had bandaged the wound with all the skill he possessed, and the blood had ceased to flow; but death was fast approaching and the Chief knew it.

"I have no time to lose," he observed, in hollow accents; " I wished but to live to bid you revenge the death of your son and mine; for we have both fallen by the same treacherous and blood-thirsty-villain."

Copeland groaned heavily.

"Speak—his name!" he uttered, in faltering accents.

"In this country, and among the people with whom he has been long associated, he is known by the name of Dirk," responded the dying man; "but you have known him by his true appellation, when you, too, bore another. You have not forgotten the villain Claude Giotti, he who robbed the dead, and was robbed in his turn by one more cunning and specious. Ha! I see I have you now," he continued, half raising himself up, with the wild fury of a demon gleaming in his eyes, " swear, then, that you will pursue him to the scaffold—swear that you will revenge your murdered son, and me, still more foully murdered; for the rash boy sought his fate, while I had more than once perilled my own life to save the villain from his merited punishment."

The Gipsy Chief sank back into the arms of Zekiel, groaning with pain, and exhausted by the exertion he had made; and Copeland, motionless and paralysed, as it seemed, by terror, in vain attempted to utter a word, until Annie approached to offer him succour.

"Go, girl," he exclaimed, with vehemence, pushing her from him. " Go, you must not hear the black tale of your father's guilt, or the heavy vengeance that has fallen upon him. And yet it is just that you should be taught to hate me. My other children are lost to me, and you—you will scorn, despise——"

"No, father, no," interrupted Annie, extricating herself from his embrace; for he had thrown his arms around her neck, and strained her to his bosom. "Let me hear nothing that you would wish concealed. To me you have ever been the kindest and best of parents; and Heaven prosper me as I fulfil my duty towards you."

She quitted the room, and Dangerfield once more raised his heavy eyes.

"My time for restitution, if I could ever have made it, is cut short by the hand of violence," he observed, "but let me at least do one act of justice. The youth whom you knew by the name of Edward Hatherleigh was innocent of even the remotest knowledge of the murder of your son. This boy, this simple boy, was witness of the deed. He knows that Dirk's hand struck the blow. Zekiel, my dying blessing or my curse be upon you, as you are faithful. You can trace his haunts, you can track him to his lair——"

"Trust me for that," interrupted Zekiel, his eyes sending forth flashes of the same unholy fire that glowed in the faded orbs of the dying Chief. "I will never leave him," continued the half-maniac boy, "till I see his bones whitening on the gibbet."

"My boy, my own spirit, my son!" exclaimed the Chief, raising himself up, and clasping the poor neglected child of misery in the strong embrace of death.

It was the last effort. In a few moments that firm and nervous grasp relaxed, his arms fell powerless, and, with one deep sigh, and a half uttered prayer for the mercy which he had but the moment before denied to others, he closed his eyes in death.

"You will lay him in a decent grave, and let prayers be said over him; for he was once a gentleman and a Christian. And I shall walk next the coffin, because I was his only son," observed Zekiel, as, after long and breathlessly watching by the ghastly corpse, he rose from his knees, convinced that his further cares were useless. "Do not grudge money," he continued, with a significant nod of his head; "for Master Ned will pay it all, though he was not his son."

"And who is Master Ned, boy?" demanded Copeland, who, relieved from his immediate fears of the betrayal of the secret of his life by the death of the Chief, had returned in a great measure to his natural habits of selfish parsimony.

" Who is he ?" returned Zekiel, with a significant smile, " you ought to know. But I forget, he is not now Master Ned, but Lionel Moreton, the son of a grand, rich gentleman; and Elinor, the girl whom you would have hunted to death, is——"

" Elinor, what know you of Elinor ?" exclaimed Copeland, in a tone of alarm, as Zekiel paused, struck with the expression of the old man's countenance.

It was the invariable practice of the half-witted boy never to reply to direct interrogation. Copeland's question, therefore, was only at first answered by a significant shake of the head; and then, suddenly a recollection occurring to his mind, that he had it in his power to indulge his malicious propensity to teaze, he observed,

" You'll hear fast enough, when she comes with her grand friends and relations; for she will not be afraid of you, nor obliged to hide from you now,"

Zekiel in this spoke only at random, nor knew how near it was to the truth; but Mr. Copeland instantly believed that the secret so many years hidden, and from his long course of prosperity until lately almost forgotten even by himself, was now revealed to the whole world; and leaning back in his chair, he murmured,

" God help me; I shall then be in my old age disgraced, a beggar! And yet, how can they prove—how can they prove ——No, no, I can set them at defiance—they can prove nothing."

" Dirk has told everything," muttered Zekiel, with a cunning leer of mischief.

" Dirk—Dirk is a felon! a murderer! a wretch whom none can listen to, none dare believe !" exclaimed the old man, with vehemence. " No, no," and he burst into a forced and unnatural laugh; " I need not fear what Dirk can say of me."

" You need not, if I once come up with him," returned Zekiel; " but I must go, to let our people know that the Chief is dead," he added, in a mournful voice. " There will be weeping to-night in the tents."

Mr. Copeland would have prevented his departure; for how without him was he to explain the cause of the violent death the wretched man had met with? But Zekiel was not to be restrained from his purpose by argument or persuasion; and merely observing, in reply, " I shall be back in time, I tell you, to follow him to the grave," he rushed out of the house.

Not many hours had elapsed from that time, ere the boy

presented himself at the door of Lionel Moreton's residence, and was instantly admitted; for the servants had been warned, on Mrs. Clifford's first arrival, in the expectation that he would, some time or other, of his own accord, seek his former friends.

The recent melancholy event—the death of Isabel, had clouded all their spirits; yet he was received with a hearty welcome.

"You are tired of wandering, I hope, at last, Zekiel," observed Lionel, "or perhaps (and he looked keenly at him) you did not succeed in finding the friend you sought."

"If you mean Paul," returned the boy, with solemnity, "I have found him, and lost him for ever; Paul is dead!"

Dead! The word seemed to have an electrical effect upon all present, but on none more than Mr. Moreton, who was sitting, unnoticed by Zekiel, in the corner of a sofa, earnestly surveying the youth of whom he had heard so much, and who instantly comprehended of whom he spoke.

"Dead!" he repeated, in a tremulous voice. "Tell me where—how did he die? Did he speak of me!—did he repent?"

"Repent!" repeated Zekiel, disdainfully. "No, he spoke of nobody but Dirk, the villain; and he repented only that he could not live to see him brought to the gallows, as he will be, and shall be; for I have sworn it, and I am Paul's own son. None ever escaped him who had injured him, and Dirk shall not escape me."

By degrees the whole particulars of the Gipsy Chief's tragical death were revealed; for Zekiel had learned in what relation Mr. Moreton stood to the wretched man, and he no longer thought it necessary to affect reserve.

It appeared that by some means Paul, as the boy persisted in calling him, had discovered Mr. Copeland's present residence. What had been his motive in making a journey thither, Zekiel knew not; but it might be readily guessed by those who understood his character, that he expected to extort a sum of money, by discovering to him that he was in possession of the secrets of his early life. There had long existed a deadly feud between the Chief and his former friend, and it was probable that Dirk suspected that it was the intention of the Chief to betray to Copeland the murderer of his son. Under this impression, he had dogged the steps of the Chief from the time he left the tents, which he had on the pretext that he was going a different route.

"Paul had appointed me to follow him by another road, and to join at a place where we had been before, about three miles from Farmer Copeland's house," continued Zekiel, "for he said I might be useful, and he did not wish our people to know that we were gone together. But I missed my way; and Paul, tired with his long walk, had laid himself down in the grass to sleep, little thinking the blood-thirsty tiger was waiting to spring upon him. Dirk dared not attack him openly; for he knew he was not a match for Paul; and so he crept upon him while he slept, and, like a base coward as he is, stabbed him, as he thought, no doubt, to the heart. But he missed his aim; and Paul came to himself in time to see who the villain was, who was flying away for his life. I came in sight directly afterwards," continued the boy, in a tone of deep dejection, "but it was too late to save him."

Zekiel paused for a few moments, and then proceeded to relate the circumstances of the Chief's death, which have been already narrated.

To say that there were any who listened to this detail who regretted that the career of fraud and villainy and vice was closed, from which it was hopeless that Oliver Moreton would ever have been reclaimed, would be to assert that which could not be true. Yet the circumstances of his death were such as none concerned could think of without shuddering, and tended greatly to damp the joy and exultation which Lionel's complete exculpation from the unjust accusations of Mr. Copeland were calculated to produce. To Mr. Moreton it was a sad blow to learn for the first time that such an accusation had ever been brought against his son; and he agreed with Lionel that every means that could possibly be devised should be immediately taken to trace and bring to justice the murderer Dirk.

Zekiel smiled contemptuously as he listened to their consultation on this subject.

"If you think to trap a cunning fox like him, that way, you are mistaken," he observed. "It must be those who know where he earths——"

"But the gipsies will not protect the murderer of their Chief, Zekiel," observed Lionel, "some of them will betray him."

Zekiel shook his head with an air of dejection.

"Dirk has made his story good with most of them," he replied, "for they believe that Paul was treacherous, and deserved his doom. Do you think, if he had been to them what he once was, that they would leave him to be buried by strangers? No, they have never trusted or honoured him as they used to do, since he left them to go over the seas; and he has long thought that one day or other he should meet his fate from them. But Dirk, he was the last that——"

" Then Dirk is now with them, and you know where they are encamped," observed Lionel.

" I did not say so," returned Zekiel, " and, if he were, that is not the place to seek him. Stop a while, and you shall see whether I keep my word to the Chief or not."

" But you must expose yourself to danger, Zekiel," observed Mrs. Clifford.

" Danger!" he repeated, scornfully, " what do you know of danger? But I must away again, before the sun rises, and I want rest and food."

" You shall have all you want," returned Lionel ; " but whither do you go now ?"

" To the funeral of the Chief, to be sure," he replied, with an air of importance. " I am his son, his only son; he owned it when he was dying; and they cannot bury him without me. I thought our people," he continued, in a mournful tone, " would all have followed as they should do; but they say he was a traitor, and should be buried as a dog. But he shall have a proper Christian burial; and that is why I have come to you for money to pay for it; for yon old stingy hound, old Cope-land——"

" Saville will take upon himself the direction of the funeral," observed Mr. Moreton to Lionel, in a tremulous voice, " none can be more proper than he for——"

" Then I am not to be trusted," interrupted Zekiel, passion-ately. " Do you think I would steal the money, old man ?"

Lionel interfered to pacify him. A larger sum than probably he had ever seen was put into his possession; and, with the assurance that nothing should be done but according to his wishes he was dismissed to the rest and refreshment he evidently needed.

The remains of the Gipsy Chief were, under the superintendence of Mr. Saville, consigned to their last dwelling-place, in a manner that befitted rather his birth and the respectability of his surviving relatives than the wretched, vagrant life he had so long led. It was not until after this melancholy ceremony was concluded, that Mr. Saville disclosed to Copeland, who was evidently rejoiced to be relieved from all trouble and responsi-bility on the score of the funeral, that he had another and more important errand to fulfil.

It had been arranged that the melancholy death of Isabel

should be concealed from him until the first shock was over, of the discovery of Dirk's connection with his former life, and the concealment of Elinor's birth; but the stubborn and hard denial with which he met Mr. Saville's questions on the subject, his positive assertion that Elinor was the child of his sister, and that he knew not even the names of George Blandford or Anna Warwick, irritated Mr. Saville, and rendered him indifferent to the sufferings he might inflict.

"Are you, then, still so insensible to the punishment—the righteous punishment that has fallen upon you, old man," observed the latter, "as to still persevere in fraud and falsehood which can now answer no purpose, since, as I have before observed, Elinor—now Mrs. Lionel Moreton—seeks no restitution at your hands, but that of her birthright? Let me then try whether gratitude can influence your hard heart. You had a daughter—Isabel."

The old man gasped for breath,

"What of her?" he tremulously demanded. "She has deserted me—disgraced——"

"She has expiated all her errors in death," returned Mr. Saville, solemnly, "the second violent death that has befallen the offspring of him who robbed the orphan of even her name, and would have pursued her to destruction, had not that Providence which ever watches over innocence——"

"Death!—a violent death!" repeated the old man, with quivering lips, "another lost! It is true—the hand of Heaven is on me. The children are punished for the guilt of the father! Tell me—my Isabel, where, how did——"

"She died in the arms of Elinor," returned Mr. Saville, "that Elinor whom you robbed, vilified——but I will tell you all the circumstances, and leave to your own heart the course you ought to pursue."

In silence, uninterrupted except by his convulsive sobs, the old man listened to the detail of Isabel's tragical death, the noble effort made by Lionel to save her, and Elinor's affectionate attention to her to the last moment of her life.

There was evidently a hard struggle in the old man's mind, before he could utter a word, when the melancholy tale was concluded; but at length he spoke.

"Heaven will reward them—I cannot," he observed, "but such restitution as I can make, I will. It is true, Elinor was the child of Captain and Mrs. Blandford, the register of whose marriage will be found in the parish-church of Charlton, in

Kent. My deceased wife, who was then Miss Warwick's maid, and Giotti, the captain's valet, witnessed the ceremony. I was then house-steward to Mrs. Clifford; but circumstances occasioned me soon after to leave, and I went abroad with a family."

The circumstances which he thus slightingly passed over Mr. Saville knew were, that he had lost at a low gaming-table a sum of money with which he had been entrusted by Mrs. Clifford; but the former said nothing, and the old man proceeded to state, that he had in Paris again renewed his acquaintance with the Italian valet of Captain Blandford, and the female attendant of Mrs. Blandford, to whom he had long been attached, though she was too prudent, he said, to marry without some certain provision.

Giotti was his rival, that he well knew; but the wily and mercenary woman contrived to keep them friends, and lulled both into security, by assuring each in secret of her attachment. The opportunity which she had so long and anxiously, though vaguely sought, at length arrived. The intelligence of Captain Blandford's death was fatal to his adoring wife.

Her constitution was previously undermined by the many conflicts she had undergone, and the anxieties she had suffered; and she had died a few hours after the fatal intelligence reached her, having given birth again prematurely to a dead child, and leaving to the mercy of her treacherous domestics the only surviving issue of her marriage, Elinor, then an infant.

All that Captain Blandford possessed in the world besides his profession, amounting to nearly three thousand pounds, had been invested in the hands of an agent in Paris, in the name of his wife and child. To become possessed of this sum became now the object of the dishonest and ungrateful domestics.

According to Copeland's account, the plan was concocted between Giotti and the female, and they succeeded; but, be that as it might, it was plain that Copeland and the woman, to whom he had been long before secretly united, had made the Italian their dupe, and had fled to England, bringing with them Elinor, who had been disposed of as before related—disposed of in such a manner as effectually, as Copeland—or Leonard, for that, it seemed, was his real name—and his wife had supposed, to prevent all possibility of her real birth or history being ever discovered.

All his undertakings had prospered, and he had become, in appearance at least, a happy and a wealthy man; but the constant sight of Elinor, the living image of her mother, had kept before him, as he now acknowledged, the constant recollection of his cruel dishonesty, and made him hate her.

Of Giotti, or the life the latter had led, he had never heard, until the dying declaration of the Gipsy Chief pointed him out as the murderer of his son, under the name of Dirk; and thus first awakened his conscience to the conviction that the sorrows that had befallen him were but a just retribution for his evil deeds.

CONCLUSION.

Two years had passed, and the stern and crafty Copeland reposed in the same grave with Isabel. Annie was now the treasured and cherished companion of Elinor and Lionel, who in their present happiness endeavoured to forget the sorrows and misfortunes of their early days.

The stormy passions, the crimes and miseries, which had marked the career of the Gipsy Chief, were buried in oblivion, under the plain stone inscribed merely with the name of Oliver Moreton, in the humble churchyard of an obscure village in Surrey; and except that the murderer Dirk was still undiscovered, and at liberty, and that Zekiel still continued his wild and wandering life, in spite of all persuasion or attempt to domesticate him, nothing would have existed to excite a painful feeling in the bosom of the happy and domestic party, including Mrs. Clifford and Mr. Moreton, who divided their time between a beautiful mansion and estate which Lionel had purchased, on the banks of the romantic and picturesque river Wye, and their splendid residence in the metropolis.

Thither Zekiel often came, and sojourned with them for a few days at a time; sometimes only a few hours, according to his wayward fancy, but ever receiving a most bountiful supply from his friends, to prevent his being tempted to return to his former mendicant and predatory habits.

The second summer of their residence in Monmouthshire had passed, and they had just returned to May Fair, when the boy, whom they had heard nothing of for the last two months, suddenly made his appearance.

"I have him at last!" he wildly exclaimed. "Yes, I have tracked him from spot to spot, and still he has escaped me; but now come with me, and you shall see the villain, and hear how I will taunt him."

The females of the family were absent; and Lionel, scarcely reflecting what he was doing, yielded to the vehemence and impetuosity of the boy, or, rather, now man—for Zekiel had wonderfully increased in stature—and left the house with him, without inquiring whither he was leading him.

"It is a long way, and you cannot walk fast enough," observed Zekiel, "for every minute that is lost burns my heart."

"I will call a coach," returned Lionel, "but what prison is he in?"

"Prison!" repeated Zekiel, "he is not in any prison. Yet— no, no, they would not listen to my story; for they say I am mad and foolish. No, it is you that must send him to prison, but not till——"

"Had we not better, then, take assistance with us?" demanded Lionel. "He is a desperate fellow."

"Assistance!" repeated Zekiel, contemptuously, "what for? Are we not two to one, and young and strong? while he—— but if we want assistance, there is plenty to be had on the spot."

Lionel was ashamed to seem to shrink from the encounter which Zekiel thought so lightly of; and he entered the coach, which the latter ordered to be driven to an obscure place in Southwark.

They alighted at the end of a wretched and squalid lane; and, heedless of the observation their appearance excited among the miserable inhabitants, proceeded to one of the most ruinous and dilapidated of the habitations. A haggard-looking woman was seated on the door-step, with her arms folded under her apron, and a short, black pipe in her mouth; but she instantly arose at their approach.

"So you are come, then, honey?" she observed, in a broad Irish accent. "Well, all is right, he is up stairs."

Zekiel nodded, and rushed forward in the direction to which she pointed; and Lionel followed. But the stairs were dark and narrow; and before the latter reached the top, Zekiel had burst into the room.

"Now then, villain—murderer, I have you," he exclaimed, throwing himself upon Dirk, who was seated by a miserable fire, his head resting on a table, on which stood a bottle and glass.

There was a deadly struggle; for each had seized the other with the grasp of desperation. Lionel rushed forward in time to avert the blow which Dirk was meditating with his usual weapon, a knife, or stiletto, which he constantly wore in his bosom; but all his strength failed in separating the deadly combatants. Nor did he succeed until, at length, Dirk's hold relaxed, and he fell back exhausted; while Zekiel, equally overpowered, staggered to a seat, unable, for some moments, to utter a word.

In a short time, however, his eye again lighted up with almost supernatural brilliancy, and he burst into a laugh of bitter derision of his enemy.

"Ha! ha! ha!" he exclaimed, "you forgot, Dirk, when you treacherously murdered the Chief, that there was still one of his blood left to revenge him. You killed the noblest animal of the forest; but there was a cub left of the true breed. I have you now, coward! treacherous coward! Do you not feel the hangman's noose already round your neck? Do you not hear the groans and hisses of thousands that will come to see you die the death of a dog? Do you not hear the creak of the irons which will hold your bones together, as you swing backward and forward on the high gibbet that will be built for you on the spot where you did the deed of blood? You will have no grave, Dirk, they will say no prayers over you, or bid God rest your soul, as they did over him you murdered. He lies under the smooth, green turf, and the sun shines upon his resting-place, and flowers will grow over it. And none can ever disturb his bones; for they are laid in holy ground; but your worthless carcase, the very dogs will bark at it, and birds of prey—aye, even the filthy carrion crow——"

"What does the idiot mean?" exclaimed Dirk, who had now recovered his recollection. "What is it that has brought you here?" he continued, looking at Lionel, "to encourage, as it seems, the wild ravings and violence of that poor fool who——"

"Fool, am I?" repeated Zekiel, with his peculiar, deriding, unnatural laugh. "Dirk, when the cap is drawn over your face, and you are kicking in the air, never again to touch the earth that you have stained with blood, till your flesh is withered and your bones drop piecemeal from their iron gyves, who will look the fool then? Will it be you, or I? who will be there to laugh at you, to spit upon you, as I do now, to howl in your ear— Remember Paul Dangerfield, and that poor boy, too, Walter Copeland. His father knew it all, knew whose ruffian hand struck that blow; and though he cannot leave his grave to see his son's murderer brought to his just punishment——"

"Copeland dead!" exclaimed Dirk, thrown off his guard, while a gleam of fierce and savage exultation passed across his livid features. "But what is that to me?" he added, recollecting himself. "You dare not accuse me of the murder of that boy; and, if you should, who would believe the tale, or listen to the frantic ravings of a madman?"

"There are other witnesses living, Claude Giotti," observed Lionel. "Do not flatter yourself that you can escape the overwhelming evidence that can be brought against you of the double murder that has crimsoned your guilty hands. But I came not here to waste words with you. For your deeds you must answer at a proper tribunal. You stir not hence," he continued, as Dirk, with desperation in his look, started on his feet, and glanced towards the door, which was now crowded with a motley assemblage of both sexes, who had been drawn thither by the noise, and probably the report of the woman they had seen at the door, who well knew their errand thither.

The woman now thrust her head forward into the room with a look of malicious triumph.

"Och, then, you may make yourself aisy, honey dear," she exclaimed, "for here's the gentleman offishers comin' up wid the darbies to clap on ye; and thin I'm even wid ye for the good turn ye did my poor boy that's lying in Newgate, bad luck to them, and the likes of them, that sint him there."

"It was you then that betrayed me, hag," exclaimed Dirk, making a desperate rush towards the woman. She eluded him, however, and Lionel's firm grasp withheld his further movement, until the officers, who, as she had said, were already on the stairs, having been sent for at her instigation, entered.

A brief explanation from Lionel of the cause for which their presence was required was sufficient; and Dirk, whose every faculty seemed to have deserted him from the moment he beheld the officers of justice, was in a few minutes manacled, and taken away, amid the taunts of the old woman, who, it appeared, attributed to him the betrayal of her son, and the hootings of those who espoused her cause.

Conscious that right and justice were on his side, it had never occurred to Lionel that there might be a legal difficulty in proving that guilt which was to his own satisfaction so undeniably established. Nor did it ever enter his mind, that Zekiel if his tale were believed as to the murder of Walter Copeland would be himself placed in jeopardy. Yet so, alas! it proved.

With regard to the death of Paul Dangerfield, there existed no proof beyond his dying declaration that Dirk was his murderer; and it was therefore judged most expedient to prefer in the first place the charge against him for the murder of Walter Copeland. But what was the consternation and dismay of

ELINOR CLARE.

"GO! YOU ARE DOOMED, I TELL YOU!"

Zekiel's friends, when they found that the latter's plain and straightforward narration of that tragical event subjected him to the imputation of having been an accomplice in the crime; and that, in spite of their utmost exertions in his favour, it was considered imperative by the magistrates that the gipsy boy should be committed to prison, with the understanding, however, that he would upon the trial be admitted as evidence against the murderer.

To describe the astonishment — the rage — the despair that seized upon Zekiel, when he became aware of this fact, would be impossible. That he who had so long devoted his thoughts—his time—his every energy, to bring the murderer to justice, should now be included in the same charge, should be treated as a felon, and placed on an equality with the object of his hate and detestation, seemed to him such a perversion of justice, that nothing could reconcile him to bear it with patience. He indignantly spurned all Lionel's soothings, and representations that the evil world not be of long continuance.

"Is it nothing to wear these even for a day?" he observed, lifting his fettered hands. "Is it nothing to hear that I am called a murderer, when I would have given my own life to have saved *his* victims? Is it nothing to receive, instead of praise for all I've done to bring the villain to justice, to hear that I too am guilty, and should be thankful for the mercy shown to me? Would (and he gnashed his teeth with vengeance) would that I were free, and Dirk, too. I would set at defiance all your cursed laws, that confound the innocent with the guilty, and revenge with my own hand the foul murder of the Chief. What had I to do with Walter Copeland? It was Paul Dangerfield. It was my father that I swore to revenge, and fool that I was to listen to your persuasions, and tell what I knew about the boy. But go, I have no more to do with you, or any one. Let me only live to see Dirk on the scaffold, and they may do what they will with me."

Lionel, however, though thus repulsed, failed not to exert every means that wealth and influence afforded to render Zekiel's confinement as little irksome as possible; but vain was every attempt to remove the sullen desperation that had seized him; and whenever the former visited him in the period that elapsed before the trial, he found him in the same mood, resentful to the utmost against those who he considered had brought him into his present circumstances, and only to be roused by the still cherished hope of vengeance upon Dirk.

"If it were not for that," he would observe, while his eyes beamed fire, "think you I would bear this life an hour? No, but I know he would escape, if I——I swore to Paul that I would bring him to the scaffold, that I would see him die a dog's death; else think you I could not long since have stolen upon him, and stabbed him in his sleep, as he did the Chief? Yes, I will keep my word; and then I care not what becomes of me."

And he did keep his word. At the assizes for the county in which the crime was committed, Claude Giotti, otherwise Dirk was arraigned for the murder of Walter Copeland; and with a calmness and composure that strongly contrasted with his usual violence and impatience, Zekiel, who had formally been admitted as evidence, related all the particulars of that tragical event, which was further corroborated by a long chain of circumstances; and many were there present of his former friends, who, when the verdict of guilty was uttered, and the awful sentence of the law pronounced, would have rushed forward to congratulate Lionel, who was present, on the public manifestation of his entire innocence of the charge which had once threatened to overwhelm him. But Lionel's attention was entirely engrossed by Zekiel, whose eyes gleamed with the wild fire of revengeful triumph, as he turned them on the livid and cadaverous face of the drooping culprit, who, sinking beneath his terrors, was compelled to be supported from the bar. Zekiel watched him till he disappeared; and then he looked wildly and unsteadily around him, as if not knowing where to go or what to do.

"You are at liberty, why do you not depart?" uttered one of the persons who stood near him; and Lionel hastily stepped forward, to lead him from the place; but Zekiel still stood, his eyes were riveted on the face of a woman who had pressed as near as she could to him, and his lips faintly uttered the name of Minna.

"Yes, it is Minna," uttered the old woman, in a stern tone; "but who are you? not Zekiel, not the son of Minna's daughter, or of the Gipsy Chief, for he hated traitors, and would have doomed to death the villain who betrayed one of his own people; and you are doomed. Yes, even Minna dooms you. Go, then, with your rich friends, go with those who brought you to this shameful spectacle, a gipsy witnessing against one of his brethren, one who has eaten of the same bread, and slept in the same tents. Go, you are doomed, I tell you, and branded for ever as a traitor. Your name will be told to children yet unborn——"

"But he murdered the Chief," exclaimed Zekiel, suddenly recovering his energy; "and I swore to Paul that I would revenge him."

"Then you should have revenged him as became a man," returned Minna, with vehemence, "but it is a lie, a false lie. He who can be a traitor will be a liar. Paul met not with his death by Dirk's hands, but by some of the pale-faced tribe for whom you have deserted your own people. If it had been so, why did you not to-day bear witness to that deed, and not betray that with which you had no concern? But go, I have done with you; and now here I pray the Great Power of vengeance that I may live to see you punished, and Dirk revenged; and then I care not how soon the earth hides the shame you have brought upon me."

Lionel watched with deep interest the effect this denunciation had upon the unfortunate gipsy boy. The fire which had lighted his eyes faded into utter vacancy; and when Minna, forcing her way through the crowd, disappeared, faintly muttering "traitor," "liar," he would have fallen on the ground, had not Lionel supported him.

In a few minutes he partially recovered, and yielded without any opposition to Lionel's proposition that he should go home with him.

"It matters little whither I go now," he observed, with a deep sigh, when he was seated in the carriage, "I am doomed, *she* said so, and Minna would not lie. And she was right. What had I to do with the murder of that boy? It was Paul whom I sought to revenge; and yet they would not let me even tell the tale of his foul death to the world. Think you if Minna and the rest of the tribe who were there watching the words that fell from my lips; think you, I say, if they had heard me tell, upon my solemn oath, how Dirk stole upon the Chief in his sleep and stabbed him like a coward, think you, if they had heard that I swore to Paul in his dying moments that I would hurl the treacherous villain to justice, and that the Chief's last words acknowledged me his own, his only son, think you, I say, that they would have branded me as a traitor and a coward? No, but I let your counsels prevail, I betrayed the secrets of my people, and I deserve to suffer."

Vain were all the attentions, the soothings, the cares bestowed upon the wild and wayward youth by the friends who anxiously sought to obliterate from his mind these painful impressions. Daily and hourly he declined. The curse of Minna, and through her of the whole tribe, as he said, clung to him, and withered his heart; and on one occasion only a ray of his former fierce and untameable spirit seemed to reanimate his sinking frame, this was the execution of Claude Giotti, who deservedly expiated on a scaffold his numerous crimes. In spite of every care and caution to prevent it, Zekiel was present at that awful scene; and the last sound that met the ears of the trembling, shrinking wretch, at the moment he was launched into eternity, was the wild, piercing, unnatural shriek of exulting laughter which burst from the lips of the half-maniac boy.

Scarcely, however, was that frantic sound heard, before Zekiel was forcibly seized, and hurried from the spot. It was Lionel's care, and anticipation of the consequences that were likely to result to the headstrong youth, that had pursued him, and now bore him from the spot amid the execrations of the tribe, who were only intimidated by a strong party, whose assistance Lionel had secured, from wreaking their revenge on him whom they regarded as a traitor to his own people.

"I have revenged Paul, however," uttered Zekiel, with difficulty, "though I shall not live to have the satisfaction of seeing the murderer's bones whiten on a gibbet."

He was conveyed home, but all energy, all vitality had faded; and from that time the world and the world's business seemed over with him, and in a few months the maniac boy was laid in the grave of his father.

THE END.